JIM THOMPSON

James Meyers Thompson was born in Anadarko, Oklahoma, in 1906.
He began writing fiction at a very young age, selling his first story to
True Detective when he was only fourteen. In all, Jim Thompson
wrote twenty-nine novels and two screenplays. Four of his novels are
collected in the first *Jim Thompson Omnibus: The Getaway, The Killer
Inside Me, The Grifters* and *Pop. 1280*, also published by Picador.

Also available in Picador

THE JIM THOMPSON OMNIBUS

The Getaway

The Killer Inside Me

The Grifters

Pop. 1280

THE SECOND
JIM THOMPSON
OMNIBUS

SAVAGE NIGHT

A SWELL-LOOKING BABE

AFTER DARK, MY SWEET

NOTHING MORE THAN MURDER

A HELL OF A WOMAN

PICADOR

First published 1997 by Picador

an imprint of Macmillan Publishers Ltd
25 Eccleston Place, London SW1W 9NF
and Basingstoke

Associated companies throughout the world

ISBN 0 330 34451 X

A CIP catalogue record for this book is available from
the British Library

Typeset by CentraCet, Cambridge
Printed by Mackays of Chatham PLC, Chatham, Kent

CONTENTS

SAVAGE NIGHT

ONE

I'd caught a slight cold when I changed trains at Chicago; and three days in New York—three days of babes and booze while I waited to see The Man—hadn't helped it any. I felt lousy by the time I arrived in Peardale. For the first time in years, there was a faint trace of blood in my spit.

I walked through the little Long Island Railway station, and stood looking up the main street of Peardale. It was about four blocks long, splitting the town into two ragged halves. It ended at the teachers' college, a half-dozen red brick buildings scattered across a dozen acres or so of badly tended campus. The tallest business building was three stories. The residences looked pretty ratty.

I started coughing a little, and lighted a cigarette to quiet it. I wondered whether I could risk a few drinks to pull me out of my hangover. I needed them. I picked up my two suitcases and headed up the street.

It was probably partly due to my mood, but the farther I got into Peardale the less I liked it. The whole place had a kind of decayed, dying-on-the-vine appearance. There wasn't any local industry apparently; just the farm trade. And you don't have commuters in a town ninety-five miles from New York City. The teachers' college doubtless helped things along a little, but I figured it was damned little. There was something sad about it, something that reminded me of bald-headed men who comb their side hair across the top.

I walked a couple blocks without sighting a bar, either on the main drag or the side streets. Sweating, trembling a little inside, I set the suitcase down and lighted another cigarette. I coughed some more. I cursed The Man to myself, calling him every kind of a son-of-a-bitch I could think of.

I'd have given everything I had just to be back at the filling station in Arizona.

But it couldn't be that way. It was either me and The Man's thirty grand, or no me, no nothing.

I'd stopped in front of a store, a shoe store, and as I straightened I caught a glimpse of myself in the window. I wasn't much to look at. You could say I'd improved a hundred per cent in the last eight or nine years, and you wouldn't be lying. But I still didn't add up to much. It wasn't that my kisser would stop clocks, understand, or anything like that. It was on account of my size. I looked like a boy trying to look like a man. I was just five feet tall.

I turned away from the window, then turned back again. I wasn't supposed to have much dough, but I didn't need to be rolling in it to wear good shoes. New shoes had always done something for me. They made me feel like something, even if I couldn't look it. I went inside.

There was a little showcase full of socks and garters up near the front, and a chubby middle-aged guy, the proprietor, I guess, was bending over it reading a newspaper. He barely glanced up at me, then jerked his thumb over his shoulder.

"Right up the street there, sonny," he said. "Those red brick buildings you see."

"What?" I said. "I—"

"That's right. You just go right on up there, and they'll fix you up. Tell you what boarding house to go to and anything else you need to know."

"Look," I said. "I—"

"You do that, sonny."

If there's anything I don't like to be called, it's sonny. If there's a goddamned thing in the world I don't like to be called, it's sonny. I swung the suitcases high as I could and let them drop. They came down with a jar that almost shook the glasses off his nose.

I walked back to the fitting chairs and sat down. He followed me, red-faced and hurt-looking, and sat down on the stool in front of me.

"You didn't need to do that," he said, reproachfully. "I'd watch that temper if I were you."

He was right; I was going to have to watch it. "Sure," I grinned. "It just kind of gets my goat to be called sonny. You probably feel the same way when people call you fatty."

He started to scowl, then shifted it into a laugh. He wasn't a bad guy, I guess. Just a nosy know-it-all small-towner. I asked for size five double-A elevators, and he began dragging the job out to get in as many questions as possible.

Was I going to attend the teachers' college? Wasn't I entering a little late in the term? Had I got myself a place to stay yet?

I said that I'd been delayed by sickness, and that I was going to stay at the J. C. Winroy residence.

"Jake Winroy's!" He looked up sharply. "Why you don't—why are you staying there?"

"Mainly because of the price," I said. "It was the cheapest place for board and room the college had listed."

"Uh-huh," he nodded, "and do you know why it's cheap, son—young man? Because there ain't no one else that will stay there."

I let my mouth drop open. I sat staring at him, worried-looking. "Gosh," I said. "You don't mean he's *that* Winroy?"

"Yes, sir!" He bobbed his head triumphantly. "That's just who he is, the very same! The man who handled the payoff for that big horse-betting ring."

"Gosh," I said again. "Why I thought he was in jail!"

He smiled at me pityingly. "You're way behind the times, s—what'd you say your name was?"

"Bigelow. Carl Bigelow."

"Well, you're way behind on your news, Carl. Jake's been out for—well—six–seven months now. Got pretty sick of jail, I reckon. Just couldn't take it even if the big boys were paying him plenty to stay there and keep his mouth shut."

I kept on looking worried and kind of scared.

"Understand, now, I'm not saying that you won't be perfectly all right there at the Winroy place. They've got one other boarder—not a student, a fellow that works over to the bakery—and he seems to do all right. There hasn't been a detective around the house in weeks."

"Detectives!" I said.

"Sure. To keep Jake from being killed. Y'see, Carl"—he spelled it out for me, like someone talking to an idiot child—"Y'see Jake is the key witness in that big bookie case. He's the only one who can put the finger on all them crooked politicians and judges and so on who were taking bribes. So when he agrees to turn state's evidence and they let him out of jail, the cops are afraid he might get killed."

"D-did—" My voice shook; talking with this clown was doing me a lot of good. It was all I could do to keep from laughing. "Did anyone ever try it?"

"Huh-uh ... Stand up a minute, Carl. Feel okay? Well, let's try the other shoe ... Nope, no one ever tried it. And the more you think about it, the easier it is to see why. The public just ain't much interested in seeing those bookies prosecuted, as things stand now. They can't see why it's so wrong to bet with a bookie when it's all right to bet at the track. But taking bets is one thing, and murder is another. The public wouldn't go for that, and o'course everyone'd know who was responsible. Them bookies would be out of business. There'd be such a stink the politicians would *have* to stage a cleanup, no matter how they hated to."

I nodded. He'd hit the nail right on the head. Jake Winroy couldn't be murdered. At least he couldn't be murdered in a way that looked like murder.

"What do you think will happen, then?" I said. "They'll just let Ja—Mr. Winroy go ahead and testify?"

"Sure," he snorted, "if he lives long enough. They'll let him testify when the case comes to trial—forty or fifty years from now ... Want to wear 'em?"

"Yeah. And just throw the old ones away," I said.

"Yep, that's the way it's working out. Stalling. Getting the case postponed. They've already done it twice, and they'll keep right on doing it. I'd be willing to bet a hundred dollars that the case never does get into court!"

He'd have lost his money. The trial was set for three months from now, and it wouldn't be postponed.

"Well," I said, "that's the way it goes, I guess. I'm glad you think it'll be all right for me to stay with the Winroys."

"Sure," he winked at me. "Might even have yourself a little fun. Mrs. Winroy is quite a stepper—not that I'm saying anything against her, understand."

"Of course not," I said. "Quite a—uh—stepper, huh?"

"Looks like she could be, anyways, if she had the chance. Jake married her after he left here and moved to New York—after he was riding high, wide and handsome. It must be quite a comedown for her, living like she has to now."

I moved up to the front of the store with him to get my change.

I turned left at the first corner, and walked down an unpaved side street. There were no houses on it, only the rear end of the corner business building on one side of the alley, and a fenced-in backyard on the other. The sidewalk was a narrow, rough-brick path, but it felt good under my feet. I felt taller, more on even terms with the world. The job didn't look so lousy any more. I hadn't wanted it and I still didn't. But now it was mostly because of Jake.

The poor bastard was kind of like me. He hadn't been anything, but he'd done his damnedest to be something. He'd pulled out of this hick town, and got himself a barber's job in New York. It was the only work he knew—the only thing he knew anything about—so he'd done that. He'd got himself into exactly the right shop, one down around City Hall. He'd played up to exactly the right customers, laughing over their corny jokes, kissing their tails, making them trust him. When the smashup came, he hadn't swung a razor in years and he was handling a million-dollar-a-month payoff.

The poor bastard, no looks, no education, no nothing—and he'd pulled himself up to the top. And now he was back on the bottom again. Running the one-chair barber shop he'd started with, trying to make a little dough out of the Winroy family residence that was too run-down to sell.

All the jack he'd made in the rackets was gone. The state had latched onto part of it and the federal government had taken another big bite, and lawyers had eaten up the rest. All he had was his wife, and the dope was that he couldn't get a kind word out of her, let alone anything else.

I walked along thinking about him, feeling sorry for him; and I didn't really notice the big black Cadillac pulled up at the side of the street nor the man sitting in it. I was just about to pass on by when I heard a *"Psst!"* and I saw that it was Fruit Jar.

I dropped the suitcases, and stepped off the curb.

"You stupid pissant," I said. "What's the idea?"

"Temper." He grinned at me, his eyes narrowing. "What's *your* idea, sonny? Your train got in an hour ago."

I shook my head, too sore to answer him. I knew The Man hadn't put him on me. If The Man had been afraid of a runout, I wouldn't have been here.

"Beat it," I said. "Goddam you, if you don't get out of town and stay out, I will."

"Yeah? What do you think The Man will say about that?"

"You tell him," I said. "Tell him you drove down here in a circus wagon and stopped me on the street."

He wet his lips, uneasily. I lighted a cigarette, dropped the package into my pocket and brought my hand out. I slid it along the back of the seat.

"Nothing to get excited about," he mumbled. "You'll get into the city Saturday? The Man'll be back, and—*oof*!"

"That's a switchblade," I said. "You've got about an eighth of an inch in your neck. Like to have a little more?"

"You crazy bas—*oof*!"

I laughed and let the knife drop down upon the seat.

"Take it with you," I said. "I've been meaning to throw it away. And tell The Man I'll look forward to seeing him."

He cursed me, ramming the car into gear. He took off so fast I had to jump back to keep from going with him.

Grinning, I went back to the walk.

I'd been waiting for an excuse to hand one to Fruit Jar. Right from the beginning, when he'd first made contact with me in Arizona, he'd been picking at me. I hadn't done anything to him—but right away he was riding me, calling me kid, and sonny. I wondered what was behind it.

Fruit Jar needed dough like a boar hog needs tits. He'd dropped out of the bootleg racket before the war and gone into used cars. Now he was running lots in Brooklyn and Queens; he was making more money legit—if you can call used cars legit—than he'd ever made with the booze.

But if he hadn't wanted to come in, why was he coming in so much farther than he had to? He hadn't needed to come down here today. In fact, The Man wasn't going to like it a bit. So . . . So?

I was still thinking when I reached the Winroy residence.

TWO

If you've been around the East much, you've seen a lot of houses like it. Two stories high but looking a lot taller because they're so narrow in depth; steep-roofed with a chimney at each end and a couple of gabled attic windows about halfway down. You could gold-plate them and they'd look like hell, but they're usually painted in colors that make them look twice as bad as they normally would. This one was a crappy green with puke-brown trimming.

I almost stopped feeling sorry for Winroy when I saw it. A guy who would live in a place like that had it coming to him. You know—maybe I'm a little nuts on the subject—you know, there's just no sense to things like that. I'd bought a little shack in Arizona, but it sure didn't stay a shack long. I painted it an ivory white with a blue trim, and I did the window frames with a bright red varnish . . . Pretty? It was like one of those pictures you see on Christmas cards.

. . . I pushed the sagging gate open. I climbed the rickety steps to the porch, and rang the bell. I rang it a couple of times, listening to it ring inside, but there wasn't any answer. I couldn't hear anyone stirring around.

I turned and glanced around the bare yard—*too goddamned lazy to plant a little grass*. I looked at the paint-peeled fence with half the pickets knocked off. Then my eyes came up and I looked across the street, and I saw her.

I couldn't let on, but I knew who she was. Even in a jersey and jeans, her hair pulled back in a horse's tail. She was standing in the door of a little bar down the street, not sure whether I was worth bothering with.

I went back down the steps and through the gate, and she started hesitantly across the street.

"Yes?" she called, while she was still several steps away. "Can I help you?" She had one of those husky well-bred voices—voices that are trained to sound well bred. One look at that frame of hers, and you knew the kind of breeding she'd had: straight out of Beautyrest by box-springs. One look at her eyes, and you knew she could call you more dirty words than you'd find in a mile of privies.

"I'm looking for Mr. or Mrs. Winroy," I said.

"Yes? I'm Mrs. Winroy."

"How do you do?" I said. "I'm Carl Bigelow."

"Yes?" That broad-A yes was getting on my nerves. "Should that mean something to me?"

"That depends," I said, "on whether fifteen dollars a week means anything to you."

"Fif—Oh, of *course!*" She laughed suddenly. "I'm terribly sorry, Car—Mr. Bigelow. Our hired girl—our maid, that is—had to go home to her folks—a family crisis of some kind—and we were really expecting you last week and—and things have been in such a turmoil that—"

"Surely. Of course—" I cut her off. I hated to see anyone work so hard for a few bucks. "It's my fault, entirely. Can I make up for it by buying you a drink?"

"Well, I *was*—" She hesitated, doubtfully, and I began to like her a little better. "If you're sure you—"

"I can," I said. "Today's a celebration. Tomorrow I'll start tightening up."

"Well," she said, "in that case—"

I bought her two drinks. Then, because I could see she wanted to ask for it, I gave her thirty dollars.

"Two weeks in advance," I said. "Okay?"

"Oh, now," she protested, huskily, that well-bred voice hitting on all cylinders. "That's entirely unnecessary. After all—we—Mr. Winroy and I aren't doing this for money. We felt it was more or less our duty, you know, living here in a college town to—"

"Let's be friends," I said.

"Friends? I'm afraid I don't—"

"Sure. So we can relax. I hadn't been in town more than fifteen minutes before I knew all about Mr. Winroy's trouble."

Her face had gotten a little stiff. "I wish you'd told me," she said. "You must have thought I was a terrible fool to—"

"Will you," I said, "relax?" And I gave her my best grin, big and boyish and appealing. "If you keep talking about being in turmoil and a terrible fool and all that stuff, you'll get me dizzy. And I'm dizzy enough just looking at you."

She laughed. She gave my hand a squeeze. "Listen to the man! Or did you mean that the right way?"

"You know how I meant it," I said.

"I'll bet I look a fright. Honest to Hannah, Carl, I—Oop, listen to me. Calling you Carl, already."

"Everybody does," I said. "I wouldn't know how to take it if anyone called me mister."

But I'd like to try, I thought. And I'd sure try to take it.

"It's been such a mess, Carl. For months I couldn't open a door without a cop or a reporter popping out at me, and then just when I think it's finished and I'm going to have a little peace, it starts all over again. I don't like to complain, Carl—I really don't—but—"

She did like to, naturally. Everyone does. But a dame who'd lived on the soft money so long was too smart to do it.

She let her hair down just far enough to be friendly.

"That's certainly tough," I said. "How long do you plan on staying here?"

"How long?" She laughed shortly. "The rest of my life it looks like."

"You don't mean that," I said. "A woman like you."

"Why don't I mean it? What else can I do? I let everything slide when I married Jake. Gave up my singing—you knew I was a singer?—well, I gave that up. I haven't been in a night club in years except to buy a drink. I just let everything slide, my voice, my contacts; everything. Now, I'm not a kid any more."

"Now stop that," I said. "You stop that right now."

"Oh, I'm not complaining, Carl. Really I'm not ... How about another drink?"

I let her buy it.

"Well," I said, "I don't know too much about the case, and it's easy for me to talk. But—"

"Yes?"

"I think Mr. Winroy should have stayed in jail. That's what I'd have done."

"Of course, you would! Any *man* would."

"But maybe he knows best," I said. "He'll probably work out some big deal that'll put you higher on the heap than you were before."

She turned her head sharply, her eyes blazing fire. But I was all wide-eyed and innocent.

The fire died, and she smiled and squeezed my hand again.

"It's sweet of you to say that, Carl, but I'm afraid ... I get so damned burned up I—well, what's the use talking when I can't *do* anything?"

I sighed and started to buy another drink.

"Let's not," she said. "I know you can't afford it—and I've had enough. I'm kind of funny that way, I guess. If there's anything that gets me, it's to see a person keep pouring it down after they've had enough."

"You know," I said, "it's funny that you should mention that. It's exactly the way I feel. I can take a drink or even three or four, but then I'm ready to give it a rest. With me it's the companionship and company that counts."

"Of course. Certainly," she nodded. "That's the way it should be."

I picked up my change, and we left the place. We crossed the street, and I got my bags off the porch and followed her to my room. She was acting a little thoughtful.

"This looks fine," I said. "I'm sure I'm going to like it here."

"Carl—" She was looking at me, curiously, friendly enough but curious.

"Yes?" I said. "Is there something wrong?"

"You're a lot older than you look, aren't you?"

"Now, how old would that be?" And, then, I nodded soberly. "I must have tipped you off," I said. "You'd never have known it from looking at me."

"Why do you say it that way? You don't like—"

I shrugged. "What's the use not liking it? Sure, I love it. Who wouldn't like being a man and looking like a kid? Having people laugh every time you act like a man."

"I haven't laughed at you, Carl."

"I haven't given you the chance," I said. "Suppose things had been different. Suppose, say, I'd met you at a party and I'd tried to kiss you like any man in his right mind would. Why, you'd have laughed your head off! And don't tell me you wouldn't, because I know you would!"

I jammed my hands into my pockets and turned my back on her.

I stood there, head bowed, shoulders slumped, staring down at the threadbare carpet ... It was raw, corny as hell—but it had almost always worked before, and I was pretty sure it would with her.

She crossed the room and came around in front of me. She put a hand under my chin and tilted it up.

"You know what you are?" she said, huskily. "You're a slicker."

She kissed me on the mouth. "A slicker," she repeated, smiling at me slant-eyed. "What's a fast guy like you doing at a tank-town teachers' college?"

"I don't really know," I said. "It's hard to put into words. It's— well, maybe you know how it is. You've been doing the same thing for a long time, and you don't think you're getting ahead fast enough. So you look around for some way of changing things. And you're probably so fed up with what you've been doing that anything that comes along looks good to you."

She nodded. She knew how that was.

"I've never made much money," I said, "and I figured a little education might help. This was cheap, and it sounded good in the catalogues. At that, I almost got right back on the train when I saw what it looked like."

"Yes," she said, grimly, "I know what you mean. But—you are going to give it a try, aren't you?"

"I kind of think I will," I said. "Now, will you tell me something?"

"If I can."

"Are those real?"

"Those? What—Oh," she said, and laughed softly. "Boy, *are* we slick! ... Wouldn't you like to know, though?"

"Well?"

"Well—" She leaned forward, suddenly. Eyes dancing, watching my face, she moved her shoulders from side to side, up and down. And then she stepped back quickly, laughing, holding me away with her hands.

"Huh-uh. No, sir, Carl! I don't know why—I must be losing my mind to let you get away with that much."

"Just so you don't lose anything else," I said, and she laughed again.

It was louder and huskier than any of the others. It was like those laughs you hear late at night in a certain type of saloon. You know.

The people are all in a huddle at one end of the bar, and they're all looking at this one guy, their lips pulled back a little from their teeth, their eyes kind of glassy; and all at once his voice rises, and he slaps his hand down on the counter. And you hear the laughter.

"Sweet"—she gave me another quick pat on the cheek—"just as sweet as he can be. Now, I've got to get downstairs and throw something together for dinner. It'll be about an hour from now in case you'd like to take a nap."

I said I might do that, after I'd unpacked, and she gave me a smile and left. I started stowing my things away.

I was pretty well satisfied with the way things were going. For a minute or two, I'd thought I was moving too fast, but it seemed to have worked out okay. With a dame like her, if she really liked you, you could practically throw away the brakes.

I finished unpacking, and stretched out on the bed with a true-detective story magazine.

I turned through the pages, locating the place I'd left off:

... thus the story of Charlie (Little) Bigger, the deadliest, most elusive killer in criminal history. The total number of his slayings-for-hire will probably never be known, but he has been officially charged with sixteen. He is wanted for murder in New York, Philadelphia, Chicago and Detroit.

Little Bigger vanished as from the face of the earth in 1943, immediately following the gangland slaying of his brother and contact-man, "Big Luke" Bigger. Exactly what became of him is still a topic for heated discussion in police and underworld circles. According to some rumors, he died years ago of tuberculosis. Others would have it that he was a victim of a revenge murder, like his brother, "Big." Still others maintain that he is alive. The truth, of course, is simply this: No one knows what happened to Little Bigger, because no one knew *him*. No one, that is, who survived the acquaintance.

All his contacts were made through his brother. He was never arrested, never fingerprinted, never photographed. No man, naturally, who was as murderously active as he could remain completely anonymous, and Little Bigger did not. But the picture we get, pieced from various sources, is more tantalizing than satisfying.

Assuming that he is still alive and unchanged, Little Bigger is a mild-looking little man, slightly over five feet tall and weighing approximately one hundred pounds. His eyes are weak, and he wears thick-lensed glasses. He is believed to be suffering from tuberculosis. His teeth are in very bad condition, and many of them are missing. He is quick-tempered, studious, a moderate smoker and 'drinker. He looks younger than the thirty to thirty-five years which, according to estimates, he is now.

Despite his appearance, Little Bigger can be very ingratiating, particularly in the case of women...

I tossed the magazine aside. I sat up and kicked off the elevator shoes. I walked to the high-topped dresser, tilted the mirror down and opened my mouth. I took out my upper and lower plate. I pulled my eyelids back—first one, then the other—and removed the contact lenses.

I stood looking at myself a moment, liking the tan, liking the weight I'd put on. I coughed and looked into my handkerchief, and I didn't like that much.

I lay back down on the bed, thinking I was sure going to have to watch my health, wondering if it would do me much damage when I started making love to her.

I closed my eyes, thinking ... about her ... and him ... and The Man ... and Fruit Jar ... and this crappy-puke looking house and the bare front yard and the squeaking steps and—and that gate.

My eyes snapped opened, then drooped shut again. I'd have to do something about that gate. Someone was liable to walk by the place and snag their clothes on it.

THREE

I met Mr. Kendall, the other boarder, on the way down to dinner. He was a dignified, little old guy—the kind who'd remain dignified if he got locked in a nickel toilet and had to crawl under the door. He said he was very happy to meet me, and that he would consider it a privilege to help me get settled in Peardale. I said that was nice of him.

"I was thinking about work," he said, as we went into the dining room. "Coming in late this way, it may be a little difficult. The part-time jobs are pretty well sewed up, by now. But I'll keep my eyes open at the bakery—we employ more student help than any place in town, I believe—and it's just possible that something can be worked out."

"I wouldn't want you to go to any trouble," I said.

"No trouble. After all, we're all living here together, and—ah, that looks very good, Mrs. Winroy."

"Thanks." She made a little face, brushing a wisp of hair out of her eyes. "We may as well see how it tastes. Heaven only knows when Jake will get here."

We all sat down. Mr. Kendall more or less took over the job of passing things, while she slumped in her chair, fanning her face with her hand. She hadn't been just kidding about throwing dinner together. Apparently she'd dashed out to the store for an armload of canned goods.

It wasn't bad, you understand. She'd bought a lot of everything, and it was all topgrade. But she could have done twice as well with half the money and a little more effort.

Mr. Kendall sampled his asparagus and said it was very good. He sampled the anchovies, the imported sardines and the potted tongue and said they were very good. He tapped his mouth with his napkin, and I was expecting him to say that *it* was very good. Or maybe he'd give her a nice juicy compliment on her can opener. Instead he turned and glanced toward the door, his head cocked a little to one side.

"That must be Ruth," he said, after a moment. "Don't you think so, Mrs. Winroy?"

Mrs. Winroy listened. She nodded. "Thank God," she sighed, and began to brighten up. "I was afraid she might stay away another day."

"Ruth is the young lady who works here," Mr. Kendall told me. "She's a student at the college, too. A very fine young woman, very deserving."

"Yeah?" I said. "Maybe I shouldn't say so, but it sounds to me like she's got a broken piston."

He gave me a blank look. Mrs. Winroy let out with the guffaw again.

"Silly!" she said. "That's her father's car, her Pa, she calls him. He drives her back and forth from their farm whenever she goes home for a visit."

There was a slight mimicking note to her voice, a tone that wasn't so much nasty as amused and contemptuous.

The car stopped in front of the house. A door opened and closed—slammed—and someone said, *"Now, you take keer o' yerself, Ruthie,"* and that broken piston began to clatter, and the car pulled away.

The gate squeaked. There was a footstep on the walk; just one footstep, and a tap; a kind of thud-tap. It—She—came up the walk, stepping and thud-tapping. She came up the steps—*thud-tap, thud-tap*—and across the porch.

Mr. Kendall shook his head at me sadly. "Poor girl," he said, dropping his voice.

Mrs. Winroy excused herself and got up.

She met Ruth at the front door and hustled her right down the hall and into the kitchen. So I didn't get a good look at her; rather, I should say, one good look was all I did get. But what I saw interested me. Maybe it wouldn't interest you, but it did me.

She had on an old mucklededung-colored coat—the way it was screaming Sears-Roebuck they should have paid her to wear it—and a kind of rough wool skirt. Her glasses were the kind your grandpa maybe wore, little tiny lenses, steel rims, pinchy across the nose. They made her eyes look like walnuts in a plate of cream fudge. Her hair was black and thick and shiny, but the way it was fixed—murder!

She only had one leg, the right one. The fingers of her left hand, gripping the crosspiece of her crutch, looked a little splayed.

I heard Mrs. Winroy ordering her around in the kitchen, not mean but pretty firm and fussy. I heard water running into the sink and pans clattering, and the *thud-tap, thud-tap, thud-tap*, moving faster and faster—humble, apologetic, anxious. I could almost hear her heart pounding with it.

Mr. Kendall passed me the sugar, then spooned some into his own coffee. "Tsk, tsk," he said. I'd been hearing people say that in books for years, but he was the first real-life guy I'd ever heard say it. "Such a sad thing for a fine young woman."

"Yeah," I said, "isn't it?"

"And there's nothing to be done about it, apparently. She'll have to go through life that way."

"You mean she can't raise the dough for an artificial leg?" I said. "There's ways of getting around that."

"We-el"—he looked down at his plate uncomfortably—"of course, the family *is* impoverished. But it's—well, it's not a question of money."

"What is it a question of?"

"Well—er—uh"—he was actually blushing—"I have no—uh—personal knowledge of the—er—situation, but I understand it's a—It's due to a very—uh—peculiar malformation of the—er—"

"Yeah?" I encouraged him.

"—of the left limb!" he finished.

He came out with it like it was a dirty word. I grinned to myself, and said "Yeah?" again. But he wasn't talking any more about Ruth's—uh—er—limb, and I didn't press him any. It made it more interesting not to know.

I could look forward to finding out about it myself.

He stuffed his pipe and lit up. He asked me if I'd ever noticed how so many deserving people—people who did their best to be decent—got so little out of life.

"Yes," I said.

"Well," he said, "I suppose every picture has its bright side. Ruthie couldn't get employment in any other household, and Mrs. Winroy couldn't—uh—Mrs. Winroy was having some difficulty in finding anyone. So it all works out nicely. Mrs. Winroy has a grateful and industrious servant. Ruth has her board and room and spending money. Five dollars a week now, I believe."

"No kidding!" I said. "Five dollars a week! That must put an awful strain on Mrs. Winroy."

"I suppose it does," he nodded seriously, "things being as they are. But Ruth's an unusually good worker."

"I should think she would be for that kind of money."

He took his pipe out of his mouth, and looked into the bowl. He glanced up at me, and he chuckled.

"I'm not much of a man to recite personal history, Mr. Bigelow, but—well, I was a teacher for a great many years. English literature. Yes, I taught here at the college for a time. My parents were living then, and I couldn't stretch my salary over the needs of the three of us; so I entered and remained in a more remunerative trade. But I've never lost my interest in literature, particularly in the satirists—"

"I see," I said, and it was my turn to blush a little.

"It's always seemed to me that satire cannot exist outside the rarefied atmosphere of excellence. It is either excellent or it is nothing ... I should be very glad to lend you my *Gulliver's Travels*, Mr. Bigelow. Also the collected works of Lucilius, Juvenal, Butler—"

"That's enough. That's more than enough." I held up a hand, grinning. "I'm sorry, Mr. Kendall."

"Quite all right," he nodded placidly. "You had no way of knowing, of course, but a student who earns five dollars a week and her board and room in a college town—*this* town, at least—is doing very well for herself."

"Sure," I said. "I don't doubt it a bit."

All at once I'd had a crazy idea about him, one that kind of gave me the whimwhams. Because maybe everyone doesn't have a price, but if this dull, dignified old guy *did* have one ... Well, he'd be worth almost anything he asked as an ace in the hole. He could throw in with me, in case of a showdown: back me up in a story, or actually give me a hand if there was no other way out. Otherwise, he'd just keep tabs on me, see that I didn't try a runout ...

But that was crazy. I've already said so. The Man knew I couldn't run. He knew I wouldn't fluff the job. I shoved the idea out of my mind, shoved it damned good and hard. You just can't play around with notions like that.

Mrs. Winroy came in from the kitchen, picking up her purse from the sideboard. She paused at the table.

"I don't want to rush you gentlemen, but I think Ruth would like to clear up here whenever you're through."

"Certainly, certainly." Mr. Kendall pushed back his chair. "Shall we take our coffee into the living room, Mr. Bigelow?"

"Why don't you take Carl's cup for him?" she said. "I'd like to speak to him for a moment."

"Certainly. Of course," he said.

He took our cups and crossed the hall into the living room. I followed her out onto the porch.

It was dark out there. She stood up close to me. "You stinker," she said accusingly, half laughing. "I heard you giving him the rib ... So I'm putting a strain on myself, am I?"

"Hell," I said, "you couldn't expect me to pass up an opening like that. As a matter of fact, when it comes to an attractive opening I—"

She snickered. "But look, Carl—honey ..."

"Yeah?" I said. I brought my hands up to her hips.

"I've got to run downtown for a while, honey. I'll get back as soon as I can, but if Jake shows up while I'm gone, don't—well, don't pay any attention to him."

"That could be quite a job," I said.

"I mean he's almost sure to be drunk. He always is when he's late this way. But it's all talk with him; he hasn't got any real guts. Just don't pay any attention to anything he says, and everything will be all right."

I said I'd do my best. There was nothing else I could say. She gave me a quick hard kiss. Then she wiped my mouth with her handkerchief and started down the steps.

"Remember, Carl. Just don't pay attention to him."

"I'll remember," I said.

Mr. Kendall was waiting, worriedly, afraid that my coffee would be cold. I said it was fine, just the way I liked it, and he leaned back and relaxed. He started talking about finding a job for me—he'd taken it for granted that I'd need one. He moved from the subject of a job for me to that of his own job. As I got it, he was the manager of the place, the kind of manager who doesn't have the title and who works all hours for a few bucks more than the regular hired hands get.

I believe he was all set to take the night off by way of giving me a full and complete history of the baking industry. As it worked out, though, he hadn't been spouting for more than ten or fifteen minutes when Jake Winroy arrived.

You've seen pictures of Jake, of course; anyone who reads the newspapers has. But the pictures you've seen were probably taken when he was still in there punching. For the Jake you've seen and the one I saw were two different people.

He was a tall guy, around six feet, I guess, and his normal weight was around two hundred pounds. But he couldn't have weighed more than a hundred and forty now. The skin on his face hung in folds. It seemed to tug at his mouth, drawing it downward; it tugged down at the pouches of his eyes. Even his nose dropped. It sagged out of his face like a melting candle in a pan of dirty tallow. He was stooped, curve-shouldered. His chin almost touched his neck, and his neck seemed to bend and wobble from the weight of his head.

He was very drunk, of course. He had every right to be. Because he was dead, the same as; and I guess he knew it.

He got snagged coming through the gate—I'd known damned well that gate would snag someone—and when he yanked himself free he went sprawling and stumbling almost to the porch. He got up the steps, falling back two for every one he took, it sounded like. He came across the porch in a kind of staggering rush. He staggered into the hall. He stood weaving and swaying there a moment, blinking his eyes and trying to get his bearings.

"Mr. Winroy!" Mr. Kendall edged toward him nervously. "Would you—uh—may I help you to bed, Mr. Winroy?"

"B-bed?" Jake hiccuped. "W-hhh-hoo y-you?"

"Now, you know very well who I am, sir!"

"S-sure. I k-now, but duh-duh duh d-you? Betcha c-can' tell me, can you?"

Mr. Kendall's mouth tightened. "Would you like to come over to the bakery with me for a while, Mr. Bigelow?"

"I think I'll go up to my room," I said. "I—"

And Jake jumped like he'd been shot.

He jumped and whirled at the sound of my voice. He looked at me, wild-eyed, and one of his long, veined hands came up pointing. "W-who y-you?"

"This is Mr. Bigelow," said Mr. Kendall. "Your new boarder."

"Oh, yeah? Yeah!" He took a step backward, keeping his eyes fixed on me. "B-boarder, huh? So h-he-s the new b-boarder, huh? Oh, y-yeah?"

"Of course, he's the new boarder!" Kendall snapped. "A very fine young man, and you're certainly doing your best to make him uncomfortable! Now, why—"

"Oh, yuh-yeah? Yeah!" He kept on edging toward the door, edging backward in a sort of half crouch. His eyes peered out at me wildly through the tumbled strands of his greasy black hair. "N-new b-boarder. Makin' h-huh-him uncomfortable. *Huh—him* uncomfortable! Oh, y-yeah?"

It was like a broken record—a broken record with a rasping, worn-out needle. He made me think of some wild sick animal trapped in a corner.

"Oh, y-yeah? Yeah!" He didn't seem to be able to stop it. All he could do was back up, back, back, back . . .

"This is disgusting, sir! You know quite well you've been expecting Mr. Bigelow. I was present when you talked about it with Mrs. Winroy."

"Oh, y-yeah? Yeah! 'S-spectin' Mr. Bigelow, yeah? 'S-spectin' Mr. B-Bigger-low . . ."

His back touched against the screen door.

And he tripped on the lintel, plunged stumbling across the porch and went crashing down the steps. He turned a complete somersault on the way down.

"Oh, my goodness!" Mr. Kendall snapped on the porch light. *"Oh,* my goodness! He's probably killed himself!"

Wringing his hands, he scuttled across the porch and started down the steps. And I sauntered after him. But Jake Winroy wasn't dead, and he didn't want any help from me.

"Nnnnuh-NO!" he yelled. "N-NUHNUH—NO . . . !"

He rolled to his feet. He sprang awkwardly toward the gate, and he tripped and went down again. He picked himself up and shot staggering into the road.

He took off right down the middle of it toward town. Arms flapping, legs weaving and wobbling crazily. Running, because there was nothing to do but run.

I felt pretty sorry for him. He didn't need to let his house look like it did, and I couldn't excuse him for it. But I still felt sorry.

"Please don't let this upset you, Mr. Bigelow." Kendall touched my arm. "He simply goes a little crazy when he gets too much liquor in him."

"Sure," I said. "I understand. My father was a pretty heavy drinker . . . Let's get the light off, huh?"

I jerked my head over my shoulder. A bunch a yokels had come out of the bar and were staring across the street at us.

I turned the light off, and we stood on the porch talking a few minutes. He said he hoped Ruthie hadn't been alarmed. He invited me to the bakery again, and I turned him down.

He stuffed tobacco into his pipe, puffed at it nervously. "I can't tell you how much I admired your self-possession, Mr. Bigelow. I'm afraid I—I've always thought I was pretty cool and collected, but—"

"You are," I said. "You were swell. It's just that you're not used to drunks."

"You say your—uh—your father—?"

It was strange that I'd mentioned it. I mean, there wasn't any harm in mentioning it; but it had been so long ago, more than thirty years ago.

"Of course, I don't remember anything about it," I said. "That was back in 1930 and I was only a baby at the time; but my mother—" That was one lie I had to pound home. My age.

"Tsk, tsk! Poor woman. How terrible for her!"

"He was a coal miner," I said. "Over around McAlester, Oklahoma. The union didn't amount to much in those days, and I don't need to tell you there was a depression. About the only work a man could get was in the wildcats, working without inspection. Stripping pillars—"

I paused a moment, remembering. Remembering the stooped back, and the glaring fear-maddened eyes. Remembering the choked sounds at night, the sobbing screams.

"He got the idea that we were trying to kill him," I said. "If we spilled a little meal, or tore our clothes or something like that, he'd beat the tar out of us ... Out of the others, I mean. I was only a baby."

"Yes? But I don't understand why—"

"It's simple," I said. "Anyway, it was simple enough to him. It seemed to him that we were trying to keep him in the mines. Keeping him from getting away. Using up stuff as fast as we could so that he'd have to stay down there under the ground ... until he was buried under it."

Mr. Kendall tsk-tsk'ed again. "Wretched! Poor deluded fellow. As if you could help—"

"We couldn't help it," I nodded, "but that didn't make it any better for him. He had to work in the mines, and when a man has to do something he does it. But that doesn't make it any easier. You might even say it was twice as hard that way. You're not brave or noble or unselfish or any of the things a man likes to think he is. You're just a cornered rat, and you start acting like one."

"Mmm. You seem to be an unusually introspective young man, Mr. Bigelow. You say your father died of drink?"

"No," I said. "He died in the mines. There was so much rock on top of him that it took a week to dig him out."

Mr. Kendall shoved off for the bakery after a few more tsks and how-terribles, and I went back in the house. Then I sauntered on back to the kitchen.

She was bent over the sink, the crutch gripped under her armpit, washing what looked like about a thousand dishes. Apparently, Mrs. Winroy had saved them up for her while she'd been away—them and every other dirty job.

I hung my coat over a chair and rolled up my sleeves. I picked up a big spoon and began scraping the pans out.

I got them all scraped into one pan, and started for the back door with it.

She hadn't looked at me since I'd come into the room, and she didn't look at me now. But she did manage to speak. The words came out in a rush like a kid who's nerved to recite a poem and has to do it fast or not at all.

"The g-garbage can's at the side of the porch—"

"You mean they don't have any chickens?" I said. "Why, they ought to have some chickens to feed it to."

"Y-yes," she said.

"It's a shame to waste food this way. With all the hungry people there are in the world."

"I—I think so, too," she said, sort of breathless.

That was all she was up to for the moment. She was blushing like a house afire, and her head was ducked so far over the sink I was afraid she would fall in. I took the garbage outside and scraped it out slowly.

I knew how she felt. Why wouldn't I know how it felt to be a kind of joke, to have people tell you off kind of like it was what you were made for? You never get used to it, but you get to where you don't expect anything else.

She was still pretty shocked by the idea of having talked to me when I went back inside. But being shocked didn't keep her from liking it. She said I s-shouldn't be helping her wipe the dishes—then, pointed out a towel to me. She said h-hadn't I better put an apron on; she did it for me, her fingers trembling but lingering.

We stood wiping the dishes together, our arms touching now and then. The first few times it happened, she jerked hers away like she'd brushed against a hot stove. Then, pretty soon, she wasn't jerking away. And, once, when my elbow brushed her breast, it seemed to me that she sort of leaned into it.

Studying her out of the corner of my eyes, I saw that I'd been right about her left hand. The fingers *were* splayed. She didn't have the full use of it, and she kept trying to hide it from me. Even with that, though, and her leg—whatever was wrong with her leg—she had plenty on the ball.

All that hard work and deep breathing had put breasts on her like daddy-come-to-church. And swinging around on that crutch hadn't done her rear end any harm. If you saw it by itself, you might have thought it belonged to a Shetland pony. But I don't mean it was big. It was the way it was put on her: the way it hinged into the flat stomach and the narrow waist. It was as though she'd been given a break there for all the places she'd been shortchanged.

I got her to talking. I got her to laughing. I draped another dishtowel over my head and started prancing around; and she leaned back against the drainboard, giggling and blushing and protesting.

"S-stop, now, Carl—" Her eyes were shining. The sun had come up behind them, and was shining out at me. "Y-you stop, now—"

"Stop what?" I said, pouring it on all the harder. "What do you want me to stop, Ruth? You mean *this* or *this?*"

I kept it up, sizing her up while I did it, and I changed my mind about a couple of things. I decided I wasn't going to give her any tips on dressing. I wasn't going to fix her up with a compact and a permanent. Because any dolling up she did need, she'd do for herself, and she didn't really need any.

Then, suddenly, she wasn't laughing any more. She stopped and stood staring over my shoulder.

I knew what it must be. I'd had a hunch it was coming. I turned slowly around, and I was damned careful to keep my hands away from my sides.

I can't say whether he'd rung the doorbell and we hadn't heard him, or whether he'd just walked in without ringing. But there he was—a tall rawboned guy with sharp but friendly blue eyes, and a graying coffee-stained mustache.

"Havin' quite a time for yourself, hey, kids?" he said. "Well, that's fine. Nothing I like better'n to see young folks enjoying themselves."

Ruth's mouth opened and closed. I waited, smiling.

"Been meaning to get out and see your folks, Miss Dorne," he went on. "Hear you got a new baby out there . . . Don't believe I've ever met you, young fellow. I'm Bill Summers—Sheriff Summers."

"How do you do, sheriff," I said, and I shook hands with him. "I'm Carl Bigelow."

"Hope I didn't startle you folks just now. Dropped over to see a fellow named—*Bigelow*! You say *you're* Carl Bigelow?"

"Yes, sir," I said. "Is there something wrong, sheriff?"

He looked me over slowly, frowning, taking in the apron and the dishtowel on my head; looking like he couldn't decide whether to laugh or start cussing.

"I reckon we've got some talking to do, Bigelow . . . Darn that Jake Winroy's hide, anyway!"

FOUR

We were in my room. Mrs. Winroy had come in a couple of minutes behind him, and she'd blown her lid so high we'd had to come upstairs.

"I just can't understand it," I said. "Mr. Winroy's known I was coming for several weeks. If he didn't want me here, why in the world didn't—"

"Well, o'course, he hadn't seen you then. What with seein' you and connecting you up with a name that sounds kinda like yours—well, I can see where it might give him a little start. A man that's in the fix Jake Winroy's in."

"If anyone's got a right to feel upset, it's me. I can tell you this, sheriff. If I'd known that James C. Winroy was Jake Winroy, I wouldn't be here now."

"Uh-huh, sure." He shook his head sympathetically. "But I was kind of wonderin' about that, son. Why did you come here, anyway? All the way from Arizona to a place like Peardale."

"That was it partly," I shrugged. "Because it was a long way from Arizona. As long as I was making a fresh start, I thought I'd better make a clean break of it. It's not easy to make something out of yourself around people who remember you when you weren't anything."

"Uh-huh. Yeah?"

"That was only part of it, of course," I said. "This was cheap, and the school would accept me as a special student. There aren't many colleges that will, you know. If you don't have a high-school education, you're out of luck." I laughed shortly, making it sound pretty grim and dispirited. "It seems pretty crazy to me, now. I'd dreamed about it for years—getting myself a little education and landing a good job and—and—But I guess I should have known better."

"Aw, now, son"—he cleared his throat, looking troubled—"don't take it that way. I know there ain't no sense to this, and I don't like it a bit better than you do. But I ain't got no choice, Jake Winroy being what he is. Now you just help me out and we'll get this settled in no time."

"I'll tell you anything I can, Sheriff Summers," I said.

"Swell. What about kinfolks?"

"My father's dead. My mother and the rest of the family—I don't know about them. We started splitting up right after Dad died. It's been so long ago that I've even forgotten what they looked like."

"Uh-huh?" he said. "Yeah?"

I started talking. Nothing I told him could be checked, but I could see he believed me; and it would have been strange if he hadn't. The story was pretty much true, you see. It was practically gospel, except for the dates. There was a hell of a depression in the Oklahoma coal fields in the early twenties. There were strikes and the militia was called in, and no one had money enough for grub, let alone doctors and undertakers. And there was plenty to think about besides birth and death certificates.

I told him how we'd drifted over into Arkansas, picking cotton, and then on down into the Rio Grande Valley for the fruit, and then over into the Imperial for the stoop crops ... Sticking together, at first, then splitting up for a day or two at a time to follow the work. Splitting up and staying split up.

I'd sold newspapers in Houston. I'd caddied in Dallas. I'd hustled programs and pop in Kansas City. And in Denver, in front of the Brown Palace Hotel, I'd put the bite on a big flashy-looking guy for coffee money. And he'd said, "Jesus, Charlie, you don't remember me? I'm your brother, Luke—"

But I left that part out, of course.

"Uh-huh"—he cut in on me. I'd given him so much he was getting tired. "When did you go to Arizona?"

"December of '44. I've never been real sure of my birthdate, but I'd just turned sixteen as near as I can figure it. Anyway"—I made a point of being careful about it—"I don't see how I could have been more than seventeen."

"Sure," he nodded, scowling a little. "Anyone'd know that. Don't see how you could even have been sixteen."

"Well, the war was still on and any kind of help was hard to get. This Mr. Fields and his wife—awfully nice old couple—gave me a job in their filling station, and it didn't pay much, because it didn't make much, but I liked it fine. I lived with them, just like I was their son, and saved everything I did make. And two years ago, when Da—I mean, Mr. Fields died, I bought the place from her ... I guess"—I hesitated—"I guess that's one reason I wanted to get away from Tucson. With Dad Fields dead and Mom moved back to Iowa, it just didn't seem like home any more."

The sheriff coughed and blew his nose. "Dang that Jake," he growled. "So you sold out and came back here, eh?"

"Yes, sir," I said. "Would you like to see a copy of the bill of sale?"

I showed it to him. I also showed him some of the letters Mrs. Fields had written me from Iowa before she died. He paid a lot more attention to them than he had to the bill of sale, and when he was through he blew his nose again.

"Goldarn it, Carl, I'm really sorry to 've put you through all this, but I reckon I'm not through yet. You won't mind if I do a little telegraphin' out there to Tucson? I just about got to, you know. Otherwise Jake'll keep kickin' up a fuss like a chicken with its head off."

"You mean"—I paused—"you want to get in touch with the chief of police in Tucson?"

"You ain't got no objections, have you?"

"No," I said. "I just never got to know him as well as I did some of the other folks. Could you send a wire to the sheriff, too, and County Judge McCafferty? I used to take care of their cars for them."

"Goldang it!" he said, and got to his feet.

I stood up also. "Will this take very long, sheriff? I hardly feel like enrolling at the college until it's settled."

"O'course, you don't," he nodded sympathetically. "We'll have it all straightened out, so's you can start in next Monday."

"I'd have liked to get into New York first," I said. "I won't go, naturally, until you say it's all right. But I bought a new suit while I was there, and the alterations were supposed to be done by this Saturday." I walked to the bedroom door with him, and it seemed to me I heard a faint creak from the door across the hall.

"A man's kinda got to get along with everyone in a job like mine, so I wouldn't want you to repeat anything. But these Winroys—well, it ain't good economy to stay with 'em, no matter how cheap it is. You take my advice, an'—"

"Yes?" I said.

"No"—he sighed, and shook his head—"I guess you can't very well do that. Jake kicks up a big fuss, and then you move out, an' no matter what I say or you say it looks bad. Makes it look like you had to move, like maybe there was somethin' to his crazy carryin' on."

"Yes, sir," I said. "I surely wish I'd known who he was before I came here."

I saw him out the door, and closed it again. I stretched out on the bed with a cigarette, lay with my eyes half closed, puffing smoke at the ceiling. I felt all wrung out. No matter how well prepared you are for a deal like that, it takes a lot out of you. I wanted to rest, to be left alone for a while. And the door opened and Mrs. Winroy came in.

"Carl," she said huskily, sitting down on the edge of the bed. "I'm so sorry, darling. I'll murder that Jake when I get my hands on him!"

"Forget it," I said. "Where is he, anyway?"

"At his shop, probably. Probably'll spend the night there. He'd better if he knows what's good for him!"

I walked my fingers up her thigh, and let them do a little wandering around. After a moment or two, she squeezed them absently and laid my hand back on the bed.

"Carl . . . You're not angry?"

"I didn't like it," I said, "but I'm not angry. Matter of fact, I feel pretty sorry for Jake."

"He's losing his marbles. Why, they wouldn't dare kill him! It would hurt them twice as much as having him testify."

"Yeah?" I said. "I guess I don't know much about those things, Mrs. Winroy."

"They—Why don't you call me Fay, honey? When we're alone like this."

"Fay honey," I said.

"They wouldn't dare to, would they, Carl? Right here in his home town where everyone knows him and he knows everyone? Why— why"—she laughed irritably—"my God! this is the one place in the world where he's safe. No stranger can get near him—no one he doesn't know, and—"

"I got near him," I said.

"Oh, well," she shrugged. "I'm not counting you. He knows that anyone the college sent here would be all right."

"Yeah? He didn't act much like it."

"Because he's full of booze! He's beginning to see things!"

"Well," I said, "whatever he does, you can't blame him much."

"I can't, huh?"

"I don't think you should," I said.

I raised up on one elbow and tamped out my cigarette.

"Here's the way I might look at it, Fay," I said, "if I were in Jake's shoes. Practically all I know about crime is what I read in the papers. But I'm pretty good at putting myself in the other fellow's place, and here's the way I'd feel if I were Jake. I'd figure that if they took a notion to kill me, there wouldn't be any way I could stop them. Nothing I could do, no place I could go. I—"

"But, Carl—"

"If they didn't get me in one place, they'd do it in another. Some place, somehow, and no matter how tough it was. I'd know they'd get me, Fay."

"But they won't! They can't afford to!"

"Sure," I said.

"The case won't ever come to trial. Everyone says it won't!"

"Well, they probably know," I said. "I was just talking about how Jake would feel if he thought they *did* want to kill him."

"Yes, but you said—I mean, when he knows they won't do it, why—?"

"He knows it, but do they know it? See what I mean? He knows they've got plenty of brains and plenty of money. He knows they'd find an angle, if they wanted to get him badly enough."

"But they—"

"They don't," I said. "But if they did? There wouldn't be anyone Jake could trust. Why, they might even try to get to him through old man Kendall."

"Oh, Carl! That's ridiculous!"

"Sure, it is," I said, "but you get the idea. Some guy who would never be suspected."

"Carl—"

She was looking narrow-eyed, interested, cautious.

"Yeah, Fay?" I said.

"You ... What if—if—"

"What if what?" I said.

She kept on staring at me in that puzzled cautious way. Then, she laughed suddenly and jumped up. "God," she said. "Talk about Jake losing *his* marbles! Look, Carl. You're not going to school this week?"

I shook my head. I didn't bother to rib her about snooping.

"Well, Ruth has a nine o'clock class, so you ought to be downstairs by eight if you want her to fix your breakfast. Or you can just help yourself to coffee and toast or something whenever you get up. That's what I usually do."

"Thanks," I said. "I'll see how I feel in the morning."

She left, then. I opened a window and stretched back out on the bed. I needed a bath, but I wasn't up to it yet. I wasn't up to such a little thing as undressing and walking a few steps down the hall to the bathroom.

I lay still, forcing myself to lie still when I felt the urge to get up and look in the mirror. You've got to take it easy. You can't run for the big score with sand in your shoes. I closed my eyes, looking at myself in my mind's eye.

It gave me a start. It was like looking at someone else.

I'd seen myself that way ten thousand times and each time it was a new experience. I'd see what other people seemed to see, and I'd catch myself thinking, "Gosh, what a nice little guy. You don't need anyone to tell you *he's* all right—"

I thought that, now, and somehow it sent a shiver through me. I started thinking about the teeth and the other chances, and I knew that they really didn't matter. But I made myself think about them.

I felt safer, some way, believing it was those things instead of—instead of?

... The teeth and the contact lenses. The tanned, healthy-looking face. The extra weight. The added height ... and only part of it was due to the elevator shoes I'd worn since 1943. I'd straightened up when I shook the bug, and—but had I shaken it? Suppose I took sick now, so sick I couldn't go through with this? The Man would be sore, and—the name? *Charles Bigger*—Carl Bigelow? Well, it was as good as any. It wouldn't have been any better to call myself Chester Bellows or Chauncey Billingsley; and it would have had to be something like that. A man can't get too far away from his own name, you know. He may try to but he's asking for trouble. There's laundry markings. There's answering when you're spoken to. So ...

So I hadn't made any mistakes. I ... But The Man had found me. He'd never seen me before either but he'd known right where to send for me. And if The Man could do it ...

I lighted a cigarette, jabbed it out immediately, and threw myself back on the pillows.

The Man—you couldn't count The Man. I hadn't made any mistakes, and I wouldn't make any. I'd make the score, and I'd make the afterwards, the hard part. Because no matter how smoothly it was done, there was bound to be some heat. And the surest way of getting cooked was to try to run from it. You'd screw things up for The Man. If they didn't get you, he would.

So ... I felt drowsy.

No mistakes. No letting down for even a second. No getting sick. And use them all, Mrs. Winroy directly, the others indirectly. They'd have to be on my side. They'd have to *know* that I couldn't do what I had to do. The Man didn't need to watch me. They would. They were all watching to see that I did it right, and . . . watching . . . always watching . . . and me . . .

. . . They crowded the sidewalks of that dark narrow street, that narrow and lonely street. And they were going on about their business, laughing and talking and enjoying life; but still they were watching me. Watching me follow Jake and watching The Man follow me. I was sweating and all out of breath, because I'd been in the street a long time. And they kept getting in my way, getting between me and Jake, but they never got in The Man's way. Me, ME, they had to screw up. And . . . I could taste the black damp in my mouth and I could hear the pillars cracking and crumbling and the lamp on my cap began to flicker and . . . I grabbed one of the bastards. I grabbed him/her, and yanked and rolled and . . .

I had her on the bed. She was under me, and I had the crutch across her throat, pinned down with my arms.

I blinked, staring down at her, fighting to come out of the dream. I said, "Jesus, kid. You don't want to ever—"

I slid the crutch to one side and she started breathing again, but she still couldn't talk. She was too scared. I looked into the great scared eyes—*watching me*—and it was all I could do to keep from slugging her.

"Spill it," I said. "Spit it out. What were you doing here?"

"I—I—I—"

I dug my hand into her side, and twisted. And she gasped.

"Spill it."

"I—I—I w-was a-afraid for you. I—I w-was w-worried about . . . *Carl!* D-don't—"

She began to struggle, then, and I lay flat against her. I held her, twisting her, and she gasped and moaned. She cried to pull at my hand, and I twisted harder.

"D-don't! . . . I've n-never . . . C-Carl, I've never . . . it's n-not n-n-nice and *Carl!* Carl! Y-you've g-got to . . . I'll have a b-baby, and—"

. . . She'd stopped begging.

There was nothing left to beg for.

I looked down, my head against hers so that she couldn't see that I was looking. I looked, and I closed my eyes quickly. But I couldn't keep them closed.

It was a baby's foot. A tiny little foot and ankle. It started just above the knee joint—where the knee would have been if she had one—a tiny little ankle, not much bigger around than a thumb; a baby ankle and a baby foot.

The toes were curling and uncurling, moving with the rhythm of her body . . .

"C-Carl . . . Oh, *C-Carl!*" she gasped.

After a long time, what seemed like a long time, I heard her saying, 'Don't. Please don't, Carl. It's a-all right, so—so, please, Carl . . . Please don't cry any more—"

FIVE

I was a long time getting to sleep, and thirty minutes after I did I woke up again. I woke up exhausted, but with the feeling that I'd been asleep for hours. You know? It went on like that all night.

When I woke the last time it was nine-thirty, and sunlight was streaming into the room. It was shining right on my pillows, and my face felt hot and moist. I sat up quickly, hugging my stomach. The light, hitting into my eyes suddenly, had made me sick. I clenched my eyes against it, but the light wasn't shut out. It seemed to be closed in, under the lids, and a thousand little images danced in its brilliance. Tiny white things, little figure-seven-shaped things: dancing and twisting and squirming.

I sat on the edge of the bed, rocking and hugging myself. I could taste the blood in my mouth, salty and sour, and I thought of how it would look in the sunlight, how yellow and purplish, and . . .

Somehow I got to the dresser and got the lenses and teeth into place. I staggered down the hall, kicked the bathroom door shut behind me, and went down on my knees in front of the toilet bowl. I threw my arms around it, bracing myself, looking down at the wavering water in the faintly brown-stained porcelain. And then my whole body swelled and shook, and I heaved.

The first one, the first heave, was the worst. It seemed to pull me two ways, forcing the stuff back and throwing it up at the same time. After that it was easier; the hard part was getting my breath, keeping from strangling. My heart pounded harder and harder. The sweat of weakness streamed down off my face, mixing with the blood and the vomit. I knew I was making a hell of a racket, but I didn't care.

There was a rap on the door, and Fay Winroy called, "Carl. Are you all right, Carl?" I didn't answer. I couldn't. And the door opened.

"Carl! What in the world, honey—?"

I gestured with one hand, not looking around. Gestured that I was all right, that I was sorry, to get the hell out.

She said, "I'll be right back, honey," and I heard her hurrying back up the hall and down the stairs.

I flushed the toilet, keeping my eyes closed.

By the time she came back I'd got some cold water dabbed on my face and was sitting on the toilet seat. I was weak as all hell, but the sickness was gone.

"Drink it down, baby," she said. And I drank it down—a half glass of straight whiskey. I gasped and shuddered, and she said, "Here. Take a deep drag." And I took the cigarette she handed me, and dragged on it deeply.

The whiskey stayed down, warming me and cooling me in all the places where I needed warming and cooling.

"My God, honey!" . . . She was down on her knees in front of me; why she bothered to wear that nightgown I didn't know, because it didn't conceal anything. "You get that way very much, Carl?"

I shook my head. "I haven't had a spell like that since I was a kid. Don't know what the hell brought it on."

"Well, gosh, I didn't know what to think. You sounded worse than Jake does sometimes."

She was smiling, concerned for me. But there was a calculating look in the reddish brown eyes. Was I a sharp guy, a guy who could give her a lot of kicks? Or was I just a sick punk, someone good for a lousy fifteen a week and no laughs to go with it?

Apparently she made up her mind. She stood up and locked her arms around mine, holding them. She said, "Mmmmmmmmph!" and kissed me open-mouthed. "You tough little bastard!" she whispered. "Oh, you tough little bastard! I've got half a notion to—"

I didn't want that. Yet. I wasn't up to it. So I started a little rough-house, and that broke the mood.

"Stinker!" she laughed, leaning against the wall of the hallway. "Don't you dare, you naughty bad boy!"

"Flag me down, then," I said. "I only stop for red flags."

I looked at her standing there laughing, everything she had on view. And all the time telling me not to look, not to dare. I watched her, listened to her. I watched and listened to myself, standing outside myself. And it was like seeing a movie you've seen a thousand times before. And ... and I guess there wasn't anything strange about that.

I shaved and took the bath I'd missed the night before. I got dressed, hurrying it up a little when she called up the stairs to me, and went down to the kitchen.

She'd fixed bacon and eggs and toast, some sliced oranges and french fries. And she'd dirtied up about half the pans and dishes in the place to do it, but it was all well prepared. She sat across from me at the kitchen table, kidding and laughing, keeping my coffee cup filled. And I knew what she was—but I couldn't help liking her.

We finished eating, and I passed her a cigarette.

"Carl—"

"Yes?" I said.

"About—about what we were talking about last night—"

She waited. I didn't say anything.

"Oh, hell," she said, finally. "Well, I suppose I'd better go downtown and see Jake. He can stay away as long as he wants to, but he's got to give me some money."

"Too bad you have to look him up," I said. "You don't think he'll be home?"

"Who knows what he'll do?" She shrugged angrily. "He'll probably stay away until they find out about you."

"I'm sorry," I said. "I hate to have him put himself out on my account."

She gave me another of those thoughtful looks, her eyes narrowed behind the smoke. "Carl. It will be all right, won't it? The sheriff—he—it'll be all right?"

"Why not?" I said.

"You're going to go to school here?"

"It would be pretty foolish not to," I said. "Wouldn't it?"

"Oh, I don't know. Skip it!" She laughed, irritably. "I guess I'm kind of goofy this morning."

"It's this town," I said. "Sticking around a hole like this with nothing to do. You just weren't built for it. You've got too much stuff for the place. I knew it the minute I saw you."

"Did you, honey?" She patted my hand.

"I should think you could get some kind of singing job," I said. "Something that would give you a better life."

"Yeah. Maybe. I don't know," she said. "If I had some clothes, the dough to look around with. Maybe I could, but I don't know, Carl. I've been out of things so long. I don't know whether I could work any more, even to get away from this."

I nodded. I took another step. It was probably unnecessary, but it wasn't any trouble and it could save a lot.

"You're afraid, too, aren't you," I said, "that things might be made a little unpleasant for Jake Winroy's wife?"

"Afraid?" She frowned, puzzledly. "Why should—?"

It had never occurred to her, apparently. And I could see it sink in on her now, sink and build and spread. It pushed the color out of her face, and her lips trembled.

"B-but it wasn't my fault. They can't blame me, Carl! H-how could they—they wouldn't blame me, would they, Carl?"

"They shouldn't," I said. "I don't suppose they would, if they knew how you felt."

"Carl! What can I—My God, honey, I don't know why I didn't see that—"

I laughed softly. It was time to call a halt. Her imagination could talk a lot better to her than I could. "Gosh," I said, "look at the time. Almost eleven o'clock, and we're still fooling around with breakfast."

"But, Carl. I—"

"Forget it." I grinned at her. "What would I know about things like that? Now you run on to town."

I stood up and began clearing away the dishes. After a long moment she got up, too, but she didn't make any move toward the door.

I took her by the shoulders and gave her a little shake. "It's like I said," I told her. "The town's getting on your nerves. You ought to run into the city for the weekend."

She smiled weakly, still pale around the gills. "Run is right. I sure as hell couldn't ride."

"Maybe you could," I said. "You got any kinfolks there? Anyone you ever visit?"

"Well, I have a sister over in the Bronx, but—"

"She'd yes for you? Give you an alibi in case Jake tried to check up?"

"Well, I don't—Why should I—?" She frowned at me, blinking; and I thought maybe I'd figured her wrong or had crowded her too hard. Then she laughed softly, huskily. "Boy!" she said. "Did I say he was slick? But look, Carl. Won't it look kind of funny if we both—?"

"We won't," I said. "You let me figure it out."

"All right, Carl." She nodded quickly. "You don't—you won't think I'm a tramp, will you? It's just that—"

"No," I said. "You're not a tramp."

"I'll go along as long as I can with a person, but when I'm through, well, I'm through. I just don't want any part of 'em any more. You understand Carl?"

"I understand," I said. "Now, beat it, will you? Or you stay here and I'll clear out. It doesn't look good for the two of us to be hanging around here alone."

"All right, honey. I'll go right now. And—oh, yes, don't bother about the dishes. Ruth can do them."

"Will you get out of here?" I said.

And she laughed and kissed me, and got out.

I cleared up the dishes and put them away. I uncovered an old rusty hammer and went out into the back yard. There was part of a packing crate lying against the alley fence. I knocked some nails out of it, walked around to the front, and went to work on that gate.

There hadn't been much of anything wrong with it in the beginning; a couple of nails in the hinges would have fixed it up fine. But just letting it go—trying to slam it when it couldn't slam had damned near wrecked it.

I was still hard at it when Kendall came home from the bakery to lunch.

"Ah," he said, approvingly, "I see you're like me, Mr. Bigelow. You like to keep busy."

"Yeah," I said. "It's something to pass the time."

"I heard about your—uh—little difficulty last night. I'm glad to see you're taking it in your stride. I—uh—don't want to seem presumptuous, but I've taken a strong personal interest in you, Mr. Bigelow. I'd have been very disappointed if you'd allowed your plans to be upset by a drunken bum."

I said, yeah, or thanks, or something of the kind.

"Well," he said, "shall we go in? I think lunch must be ready."

I told him I'd just finished breakfast. "I guess you'll be the only one eating lunch, Mr. Kendall. Mrs. Winroy's gone to town, and I don't imagine Mr. Winroy will be here either."

"I'll tell Ruthie," he said, quickly. "The poor child's liable to go to a lot of trouble for nothing."

He went on inside, and I went back to work. After a moment he came out again.

"Uh, Mr. Bigelow," he called. "Do you know where Ruth might be?"

"I haven't seen anything of her," I said. "I didn't know whether she was supposed to come home at noon."

"Of course she is! Certainly." He sounded a little annoyed. "She gets out of her last morning class at eleven, and she's always here by eleven-thirty to start fixing lunch."

"Well," I said, and picked up my hammer again. He fidgeted on the porch uncertainly.

"I can't understand it," he frowned. "She's always here by eleven-thirty. She has to be to fix lunch and get the beds made before she goes back to school."

"Yeah," I said. "I can see how she would."

I finished working on the gate. I lit a cigarette, and sat down on the steps to rest.

Ruth. Ruthie. I'd dreaded facing her after last night. She'd asked for it, creeping in on me that way, and yeah, yeah, she'd wanted it, and she'd said it was all right. But someone defenceless, someone—a *baby* . . .

But now I wanted to see her. I wanted to see her more than anything in the world. It was like part of me was missing.

I puffed at the cigarette. I flipped it away, and lit up another one. I thought about her—me—swinging along on that crutch, head down, afraid to look at people, afraid to see them looking. You do all you can, and it's still not enough. You keep your head down, knocking yourself out. You take all the shortcuts ...

I got up and started around the house. I almost ran ... Kendall had said she was always here by eleven-thirty. She had to be to do the things she had to do. And she'd have to race to do it. She'd have to take all the shortcuts.

I jerked the alley gate open, and looked up the line of high board fence. I looked just as she turned into the alley, pulling herself along on the fence, using the crutch as a cane.

For a moment I was sicker than I'd been when I first got up. Then, the sickness went away, gave way to anger. I ran to meet her, cursing the whole world and everybody in it.

"For Christ's sake, honey!" I took the crutch out of her hand, and drew her arm around my shoulder. "Are you hurt? Stop a minute and get your br—"

"N-no!" she panted. "J-just let me l-lean on you s-so—"

Her face was smudged, and the left side of her coat was all dusty and dirty. Apparently the end piece of the crutch had worked loose, and she'd taken a hell of a fall.

"Where did it happen?" I said. "Why didn't you ask someone for help? My God, baby, you shouldn't—"

"H-hurry," she gasped. "Please, C-Carl."

I hurried, letting her use me as a crutch. And I didn't ask any more foolish questions. What difference did it make where the accident had happened, whether she'd been struggling for two blocks or six—two thousand miles or six thousand?

I got her across the back yard and up the steps. Hurrying, hurrying, the two of us one person. And her pounding heart, pounding so hard that it seemed to come right out through the skin, was my pounding heart.

I helped her into the kitchen and pushed her into a chair. She struggled to get up, and I pushed her down into it hard.

"Stay there!" I said. "Goddammit, stay there! If you don't sit still, by God I'll slough you!"

"I c-can't! Mrs. W-Winroy—"

"Listen to me!" I said. "Will you listen, Ruth? Everything's going to be all right."

"It w-won't!" She was rocking in the chair, weeping helplessly. "Y-you don't understand. Y-you don't know how it is. She'll f-fire me, and I j-just can't—I've g-got t-to—"

I slapped her across the face, two quick hard slaps with the palm of my hand and the back of it.

"Want to listen?" I drew my hand back, ready to swing at her again. "Just tell me what you want to do. You want to listen or do I knock your head right off of your shoulders?"

"I—I'm"—she shuddered and gulped down a sob—"I'm l-listening, Carl."

I found the whiskey bottle in the cupboard and poured out a stiff shot. I stood over her, watching her to see that she drank every last drop.

"Better, huh?" I grinned. "Now you're going to eat something, and then you're going to lie down."

"No! I—"

"You have to be at school this afternoon? Have to? Sure, you don't, and you're not going to. Everything's jake here. No one showed for lunch but Kendall and he won't say anything. I'll talk to him and see that he doesn't."

"Y-you don't know! Mrs. Winroy—"

"She went downtown to get some money. She'll get it if she has to take it out of Winroy's hide, and after she gets it she'll have to spend it. She won't be home for a long time. I know, get me? I know exactly what she'll do."

"B-but"—she looked at me, curiously, a faint frown on her face—"I h-have to make—"

"Make the beds. What else?"

"Well. P-pick up the rooms a little."

"What time do you usually get out of school?"

"Four."

"Well, today maybe you cut a class. See what I mean? If she gets home before I think she will. You're home early, and you're hard at it when she gets here. Okay?"

"But I have to—"

"I'll do it," I said. "And don't tell me I can't. I'm a whiz at making beds and picking up. Now, I'll fix you a little lunch and help you upstairs, and—"

"No, Carl! Just—just do the other. I'll fix my own lunch. Honest, I will. I'll do anything you say, but p-please—"

"How are you going to do it? What about your crutch?"

"I'll fix it! I've done it before. I can tighten the screws with a case knife, and there's some tape here and—Please, Carl!"

I didn't argue with her. It was better to let her do a little something than to have her go hysterical again.

I gave her the crutch and a knife and the roll of tape.

There were two bedrooms downstairs, Ruth's and an unoccupied one—I didn't have to bother with them, of course. Upstairs there were four bedrooms, or, I should say, four rooms with beds in them. Because you couldn't call the place Jake slept a real bedroom. It was more like a long, narrow closet, barely big enough for a bed and a chair and a lopsided chest of drawers. I guessed it had been a closet before Fay Winroy had stopped sleeping with him.

Since he hadn't slept there the night before, there wasn't much of anything to do to it. Nothing at all, in fact. But I went in and looked around—after I'd put my gloves on.

There was a half-empty fifth of port on the chest of drawers. Six-bits a bottle stuff. In the top drawer of the chest was a small white prescription box. I rocked it a little with the tip of one finger. I studied the label. *Amyt. 5 gr. NO MORE THAN ONE IN ANY SIX HOUR PERIOD.*

Five-grain amytal. Goofballs. Tricky stuff. You take one, and you forget that you've done it. So you take more … A few of those in that rotgut wine, and—?

Nothing. Not good enough. He might drink too little, and you'd only tip your hand. He might toss down too much, and throw it up.

No, it wasn't good enough, but the basic idea was sound. It would have to be something like that, something that could logically happen to him because of what he was.

In the bottom drawer, there was a forty-five with a sawed-off barrel.

I looked it over, moving it with my finger tips, and saw that it was cleaned and loaded. I closed the drawer and left the room.

You didn't really have to aim that gun for close-range shooting. All you had to do was pull the trigger and let it spray. And if you happen to be cleaning it when …

Huh-uh. It was too obvious. Whenever a man's killed with something that's made for killing—well, you see what I mean. People get ideas even where there's nothing to get ideas about.

Mrs. Winroy's room looked like a cyclone had struck it; it looked like she might have tried to see how big a mess she could make. I did a particularly good job on it, and went on to Mr. Kendall's room.

Everything there was about as you'd expect it to be. Clothes all hung up. Bookcases stretching along one side of the room and halfway down another. About the only thing out of place was a book lying across the arm of an easy chair.

I picked it up after I'd finished doing the little work that had to be done, and saw that it was something called *Mr. Blettsworthy on Rampole Island* by H. G. Wells. I read a few paragraphs at the place where it had been left open. It was about a guy who'd been picked up by a bunch of savages, and they were holding him prisoner down in a kind of canyon. And he was pretty worried about getting to be as crummy as they were, but he was more worried about something else. Just staying alive. I only ready those few paragraphs, like I've said, but I could see how it was going to turn out. When it came to a choice of being nice ahd dead or crummy and alive, the guy would work overtime at being a heel.

I crossed the hall to my own room. I was just finishing it up when I heard Ruth coming up the stairs.

She looked in all the other rooms first, making sure, I guess, that I'd done them up right.

I asked her how she was feeling. She said, "J-just fine," and, "C-Carl, I can't tell you how much I—"

"What's the use trying, then?" I grinned. "Come on, now, and I'll help you downstairs. I want you to get some rest before Mrs. Winroy shows up."

"But I'm all—I don't need any—"

"I think you do," I said. "You still look a little shaky to me."

I took her back downstairs, making her put most of her weight on me. I made her lie down on her bed, and I sat down on the edge of it. And there wasn't anything more I could do for her, and I couldn't think of anything to say. But she lay there, looking at me as though she expected something more; and when I started to get up she put her hand over mine.

SIX

"I think I'd better shove off," I said. "I want to tell Mr. Kendall not to say anything about missing his lunch."

"C-Carl. Do you—?"

"What about him, anyway?" I said. "How long has he been boarding here?"

"Well"—she hesitated—"not very long. They didn't start keeping boarders until this last fall."

"And he moved in right away?"

"Well—yes. I mean, I think he was the one who gave them the idea of running a boarding house. You see, the way it is here, in a college town, you can't have both girls and boys—men—living in the same place. So the place where he was living, all the boarders were boys and they were awfully noisy, I guess, and—"

"I see. The Winroys had plenty of room, so he asked them to take him in. And as long as they had the one boarder, they decided to go after some others."

"Uh-huh. Only no one else would stay with them. I guess Mr. Kendall knew it would never be crowded here."

"Yeah," I said. "I imagine he did. Well, I think I'll go and see him, and—"

"Carl." Her hand tightened on mine. "About last . . . I'm not sorry, Carl."

"All right," I said, trying to be firm and gentle at the same time. "I'm glad you're not sorry, Ruthie, and there's nothing for you to worry about. Now let's just leave it at that, huh? Let's make like it never happened."

"B-but I—I thought—"

"It's better that way, Ruthie. Mrs. Winroy might catch on. I've got an idea she wouldn't like it."

"B-but she didn't last night. If w-we were careful and—"

She was blushing; she couldn't look at me straight.

"Look," I said. "That stuff won't get you anything, kid. Nothing but trouble. You were doing all right before, weren't you? Well, then—"

"Tell me something, Carl. Is it because of my—because I'm like I am?"

"I've told you why," I said. "It's just damned bad business. I haven't got anything. I don't know how long I'm going to be here. You can't win, know what I mean? You ought to be doing your stepping out with one of the local boys—some nice steady guy you can marry some day and give you the kind of life you ought to have."

She bit her lip, turning her head on the pillows until she was staring at the wall.

"Yes," she said, slowly. "I suppose that's what I'd better do. Start stepping out. Get married. Thank you."

"Look," I said. "All I'm trying to do is—"

"It's my fault, Carl. I felt different around you. You seemed to like me, and you didn't seem to notice how—notice anything. And I guess I thought it was because you—I don't mean there's anything wrong with you—but—"

"I know," I said. "I felt the same way."

"And"—she didn't seem to have heard me—"you were just trying to be nice, weren't you?"

"Ruth," I said.

"It's all right, Carl. Thanks for everything. You'd better go, now."

I didn't go, of course. I couldn't after that. I lay down at her side, pulling her around facing me, holding her when she tried to pull away. And after a moment, she stopped trying; she was holding me twice as hard.

"Don't go away, Carl! Promise you won't go away! I've n-never had anyone, and if you went away I—"

"I won't," I said. "Not for a long time, anyway. I'm going to stay right here, Ruthie."

"Was it g-g—" She was whispering, whispering and shivering, her face pressed close to mine. "Did you l-like—me?"

"I—Look," I said. "I just don't think—"

"Please, Carl. P-please!" she said, and slowly she turned her body under mine. And there was just one way of telling her that it was all right.

It was all right. It was better than all right. I didn't look down at that little baby foot, and nothing could have been any better.

We went up to the bathroom together. Then I left the house and headed for the bakery.

It was a long one-story, buff brick building, about a block and a half up the street toward the business section. I passed up the offices, and went around to the side where a couple of guys were loading bread into trucks.

"Mr. Kendall?" One of them jerked his head at the side door. "He's probably in on the floor. Just keep going until you spot him."

I went in. I went down a long corridor, crowded with wire racks of bread, and came out into a big room where about fifty guys were working. Some of them were throwing long ropes of dough over hooks in the wall, throwing it and pulling it back and throwing it again. And others were carrying the dough away from the hooks and laying it out on long wooden tables.

One side of the room was made up of a row of brick ovens, and the guys working in front of them were stripped to the waist. They'd flick the door of the oven open, and reach inside with a kind of flat-bladed shovel; they'd reach about sixty times to the second, it looked like. I was watching them, thinking that that kind of work I could do without, when Mr. Kendall came up behind me.

"Well," he said, touching me on the arm. "What do you think of us, Mr. Bigelow?"

"It's quite a place," I said.

"Not completely modern," he said. "I mean, it's not mechanized to the extent that big-city bakeries are. But with help so cheap there's no reason why it should be."

I nodded. "I came over to explain about Ruth, Mr. Kendall. She had an accident on the way home at noon, and—"

"An accident! Was she badly hurt?"

"Just shaken up. Her crutch gave way under her, and she took a spill."

"The poor child! You're not in any hurry? Well, let's get out of this noise for a moment."

I followed him across the room, a fussy polite little guy in white overalls and a white sailor cap.

We entered another room, about a third of the size of the first one, and he pushed the connecting door shut. He boosted himself up on a table and gestured for me to sit beside him.

"It's clean, Mr. Bigelow. We don't keep flour in here, just the more or less precious commodities. Looks a little like a grocery store, doesn't it, with all these shelves?"

"Yeah," I said. "Now, about Ruth. I wanted to ask you—"

"You don't need to, Mr. Bigelow." He took out his pipe and began filling it. "Naturally, I won't say anything to Mrs. Winroy. But thank you for letting me know what the situation was."

"That's all right," I said. "I helped her set the rooms straight. I mean—"

I let my voice trail away, cursing myself. I didn't want anyone to know that I'd been through the rooms.

"Mmm," he nodded absent-mindedly. "I'm very glad you came over, Mr. Bigelow. As I said at noon. I don't want to appear presumptuous, but I've been thinking—uh—don't you believe that, instead of merely waiting around until you hear from the sheriff, it might be well for you to start putting roots down? In a word, don't you feel it would be sound psychology to demonstrate that there is not the slightest doubt in your own mind of the outcome of last night's unfortunate business?"

"Yeah?" I said. "I don't get you."

"I was referring to—" He paused. "Now that—your response just now—brings up something else I wanted to speak to you about. If, that is, you won't think I'm—uh—being—"

"Let's say, I won't," I said. "You're not being presumptuous. You just feel a friendly interest in me, and you want to give me a little fatherly advice."

I'd said it the right way, and there wasn't anything in my face to show that I didn't mean it.

"I'm glad you understand, Mr. Bigelow. To take the second matter first, I was going to suggest that you be a little more careful about the language you use. I know most young men talk rather slangily and—uh—tough these days, and no one thinks anything of it. But in your case, well, don't you see?"

"I understand. And I appreciate the advice," I said. "After all, regardless of what's happened, it won't hurt me to talk a little better brand of English."

"I'm afraid I put things rather badly," he said. "Badly or baldly, if there's any difference, I suppose I'm so used to ordering these student workers around that—"

"Sure—surely," I said. "Don't apologize, Mr. Kendall. Like I say, I appreciate your interest."

"It's a very warm interest, Mr. Bigelow." He bobbed his head seriously. "All my life, I've had someone to look after, and now with my parents dead—God rest them—and nothing to occupy me but my job and my books, I—I—"

"Sure. Surely," I repeated.

He laughed, a shamed sad little laugh. "I tried to take a vacation last year. I own a little lakeside cabin up in Canada—nothing pretentious, you understand; the site is too isolated to have any value, and we, my father and I, built the cabin ourselves—so I bought a car and started to drive up there. Two days after I left town, I was back here again. Back here working. And I've hardly had my car out of the garage since."

I nodded, waiting. He chuckled halfheartedly. "That's an explanation and an apology, if you can unravel it. Incidentally, if you'd like to use the car some time, you'll be entirely welcome"

"Thanks," I said. "I'd be glad to pay you for it."

"You'd only complicate my life further for me." He laughed again. "I could only add it to my savings, and since they, obviously, can do me not the slightest good—I couldn't appreciate the pleasures they might buy, and the pension which will soon be due me is more than enough to provide for my wants—so—"

I said, "I understand," or something equally brilliant.

"I imagine I'm too old to acquire the habit of spending," he went on. "Thrift like work has become a vice with me. I'm not comfortable with them, but I'd be less content without them. Does that sound pretty stupid to you?"

"I wouldn't put it that way," I said. "I'd say, though, that if you had *enough* money—you know twenty or thirty thousand dollars—you might get quite a bit of fun out of it."

"Mmm. You feel the case is similar to that of having a little knowledge, eh? Perhaps you're right. But since the relative little is what I do have and I see no way of substantially increasing it—" He ended the sentence with a shrug. "Now to get back to you, Mr. Bigelow, if I may—if you won't feel that I'm trying to order your life for you—"

"Not at all," I said.

"I've felt for a long time that there should be a storeroom man in here. Someone to check these supplies out instead of merely letting the different departments help themselves. I mentioned the fact to the owner today and he gave his approval, so if you'd like to have the job you can start in immediately."

"And you think I should?" I said. "Start in immediately, I mean."

"Well"—he hesitated; then he nodded firmly—"I certainly don't see that you could lose anything by it."

I lighted a cigarette, stalling for a minute's time. I thought it over fast, and I decided that whatever he was or wasn't, I was on my own. This was my job, my game, and I knew how to play it. And if anyone was going to tell me what to do, it would have to be The Man.

"I'll tell you what, Mr. Kendall," I said. "I've had a long trip, and I'm pretty tired and—"

"The job won't be at all arduous. You can set your own hours, practically, and much of the time there's nothing at all to—"

"I think I'd rather wait," I said. "I plan on running into New York tomorrow night, or Saturday at the latest. Today would probably be the only day I could get in before Sunday."

"Oh," he said. "Well, of course, in that case—"

"I would like to have the job, though," I said. "That is, if you can hold it for me."

He said that he could, rather reluctantly, apparently not too pleased at failing to get his own way. Then his face cleared suddenly, and he slid down off the table.

"I can give it to you, now," he said. "We'll say that you're just laying off for a couple of days."

"Fine," I said.

"I know I'm overcautious and apprehensive. But I always feel that if there's any small barrier we can erect against potential difficulties we should take advantage of it."

"Perhaps you're right," I said.

We walked along the rows of shelves, with him pointing out the different cans and packages of baking ingredients and giving me a running commentary on how they were used.

"I'm having some batch cards designed—that is, requisitions for

ingredients which the various departments will submit to you. All
you'll have to do is fill them. Now, over here is our cold-storage room
where we keep perishables—"

He levered the door on a big walk-in refrigerator, the kind you see
in meat markets, and we went inside. "Egg whites," he said, tapping
a fifteen-gallon can with the toe of his shoe. "And these are egg yolks,
and here are whole eggs," tapping two more cans. "Bakeries buy these
things this way for two reasons: they're considerably cheaper, of
course, and they can be measured much more easily."

"I see," I said, trying to keep from shivering. I'd only been in the
place for a minute, but the cold was cutting me to the bone.

"Now, this door," he said, pushing it open again. "You'll notice
that I left it well off the latch. I'd suggest that you do the same if you
don't want to risk freezing to death. As"—he smiled pleasantly—
"I'm sure you don't."

"You can sing two choruses of that," I said, following him out of
the refrigerator. "I mean—"

He laughed and gave me a dignified clap on the back. "Quite all
right, Mr. Bigelow. As I said a moment ago, I'm inclined to be
overcautious ... Well, I think that will be enough for today. Uh—I
know it isn't much, but in view of the job's other advantages—uh—
will twelve dollars a week be all right?"

"That will be fine," I said.

"You can set your own hours—within reason. The ingredients for
the various dough batches can be checked out before they're ready for
use, and then you'll be free to study or do—uh—anything else you
like."

We left the main storage room and entered a smaller one, an
anteroom, stacked high with sacks of salt, sugar and flour. At the end
of a narrow corridor between the sacks, there was a door opening
onto the street. Kendall unlocked it, winking at me.

"You see, Mr. Bigelow? Your own private entrance and exit. No
one is supposed to have a key to this but me, but if you should be
caught up on your work and feel the need for a breath of air, I see no
reason why—uh—"

He gave me one of his prim, dignified smiles, and let me out
the door. I paused outside and lighted another cigarette, glancing
casually up and down the street. The door—the one I'd just come

out of—was well to the right of the entrance to the office. Even if there was someone in there working late, as I would be on an after-school job, I could go in and out without being seen. And straight down the street, a matter of a hundred and fifty yards or so, was the house.

With Fay Winroy to set him up for a certain time—a good dark night—it would be a cinch. I could stand there at the door and watch until he went by, and then . . .

It was too much pie. It was so good that I couldn't make up my mind whether I liked it.

I sauntered on down the street, turning in at the bar across from the house. I ordered an ale, and sat down.

Kendall. Was he just a nice old busybody, a man who'd taken a fancy to me like a lot of elderly people had, or had The Man got to him? I couldn't make up my mind about him. Twice now, well, three times, I'd thought I'd had him figured. And each time, even now, right after he'd practically told me where he stood and handed me the deal on a platter, I began to doubt my figuring. I still wasn't sure.

He just didn't fit the part. No matter what he said or did, I just couldn't hold a picture of him as a guy who'd get mixed up in a gang murder. And yet . . . well, you see? That was what made him an almost sure-fire bet. If—*if* The Man was a little leery of me, *if* he did have an ace in the hole—little old man Kendall would be his boy. It would have to be him or someone like him.

I kicked it around in my mind, pulling myself first one way then the other . . . Whatever he was, Kendall was a long way from being stupid. He wouldn't do the job himself, assuming that it was something that an amateur could handle. He wouldn't work with me as an accomplice. He'd handle his end without doing a thing that could be pinned on him. And if I didn't handle mine, if I fell down on the job or screwed it up . . .

I didn't like to think about it. Because if I fell down or screwed it up, I'd never live to fumble another one. Maybe I wouldn't, anyway, but I'd have a chance. I'd done the vanishing act before, and I'd stayed hidden for more than six years. But with Kendall keeping tabs on me—if he *was*—with him tipping off The Man the moment I went sour on the deal or it went sour on me . . .

Huh-uh. The Man didn't take excuses. He didn't let you quit. I wouldn't run far enough to work up a sweat.

I bought another ale. So what if it was that way? I'd agreed to do the job, and as long as I did it I'd be all right. Since that was the way things stood, what difference did it make about Kendall?

It made plenty. It showed that The Man didn't trust me—and it wasn't good when The Man didn't trust you. It was either that or he was leery of the job—and that wasn't good either. The Man didn't operate on hunches. If he was leery, he had good reason to be.

I wondered what he'd say if I asked him point-blank about Kendall. And I didn't need to wonder long about it; I was through wondering almost before I began.

He'd laugh it off. He'd put his arm around my shoulder and tell me how much he liked me ... and that would be the beginning of a damned fast end. He'd have to get rid of me. He'd be afraid not to. Afraid I might be getting panicky or worrying about a double-cross.

I finished my ale, and started out of the bar. Just as I reached the door, Fay Winroy came in.

"Oh, there you are, hon—" she caught herself. "I thought you might be over here. The sher—there's someone at the house to see you."

She drew me outside, lowering her voice. "It's the sheriff, honey. Maybe you'd better go on over by yourself, and I'll stay here for a drink."

"All right," I said. "Thanks for hunting me up."

"Carl"—she looked at me anxiously—"are you sure that everything's all right? Is there anything that—?"

"Not a thing," I said. "Why?"

"Nothing. No reason. He said it was all right, but—"

"Yeah?" I said.

"He acts so funny about it, Carl. So ... so awfully funny—"

SEVEN

He was waiting for me in the living room. When I came in, he eased himself up out of his chair a few inches, as though he was planning on shaking hands. Then, he let himself down again, and I sat down across from him.

"I'm sorry I kept you waiting," I said. "I've been down at the bakery lining up a part-time job."

"Uh-hah," he nodded. "Miss Ruth told me she thought you might be there, but you was already gone when I stopped by. Got you a job, eh?"

"Yes, sir," I said. "I haven't started to work yet, but—"

"Uh-hah. You're plannin' on staying here, then? Going to school and all."

"Why, yes," I said. "That's why I came here."

"Uh-hah, sure," he drawled again. "Well, I hope it works out all right. We got a nice little town here. Nice little college. We'd like to keep it that way."

I frowned at him, looking him straight in the eye. "I don't particularly like it here, sheriff," I said. "In fact, I wish I'd never seen your town or your college. But now that I'm here I plan on staying. And if you can think of any reason why I shouldn't, perhaps you'd better tell me."

He swallowed heavily. He wasn't used to being talked to that way. "Didn't say there was any reason, did I? Maybe you better tell me if you can think of any."

I didn't even bother to answer him.

He cleared his throat, uncomfortably. After a moment, his glance wavered and he gave me a sheepish grin. "Pshaw," he mumbled. "Now how the heck did I ever get started talkin' to you that-a-way? Must be I had to hold in the good news I had for you so long it kinda clabbered on me. Ever have that happen to you? You got somethin' nice to pass on to a fella, and when you can't find him—"

"Good news?" I said. "What good news?"

"The answers to them wires I sent to Arizona. Don't know when I've seen so many good things said about a man. Looked like the judge an' the chief o' police was trying to outdo each other."

"They're very fine gentlemen," I said.

"Must be. Don't see how they could be anything else," he nodded firmly. "And with two high-placed people like that speakin' up for you, I don't see—"

"Yes?" I said.

"Nothin'. Just sort of talkin' to myself, more or less. Kind of a bad habit of mine." He stood up, slapping his hat against the side of his pants. "Let's see, now. You was saying you planned on running into the *city* this weekend?"

"Tomorrow or Saturday," I said. "If it's all right."

"Sure, sure it's all right. You just go right ahead."

He put out his hand, and gave mine a firm hard grip.

I went upstairs and my head had hardly touched the pillows before Fay Winroy slipped into the room.

"Carl. Was it—what did he want?"

"Nothing much." I moved over on the bed to let her sit down. "Just came to tell me that I'd gotten a clean bill from Arizona."

"Oh? But he acted so strange, Carl. I thought—"

"How about it?" I said. "You didn't give him a bad time when he came here looking for me."

"N-no." She hesitated. "I mean, naturally I don't like cops hanging around with their cars parked in front of the house, but—well, I'm sure I didn't say anything out of the way."

I wouldn't have bet money on it. "I don't imagine Kendall liked having him come to the bakery, either," I said. "That must have been the trouble. The guy had his feelings hurt."

"You can't think of anything else?"

I shrugged. "I don't know what it would be. How did you make out with Jake?"

Her eyes flashed. "I don't want to talk about him."

"Neither do I," I yawned. "In fact, I'd just as soon not talk at all. I think I'll take a nap."

"Well," she laughed, getting up. "Here's my hat, what's my hurry, huh? But it's almost dinnertime, honey."

"I'm not hungry," I said.

"You could have something up here. Would you like to have me bring you up a tray in about an hour?"

"Well—" I frowned.

"It'll be all right. Kendall will be gone back to the bakery—you'd think the guy would move his bed over there—and Ruth will have plenty to keep her busy in the kitchen. I'll see that she does."

I nodded. "In about an hour, then."

She left. I closed my eyes and tried to forget about Kendall, and the sheriff, and The Man and Fruit Jar and . . .

I was still trying an hour later when she pushed the door open and came in with the tray.

She had a glass half full of whiskey on it, covered up with a napkin. I drank it down, and began to feel hungry.

It was a good dinner—a beef stew with vegetables, and apple pie for dessert. Fay lay back on the bed while I ate, her hands clasped under the back of her head.

I drank the last of my coffee. I lay down crosswise on the bed with her, pulling her around in my arms.

"Carl—"

"That's me," I said.

"Did you really mean what you said this morning? About us—me—going into New York?"

I reached the wallet out of my pocket, and took out two twenties. I tucked them into the front of her brassiere.

"Oh, Carl, honey," she sighed. "I can hardly wait."

I told her where to meet me, a hotel on West Forty-seventh where the fix was in strong.

"I'll go in tomorrow afternoon," I said, "and come back late Saturday night. You come in Saturday morning, and come back here Sunday night. And don't forget to fix things up with your sister."

"I won't, honey!" She sat up eagerly. "I'll be very careful about everything. I'll tell Jake that sis sent me the money to come on, and—"

"All right," I said. "Just be careful, and let it go at that."

She took the bills out of her brassiere, and smoothed them over her knee. Then, she folded them neatly and tucked them back between her breasts.

"Sweet," she said, huskily, laying her head against my shoulder. "You don't mind waiting, do you, honey?"

I didn't mind. I wanted it—who the hell wouldn't have—but I wasn't in any hurry. It was something that had to be done, the clincher to the bargain.

"It would do me good to mind?" I said.

"Yes," she nodded. "I'm not—well, I know I'm a long way from being what I should be—but here, well, to do it—to start off here in Jake's house ... If you say so, I will but—"

"That's okay," I said.

"You're not sore, Carl? You know what I'm trying to say?"

"I think I do," I said, "and it's all right. But I can't say how long it will stay that way if you don't beat it out of here."

She looked at me teasingly, her head cocked a little to one side.

"Suppose I change my mind," she said. "Suppose I wake up in the night, and—"

I made a grab for her. She leaped back, laughing, and ran to the door. She pursed her lips; then she whispered, "Good night, honey," and slipped out of the room.

... I slept pretty good that night. Nothing out of the way happened the next morning. I got up around nine, after Kendall and Ruth had left, and fixed my own breakfast. I lingered over it, thinking Fay might join me, but she didn't. So I cleaned up the dishes, left for the railroad station.

The Long Island was outdoing itself that day. It was only an hour late getting into New York. I picked up the suit I'd bought and checked in at the hotel. At six o'clock I called The Man from a booth telephone. Then I strolled down to the Automat near Forty-second and Broadway and waited.

Fruit Jar drove up in front of the place at seven o'clock. I got into the Cadillac, and we headed for The Man's house.

EIGHT

You've heard of The Man. Everyone has. There's hardly a month passes that the papers don't have a story about him or you don't see his picture. One month he's up before some government investigating committee. The next he's attending a big political dinner—laughing and talking to some of the very same people who were putting him through the wringer the month before.

The Man is a big importer. He controls shipping companies, and distilleries, race tracks and jobbing houses, wire services and loan companies.

He's one of the biggest open-shop employers in the country, but it's not because he's opposed to unions. He's a charter member of two old-line craft unions, and he's supported their organizational drives, and he's got letters from some of the top labor-skates thanking him for his "earnest endeavors in behalf of the American workingman."

The Man controls race tracks—but he supports anti-race-track legislation. He can prove that he's supported it, and you can't prove that he controls the tracks. He controls distilleries—but can you prove it?—and he supports temperance movements. He controls loan companies—controls the men who control them—and he backs anti-loan-shark laws.

The Man donated heavily to the defense of the Scottsboro boys. The Man went bail for bigwigs in the Klan.

No one has ever pinned anything on him.

He's too big, too powerful, too covered-up. You try to pin something on him, and you lose it along the way.

The Man lived in a big stone and brick house out in Forest Hills. He wasn't married, of course—although I don't know why I say of course—and the only servant around was the square-faced Japanese houseboy who let us in.

The boy took us into the library-drawing room where The Man was waiting. And The Man still stood beaming at me, shaking my hand and asking me about my trip East and saying how delighted he was to meet me.

"I'm so sorry I didn't get to talk to you before you went down to

Peardale," he said, in his soft pleasant voice. "Not, I'm sure, that you need my advice."

"I thought I'd better not lose any more time," I said. "The school term has already started."

"Of course. Naturally." He finally let go of my hand and waved me to a chair. "You're here, now, and that's the important thing."

He sat down, smiling, and nodded to Fruit Jar. "Perfect, wouldn't you say so, Murph? We couldn't have found a better man for the job than Little Bigger. Didn't I tell you he'd be worth any trouble we went to in locating him?"

Fruit Jar grunted.

"Would you mind telling me how you did it?" I said. "How you found me?"

"Not at all. But I didn't suppose it would be anything that would mystify you."

"Well, it doesn't exactly," I said. "I mean, I think I have it figured out. I was red hot here in the East, and I'd had a little lung trouble—"

"And your teeth and eyes were very bad."

"You figured I'd just about have to go West. I'd have to take some kind of unskilled outdoors job. I'd get my teeth and my eyes taken care of—not in the place I was living but some place nearby—and I'd be damned careful to build up a good reputation. And—and—"

"About all, isn't it?" He chuckled, beaming at me. "The teeth and the contact lenses, of course, were decisive."

"But the police knew as much about me as you did. Even more, maybe. If you could find me, why couldn't they?"

"Ah, the police," he said. "Poor fellows. So many distractions and diversions and restrictions. So many things to do and so little to do it with."

"There's the reward money. It totaled around forty-seven thousand dollars the last I heard."

"But, my dear Charlie! We can't expend public funds on the off-chance that the police may collect rewards. Of course if they wished to carry on their search on their own time and at their own expense—"

"Yeah," I said, "but—"

"Some ambitious private investigator? No, Charlie. I can under-stand the slight trepidation which you may feel, but it is absolutely groundless. What would it profit anyone—some reward-hungry or public-spirited citizen—if he did find you? He would have to prove your identity, would he not? And who would believe that you, this soft-spoken slip of a youth, was a murderer? You've never been arrested, never mugged or fingerprinted."

I nodded. He spread his hands, smiling.

"You see, Charlie? I didn't need to prove who you were. With me it was merely necessary to know. I could then place my proposition before you and ask for your co-operation—I dislike the word demand don't you?—and you were kind enough to give it. The police, the courts"—he shrugged wryly—"Paah!"

"I'd like to get just one more thing straight," I said. "I wanted this job, but I don't want any others. I don't want to pick up again where I left off the last time."

"Naturally, you don't. What . . . Murph, didn't you tell him?"

"Not more than a dozen times," said Fruit Jar.

The Man gave him a long, slow look. He turned back to me. "You have my word on it, Charlie. It wouldn't be practical to use you again, even if I wanted to."

"Fine," I said, "that's all I wanted to know."

"I'm delighted to reassure you. Now, to get down to the business at hand—"

I gave him a report on how things stacked up in Peardale—about my run-in with Jake and lining up a job at the bakery and how I'd made out with the sheriff. He seemed pleased. He kept nodding and smiling, and saying "Excellent" and "Splendid" and so on.

Then he asked me one question, and for a moment I was kind of stunned. I felt my face turning red.

"Well?" He asked it again. "You said the sheriff got his report on you yesterday afternoon. Did Jake stay at the house last night?"

"I"—I swallowed—"I don't believe he did."

"You don't *believe* he did? Don't you know?"

I should have known, of course. It was the one thing I should have known. I was pretty sure that he hadn't stayed at the house but I'd been worn out and I'd got to grab-assing around with Fay Winroy and . . .

"That's rather important," The Man said. And waited. "If he

wasn't there last night, how can you be sure that he plans on staying there at all?"

"Well," I said, "I—I don't think—"

"You can say that again!" Fruit Jar snickered. "Boy, oh, boy!" That snapped me out of it.

"Look," I said. "Look, sir. I talked to the sheriff yesterday for the second time in two days. I spent more than an hour with this man Kendall. He doesn't know anything but he's a pretty sharp old bird—"

"Kendall? Oh, yes, the baker. I see no cause to worry about him."

"I'm not worried about him or the sheriff either. But with Jake feeling the way he does, I don't have to move very far out of line to be in trouble. I can't show any interest in him. I can't do anything that might be interpreted as showing interest in him. I deliberately went to bed early last night, and I stayed there until late this morning. I—"

"Yes, yes," The Man interrupted impatiently. "I commend you for your discretion. But there should have been some way to—"

"He'll stay at the house," I said. "Mrs. Winroy will see that he does."

"Oh?"

"Yes."

He shook his head, leaning forward in his chair. "Not just yes, Charlie. Are you telling me that after only forty-eight hours, you've made a proposition to Mrs. Winroy?"

"I've been leading up to one, and she'll grab it. She hates Jake's guts. She'll jump at the chance to get rid of him and make herself a stake at the same time."

"I'm relieved that you think so. Personally, I believe I'd have taken a little more time in arriving at such a decision."

"I couldn't take any more time. She was opening up to me before I'd talked to her five minutes. If I hadn't played up to her right at the start, I might not have got another chance."

"So? And you felt you had to have her assistance?"

"I think it will come in pretty handy, yes. She can still make Jake jump through hoops. She knows her way around. She could get tough if she thought she was losing her meal ticket with nothing to take the place of it."

"Well," The Man sighed. "I can only hope your appraisal is correct. I believe she's a former actress, isn't she?"

"A singer."

"Singer, actress. The two arts overlap."

"I've got her taped," I said. "I've only known her a couple of days, but I've known women like her all my life."

"Mmm. May I assume that there's a connection between her and your arrival in town a day early?"

"She's meeting me here tomorrow. She's supposed to be visiting her sister, but—"

"I understand. Well, I'm rather sorry you didn't consult me, but inasmuch as you didn't—"

"I thought that was why you wanted me," I said. "Because I'd know what to do without being told."

"Oh, I did, Charlie. I do." He smiled quickly. "I don't at all doubt your ability and judgment. It's just that your procedure seemed rather daring—unorthodox—for such an extremely important matter."

"It seems that way here. Other things may seem that way to you. Here. What I have to go on is how things seem to me there. It's the only way I can work. If I had to ask you every time I wanted to make a move—well, I just couldn't do it. I—I'm not telling you where to get off, but—"

"Of course not," he nodded warmly. "After all, we're all intent on the same goal. We're all friends. We all have a great deal to gain ... or lose. You understand that part don't you, Charlie? Murph made it clear to you?"

"He did, but he didn't need to."

"Good. Now, about the time. You'll naturally be governed to an extent by the local factors, but the optimum date would be about a week before the trial. That will allow you to become firmly integrated into the life of the town, to allay the suspicion which always attaches to a stranger. Also, by disposing of Jake at the approximate time of the trial, the newspapers will have less to feed upon; there will only be one story instead of two."

"I'll try to handle it that way," I said.

"Fine. Splendid. Now ... Oh, yes"—his smile faded—"one more thing. Murph tells me that you pulled a knife on him. Actually stabbed him in the back of the neck."

"He shouldn't have been there in Peardale. You know he shouldn't, sir."

"Perhaps not. But that doesn't excuse your actions. I don't like that at all, Charlie." He shook his head sternly.

I looked down at the floor and kept my mouth shut.

"Would you mind waiting out in the reception room, Murph? I have quite a few things to say to Charlie."

"I don't mind," said Fruit Jar. "Take your time." And he sauntered out of the room, grinning.

The Man chuckled softly, and I looked up. He was holding out the knife to me.

"Could you use it again, Charlie?"

I stared at him—pretty blankly, I guess. He put the knife in my hand and closed my fingers around it.

"You killed his brother," he said. "Did you know that?"

"Christ no!" So that was it! "When—what—?"

"I don't know the details. It was in Detroit, 1942, I believe." Detroit, 1942. I tried to place him, and of course I couldn't. The name wouldn't have meant anything. And there'd been four—no, five in Detroit.

"I was disturbed by the way he felt toward you. I made a few inquiries . . . It won't do, Charlie. He's stupid and vengeful. He could blow things higher than a kite."

"Yeah," I said, "but . . . tonight?"

"Tonight. You haven't been here, Charlie. He was here to see me about a financial matter. I walked out to the car with him when he left. I saw him stop down there on the highway and pick up a hitchhiker. In fact, Toko and I both saw him."

He chuckled again.

"You understand my position, Charlie? I depended on Murph, and he failed me. How long would I last if I tolerated failure in the people I depend upon? I simply can't do it, Charlie, regardless of the person or cost. The whole system is based on swift punishment and prompt reward."

"I understand," I said.

"In that case—" He stood up. "How about another drink before you leave?"

"I guess not," I said. "I mean, no, thanks, sir."

He walked out to the car with Fruit Jar and me, walked between us with an arm around each of our shoulders. He shook hands with both of us, and stood at the side of the car talking a moment.

"A beautiful evening," he said, breathing in deep. "Smell that air, Charlie? I'll bet Arizona doesn't have anything finer than that."

"No, sir," I said.

"I know. There's no place like Arizona, is there? Well—" He gave Fruit Jar a playful punch on the arm. "Why don't I see more of you these days, hey? Not for business. Just a little quiet get-together?"

"Well, say"—Fruit Jar began to puff up—"just say the word, and—"

"We'll make it Sunday ... No, no I'll come to see you." He stepped back from the car beaming. "Sunday afternoon, say. I'll look forward to it—"

Fruit Jar drove away, so swelled up that he could hardly sit behind the wheel. And I wanted to burst out laughing. Or crying. Because he was a no-good son-of-a-bitch, but I felt sorry for him.

"I guess you got told off," he said, flicking a glance at me. "You're lucky he didn't do nothin' but eat you out."

"He told me off," I said. "I'm lucky."

"You think me'n him ain't like that? You think he didn't mean that about coming to see me?"

I shook my head. The Man would see him all right. He'd have a quiet get-together with him Sunday afternoon.

They'd have Fruit Jar embalmed by that time.

NINE

The trouble with killing is that it's so easy. You get to where you almost do it without thinking. You do it instead of thinking.

... I told Fruit Jar that I'd take the subway into town, and he drove me over near Queens Plaza. I had him pull up there in the shadows of the elevated, and I said, "I'm sorry as hell, Fruit Jar. Will you accept an apology?" And he was feeling good, so he stuck out his hand and said, "Sure, kid. Long as you put it that way, I—"

I jammed his right hand between my knees. I gripped the fingers of his left hand, bending them back, and I snapped the knife open.

"J-Jesus—" His eyes got wider and wider, and his mouth hung open like the mouth of a sack, and the slobber ran down his chin, thick and shiny. "W-whatcha d-doin' . . . whatcha . . . aaahhhhh . . ."

I gave it to him in the neck. I damned near carved his Adam's apple out. I took the big silk handkerchief out of his breast pocket, wiped my hands and the knife, and put the knife in his pocket. (That would give them something to think about.) Then I shoved him down on the floor of the car, and caught the train into town.

And I hadn't ridden to the next station before I saw what a fool I'd been.

Fruit Jar . . . He could have told me. I could have made him tell me—the thing that might mean the difference between my living and dying. And now he couldn't tell me.

His brother . . . HIS BROTHER HELL! I almost yelled it out; I think I did say it. But I was up in the front of the car by myself, and no one noticed. People hardly ever notice me. And maybe that's the reason I'm . . .

His brother . . . Detroit, 1942 . . . not sure of the details . . . Not sure! The Man wasn't sure! Christ Almighty. As if he'd have hauled Fruit Jar into this deal without knowing every damned last thing there was to know about him!

He'd hauled him in. Fruit Jar had been sitting pretty with no heat on him and a swell income, and The Man had hauled him in on something that could be very hot. He couldn't say no to The Man. He couldn't even let on that he didn't like it. But he didn't like it; he was sore as hell. And since he couldn't take it out on The Man, he'd taken it out on me.

That was the trouble. Just what I'd thought it was all along. It must have been that . . . I guessed.

His brother. Even if he'd had a brother, even if he'd had fifty-five brothers and I'd killed them all, he wouldn't have done anything about it. Not, anyway, until after I'd done my job. I should have known that. I did know it when I stopped to think. But The Man had shot me the line fast, and I wasn't thinking. Why think when it's so easy to kill?

The Man wanted me to believe that Fruit Jar had come down to Peardale that day on his own. He had to make me think that, or I'd think of another reason for Fruit Jar being there ... the real reason. Because he'd been sent. It might blow the job if I knew that. I might blow it and get away ... instead of getting what a guy always got for blowing or running out.

Fruit Jar wasn't very bright. He hadn't needed to be very bright for the job The Man had sent him to do—to deliver some dough, maybe, or maybe to throw in a good chill as the clincher to a deal. But he hadn't been even that bright. He'd missed connections somehow with the party he was supposed to see, and instead of beating it and trying again later he'd screwed around waiting. He'd gone out of his way to needle me.

I'd scratched him up with the knife, and he'd been a little worried when he took off for the city. He had a pretty good idea that he'd pulled a boner. And he should have known what The Man was like—when The Man was really sore at you, you never knew it—but he wasn't bright, like I've said, and ...

Or was it that way? Was I knocking myself out over nothing? Had The Man given me the straight dope?

He might have. A guy like me—well, he gets so used to looking around corners that he can't see in a straight line. The more true a thing is, the less he can believe it. The Man could have leveled with me. I was damned sure he hadn't, but he could have. He had—*he hadn't*. He hadn't—*he had:*

I didn't know. I couldn't be sure. And it wasn't The Man's fault and it wasn't Fruit Jar's. There was just one guy to blame, a stupid, dried-up jerk named Charles Bigger.

Big shot ... Bright boy ...

I could feel it. The hard glaze spreading over my eyes. I could feel my heart pounding—pounding like someone pounding on a door. Pounding like a scared kid locked in a closet. I could feel my lungs drawing up like fists, tight and hard and bloodless forcing the blood up into my brain.

There was a crowd of people waiting to get on the train at Times

Square. I went through them. I walked right through them. Giving it to them in the ribs and insteps. And no one said anything, so maybe they sensed what was in me and knew they were lucky. Because they were lucky.

There was a woman getting on, and I gave it to her in the breasts with my elbow, so hard she almost dropped the baby she was carrying. And she was lucky, too, but maybe the baby wasn't. Maybe it would have been better off down under the wheels. Everything ended.

Why not? Tell me why not.

I walked back to Forty-seventh Street, and somewhere along the way I bought a couple of newspapers. I rolled them up tight under my arm, and their hardness felt good to me. I rolled them tighter, and slapped them against the palm of my hand. And that felt good, too. I walked along, swinging them against my hand, swinging them like a club, the motions getting shorter and shorter, jerkier and jerkier, and . . .

"Temper, temper—"

Who was it that'd said that? . . . I grinned and it made my mouth hurt, and the hurt felt good . . . *"Temper, temper—"*

Sure. I knew. Have to watch the temper-temper. So I'd watch it. I liked to watch it. There was only one thing I'd like better . . . but everyone saw how lucky they were. And in a minute or two I'd be alone in my room. And it would be all right then.

I walked up the two flights of stairs. There was only one elevator and it was crowded, and I had enough sense to know that I'd better not get on it.

I climbed the stairs to the third floor, and walked down the corridor to the last room on the right. And I leaned against it a moment, panting and shaking. I leaned there, quivering like I'd been through a battle, and . . .

And I heard it. Heard the splashing and humming.

The quivering and the panting stopped. I turned the door knob. It was unlocked.

I stood in the doorway of the bathroom looking at her.

She was scooted down in the tub of suds, one arm raised up so she could soap it under the pit. She saw me, and she dropped the washcloth and let out a little squeal.

"C-Carl, honey! You scared me to death."

"What are you doing here?" I said.

"Why"—she tilted her head to one side, smiling at me lazily—"you don't recognize Mrs. Jack Smith?"

"What are you doing here?"

"Don't speak to me that way, Carl! After all—"

"What are you doing here?"

The smile began to shrink, pull in around the edges. "Don't be mad, honey. I—I—don't look at me like that. I know I was supposed to come in tomorrow, but—"

"Get out of there," I said.

"But you don't understand, honey! You see, sis and her boy friend drove out to Peardale, a-and I—it was perfectly natural for me to r-ride back to the city with them—No one could think there was anything w-wrong with—"

I didn't hear what she said. I didn't want to. I heard but I made myself not hear. I didn't want any explanations. I didn't want it to be all right. I was scared sick, so damned sick, and I was already sliding into Fruit Jar's shoes. And I couldn't pull back, I couldn't run. They were all watching and waiting, looking for the chance to trip me up.

All I could do was kill.

"Get out of there," I said.

I was slapping the newspapers into my palm. *"Get—slap—out—slap—of there—slap, slap, Get—slap . . ."*

Her face was as white as the suds, but she had guts. She forced the smile back, tilted her head again. "Now, honey. With you standing there? Why don't you go on and get in bed, and I'll—"

"Get-slap-out—slap—of there—slap, slap . . ."

"P-please, honey. I'm s-sorry if—I'll be sweet to you, honey. It's been more than a year, and h-honey you don't know—Y-you don't know how s-sweet—all the things I'll—"

She stopped talking. I had my hand knotted in her hair, and I was pulling her up out of the water. And she didn't try to pull away. She came up slowly, her neck, her breasts, the soapsuds sliding away from them like they didn't want to let go.

She stood up.

She stepped out of the tub.

She stood there on the bathmat, fighting with everything she had to fight with—offering it all to me. And she saw it wasn't enough. She knew it before I knew it myself.

She raised her arms very slowly—so slowly that they hardly seemed to move—and wrapped them around her head.

She whispered, "N-not in the face, Carl. J-just don't hit me in the—"

I flicked the newspapers across her stomach. Lightly. I flicked them across her breasts. I drew them back over my shoulder and—and held them there. Giving her a chance to yell or try to duck. Hoping she'd try it . . . and stop being lucky.

There were too many lucky people in the world.

"You're a pretty good actress," I said. "Tell me you're not an actress. Tell me you haven't been leading me on, acting hardboiled and easy-to-get so you could screw me up. Go on, tell me. Call me a liar."

She didn't say anything. She didn't even move.

I let the newspapers drop from my hand. I stumbled forward, and sat down on the toilet stool, and made myself start laughing. I whooped with laughter, I whooped and choked and sputtered, rocking back and forth on the stool. And it was as though a river were washing through me, washing away all the fear and craziness and worry. Leaving me clean and warm and relaxed.

It had always been that way. Once I could start laughing I was all right.

Then, I heard her snicker, and a moment later that husky saloon-at-midnight laugh. And she hunkered down in front of me, laughing, burying her head in my lap.

"Y-you crazy tough little bastard, you! You've taken ten years off my life."

"So now you're sixteen," I said. "I'm going to count on it."

"Crazy! What in the name of God got into you, anyway?" She raised her head, laughing, but looking a little worried. "It was all right to come in, wasn't it, as long as sis and—"

"Sure, it was all right," I said. "It was swell. I'm tickled to death you're here. I've just had a hell of a hard day and I wasn't expecting you, and—Let it go at that. Let me up off this toilet before I fall in."

"Yeah, but, honey—"

I tilted her chin up with my fist. "Yeah? We leave it at that or not?"

"Well—" She hesitated; and then she nodded quickly and jumped up. "Stinker! Toughie! Come on and I'll give you a drink."

She had a pint of whiskey in her overnight bag. She opened it after she'd slipped into her nightgown, and we sat cross-legged on the bed together, drinking and smoking and talking. There weren't many preliminaries to go through. I'd broken the ice but good there in the bathroom. She knew who I was now, if she hadn't had a damned good idea before. She knew why I was in Peardale. She knew why I'd had her come into the city. And it was okay with her.

"Little Bigger," she said, her eyes shining at me. "Little Bigger. Why, my God, honey, I've been hearing about you ever—"

"Okay," I said, "so I'm famous. Now just wipe it out of your head, and leave it wiped out."

"Sure, honey. Carl."

"I don't know how I'll do it. We'll have to work that out. Now, about the dough—"

She was smart there. She might have said fifteen or twenty grand. And I might have said yes. And then I might have thought, I might have passed the word along: The dame's hungry; maybe we'd better keep her quiet . . .

"Aw, honey—" She made a little face. "Let's not talk about it like I was doing it for—for *that*. We'll be together, won't we? Afterwards? And I know you're not the kind to be stingy."

"It'll be a long time afterwards," I said. "I'll have to stay there at least until summer. You can leave any time, of course, but I couldn't get together with you before summer."

"I can wait. Where would we go, honey? I mean after—"

"We'll work it out. That's no problem. You got money, there's always some place to go. Hell, we could live here or anywhere after a couple of years, when things cool off enough."

"You won't . . . You don't think I'm awful, do you, Carl?"

"How do I know? I haven't had you yet."

"You know what I mean, honey . . . You won't think I'd—I'd do the same thing to . . . You won't be afraid of me, honey? You won't think you have to—"

I tamped out my cigarette.

"Listen to me," I said. "Listening? Then get this. If I was afraid of you you wouldn't be here. Know what I mean?"

She nodded. "I know what you mean."

"Carl, honey . . ." That husky voice; it was like having cream poured over you. "Aren't you—?"

"Aren't I what?"

She gestured toward the light.

TEN

That next week is hard to tell about. So much happened. So many things that I couldn't understand—or, that I was afraid to understand. So many things that kept me worried and on edge or scared the living hell out of me.

I had time. I knew I had to take time. The Man didn't want the job done for at least ten weeks, so I should have been able to get my bearings and plan and take things kind of easy. But after that first week—hell, before the week was halfway over—I had an idea that what I and The Man wanted didn't make any difference.

This might be the first week, but I had a damned good idea that it wasn't far from the last one.

That was the week that Kendall really began to show his hand . . . At least, it seemed he was showing it.

That was the week that Jake tried to frame me.

It was the week he tried to kill me.

It was the week Fay and I began brawling.

It was the week Ruthie . . .

Jesus! Jesus God, that week! Even now—and what do I have to worry about now?—it rips the guts out of me to think about it.

But let's take things in order. Let's go back to the Friday before the week began, to Fay and me at the hotel.

. . . She's said it had been over a year since you know what, and I kind of think it must have been an understatement.

And, then, finally, she gave me a long good-night kiss, about fifty kisses rolled into one, and turned on her side. And a minute later she began to snore.

It wasn't a real snore, one of the buzzsaw variety. It was as though there was some small obstruction in her nose where the moisture kept gathering and cutting loose in a little *pop-crack* on about every tenth breath.

I lay there, stiff and tense, counting her breaths, wishing by God that it was a faucet, wanting to grab her by the nose and twist it off. I'd lie there counting her breaths, getting set for the little *pop-crack* that stabbed through me like a hot needle. And just when I had the damned thing about timed, she broke the rhythm on me. She started *pop-cracking* on a seven count, then a nine, and finally a twelve.

It went up from there to a point where she was taking twenty breaths before it came, and finally—God, it seemed like about forty-eight hours later!—finally it stopped.

Maybe you've slept with someone like that; tried to sleep. One of those people who can't get into dreamland good unless they're lying all over you. Well, she was that way. And now that she'd got that goddamned *pop-cracking* out of her system, she started in on the other, scrounging around in the bed. It was hell.

I tried to make myself sleep; but it was no dice. I got to thinking about a guy I'd met that time I skipped out of New York. I couldn't sleep, so I began thinking.

I'd been afraid to show myself on a train or bus or plane, so I'd started hitchhiking up toward Connecticut. I planned on getting up near the Canadian border, where I could jump across fast if I had to, and swinging west from there. Well, this guy picked me up, and he had a good car, and I knew he must have dough on him. But ... well, it doesn't make sense the way it turned out; *he* didn't make sense, like you ordinarily think of a guy making it. Anyway ...

He was a writer, only he didn't call himself that. He called himself a hockey peddler. "You notice that smell?" he said, "I just got through dumping a load of crap in New York, and I ain't had time to get fumigated." All I could smell was the whiz he'd been drinking. He went on talking, not at all grammatical like you might expect a writer to, and he was funny as hell.

He said he had a farm up in Vermont, and all he grew on it was the more interesting portions of the female anatomy. And he never laughed or cracked a smile, and the way he told about it he almost made you believe it. "I fertilize them with wild goat manure," he said. "The goats are tame to begin with, but they soon go wild. The stench, you know. I feed them on the finest grade grain alcohol, and they have their own private cesspool to bathe in. But nothing does any good. You should see them at night when they stand on their heads, howling."

I grinned, wondering why I didn't give it to him. "I didn't know goats howled," I said.

"They do if they're wild enough," he said.

"Is that all you grow?" I said. "You don't have bodies on any of— of those things?"

"Jesus Christ!" He turned on me like I'd called him a dirty name. "Ain't I got things tough enough as it is? Even butts and breasts are becoming a drug on the market. About all there's any demand for any more is you know what." He passed me the bottle, and had a drink himself, and he calmed down a little. "Oh, I used to grow other things," he said. "Bodies. Faces. Eyes. Expressions. Brains. I grew them in a three-dollar-a-week room down on Fourteenth Street and I ate aspirin when I couldn't raise the dough for a hamburger. And every now and then some lordly book publisher would come down and reap my crop and package it at two-fifty a copy, and, lo and behold, if I praised him mightily and never suggested that he was a member of the Jukes family in disguise, he would spend three or four dollars on advertising and the sales of the book would swell to a total of nine hundred copies and he would give me ten per cent of the proceeds ... when he got around to it." He spat out the window and took another drink. "How about driving a while?"

I slid over him, over behind the wheel, and his hands slid over me. "Let's see the shiv," he said.

"The what?"

"The pig-sticker, the switchblade, the knife, for Christ's sake. Don't you understand English? You ain't a publisher, are you?"

I gave it to him. I didn't know what the hell else to do. He tested the blade with his thumb. Then he opened the pocket of the car, fumbled around inside and brought out a little whetstone.

"Christ," he said, drawing the blade back and forth across it. "You ought to keep this thing sharp. You can't do any good with a goddamn hoe like this. I'd sooner try to cut a guy's throat with a bed slat ... Well"—he handed it back to me—"that's the best I can do. Just don't use it for nothing but belly work and it may be all right."

"Now, look," I said. "What—what—"

"You look," he said. He reached over and took the Lueger out of my belt. He held it down under the dashlight and looked at it. "Well, it ain't too bad," he said. "But what you really need is a rod like this." And he reached into the pocket again and took out a .32 Colt automatic. "Like to try it? Come on and try it on me. Stop the car and try them both."

He shoved them at me, reaching for the switch key, and—and, hell, I don't know what I said.

Finally, he laughed—different from the way he'd laughed before, more friendly—and put the Lueger back in my belt and the Colt back into the car pocket.

"Just not much sense to it, is there?" he said. "How far you want to ride?"

"As far as I can," I said.

"Swell. That'll be Vermont. We'll have time to talk."

We went straight on through, taking turns about driving and going in places for coffee and sandwiches, and most of the time he was talking or I was. Not about ourselves, nothing personal, I mean. He wasn't nosy. Just about books and life and religion, and things like that. And everything he said was so kind of off-trail I was sure I could remember it, but somehow later on it all seemed to boil down pretty well to just one thing.

"Sure there's a hell..." I could hear him saying it now, now, as I lay here in bed with her breath in my face, and her body squashed against me ... *"It is the drab desert where the sun sheds neither warmth nor light and Habit force-feeds senile Desire. It is the place where mortal Want dwells with immortal Necessity, and the night becomes hideous with the groans of one and the ecstatic shrieks of the other. Yes, there is a hell, my boy, and you do not have to dig for it ..."*

When I finally left him, he gave me a hundred and ninety-three dollars, everything he had in his wallet except a ten-spot. And I never saw him again, I don't even know his name.

Fay started snoring again.

I got the whiskey bottle and my cigarettes, and went into the bathroom. I closed the door, and sat down on the stool. And I must have sat there two or three hours, smoking and sipping whiskey and thinking.

I wondered what had ever happened to that guy, whether he was still in Vermont growing those things. I thought about what he'd said about hell, and it had never meant more to me than it did right now.

I wasn't an old man by a hell of a long ways, but I got to wondering whether the way I felt had anything to do with getting older. And that led into wondering how old I really was, anyway, because I didn't know.

About all I had to go on was what my mother told me, and she'd told me one thing one time, and another thing another time. I doubt that she really knew, offhand. She might have figured it out, but with all the kids she'd had she didn't get much figuring done. So . . .

I tried to dope it out, a screwy thing like that. I added up and subtracted and tried to remember back to certain times and places, and all I got out of it was a headache.

I'd always been small. Except for those few years in Arizona, it seemed like I'd always been living on the ragged edge.

I thought way back, and if things had ever been very much different or I'd ever been very much different, I couldn't remember when it was.

I sipped and smoked and thought, and finally I caught myself nodding.

I went back into the bedroom.

She was sleeping in a kind of loose ball, now, with her rear end way over on one side of the bed and her knees on the other. That left some space at the foot of the bed, so I lay down across that.

I woke up with her feet on my chest, feeling like my ribs had been caved in. It was nine o'clock. I'd had less than four hours' sleep. But I knew I wasn't going to get any more, so I slid out from under her and got up.

I went to the toilet and took a bath, being as quiet about it as I could. I was standing in front of the bathroom mirror, fitting the contact lenses into place, when I saw her looking in the doorway.

She didn't know that I saw her. It's funny how people will watch you in a mirror without thinking that you're bound to be watching them. She was looking at the lower part of my face, my mouth, and I saw her grimace. Then, she caught herself, catching on to the fact, I guess, that I might be able to see her. She moved back into the bedroom, waited a moment, and headed for the door again, making enough noise for me to know that she was up.

I slipped my teeth into place. I guess my mouth did look bad without them—kind of like it belonged in another location. But I didn't give a damn whether she liked it or not.

She came in yawning, drowsily scratching her head with both hands. "Gosh, honey," she said. "What'd you get up so early for? I was sleeping sooo-ahh—'scuse me—so good."

"It's after nine," I said. "I figured I'd been in bed long enough."

"Well, I hadn't. You woke me up with all your banging around."

"Maybe I'd better go stand in the corner."

Her eyes flashed. Then she laughed, half irritably. "Grouchy. You don't have to snap me up on everything. Now, get out of here and let me take a bath."

I got out, and let her. I dressed while she bathed and started brushing her teeth—washing her mouth out a thousand and fifty times, it sounded like, gargling and spitting and hacking. I began getting sick at my stomach; rather, I got sicker than I already was. I threw down the rest of the whiskey fast, and that helped. I picked up the phone and ordered breakfast and another pint. And I knew how bad the whiz was for me—I'd been told not to drink it at all—but I have to have it.

She was still horsing around in the bathroom when the waiter came. I got down another fast drink; then, I gulped and coughed and a whole mouthful of blood came up in my handkerchief.

I raised the bottle again. I lowered it, holding my breath, swallowing as rapidly as I could. And there wasn't any blood that time—none came up—but I knew it was there.

I'd already been damned sick in front of her once. If I was sick very much; if she thought I might be on the way down ... down like Jake ...

ELEVEN

She came out of the bathroom feeling a lot better than when she
went in, and with a fresh half pint of whiskey in me I wasn't feeling
so bad myself. We ate all the breakfast, with her helping out quite a
bit on my share. I lighted cigarettes for us, and she lay back on the
pillows.

"Well?" she crinkled her eyes at me.

"Well, what?" I said.

"How was it?"

"Best coffee I ever drank," I said.

"Stinker!" She let out with that guffaw again. I was getting to
where I waited for that, too, like I'd waited for her snoring. "Mmm?"
she said. "I do if you do. Want to come back to bed with mama?"

"Look, baby," I said. "I'm sorry as hell, but—well, you'll have to
be starting back."

"Huh!" She sat up. "Aw, now, honey! You said—"

"I said we'd stay overnight. We've done it. It doesn't make any
difference whether—"

"It does too make a difference! You haven't been stuck in that
God-forsaken hole as long as I have! I ... Why don't we do it like
we planned, honey? I can go back tonight, and you can come
tomorrow ... that'll give us a whole day together. Or I can stay—I'll
go over and stay with sis tonight—and come tomorrow, and you
can—"

"Look, baby; look, Fay," I said. "I guess I hadn't thought the thing
through. I've had plenty of things to think about, and I couldn't see
that it mattered much whether—"

"Of course, it matters! Why wouldn't it matter?"

"You've got to go back," I said. "Now. Or I'll start back and you
can come later on in the day. I can't stay at the house overnight unless
you're there. I've got to have you there to yes me, in case something
pops with Jake. If he should get out of line like he did the first
night—"

"Pooh! For all we know he may not even come home."

"That's another thing. He's got to start staying there. All the time.

You'll have to see that he does. He can't just be there on the one night that something happens to him."

"Hell!" She stamped out her cigarette angrily, and reached for the bottle. "Just when I think I'm going to ... Well, gosh, honey. You could go back tomorrow, and I could go back tonight. Why wouldn't that be all right?"

"I'm afraid of it. I'm not supposed to have much dough. It doesn't look right for me to take damned near three days to pick up a suit."

She slammed the whiskey bottle down angrily.

"I'm sorry as hell, Fay," I said.

She didn't say anything.

"We just can't take chances now. We've got too much to lose—" I went on talking and explaining and apologizing; and I knew she'd better snap out of it fast or she wouldn't be able to get back to Peardale.

Finally, she turned back around; maybe she noticed the tightening of my voice. "All right, honey," she sighed, half pouting. "If that's the way it is, why that's the way it is."

"Fine. That's my baby," I said. "We'll have our good times. Just you and me and thirty grand; maybe five or ten more if it's an A-1 job."

"Oh, I know, Carl," her smile was back. "It'll be wonderful. And I'm awfully sorry if I—I was just kind of disappointed and—"

"That's okay," I said.

She wanted me to go back to Peardale first. She wanted to laze around a while, and take her time about dressing. I said it would be all right. Just so she showed before night.

We chewed the fat a while longer; just talking without saying much. After a while, she said, "Mmmmm, honey?" and held out her arms to me; and I knew I couldn't do it. Not so soon, not now. God, Jesus, I knew I couldn't do it.

But I did!

I struggled and strained, aching clear down to my toenails; and I kept my eyes closed, afraid to let her see what she might see in them, and ... *and I was in that drab desert where the sun shed neither heat nor light, and* ...

*

... What about that afterwards, anyway? If there was an after-wards. What about her?

I stared out the dirty window of the Long Island train, half dozing, my mind wandering around and around and drifting back to her. What about her?

She was stacked. She was pretty. She was just about everything you could want in a woman—as long as you were on top or you looked like you might be on top.

But I couldn't see it, the one big long party which was what it would be like with her. I couldn't see it, and couldn't take it. What I wanted was ... well, I wasn't sure but it wasn't that. Just to be by myself. Maybe with someone like—well, like Ruthie—someone I could be myself around.

Ruth. Fay. Fay, Ruth. Or what? I didn't know what I wanted. I wasn't even real sure about what I didn't want. I hadn't wanted to be dragged in on this mess, but I had to admit I'd been getting pretty fed up out there in Arizona. I'd kept quiet about it, but I'd had more than one babe in my shack. Hell, the last month, I'd had two or three a week, a different one each time. And they were all okay, I guess, they all had plenty on the ball. But somehow none of them seemed to be it—whatever it was I wanted.

Whatever it was I wanted.

My eyes drifted shut, and stayed shut. The Man would probably have something to say about Fay. He might see a spot where he could use her again, or he might decide that she was a bad risk. He'd talk to me about it, of course. And if I wanted her, and was responsible for her ...

I didn't know. I didn't want her now, her or anyone else. But that was natural enough. Tomorrow, the next day ... afterwards? I didn't know.

My head fell over against the window, and I went to sleep.

It was hours later when I woke up.

I was way the hell out to the end of the line, and the conductor was shaking me.

Somehow I managed to keep from punching the stupid bastard in the face. I paid the extra fare, plus the fare back to Peardale. It was still early afternoon. I could still get back to Peardale well ahead of her.

I went to the john and washed my face. I came back to my seat, studying the minute hand on my watch, wondering what the hell was holding us up. And then I glanced out the window, and started cursing.

Mr. Stupid, the conductor, who should have picked up my seat check and put me off at Peardale—he and all the other trainmen were sauntering up the street together. Taking their own sweet time about it. Shoving and grab-assing with each other, and braying like a bunch of mules.

They turned in at a restaurant.

They stayed in there, doing what God only knows, because they couldn't have been eating that long. They must have stayed in the place two hours.

Finally, when I was just about ready to go up into the locomotive and drive off by myself, they got through doing whatever they were doing and sauntered back to the station again. They got there, eventually, back to the station. But, of course, they didn't climb on the damned train and get going.

The had to stand around on the station platform, gabbing and picking their teeth.

I cursed them to myself, calling them every dirty name I could think of. They were trying to screw me up.

They broke it up at last, and began climbing on the train.

It was dark when we got into Peardale. A train from the city was just pulling out. I looked through the station door and saw a taxi on the other side—the only taxi there.

He swung the door open, and I climbed in. And—but I guess I don't need to tell you. I'd tried to be so damned careful, yet here she was, here we were, riding home together.

She gave me a startled, half-scared look. I said, "Why, hello, Mrs. Winroy. Just come out from New York?"

"Y-yes." She bobbed her head. "Did—did you?"

I laughed. It sounded as hollow as that conductor's head. "Not exactly. I left the city this morning but I fell asleep on the train. They carried me out to the end of the line, and I'm just now getting back."

"Well," she said. Just well. But the way she said it, she was saying a whole lot more.

"I was all worn out," I said. "A friend I stayed with in New York snored all night, and I didn't get much sleep."

She turned her head sharply, glaring at me. Then she bit her lip, and I heard a sound that was halfway between a snicker and a snort.

We reached the house. She went on inside, and I paid off the driver and went across the street to the bar.

I drank two double shots. Then I ordered a ham and cheese sandwich and a bottle of ale, and sat down in one of the booths. I was easing down a little. It was a stupid mixup, but it was just one, and it would be hard for anyone to make anything out of it. Anyway, it was done, and there wasn't any use worrying.

I ordered another ale, easing my nerves down, arguing away the worry. I almost convinced myself that it had been a good break. It could be, if you looked at it in the right way. Because any damned fool ought to know that we wouldn't be goofy enough to lay up in town, and then ride home together.

I finished the ale, started to order a third one, and decided against it. I'd had enough. More than enough. Or I never would have. You take just so much from the bottle, and then you stop taking. From then on you're putting.

I picked up my suit box and crossed the street to the house. Half hoping that Jake was on hand.

He was.

He and Fay and Kendall were all in the living room together, and she was laughing and talking a mile a minute.

I went in, giving them a nod and a hello as I headed for the stairs. Fay turned and called to me.

"Come in, Mr. Bigelow. I was just telling about your train ride—how you went to sleep and rode to the end of the line. What did you think when you woke up?"

"I thought I'd better start carrying an alarm clock," I said.

Kendall chuckled. "That reminds me of an occasion several years ago when—"

"Excuse me"—Fay cut in on him—"Jake—"

He was bent forward in his chair, staring at the floor, his big bony hands folded across each other.

"Jake ... Just a moment, Mr. Bigelow. My husband wants to apologize to you."

"That's not necessary," I said. "I—"

"I know. But he wants to ... don't you, Jake? He knows he made a very foolish mistake, and he wants to apologize for it."

"That's right," Kendall nodded primly. "I'm sure Mr. Winroy is anxious to rectify any misunderstandings which—uh—can be rectified."

Jake's head came up suddenly, "Oh, yeah?" he snarled. "Who pulled your chain, grandpa?"

Kendall looked down into the bowl of his pipe. "Your grand-parent?" he said, musingly. "I believe that is just about the foulest name anyone ever called me."

Jake blinked stupidly. Then it registered on him, and he dragged the back of his hand across his mouth like he'd been slapped. All the fight in him, the little he had left, went away again. He looked from Kendall to Fay and then, finally, at me. And I guess mine was about the friendliest face there.

He got up and sagged toward me, a big drained-empty sack of guts. He came toward me, holding out his hand, trying to work up a smile, the sly, sick look of a beaten dog on his face.

And I couldn't help feeling sorry for him, but the flesh crawled on the back of my neck. He'd had too much. He was too beaten. When they get that far gone, you'd better get in the final licks fast.

"S-sorry, lad. Musta had one too many. No hard feelings?" I said it was okay, but he didn't hear me. He clung to my hand, turning to look at Fay. He stared, frowned puzzledly, then turned back to me again. "Glad to have you here. Anything I can do I—I—I—"

That was as much of his speech as he could remember. He dropped my hand, and looked at her again. She nodded briskly, took him by the arm, and led him out of the room.

They went out to the porch, and the door didn't quite close; and I heard her say, "Now, you'd better not disappoint me, Jake. I've had just about—"

Kendall pushed himself up out of his chair. "Well, Mr. Bigelow. You look rather tired if I may say so."

"I am," I said. "I think I'll turn in."

"Excellent. I was just about to suggest it. Can't have you getting sick at a time like this, can we?"

"At a time like this," I said. "How do you mean?"

"Why"—his eyebrows went up a trifle—"just when you're on the threshold of a new life. Your schooling and all. I feel that great things are in store for you here if you can just keep your original objective in mind, keep forging ahead toward it despite divertissements of the moment."

"That's the secret of your success, huh?" I said.

And he colored a little but he smiled, eyes twinkling. "That, I believe, is what might be called leaving one's self wide open. The obvious retort—if I cared to stoop to it—would be an inquiry as to the secret of *your* success."

We said good night, and he went back to the bakery. I started up the stairs.

Fay had seen Jake off for town or wherever he was going, and was out in the kitchen with Ruth. I stood at the foot of the stairs a moment, listening to her lay down the law in that husky, what-are-you-waiting-on voice. Then I cleared my throat loudly, and went on up to my room.

About five minutes later, Fay came in.

She said there wasn't a thing to worry about. Kendall and Jake had swallowed the story whole.

"And I'd know if they hadn't, honey. I was watching, believe you me. They didn't suspect a thing."

She was feeling pretty proud of herself. I told her she'd done swell. "Where's Jake gone?"

"To the liquor store. He's going to get a fifth of wine, and he'll probably pick up a couple of drinks in a bar. He damned sure won't get any more than that. I got all his money away from him but two dollars."

"Swell," I said. "That's my baby."

"Mmmmm? Even if I do snore?"

"Ahhh, I was kidding. I was sore about that goddamned train ride."

'We-el, just so you're sorry—" She leaned against me.

I gave her a poke and a kiss, and pushed her away. "Better beat it, now, baby."

"I know. I'm just as anxious to be careful as you are, honey." She reached for the doorknob, then she clapped her hand over her mouth suddenly, stifling a giggle. "Oh, Carl! There's something I just have to tell you."

"Yeah?" I said. "Don't take too long about it."

"You'll die laughing. I don't know why I didn't see it before, but she's just not the kind of person you pay much attention to and—And of course it may have just happened. I—You just won't believe it, honey! It's just so—"

"That is funny," I said. "Better not tell me any more or I'll be laughing all night."

"Stinker! Just for that . . . It's Ruthie, honey. Would you believe it? I swear to God someone's gotten to her."

TWELVE

I laughed. I did a pretty good job of it, considering. "No fooling. How did she happen to tell you about it?"

"She didn't, silly. You can see it. It sticks out all over her."

"That should be something to see," I said.

"Crazy!" She buried her head against my chest, giggling. "B-but—but, honestly, Carl! Who in the world would want to . . . Carl! I bet I know."

"Yeah?" I said. "I mean, you do?"

"Why, of course. It couldn't be anyone else. She went home last night. I'll bet it's someone in her own family."

I swallowed. I was relieved, in a way, but I wished she hadn't said it. I felt shamed, embarrassed.

"They're . . . they're that kind of people?"

"They're trash. You ought to see how they live! They've got about fourteen kids, and— "

"Maybe I ought to tell you," I said. "There were fourteen children in my family."

"Oh—" She hesitated, uncomfortably. "Well. Of course, I didn't mean that—that—"

"Sure. Forget it," I said.

"But it isn't the same, Carl. You didn't just put up with it like they do. You did something about it."

"Well," I said. "Isn't she doing something?"

"Oh, pooh! What good will it do her if she does manage to squeeze through college? Who's going to give *her* a job that's worth having?"

I shook my head. Ruthie looked pretty good to me, but she'd just about have to. She was me, in a way, and I was seeing myself in her.

"... you know I'm right, Carl. She's trash, stupid, like all the rest of her family. If she really had any brains or guts, she'd—she'd— Well, she'd do *something*!"

"Well, maybe she's working on it now. Maybe she's going to grow herself a gang of kids and put them all out to picking cotton."

"All right," she laughed good-naturedly. "I guess my own family didn't amount to much, for that matter, but I did *do*—"

"You'd better start doing something else," I said, "before someone catches you in here."

She kissed me, patted me quickly on the cheek and slipped out of the room.

I went to bed.

It was only a little after nine when I turned in, and I couldn't have slept better if I hadn't had a worry in the world. I woke at six with nine good hours under my belt, the best night's sleep I'd had since I left Arizona. I had a hangover, but nothing bad. I coughed and spit blood, but nothing bad. That rest had done me a world of good.

Well, anyway, I'd had that much.

I smoked a couple of cigarettes, wondering what I'd better do. Whether I'd better get up and get out on the town—stay away from the house until the others were up. Or whether I should just stay here in my room until they were up.

It would have to be one way or another. Otherwise, unless I missed my guess, I'd have Ruthie on my neck. And all Ruthie was getting from me, from now on, was the cold shoulder. I wasn't going to get caught alone with her. Any time I saw her, there'd be someone else around. Pretty soon she'd get the idea, and then maybe it would be safe to be friendly with her ... just friendly.

... I found a little lunchroom open down near the railroad station and got some coffee. Afterwards, I sauntered back up the street.

It was Sunday—somehow that fact kept slipping in and out of my mind. You know how that is, maybe, when a lot's been happening to you, and you lay off on days you're used to working and so on. The church bells were starting to ring, booming out over the town. Practically every business house was closed; nothing was open but a few cigar stands, lunch counters and the like. I began to feel kind of conspicuous.

I stopped at an intersection to let a car go past. But instead of passing it pulled even with me and stopped.

Sheriff Summers rolled the window down and leaned out.

"Hey, there, young feller. Give you a lift?"

He was all duked out in a hard-boiled collar and a blue serge suit. There was a hatchet-faced dame with him—a dame in a stiff black satin dress and a hat that looked like a lamp shade. I took off my hat and smiled at her, wondering why some dairy hadn't snapped her up to sour their cream for them.

"What about the lift?" he said, shaking hands. "'Spect you're headin' for church, eh? Glad to take you t' any one you say."

"Well," I hesitated. "As a matter of fact, I'm not a—I've never affiliated—"

"Just lookin' around, huh? Well, come on and go with us."

I went around to the other side, and he started to open the front door. I opened the back door, and climbed in ... How dumb can you be anyway? How little can you know about women? Muss 'em up when they've got their clothes off, that's my motto. When they're dressed up—maybe in the only good thing they've got—give them room.

He drove on. I cleared my throat. "I don't believe I've met your— is it your daughter, sheriff?"

"Huh?" He looked up into the rear-view mirror, startled. Then, he gave her a poke in the ribs with his elbow. "You hear that, Bessie? He thinks you're my daughter."

"And who am I, pray tell?"

"Why—uh—my wife."

"Thank you. I was afraid you'd forgotten."

She half turned in the seat, brushing at the place where he'd poked her, and the way she looked then she wouldn't have stood a chance at that milk-souring job.

"Thank you for the compliment, young man. It's about the first one I've had since Bill came home from the war. World War One, that is."

"Aw, now, Bessie. I ain't that—"

"Be quiet. Mr. Bigelow and I are thoroughly disgusted with you, aren't we, Mr. Bigelow? There is nothing he can say that we care to hear."

"Not a thing," I grinned. "That's an awfully pretty hat you're wearing, Mrs. Summers."

"Do you hear that, Your Highness? Did you hear what this *gentleman* said about my hat?"

"Well, heck, Bessie. It does look kinda of like a lamp—"

"Hush. Just be quiet, and Mr. Bigelow and I will try to ignore you."

They kept it up all the way to church, and practically up to the door. And they seemed to enjoy it in a way, but I wondered if they wouldn't have enjoyed some other way better. I mean, arguing is arguing, and quarreling is quarreling, and it's still that regardless of how you laugh and kid around about it. You don't do it unless something is eating on you. You don't do it when things are like they should be.

I opened the car door for her and helped her out ... and she looked at him. I took her elbow and helped her up the steps of the church ... and she looked at him. I stood aside at the door and let her go in first ... and she looked at him.

We stayed through Sunday school and church, and you probably know a lot more about those things than I do, so I won't describe them to you. It was better than wandering around the street. It was as good a way as any of killing the morning. I felt safe and peaceful, like a guy has to feel if his brain is going to work at its best. I sang and prayed and listened to the sermon—just sort of letting my mind wander. Letting it go where it wanted to. And by the time church was over, I had it. I'd figured out how I was going to kill Jake Winroy.

Not completely, you understand. There were a few details to iron out, my alibi and setting him up and so on. But I knew they'd come to me.

Mrs. Summers glanced at me as we went back up the aisle together. "Well, young man. You're looking very happy."

"I'm glad you let me come with you," I said. "It's done me a lot of good."

They stopped at the door to shake hands with the minister, and she introduced me. I told him his sermon had been very inspiring ... which it was. I'd doped out the plan for Jake while he was spieling.

We started on out to the car, she and I walking together and the sheriff trailing along behind.

"I was wondering, Mr. Big—Oh, I think I'll call you Carl. If you don't mind."

"I wish you would," I said. "What were you wondering, Mrs. Summers?"

"I was going to ask you if—"We'd reached the curb, and she turned and motioned impatiently. "Oh, do come on, Bill. You're slower than molasses in January. I was about to ask Carl to come home to dinner with us."

"Yeah?" he said. "How come? I mean—uh—you were?"

Her mouth tightened. Untightened. I think she was just about to open up on him when he headed her off.

"Well, fine, great!" He clapped me on the back. "Tickled to death to have you, son. Meant to ask you myself."

He hadn't meant to. He didn't even halfway like the idea. He could take me to church, sure. But to take me into his home—pal up with me—when there was any kind of a chance that I might mean trouble ...

There *was* something about me that bothered him. There was something he wasn't quite satisfied about.

"Thanks very much," I said. "I don't think I'd better today. They're expecting me at the house, and I've got a lot of things to get ready for school and—and all."

"Uh-huh. Sure," he nodded. "Well, if you can't make it, you can't ... guess we'll have to eat by ourselves, Bessie."

"You," she said. "I'll swear, Bill Summers, I—I—!"

"Now, what'd I do? I asked him, didn't I? You heard him say he couldn't come. Didn't I"—he turned to me—"Didn't you say you couldn't come?"

"Hush. You're impossible. Utterly impossible ... Carl, I'd ask you to let us drive you home, but I imagine His Highness would find some way to keep you from accepting."

"Now, I wouldn't neither! Heck, I—why'd I do a thing like that?"

"Why do you do anything, pray tell?"

It was getting embarrassing. I put a stop to it. I said I honestly couldn't take dinner with them today—maybe some other time—but I would appreciate a ride home.

Neither of them said anything until we reached the house. Then, while I was thanking them and saying good morning, he squinted at the coupé pulled in at the gutter.

"Hey," he frowned, "that's Doc Dodson's car, ain't it? You got some sick folks here, son?"

"Not that I know of," I said. "I left the house before anyone was up this morning."

"Must be someone sick. Doc wouldn't be payin' no social calls on the Winroys. Wonder who it could be?"

"Why don't you go in and ask?" Mrs. Summers glared at him. "Shake hands with all of them. Call them all by their first names. Ask about their families. Never mind about *me*, or how *I*—"

He jammed the car into gear, cutting her off. "I'm goin', ain't I? Doggone it, can't you see I'm goin'? . . . son, I'm—I—"

I hopped out fast. He drove off, the engine roaring, and I went up the walk and into the house.

Fay met me in the hall. She was breathless. The reddish-brown eyes blazed with fear against the dead white of her face. I looked past her, into the dining room.

Ruth was in there. Ruth and Kendall and Jake and a potbellied, bald-headed little guy I knew was a doctor. Jake was sprawled on the floor on his back, and the doctor was stooped down over him, holding a stethoscope to his chest.

Fay whispered to me, her lips barely moving.

"His wine. Poisoned. Doped. Did you—?"

THIRTEEN

I pushed past her, flipping my fist against her groin. God-dammit, of course she was scared, but she didn't need to hang a sign on me. She followed me into the dining room and stood beside me. I moved away from her, over between Kendall and Ruth.

Jake's eyes were closed. He was mumbling, rolling his head from side to side. The doc leaned back, letting the stethoscope swing free, and frowned down at him.

He picked up Jake's wrist and felt the pulse. He let the hand drop back to the floor.

"Hold still," he said curtly.

"... Slee-py ... s-so—" Jake kept on rolling his head, breathing in great shuddering breaths "... S-save me .. I-lookit ... w-wine—"

"Stop that! Stop it this minute!" The doctor gripped him by the head with one hand. "Hold still!"

Jake held still. He had to. The way the doc was gripping him, he might have got his scalp peeled off.

The doctor pulled back first one eyelid, then, the other. He stood up, brushing at the knees of his pants, and nodded to Kendall.

"You tell me how this happened, Phil?"

"Why, yes, Doc." Kendall took the pipe out of his mouth. "I don't know as I can add anything to what Mrs. Winroy—"

"Mrs. Winroy was somewhat excited. You tell me."

"Well, let's see. She and I—Mrs. Winroy and I—were in the living room, reading the Sunday papers, and Miss Dorne was in the kitchen preparing dinner. Isn't that right, Ruth?"

"Y-yes, sir."

"Never mind all that. Just the essentials." The doctor glanced impatiently at his watch. "I can't spend all morning on—on—You heard Winroy coming down the stairs, making plenty of noise about it. Go on."

"I got up. We both got up, I believe. We supposed that—uh—he was just—"

"Drunk. Go on."

"We went out into the hall and he staggered past us mumbling that he'd been doped—that the wine had been doped, or something of the kind. His speech was very unclear. He came into the dining room and collapsed, and we—Mrs. Winroy—called—"

"He was carrying the wine bottle with him, eh? Very carefully corked?" The doctor's face was flushed; the red seemed to go clear up into his eyes. "Let me see it again."

Kendall took the bottle from the table and handed it to him. He sniffed it, tasted it, took a man-size swallow of it. He brushed his mouth sourly, glancing at Fay.

"He take sleeping pills? How many—how often?"

"I—I don't kn-know, doctor."

"Know how many he has? Whether any great number is missing?"

"No, I—" Fay shook her head "—I brought him some back from the city, but I don't know how many he had—"

"Did, eh? Have a prescription? No? Know that's illegal? Never mind. No bearing here."

"He's n-not—?"

The doctor grunted. He dug the toe of his shoe into Jake's ribs. "Cut it out. Stop it. Get up from there," he snapped.

Jake's eyes wavered open. "S-something . . . in the—"

"There's something in it, all right. Alcohol. Twenty per cent by volume."

He reached for his medicine kit, nodding grimly at Fay. "Nothing wrong with him. Not a thing in the world. Throw a pail of water on him if he doesn't get up."

"But, I—" Her face was red, too, now. Even redder than his. "Why . . . I just don't understand—"

"Exhibitionism. Wants attention, sympathy. They hit that stuff long enough they don't make much sense . . . No, he's not drunk. Hasn't had enough."

Fay grimaced, trying to smile. "I'm terribly sorry, doctor. I'll . . . if you'll send a bill—"

"I will. And don't call me again, understand? I have sick people to take care of."

He slapped his hat on his head, shook hands with Kendall and slammed out of the house.

Jake sat up. He pushed himself up to his feet, stood weaving, his head sagged, staring at the floor.

"Ruth"—Fay kept her eyes on him—"haven't you some work to do?"

"I—Yes, ma'am." Ruth pivoted on the crutch and scuttled back to the kitchen.

"Jake." Fay moved toward him slowly. "Jake. Look at me!"

"Somethin' . . . something wrong," he mumbled.

"Oh." She said hoarsely. "Something was wrong, huh? Something wrong. You—you frightened us all half to death—make a big scene here on Sunday—and a-and let me in for a bawling out from that damned snotty Dodson, and—and something's wrong! Is that all you've got to say? Look at me, Jake Winroy!"

He kept his eyes on her feet, mumbling that something was wrong. Moving backward as she came toward him.

He reached the door, and there, as he had that first night, he whirled and made a break for it. I heard him trip and stumble on the steps, but he didn't fall as he had the other time. He got through the gate, and glancing out the window I saw him heading for town at his sagging, loping walk.

Fay turned back toward us. Her lips were trembling, her hands clenching and unclenching. She shrugged—or tried to. She tried to smile. She said, "Well, I g-guess that's th-tha—" Then she sank down into a chair at the table, and buried her head in her arms.

Kendall touched me on the elbow and we went out in the hall together. "Not the most pleasant way to spend the Sabbath, eh? You look like you might be able to use a small libation, Mr Bigelow."

"I could," I said. "It wouldn't even have to be small."

"So? You will do me the honor, then."

We crossed the street to the bar. There were quite a few people in the place, but the bartender came around from behind the counter fast and showed us to a booth.

He'd never done that for me. I'd never seen him do it for anyone else. Kendall seemed to take it as a matter of course. I wondered about it—this and the way the doctor had kind of kowtowed to him—and I guess I showed it.

"I've lived here the better part of my life, Mr. Bigelow. Or should I say the larger part of it? I grew up with many of these people. I taught school to many."

The bartender brought our drinks, double Scotches. Kendall

rocked the ice in his glass, looked up at me slowly. His eyes were twinkling.

"Odd about Winroy, isn't it? Now, he above all people should know that if you *had* been sent here to kill him—*if* you had, Mr. Bigelow—"

"That's not a very pleasant if," I said.

"Sorry. Thoughtless of me. Make it a hypothetical person, then. What good would it do for Winroy to dispose of him? He'd only be postponing the inevitable."

"Yeah?" I said. "I guess I don't know much about those things."

"But it's so elementary! They—his former associates, that is— would be even more determined, if anything. Suppose the officers charged with executing our laws allowed a malefactor to go unpunished, merely because punishment was difficult or dangerous to render him. We'd have chaos, Mr. Bigelow. It simply couldn't be allowed."

I raised my glass and took a drink. "I guess you're right," I said. "It would be that way, wouldn't it? But a mal—a criminal usually does try to get away. He may know it won't do him any good, but he's got to try; he can't just sit."

"Yes. Yes, I suppose so," he nodded. "While there's life there's hope, et cetera. But Winroy—"

"I—I don't know what all this has to do with me," I said. "What you said a moment ago; it sounded like you thought he'd tried to get me in trouble."

"And? Surely you were aware of that."

"Why, no." I shook my head. "I thought it was like the doctor—"

"Tell me, Mr. Bigelow. What do you think the doctor's reaction would have been if there had been a quantity of amytal in the wine? What do you think would have been the end result of the ensuing course of events?"

I stared at him. What did I think? Jesus Christ, I didn't have to think!

He nodded slowly.

"Yes. He tried to—uh—frame you ... that's the expression, isn't it? You are here by the grace of God, and, I might say, due to my innate distrust of and dislike for the man. Here, instead of in custody on a charge of attempted murder—or worse."

"But—for God's sake!" I said. "How—?"

"Winroy is not notably an early riser. Neither is he inclined to show consideration to others in the matter of quiet. So, when I heard him moving about early this morning—moving with attempted but not too successful stealth—I was disturbed. I got up and listened at my door. I heard him creep out of his room and enter yours. When he came out and went downstairs, I investigated. I—I hope you don't think it was presumptuous of me to enter your room, but my thought was that he might have harmed—"

"I don't. That's all right," I said. "Just—"

"He was too obvious about it. If he'd used any subtlety at all, but ... It was a box of amytal, Mr. Bigelow. He'd emptied six of the capsules and left the empty ones in the box with the full ones. And he'd placed the box behind the window curtain, where anyone who suspected wrongdoing would have no difficulty in finding it. Well, I suspected. I saw what he must intend. I went into his room and examined his wine with a result which you are, of course, aware of. I might have simply called him to account, but it seemed best to thwart him. To make him appear so painfully ridiculous that any future similar attempt would be knocked in the head at the outset . . . You see that, do you not?"

I saw it. Jake wouldn't pull another stunt like that.

"I disposed of the amytal capsules in the toilet along with the wine. Then, I washed the bottle out, and refilled it to its former level from a bottle I had. I am not what is ordinarily thought of as a drinking man, but a small glass of wine, sometimes, when I am turning through a book—"

"He had to take a drink of it," I said. "He'd want to have at least a little of the amytal in him. It's a wonder he didn't—"

"Notice the taste?" Kendall chuckled, his eyes twinkling. "Well, I don't imagine he's accustomed to drinking amytal and liquor, so he'd hardly know what taste to expect. And I imagine it did taste rather peculiar to him. It's much better wine than he's accustomed to drinking."

I looked down at the table. "Gosh," I said. "I hardly know what to say. Except thanks. I don't like to think what would have happened if—"

"Then don't. And I enjoyed doing it, Mr. Bigelow. I can't remember when I've had such an interesting experience."

"What do you think?" I said. "Do you think I should move out?"

"What do *you* think?"

I hesitated. Was he or wasn't he? If he was tied up with The Man, I'd better not be thinking about moving. But if he wasn't, well, moving would be the first thing I'd think of.

"I've been trying to make up my mind," I said. "I'd hate to. People would naturally wonder about it, and it's reasonable there—the price, I mean. And with us working together and the bakery so nearby, it's—"

"I don't believe I'd move, if I were you."

"Well," I said. "I certainly wouldn't want to."

"I hope you don't. I very much hope so. Of course, I wouldn't want you to let me influence you against your better judgement."

"Sure. I understand."

"I admired you a great deal at your first encounter with Winroy. Your complete self-possession. Your self-control, nerve, in the face of an alarming and awkward situation. Frankly, I was a little envious of you; you shamed me. I had just about arrived at a point where I was ready to move myself. In other words, I was going to allow this drunken lout, a convicted gangster, to dictate to *me*. That would have been wrong of me, Mr. Bigelow. Very wrong. But I needn't tell you that, of course. I can't tell you how disappointed I'd be, if you should—well, it sounds rather harsh but I'll say it. If you should turn tail and run."

"I'm not going to," I said. "I'm going to stay, all right."

"Good. Excellent. We shall stand shoulder to shoulder in this matter. You may depend on my fullest support, moral and otherwise. In case of difficulty, I believe you will find that my word carries far more weight in this community than Winroy's."

"I'm sure it does," I said.

"Well—" He raised his glass. "By the way, am I mistaken or did Sheriff and Mrs. Summers drive you home?"

"I ran into them downtown this morning," I said. "I went to church with them."

"Splendid! Those seemingly small things—they mean a great deal in a town like this ... Another drink?"

I shook my head. I wanted one, but I didn't think I'd better take it.

He might get the idea that I needed the stuff to keep going.

We went back to the house, and he and I had dinner together alone. Fay was in her room, I guess, still too upset and sore to eat.

We finished eating, and he went to the bakery. And I went right along with him. We came back at seven for sandwiches and coffee and so on—what they usually feed you for Sunday night supper wherever you are. Then we returned to the bakery, and I stuck with him until he knocked off at ten o'clock.

I was afraid to be there in the house with Ruth when all the others were out of the way. I hoped she got the idea fast that I didn't know her from now on.

Sunday is a big night in a bakery, Kendall explained. On Saturday there's practically nothing to do, since most retail outlets are closed the following day. But on Sunday you're baking for Monday, and with almost everyone run out of stuff over the weekend, it's the busiest day of the week.

He had plenty to do out on the floor, and most of the time I was by myself in the stockroom. I kept busy, as busy as I could. It would have looked funny to loaf around for seven or eight hours. He gave me a set of his whites to wear—we were about the same size—and I went all through the stock, getting familiar with it and taking inventory of everything but the bulk stuff.

"You can inventory that tomorrow," Kendall said, when he dropped in on me during a lull. "You'll need someone to help you weigh it, and give you the tare—the weight of the various containers. That would have to be deducted from your gross weight, understand, to give you the net."

I nodded, and he went on:

"These bulk items, they're the things that have given us trouble. Not at all surprising, either, with everyone chasing in and out of here, tossing their batches together by guess and by golly. Now here"—he tapped a heavily insulated barrel—"is a plaster-of-Paris compound—"

"Plaster of Paris," I said. "You put that stuff in—in—?"

"In bread. A few ounces in a large batch of bread does wonders for the texture, and of course it's completely harmless. A very little more than a few ounces, well, you'd have something resembling paving blocks." He smiled, his eyes gleaming behind the glasses. "Your dough would be wasted unless, say, you cared to pelt our friend Winroy in the head with it."

"I see," I laughed. "Yeah."

At ten o'clock we dressed out together. Quite a few of the other workmen were changing clothes at the same time, but he didn't introduce me, as I kind of thought he should. We started up the stairs to the street. And the locker room had been plenty quiet a moment before, but the minute we left you could hear the talk starting up.

"By the way," he said, as we walked home. "I was very favorably impressed by your industry tonight, Mr. Bigelow. I felt justified in beginning your pay instead of waiting until tomorrow."

"Well, thanks," I said. "Thanks very much, Mr. Kendall."

"Not at all, Mr. Bigelow."

"About"—I hesitated—"about my name, Mr. Kendall. It seems kind of funny for you to be mistering me. Wouldn't you rather call me Carl?"

"Would you prefer that I did?"

"Well, I—it would be all right," I said.

"I'm sure it would. But I think we might well leave things as they are." He paused to knock out his pipe on the gate-post; then we went on up the walk together. "Man is forced to give up so much of his dignity by the mere exigencies of existence. It seems to me that he should cling sturdily to the few shreds that are left to him."

"I see," I said. "I just didn't want you to feel—"

"Moreover, as a somewhat more than casual student of human nature, I believe you resent being called by your first name, at least on short acquaintance. I think our reactions are much the same in that respect."

The house was quiet, dark except for the hall lights. We said good night, whispering, and he went to his room and I went to mine.

I took out my contact lenses. I took out my teeth, and stood in front of the mirror massaging my gums. They ached; they always did. There was something wrong with the jawbones—they were soft and they weren't shaped right. I'd never had a set of teeth that didn't make my mouth hurt. Not too bad, understand. Just a steady nagging ache that chewed away at you a little at a time.

I put the teeth back in, and went to bed.

It was after midnight when she slipped into my room. She said that Jake had come home early and gone straight to bed, and that if he knew what was good for him he'd stay there.

It was funny, her ordering him around. We were going to kill him, yet she was going right ahead scolding and fussing, threatening what she'd do if he didn't behave himself.

"Damn him, anyway," she whispered angrily. "I was never so scared in my life, Carl."

"Yeah," I said. "It gave me quite a jar, too."

"Why in the world do you suppose he did it?"

"Oh, I don't know. Like the doctor said probably, so mixed up and screwed up he doesn't know what he's doing."

"Yeah, but . . . but gosh! Whew, I was scared!"

I didn't tell her about Kendall. I had nothing to gain by it, and a hell of a lot to lose. She might say something or do something that would tip him off. Or she might . . . well, I didn't like to think about that but I had to: The fact that she might not be on, or stay on, the level with me.

Kendall had saved my neck this morning. He couldn't have done it if Jake had been wise to him. And if I needed help from Kendall in the future and Jake *was* wise to him . . .

You see? Kendall was The Man's ace in the hole . . . *dammit, he just about had to be.* But he was mine, too, up to a point. As long as I kept my nose clean with The Man Kendall was on my side . . . *he didn't have to be; he could be leading me on, trying to get me to tip my hand.* I couldn't open up with him. I couldn't lay it on the line with her.

The only person I could trust was Charlie Bigger, Little Bigger. And that sawed-off son-of-a-bitch, I was beginning to have some doubts about him.

Talk about Jake being on a spot. Compared to me, Jake didn't have anything to worry about.

. . . It was a pretty chilly night, and she'd gotten into bed with me. We lay close together, whispering when we had anything to say, her head pillowed on my arm.

"I'd better start getting used to doing without you," I said. "We can't keep this up, baby. If there's something we have to talk over, sure; we'll risk it. Otherwise, we stay out of the clinches."

"But ... but it'll be months, Carl! You mean we've got to wait all that time until—"

"Maybe not. I guess not," I said. "Like I said, there'll be times we have to get together. But we'll have to hold 'em down, Fay. The more we're together, the more chances that someone will find out about it."

"I know, honey. I know we have to be careful."

"Another thing"—I suddenly remembered something. "Those amytal capsules. Why in the name of God did you buy them, kid?"

"Well ... he uses so damned many of them, and they cost so much if you go to a doctor and get a prescription—"

"Don't try to save dough that way again," I said. "The stuff is poison. You buy it without a prescription, and he accidentally takes an overdose—"

"Whew!" she shivered. "Why—why someone else might slip him a load and I—I'd—"

She left the sentence unfinished.

At last she snickered softly. I gave her a pat ... and took a long deep breath.

"Something funny?"

"That Ruth! Every time I think about it I want to burst out laughing."

"Yeah," I said. "That's a riot, all right."

"Ugh. It makes me kind of sick to think about it. What in the world would anyone—what could he be like, Carl?"

"I wonder," I said.

FOURTEEN

I was up and dressed early the next morning, but I didn't go downstairs right away. I'd started to when I remembered about Ruth, about being alone with her—and I *would* have been alone with her at that hour. So I sat down on the edge of the bed and waited. Smoking and fidgeting. Feeling pretty queasy and nervous about getting started in school—Christ, imagine me in school!—but wanting to get it over with.

I waited, listening for Kendall's door to open. Then, I waited a few seconds more, so it wouldn't look like I *had* been waiting for him, and headed for my door.

He knocked on it, just as I turned the knob.

"Ah, good morning, Mr. Bigelow," he said. "All ready to begin your college career?"

"Yes, sir. I guess I am," I said.

"Such enthusiasm," he laughed sympathetically. "A little nervous, eh? A feeling of strangeness and unreality? Well, that's natural enough. Do you know, I have half a notion to—uh—"

"Yes, sir?"

"Would you regard it as—uh—presumptuous if I accompanied you? I am rather well acquainted with the faculty, and possibly as my—uh—er—protégé you might feel somewhat more—"

"I wish you would," I said. "I can't think of anything I'd like better."

"Really?" He seemed pleased as all get out. "I—I feel very flattered, Mr. Bigelow. I was going to suggest it last night, but I was afraid it might seem an intrusion."

"I wanted to ask you," I said. "But it seemed like a pretty nervy thing to do."

"Tsk, tsk," he beamed. "We must be less—uh—diffident with one another from now on. How about breakfast, eh? I seem to have an unusually hearty appetite this morning."

I didn't know. I'd been practically sure yesterday, but now he had me wondering again.

He could be both things. The nice, dignified, little old guy and the other, too. You can do that, split yourself up into two parts. It's easier than you'd think. Where it gets tough is when you try to get the parts back together again, but ... He didn't need to be pretending. Most of the time I'd never pretended I'd really like a guy or want to help him along, but I'd go right ahead and—and do what I had to.

Well, anyway, I was damned glad he was going with me. It seemed funny, with all the other things I had to worry me, that I'd been uneasy about getting enrolled in a hick college. But I just couldn't help it. I guessed maybe it went back to the days when Luke and me and the rest of us had been crop tramps, and maybe you'd get two days in a school one week and three days a month in another. You never knew a thing about the lessons, and you smelled kind of bad and maybe you had a head full of lice, and you'd get put way off somewhere by yourself. You couldn't see worth a damn and your teeth had screwed up your hearing, and there was nothing you could do that someone didn't laugh at you or lay into you. And . . .

Skip it. Forget it. I was just trying to explain why I felt like I did.

Ruth served breakfast to us, and the way she kept trying to catch my eye I had a notion to take it out and hand it to her.

If she hadn't been kind of awed by Kendall, I think she might have suggested walking to the college with me. Shy as she was, much as she hated to show herself on that crutch.

She seemed to have it that bad.

I wondered whether there wasn't some safe way of getting Fay to give her the gate. And I guessed there was, probably, but I knew I wasn't going to do it. I'd tell her where to head in if I got the chance—if I had to.

But I wouldn't get her fired.

Kendall finally finished eating—I'd just been dragging my break-fast out, waiting for him—and we got started. I hadn't thought much about what courses I would take. I didn't know the score on those things, naturally, and I'd just supposed that you wouldn't have much say-so about your studies.

Kendall said it wouldn't be that way.

"That would be somewhat the case if you were a regular member of the freshman class or if you were majoring in a specific subject. But since you'll be classified as a special student—you're attending as a matter of self-improvement and for, I assume, the prestige value of college study—you have a great deal of latitude as to subjects. Now if you wouldn't—uh—if you would like my suggestions—"

"I certainly would," I said.

"Something, then, which would not point up any shortcomings in your past schooling. Something that is not predicated upon earlier studies in the same field . . . English literature. One can appreciate Pope without ever having read a line of Dryden. Political Science— more a matter of common sense than doctrinaire. History—merely another branch of literature ... How does that sound to you, Mr. Bigelow?"

"Well—it sounds pretty—"

"Impressive? Impressive is the word." He chuckled, pleased with himself. "With such a course, no one could doubt your seriousness as a student."

Impressive wasn't the word I'd been thinking of. I'd been about to say it sounded pretty damned tough.

"Whatever you say," I said. "If you think I can get by in those things."

"You can and shall ... with perhaps some slight assistance from me. You may depend upon it, Mr. Bigelow, I would not suggest subjects for you in which you could not—uh—get by."

I nodded. I didn't think I'd have much trouble getting by either. With someone like Kendall to steer me—someone who knew the ropes—I couldn't miss.

I imagine I could have got the enrollment over in thirty minutes, and I did get my registration over and my fees paid in about that time. But Kendall wasn't through when that was done. He introduced me to the president and the chancellor and the dean of men—and they were all polite and respectful to him. Then, he took me around and introduced me to each of the instructors I'd have.

When noon came we still had one more guy to see, so we ate in the school cafeteria and looked him up after lunch. By the time we got through with him it was two o'clock, and Kendall said there wasn't much point in starting any classes that day.

"Let's see, now"—he glanced at his watch as we left the campus—"why don't you use the rest of the afternoon to pick up any books or supplies you need? Then, after dinner, around six-thirty, say . . . Would that be agreeable, Mr. Bigelow? I was thinking we might set your working shift at, loosely, six-thirty to eleven."

"Couldn't I come in earlier than that?" I said. "I won't need more than an hour or so to do my shopping, and after today I'll be out of my class at three. I'd like to come in earlier, Mr. Kendall. For a while, anyway."

I sounded plenty sincere—like maybe Dick Doordie, fighting through to fortune—and that's just how I felt. Until Ruthie cooled off, I had to have some place to hang out.

"Well—uh—of course, there wouldn't be any more money for you, but ... "

"I don't care about that," I said. "I just like to be doing something, learning something."

He turned his head slowly and looked at me, and for a moment I thought he was going to ask who the hell I was kidding. And when he finally got around to speaking, he seemed so pleased he was all choked up.

"Mr. Bigelow, I—I can't tell you how glad I am that you came to Peardale. My only regret is that we could not have met—that the circumstances of our association could not have been—uh—"

He broke off, blowing his nose, and we walked a block before he said anything more.

"Well, we must take things as we find them, eh? We must look on the bright side. You are industrious, you have fortitude, the will-to-do, and now you are doing all that can be done to round out your education ... A powerful triumvirate, my s—Mr. Bigelow, flawed and shadowed as it may be. When you consider someone like poor Ruth, whose sole assets virtually are ambition and a quick mind—and handicapped as she is they are doubtful assets indeed—your own situation seems one of great good fortune."

"I'm not complaining," I said. "You say Ruth's pretty smart?"

"Brilliant. Far from worldly-wise, of course, but an exceptionally keen intelligence. An honor student at the college. She's very well thought of there, incidentally. If you should encounter some difficulty with the curriculum, I'm sure she'd be glad to—"

"I wouldn't want to bother her," I said. "She gets embarrassed so easily. I don't want to pester you either, of course, but if I do have any trouble I'd rather talk it over with you. I feel more—well, more at home with you."

"Hem!" He swelled up like a poisoned pup. "Splendid—uh—that is to say, excellent! A pleasure, Mr. Bigelow."

We separated down near the middle of town. He headed for the bakery, and I picked up my school supplies, taking a fast gander at Jake's barber shop as I passed it. It was a two-chair joint, but a cloth was draped over the front chair. Jake was dozing in the rear one, his head drooped forward on his chest.

I finished my buying, and had some coffee in a drugstore. Going out the door, I ran head on into Sheriff Summers.

"Howdy there, son." He stood back from me a little. "Thought you'd be in school today."

"I've been there most of the day," I said. "Mr. Kendall went with me to see that I got off on the right foot, and we met so many of his friends I was all day in registering."

"Well, well. Kendall went with you, eh? Didn't think nothin' short of a three-ring circus could get him away from that bakery."

"I'm on my way to work there now," I said. "I've just been picking up some things I need at school."

"Swell. Good boy." He clapped me on the back. "Uh—kinda hopin' I might run into you. Bessie's been—I mean, how about eatin' with us this Sunday?"

"Well"—I hesitated—"I ... If you're sure it wouldn't be any trouble for you, sheriff."

"Nothin' like it," he said heartily. "Tickled to death to have you. How'd it be if we meet you at church and go right from there?"

I said that would be fine.

"We'll be lookin' forward to it, then. I'm doggone glad you're gettin' lined up so well, son, after that—after all that mess at the beginning. Just keep up the good work, huh?"

"Thank you," I said. "I certainly intend to, sheriff."

I passed Jake's shop again on the way to the bakery. And there he was, standing right up against the glass, staring straight out at me.

I could feel him watching me all the way up the street.

I put my books in my locker at the bakery, and changed clothes. I went up the stairs, whistling, feeling about as happy as a guy like me could feel. I knew I had plenty to worry about, and it wasn't any time to be getting cocky and careless. But the way things had gone today—getting squared away at school and the sheriff warming up to me and ... and everything—I just couldn't worry much.

Kendall spotted me the moment I hit the floor, and he was all business now.

"Come along, Mr. Bigelow," he said, herding me toward the stockroom. "I'll get you started off, and then I'll have to leave you."

We entered the stockroom, the main one, and he handed me the batch cards. There were fourteen of them—cardboard oblongs a little wider than a cigarette package and about three times the length. Each one listed the quantity and kind of ingredients wanted for a dough batch: bread, cake, piecrust, doughnuts and so on.

"Read them all, all right, Mr. Bigelow? Everything clear to you? Let me see you set up the sponge on that whole-wheat bread mix."

I picked out the card, and shoved the others into my pocket. I looked at the list of ingredients and started for the substoreroom. Then, I remembered and picked up a pail instead.

"That's right," he smiled briskly. "The flour's just there for the record; they can draw that themselves. Pretty hard to over or under-draw on sacked flour. All you're concerned with is the sponge. Sugar, first, remember. Then—"

I remembered.

I scooped sugar from a barrel and weighed it on the scales. I dumped it into the pail, and weighed in salt and powdered milk. I wiped the scales clean, dribbled some of the plaster-of-Paris compound on them, and emptied it into a glassine bag. I tucked the bag into the pail, up against the side of it. Then I carried the pail into the cold-storage room.

I'd worked up a light sweat, but it was gone the second I stepped inside. He stood watching me, holding the door open.

There was another set of scales in there. I weighed lard onto them and dumped it into the pail. I punched a depression in the lard with my fist, measured a pint of malt syrup into the depression, and carried the pail outside. Kendall let the door slam shut, nodding approvingly

"Very good, Mr. Bigelow. Just drop the batch card in at the side, there, and you have it done ... Now about that door—you can't be too careful about that. Be very sure it's off the latch when you go in, or better still block it open slightly. One of those barrel scrapers should do the job."

"I'll be careful, all right," I said.

"Please do. You'll be here alone most of the time. You could be locked in there several hours before you were discovered, and it would be of very little use to discover you even after a much briefer lapse of time. So ... Oh, yes. Speaking of doors."

He motioned to me, and I followed him into the substoreroom. He led me to the street door—the one he'd hinted I might use as a private entrance—pulling out a key ring.

"I've had a key made for you"—he took it off the ring. "We receive flour and other supplies through this door, so regardless— uh—So you'll doubtless find use for it. We'll just see how it works, now, and—"

It didn't fit too well, apparently. Kendall had to twist it back and forth and push up on the knob before the door finally opened.

"Well," he frowned. "I suppose we'll have to make it do for the time being. Perhaps with use—"

His mouth came shut, tightening with distaste. I looked across the street where he was looking—staring—and I saw Jake Winroy duck his head quickly and speed up that sagging, lopsided lope of his by a notch or two.

He passed out of viewing range.

Kendall slammed the door, jerked on the knob, testing it, and handed me the key.

"I don't know"—he shook his head—"I don't know that I've ever met anyone I so thoroughly detested. Well, we can't waste our valuable time on him, can we? Any questions? Anything that's not clear to you? If not, I'll get back to the floor."

I said I thought I had everything down pat, and he left.

I went back to the main stockroom.

I lined up all the sponge pails in a row, measured the dry ingredients into each of them, and carried them into the cold-storage room. I measured in the lard and malt, tucked in the batch cards, and set the pails just outside the entrance to the baking room.

I came back into the stockroom, studying the cards for the sweet doughs.

I was kind of breathless. I didn't need to, but I'd been rushing my head off. Not out here, but in there. In the cold-storage room.

I lighted a cigarette, telling myself I'd better take it easier. I wouldn't last long, rushing. Hard work—steady hard work—well, I'd given my lifetime quota on that a long time ago.

Aside from that, it would be easy to screw things up if I hurried too fast. I didn't know the job good yet. Working with all those different ingredients and measurements, a guy wouldn't have to be even pretty careless to get a little too much of one thing and not enough of another. And there wouldn't be any way of spotting the mistake until the stuff came out of the ovens—as hard as brick-bats maybe or as tough as shoe leather.

I glanced at the cold-storage room, and I shivered a little. So it was cold. What of it? I didn't need to stay in there, like I'd done on the sponges, wrapping up everything at one time. I could stay in, say, for five minutes, come out and go back in again for another five. Why stay in there, freezing my tail off, trying to do everything at once?

I knew why, and I made myself admit it. The goddam place kind of gave me the creeps. I wanted to get through in there as fast as I could. It was so damned quiet. You'd hear a noise and sort of start, and then you'd realize that you'd gulped or one of your muscles had creaked and that was the noise you'd heard.

The door was so thick and heavy that you seemed locked in even when you knew you weren't. You kept looking at the scraper to see if it was still in place. And everything was kind of greasy and damp in there—everything seemed about the same shade—and you could look two or three times and still not be sure.

If you could have propped the door wide open—but you couldn't do that. Kendall had warned me about keeping the door open any more than was necessary. It would be a hell of a cold-storage room if you did that much.

I coughed, choked back another cough. The bug wasn't active again, I was sure of that, but I was glad I hadn't had to produce a health certificate.

I dropped the cigarette butt, stepped on it, and looked at the cards for the sweet doughs. They were more complicated than the others, the sponge mixes, and the extra-refined flour had to be weighed out with the other ingredients. They didn't just draw what they wanted as they did on the bread.

If I took my time on this stuff—and I'd damned well better—I probably wouldn't have it ready a hell of a lot sooner than I had to.

I took the scraper out of my pocket. I pulled the cold-storage-room door open, and went inside. I laid the scraper handle against the jamb, letting the door settle against it. Then I turned my back on the damned thing and got busy.

There were eight batches in all. I decided to do two, and go out and get the dry stuff ready for them. Then, I'd come back and do two more, and so on until I was through. And if I didn't like it in here, I knew what to do about it. There was an easy way to save time. I could snap out of the creeps and stop checking on the door every ten seconds.

I got busy, I put two pans on the work table, leaned their batch cards against them, and began pouring and dumping and weighing. And the creeps stayed right with me, but I didn't give in to them. I never looked once at the door.

The work went pretty fast. It didn't seem to, but according to my watch it did. I finished the first two batches—the wet part of them— took them out and set up the dry stuff, and came back in again.

I did another two and another two. And started on the fourth pair. The last two I had to do.

I got them done, and somehow they seemed to take longer than the others. It seemed like I'd never get through with them. Finally, though, they were ready, and I tucked the batch cards into the slits at the end of the pans.

Then, I picked them up and turned around and pushed against the door.

I pushed—pretty easy at first. Easy because I couldn't bring myself to push hard. I just sort of leaned against it, because if I did more than that—if I pushed hard and it *didn't* . . .

I put a little more steam into it, just a little. And then a little more . . . and a little more.

And then suddenly I wasn't pushing, hard or any other way. I was throwing myself at it, giving it everything I had. And I was still holding onto those mixes, why the hell I don't know, and they were slopping all over me and the floor. And I hit that door like I was going to drive straight through it. And I bounced and skidded and slipped. And I did a belly whopper to the floor.

The wind went out of me like a popped balloon. I gagged and retched but nothing came up. I lay on the floor, writhing, squeezing my head between my hands, trying to squeeze the pain away. And after a while I could breathe again, and I could get my eyes to focus.

I looked. The door was closed tight.

The scraper wasn't there, and it hadn't slipped inside.

Someone had taken it away.

FIFTEEN

I laughed. I got ahold of the table and pulled myself up. I laughed and laughed, brushing at the crap on my clothes, feeling it cling and stick and stiffen against my fingers.

Because what was the sense to it anyway? How in the hell could you win? You were right on the beam—playing all the angles, doing things twice as well as you thought you could and getting some breaks thrown in. Everything was swell, and you were a bright boy and a tough boy.

And a punchy booze-stupe without enough guts to string a uke could come along and put the blocks to you.

He could do it because he *didn't* have anything. Nothing to lose. He didn't need to be smart, to cover his tracks. You had to cover them for him. He could make one dopey move after another, and all you could do was duck and keep your mouth shut. He didn't need guts. He could run from you, but you couldn't run from him. He could pick you off any way, any time, and if he got caught...? I had to choose between times and ways, and if I got caught...? Not responsible? Not a chance. If you beat the law there was still The Man.

I laughed and choked and coughed. It was such a hell of a good joke, me feeling sorry for Jake.

That was my first reaction—that it was the damnedest funniest thing in the world and it was a relief to get it all over. It hadn't made any sense from the beginning. I'd go right on looking for whatever I was looking for, and I wouldn't stand any better chance of finding it than I ever had.

So it was funny. It was a relief.

Then that cold really began to gnaw into me, and I stopped laughing and I wasn't relieved any more.

It was too simple, too clear-cut and easy. I'd been swimming in muck all my life, and I could never quite sink in it and I could never quite get to the other side. I had to go on, choking to death a little at a time. There wouldn't be anything for me as clean and easy as this.

I looked at my watch. I got up and started walking back and forth, stamping my feet, rubbing my hands and slapping them against my body.

Four-thirty. It seemed like it ought to be hours later than that, I'd done so much that day and got started so early, but it was only four-thirty . . . Kendall would knock off at a quarter of six to go to the house for dinner, and he'd come in after me. And then I'd get out of here.

No one would come in before then. There wasn't any reason for them to, and—and they just wouldn't. And Kendall wouldn't dress out without me, and go on to the house by himself.

Either way, see, would make it easy for me, and that was against the rules. I wouldn't be found soon enough to really help, or late enough to . . . to do any good.

Four-thirty to five-forty-five. An hour and fifteen minutes. That would be the score. No more, no less. Not enough to kill me; too much, a hell of a lot too much, to leave me unharmed. Just the right amount to knock me on my ass.

I should have given up, just relaxed and stopped trying to do anything about it. Because whatever I did or didn't do, I wasn't going to change a thing. I'd still be just *so* sick, *almost* completely screwed up, not *quite* stripped of everything I had. Right at the time when I needed everything I had and I couldn't be screwed up at all.

No, I couldn't change a thing. But I had to try.

Relaxing, giving up, those were against the rules, too.

I walked back and forth, stamping and slapping and pounding, hugging my arms across my chest, sticking my hands between my crotch and clasping my legs on them. And I kept getting colder and stiffer, and my lungs began to feel like I was breathing fire.

I climbed up on the table, trying to warm my hands against the light in the ceiling. But there was a wire guard around it, and it was just a little globe, and it didn't do any good.

I climbed back down and started walking again. Trying to think . . . A fire? Huh-uh. Nothing to burn, and it wouldn't do anyway. It wouldn't even be smart to smoke. The air wasn't too good now.

I looked along the rows of shelves, looking—for anything. I studied the labels on the thick jugs: Extract of Vanilla, Extract of Lemon . . . *Alcohol 40 per cent* . . . But I knew better than that, too.

You'd feel warmer for a few seconds, and then you'd be colder than ever.

I began to get sore. I thought, for Christ's sake, what kind of a dope are you, anyway? You're suppose to be smart, remember? You don't just take things. You don't like something, you do something about it. Locked up, not locked up. It's still the same, isn't it, except for the air. Suppose...

Suppose you were riding that manifest out of Denton, the fast meat train that balls the jack all the way into El Reno. It's November and all the goddamned reefer holes are locked, so you're riding the top, in the goddamn cold wind. And you can't die, and you'd better not get down. Because you remember that kid in the jungle at St. Joe, the color of the weeds he was lying in; taking on the boes for a dime or a nickel or a cart of coffee or ... So?

I remembered. I didn't invent the trick but it's a good one:

You crawl down inside your cotton sack, the sack you pick cotton into. It's nine feet long and made out of canvas, and you kind of flap the end over itself so that just a tiny bit of air comes in. And you breathe practically the same air in and out, but you warm up fast. After a while your lungs start itching and smarting and your head begins to hurt. But you stay there, keeping your mind on warm things, warm and soft, and safe...

I didn't have a cotton sack now, of course, or anything in the way of a big piece of cloth. But if I could get inside of something, pull something over me, and put my breath to work ... well, it would help. I took a long careful look around the room.

Egg can? Too small. Lard barrel? Too big; it would take too long to dig the lard out. Mincemeat...?

The keg was only about a fourth full. I squatted down, trying to measure myself against it, and it was pretty small—not really what I ought to have. But it was the only thing I did have.

I turned it upside down, then got my arms around it and banged it up and down, dumping the sweet-smelling, semifrozen slush on the floor. I scraped the inside with a scoop, and I knew I could scrape all night and not get it completely clean. So I gave up and got it over me.

I sat down on the floor with my arms at my sides, and stuck my head and shoulders into it. Then, I sat up and let it slide down over me. It only came down to my hips, and little gobs of that goo kept letting go and trickling down onto me. But that had to be it—it and me was all I had. So I breathed hard and tried to concentrate on . . . on warmness and softness, comfort and safety.

I got to thinking about the farm that guy had up in Vermont, where he grew all those things. And I remembered how he'd said that he didn't have any demand any more except for just the one thing. I closed my eyes, and I could almost see them, the long rows of them. And I grinned and laughed to myself, beginning to feel kind of good and pretty warm. And then I thought, I began to see:

. . . *the goats were going up and down the rows, walking sideways on their hind feet. And every time they came to one they'd raise their tails and cut loose with the fertilizer. And each time they came to the end of a row they'd stand on their heads and howl. They had to do it. They knew it wasn't going to get them anything because there was nothing there to get, but they kept right on. Moving sideways and backwards—because that was the way the rows were laid oat. And at the end they stood on their heads, howling . . .*

I stopped thinking about it.

There was no warmth in it.

I brought my mind back to Kendall, him and Fay. Wondered what I'd better tell them. And I knew I'd better not tell the truth.

She might blow up—jump Jake about it or give it away to someone else. She might scare off. If she got sore or shaky, if she thought Jake could take the ball away from me . . .

And Kendall. If he was on the level, he'd have Jake in jail so fast it would make his head swim. He'd gotten a bang out of the other, the frame-up, because nothing had come of it and he'd outsmarted Jake. But if he thought Jake had tried to kill me, and *if* he was on the level, he couldn't let it slide. He'd have to crack down to protect the bakery.

If he was with The Man—that would be worse yet. The Man already thought I might have a few rocks in my head. He'd been sore about me dragging in Fay and . . . *why in hell had I done that, anyhow? I could have got along without her* . . . He probably had a hunch that I might have seen through that Fruit Jar frammis and didn't trust him as much as I had to trust him. And if he thought I couldn't do any better than this, get it thrown into me by the guy I was supposed to throw it into . . .

No, it had to be an accident. That would be bad enough.

... I twisted my wrist and looked down. Five-twenty. About twenty-five minutes to go. An hour and fifteen minutes plus the time before I'd got locked in. It wouldn't be enough for a guy in good health. He'd have the sniffles and a sore throat, and that would be about the size of it. With me, though, it would be exactly enough. I couldn't have timed it better if I'd been trying to knock myself out.

Twenty-four minutes ...

Ruth. As long as I'd known I was going to use Fay, why had I made a play for Ruth?

And Fay; getting back to Fay. It wouldn't have been any wonder— I wouldn't have blamed The Man much—if he'd given Fruit Jar that knife instead of me.

Sure, Fay could be a big help. Sure, she could make things a lot easier for me. So what? She could do something else, too. If she was smart enough to see it. Because how can you really trust a dame who'll help kill her own husband?

The Man had told me what she could do; he'd pointed out the spot where I could go down and never come up. He'd just mentioned it once, then he'd let it lay and gone on. Fay was already in or as good as in, and there was nothing to do but like it. But he wouldn't have been The Man if he *had* liked it. Brother, he must have thought I was a goof!

Me—Little Bigger—putting the one rope in the world around my neck that would hang me!

I didn't have a record, none that they could pin on me. I could line up before every cop in the country and there wasn't a one that could say, yes, that's our Bigger boy. No one could say it and prove it.

No one could, now.

But if I could be caught in the act of trying to kill Jake Winroy— if they had that much to go on, and could work back from it ...

All those rewards, all for Fay. Forty-seven thousand dollars for Fay ... and no half-blind runt with a mouth like a dog's behind to get in her hair.

... I got out just about on schedule. Kendall found me around ten minutes of six, and he and one of the bakers got me home. By six-thirty I was in bed with two hot-water bottles, feeling sort of drowsy and dopey from something the doctor had given me.

It was the same doctor—Dodson—that Fay had called for Jake. But he wasn't at all crusty and tough with me like he'd been with him and her. My own moth ... you couldn't have wanted a guy to be nicer.

He pulled the blankets back up over my chest, and tucked them under my chin.

"So you're feeling fine, huh? No pain at all ... Never mind. I don't want you talking with that throat."

I grinned at him, and my eyelids began to droop shut. He turned and gave Fay a nod.

"I want this boy to rest. He is to have complete quiet, understand? No nonsense. No disturbance such as occurred here yesterday."

"I"—Fay bit her lip, blushing—"I understand, doctor."

"Good. See that your husband does. Now, if you'll get that bedpan I spoke to you about a quarter of an hour ago—"

She went out.

The doctor and Kendall moved over near the door.

And I wasn't quite asleep yet, I was just drifting off. And I got a little of what they said.

"... all right?"

"This time. Stays in bed, and ... Ought to be up by ..."

"... relieved to ... strong personal interest ..."

"Yep. This time ... wouldn't bet a nickel on ..."

"... pessimist, Dod. Why a next ..."

"... teeth out ... lens. No, better do it my ..."

"... don't mean he ...?"

" ... everything. Straight across the board ... nothing really right ... no good to begin ..."

That was the last I heard.

SIXTEEN

I was in bed until Friday. Or, I should say, I didn't leave the house until then, because I didn't stay in bed all the time. When I had to vomit or use the toilet I went to the bathroom, and I made sure that everything was flushed down good.

I told everyone that I felt all right—that I was just sort of weak and tired. And aside from all that blood and phlegm, which began tapering off about Thursday, there *didn't* seem to be a hell of a lot wrong with me. I didn't have much pain. Like I said, I was just weak and tired. And I had a funny feeling that a lot of me had been taken away.

What there was of me was all right, but there wasn't much of me any more.

Fay spent a lot of time in my room. And that was okay, of course, since she was supposed to take care of me. We had plenty of time to talk.

She said that Jake had been in the house and in bed every night by eleven o'clock. As she put it, he was behaving like a perfect lamb.

"How about that, anyway?" I asked her, making it sound casual. "I mean, how come he lets you boss him around? What's he afraid of?"

She shrugged. "Gosh, I don't know, honey. Afraid I'll leave him, I guess."

"It's not doing him a hell of a lot of good for you to stay."

"No?" She laughed huskily, slanting her eyes at me. "Now how would you guess a thing like that?"

I let the talk drift off onto other things—what a funny little guy Kendall was and who in the hell could have seduced Ruthie—and after a while I let it drift back to Jake again.

"This board money doesn't amount to anything," I said, "and I don't see how he can make any dough in that shop of his. How do you keep going?"

"You call this going?"

"It takes dough. Quite a bit with Jake hitting the whiz so hard."

"We-el, he does have *some* business, Carl. Me"—she guffawed and put her hand over her mouth—"I'd be afraid I'd get scalped. But everyone knows him and knew his folks, and he has some trade. On Fridays and Saturdays, you know, when all the shops are busy. And he's usually hanging around there, at night, staying open, when the other shops are closed."

One day—Wednesday, I think it was, when she brought my lunch up—I asked her if Jake had ever mentioned going back to jail.

She shook her head firmly. "For ten years? He couldn't take it when he was being paid off heavy—when he knew he'd be taken care of when he got out. They wouldn't play with him any more, would they, Carl? If he was willing? He'd just do his time and they'd get him when it was over?"

I nodded. "If they couldn't arrange to get him inside ... Why in hell did he do it anyway, Fay? I know the cops probably shot him a big line about how they'd protect him and no one would dare touch him because it just wouldn't be good business, but—"

"And how! I hated to lose out on that payoff money, but I didn't think—no one seemed to think that—"

"Jake must have known how it would be. Hell, look at the way he started slipping. Hitting the jug and letting himself go. Look at the way he blew up when he spotted me."

"Yeah. Well—" She shook her head again. "Why do we do anything? He was going nuts in jail. He felt like he'd been the fall guy for the rest of the crowd, and the money he was getting wasn't doing *him* any good. So—"

That was about the size of the matter. I knew it. I'd been briefed on every phase of the deal, just what had happened and why and how it had happened.

But I wanted her to tell me, anyway.

"Why doesn't he turn himself into custody? Stay in the jug until after the trial is over?"

"Why?" She frowned at me, puzzled.

"That's what I said. If he's so sure I'm—someone's going to bump him off to keep him from talking, why—?"

"But, honey. What good would that do? They'd get him afterwards."

"Yeah, sure," I said. "That's the way it would be, all right."

Her frown deepened a little.

"Honey . . . You're not—not getting nervous, are you?"

"About him?" I forced a laugh. "Not a chance. He's in the bag and I'm all set to sew it up."

"How? Tell me, Carl."

I hadn't meant to tell her so soon. The safest way would have been to keep it to myself right up to the last minute. But—well, I'd got her a little worried with all that questioning. And it looked to me like I'd better show her I was right on the ball before she got more worried.

"Here's the deal," I said. "We'll pick a weekend night when Ruth's gone home to her folks, and—"

She, Fay, would set Jake up. She'd meet him downtown earlier and see that he didn't get too much to drink. Then she'd go on home, after she had him good and teased up, to get ready for what she'd promised to give him.

"Make him believe it," I said. "Make him want it so bad he can taste it. Know what I mean?"

"I know. Go on, Carl."

"Okay. You go on home. He gives you a few minutes, and then he follows you. I'll be watching at the door of the bakery, and I follow him. I catch up with him at the steps, pop his neck and drop him off on his head. I beat it back to the bakery, and you discover him. You heard him stumble, see, like he's always stumbling on those steps. That's it."

"How will you—his neck—?"

"It's easy. You don't have to worry about that."

"Well, gosh. It—it sounds so . . . so simple!"

"You want it hard?"

"Well, no—" Her frown went away and she laughed. "When do we do it, Carl?"

"I'll let you know. Not for weeks yet."

"Gee," she said, wonderingly. "Imagine me thinking you might be getting a little sca—worried!"

"Are you kidding?" I said.

"Gee," she said, again. "You tough little bastard, you!"

. . . Kendall was in to see me at least twice a day. He fussed around over me like I was a two-year-old kid, feeling my forehead and asking me if I didn't want this or that or the other, then kind of scolding me about smoking too much and not taking better care of myself.

"You really must, Mr. Bigelow. So much depends on it," he'd say.

And I'd say, "Yes, sir, Mr. Kendall. I understand."

It seemed that quite a few guys had got themselves locked into the cold-storage room at one time or another, and he took it for granted that I'd done the same. He also took it for granted that I'd opened that side door of the bakery for some reason, and left it unlocked.

And, of course, I didn't correct him. I didn't point out that he'd done it himself when he was trying out the new key.

Kendall usually managed to be around when the doctor came to see me, but he and the doc didn't do much talking after the first couple visits. Kendall didn't want to be told that I was in bad shape, and Dodson apparently wasn't a guy to pull his punches. So, after the first couple visits, when Kendall argued with him and kept calling him a pessimist, the doctor got sort of grim and clammed up. About all he'd say was I'd be all right this time—*but*. "But," he'd say, and let it go at that.

And Kendall would be pretty red-faced and huffy, and almost glare at him until he got out of my room.

"A pessimist," he'd say, huffily. "Always looking on the dark side of everything ... You *are* feeling better, aren't you, Mr. Bigelow?"

"Sure. Sure, I feel fine, Mr. Kendall," I'd say.

Thursday evening, he asked me about a dozen times if I was feeling better and if I was sure I should get up the next day ... after that he got pretty quiet for a time. And when he spoke again it was about that little cabin he had up in Canada.

"It might be just the thing for you, Mr. Bigelow. In case, that is, that your health should worsen and you should not—uh—be able to carry out your plans here."

"I'm all right," I said. "I'll be able to carry them out, Mr. Kendall."

"I'm sure of it. It would indeed be tragic if you could not. But, in case ... It would be ideal for you, Mr. Bigelow. You could take my car, and living would be very cheap and—I assume you have some money but I would be very happy to help—"

"I have most of what I got from my filling station," I said. "But it's awfully nice of you to offer—"

"Not at all. You're more than welcome to any help I can give you
. . . What do you think about it, Mr. Bigelow, as a more or less
pleasant solution to an unpleasant eventuality? You'd have complete
quiet, the most favorable conditions for rest and study. The nearest
town is forty miles away, accessible enough by car but far enough
distant to insure your privacy. How does it sound to you, anyway?"

It sounded swell. I'd never heard of a better place to knock a guy
off—as I was going to be knocked off if I fell down on the job here.

"That sounds nice," I said. "But I don't imagine I'll be going. I'm
staying right here and going to school and—and do everything else I
planned."

"Of course. Certainly," he nodded, and stood up to go. "It's just
something to think about."

I thought about it.

It was almost one o'clock in the morning before I could get to
sleep.

The next day, the day after that night, rather, was Friday. And I
was still awfully weak and wrung out, but I knew I'd better not lie
around any longer. Fay would start to worrying again. Kendall would
start to wondering whether I could carry on or not. And if he had
any doubts, it wouldn't be long until The Man had them.

I got up early, so that I could take my time about dressing, and ate
breakfast with Kendall. I left the house when he did, and headed for
the college.

That first morning—Monday morning—I hadn't paid any attention to the other students. I'd seen them, of course; some of them
were passing us or we were passing them all the way to the school.
But they hadn't made any impression on me. I mean, I hadn't been
bothered by them. Kendall had been so free and easy that I'd felt the
same way.

This morning, it was different. I felt like a jerk.

There was a regular parade of students going toward the college,
and I was right in the middle of it. But somehow I wasn't part of it. I
was always by myself, with the others in back or ahead of me,
nudging each other when they thought I wasn't looking; laughing
and whispering and talking. About my clothes, about the way I
looked, about—everything. Because nothing about me was right . . .

I went to my first class, and the instructor acted like he'd never seen me before. He wanted to know if I was sure I was in the right class and why I was starting to school so late in the term. And he was one of those goofs who keep asking you questions without listening to your answers; and I had to explain, over and over, while the others sat grinning and watching me.

Finally, it sank in on him. He remembered about Kendall introducing me, and he halfway apologized for his forgetfulness. But things still weren't squared away. I'd been absent for three days, so I had to go to the dean of men for an okay before I could be admitted to classes.

I got it—a cut slip, I think they called it—and got back just about thirty seconds before the class was over. I was just sitting down in my seat when the bell rang.

Everyone got a big bang out of it. You'd have thought it was the funniest thing that ever happened.

In one class, I guess I must have moved a dozen times before I found a seat that didn't belong to someone else. I'd just get sat down when some dope would trail up and say it was where he sat. And, yeah, I think they were making a game out of it, trying to make me look dopier than I felt, but all I could do was keep moving until the instructor woke up and assigned me to a desk.

The third class, the one just before lunch, was the worst one. It was English literature, and everyone was taking turns at reading a few paragraphs aloud. So it came my turn, and the way I was looking down and talking at the same time, my teeth slipped a little bit. And everything I said sounded sort of like baby talk. The snickers and giggles got louder and louder, and finally the instructor told me to sit down.

"Very amusing, Bigelow," he said, giving me a glare that would have frosted an orchard. "Is Mr. Kendall acquainted with your talent for mimicry?"

I shrugged and smirked—what the hell could I do or say? And he frowned and nodded for another student to start reading. A little bit later—although it didn't seem like a little bit—the noon bell rang.

I stopped by his desk on the way out, and explained about the teeth. He was pretty nice about it, said he was sorry he'd misunderstood the situation and so on. So that was taken care of: he wouldn't knock me to Kendall. But ...

I walked down the corridor to the building entrance, and everyone seemed to be laughing and talking about me. And part of it was imagination, of course, but not all of it. It was a small college, and I guess the students were pretty hard up for kicks, and news traveled fast.

I headed toward the house, wondering why in hell I bothered when I knew I wouldn't be able to eat anything. I tried to keep to the side streets, dodging people whenever I could and cursing myself for doing it.

She ducked out of an alley just as I was ducking across it. Looking back, now, I'd say that she'd been waiting for me to pass.

I said. "Oh, hello, Ruth," and started to go on.

She said, "C-Carl. Wait a minute."

"Yeah?" I said. I paused, waiting

"I kn-know you're mad at me about something, but—"

"Mad?" I said. "I don't even know you're alive."

"Y-yes," she said, "I know that, too. I didn't want to talk to you about that. All I wanted to say was about … about school. D-don't mind the way they act. Just go ahead, and after a while you get used to it."

She smiled, tried to. She nodded her head, and pivoted on her crutch.

And I knew that I should let her go like that, a clean hard break. But I couldn't do it. I stepped in front of her.

"I know you're alive, Ruthie," I said. "I know it plenty."

"N-no … I mean, it's all right, Carl. I—I guess, I just—"

"I've been trying to give you a break. I'm no good for you. I'm no good, period. But—"

"You are, too!" Her eyes flashed. "You're nice!"

"And there's Mrs. Winroy," I said. "I think she might be a little suspicious. If she thought there was anything going on between us, she'd probably fire you fast."

"Oh," she said, and her voice quavered a little. "I d-didn't … has she said anything? I couldn't lose my job, Carl! If I—"

"You'll have to watch it, then," I said. "That's why I've acted the way I have, Ruthie. It's the only reason. I like you a lot."

She stood blushing and trembling, the splayed hand gripping the brace of the crutch.

"That's the way it is, Ruth. Keep it in mind. I think you're pretty swell. If I don't show it, it's because I can't."

She nodded, looking like she was a dog and I owned her.

"Now, you can do me a little favor," I said. "If you want to. I'm feeling a little rocky, but I don't want to go back to the house and have everyone worrying over me, so—"

"Shouldn't you, Carl? I mean, don't you think you should stay in bed for another day?"

"I'm all right," I said, "but I don't think I feel up to school this afternoon. If you'll tell Kendall, or anyone else that asks, that I'm eating lunch at the cafeteria—don't let on, you know, that everything isn't okay—"

"It will be, Carl. You'll get used to it."

"Sure, I will," I said. "But I've had enough for today. I think I'll just loaf around town for a couple of hours, get myself pulled together before it's time to go to work."

She hesitated, frowning sort of troubled. "You're not ... not awfully discouraged, Carl? You don't intend to drop out of school, and—?"

"Not a chance," I said. "Peardale's stuck with me, and I'm sticking with it. I just don't feel up to it this afternoon."

She went on, then, on down the alley, and I went on up the street to a nice quiet bar I'd spotted the day I was with Kendall. I settled down in a rear booth, and I didn't move out of it until three o'clock.

I wouldn't have cared much if the sheriff or someone had spotted me there; they'd have had a hard time making anything out of the fact that I was taking things easy my first day out of bed. But no one came into the place that I knew. Hardly anyone came in at all, for that matter. So I just sat there, feeling more relaxed and rested the longer I sat, thinking and smoking and drinking.

I felt pretty good by the time I left.

What there was of me felt pretty good.

I got through my shift at the bakery. I put in a full eight hours there the next day, Saturday, and I got through them all right, too. So I got by all right. Just barely.

Because, like I said, there just wasn't a whole lot left of me.

I wondered what would happen if something tough came up,

something really hard to take. Something that I couldn't handle in my own way, a little at a time, like I did the job.

And then it was Sunday, and I began to find out.

SEVENTEEN

Sheriff Summers belched, and leaned back in his chair. "Fine dinner, Bessie," he said. "Can't remember when—*ughahh*—I et so much."

"At breakfast," said Mrs. Summers, wrinkling her forehead at him. "More coffee, Carl? I think, from the sound of things, that His Highness will have to settle for some baking soda and water."

"Aw, now, Bessie. Why—?"

"No, sir. Not another drop. And kindly stop picking at the meringue on that pie!"

The sheriff grinned sheepishly, and winked at me. "Ain't she a terror though, son? 'Bout the bossiest one woman you ever seen, I'll bet."

"I don't think I'd say that," I laughed.

"Certainly you wouldn't. Only His Highness is capable of it."

"He's just being polite." The sheriff winked at me again.

"But you're not, are you? Quiet. Carl and I do not care to talk to you, do we, Carl?"

"No, ma'am," I said, smiling.

And he and she laughed and smiled at me.

It was a nice day, any way you looked at it. Cool but sunny, just enough breeze to ripple the green-brown leaves of the trees. And it had got off to a good start. Kendall had let me set up most of my Sunday batches the day before and leave them in cold storage, and he'd insisted that I take all of today off. He'd really insisted, not in the way people do when they expect you to talk 'em out of it.

I was beginning to feel almost as much at home with the sheriff and his wife as I had with that old couple out in Arizona.

Sheriff Summers said he guessed he'd take a little nap, and Mrs. Summers told him by all means to go ahead. He went up to the front of the house where his bedroom was. She and I sat at the table a while longer, drinking coffee and talking. Then she took me outside to show me the yard.

Their house was one of those rambling old cottages which never seem to go out of date no matter how old they are. The yard was almost a half block wide and a block deep, and she'd tried to doll it up with flower beds and a rock garden in the rear.

I told her how I'd fixed up my little place in Arizona, and she said she could just see it and it sounded wonderful. We went from that to talking about the yard here, and hell, it had all kinds of possibilities. So I gave her a few suggestions, and she was tickled pink.

"That's marvelous, Carl! Will you come over and help me some time—some weekend, perhaps—if I pay you?"

"No, ma'am, I said. "Not if you pay me."

"Oh. But really—"

"I'd enjoy doing it. I like to see things looking nice. I started to do a little work on the Winroy place—there's quite a few things, you know, that need—"

"I do know. Yes, indeed!"

"But I haven't felt like it was appreciated—more like I might be butting in. So I fixed the gate and let the other things slide."

"Those people. I'll bet they never even said thank you, did they?"

I shook my head. "For that matter, I guess I wanted to do the work more on my own account than theirs. The gate was the worst off, but those front steps have me worried too. Someone could get killed on those steps."

It was true. They were in lousy shape, and someone *could* get killed on them without any help. But I felt ashamed of myself for mentioning it. It was just that I always had to keep pointing so hard at one thing that everything coming out of me—everything I said or did—pointed at the one thing, also.

"Well," I said. "Speaking of work, I think it's time I was getting busy on those dinner dishes."

We'd been sitting on the back steps while we talked. I stood up and held out my hand to her.

She took it, and drew me back down on the steps.

"Carl—"

"Yes, ma'am," I said.

"I—I wish I could tell you how much I—" She laughed sort of crankily, as though she was scolding herself. "Oh just listen to me! I guess I've gotten like Bill, completely out of the habit of handing out bouquets. But . . . you know what I mean, Carl."

"I hope I do," I said. "I mean, I enjoy being with you and the sheriff so much I hope you—"

"We do, Carl. We've never had any children, no one but ourselves to think about. Perhaps that's been the . . . well, no matter. What can't be cured must be endured. But I've thought—I seem to have had you on my mind ever since last Sunday, and I've thought that if things had been different, if we'd had a son, he'd have been just about your age now. H-he—he'd be like . . . if he was like I've always pictured him . . . he'd be like you. Someone who was polite and helpful and didn't think I was the world's biggest bore, and—"

I couldn't say anything. I didn't trust my voice . . . Me, *her* son! *Me!* . . . And why couldn't it have been that way, instead of the way it was?

She was talking again. She was saying that she'd been "so angry at the way Bill acted last Sunday."

"It was all right," I said. "He has to be pretty careful in the job he's got."

"Careful, fiddlesticks!" she snapped. "It was not all right. I was never so angry in my life. I gave that man fits, Carl! I told him, 'Bill Summers, if you're going to be swayed by those Fields—someone who is obviously malicious and petty—instead of believing the evidence of your own eyes and ears, I'm—'"

"The Fields!" I turned and looked at her. "What Fields? The only Fields I know are dead."

"I'm talking about their son, him and his family. The relatives she lived with when she went back to Iowa. Bill wired them, you know, at the time he wired—"

"No," I said, "I didn't know. And maybe you'd better not tell me about it, Mrs. Summers. As long as the sheriff didn't, I don't think you should."

She hesitated. Then she said, softly, "You mean that, don't you, Carl?"

"I mean it," I said.

"I'm glad. I knew you'd feel that way. But he knows that I planned to tell you, and he doesn't object at all. The whole thing was so completely ridiculous in the first place! Even if he couldn't see the kind of young man you were at a glance, he had those wonderful wires about you from that judge and the chief of police and—"

"I don't understand," I said. "I don't know why this son would say anything against me. I couldn't have thought any more of a mother and father than I did of them. Why, Mrs. Fields wrote me right up to the time she died, and—"

"I imagine that was a large part of the trouble. Jealousy. And you know how kinfolk can be when it comes to elderly people. No matter what you do, how much you do, they're always convinced that you've abused the old folks. Imposed on them or swindled them or worse."

"But I—I just don't see how—"

"Honestly, Carl! Without ever having met you, I knew it was preposterous. They sent a five-hundred-word telegram back here, and it was simply filled with the worst possible ... And, of course, Bill didn't just swallow it whole, but he didn't feel that he could disregard it completely. So—Oh, I suppose I shouldn't even have mentioned it. But it was so unfair, Carl, it made me so angry that—"

"Maybe you'd better tell me about it," I said. "If you don't mind."

She told me about it. I listened, sore at first, and then just sick. And I got sicker and sicker.

They—this Fields character—had said that I'd stolen his mother and father blind all the time I was working for them, and then I'd gypped her out of the station, paid her about half what the place was worth. He said I'd just moved in on his folks and taken over, and they'd been too scared of me to complain. He said—he hinted—that I'd actually killed Mr. Fields; that I'd made him do all the hard heavy work until he keeled over from heart failure. He said I'd planned to do the same thing to the old lady, but she'd taken what I offered her so I'd let her go "completely broken in health." He said ...

Everything. Every lousy thing that a smalltime stinker could think of to say.

It was a lie, of course, every word of it. I'd worked for those people for peanuts, and I'd have stolen from myself quicker than I would have from them. I'd paid Mrs. Fields more than anyone else had offered when she put the place up for sale. I'd even done a big part of the housework for Mrs. Fields. I'd made Mr. Fields stay in bed, and

I'd waited on him and done the other work besides. He'd hardly been out of bed for a year at the time he died, and she'd hardly stirred a hand, and . . .

And this character said things like that about me.

It made me sick. These people—those two people I'd cared more about than anything in the world, and . . . And this was the way it turned out.

Mrs. Summers touched my arm. "Don't feel badly, Carl. I know you were just as good and kind to those people as you could be and what *he* says doesn't change the facts."

"I know," I said. "I—" I told her how much I'd thought of the Fields and how I'd tried to show it, and she sat nodding sympathetically, murmuring an occasional, "Of course," and, "Why, certainly you did," and so on.

And pretty soon it seemed like I wasn't talking to her, but myself. I was arguing with myself. Because I knew what I'd done, but I wasn't sure why I had done it. I'd thought I was, but now I didn't know.

He was lying, of course; the way he'd put things had been a lie. But a lie and a truth aren't too far apart; you have to start with one to arrive at the other, and the two have a way of overlapping.

You could say I had moved in on the Fields. They hadn't really needed any help, and if they'd been younger and less good-hearted they probably wouldn't have given me a job. You could say that I had made them work hard. Two people could get by fine on the little business their station was doing, but three couldn't. And I'd saved them all the work I could, but still they'd had to work harder than they had before I came. You could say that I had stolen from them— just being there was stealing. You could say I had cheated Mrs. Fields on the price. Because all I had I'd got from them, and the place was worth a lot more to me than it would have been to an outsider. You could say . . .

You could say that I'd planned it the way it had turned out; maybe without knowing that I was planning it.

I couldn't be sure that I hadn't. All I could be sure of was that I'd been fighting for my life, and I'd found the perfect spot—the one place—to take cover. I'd had to have what they had. In a way, it had been me or them.

Those six years I'd spent with them . . . Maybe they were like all the other years. Just crap. Nothing to feel kind of proud of or good about.

"Carl . . . Please, Carl!"

"I'm all right," I said.

"You're sick. I can see it. Now, you're coming right into the house with me and I'm going to fix you a cup of coffee, and you're going to lie down on the lounge until—"

"I think I'd better go home," I said.

I stood up and she stood up with me. And she looked almost as sick as I probably did. "Oh, I wish I hadn't told you, Carl! I might have known how upset you'd be."

"No, it's—I just think I'd better be going," I said.

"Let me call Bill. He can drive you."

"No, I'd rather you didn't," I said. "I—I want to walk around a little first."

She argued about it, looking and sounding like she might burst out crying any second. But finally she walked to the gate with me, and I got away.

I walked toward the house, the Winroys', my eyes stinging behind the contact lenses; and it didn't seem sunny or pleasant any more.

I could hear Ruthie out in the kitchen. No one else seemed to be around. I went out there, reached the whiskey out of the cupboard and took a long drink out of the bottle. I put it back in the cupboard, and turned around.

Ruthie was staring at me. She'd taken her hands out of the dishwater and was starting to reach for a towel. But somehow she never made it. She stared at me, and her face twisted as though a knife had been twisted in her; and she took a swing and a step on the crutch. Then her arms were around me and she was pressing me to her.

"C-Carl . . . oh, darling. What's the—"

"Nothing," I said. "Just a little sick at my stomach."

I grinned and pulled away from her. I gave her a little spank on the thigh, and I started to say, I *did* say, "Where's—?" But I didn't get a chance to finish the sentence. I heard Fay coming up the front steps, that firm I'm-really-something walk of hers. And by the time she got the front door open, I was in the hallway.

I winked and jerked my head over my shoulder. 'Just borrowed a drink of your whiskey, Mrs. Winroy. Had a sudden attack of stomach sickness."

"It's perfectly all right, Carl." She gave me back the wink. "Sick at your stomach, huh? Well, that's what you get for eating with cops."

"That's it," I laughed. "Thanks for the whiskey."

"Not at all," she said.

I started up the stairs. About halfway up, I suddenly turned around.

I wasn't quite sick enough to catch her at it; she was already entering the dining room. But I knew she'd been looking at me, and when I got to my room I found out why.

The back of my coat. The two white soapsuds prints of Ruthie's hands.

EIGHTEEN

Fay was an actress. The Man had been right about that. I didn't know how much she'd been acting up until now, but she could have been doing it all the time. She was good, what I mean. A whole week had passed since she'd seen those handprints, and if I hadn't known that she *had* seen them, I'd never have guessed that there was anything wrong.

She'd come up to my room that night, that Sunday, and we'd kicked the gong around for almost an hour; and she'd never let on. We'd been together again on Wednesday—and I mean, *together*— and there still wasn't any indication that she knew. She'd never done or said anything to show that she was hell-hot sore.

She was waiting. She was going to let it all slide, convince me that she hadn't seen anything, before she made her move.

She waited a whole week, until the next Sunday night and . . .

That week.

I'd thought that school couldn't be any worse than it'd been that Friday, but it was. Maybe it just seemed worse because there was so much more of it and so much less of me.

That wire Mrs. Summers had told me about. This trouble with Fay. Ruthie. Kendall. Jake . . .

Jake was at the house for almost every meal. A couple of mornings he even ate breakfast with Kendall and me. He was still hitting the jug pretty hard, but he didn't seem to sag so much.

He seemed to be getting bigger, and I was getting littler. Every day there was a little bit less of me.

I said he was hitting the bottle pretty hard. But he wasn't even in it with me. I had to nail down my breakfast every morning with a few drinks before I could go to school. And I had to have more in the afternoon before I could get to work, and at night . . .

Thursday night I took a bottle up to my room with me, and I got half cockeyed. I got a notion in my head to go over and wake Kendall up and tell him I was too sick to go on. I'd tell him I wanted to take him up on that business of going to Canada in his car, and I knew he'd argue a little but not much, because if a guy was that far gone, there wasn't much use in trying to use him. So he'd let me do it, and I'd go there, and in a few days someone from The Man would show up and . . .

But I couldn't get that drunk. It would have been too easy, and there was still a little hope left in me.

I had to go on waiting and hoping, losing more of the little that was left of myself.

It didn't seem possible that I'd slipped so far, that so much had gone wrong in such a short length of time. I guess I'd been walking on the edge of a cliff for a long time, and it didn't take a very big breeze to start me sliding.

It was almost a relief to slide.

Well . . .

I got through the week. Sunday came again, and I kind of wanted to go to church and see Mrs. Summers again but I couldn't bring myself to do it. I got to thinking *why* about her—why I wanted to please her and make her face light up—and all I could think of was that I might be trying to pull something on her like I had on Mrs. Fields.

I spent almost the whole day at the bakery; not just my shift but the day. I was actually there longer than Kendall was, and you had to go some to beat him.

Finally, though, it was ten o'clock, and I hadn't done anything but loaf for a couple of hours. So when he suggested knocking off, I didn't have any excuse for staying.

I showered and changed clothes. We walked home together.

He said I was doing fine. "I've been able to turn in a very good report on you, Mr. Bigelow," he said.

"Swell," I said.

"Studies going satisfactorily? Nothing I can help you with? After all, we mustn't lose sight of the fact that your job is only a means to an end. If it interferes with your school—the reason for your being here—why—"

"I understand," I said.

We said good night and I turned in.

I woke up a couple of hours later when Fay crawled into bed with me.

She'd taken off her nightgown, and she snuggled up close to me, warm and soft and sweet-smelling.

A little moonlight sifted past the edge of the window shades. It fell across the pillows, and I could see into her eyes. And they didn't tell me a thing, as they should have. And because they didn't, they told me a lot.

I knew she was ready to spring it.

"Carl—" she said. "I—I've got something to tell you."

"Well?"

"It's about Jake. H-he—he's going to go back to jail until after the trial."

My guts sank into my stomach like a fist. Then a little laugh came out of me and I said, "You're kidding."

She rolled her head on the pillows. "It's the truth, honey, if he's telling me the truth. Is it—is it bad?"

"Bad," I said. "Is it bad!"

"I don't mean he's going right away, honey. Tonight's the first time he's mentioned it, and the way he hates jail it'll probably take him a week to work himself up—"

"But," I said, "what—why is he doing it?"

"Gosh, I just don't know, honey."

"You told me he couldn't take jail. You told me he'd never go back. He knew it wouldn't change a damned thing."

"You told me that, too, honey. Remember?" She squirmed lazily against the sheets. "Scratch my back, will you, baby? You know. Down low there."

I didn't scratch it. If I'd got a grip on her hide right then, I'd have pulled it off of her.

"Fay," I said. "Look at me."

"Mmmm?" She tilted her head and looked. "Like this, Carl?"

"Jake's been getting his nerve back. He's in a lot better shape than he was when I came here. Why this sudden notion to go back to jail?"

"I told you, honey, I don't know. It doesn't make sense."

"You think he means it?"

"I'm pretty sure he means it. Once he gets an idea in his head, like he did about you, you know, he never lets go."

"I see," I said.

"Is it ba—we can do it, now, can't we Carl? Let's kill him now and get it over with. The quicker it's done the sooner we can be together. I know you'd probably rather go on like this as long as you can, but—"

"Why?" I said. "Why do you think I'd rather?"

"Well, you would, wouldn't you? You're having a good time. You and your dear sweet little—t-trashy little—"

I said: "What the hell are you talking about?"

"Never mind. The point is I'm not going to go on like this any longer. Even if you do want to."

She wouldn't come all the way out with what was eating on her, and anyway I already knew. It would only lead to a brawl, and things were bad enough as they were.

"I'll tell you why I'd rather wait," I said. "I was told to. And the guy who told me wasn't talking to exercise his lungs."

"W-what do—" Her eyes shifted nervously. "I don't see what difference it makes if—"

"I told you. I spelled it out for you."

"Well, it doesn't make any difference! I don't care what anyone says. We can do it now just as well as not."

"All right. It doesn't make any difference," I said. "You said it doesn't, so that settles that."

She looked at me sullenly. I reached across her to the reading stand and got a cigarette lighted.

I let the match burn until the flame was almost to my finger tips. Then I dropped it, squarely between her breasts.

"*Oooof!*" She slapped and brushed at the match, stifling the instinctive scream into a gasp. "Y-you!" she whispered. "W-why did you—?"

"That's the way acid feels," I said. "Just a little like that. I imagine they'd start there and work up."

"B-but I—I haven't—"

"You're in with me. If I get it, you get it. Only you'd be a lot more interesting to work on."

That was wrong, to throw that kind of scare into her. I shouldn't make her think she had nothing to lose by pulling a doublecross. But ... well, you see? For all I knew, she was already pulling one. Or on the point of doing it. And if I could make her see what it would cost her ...

"You're sure about it?" I said. "You didn't misunderstand him, Fay? If you did, you'd better tell me."

'I—I—" She hesitated. "W-well, maybe I—"

"No lies. If that's the way it is I've got to know."

Her head moved shakily. "Th-that's the way it is."

"I see," I said.

"I—I'll talk to him, Carl! I'll m-make him—he'll listen to me. I'll try to make him change his mind."

"You talk him into it," I said. "Then you try to talk him out of it. Huh-uh, baby. You're not that good."

"B-but I—what makes you think I—?"

"Don't kid me," I said. "How was it supposed to be, anyway? Jake's a nice boy, so they give him plenty of privileges in the jug, huh? He'll be safe and you can go right on seeing each other, and he won't be missing a thing. Is that it?"

She bit her lip. "M-maybe he doesn't mean it, Carl. Maybe he knows I didn't intend to—"

"Maybe," I nodded. "Maybe a couple of times. But like you said he's got the idea, and he doesn't let go of his ideas."

"B-but if ... Oh, Carl, honey! W-what will they—?"

"Nothing," I said, and I lay down again and pulled her into my arms. "I'll straighten it out. We should have waited, but as long as we can't—"

"You're sure it'll be all right? You're sure, Carl?"

"I'm sure," I lied. "I'll fix it up. After all, Jake could have got the idea by himself. They won't know that he didn't."

She sighed and relaxed a little. I kept on soothing her, telling her it would be all right, and after a while I got rid of her. She slipped back to her room.

I uncorked a pint I had, and sat on the edge of the bed drinking. It was around daylight when I went to sleep.

... I called The Man from a booth in that quiet little bar I'd found. He answered right away, and the first thing he asked me was where I was calling from. He said that was good, splendid, when I told him. And, dammit, it *was*; it was as good as I could do. So many drunks phone from bars that no one pays any attention to the calls.

But I knew he didn't think it was good. He didn't think I should be calling him at all.

He told me he'd call me back. I hung up and had a couple of drinks while he went to another phone.

"All right, Charlie—" his voice came over the wire again. "What's on your mind?"

"Our—that merchandise," I said. "It looks like it was going off the market. We'll have to act fast to get it."

"I don't understand," he said. "You'd better speak plainly. I hardly think that our conversation can be completely camouflaged and comprehensible at the same time."

"All right," I said. "Jake's talking about going to jail until after the trial. I'm not sure whether he means it or not, but I thought I'd better not take any chances."

"You want to do it now, then. Soon."

"Well"—I hesitated—"I can't do it after he's in jail."

"That isn't what we agreed on, Charlie."

"I know," I said, "but I—"

"You said he'd been talking about it. To whom?"

"To Mrs. Winroy."

"I see. And does she still have your fullest confidence, Charlie? You'll recall, I believe, that I had some few small doubts about her myself."

"I think she's telling the truth," I said.

"Why does she say Jake's going to jail?"

"She doesn't say. Jake didn't tell her."

"Strange." He paused. "I find that slightly puzzling."

"Look," I said. "I know it doesn't seem right, but Jake's halfway off his rocker! He's running around in circles."

"A moment, please. Am I wrong or wasn't it Mrs. Winroy's job to keep Jake available? You were very sure she could do that, weren't you? And now the opposite has happened."

"Yes, sir," I said.

"Why, Charlie?"

"I don't know," I said. "I don't know whether he's really going to do it."

He was silent for a long time. I'd about decided he'd hung up. Then, he laughed softly and said:

"You do whatever you think is necessary, Charlie. As soon as you think it's necessary."

"I know how you feel," I said. "I haven't been here very long, and . . . I know it would look better if I could have waited."

"Yes. And there's the matter of publicity, having the story kept alive for weeks. Or perhaps you've forgotten that in the press of your other affairs?"

"Look," I said. "Is it all right or not? I want to know."

He didn't answer me.

That time he *had* hung up.

I picked up my books off the bar and went on to school. Cursing Fay, but not putting much heart into it. It was my fault for bringing her into the deal.

The Man hadn't wanted her in. If she hadn't been in and Jake had got this jail idea on his own, I wouldn't have been held responsible. As it was . . .

Well, a lot depended on how things worked out. If it all went off all right they'd go easy on me. No money, of course. Or, if I had the guts and was stupid enough to ask for money, a few bills and a beating. They'd leave me here—that would be my payoff. I'd be left here to rot, with no dough but the little I had and no way I could get any more. Just barely scraping by on some cheap job, as long as I could hold a job and then . . .

The Man would get a kick out of that. Hell—*the hell*—he knew you didn't have to dig for it, too.

And if the job didn't go right . . .

It didn't make much difference. I couldn't win.

NINETEEN

It was Sunday when Fay had given me the bad news.

We set Jake up for Thursday night.

So there were four days there, between the first thing and the second. Four whole days. But it didn't seem that long. It seemed like I'd walked out of the bar, after I'd talked to The Man, and stepped straight into Thursday night.

I was through, washed up. I wasn't living; I was just going through the motions.

Living is remembering, I guess. If you've lost interest, if everything is that same shade of gray, the kind you see when you look into light with your eyes closed, if nothing seems worth storing away, either as bad or good, reward or retribution, then you may keep going for a while. But you don't live. And you don't remember.

I went to school. I worked. I ate and slept. And drank. And . . . Yes, and Ruthie. I talked to her a few times on the way to and from school. I remembered—yes, I *did* remember her. I remember wondering what would become of her. Wishing I could help her some way.

But aside from Ruthie, nothing.

Except for the few minutes I was with her, I moved straight from Monday into Thursday. Thursday night at eight o'clock.

I snapped out of it then, and came back to life. You have to at a time like that whether you want to or not.

It was a slow night on the job, one of the slowest in the week. I was all caught up on my work, and no one had any reason to come into the stockroom.

I stood in the outer storeroom with the light turned off, watching the other side of the street.

Fay went by, right on the dot at eight.

I studied my watch, waiting. At eight-fifteen, Jake went by.

I unlocked the door and stepped out.

It was a good dark night. He was moving in a beeline for the house, not looking to right or left.

I sauntered down the side of the street the bakery was on, until he'd passed the intersection. Then I crossed over and followed him, walking faster because he'd got quite a way ahead of me.

I was about fifty feet behind him when he started across the parallel street to the house. Just about the right distance, allowing for the time he needed to open the gate. He fumbled with it, unable to find the catch, and I slowed down to where I was barely moving. At last he got it open, and I . . .

I froze in my tracks.

He—this guy—was a drunk, I found out later. He'd come out of that little bar catercornered to the house and wandered across the road, and I don't know how the hell he'd managed it but somehow he'd fallen over inside the fence. He was lying there when Jake came along, inside and up against the fence. As Jake opened the gate, he rose up and sort of staggered toward him. And Jake let out a yell.

And that front yard was suddenly as bright as day.

Two big floodlights struck it from the vacant lots on each side of the house. Cops—deputy sheriffs, rather—swarmed up from everywhere.

I stood frozen for a second, unable to move. Then I turned around and started walking back to the bakery.

I'd gotten almost to the corner when I heard a yell from the sheriff rising above the other yells. *"Wait a minute, dang it! This ain't the right—"*

I kept right on going, and I was crossing the street to the bakery before the shout came. *"You there! Halt!"*

I didn't halt. What the hell? He was almost two blocks away. How should I know he was hollering at me?

I went right on into the bakery, locking the door behind me. I went into the main stockroom, closed the connecting door, and sat down at my work table.

I picked up the batch cards for the night, and began checking them off against my perpetual inventory.

Someone was banging on that outside door. I stayed where I was. What the hell again? I couldn't let anyone in that door this time of night. Why, it might be a robber, someone trying to steal a sack of flour!

The banging stopped. I grinned to myself, flipping through the cards. I was alive again. I'd have laid down for them, but since I couldn't do that, I'd make them lay me.

The door to the baking room slammed open. Kendall and the sheriff and a deputy came in, the sheriff in the lead.

I stood up. I went toward him, holding out my hand.

"Why, how are you, sheriff?" I said. "How is Mrs. Sum—"

He swung his hand, knocking mine aside so hard that it almost spun me around. His fingers knotted in my shirt, and he yanked me clean off the floor. He shook me like a dog shakes a rat. If ever I saw murder in a mug it was his.

"You snotty little punk!" He shook and swung me with one hand and began slapping me with the other. "Think you're cute, huh? Think it's smart to go around so danged nice an' lovey-dovey, gettin' people to trust you and then—"

I didn't blame him for being sore. I guess no one can ever be as sore at you as the guy who's liked and trusted you. But that hand of his was a hard as a rock, and Kendall couldn't get past the deputy to stop him like he was trying to do.

I passed out.

TWENTY

I wasn't out very long, I guess, but it was long enough for Dr. Dodson to get there. I came to, stretched out on the floor with my head on some flour sacking and the doc bent over me.

"How are you feeling, son?" he said. "Any pain?"

"Of course, he's in pain!" Kendall snapped. "This—this creature beat him within an inch of his life!"

"Now, wait a minute, dang it! I didn't—"

"Shut up, Summers. How about it, son?"

"I—I feel all right," I said. "Just kind of dizzy, and—" I coughed and began to choke. He raised my shoulders quickly, and I bent over, choking and coughing, and blood spilled down on the floor in a little pool.

He took the handkerchief out of his breast pocket and wiped my mouth with it. He lowered me back to the floor again, and stood up, staring at the sheriff.

The sheriff looked back at him, sullen and sheepish.

"Kinda lost my temper," he mumbled. "Reckon you would've, too, doc, if you'd been in my place. He was all set t'do Winroy in, just like the note said he'd be, and then this danged drunk gets in the way an' he comes saunterin' back here, just as pretty as you please, and—"

"You know," the doctor cut in, quietly. "You know something, Summers? If I had a gun I think I'd blow that fat head of yours right off your shoulders."

The sheriff's mouth dropped open. He looked stunned, and sort of sick. "Now, now looky here," he stammered. "This—you don't know who this fella is! He's Charlie Bigger, Little Bigger, they call him. He's a killer, an'—"

"He is, eh? But you took care of him, didn't you?"

"You want to know what happened or not?" Sheriff Summers' face turned a few shades redder. "He—'

"I'll tell you what happened," Kendall spoke up coldly. "Carl stepped out for a little walk, as he has my permission to do when his work is caught up. In fact, I've encouraged him to do it since his illness. He was in the vicinity of the Winroy house when this ruckus broke out, and having something better to do with his time than gawk and gape at matters which did not concern him—"

"The heck they didn't concern him! How come the note said he—"

"—he came back here," said Kendall. "A few minutes later, Summers came storming into the bakery with this—uh—hireling and started babbling some nonsense about Carl's having tried to murder someone and failing to stop when he was ordered to. Then he rushed in here and attacked him, beat him into unconsciousness. I've never seen such savagely inexcusable brutality in my life, Dod!"

"I see," the doctor nodded, and turned to the sheriff. "Well?"

Sheriff Summers' lips came together in a thin hard line. "Never mind," he grunted. "You want it that way, you have it that way. I'm takin' him to jail."

"On what charge? Taking a walk?"

"Attempted murder, that's what!"

"And what are your grounds for such a charge?"

"I already told—!" The sheriff broke off, his head lowered like a mad bull. "Never you mind. I'm takin' him in."

He started toward me, the deputy hanging back like he was pretty unhappy, and Kendall and the doc stepped in his way. In about another ten seconds, I think he'd have had a knockdown drag-out fight on his hands. And there wasn't any sense in that, so I got up.

I felt all right, everything considered. Just a little smaller and weaker than I had felt.

"I'll go," I said.

"We can settle it; you don't need to go," the doctor said, and Kendall added, "No, he certainly does *not* need to!"

"I'd rather go," I said. "Sheriff Summers and his wife have been very nice to me. I'm sure he wouldn't be doing this if he didn't think it was necessary."

There was some more argument from Dodson and Kendall, but I went. We all went.

We got to the courthouse just as the county attorney was going up the steps, and the deputy took us into the c.a.'s office while he and the sheriff stood in the corridor talking.

The sheriff had his back to the door, but the county attorney was facing it, and he looked weary and disgusted. All the time the sheriff was talking, he just stood there with his hands shoved into his pockets, frowning and shaking his head.

Finally, they came inside, and he and the sheriff started to ask a question at the same time. They both stopped, one waiting for the other, then they started again, both at once. They did that about three times, and the doctor let out a snort and Kendall sort of half smiled. The county attorney grimaced and leaned back in his chair.

"All right, Bill," he sighed. "It's your headache, anyway."

Sheriff Summers turned to me.

"What's your name? Your right name?"

"You know what it is, sheriff," I said.

"It's Charlie Bigger, ain't it? You're Little Charlie Bigger."

"Suppose I said, yes," I said. "Then what? I'd like to accommodate you, sheriff, but I don't see how that would help."

"I asked you what your—!" He broke off as the county attorney caught his eyes. "All right," he grunted. "What was you doin' sneaking along behind Jake Winroy tonight?"

"I wasn't sneaking anywhere. I was walking."

"You always go for a walk at that time o'night?"

"Not always. Often. It's a slack time for me."

"How come you was walkin' toward the Winroy place instead of the other way?"

"These work clothes. Naturally, I wouldn't want to walk up toward the business district."

"I got a note about you. It had you right down to a *t*. Said you was gonna do just what you—what you tried to do."

"What was that?" I said.

"You know what. Kill Jake Winroy!"

"Kill him?" I said. "Why, I didn't try to kill him, sheriff."

"You would have! If that danged drunk—"

Dr. Dodson let out another snort. "Anonymous notes! What next? "

"He was there, wasn't he?" The sheriff whirled on him. "How come I got that note if—"

"I believe it has been established," the county attorney sighed, "that he is in that vicinity almost every night at approximately that time."

"But Winroy ain't! It ain't been established how I—"

Kendall cleared his throat. "Since you seem to be unwilling to accept the note as the work of some crank who has observed Mr. Bigelow's movements and who profited by an unfortunate but by no means extraordinary coincidence—"

"It's too danged extraordinary for me!"

"As I was saying, then, the note can only be explained in one way. This shrewd and crafty killer"—he smiled apologetically at me—"the most elusive, close-mouthed criminal in the country, went around town confiding his plans . . . Something wrong, sheriff?"

"I didn't say he done that! I—I—"

"I see. It's your theory, then, that he wrote you—or I believe it was printed, wasn't it?—he sent you the note himself. So that you'd be on hand to apprehend him."

Doc Dodson burst out laughing. The county attorney tried not to laugh, but he couldn't quite hold it back.

"Well," he said, bringing his hands down on the desk. "Bill, I think the best thing we can do is—"

"Now, wait a minute! He could have had someone workin' with him! They could've given him away!"

"Oh, come now." Kendall shook his head. "He's a stranger here. I live with him and work with him, and I can assure you he has no intimates aside from me. But perhaps that's what you had in mind, sheriff? You think I was involved in this matter."

"I didn't say so, did I?" The sheriff glared at him helplessly. "I—anyway, that ain't all I got on him. I got a wire from the kin of some folks he used to live with. They said he swindled and abused these old people, and—"

"I believe you got two other wires about me, also," I said. "From a chief of police and a county judge. What did they say about me?"

"I—well—why'd you run away tonight?"

"I didn't do any running, sheriff."

"Why didn't you stop when I hollered? You heard me."

"I heard someone, but they were a couple of blocks away. I didn't know they were hollering at me."

"Well—uh—why—?"

He paused, trying to think of something else to ask me. He wet his lips, hesitating. He slanted a glance at Kendall and Dodson and the county attorney, and in his mind's eye, I guess, he was also looking at his wife, wondering how he was going to explain and excuse himself to her.

The county attorney yawned and massaged his eyes. "Well," he said, "I suppose we'll have an army of city cops moving in on us now. Ordering us around and telling us how to run our business like they did last time."

"Now, I—I—" The sheriff gulped. "I don't reckon we will. My boys ain't letting out anything."

"He'd probably like that," said Dr. Dodson. "Likes to get his picture in the papers. If I didn't think you'd suffer enough without it, I'd file a complaint against you with the county commissioners."

"You will, hey?" The sheriff jumped to his feet. "Hop right to it! Go ahead and see if I give a dang."

"We'll see," Dodson nodded, grimly. "Meanwhile, I'm going to take this boy to my clinic and put him to bed."

"You are, huh? He ain't going anywhere."

"Very well. He needs rest and medical attention. I've said so. These gentlemen are my witnesses. And I'll tell you something, Summers—" He slammed on his hat. "Don't be too surprised if you find them testifying against you on a charge of murder by criminal neglect."

"Pshaw." The sheriff's eyes wavered. "How come he gets around like he's been doin' if he's so sick? You can't tell me—"

"I could but I doubt that you'd understand . . . Coming, Phil?"

Well . . .

I went to the clinic.

The doctor checked me over from head to foot, shaking his head and grunting now and then in a kind of baffled way. Then he gave me a shot glass of some yellowish stuff, and three hypodermic injections, one in each hip and the other right over my heart; and I went to sleep.

But Sheriff Summers still hadn't given up. He posted a deputy on my door at the clinic that night. And the next morning, around eleven, he came in and threw some more questions at me.

He didn't look like he'd got much sleep. I'd have bet dough that Mrs. Summers had eaten him out to a fare-you-well.

He was still at it, going through the motions of playing cop, when Kendall showed up. Kendall spoke to him pleasantly. He suggested that they take a little walk, and they left together.

I grinned and lighted a cigarette. Kendall was starting to earn his money, if he hadn't already earned it. It was the first real chance he'd had to get the sheriff alone.

The next thing he'd do, now . . .

The rest and the stuff the doctor had given me seemed to have perked me up quite a bit. And I guess a guy always fights best just before he's through fighting. I didn't think I could beat The Man— no one ever beat The Man—but I figured I could give him plenty of trouble. It might be a year or two before he could hunt me down, and if I could hold out that long . . . well. Maybe I could find the place or the thing or whatever it was I'd always been looking for.

I had almost five hundred dollars—more in the bank in Arizona, but I might as well forget about that. With five hundred bucks and a good car—and there was a drop in Philly where I could turn that car fast for another one—well, it was worth a try. I couldn't lose anything.

... It was almost two o'clock when Kendall came back. And I was sure of what he was going to say, but he led into it so gradually that I almost got unsure.

Mrs. Winroy had gone to New York, he said. Her sister had taken sick and she'd had to leave suddenly.

"Poor woman. I've never seen her quite so agitated."

"That's too bad," I said, wanting to laugh so bad it hurt me. She'd probably worry herself to death before they could get to her. "When is she coming back?"

"She wasn't able to say. I gathered, however, that it might be quite some time."

"Well," I said, "that's certainly too bad."

"Yes. Particularly with nothing better than Winroy to depend on. I wanted to talk to him—straighten out our accounts since Mrs. Winroy isn't available, but Ruthie hasn't seen anything of him since lunchtime and he's not at his shop. I suppose, now that the last restraining influence is gone, he intends to get drunk and stay drunk."

I nodded. And waited. He went on.

"An awkward situation. Poor Ruthie; it's really a tragedy in her case. There's no other place she can get a job, and, with Mrs. Winroy gone indefinitely, she can't stay there. I'd like to help her, but—uh—a man my age, giving financial assistance to a girl who obviously could not repay it . . . I'm afraid it would do her more harm than good."

"She's dropping out of school?"

"I'm afraid there's no alternative. She seems to be bearing up very well, I'm happy to say."

"Well," I said. "It looks like we—like you'll have to be finding another place to live."

"Uh, yes. Yes, I suppose I will. Uh—er—incidentally, Mr. Bigelow, the sheriff is satisfied to—uh—abandon this Winroy matter. I've brought your clothes from the bakery, your pay to date also since it seemed doubtful in view of your health, and—uh—the situation in general—that you would care to continue there."

"I see," I said. "I understand."

"About Sheriff Summers, Mr. Bigelow. His attitude is by no means as compromising as I would like to have it. I suspect that he would need only the slightest pretext, if any, to—uh—cause you serious embarrassment."

I thought it over; rather I appeared to be thinking it over. I laughed, kind of hurt, and said, "It looks like I'm out of luck all the way around, Mr. Kendall. No place to live. No job. The sheriff all set to make trouble. The—I don't suppose the college will be exactly happy to have me around either."

"Well—uh—as a matter of fact—"

"It's all right," I said. "I don't blame them a bit."

He shook his head sympathetically, clucking his tongue a few times. Then he looked up sharply, eyes sparkling, and came out with it. As though it had just then popped into his mind.

"Mr. Bigelow! This may turn out to be a stroke of good fortune in disguise! You can go up to my place in Canada for a few months, use the time for studying and rebuilding your health. Then, when all this business is forgotten—"

"Gosh," I said. "You mean you'd still be willing to—?"

"Certainly, I would! Now, most of all. Of course, we'll have to see what the doctor has to say about you, but—"

... The doctor didn't like it much. He fussed quite a bit, particularly when he found out that I wanted to leave town that day. But Kendall fussed right back, calling him a pessimist and so on. Then he took him to one side, explaining, I guess, that I didn't have much choice about leaving. So ...

We drove to the house in Kendall's car, me driving since he didn't like to. He asked me if I'd mind driving Ruthie to her folks' farm on my way, and I said I wouldn't mind at all.

I stopped in front of the house, and we stood at the side of the car for a few minutes, talking but not getting much said.

"By the way, Mr. Bigelow," he said, hesitantly, "I know I've seemed inexcusably dictatorial during our all too brief acquaintance. I'm sure there must have been a great many times when you must have felt like telling me to mind my own business."

"Oh, no," I said. "Not at all, Mr. Kendall."

"Oh, yes." He smiled at me. "And I'm afraid my reasons were

extremely selfish ones. Do you believe in immortality, Mr. Bigelow? In the broadest sense of the word, that is? Well, let me simply say then that I seem to have done almost none of the many things which I had planned on doing in this tearful vale. They are still there in me, waiting to be done, yet the span of time for their doing has been exhausted. I ... But listen to me, will you?" He chuckled embarrassedly, his eyes blinking behind their glasses. "I didn't think myself capable of such absurd poeticism!"

"That's all right," I said, slowly, and a kind of chill crept over me. "What do you mean your span—"

I was looking straight into him, through him and out the other side, and all I could see was a prim, fussy old guy. That was all I could see, because that was all there was to see. *He wasn't working for The Man. He never had been.*

"... so little time, Mr. Bigelow. None to waste on preliminaries. Everything that could be done for you had to be done quickly."

"Why didn't you tell me?" I said. "For Christ's sake, why—"

"Tsk, tsk, Mr. Bigelow. Fret you with the irremediable? Place yet another boulder in your already rocky path? There is nothing to be done about it. I am dying and that is that."

"But I ... if you'd only told me!"

"I only tell you now because it is unavoidable. As I have indicated in the past, I am not exactly a pauper. I wanted you to be in a position to understand when you heard from my attorneys."

I couldn't say anything. I couldn't even see the way my eyes were stinging and burning. Then he grabbed my hand and shook it, and his grip almost made me holler.

"Dignity, Mr. Bigelow! I insist on it. If you must be mawkish, at least wait until I ... I—"

He let go of me, and when my eyes cleared he was gone.

I opened the gate to the yard, wondering how I could have been so wrong. But there really wasn't much to wonder about. I'd picked him because I didn't want to pick the logical person. The person who could do everything he could, and who had a lot better reason for doing it ... Ruthie.

I wasn't particularly quiet going into the house, so I guess she heard me, even if she didn't let on. The drapes to the living room were pulled back and her bedroom door was open, and I stood watching her, braced against the end of the bedstead, as she pulled on her clothes.

I looked her over, a little at a time, as though she wasn't one thing but many, as though she wasn't one woman but a thousand, all women. And then my eyes settled on that little foot with its little ankle, and everything else seemed to disappear. And I thought:

"Well, how could I? How can you admit you're screwing yourself?"

She put on her brassiere and her slip before she took notice of me. She let out a gasp and said, "Oh, C-Carl! I didn't—"

"About ready?" I said. "I'll drive you out to your folks."

"C-Carl, I—I—"

She came toward me, slowly, rocking on her crutch. "I want to go with you, Carl! I don't care what you've—I don't care about anything! Just so I can be with you."

"Yeah," I said. "I know. You were always afraid I'd go away, weren't you? You were willing to do anything you could to keep me here. Help me with the school, sleep with me ... be Johnny-on-the-spot if I needed you for anything. And you couldn't leave either, could you, Ruthie? You couldn't lose your job."

"Take me, Carl! You've got to take me with you!"

I wasn't sure yet. So I said, "Well, go on and get ready. We'll see."

Then, I went upstairs to my room.

I packed my two suitcases. I turned back a corner of the carpet and picked up a carbon copy of the note I'd sent to the sheriff.

For, naturally, I had sent the note. I'd meant to tell Ruthie about the carbon afterwards so that she could take credit for the tip and claim the rewards.

I hadn't had anything to lose, as I saw it. I couldn't help myself, so I'd tried to help her. The person who might wind up as I had if she didn't have help.

I hesitated a moment, turning the slip of paper around in my fingers. But it was no good now. They'd muffed their chance to catch me in the act of attempting to kill Jake Winroy, and I figured there was at least one damned good reason why they'd never get another one.

I figured that way, but I wanted to make sure. I burned the carbon in an ashtray, and crossed the hall to Jake's room.

I stood at the side of his bed, looking down. At him and the note Ruthie had written.

It was stupid; no one would believe that Jake had tried to attack her and she'd done it in self-defence. But, well, I could understand. The whole setup had been falling apart. Ruthie had to do it fast if at all. And I guess if a person is willing to do a thing like that, then he's stupid to begin with and it's bound to crop out on him sooner or later.

It was all wrong. The Man wouldn't like it. And getting me for him wouldn't help her any. She had to latch onto me now, of course; and you get stupider and stupider the farther you go. But excuses didn't cut any ice with The Man. He picked you because you were stupid; he *made* you stupid, you might say. But if you slipped up, *you* did it. And you got what The Man gave people who slipped.

It was done, though, and me, I was done, too. So nothing mattered now but to let her go on hoping. As long as she could hope...

I took one last look at Jake before I left the room. Ruthie had almost sawed his throat out with one of his own razors. Scared, you know, and scared not to. Angry because she was scared. It looked a lot like the job I'd done on Fruit Jar.

TWENTY-ONE

I'd never seen the place, just the road that led up to it; and I'd only seen that the one time years before when that writer had driven me by on the way to the train. But I didn't have any trouble finding it again. The road was grown high with weeds, and in some places long vines had spread across it from the bare-branched trees on either side.

The road sloped up from the Vermont highway, then down again, so that unless you were right there, right on top of them, you couldn't see the house and the farm buildings. Ruth looked at me pretty puzzled a time or two, but she didn't ask any questions. I ran the car into the garage and closed the doors, and we walked back toward the house.

There was a sign fastened to the gate. It said:

BEWARE OF WILD GOATS
"The Way of the Trespasser is Hard"

And there was a typewritten notice tacked to the back door:

Departed for parts unknown. Will supply forwarding address, if, when, and as soon as possible.

The door was unlocked. We went in.

I looked all through the house, by myself mostly because the stairs were steep and narrow and Ruthie couldn't have got around so good. I went through room after room, and he wasn't there, of course, no one was there, and everything was covered with dust but everything was in order. All the rooms were in order but one, a little tiny one way off by itself on the second floor. And except for the way the typewriter was ripped apart, even that one had a kind of order about it.

The furniture was all pushed back against the wall, and there was nothing in the bookcases but the covers of books. The pages of them and God knows how many other pages—typewritten ones that hadn't been made into books—had been torn up like confetti. And the confetti was stacked in little piles all over the floor. Arranged into letters and words:

And the Lord World so loved the god that It gave him Its only begotten son, and thenceforth He was driven from the Garden and Judas wept, saying, Verily I abominate onions yet I can never refuse them.

I kicked the piles of paper apart, and went downstairs.

We moved in, and stayed.

There was case after case of canned goods in the cellar. There was a drum of coal oil for the lamps and the two stoves. There was a water well with an inside pump at the sink. There wasn't any electricity or telephone or radio or anything like that; we were shut off from everything, as though we were in another world. But we had everything else, and ourselves. So we stayed.

The days drifted by, and I wondered what she was waiting for. And there was nothing to do ... except what could be done with ourselves. And I seemed to be shrinking more and more, getting weaker and littler while she got stronger and bigger. And I began to think maybe she was going to do it that way.

Some nights, afterwards, when I wasn't too weak and sick to do it, I'd stand at the window, staring out at the fields with their jungle of weeds and vines. The wind rippled through them, making them sway and wiggle and squirm. And there was a howling and a shrieking in my ears—but after a while it went away. Everywhere, everywhere I looked, the jungle swayed and wiggled and squirmed. It shook that thing at me. There was something sort of hypnotic about it, and I'd still be weak and sick, but I wouldn't notice it. There wouldn't be a thing in my mind but that thing, and I'd wake her up again. And then it was like I was running a race, I was trying to get to something, get something, before the howling came back. Because when I heard that I had to stop.

But all I ever got was that thing. Not the other, whatever the other was.

The goats always won.

TWENTY-TWO

The days drifted by, and she knew that I knew, of course, but we never talked about it. We never talked about anything much because we were cut off from everything, and after a while everything was said that we could say and it would have been like talking to yourself. So we talked less and less, and pretty soon we were hardly talking at all. And then we *weren't* talking at all. Just grunting and gesturing and pointing at things.

It was like we'd never known how to talk.

It began to get pretty cold, so we shut off all the upstairs rooms and stayed downstairs. And it got colder and we shut off all the rooms but the living room and the kitchen. And it got colder and we shut off all the rooms but the kitchen. We lived there, never more than a few feet away from each other. It was always right close by, that thing was, and outside ... it was out there too. It seemed to edge in closer and closer, from all sides, and there was no way to get away from it. And I didn't want to get away. I kept getting weaker and littler, but I couldn't stop. There was nothing else to think about, so I kept taking that thing. I'd go for it fast, trying to win the race against the goats. And I never did, but I kept on trying. I had to.

Afterwards, when the howling began to get so bad I couldn't stand it, I'd go outside looking for the goats. I'd go running and screaming and clawing my way through the fields, wanting to get my hands on just one of them. And I never did, of course, because the fields weren't really the place to find the goats.

TWENTY-THREE

I couldn't eat much of anything. The basement was loaded with food and whiskey, but I had a hard time getting any down. I'd eaten less and less ever since that first day when I'd raised up the trap door that was set flush with the kitchen floor and gone down the steep narrow steps.

I'd gone down them, taking a lantern with me, and I'd looked all along the shelves, packed tight with bottles and packages and canned goods. I'd circled around the room, looking, and I came to a sort of setback in the walls—a doorless closet, kind of. And the entrance to it was blocked off, stacked almost to the ceiling with empty bottles.

I wondered why in hell they'd been dumped there instead of outside, because it would be stupid of a guy to drink the stuff upstairs, where he naturally would drink it, and then bring the bottles back down here. As long as he was up there, why hadn't he ...?

TWENTY-FOUR

I said we never talked, but we did. We talked all the time to the goats. I talked to them while she slept and she talked to them while I slept. Or maybe it was the other way around. Anyway, I did my share of talking.

I said we lived in the one room, but we didn't. We lived in all the rooms, but they were all the same. And wherever we were the goats were always there. I couldn't ever catch them but I knew they were there. They'd come up out of the fields and moved in with us, and sometimes I'd almost get my hands on them but they always got away. She'd get in my way before I could grab them.

I thought and I thought about it, and finally I knew how it must be. They'd been there all along. Right there, hiding inside of her. So it wasn't any wonder I could never win the race.

I knew they were in her, where else could they be, but I had to make sure. And I couldn't.

I couldn't touch her. She didn't sleep with me any more. She ate a lot, enough for two people, and sometimes in the morning she vomited ...

It was right after the vomiting started that she began walking. I mean, really walking, not using the crutch.

She'd tuck her dress up around her waist, so that it wouldn't be in the way, and walk back and forth on one knee and that little foot. She got to where she could walk pretty good. She'd hold her good foot up behind her with one hand, making a stump out of the knee. It came just about even, then, with that little baby foot and she could get around pretty fast.

She'd walk for an hour at a time with her dress tucked up and everything she had showing, but you'd never have known I was there from the way she acted. She ...

Hell, she talked to me. She explained to me. We'd been talking all the time, and not to the goats either, because of course there weren't any goats, and ...

She walked on the little foot, exercising the goats. And at night they sat on my chest howling.

TWENTY-FIVE

I stayed in the basement as much as I could. She couldn't get me down there. She wasn't good enough on that little foot and knee to come down the stairs. And somehow I had to hang on.

The last race was over, and I'd lost them all, but still I hung on. I seemed to be right on the point of finding something ... of finding out something. And until I did I couldn't leave.

I found out one evening when I was coming up out of the basement. I came even with the floor and turned sideways on the steps, putting down the stuff I'd brought up. And I'd brought a pretty big load because I didn't want to come up any more often than I had to; and I was kind of dizzy. I leaned my arms on the floor, steadying myself. And then my eyes cleared, and there was the little foot and leg right in front of me. Braced.

The axe flashed. My hand, my right hand, jumped and kind of leaped away from me, sliced off clean. And she swung again and all my left hand was gone but the thumb. She moved in closer, raising the axe for another swing ...

And so, at last, I knew.

TWENTY-SIX

Back there. Back to the place I'd come from. And, hell, I'd never been wanted there to begin with.

"... but where else, my friend? Where a more logical retreat in this tightening circle of frustration?"

She was swinging wild. My right shoulder was hanging by a thread, and the spouting forearm dangled from it. And my scalp, my scalp and the left side of my face was dangling, and ... and I didn't have a nose ... or a chin ... or ...

I went over backwards, then down and down and down, turning

so slowly in the air it seemed that I was hardly moving. I didn't know it when I hit the bottom. I was simply there, looking up as I'd been looking on the way down.

Then there was a slam and a click, and she was gone.

TWENTY-SEVEN

The darkness and myself. Everything else was gone. And the little that was left of me was going, faster and faster.

I began to crawl. I crawled and rolled and inched my way along; and I missed it the first time—the place I was looking for.

I circled the room twice before I found it, and there was hardly any of me then but it was enough. I crawled up over the pile of bottles, and went crashing down the other side.

And he was there, of course.

Death was there.

TWENTY-EIGHT

And he smelled good.

A SWELL-LOOKING
BABE

ONE

He had dreamed about her. Now, waking to the sweaty southern night, he found both arms clasped around his pillow, the cloth wet with saliva where his mouth had pressed against it, and he flung it away from him with a mixture of disgust and disappointment. Some babe, he thought drowsily, his hand moving from bed lamp to alarm clock to cigarettes. A dream boat—and that's the way he'd better leave her. Right in the land of dreams. He had to keep the money coming in. He had to keep out of trouble. And he had been sternly advised, at the time of his employment by the Hotel Manton, that bellboys who attempted intimacies with lady guests invariably landed in serious trouble.

"This is what they call a tight hotel," the superintendent of service had explained. "A hooker never gets past the room clerk. Or if she does, she doesn't stay long and neither does he. It's just good business, get me, Rhodes? A guest may not be everything he should be himself, but he doesn't want to pay upwards of ten dollars a day for a room in a whore house."

"I understand," Dusty had said.

"We're not running any Sunday school, of course. As long as our guests are quiet about it, we'll put up with a little hanky-panky. But we don't—and you don't—mix into it, see? Don't get friendly with a woman, even if she does seem to invite it. You might be mistaken. She might change her mind. And the hotel would have a hell of a lawsuit on its hands."

Dusty had nodded again, his thin face slightly flushed with embarrassment. That had been almost a year ago, back before he had lost his capacity for being insulted, before he had learned simply to accept ... and hate. He had thought the job only temporary then, something that paid well, without the business experience and references usually required in well-paying jobs. Mom had still been alive. Dad had stood a chance of being reinstated by the school board. He, Dusty, had had to drop out of school, but it would be only for a few months. So he had thought—or hoped. He was going to be a doctor, not merely a uniform with a number on it.

He had nodded his understanding, blushing, trying to cut short the interview. And the superintendent's face had softened, and he had called him by his first name.

"Are you sure you want to do this kind of work, Bill? I can fit you in as food checker or key clerk or something of that nature. Of course, it wouldn't pay nearly as much as you can make on tips, but . . ."

"Thank you," Dusty had said. "But I think I'd better take it, the job that pays the most money."

"Don't forget what I've said, then." The superintendent became impersonal again. "It's only fair to tell you, incidentally, that periodic checks are made on all our service employees."

"Checks?"

"Yes. By women detectives—spotters, we call 'em. So watch yourself when some prize looker makes a play for you. She may be working for the hotel."

Dusty had mumbled a promise to watch himself. Until last night, he had strictly adhered to that promise. It wasn't because of any want of temptation. As the superintendent had pointed out, the Manton wasn't running a Sunday school. It was exclusive largely via its room rates. You didn't have to show a financial statement or a marriage certificate to get a room. The Manton insisted not so much on respectability as the appearance of it; its concern was for its own welfare, not the morals of its guests.

Actually, Dusty supposed, the Manton got more than its share of the fast crowd; they preferred it to hotels with lower rates and virtually no restrictions. In any event, more than one woman guest had given him some pretty broad hints, and he'd let them slide right on past. Not because they might be spotters. He just hadn't been interested. In his sea of troubles, there'd been no room for women.

Then, last night . . .

Dusty yawned, glanced at the clock, and swung his feet out of bed. For a moment he remained perched on the edge of the mattress, absently wiggling his toes against the semi-cool bare floor. Then he stood up and padded into the bathroom.

He took a quick cold shower. He came out of the shower stall, and began to shave.

Even with his face lathered, tautened and twisted to receive the strokes of the razor, he was good-looking, and, more important, intelligent-looking. As a youngster, when the other kids had dubbed him with such hateful titles as Pretty Boy and Dolly, he had detested those good looks. And while he had eventually become resigned to them, he had always resented them. They could get him nothing he wanted, nothing, with ten years of college study to complete, that he had time for. After all, he was going to be a doctor, not an actor.

A year ago he had gone to work at the Manton, and gradually, through the months since then, it had been borne home to him that he was never going back to college, that he would never be a doctor. But that had not changed his attitude about his appearance. It set him apart from the other employees, at once arousing their resentment and precluding the anonymity which he sought. It brought unwanted and dangerous attentions from certain of the women guests.

It spelled nothing but trouble, and he was already knee-deep in trouble.

Then, last night had come, and for the first time in his life he was glad that he was as he was. After he had seen her, after what had happened last night ...

He dashed water over his face, dried it, stood frowning at himself in the medicine-cabinet mirror. Silently, he advised his image to forget last night. A dame like that didn't go for bellboys. She might tease you along a little, but that would be the end of it. Or if it wasn't the end of it, if you could actually get a tumble from her, what of it? Nothing. Just a big fat headache. He might not be able to drop her, and he certainly couldn't hang onto her. For something he couldn't really have—just a taste of something that would leave him hungrier than ever—he'd risk losing his job. Maybe something a hell of a lot worse than that.

He returned to the bedroom, and started to dress: grey trousers, black-and-white sport shoes, blue shirt and black tie. He donned a blue flannel coat, tucked a white handkerchief into the breast pocket. He buttoned the second button absently, still worrying. Step by step, he thought back over last night's events.

According to her registry card, her name was Marcia Hillis and she was from Dallas, Texas. Dusty supposed that she must have hit town on the 11:55 train since she arrived at the hotel a little after midnight, a few minutes after he had gone to work. He swung the cab door open for her, lifting her luggage from the driver's compartment. Then, he stepped across the walk to the lobby entrance, at this door without its doorman, and pulled open the door there.

Smiling perfunctorily, he turned and waited for her.

She finished paying and tipping the driver. She came out of the dark interior of the cab and into the bright lights of the marquee. Dusty blinked. His heart popped up into his throat, then bounced down into the pit of his stomach. He almost dropped her luggage.

Sure, he'd seen some good-looking women before, at the Manton and away from it. He'd seen them, and they'd made it pretty obvious that they saw him. But he'd never come up against anything like this, a woman who was not just one but *all* women. That was the way he thought of her, right from the first moment. All women—the personification, the refined best of them all. She was twenty. She was thirty. She was sixty.

Her face, with the serene brown eyes and the deliciously curling lips: she was twenty in the face but without the vacuousness which often goes with twenty. Her body, compactly mature, was that of a woman of thirty but with none of thirty's sometime flabbiness. Her hair was sixty, he thought of it that way—or, rather, what sixty is portrayed as being in story and picture. Completely gray. Gray, but soft and lustrous. Not the usual dead, crackling harshness of gray.

She wore it in a long gleaming bob which almost brushed the shoulders of her tailored suit. He stared down at it as she passed him, and then still half-dazed he followed her into the lobby.

Apparently she had something of the same effect on Bascom, the room clerk, that she had on him, for he was shoving a registration card across the desk and extending a fountain pen while she was still a dozen feet away. That was so unusual as to be unheard of. Dusty couldn't remember when Bascom had rented a room to an unescorted woman. He got a kick out of turning them down. With Miss Marcia Hillis, however, he was all welcoming smiles. Moreover, he did not treat her to an icy stare, as he usually did in such cases, when she hesitated over the price of the room.

"Well, now, of course," he murmured, with unaccustomed unction. "Fifteen dollars is rather high. I believe ... yes, I do have one room at ten. I'll let you have that."

Bascom assigned her to a room with southern exposure on the tenth, the top, floor. It was at the end of the corridor, a considerable walk from the elevator, and not too large, but it was undoubtedly the best of the Manton's ten-buck rooms. The city got hot as hell at this time of year, and high-up rooms on the south were at a premium.

Dusty preceded her down the long thickly carpeted hallway. He unlocked the door, flicked on the light and gestured without looking at her. She went in, brushing against him slightly as he stooped to pick up her baggage.

He placed the luggage—a suitcase, hat box and overnight case— on a stand immediately inside the door. He turned on the bathroom light, tested the circulating ice water spigot and checked the supply of towels and soap. He came out of the bath, edged toward the corridor door.

Breathing heavily. Still not looking at her.

A little red flag in his mind was swinging for all it was worth. He didn't want any tip from her, only to get out of there before something happened that had better not happen.

"I hope you'll be comfortable, ma'am," he said, and he got his hand on the doorknob. "Good night."

"Just a moment," she said, firmly. "Don't I have a fan in this room?"

"You won't need one," he said. "You get a very nice breeze on this side of the hotel."

"Oh? Well, will you open the windows, please?"

That was just what he didn't want to do, because she was standing by the bed, between the bed and the chest of drawers, and that left very little room for him to pass her. And he knew, as well as he knew he couldn't trust himself far with this babe, that she wasn't going to move out of the way.

He hesitated for a moment, his eyes concentrating on a spot directly above that lustrous gray head, but of course he couldn't refuse. He squeezed past her hurriedly, so brusquely that her knees bent and she almost toppled backward to the bed. He flung the windows up, and the strong south breeze swept in . . . slamming the door.

He turned around, looking directly at her at last.

She was facing him now. There was a fifty-cent piece between the tapering fingers of her extended right hand.

"Thank you, very much," she said. "Who shall I call for—in case I want anything else?"

"I"—he licked his lips—"I'm the only bellboy on at night. You won't need to call by name."

She looked at him silently. She stared straight into his eyes, holding them, and came toward him. The extended hand lowered, went into the pocket of his trousers, placing the tip there. It remained there, deep in his pocket. "Dusty"—he blurted the word out. He had to do something, say something, before he exploded. "I m-mean it's Bill, but my last name's Rhodes so everyone calls me D-Dus—"

"I see." Her eyes narrowed drowsily, her hand still in his pocket. "What time do you get off work, Dusty?"

"S-seven. I work from midnight to seven"

"I'll bet you get awfully lonesome, don't you, roaming through a big hotel at night all by yourself? Don't you get lonesome, Dusty?"

"Look," he stammered. "Look, Miss. I—"

"But you wouldn't be lonesome long," she said. "Not a guy who looks like you."

She leaned into him. Suddenly, because by God he couldn't help it, his arms went around her, right around those smoothly curving hips. And just as suddenly . . .

Just as suddenly she was standing six feet away from him! Over by the windows. And her voice and face were as cool as the insweeping breeze.

"Did I give you your tip?" she said. 'I believe that will be all, then."

That brought him up short. It was as though he'd been jerked out of an oven and into an ice box. He turned toward the door, angry, disappointed, and also relieved. Nothing could come of a deal like this. She was trouble. He couldn't afford trouble.

He shivered a little, thinking of what might have happened if she hadn't turned frosty on him. Relieved that it hadn't happened. Empty-feeling and disappointed because it hadn't.

He reached the door. She spoke again, and again her voice was warm, drowsy, filled with promise.

"That will be all," she repeated. "Now."

Slowly, he turned around.

She was still standing by the windows, and the wind was swirling the long white curtains around her, draping the rich body, ruffling the lustrous white hair. There against the background of the night, molded by the wind-blown curtains, she was like one of those unbelievably beautiful manatees from the prow of some Viking vessel. Or, no that wasn't right; she was too alive for that. She was like one of those ancient goddesses who tired of their heavenly pleasures and came down to earth for the delights of Man. Venus. Ceres, the Earth Mother. All things that were woman, eternal but never aging.

"Now," she said. "Nothing else now, Dusty."

And she laughed in a gently mocking way.

He let the door slam behind him. Rather, he slammed it.

He cursed her all the way to the elevator.

It didn't seem possible, but almost fifteen minutes had passed since he'd left the lobby. Behind the long marble desk, Bascom beckoned to him grimly.

"Where have you been?" he snapped. "What were you doing up in that room all this time?"

"Had to get some towels from the linen room," Dusty lied. "I guess the maid must have slipped up."

"You're sure *you* didn't slip up?"

"Just the maid," Dusty grinned at him, "and possibly you."

Bascom's mouth tightened. His eyes shifted uncomfortably.

Like many first-class hotels, the Manton had very few rooms at its lowest advertised rate. In fact, in the case of the Manton, there were only six rooms which rented for the ten-dollar minimum. They were by way of being prizes, something to be doled out to long-time patrons of the hotel. Never, to the best of Dusty's recollection, had one been rented at night. They didn't have to be. A guest hitting town late at night could and would pay practically anything he was asked to.

Bascom had slipped, then. He'd made a double slip. He'd not only deprived the hotel of the extra revenue deriving from a more expensive room, but he'd also—potentially but inevitably—disappointed a preferred guest. The guest wouldn't like that. The day clerks wouldn't like it. The management wouldn't like it. In view of the Manton's room turnover, of course, Bascom's lapse stood every chance of going unmarked. But if Dusty should happen to mention it, very casually, needless to say . . .

Bascom turned on his heel and went up into the cashier's cage. After a moment, he called to Dusty to come help him with the transcript sheets. That was the way the matter ended.

Anyway, Dusty guessed—as he studied himself in the dresser mirror—he wasn't in any trouble. If she'd been a teaser, one of those dames who worked you into making a pass and then squawked to the management, she'd have done her kicking last night. It didn't take a woman seven hours to decide she'd been insulted.

He heard the screen door to the front porch open, and his father's dragging footsteps. He frowned, irritably, still thinking about her and hating this interruption.

Who was she anyway, this Miss Marcia Hillis, of Dallas, Texas? What was she? Not a hooker, certainly. She hadn't propositioned him, and you learned to spot a hustling woman fast around a hotel. It didn't make any difference how they dressed, how high-toned they acted. You could spot them a mile away.

She wasn't a spotter—a detective—for the hotel, either. If she had been, she wouldn't have quibbled over the room rate. There would have been no reason to since the house would pick up her bill.

A business woman, then? Nope, she didn't use the right lingo, and business people didn't arrive at a hotel late at night without reservations.

A tourist? No, again; there was nothing in this town to attract a tourist, and, at any rate, he just couldn't picture her as a sightseer.

One of the horse-racing crowd? Well, yes, she could fit in with them, the upper-class stratum of them which made Hotel Manton its headquarters. She could, but he knew she didn't. The racing season didn't start for at least two weeks.

Probably, Dusty decided, she was just a woman at loose ends. Hungering for adventure, but afraid of it. Wandering aimlessly from one place to another, with nothing to do and all the time in the world to do it in.

So . . . so what difference did it make? Whoever or whatever she was, he'd never let her get him into another spot like the one last night. If she tried anything like that again, and for all he knew she might have checked out during the day—he'd put a freeze on her that would give her pneumonia.

... There was a tired apologetic cough from the bedroom doorway.

Frowning, Dusty turned and faced his father.

TWO

Of course, the old man was sick, much, much sicker than he realized. But that still could not account for his appearance; it did not, in Dusty's opinion, excuse that appearance. He had begun to let himself go after his dismissal from the city schools; then, his wife—Dusty's foster mother—had died and he had let go completely.

He went days on end without shaving, weeks without a haircut. His soiled baggy clothes looked like they'd been slept in. He looked like a tramp—like a scarecrow out of a cornfield. And that wasn't the worst of it. The worst was what he'd let happen to himself mentally. He seemed to take pride in being absent-minded, in seeing how stupidly he could do the few things that were left for him to do.

Why, good God, Dusty thought. His father was only a little past sixty, and he was practically senile. He couldn't be trusted with the simplest task. You couldn't send him to the store after a cake of soap and have him come back with the right change.

"Well"—Dusty forced the frown from his face. "How's it going, Dad?"

"Pretty good, Bill. Did you sleep well?"

"Not bad. As good as I could in this weather."

Mr. Rhodes nodded absently. A streak of saliva curved down from the corner of his mouth, and he wiped at his chin with the back of his hand.

"I got another letter from the lawyers today, Bill. They think that—"

"Have we got anything to eat in the house?" Dusty interrupted. "Anything I can make a sandwich out of?"

"I wanted to tell you, Bill. They think—"

Dusty interrupted him again. He knew what the lawyers thought, the same thing they always thought: that his father's case should be appealed to a higher court; that he, Dusty, was a sucker who could be conned indefinitely into paying their legal fees.

"Dad!" he said sharply. "We'll talk about the lawyers another time. Right now I want to know why we don't have any food. What did you do with the money I gave you?"

"Why, I—I—" The old man's eyes were blank, childishly bewildered. "Now, what did I—"

"Never mind," Dusty sighed. "Skip it. But you did get something to eat yourself, didn't you? You did, didn't you Dad?"

"Why—oh, yes," Mr. Rhodes said quickly. Too quickly. "I've eaten very well today."

"What, for example? You bought just enough groceries for yourself—is that what you're telling me, Dad?"

"Ye—I mean, no." Mr. Rhodes' eyes avoided his son's. "I ate out. It was too hot to do any cooking, so I—"

"You ate at Pete's place?"

"Yes—no. No, I didn't eat at Pete's." His father shied away from the trap. Dusty might check at the neighborhood lunchroom. "I went to another place, down toward town."

Dusty studied him wearily. He refrained from asking the name of the restaurant. It was no use—at such times as this his father was like a sly child—and he just wasn't capable of it. No matter how provoked you got, you shouldn't badger your own dad.

"All right," he said quietly, taking his billfold from his pocket. "Here's a couple dollars. Go down to Pete's and get you a good meal. Right now, Dad, before you go to bed. Will you do that?"

"Certainly. Of course I will, Bill." Mr. Rhodes almost snatched the money from his hand. "Will it be all right if—if—?"

Dusty hesitated over the unspoken question. "Well," he said, slowly. "You know what we decided about that, Dad. We both agreed on it, that it just wasn't a good idea. When a man's out of work, when he's worried, it's pretty easy to . . ."

"But I was just going to get a beer, just sit at the bar a while and watch television."

"I know, but—"

"But what?" There was an unaccustomed sharpness in his father's voice. "I don't understand you, Bill. Why all this fuss over a bottle of beer? You know I've never been a heavy drinker. I just don't have any taste for the stuff. But the way you've harped on the subject lately, you'd think I—"

"I'm sorry." Dusty clapped him on the back, urged him toward the door. "I just get tired and worried, and I talk too much. Go on and have your beer, Dad. But get you a good meal, too."

"But I'd like to know why—"

"No reason. Like I said, I talk too much. You run along, and I'll see you in the morning"

Mr. Rhodes left, still muttering annoyedly. Dusty remained in the house a few minutes longer, giving him time to get out of sight. The old man had gotten dangerously suspicious a moment ago. It wouldn't do to feed those suspicions further by having him think he was being followed.

Dusty fixed and drank a glass of ice water while he waited. Ice, by God, was just about all there was in the refrigerator. He smoked a cigarette, pacing back and forth across the shabby living room. At last, after a nervous glance at his wrist watch, he hurried out of the house and jumped into his car.

At a drive-in restaurant, he gulped down a hot turkey sandwich and two cups of coffee. He parked his car at the rear of the Manton, hurried through the service entrance and on into the locker room. There was a sour taste in his mouth. The food he had eaten lay heavy on his stomach. He was tired, sweaty. He felt like he had never rested, never bathed.

Stripping out of his clothes, he took another shower—cold and necessarily quick. He dried himself, standing directly beneath the ceiling fan. He put on his wine-colored, tuxedo-like uniform, and hung his street clothes in his locker. He sat down under the fan, tapping the persistent sweat from his face with his bath towel. It was ten, no nine, minutes of twelve. There was time for another smoke, time to pull himself together a little before he went up to the lobby.

He lighted a cigarette moodily, broodingly, trying to escape from the feeling of sullen despair, of hopeless frustration, which crept over him more and more of late.

There was no way out that he could see. No exit from his difficulties. His mind traveled in a circle, beginning and ending with his father. The doctor's bills, the medicines, the frittering away of money almost as fast as it could be made. Two dollars, five dollars, ten dollars, whatever you gave the old man, he got rid of. And he wasn't a damned bit hesitant about asking for more.

Dusty had considered taking a day job. But day bellboys didn't make as much money, and they had to work split watches. He'd have to be away from home practically as much as he was now... Hire a housekeeper? Well, how would that help? Thirty-five or forty bucks a week in salary, and you'd have to feed her besides. Anyway, dammit, it just wasn't necessary. None of this nonsense, which kept him drained of money, was necessary. His father was sharp enough when he chose to be. He'd proved that tonight. The trouble was that he, Dusty, had just babied and humored the old man so much that...

"Hey, Rhodes! How about it?" It was the day captain, shouting down from the top of the service steps.

Dusty shouted, "Coming!" and left the locker room. But he ascended the long stairway unhurriedly, wrapped in thought.

His father couldn't be losing and mislaying and generally mismanaging to the extent that he appeared to be. He must be spending the money on something. But what in the world would a man his age—

Suddenly, Dusty knew. The answer to the riddle was so damned obvious. Why the hell hadn't he thought of it before this?

The day bellboys swept past him on the steps. Lighting cigarettes, peeling out of their jackets and collars as they hastened toward the locker room. A few spoke or nodded to him. They got no greeting in return. He was too choked up, blind with anger.

Those lawyers, those dirty thieving shysters! That was where the money was going.

Well, he'd put a stop to that. There would be no use in jumping his father about it; he couldn't really blame his father for doing what he undoubtedly had. It was their fault—the lawyers—for holding out hope to him. And they'd darned well better lay off if they knew what was good for them. He'd write 'em a letter that would curl their hair. Or, no, he'd pay them a little visit. He wanted to tell those birds off personally.

Opening the door of the service landing, he entered the lobby, his anger dying and with it the sense of frustration. He paused at the end

of the long marble desk untended now except by sour old Bascom—
and looked down at the open pages of the room-call ledger.

She was still here, he saw. A bellboy had taken cigarettes and a
magazine to her room fifteen minutes ago. Up at 11:45, down at
11.50; just long enough to complete the errand. Not long enough for
anything ... anything else. And, yes, that was the only boy to go to
her room today.

Dusty didn't know why he felt good about it, because of course—
she couldn't mean anything to him; he was shying clear of that baby.
But somehow he did feel good. Here was proof positive that she
wasn't a hooker or spotter, proof that he was the only guy in the place
that she had any interest in.

A cab honked at the side door. Grinning unconsciously, Dusty
hurried across the lobby and down the steps.

THREE

As modern hotels go, the Manton was not a large place. Its letterheads
boasted of "four hundred rooms, four hundred baths." Actually, there
were three hundred and sixty-two, and since any number of these
were linked together into suites, the baths totaled far less than three
hundred and sixty-two.

The Manton—or rather the company which operated it—had
learned the advantage in renting two rooms to one person rather than
two rooms to two persons. It had learned the vast difference in profit
between renting two rooms at five dollars and one at ten dollars. It
had learned that the man who pays five dollars for a room is apt to be
much more demanding than the one who pays ten.

The Manton was seldom rented to capacity. It did not have to be.
With only two-thirds of its rooms rented, its income was equal to that
of a larger, fully-occupied—and less "exclusive"—hotel. Also, since
the number of a hotel's employees is inevitably geared to the number
of its guests, its overhead was much lower.

Bascom was the sole front-office employee after midnight,

performing—with Dusty's assistance—the duties of room clerk, key clerk, cashier and night auditor. There was no night house detective. The coffee shop and grille room closed at one o'clock. By two, the lobby porters had completed their mopping and scrubbing and were on their way homeward. At two, the late-shift elevator operator left, and Dusty took care of his infrequent calls from then on.

It was a little before two when Tug Trowbridge came in. While his two companions—you seldom saw him alone—sauntered on a few steps, Tug stopped at the cashier's cage where Dusty and Bascom were working. He was a big, almost perpetually smiling man, with a shock of red hair and a hearty, booming voice. Now, as Dusty grinned obediently and Bascom smirked nervously, he triggered an enormous forefinger at the clerk.

"Okay, Dusty boy"—he scowled with false menace—"I got him covered. Grab the keys and clean out those safety-deposit boxes."

Dusty stretched his grin into an appreciative laugh. Tug's joke was an old one, but he was the best tipper in the Manton. "Can't do it, Mr. Trowbridge, remember? It takes two different keys for each box."

"Now, by God!" Tug slapped his forehead in a gesture of dismay. "Why can't I ever remember that!"

He guffawed, putting a period to the joke. Then, he dug a small, flat key from his vest and shoved it through the wicket. "A little service, hey, brother Bascom? Got something that's kind of weighing me down."

"Yes, sir," said Bascom obsequiously.

There was a ledger, indexing the depositors in the chilled-steel boxes which formed the rear wall of the cashier's cage. But it was unnecessary to consult this, of course, in the case of a regular like Tug Trowbridge. Bascom took a heavy ring of keys from his cash drawer, and selected one with a certain number—a number, incidentally, which did *not* correspond to the one on Tug's key. Turning to the rear of the enclosure, he found Tug's box number—and this also was different from that of either of the two keys—and unlocked its two locks. He pulled the box out of its niche, and set it in the window in front of Trowbridge.

Dusty averted his eyes, tactfully, but not before he had got a glimpse of the sheaf of bills which Tug casually tossed into the box. It was almost an inch thick, wrapped around at the ends with transparent tape. There was a thousand-dollar bill on top.

Bascom put the box back into place, and carefully relocked it. He returned Tug's key, dropping the others back into the cash drawer.

"Well, Dusty"—Trowbridge gave the bellboy a wink—"I guess you're right. No use knocking over Bascom here unless we could get ahold of the other keys."

"No, sir," Dusty smiled.

"And how we going to do that, hey? How we going to know who's got keys and whether they got anything worth getting?"

"That's right," said Dusty.

Bascom was trying to smile, but the effort was not very successful. Tug winked at Dusty.

"Looks like we're making our pal a little nervous," he said. "Maybe we better lay off before he calls the cops on us."

"Oh, no," Bascom protested. He had about as much sense of humor, in Dusty's opinion, as one of the lobby sand-jars. "It's just that when a man's alone here at night—practically alone all night long—and he's responsible for all this—"

"Sure," Trowbridge nodded good-humoredly. "Jokes about hold-ups aren't very funny."

"As a matter of fact," Bascom continued seriously, "I don't believe there's ever been a successful hold-up of a major hotel. You see—"

"No kidding," said Trowbridge, his voice faintly sarcastic. "Well, thanks for letting me know."

"Oh, I didn't mean that—"

"Sure, sure. I know." Trowbridge laughed again, but not too jovially. "Come up to the suite after a while, huh, Dusty? Make it about a half hour. Got some laundry I want you to pick up."

"Yes, sir," said Dusty.

Trowbridge rejoined his two companions. Bascom watched them as they proceeded on down the lobby to the bank of elevators beneath the mezzanine. There was a drawn look about his prim humorless face. He was breathing a little heavily, his thin pinched nostrils flaring with annoyance.

Dusty studied him covertly, grinning to himself. Bascom had better watch his step. Tug Trowbridge definitely wasn't a guy you'd want to get down on you.

Back in prohibition days, Tug had headed a statewide bootleg syndicate. His well-earned reputation for toughness was such as to make even the Capones shy away from him. During the war—though he had never been convicted—he had been the brains, and no small part of the muscle, of a group of black-market mobsters, men who specialized in the daylight hijacking of bonded whiskey trucks. At various times in his career, he had been involved—reputedly—in the loan-shark and slot-machine rackets.

These illegal and often deadly activities, or, more properly, these *alleged* activities, were now years behind him. His present and obviously profitable enterprises were confined to a juke-box company and a stevedoring firm. Still, and despite his brimming good humor, he obviously was not a man to be trifled with. Dusty knew that from the attitude of the men who accompanied him.

It wasn't likely, of course, that Tug would ever rough up Bascom. He'd be too contemptuous of the clerk, and there was an easier way of showing his displeasure.

Tug paid seven hundred and fifty dollars a month rent. His bar and restaurant bills ran at least as much more. Neither he nor his associates ever created a disturbance. He made no special demands on the hotel. In short, he was the Manton's idea of a highly desirable—a "respectable"—guest; and it would take no more than a word from him to get Bascom discharged.

... Dusty didn't get up to the Trowbridge suite within the half hour suggested. First, he had a hurry-up call for some aspirin from another room. Next, he had to unlock the check room for an early-departing guest, locate a small trunk stored therein and lug it out to the man's car. Then, there was a flurry of elevator traffic, now his responsibility since the operator had gone home.

It was Bascom, however, who was the chief cause of the delay. The clerk had insisted that Dusty give him the few minutes help he needed to complete the transcript. Then, with the task completed, he had pretended that the lock to the cashier's cage was jammed. Anyway, Dusty was convinced that it was a pretence. Bascom wouldn't let him try to work the key. He couldn't climb out of the enclosure, as he might have in any of the other front offices, because of the heavy steel netting across the top.

Finally, after almost twenty minutes had passed, the room clerk's phone rang, and, lo and behold, the lock suddenly became unjammed. Bascom gave him a shrewish, over-the-shoulder grin as he sauntered out of the cage. Dusty shoved past him roughly as the clerk began relocking the door.

It was in his mind to tell Trowbridge what had happened. But he wasn't quite angry enough for that, and, as it turned out, there was neither opportunity nor necessity to do so.

Tug and the other two men were lounging in the parlor of his suite, their coats off, brimming glasses in their hands. They were obviously unaware that Dusty was more than thirty minutes late.

"Here already, huh?" Tug beamed. "Now, that's what I call service. Sit down and have a drink with us."

"Thanks very much," said Dusty. "I don't drink, Mr. Trowbridge."

"Sure, you don't; keep forgetting," the big man nodded. "Well, have a smoke then. Shake hands with my friends. Don't believe you've met these gents."

Dusty shook hands with them, and sat down. He'd never seen them before, but he felt that he had. There was something in the manner of Tug's friends that made them all look a little alike.

"Dusty's the lad I started to tell you about," Trowbridge continued. "Ain't that hell, though? Here's a plenty smart kid, got almost four years of college under his belt, and he winds up hopping bells. Nice, huh? Some future for a guy that figured on being a doctor."

The two men looked sympathetic. Or, rather, they tried to. Tug wagged his head regretfully.

"That's about the way it stacks up, eh, Dusty? Your old man doesn't stand a chance of getting things straightened out?"

"It wouldn't do much good if he could," Dusty shrugged. "He'll never be well enough to go back to work."

"A hell of a note," mused Trowbridge. "I remember readin' about it at the time. I said to myself right then, Now, why the hell does a man want to do a thing like that? A man with a good job and a family to take care of. What's he figure it's going to get him to mix himself up with a bunch of Reds?"

"He didn't mix with any Reds," Dusty said quickly, almost sharply. "I know they tried to make it look that way, but it wasn't anything

like that. You see there was this group—the Free Speech Committee—who wanted to hold a meeting in the school auditorium, and
all Dad did was sign a petition to—"

"Sure"—Tug stifled a yawn. "Well, it was a lousy break, anyway.
Lousy for you. Of course, it was hard on your old man, too, but he'd
already lived most of his life. The way I see it, he stuck his neck out
and yours got stepped on."

"Well..." Dusty murmured. There was a casual bluntness about
Trowbridge which precluded argument. For that matter, he didn't
entirely disagree with the ex-racketeer.

Trowbridge got the bag of laundry from the bedroom, and gave
him a dollar tip. He returned to the lobby, heartened by his talk with
Tug yet vaguely ashamed of himself. His father hadn't done anything
wrong. In any event, it wasn't up to Tug Trowbridge to pass
judgment on him. Still, it was nice to have someone see your side of
things, to realize that you were making a hell of a sacrifice and
getting nothing for it. Everyone else—the doctor and the lawyers and
his father, and his mother, up until the time of her death—had taken
what he had done for granted.

Dusty couldn't remember just how he'd happened to tell Tug
about the matter. It had just slipped out somehow, he guessed, a
natural consequence of the big man's friendliness and interest.
Trowbridge was a far cry from the Manton's average guest. He
treated you like a friend, introduced you to the people he had with
him. When he said, "How's it going?" or "What's on your mind,
Dusty?" he really wanted to know. Or he certainly made it sound like
he did.

... Bascom was waiting for him when he got downstairs, frowning
and tapping impatiently on the counter. "Finally got back, did you?"
he said grimly. "How long does it take you to pick up a bag of
laundry?"

"Not too long." Dusty looked at him coolly. "About as long as it
takes you to unlock a door."

Bascom's eyes flashed. He flipped a slip of paper across the counter.
"College boys," he jeered. "There's some calls for you, college boy.
See if you can take care of them between now and daylight."

"Look, Mr. Bascom"—Dusty picked up the call slip. "What's ...
well, what's wrong, anyway? What are you sore at me about? We

used to get along so well together, but every time I turn around now
you—"

"Yes?" said Bascom. "If you don't like it, why don't you quit?"

"But I don't understand. If I've done or said anything—"

"Get moving," said Bascom crisply. "Step on it, or you won't get a
chance to quit."

Dusty made the two calls—ice to one room, a telegram pick-up
from another. This was another thing he couldn't remember: just
how his quarreling with Bascom had started. It had begun only
recently, he knew that. They'd gotten along swell for months, and
then, apparently for no reason at all, Bascom had changed. And since
then he could do nothing but scold and snarl and ridicule. Make
things tougher than they were already.

Dusty had been pretty hurt at first. He still was. But the hurt was
giving way to anger, a stubborn determination to stand up against the
clerk's injustice. He didn't know what it was all about—and he was
ceasing to care—but he knew that Bascom couldn't get him fired.
Not, anyway, without digging up much more serious charges than he
could make now. Dusty had broken various of the hotel's innumerable
rules, as in the instances, for example, of smoking behind the key
rack and working without his collar. But Bascom was guilty of some
rule-breaking himself. Bascom wasn't supposed to slip up to an empty
room for a quick shower. He wasn't supposed to trot down the street
to an all-night lunch room instead of having his food sent in. Dusty
always knew where he was, of course, and could get him back to the
desk with a phone call within the space of two or three minutes. But
that could make no difference to the hotel. Bascom was supposed to
remain behind the counter throughout his shift. That was the rule,
period. If the management ever found out—

Dusty completed the two calls, and returned to the desk. He and
Bascom resumed the night's chores, interrupted now and then when
Dusty had to leave on a room call or one of the telephones rang. They
checked off the day's charge slips against the guests' bills. They
checked the room rack against the information racks. The work went
rapidly, Dusty calling out the data, Bascom checking it. In the pre-
dawn stillness, the bellboy's clear steady monotone echoed through
the desk area:

"Haines, eight fourteen, one at twelve dollars . . . Haley, nine twelve, Mr. and Mrs., two at fifteen ... Heller, six fifty and fifty-two, one at eighteen ... Hillis, Dallas, Tex.—"

"Wait a minute!" Bascom flung down his pencil. "What kind of a room number is Dallas, Tex.? If you can't do any better than that, I'll—"

"Sorry," Dusty said quickly. "Hillis, ten oh four, one at ten."

Bascom picked up the pencil. Then, suddenly, he laughed. Softly, amusedly. Suddenly—for the moment, at least—he was the old Bascom again.

"Out of this world, wasn't she?" he said. "I don't think I've ever seen a woman who could come up to her."

"I *know* I haven't," said Dusty.

"Yes, sir, a lovely woman," mused Bascom. "Everything a woman should be. You know, Bill"—he turned on his stool and faced Dusty—"have you any idea how it feels to be my age, in the job I'm in, and to see someone like her? I've used up my chances. I'm not an old man, but I'll never amount to anything more than I do now. And that isn't enough by a million miles for a woman like that ... It's not a nice feeling, Bill. Take my word for it."

Dusty nodded, slowly, still taken aback by the clerk's sudden change in manner. He could see what Bascom was driving at, but—

"You've been here about a year," Bascom went on. "How long do you intend to stay?"

"Well"—Dusty hesitated—"I don't know. I can't say, exactly. It depends on my father, how my expenses run and—"

"Does it? I've seen you on the street, Bill, the way you dress, your car. I've got a pretty good idea of what you make here—around a hundred and fifty a week, isn't it? That's what's actually keeping you here, the money. Plenty of money with no real work or responsibilities attached to it. A nice soft job with a lot of so-called big shots calling you by your first name. You don't want to give it up. If you did, you'd have gone back to school long ago."

"Oh, yeah?" Dusty reddened. And then he checked himself. "I mean, I know you're just trying to help me, Mr. Bascom, and I appreciate it. But—"

"I know. You've got doctor bills, your father to take care of. But you could still swing it, Bill. There's such a thing as a student loan. Scholarships. You used to talk quite a bit about them when you first came here. There are part-time jobs you could get. You'd have to do plenty of scrimping and sacrificing, but if you really wanted to—"

"I couldn't. I can't!" Dusty protested. "Why the doctor bills alone, those and the medicines, take—"

"Doctors will wait for their money, if it's in a good cause. There's a city dispensary for people with low incomes. So"—Bascom's eyebrows rose—"what else is there? A place to sleep, something to eat. That's about the size of it, isn't it? Don't tell me you couldn't manage that in these times. You could squeeze by for a few years, long enough to get your education."

Dusty wet his lips, hesitantly. Bascom made things sound awfully easy. If he had to do them himself, well . . .

"It's not that simple," he said. "There are plenty of things besides—"

"There always are. But there aren't many that you can't do without. No, Bill. It wouldn't be easy, not an ideal arrangement by any means. But . . ." His voice died. The friendliness went out of his face. "Forget it," he said coldly. "Let's get back to work."

"But I was going to say that—"

"I said to forget it," Bascom snapped. "You're lazy. You feel sorry for yourself. You want something for nothing. It's a waste of time talking to you. Now, call those rooms off to me, and call 'em off right."

Dusty gulped and swallowed. Voice shaking, he resumed the calling.

The remaining three hours of the shift passed swiftly. At five-thirty, the split-watch elevator boy arrived. At six, the head baggage porter retrieved the check-room key from Dusty and began his day's duties. At seven the entire day shift came to work.

In the locker room, Dusty took another shower and changed into his street clothes. He scowled at himself in the mirror, ripped out an abrupt disgusted curse.

He's right, old Bascom's right, he thought. No wonder he doesn't have any use for me. Dad and I could manage. We—he—couldn't spend what I didn't have. He'd probably pull himself together if I went back to school, if he knew that one of us was going to amount to something. It would give him something to live for.

He finished dressing, and went out to his car. Pulling away from the curb, he gave the Hotel Manton a knowing, deprecating look. It could go to hell, the Manton could, and Marcia Hillis along with it.

FOUR

It was a shabby, rundown house, a faded-blue cottage, in a block that was barely a half-block. It was bordered on one side by a vacant lot, a hundred squarefoot jungle of weeds and Johnson grass, on the other by a crumbling brick warehouse. Facing it, across the narrow street, was a used-car lot. Dusty had rented the place shortly after his mother's death. Its chief—rather, its only—advantages were its cheapness and its distance, *per se* and socially, from the family's former neighborhood. Things had gotten pretty uncomfortable there after his father's trouble. In this section of town, there was little chance of encountering one-time friends.

Dusty ate breakfast on the way home, and it was nearly nine when he arrived. It was Wednesday, one of the two days a week that the doctor called, and a black coupé, with the letters MD on the license plate, was parked in front of the house. Dusty drew up behind it, waited until the doctor came out.

Doctor Lane was a brisk, chubby man with narrowed irritable-looking eyes. He bustled out to his car, frowning impatiently when Dusty intercepted him.

"Well, he's all right," he said brusquely. "As good as can be expected. Incidentally, can't you spruce him up a little? Can't expect a man to feel good when he goes around like a tramp."

"I'm doing the best I can." Dusty flushed. "I give him plenty of—"

"The best you can, eh?" The doctor looked him up and down. "Better try a little harder. Or else get someone in to look after him. Should be able to afford it."

He nodded curtly, and tossed his black-leather bag onto the seat of the car. His hand on the door, he paused and turned.

"Understand he's been having a little beer. Well, won't hurt him any. Won't do him any good, but there's damned little that will. Not enough alcohol in the slop they make these days to hurt a baby."

"I wanted to ask you, Doctor. If it's as dangerous as you say—'

"As I *say?*" Doctor Lane snapped. "Any considerable amount of alcohol will kill him. Stop his heart like that."

"Well, don't you think it would be better—safer—if he was told—"

"No, I don't think so. If I did I'd have told him before now." The doctor sighed wearily, obviously struggling to control his impatience. "Don't want to alarm him. You can understand that, can't you? Not the slightest need to tell him. He's a naturally careful liver. Doesn't smoke. Goes easy on the coffee. Gets plenty of rest ... By the way, he's just as well off if he doesn't eat much. Doesn't do enough to burn it up. Okay? That doesn't make you mad, does it?"

"I—" Dusty's mouth snapped shut. He stared at Lane steadily. "Just what," he said, "do you mean by that?"

"Well—uh—" The doctor cleared his throat. "No offence. I only meant that working nights, and all, it was probably difficult for you to—to—"

"I see. I thought that's what you must mean, Doctor."

Doctor Lane laughed uneasily. "Now—uh—I was saying about the liquor. Only danger in it I see is, uh, negative, largely negative. Know what I mean? Explaining why he shouldn't have it. Alarming him. Mustn't do that, understand? No reason to do it. He's never drunk the stuff, no reason why he should take on any fatal quantity now. If he had any money to throw away, he'd—" The doctor broke off abruptly. He cleared his throat again. "As I was saying. My thought in warning you was that you might, with the best of intentions, urge some on him. I mean to say that, for example, you might be having some people in, and if you were drinking yourselves you'd naturally offer your father—"

"I don't drink, Doctor. I don't do any entertaining."

"Fine. Splendid. No cause for worry, then." Doctor Lane backed away a step. "Anything else?"

Dusty shook his head. There had been something, but he couldn't mention it now. Perhaps he could do it later, but he was in no mood now to ask for favors from Doctor Lane now. Probably it wouldn't do any good if he did ask. If Lane thought he was so lowdown as to mistreat his own father, he'd hardly be inclined to wait indefinitely on payment for his services.

Going up the walk to the house, Dusty guessed that he'd mismanaged the whole interview. The doctor was always cranky, ready to leap down your throat, at this hour of the morning. If he'd had to talk to him—and he might have waited until another time— he shouldn't have disputed with him, made the doctor humble himself for a curtness that was more or less normal for him.

Mr. Rhodes was seated on the living room lounge, squinting at the morning newspaper. He smiled absently at his son, and Dusty went on back to the kitchen. The coffee pot was still warm, and there was a little coffee still left in it. Dusty poured a cup, and carried it into the living room.

"Dad," he said. Then, sharply, "Dad! I want to talk to you."

"Oh!" The old man laid the paper aside reluctantly. "Go right ahead, Bill."

"I want you to gather up all your clothes today, all your laundry. I—maybe you'd better do it right away. I'll have the stuff picked up this morning, so we can get it back tomorrow."

"All right, son," his father said, mildly. "Do you want any of your things to go, too?"

"Just yours. The hotel still does mine at half price."

Mr. Rhodes shuffled out of the room. Dusty took up a sip of coffee, and picked up the telephone. He called the laundry and cleaners. Then he consulted the telephone directory, and, swallowing the rest of his coffee, called a grocery store.

He was just hanging up when his father returned. He lighted a cigarette, motioned for the old man to sit down.

"I've just ordered some groceries, Dad. They'll be delivered within the hour—twenty-three dollars and eight cents worth—and the man will have to have his money upon delivery. Now I can leave the money with you for him, and go on to bed, if you're sure you can take care of it. Otherwise, I'll sit up and wait."

"Of course, I can take care of it," said Mr. Rhodes. "You go get your sleep, Bill."

"Another thing. While you're waiting, I'd like to have you shave. I'll put a new blade in the razor for you. Draw the water if you want me to. Will you do that, Dad?"

"Well, I—" Mr. Rhodes ran a hand over his stubbled face. "That's—it's pretty hard for me to do, son. I—I have a hard time seeing what I'm doing since I broke my glasses."

"But you ... You didn't have them fixed, Dad? After I gave you the money, and you promised—" Dusty broke off, abruptly. "All right," he said. "All right. You go in and see the optometrist tomorrow, have him give me a ring here at the house and tell me what the bill will be. I'll get a money order for you to give him when you pick up the glasses."

"Fine," the old man murmured.

"Now, I'll give you a shave myself. Or, no"—Dusty took a dollar from his wallet and added some change to it "you can use a haircut, too. This will take care of it. You run along right now, Dad."

"Well"—Mr. Rhodes looked down at the money—"hadn't I better wait until the groceries...?"

"I'll take care of them myself. I don't want to go to bed, anyway, until you get back from the barber shop."

"Well, now, there's no need to—"

"I'll be waiting," Dusty said firmly. "I want to be sure you—that they give you a good job."

His father looked at him thoughtfully, the kind of appraising look he had used to give him, back before the trouble had come up, when Dusty's conduct had fallen below standard. Curious, disappointed, but not condemnatory nor surprised.

Dusty stared back at him stolidly.

Mr. Rhodes stood up, shoved the money into the pocket of his stained baggy trousers, and left the house.

The laundry and cleaning men came, then the man from the grocery store. Dusty was in the kitchen, still unpacking and putting away the groceries, when his father returned from the barber shop.

The barber had done his work well. Except for his clothes, Mr. Rhodes might have been Professor Rhodes, principal of Central High School. Dusty was pleased by the transformation, but also annoyed. It confirmed his belief that his father could, if he only chose to, escape the slough of senility into which he seemed to be sinking.

"Well," he said, curtly, "I hope we've got enough here to last a while."

"This meat, Bill"—Mr. Rhodes shook his head. "Why did you get so much? It'll spoil before we can use it."

"I can't be waiting around here every morning while they bring a pound or two, can I?" Dusty rammed the package of meat into the refrigerator. "I can't hang around town in the morning until the stores open. I'm tired when I get off work. I want to get home and get to bed."

"Cornmeal," murmured the old man. "And flour. We never use anything like that, Bill."

"Well"—Dusty's lips pressed together—"I did the best I could. I didn't suppose there'd be any use in asking you what we needed. When I leave it to you, we usually wind up without anything."

"No coffee," said Mr. Rhodes, worriedly. "No fresh milk. Or bread. No—"

"All right!" Dusty yanked a five-dollar bill from his wallet and flung it on the table. "That ought to take care of it! Now, I'm going to bed."

"You don't want something to eat first?"

"I've already eaten. Ate downtown. I—honest to God, Dad, I—"

"You shouldn't have bought so much, Bill." The old man shook his head. "All this stuff, and you eating at home so seldom. You'd better let me do the buying after this."

"How the hell can I? Goddammit, I keep handing money out to you and—"

He broke off, choking down the angry words, ashamed of himself; seeing the futility of talk. His father's mouth had drooped open in that loose, imbecilic way. His eyes were vacantly bewildered. Swiftly, as he always did when the perplexing or troublesome loomed, he had retreated behind the barrier of helplessness.

"Sorry," Dusty said, gruffly. "Have a good day, Dad."

And he entered his bedroom, and closed the door behind him.

Well, hell, he thought, with a kind of sullen remorsefulness. Probably he can't help it; maybe it's the way it has to be. He's had too much to cope with in too short a time. He's all right, as long as things run along smoothly, but the minute any trouble starts . . .

Dusty drew the shades, and turned on the electric fan. He took a few puffs from a cigarette, tapped it out in the ash tray and stretched out on the bed. He turned restlessly, flinging himself around on the rumpled sheets ... Should have come straight home from work, he thought. Got to sleep while it was still fairly cool. Going to be a scorcher today, and that fan didn't really do any good. Just stirred up the same old air, made a lot of racket. And ... and how the hell could a guy sleep, anyway? How could you when you were knocking yourself out night after night, and never getting anywhere? When you knew you were never going to get anywhere? His father could go on living for years, and, hell, of course he wanted him to. But—

Dusty groaned, and sat up. He lighted another cigarette, smoked moodily, sitting on the edge of the bed. Dammit—the frown on his pale face deepened—it wasn't fair! It was too much to swallow. There was no excuse for it.

So the old man had lost his job. *And I suppose I didn't lose anything! He's lost his wife. Well, she was my mother, wasn't she? I lost my mother ...*

Dusty winced, unconsciously. He didn't like to think about his mother. They'd been so close at one time. He could always talk to her, and whatever his problems were she always seemed to understand and sympathize. Then, well, that rumpus over the Free Speech Committee had come up, and Dad had been kicked out of his job. And after that—everything had been different. All her thought, all her sympathy was for his father. To Dusty, she was like—almost—a polite stranger. She wasn't at all concerned about his dropping out of college. College could wait: he was young and his father was old. She took his sacrifices for granted, as something he was obliged to make, a debt that he had to pay. The trouble wasn't his, but it was. He was shut out of it—she drew further and further away from him, drew closer and closer to his father—but he was expected to pay for it. She wouldn't share it with him, this or anything else. Not really share, as she'd used to. He was just a stranger paying off a debt.

... It was almost noon before he fell asleep. Five minutes later— what seemed like five minutes—a steady ringing roused him into wakefulness. Automatically, his eyes still closed, he thrust his hand out to the alarm clock. He pressed down on the alarm button— pressed and found it already depressed. He fumbled with it a moment longer, then drowsily opened his eyes.

It was still daylight. Not quite three o'clock. The ringing continued.

He jumped up, ran into the living room and snatched up the telephone.

It was Tolliver, the Manton's superintendent of service.

"Rhodes—Bill?" he said crisply. "Sorry to bother you, but I'll have to ask you to come down to the hotel."

"Come . . . you mean *now*?"

"Sorry, yes. Mr. Steelman wants to see you, and he's not available after five. Come straight to his office, Bill. If anyone gets curious, you can say you came down to see the auditor. A mix-up in your pay or something like that."

"But I don't—is there something wrong? I certainly hope I haven't done—"

Tolliver's laugh was friendly. "Sounds like you've got a guilty conscience. No, it's nothing like that. Nothing that concerns you directly . . . We can expect you right away, Bill?"

"Just as fast as I can get there," Dusty promised.

He was on his way out of the house within ten minutes, still too grumpy with sleep to care much about the reason for the summons . . . That Steelman, he grumbled silently. You'd think he was God instead of just the Manton's manager. *He* "wasn't available" after five, Mr. Steelman wasn't, just couldn't be bothered, no matter what came up. But everyone else had to be available. He could drag *you* out of bed in the middle of the day, and that was perfectly all right.

Dusty found a parking space at the rear of the hotel, and went in the employees' entrance as usual. He rode a service elevator to the second floor, walked on past the auditor's offices and the switchboard room and entered the outer room of the manager's office. The receptionist nodded promptly when he mentioned his name.

"Oh, yes. They're waiting for you. Go right on in."

She gestured toward the door marked PRIVATE. Dusty opened it and went in.

The manager was seated behind his desk, crisp and cool looking in a white linen suit. Tolliver, the superintendent of service, sat a little to one side of him, his fumed-oak chair pulled up at the end of the desk. They were studying some papers when Dusty entered, and they continued to study them for a few moments longer. Then, Steelman murmured something under his breath and Tolliver laughed unctuously, and the two of them looked up.

"Sit down, Bill." Tolliver motioned to a chair. "No, better pull it up here. We'll get this over with as quickly as possible."

Dusty sat down, a faint feeling of nausea in his stomach. It was almost a physical shock to come into this air-conditioned, indirectly-lighted room from the blinding heat outside.

Tolliver went on. "Now this is strictly confidential, Bill. Not a word about it to anyone, you understand? Good. Here's what we want to know. You've been working with Mr. Bascom for about a year. You've been around him more—presumably talked with and observed him more—than any of the rest of us. What can you tell us about him?"

"Tell you?" Dusty smiled puzzledly. "I guess I don't understand what—"

"Put it this way. Has he done or said anything that would lead you to believe he wasn't strictly on the level?"

"Why—why, no, sir." Dusty shook his head. "I mean, well, I don't believe that he has."

"Has he told you anything about his past, what he did before he came here? Any of his experiences, say, at other hotels?"

"No."

"To the best of your knowledge, he's an honest man who does his work as it should be done?"

"Yes, sir." Dusty looked from Tolliver to Steelman. "I'm not being inquisitive, but maybe if you could tell me what the trouble is I might—"

"Here's the trouble," the manager said crisply. "We've received an anonymous letter about Mr. Bascom. It's not at all specific, doesn't give us any details, but it does indicate that Mr. Bascom's character leaves something to be desired. Ordinarily, we'd pay no attention to such a communication. If one of our other clerks was involved, someone we knew something about—"

"Someone you knew something about?" Dusty frowned. "You mean, you don't know anything about Mr. Bascom?"

"Practically nothing. According to his application blank, he'd always been self-employed, kind of a small-time jobber. He bought novelties and candy and the like from wholesale houses and resold them to retailers. Now, there's nothing wrong with that, of course, but it doesn't tell us much about him. Doesn't give us anything we can check on. And it's the same story with his character references—the director of a YMCA where he lived a few months, the minister of a church he attended. Virtually meaningless. Those people hand out references right and left."

"But"—Dusty spread his hands—"but why did you hire him, then?"

Tolliver laughed wryly. "Doesn't sound much like the Manton, does it, Bill? But you see, Bascom was hired during the war, right back at the beginning of it. We had to take what we could get, and very few questions asked. Afterwards, since he seemed to have worked out very well, we simply let matters ride. We can't very well start questioning him about his background at this late date. Always assuming, of course, that questioning would do any good."

"It wouldn't," said Steelman. "When a man's applying for a job, he tells everything he can that will be a credit to him. No, we have to go on accepting Bascom at his word, which is just about what it boils down to. Or we have to let him go."

"I'd hate to do that," Tolliver said, "with nothing more against him than an anonymous note. I—yes, Bill?"

"I was just going to say that the bonding company must have investigated him. As long as they feel—"

"He isn't bonded. We've never felt it necessary to bond the night clerk. He carries a very small change bank, doesn't handle much cash. He doesn't have access to any valuables. So . . ."

"Let's see," said Steelman. "Do you have many one-shift guests, Rhodes? People who arrive after midnight and leave before seven?"

"Not very many. If you wanted to check the transcript—"

"We already have. I was wondering whether Mr. Bascom ever ordered you to make up those checked-out rooms instead of leaving them for the maids."

"You mean have I helped him steal the price of the room?" Dusty said. "No, sir, I haven't."

"Now, Bill"—Tolliver frowned. "That wasn't Mr. Steelman's question."

"I'm sorry," Dusty said. "No, sir, Mr. Bascom has never told me to do anything like that. He knows that I wouldn't do it if he did ask me. If he was going to pull anything crooked, he'd get rid of me before . . ."

His voice trailed away, leaving the sentence unfinished. Steelman glanced at him shrewdly.

"Go on, Rhodes. He's been riding you, trying to get rid of you?"

"Well," Dusty hesitated. "Yes, sir, he has. But I'm not sure he doesn't mean it for my own good. You see he thinks—he seems to think—that I ought to go back to college."

"Mmm. I wonder," said Steelman. "If he could get another bellboy on the job, work out a deal with him ... Tolly, do you remember that night team they caught out in Denver a while back? Stealing rent. Refunding—right into their own pockets. Carting out linens and supplies by the armload. God only knows how many thousands of dollars they cleaned up."

"I remember," Tolliver nodded. "But with nothing more against the man than this one letter, which doesn't really tell us anything, I'd be very reluctant to jump to any conclusions. After all, Bascom worked with a number of other bellboys before Bill came here. His work is audited daily, and we run comparison reaudits from month to month. It seems to me that if he was pulling anything, we'd have found out about it in ten years' time."

"Perhaps he hasn't pulled anything. Maybe he's just getting ready to."

"Well," said Tolliver. "Maybe."

"I don't like it, Tolly." Steelman's lips thinned fretfully. "A letter like this concerning the one man we know nothing about. If a man's been a crook once—and this indicates that he has—he's very apt to be one again. He feels a sudden pinch, has to get money in a hurry, and he's off to the races."

"Yes, I suppose so," Tolliver nodded. "What about that, Bill? Does Mr. Bascom have any money problems that you know of?"

"No, sir. He's never mentioned any."

"Well, there's still another angle," the manager went on. "Suppose the author of this letter is trying to blackmail Bascom. He doesn't want him dismissed from his job, so he says just enough to disturb us. As he sees it, we'll be impelled to make some mention of the matter and Bascom will be frightened into paying off. Otherwise, there'll be another letter with more details."

Tolliver frowned solemnly. Then, suddenly, his mouth twisted and he bent forward laughing. "Excuse me, John, but—ha, ha, ha—when I try to picture poor old Bascom in the toils of a blackmailer, I—ha, ha—I—"

"Well," Steelman grinned a trifle sheepishly. "Maybe I'd better start reading westerns instead of detective stories. I can't see the prim old boy in the role myself. Seriously, however..."

"We've gotten crank letters before, John. It's not unnatural, after all the years he's been with us, that one should eventually crop up about Bascom. If we get another one, we certainly ought to take some action, but I don't see how we can at this point. For the present, we can just keep our eyes and ears open—that means you particularly, Bill—and—"

"What about putting Bascom on a day shift?"

"If you say so, but I wouldn't like to. He doesn't have the zip, the polish for a front-office day job. Aside from that, it takes a long time to break a man in on the night paper work.

Steelman nodded. "All right, Tolly. I'll leave it up to you. You don't think you should mention the letter to Bascom? Very casually, of course. If he's on the level, there's no harm done, and if he isn't, well, it might keep him out of trouble."

"Except with that blackmailer, eh?" Tolliver laughed. "But I think you may be right, John. Now..."

They discussed the matter for a minute or two longer. Then, Tolliver looked at Dusty and stood up. "There's no reason to keep Bill around for this, is there? There's nothing more you have to say to him?"

"Can't think of anything." The manager shook his head. "Thanks for coming down, Rhodes."

"And remember," Tolliver said, "under your hat, Bill. You don't know anything about this matter."

"Yes, sir," said Dusty.

... Later, when it was too late to do much about it, it seemed to him that he should have seen the connection between the letter and Marcia Hillis and Tug Trowbridge and Bascom ... and the threat they represented to himself. Later, he did not know he had been so blind as to fail to see. It was all so simple, simple and deadly. All the parts to the puzzle had been in his hands, and he had only to look at them.

That, however, was later. At the time, it was only an annoyance and one for which there was little excuse. His sleep had been broken into. He had been dragged downtown on a hot afternoon. And all because some nut, some guest probably with a hangover grouch, had written an anonymous note. That was all it amounted to when you got right down to it. If the hotel had any real doubts about Bascom, he wouldn't have stayed there ten years.

Dusty went home, found that his father had returned from his stroll or wherever he had been, and went to bed. It was now nearing six o'clock, but he was too tired and hot to eat. Too tired to sleep, for that matter. He heard his father moving about in the kitchen, closing and reclosing the refrigerator, rattling ice trays, setting a pan on the stove. It went on and on, it seemed. Interminably. It would—*he began to drift into sleep*—always go on. The heat and the noise ... and ... and his father. And nothingness.

A vivid image of his mother flashed into his mind, and he tossed restlessly. The image changed, a line here, a line there, and it was another woman: alluring, youthful, and above all warm and interested ... and understanding.

He fell asleep, half-frowning, half-smiling.

FIVE

The night was about average for the Hotel Manton. Bascom seemed about the same as always, with little to say and that cranky and carping. If Tolliver had shown him the letter, and if it meant anything to him, he gave no sign of the fact.

Dusty drove straight home from work. Or, rather, he started to. Halfway there he remembered that his father was to see the optometrist and that he had no clean clothes. Wearily, cursing, he let the car slow. Of course, the cleaning and laundry might get back early today, but it also might not. And now that he'd taken a firm stand with his father, he'd better carry through with it. There was going to be no more of this putting off, letting him go on with his expensive and embarrassing shiftlessness. He'd been told to see the optometrist today, so today it would be.

Dusty drove back to town, eating breakfast while he waited for the stores to open. He bought a pair of summer trousers, a shirt and underwear, and started home again.

Mr. Rhodes was in the kitchen, dabbling ineffectually at the suds-filled sink. He lifted a platter from the dishwater, peering at his son reproachfully as he began to scrub it.

"Had a nice breakfast fixed for you, Bill," he said. "Bacon and eggs and toast, and—"

"Sorry," Dusty said, shortly. "Wash up, and put these on, Dad. I'll drive you down to the optometrist."

"Thought sure you'd be here," the old man went on. "After buying all that stuff yesterday. If you'd told me you were going to be late, I'd—"

"I'm telling you now!" Dusty snapped. "I mean, I'm sorry, but please hurry, Dad. I want to get to sleep. I'll drive you down, and you can come home by yourself."

Mr. Rhodes nodded mildly, and put down the platter. "This night work, son—do you really think it pays? You don't get your proper rest, and it costs more to—"

"I know. We'll talk about it another time," Dusty cut in. "Now, please hurry, Dad."

He waited in the car while the old man got ready. Impatiently. Trying to stifle his irritation. Probably, he decided, his father was right. He made more money by working nights, but his expenses were higher. There was this car, for example; bus service was slow and irregular late at night, so the car was virtually a necessity. And that was only part of the story. There were usually two sets of meals to fix—or to buy away from home. There was his father, free to do as he chose and always in need of money. Still . . .

Dusty shrugged and shook his head. He wouldn't change jobs for a while, anyway. Not anyway until—and if—he went back to college. He didn't sleep well at night. He hadn't slept well since his mother's death, and, yes, even before that. Of course, it was hard sleeping in the daytime, but that was different. It wasn't like lying alone in the darkness and quiet, thinking and worrying and—and listening.

... He drove the old man downtown, and opened the car door for him. Mr. Rhodes started to slide out of the seat, hesitated.

"You know, Bill, we never did get around to talking about my case. I mentioned that letter the other night, and you said—"

"I haven't forgotten," Dusty said. "We'll see about it."

"Well..." Mr. Rhodes looked at him thoughtfully, sighed and put a foot on the sidewalk. "I thought I might go to a show after I get through here, Bill. If that's all right with you."

"You do that," Dusty nodded. "Pick some place with air-conditioning."

"Well, I-I'm not sure that—"

"I am," Dusty said firmly. "You must have enough money, Dad. You couldn't help but have."

"Well ... well, maybe," the old man mumbled. "I guess I have at that."

He got out and trudged away. Dusty drove home, and went to bed. This was one day, he thought, he'd really get some sleep. He was so tired that ... that ...

He was asleep almost the moment that he climbed into bed. An hour later he was aroused by the laundry man.

He put the laundry away, and went back to sleep. Another hour passed—roughly an hour. And the man from the cleaner's came.

This time it was harder returning to sleep. He smoked a couple of cigarettes, got a drink of water, tossed and turned restlessly on the bedclothes. Finally, at long last, he drifted off into unconsciousness. And the phone rang.

He tried to ignore it, to pretend that it was not ringing. It rang on and on, refusing to be denied. Cursing, Dusty flung himself out of bed and answered it.

"Mr. Rhodes? Hope I didn't interrupt anything, but your father said I was to be sure to ..."

It was the optometrist.

Dusty learned the amount of his bill, muttered a goodbye and slammed the phone back in its cradle. He returned to bed, but now, of course, sleep was impossible. His eyes kept popping open. His head throbbed with a surly, sullen anger. Unreasoning, focusing gradually on just one object ... Why the hell did *he* have to go to a show today?

Why couldn't *he* ever do anything except make a damned nuisance of himself? All *he* thought of was his own comfort, his own welfare. Lying and sponging to get money for those—

Abruptly, Dusty got up. Sullenly ashamed, vaguely alarmed. He didn't really feel that way about his father. He couldn't be blamed much if he did, but he didn't. He didn't feel at all that way. He was just grouchy with the heat and work and not being able to sleep.

There was still some coffee on the stove. He drank a cup, smoking a cigarette with it, and went into the bathroom. Today was as good a time as any to see those lawyers. A good time to get it over with, since he couldn't sleep. He came out of the bathroom, dressed and headed for town.

... The building was an old faded-brick walkup, squatting almost directly across the street from the county courthouse. Dusty climbed the worn stairs to the second floor, and proceeded past a series of doors with the legend:

McTeague & Kossmeyer
Attorneys at Law
Entrance 200

Room 200 was at the end of the corridor, uncarpeted, high-ceilinged, barren of everything—it seemed to Dusty—except spittoons and people. A low wooden rail with a swinging gate enclosed one corner of the room. Dusty made his way to the barrier, and gave his name to a graying, harried-looking woman.

"McTeague?" she said. "Something personal? You a friend of his? Well, you don't see Mac then. Kossy does all the seeing in this firm."

"Well..." Dusty hesitated. He didn't want to see Kossmeyer— "Caustic" Kossmeyer, as the newspapers called him. From what he had observed of the attorney, it would not be easy to say the things to him that he had come to say.

"Well," the woman said. "Kossmeyer?"

"You're sure I can't—?"

"Kossmeyer," she said grimly. With finality. And jabbed a plug into her switchboard. "Now sit down and stay put, will you? Don't go wandering off someplace where I can't find you."

She kept her eyes on him until he sat down—on a bench between a middle-aged Mexican in soiled khakis and a middle-aged matron in crisp cretonne. Dusty started to light a cigarette, then noting the sidelong glance the matron gave him, dropped it into one of the ubiquitous spittoons. Uncomfortably, he looked around the room.

A young, scared-looking couple sat in one of the windows, holding hands. A few feet away from them, a paunchy man in an expensive suit talked earnestly to a bosomy, flashily dressed blonde. Two men with zoot coats and snapbrimmed hats were playing the match game. Three Negroes, obviously mother, father and son, huddled in a corner and conversed in whispers ... It was as though a cross-section of the city's population had been swept up and set down in the room.

Dusty stood up, casually. The receptionist wasn't looking at him. He'd just saunter on out. Tomorrow he'd write a letter to the firm. A letter would do just as well as a personal talk—almost as well, anyway—and ...

The door inside the barrier opened, and Kossmeyer came out. Rather, he lunged out, pushing a sharp-faced oldish young man ahead of him. His voice rasped stridently through the suddenly stilled room.

"All right," he was saying. "Suit yourself. Be your own lawyer. But don't come crying to me afterwards. You want to go to the jug, it's your funeral, but I ain't sending any flowers."

"Now, look, Kossy"—the man's eyes darted around the room. "I didn't mean—"

"You look,' said Kossmeyer. "You ever see yourself in a mirror? Well, take a good gander ..."

Dusty watched, fascinated.

Kossmeyer didn't look anything like the other man; he was barely five feet tall and he couldn't have weighed more than a hundred pounds. But now, despite their facial and physical dissimilarity, he looked strikingly like him. In an instant, he had made himself into a hideous caricature of the other. His eyes had become shifting and beady, his face sinisterly slack-jawed. He had called in his chest, simultaneously squaring his shoulders so that his elbows were forced out from his sides. His pants were drawn high beneath his armpits. He wore no coat, but he seemed to, a coat that hung almost to the knees like the other man's. Eyes darting he slowly revolved, not moving a muscle of his dead-pan face ...

He was preposterous. Preposterous yet somehow frightening. A cartoon labelled CRIME. And, then, suddenly, he was himself again.

"You see, Ace? You got three strikes called the minute they look at you. Just handing it to 'em straight ain't good enough. We got to knock 'em over, know what I mean? Pile it around 'em so high they can't see over it."

The man nodded. "You got me sold. Now, how about—"

"Beat it. Come back tomorrow." Kossmeyer gave him a shove through the gate, and bent over the receptionist. He said, "Yeah? Where?" and glanced up. Then Dusty heard him say, "Oh ... the son ... junior ..."

And the next instant he was out of the enclosure and gripping Dusty's hand.

"Glad to see you, Rhodes, Bill ... No, I bet they call you Dusty, don't they? Come on in."

Dusty hung back. Or tried to. "I—it's nothing important, Mr. Kossmeyer. I can come back some other—"

"Nonsense." The attorney propelled him through the throng. "Been hoping you'd drop in. Let's see, you're over at the Manton, right? Nice people. Done a little work for them myself. How's your father? How you like this weather? What...?"

Talking rapidly, answering his own questions, he ushered Dusty into his office and slammed the door.

Except for the bookcases, the room was practically as barren as the one outside. Kossmeyer waved Dusty to a chair, and perched on the desk in front of him.

"Glad you came in," he repeated. "Wanted to ask you, but I knew you worked nights. How about a drink? You look kind of tired."

"Thanks. I don't drink," Dusty said.

"Yeah? Well I was saying—I'm damned glad you came in. I got a pretty good idea how you feel, Dusty. We've been on this thing about a year now, and we seem to be getting nowhere fast. Your father still out of a job. You stuck with a lot of expenses. You're asking yourself, what the hell, and I don't blame—"

"About that"—Dusty cleared his throat. "About the expenses, Mr. Kossmeyer. I'm afraid I can't—I mean, it seems to me that—"

"Sure." The little man nodded vigorously. "They've been high. Just the costs alone on a deal like this can hit a guy pretty hard. I—"

he paused. "You know that's all we've taken, don't you? Just the actual expense of filing briefs and serving papers, and so on."

"Well, no," Dusty said. "I didn't know it. But—"

"But it's still too much," Kossmeyer interrupted. "Anything's too much when it ain't buying anything. But that's just the way it looks to you, y'know, Dusty? It's just the way it looks from the outside. Actually, we're making a lot of headway. We've been pouring in the nickels, and now we're just about to hit the jackpot. I—"

"Mr. Kossmeyer," said Dusty, "I want you to drop the case."

"Huh-uh. No, you don't," the lawyer said. "You just think you do. Like I've been telling you, kid, we're just about to pick up the marbles. Give me two or three more months, and—"

"It won't do any good if Dad does win. He's not going to be able to go back to his job. He's not—well, he's just not himself any more."

"Who the hell is?" Kossmeyer shrugged. "But I know what you mean, Dusty. I've seen him myself, y'know. This knocked the props out from under him, and he's still going around in a daze. I'd say the best way to snap him out of it is to—"

"He's not physically well either. He's—"

"Sure, he's not," Kossmeyer agreed. "A man's sick, he's sick all over."

"I want you to drop it," Dusty said stubbornly. "Winning the case won't really change anything. People will go right on thinking that— what they've been thinking. It would be impossible for him to work."

"Yeah, but, kid ..." Kossmeyer paused, a puzzled frown on his small, sharp-featured face. "Let me see if I got you right, Dusty. We're supposed to have free speech in this country; it's guaranteed by the constitution. So a man does something in support of that guarantee, and a bunch of know-nothings and professional patriots do a job on him. He's right and they're as wrong as teeth in a turkey, but he's supposed to take it. Just crawl in a hole and stay there. Don't give 'em no trouble, so they can go on and do the same kind of job on another guy. Is that what you mean?"

"I'm sorry," Dusty said doggedly. "I can't help it that things are the way they are. It's not right, of course, but—"

"I think you're low-pricing your dad," Kossmeyer said. "He thought enough of this issue to go to bat on it. I don't see him running for the dugout just because they're tossing pop bottles. If he gets his job back—*when* he gets it back, I should say—he won't let 'em smoke him out. He'll be right in there pitching a long time after these bastards are ducking for cover themselves."

He nodded firmly. Dusty shook his head. "I don't think he felt that way. I mean, well, like he was fighting for something. I doubt that he even knew what he was signing. Someone handed him a petition and he just..."

"Yeah?" Kossmeyer waited. "Why didn't he say so, then? That it was all a misunderstanding? That would have let him off the hook."

"Well," Dusty hesitated. "I ... he probably thought they wouldn't believe him."

"I see," said Kossmeyer. "Well, possibly you're right. After all, if a son doesn't know his father, who does?"

He stared at Dusty blandly, his bright black eyes friendly and guileless. And yet there was something about him, there had been something for several minutes now, that was vaguely disturbing. He was like some small deadly bird, coaxing a clumsy prey within striking distance.

Dusty took out his cigarettes, fumbled one from the package. Instantly, Kossmeyer was holding a match for him.

"Had a pretty rough time of it, haven't you, kid? Losing out on your schooling. Losing your mother. Working and trying to take care of a sick old man at the same time."

"I don't mind," Dusty said. "I'm glad to do what I can."

"Sure, you are, but it's plenty tough just the same. Well, I thought we'd gone pretty easy with you on money, but maybe we can make it a little lighter still. That's your only objection to going on with the case, isn't it? The expense. If we can take care of that, you'd just as soon we went ahead."

"Well, I—I wouldn't want you to—"

"We'll work something out," Kossmeyer said. "Maybe—y'know, it's just possible we can get by without any more expenses. If I can get your father to cooperate."

"If ...?" Dusty's head was beginning to ache. "I don't understand."

"You gave me an idea a minute ago. About your father signing that petition without knowing what he was doing. Now, that might be pretty hard for people to swallow, particularly at this late date. And I kind of think he wouldn't want to make such an admission, anyway. If he wasn't any brighter than that, he shouldn't have been holding the job he was in . . ."

"But what—"

"That petition was floating around everywhere. Different copies of it. Maybe someone signed your dad's name to it. You . . . Here! You're about to burn your fingers, kid."

Kossmeyer reached behind him and procured an ashtray. He extended it in a lean, steady hand.

Dusty ground out his cigarette. "Why would anyone sign his name?"

"Some joker maybe. Some guy who wanted to get him into trouble."

"But why wouldn't Dad have said so if—"

"We-el"—Kossmeyer pursed his lips—"now, that's a question, ain't it? Ordinarily, I'd say he was standing on the principle of the thing. He had a right to sign it, and regardless of whether he did or not isn't important. It's the principle involved, not the physical action itself. But you say he doesn't feel that way, so—That *is* what you said, isn't it?—so I guess he must have another reason."

He continued to stare at Dusty, frowning thoughtfully, interested and sympathetic: a man helping a friend with a puzzling problem. He waited, watched and waited, and Dusty could only look back at him wordlessly, his throat dry, a slow hot flush creeping over his face. The silence mounted. It became unbearable.

And then Kossmeyer shrugged, and grinned deprecatingly. "Listen to me rave, huh? Who the hell would forge your old man's signature? It don't make sense any way you look at it. All your dad would have to do is call in a handwriting expert, and he'd be in the clear like that."

He snapped his fingers, demonstrating. He slid off the desk, and held out his hand. "Don't want to rush you off, kid, but I got a lot of people waiting and . . ."

"I've got to run along, anyway." Dusty stood up hastily. "I'll— thanks very much for seeing me, and—"

It wasn't what he wanted to say. He hadn't said anything he'd wanted to say. He'd gotten all twisted around, and all he could think of now was release. All he wanted now was to escape from this friendly, helpful and terrifying little man.

"I'll—I hope I see you again," he mumbled weakly.

"Sure you will." Kossmeyer gave him a hearty clap on the back. "Any old time, kid. If it ain't convenient for you to come in, I'll look you up."

He held the door open, beaming, ushered Dusty through it. He shook hands again. "Yes, sir," he said. "I'll keep in touch. You can depend on it, Dusty."

SIX

As it often did, after a scorching day, the night brought rain. It had started a few minutes before Dusty came to work; now, at three in the morning, it had settled down to a slow steady drizzle.

It was a quiet shift. No guests had come in on the late train, and there had been hardly a dozen room calls thus far. He and Bascom were practically through with their paper work; at least, there was little remaining that he could help with. Lounging at the side of the door of the lobby, he drank in the wonderfully cool clean air, watching the curtain of rain flow endlessly into the oily black pavement.

He was feeling good, all things considered, considering that he had had almost no sleep. It was cool, and Kossmeyer hadn't guessed anything—what the hell was there for him to guess, anyway?—and Bascom was being decent for a change. Bascom had been taking a lot out of him, Dusty decided. You were bound to be nervous and depressed when you had some guy riding you night after night.

Dusty flipped his cigarette into the street, and went back into the lobby. Bascom called to him pleasantly from the cashier's cage.

"How does it look, Bill? Still coming down pretty hard?"

"Not too bad. You can make it all right if you take an umbrella."

"Good. Think I'll go get a bite to eat, then."

Dusty went behind the desk. Bascom came out of the cashier's cage, locked the door behind him and got an umbrella. He opened the door at the rear of the keyrack, and emerged into the lobby.

"Well"—his voice was casual; he spoke almost over his shoulder—
"I guess you're not going to go back to college?"

"I'm still thinking about it," Dusty said. "I want to, but it'll take
time to work it out."

"I see," Bascom nodded. "At any rate, I don't suppose you could go
back before the fall term."

"No, sir. Not very well."

"I'll be back in a few minutes," Bascom said. "You know where to
reach me if anything comes up."

He went out the side door, raising the umbrella as he stepped
under the marquee. Dusty leaned his elbows on the marble desk top,
and let his eyes wander around the lobby. He yawned pleasurably. A
good night, any way you looked at it. Bascom, the weather, money-
wise. Tug Trowbridge had given him a ten-dollar tip. If he didn't
make another nickel between now and quitting time, he'd still have a
good shift.

At his elbow, the bell captain's phone rang suddenly. Dusty
jumped, startled, then picked up the receiver.

It was her, Marcia Hillis. He recognized her voice instantly, and
she recognized his.

"Dusty? Can you bring me some stationery?"

"Yes, ma'am. Right away, Miss—I mean, I can bring them in a
few minutes, Miss Hillis. The room clerk's gone out to eat, and I have
to watch the desk."

"Oh? Are you afraid it will run away?"

"No, ma'am, I—"

She laughed softly. "I was teasing ... As soon as you can,
then."

"Yes, ma'am."

He hung the receiver up clumsily. Opening a drawer, he took out
a stack of stationery, small and typewriter size, and laid it on the
counter. He went behind the keyrack to the lavatory and combed his
hair. He came out front again, and looked at the clock. Bascom had
been gone ... well, he'd been gone long enough. Should be back any
minute. He looked at the stack of stationery, shook his head
judiciously, and returned two thirds of it to the drawer.

Something in the action stirred his memory. Or, perhaps, it was
the other way around: memory, a recollection, brought about the

action. Something the superintendent of service had lectured him about at the time of his employment.

"*... Very careful about waste, Bill. Lights not in use, leaky water taps, two trips with the elevator when one might suffice, more soap and towels and stationery than a guest can legitimately use. Little things ... but they aren't little when you multiply them by several hundred. It's those little things that count. They make the difference between profit and loss...*"

Dusty glanced at the clock again. For no reason that he could think of, merely to kill time, he walked up the aisle to the room rack. There was nothing to be learned there, of course. She was just another one of hundreds of small white slips ... a capital-lettered composite name, place of residence, rate and date ... He returned to the bell captain's section, drummed nervously on the neat stack of stationery.

He picked up the outside phone, dialed the first two numbers of the lunch room, and replaced the receiver. This wasn't important enough to have Bascom come rushing back. If she waited until this time of night to write letters, she could wait a little longer. That's the way Bascom would look at it. That was the way he looked at it. She was just another guest, good for a two-bit tip, perhaps. So what was the hurry?

Dusty leaned over the counter, and looked up the expanse of lobby to the front entrance. He went out the door and waited in front of the counter.

Stationery at three in the morning. Not usual, but it wasn't extraordinary either. A guest couldn't sleep, so to pass the time, he or she wrote letters. It happened. Every few nights or so there'd be a room call for stationery. As for the way she'd talked over the phone, the way she'd acted that first night ...

Well ...

He shrugged and ended the silent argument. Why kid himself? She'd been interested in him from the beginning. Now, she'd worked herself up to the point of doing a little playing. And so long as she wasn't a spotter—and she wasn't—so long as he let her take all the initiative and he damned well would—it would be okay. No trouble. Not a chance of trouble. He'd never done anything like this before, and he never would again. Just this once.

Bascom came in the front door. Dusty signaled to him, jabbing a finger into the air. The room clerk nodded, and Dusty picked up the stationery and trotted off to the elevator.

At the tenth floor, he opened the door of the car and latched it back with a hook. He started down the long semidark corridor. There was a low whistle from behind him, then a:

"Hey, Dusty!"

Dusty turned. It was Tug Trowbridge, standing in the door of his suite in undershirt and trousers. Two men—the two he had met a few nights before—were with him.

"In a big hurry? How about running my friends downstairs?"

"Well"—Dusty hesitated—"yes, sir," he said. "Glad to." It had to be done. He couldn't leave them waiting indefinitely for an elevator.

He took them downstairs, said good night and went back to the tenth floor. He latched the door back quietly, and started down the hall again.

Slowly, then more slowly.

Now that he was here, rounding the corner of the corridor, approaching her door, standing in front of it—now, his nervousness, his sense of caution, returned. An uneasy premonition stirred in him, a feeling that once before he had done something like this with terrifying, soul-sickening results. There had been another woman, one who like this one was all woman, and he—

He shook himself, driving the memory deep down into its secret hiding place. It had never happened, nothing like this. There had been no other woman.

He raised his hand, tapped lightly on the door. He heard a soft, rustling sound, then, dimly, "Dusty?"

"Yes."

"Come in."

He went in, let the door click shut behind him. He stood there a moment, his eyes still full of the light outside, seeing nothing in the pitch black darkness. His hand unclasped, and the stationery drifted to the floor.

She laughed softly. She murmured . . . a question, an invitation. He felt his way forward slowly, guided by the sound of her voice.

His knee bumped against the bed. A hand reached up out of the darkness. He sat down on the edge of the bed, and her arms fastened around his neck.

There was one savagely delightful moment as his mouth found hers, as he felt the cool-warm nakedness of her breasts. Then, suddenly, he was sick, shivering with sickness and fear. It was all wrong. It wasn't like it should have been.

Her mouth was covered with lipstick. He could taste its ugly flatness in his own mouth, feel the sticky smears upon his face and neck. And she wasn't naked. Only part of her was nude, and there the nakedness was not complete. It was as though her night clothes had been torn. It—

She didn't speak. She was still clinging to him, smearing him, digging her nails into his face. She didn't speak, but there was a voice:

"Y-you filthy, sneaking little bastard! Yes, bastard, do you hear? We got you out of a foundling asylum! And God curse the day we ... No, I won't tell him. I won't do that to him. But if you ever—"

He was almost motionless for a moment, paralyzed by the unbearable voice. But it had never happened. It was only a bad dream. And this ...

There was a roll of thunder. The drawn curtains whipped back in a sudden gust of wind, and lightning illuminated the room just for a second, but that was long enough for him to see:

The over-turned chairs. The upset lamp. The deliberate disorder. The night-gown, half ripped from her body. And the smeared red mouth, opened to scream. He hit her as hard as he could.

SEVEN

The next thirty minutes was a nightmare. A confused and hideous dream, the incidents of which piled terrifyingly, bewilderingly, one atop another. He was bent over her—pleading and apologizing— hysterically trying to bring her back to consciousness. Then, he was leaving her room, running blindly down the hall, bursting into Tug Trowbridge's suite. And Tug was gripping him by the shoulders, slapping him across the face, forcing him into a semi-calm coherence ... *"So okay, kid. I'll try and square the dame some way. Now straighten up and beat it back downstairs. Before old Bascom sends out an alarm for you."*

He was washing his face, combing his hair, under Tug's supervision. He was in the elevator, then crossing a seemingly endless expanse of the lobby. With Bascom's eyes on him every step of the way. And at last—at last, immediately—he was facing Bascom across the marble counter.

Trying to explain the inexplicable.

"Bill! Answer me, Bill!"

"Y-yes, sir . . .?"

"What took you so long? What have you been doing up there in Miss Hillis' room?"

"I—I—"

It made no impression on him at the time: the fact that, illogically, Bascom knew where he had been. He was still too frightened, too conscience-stricken, to raise even a silent question.

"Bill!"

"N-nothing, sir. The—the window in her room was stuck. I had to pry it open for her. P-prop it open."

"And that took you thirty minutes? Nonsense! What were you doing up there? What have you done to—to—"

Bascom's voice trailed away. Eyes fastened on Dusty's face, he picked up the telephone. Gave a room number to the operator.

Dusty would have run, then. He would have, but his legs refused to obey the frantic signaling of his mind. He could only stand, paralyzed, wait and listen as Bascom spoke into the phone.

". . . uh, Miss Hillis? This is the night clerk. The bellboy tells me that you were having some trouble—that there was some trouble with your window, and . . . I see. You're all right—I mean, everything is taken care of, then? Thank you very much, and I hope I haven't disturbed you."

He hung up the phone. Incredibly, he hung it up . . . without summoning the police or the house detective. And, seemingly, the nightmare began to draw to a close.

Dusty could breathe again. He could talk—and think—again.

Tug had squared the dame some way. He'd bought her off. Or, more likely, he'd frightened her away from whatever stunt she'd been attempting. Probably he'd been there in the room with her when

Bascom called. Letting her know—making her believe—that she'd get her teeth slapped out if she pulled anything funny.

At any rate, everything was all right. A miracle had happened, and he was too grateful to inquire as to its creation or authenticity.

"I told you," he said—he heard himself saying. "What the hell did you think I was doing?"

Bascom frowned at him puzzledly. He gave him a long, level look, and at last turned back to his work on the transcript sheets.

"I'll tell you what I think," he said. "What I've been thinking for quite a while. You don't belong here in this job. Sooner or later, if you stay on, you'll find yourself in very serious trouble."

Dusty laughed. Almost steadily. "What have you got it in for me about, anyway? I can't turn around any more without you making a production out of it."

"Come around the desk," said Bascom. "Give me some help. Do a little something to earn your pay."

"Sure," Dusty grinned. "Why not?"

He and the clerk finished the few remaining two man chores. Then, Bascom retired to the cashier's cage, and Dusty sauntered back to the bell-captain's area. Elbows propped on the marble counter, he wondered—without really caring—how Tug had managed to square Miss Marcia Hillis, of Dallas, Tex.

A little slapping around, he supposed, not enough to mark her up, but more than enough to scare hell out of her. She hadn't counted on his having a friend like Tug. She'd framed him into a case of seeming attempted rape, the objective a hefty lawsuit against the hotel. But now that she'd seen what she was up against, that the only thing she was likely to collect was a broken neck . . .

Dusty frowned, still not actually caring or worrying about her, but continuing to wonder. He'd have sworn that she wasn't a shakedown artist. How could he have been so wrong? And if she was one—*since* she was one—why had she waited so long to pull this rape setup?

A dame as smart as she seemed to be would have made the try right away. She'd have known that the hotel might become suspicious, decide that her room was subject to "previous reservation" and that, regrettably, no others were available.

She should have know that. Anyone who knew anything at all about hotels, *had* to know it. And yet . . . Dusty's face cleared, and he smiled almost pityingly. Despite the ordeal she'd put him through, he felt a little sorry for her.

She *didn't* know anything about hotels: that was the answer to the riddle. She was a swell-looking babe, and doubtless smart enough in other respects, but what she didn't know about hotels was everything. As little as she knew about the rackets.

He'd been right about her. She wasn't a shakedown operator. This was her first attempt. She'd been rocking along somewhere, respectably enough, and then she'd gotten this big idea—one she thought was completely original. So she'd gone to work on it. And made every blunder in the book.

The Manton itself had been blunder number one. A professional would have chosen a really big house with heavy turnover in personnel and guests. Then, there was error number two—a thing to make a real pro wince. That was her biggest bonehead, checking in in the middle of the night, without a reservation for God's sake! And demanding a low-priced room! And making a play, arousing the suspicions of an employee, before she was ready to carry through with it...

One mistake after another. In a way, her many and incredible blunders had protected her. Ignorance had masqueraded as innocence, and while he had been disturbed by her, he had had no strong suspicions.

Well ... Dusty sighed regretfully. She wasn't the only one who'd been stupid. If he'd seen the simple truth sooner, he could have avoided tonight's terrifying experience. Replaced it with one exceedingly more pleasant. He could have said, Look, honey. You're trying this in the wrong place and on the wrong guy ... And doubtless she would have been grateful. Very grateful.

As things stood now—well, just where did things stand now? Covertly, he glanced down the long aisle toward Bascom, hesitated, then sighed again. The clerk was already suspicious. Aside from that, a call or a visit to her room was out of the question. She'd be frightened and angry, afraid of and ready to repel any overtures he might make. Also, Tug might still be with her ... and so occupied as to make him resent an intrusion. That would be like Tug. She had made trouble for the big man; in a word, she owed him something. And he would collect as a matter of course.

Dusty wished he could get her out of his mind. He wished he could feel more relieved, grateful, for escaping from what had seemed an inescapable mess. But as the long night drew to a close, he felt only one thing: a sense of irreplaceable loss. He had lost her *again*. For the second time, he had lost the only woman in the world.

The vanguard of the day shift began to arrive. The first elevator boy went to work, the first mezzanine maid, the first lobby attendant. The head baggage-porter retrieved the checkroom key, unlocked it under the drowsy gaze of a black-shined subordinate.

As dawn spread into daylight, Dusty was forced out of his reverie. With the calls piling on top of each other he was kept too busy to think about her.

He raced up and down on the service elevator, *de rigueur*, when in use, for the hotel's employees. He raced up and down the long, deeply carpeted hallways. Tapping on doors. Delivering cigarettes and morning papers and toilet articles and a dozen-odd things. Everything moved in a blur of automatic action. There were no people, only room numbers. And the numbers themselves soon lost meaning. They were connected with the transitory moment's errand, and beyond that they had no existence.

... He said, "Thank you, very much, sir," and pocketed a quarter tip. He rounded the corner of the corridor, moving at a fast trot.

He looked up, just in time to keep from piling into them.

The baggage porter was in the lead, her overnight case under one arm, her hatbox and suitcase in his hands. Sauntering along behind him was one of Tug's men, and at the rear of the procession was another. She was walking between the two. Knotted at the back of her head were the cords of a heavy black veil.

Dusty gulped. He turned and darted back around the corner. He couldn't say why the scene was such a shock to him, why it sent waves of sickness through his brain. Because, naturally, he should have expected something like this. Tug would feel that he had to get her out of the hotel. Nothing less would be safe—absolutely safe— and Tug was not the kind to take unnecessary chances. So ... so there was nothing wrong. Tug, or, rather, Tug's boys would see that she checked out. They'd slip her a little money and load her on a train, and—and that was all they would do. Just enough to insure Tug's safety and his, Dusty's, own.

Everything was as it should be, then. As he should have expected it to be. But still he was sick, and getting sicker by the moment. It was as though he'd witnessed a death procession, a criminal being led to the execution chamber.

He ran down the service stairs to the next landing. He raced down that corridor, and around to the service elevator. Why, he couldn't have said, because certainly he couldn't interfere. It would be his own neck if he did, and ... and why should he, anyway?

Why, he demanded furiously. She tried to get me, didn't she? They won't do anything to her, but why should I care if they did?

The sickness mounted. It disintegrated suddenly, still in him but spread through his body, no longer a compact, centralized force. And mixing with it, adulterating it, was a strange feeling of pride. Tug Trowbridge. He and Tug. She'd stepped on Dusty's toes, and now, by God, she was learning a lesson. They were showing her, her and the Manton and the rest of the world. She had everything on her side, all the forces of law and order. And against him and Tug, they didn't mean a thing. She was being kidnaped in broad daylight from one of the biggest hotels in town.

They were bolder than the others, see? They could think faster than the others. Sure, everyone knew who Tug's boys were, but the boys weren't with her, understand? They just happened to be around when she decided to check out.

They made her call for a porter. Then, they set her baggage out in the hall, and told her to wait there until the porter arrived. And when he did, well, they were just down the hall a few steps, just coming out of another room—it appeared. And very casually, oh, so innocently, they all headed for the elevator together. True, one got ahead of the other, but what of it? Doubtless the second guy had had to pause to tie a shoelace.

Dusty stepped off the elevator, hurried toward the entrance to the lobby. He was panting unconsciously; the pounding of his heart grew wilder and wilder. The next step, now—how would he and Tug manage that! She'd have to pay her own bill. She'd have to leave the hotel alone. They wouldn't dare let her, but they'd have to. God, what else could they do? And once she got out on the street—or, Christ, even before she got to the street even here in the lobby ...!

They couldn't hold a gun in her back down here. They couldn't follow her right up to the cashier's cage, wait until she paid her bill, and then march her out to the street. They couldn't, but they had to! They had to without letting anyone know they were doing it. And how the hell could they manage that?

Blindly, Dusty entered the lobby. The swelling pride was gone, now; disintegrated as suddenly as the sickness. And the sickness was coagulating and mounting again, taking charge of his every fiber and cell.

He and Tug, rather, Tug and his boys would never get away with it. They were a bunch of stupid stumblebums, and they'd got him in twice the mess he'd already been in, and—

The four were just emerging from the elevator. They passed within inches of him as he paused near the check stand, too stricken to proceed into the lobby proper. Blinded, choking with sickness and terror.

Hell, why had they had to do it like this? Why try to do it so damned right that it was bound to be wrong? They shouldn't have bothered with her baggage or her bill. Just left the bags in her room, and let the bill go unpaid. Of course, that would cause troublesome inquiries eventually. The hotel would chalk her up as a skip, and her name and description would be circularized in every hotel in the country. Her baggage would be opened and examined. Her hometown police would be notified. And if it appeared that she was a responsible person—that she'd simply dropped out of sight in this city—well, it could be tough for anyone who'd had contact with her. But that would be better than this, wouldn't it? You'd stand a chance that way, and this way there was no chance. You were licked before you started.

. . . The baggage porter was heading toward the taxi entrance. She was proceeding up the lobby toward the cashier's cage. Quite alone, now, for the two men had dropped well behind. They had paused to talk, casually, letting her go on alone. Leaving her to scream or run— to appeal to that blurred figure who stood in front of the cashier's cage.

She went forward slowly, stiffly, like a person walking in her sleep. She was almost there, almost safe, completely beyond the reach of her guards.

Why doesn't she do it? Dusty though angrily. Just do it and get it all over with.

A voice rang in his ears, booming, familiar. Tug Trowbridge's confident, ever-cheerful bellow. It penetrated the chaos of Dusty's mind, clearing his terror-blurred vision.

Tug. It was he who stood at the cashier's window. Now, he stepped back politely, making room for the woman, and called again to the two men:

"Hey, you guys! Been waiting for you"

They looked up. They allowed themselves to discover him. They joined him.

The three of them stood in a semi-circle, only a few feet withdrawn from the cashier's cage. Ringing her in (although no one would have suspected it), while they held inaudible but patently earnest conversation.

She finished paying her bill. She picked up her change awkwardly, and turned away from the wicket. And Tug put an end to the conversation with another bellow.

"Well, that's that," he announced to the lobby at large. "We'll get busy on it right way, and—hey, you lug! Get out of the lady's way, will you?"

The man addressed stepped out of the "lady's" way. They all stepped out of her way, gesturing and murmuring politely.

She stood motionless for a moment Then, head bowed a little, she started toward the taxi entrance. The three men fell in behind her.

They followed her down the steps, and out to the street. They lingered on the walk while she tipped and dismissed the porter. Then . . .

Heart pounding with relief, his exultation growing again, Dusty moved out into the lobby at last. He stepped over to the front post, with its direct view of the sidewalk, and watched this final and most important step.

Not that he doubted its success. He and Tug had swung the deal this far, and they could swing this. But just how—*now* was something he hadn't thought through. It was a fearful stumbling block which only Tug knew how to surmount.

She had a cab waiting. It was her cab, called for her by the porter, and her baggage was loaded into it. And if they tried to pile in with her . . .

They *did* pile in with her. They almost shoved her inside and climbed in themselves. The door slammed, and the plain black vehicle pulled away from the curb, disappeared in the traffic. And Dusty was puzzled for a moment, but only a moment.

Naturally, the driver hadn't squawked. He was one of Tug's boys. He'd been posted at the entrance in advance, and with a cab already there, why should the porter have called another one?

Dusty grinned. He turned back around, grinning, and looked straight into Bascom's eyes.

His throat went suddenly dry; his contorted lips felt as stiff as stone. For, obviously, Bascom knew. He had seen it all, and he knew what it was all about. He didn't know why it had happened, perhaps, but he knew what had happened. The fact of his knowledge was spread like a picture over his pale, old face.

"W-well?" Dusty said. And then louder, boldly, "Well?" for something else was spread over the room clerk's face: Terror and sickness far greater than he, Dusty, had known that night.

"Bill ..." Bascom's voice was quaveringly servile. "I—you don't hold any grudge against me, do you, Bill? I know I may have appeared to give you a pretty rough time, but it was only because I—"

"Yeah?" Dusty's grin was back. "What are you driving at?"

"I don't want anyone else to suffer for it, Bill. For the way you might feel about me. You wouldn't do that, would you? You wouldn't try to put me on a spot by—by—" Dusty's grin widened. Bascom was scared out of his wits, and he damned well should be. The woman was his responsibility. He'd been flagrantly stupid in ever letting her have a room. Now, if something happened to her—if, through her, the hotel became involved in a scandal—Bascom's name would be mud.

Dusty stared at the clerk. He shrugged contemptuously. "I don't know what you're talking about," he said.

"Please, Bill. I know how you feel about me, but—"

"Do you? Well, that's good."

The old man's eyes blazed. Then all the fire went out of them, leaving nothing but lifeless ashes.

"I've got some calls here for you, Bill. I took care of them for you while you were gone."

"Well," said Dusty, ironically. "Well, well. Now, that was certainly thoughtful of you, *Mister* Bascom!"

He shuffled through the call slips, then glanced at the lobby clock. Yawning, he flicked the slips with a finger, scattering them over the counter, sending some of them down behind the counter. "Save them for the day shift," he said. "I'm about due to knock off."

EIGHT

The exalted mood lasted until he reached home. It began to fade as he ascended the steps of the shabby old house. After five minutes with his father it was gone completely.

Dusty could not say what it was about the old man that wrought such a sudden and sharp change in his mood. Perhaps, he admitted glumly, a little guiltily, there was really nothing. Mr. Rhodes had made himself fairly presentable. He looked and talked almost as well as he had in the old days, and for once—for once!—he did not need money. Still, there he was; that he *was* at all was the trouble. Someone who provided nothing, yet had to be provided for. Someone to be accounted to. Someone who served as a reminder of things that were best forgotten.

Feeling ashamed, Dusty gave the old man five dollars. ("Spend it on anything you want to, Dad.") But the gift, admittedly made for his own sake and not his father's, did nothing to dispel the pangs of conscience. He retired to his room, writhing inwardly, gripped in the black coils of an almost unbearable depression.

He undressed quietly. He turned on the electric fan, and lay back on the bed. He lighted a cigarette ... and as the minutes ticked by he continued to light them. One from the butt of another.

The humid summer air moved back and forth across his body. It did not actually cool, but it dried. And always there was more to dry. He thought, forcing himself to think back to the beginning—the only beginning he was aware of—and the perspiration rolled out of his pores, dried under the lazy exhalations of the fan.

... Yes, he remembered. He had been five at the time of the adoption. He knew that they were not actually his parents. But it had been an easy thing to forget. She made it easy, starved as she was for the motherhood she could not naturally achieve.

He was her own-est, dearest baby, Mama's very own darling-est sweetest boy. The days were one long round of petting and coddling, of wild outpourings of affection. She could not do enough for him. She would bathe him over and over, change his clothes a dozen times a day.

The old man—not an old man, then, but much older than she was—had protested mildly. But he never actually interfered. He was very much in love with her, very happy in the status of family man. And it took no more than a few tears or a hurt look from either of them, woman or boy, to silence him immediately.

Only once, to Dusty's recollection, had his Dad (call him that; he had always called him that) demonstrated anything resembling firmness. That was when he, Dusty, was about nine. He had insisted that the boy have his own room and his own bed; he simply had to, he declared, and that was that.

But that, as it turned out, was not that. Mr. Rhodes was away from home a great deal during those days—lecturing in winter, attending college for doctorate credit in summer. And during these absences, his edict was generally ignored.

They would start off to obey, go through all the preliminaries. She would see him to his room, turn on the nightlamp, tuck him under the bedclothes. She would tuck him in very firmly, moving the bedclothes this way and that, adjusting and readjusting the lamp. She would look down at him, primly, her voice faltering a little as she explained why things had to be as they were. "You understand, don't you, darling? Dad's so awfully good to us and he knows what's best, and if he asks us to do something even if it doesn't make any sense— well, we simply must! It's not because Mother doesn't love you any more. She l-loves her boy s-s-so much that ... Oh, darling, dar- ling!"—a wail. "I can't! I *won't*. N-not tonight. Tomorrow but not tonight..."

He liked their bed best. It was larger than his, of course, and he derived a strangely satisfying sense of security from being in it. He did not always feel secure, otherwise, despite the daily demonstrations of her and his father's love. Almost always there was a feeling of unsatisfied want, of something withheld. Of incompleteness. But there with her in the big bed, just the two of them alone, he at last knew absolute safety: the haunting, indefinable hunger was fed. And he wanted for nothing.

He believed he had been about eleven when it happened. It was on a Sunday morning, and she had been awakened early by a rainstorm, and so she had awakened him (not intentionally) with drowsy kisses and hugs. He burrowed close to her. He moved his head, sleepily, feeling an unusual softness and warmth. And suddenly he felt it withdrawn, or, rather, since he did not release his hold, an attempt at withdrawal.

"Bill! Let go, darling!"

"Huh?" He opened his eyes, unwillingly. "What's the matter?"

"Well, you can see, can't you?"—her voice was almost sharp. "I mean, Mother has to fix her nightgown."

She fixed it hastily, blushing. She lay back down, rather stiffly, and then, seeing the innocence of his expression, she drew him close again.

"I'm sorry, darling. Mother didn't mean to sound cross to her baby."

"I'm not your baby," he said, and this time it was he who drew away from her.

"You're—? Oh, well, of course, you're not. Now you're Mother's big boy, her little man."

"I never was your baby," he said.

"B-but, sweetheart"—she raised up on one elbow, looked down troubledly into his face. "Of course, you were my baby. You still are. Has someone—did someone tell you that—"

"I know," he said. "I know what those are for. They're for babies, what Mamas feed babies with, and you never did so I'm not."

"But"—she laughed uncomfortably. A faint crimson was tinging the pale gold of her face, spreading down over her neck and into the deep shadowed hollow of her breasts. "But, sweetheart"—there was a catch to her laugh. "Of course, I did. You just don't remember!"

"No," he said, "I wasn't your baby, so you wouldn't want me to."

"But I would! I mean, I did! When you were a baby, I always— well, I always did!"

He turned his body, turning his back to her. She tried to put her arms around him, and he jerked away roughly.

"Darling! It's true, darling. You don't think Mother would lie, do you?"

He didn't answer her.

"You've g-got to believe me, dearest. You were always my baby, no one's but mine. Why whose baby would you be if . . . if . . ."

He didn't answer her.

"Now listen to me, Bill! I will not let you carry on like this! It's an extremely foolish way for you to act, and . . . Oh, darling! My poor darling! What can I say to you?"

Silence.

"Darling . . . honey lamb . . . Mother wasn't angry a moment ago. She didn't really mind. She wouldn't have minded a bit if you were still a little baby l-like . . . You understand, don't you, darling?"

Silence.

"If I . . . Would it be all right, darling, would you believe me if I—we—If now . . . ?"

He was still silent, but it was a different kind of silence. Warm, expectant, deliciously shivery. They lay very still for a moment, and then she sat up, and there was the sound of soft silk against silken flesh.

She lay back down. She whispered, "B-baby. Turn around, baby . . ." And he turned around.

Then, right on the doorstep of the ultimate heaven, the gates clanged shut.

She lay perfectly still, breathing evenly. She did not need to push him away, not physically. Her eyes did that. Delicately flushed a moment before, the lovely planes of her face were now an icy white.

"You're a very smart boy, Bill."

"Am I, Mother?"

"Very. Far ahead of your years. How long have you been planning this?"

"P-planning what, Mother?"

"You had it all figured out, didn't you? Your—poor old Dad, sick and worn out so much of the time. And me, still young and foolish and giddy, and loving you so much that I'd do anything to save you hurt."

"I—you mad at me about somethin', Mother?"

"Stop it! Stop pretending! Don't deceive yourself, Bill. At least be honest with yourself."

"M-Mother. I'm sorry if I—"

"Not nearly as sorry as I am, Bill. Nor as shocked, or frightened . . ."

She was frightened. And being unable to live with her fear, she tried to deny its existence. It had never happened, she told herself—and she told him. That rainy Sunday morning was a bad dream, or at worst no more than a misunderstanding, exaggerated out of true and innocent proportion by sleep-drugged minds. It had no reality, she said, and should be forgotten completely. And he did forget—almost. His conscious memory forgot.

He was her son. He understood the importance of believing that, and so he believed. And ostensibly—even in the eyes of Mr. Rhodes—there was no change in their relationship. No untoward change. She was still lovingly affectionate with the boy, absorbed in his welfare. He was still mutely adoring in her presence. True, there was no longer any pouting and arguing about Bill's sleeping arrangements. And, true, the caresses exchanged between woman and boy seemed considerably less fervent. But that, those things, were as they should be. Bill was growing up. Naturally he was pulling away from his mother's apron strings.

Dusty rolled restlessly on the bed, still thinking. His disinterest in girls, his "lack of time" for them: was she the reason? She was. He admitted it now. She had been the woman, the only one. Until he met her counterpart, in Marcia Hillis, there could be no other.

So the years passed, and everything *was* forgotten. As far as it is within human capacity to forget. Mr. Rhodes remained active, but his health was failing. Their concern for him, and the necessity to take care of him, drew the two well members of the family closer and closer together.

There were long, almost nightly discussions in the living room after the old man had retired. Conferences held in whispers, lights dimmed, so as not to disturb him. There were cups of coffee shared, and cigarettes passed back and forth. There was an intimacy of silences and sighs. Occasionally there were tears, with Dusty soothing her, drawing her head against his shoulder and stroking the thick lustrous gray hair.

All the awkwardness between them disappeared. The bond of

trust and interdependence strengthened. Some nights she fell asleep, and he carried her up to her room ... a room no longer shared with her husband.

The first night it happened, she had waked up. She kept her eyes closed but he knew she was awake, and for a terrible moment he was afraid she might scream or strike out at him. Still, since there was nothing to do but go ahead he went ahead, slipping off her robe, laying the thin-gowned body between the covers and carefully tucking them around its curving richness. Then, very gently, he had given her a chaste kiss on the forehead. And started to tiptoe from the room.

So I knew what I was doing. What of it? Was I supposed to make myself look like a heel?

She whispered, "Bill ..." and he went back. She stretched out her arms, and he went down on his knees at her bedside, and the arms locked around him. "Bill, my darling Bill ..." Her lips moved over his face. "How could I ever have—what would I ever do without you? You've been so good, so wonderful!"

"You're pretty wonderful yourself," he said. "And now you're going to sleep. Right now, young lady, understand?"

With superhuman effort, he forced himself to disengage her arms, to stand up and walk out of the room. It left him unnerved, sleepless throughout the night, but it proved worthwhile. The last shred of her caution was struck away. Carrying her to her room became an almost nightly happening, even when she did not fall asleep. She would demand it, playfully, moving drowsily into his embrace. "S-oo tired, Bill. Help the old sleepy-head upstairs, hmm ...?"

Her weariness was not pretended, he knew. She had worried herself into exhaustion, and the long years of sexual starvation, or near-starvation, had robbed her of vitality. Now, at last, she had someone to lean upon, someone who loved as unselfishly as she. So she leaned willingly, anxiously.

The Free Speech petition ... well, the old man had reacted exactly as he thought he would about that. He wasn't sure that he hadn't signed. In any event, he would not deny that he had and thus indirectly damn a cause he had believed in. He had stood pat, and, of course, the school board had promptly booted him out of his job. And with his failing health, the blow was almost fatal.

But, no. NO—Dusty almost shouted the word. That wasn't the way it was. It had worked out that way, but he hadn't planned it. A street-corner solicitor had offered him the petition, and he had signed it ... without even thinking of the consequences. He had signed it simply William Bryant Rhodes, because there had not been enough space to add the Jr. (That was the only reason.) And he definitely had not faked his father's signature. Dad had taught him how to write. It was only natural that their signatures should be very similar.

She had been almost hysterical that night. She had been denied so much, real motherhood, real wifehood; she had had so little, and now that little—the modest security—had been lost. She was frightened; she was bewildered. In the dimly lit living-room, she lay sobbing in Dusty's arms, weeping and clinging to him like a lost child. Slowly drawing strength from his strength, reassurance from his softly whispered words.

She sniffled, and began to smile. He held a handkerchief to her nose and she blew obediently.

"J-just look at me," she smiled tremulously. "What a big cry-baby!"

"My baby," he said. "My little baby. And you just cry all you want to."

"Oh, B-Bill! Darling! W-what would I ever do without—"

"Nothing. Because I'll always be with you. Now. Hold still a minute and ..."

He took the handkerchief and tapped the tears from her face. Very business-like, he tapped them from her neck ... From her half-exposed breasts.

"My," he said, "a little bit more and you'd have been soaking." And he cupped one of his hands over the bare flesh. "You just ought to feel yourself."

He looked up, then, forced himself to, and he saw the shadows in her eyes. Then, his eyes narrowed, lazily, and she buried her face against his chest. And she whispered, "You shouldn't do that, Bill. You know you shouldn't. Never ever."

"Why not?" he said. "If you knew how much I loved you ..."

"I know. I love you, too, darling. You've been so wonderful, so good to me that—Oh, Bill, sweet"—she tightened her arms desperately—"I wish I could tell you how much you mean to me."

Her body stiffened and went limp. He withdrew his hand, shifted her gently from his lap to the lounge. She lay there, motionless, hardly seeming to breathe, one arm flung across her face.

He hesitated. Then, kneeling, he turned back her robe, and pulled up her nightgown, and . . .

Her open palm exploded against his face.

It rocked him back on his heels, and he sat down on the floor. She sat up, readjusting her nightclothes.

"I had to be sure," she said, quietly. "I couldn't believe that you meant what you seemed to—I hated to believe it. But I had to be sure . . ."

. . . Then, she had begun to scream at him . . . bastard . . . filth . . . monster . . . pouring out her hatred and disgust.

Fortunately, Mr. Rhodes had taken a heavy sedative before retiring.

. . . The fan hummed drowsily. Stretched out before its warm, narcotic breeze, Dusty relived that terrible scene with his foster mother and found it not so terrible after all. He was glad that he had done this, forced himself to honestly re-examine the past. Taken bit by bit, looked at in the light of background happenings, he had only reacted normally to an abnormal situation. It was her fault, not his. She had been the aggressor, not he. Probably, if he had been a little more adroit, a little less clumsy, she would have done what he wanted her to. And what she undoubtedly wanted him to do to her.

No, it wasn't so bad, and he wasn't so bad. On the whole, he had behaved, and was behaving, a lot more decently than most guys.

He didn't hate Dad. He got a little annoyed with him, depressed when he thought of being saddled with him for years to come—but who wouldn't? He didn't hate him, certainly, and most certainly he didn't wish him dead.

And Bascom. He didn't hate Bascom, nor wish him dead . . . even if it was possible to bring his death about. Bascom had rubbed his nose into the dirt for months. Now, the old guy was scared out of his wits, and it was his, Dusty's, turn to do some rubbing. And why should he have been disturbed about doing it?

Tug Trowbridge. He felt no admiration for Tug, no identification with him. It had been up to Tug to rescue him from a trap. Naturally, since the matter was vital to him, he had been keenly interested in its success. That was all there was to it.

Marcia Hillis ...

Well, his attitude toward her was harder to analyze. First, he had been sick with concern for her. Then, the concern had shifted to something that was almost hate. She had been the prey, and they the hunters, and when it seemed that she might escape—as he had hoped she would a moment before—he had almost hated her.

Well. But was that so odd, after all? He had much the same mixed feelings about that other *her*, his foster mother. And there had been a parallel situation in that case. He had been afraid that she might tell Dad—dreadfully, sickeningly afraid. So loving her, unable to keep from loving her, he had also hated her. He had wanted her punished for the terror she had caused him.

Now, well, now, of course, he only loved her; he would have loved her if she had still been alive. And now that the danger to himself was past, he felt only love—he could think of no other way to describe his feelings—for Marcia Hillis. He would talk to Tug tonight. Find out where she had gone. Then, when Dad died ... if he died ... or sometime, somehow, he would get in touch with her. Go to her or have her come back here. She liked him. He was sure of that, despite this thing she had tried to do for financial gain. So ... so they would be together, and this time it would be different The scene would be the same but this time ...

... *no sudden, terrifying blow in the face. No icy voice, no hatefully screamed reproaches. Only the yielding ivory body, the warm welcoming arms, the mass of hair tumbling silkily over his face ... And, at last, fulfillment.*

Dusty stirred restlessly. His eyes dragged open, and after a minute's more tossing, he sat up. He lighted a cigarette, blew the smoke out in nervous, excited puffs.

It would be like that. It *had* to be, he realized now. Through the years, he had been so formed that he could accept only one woman. And without her there could be nothing—no rest, no peace, no completion. Only an aching void where strange fears dwelled and multiplied, and gnawed unceasingly.

He had to have her, and he would. She liked him. He made good money—and there were ways of making more—and if she'd been desperate enough to attempt ...

Dimly, he heard the phone ring. Then, his father's voice answering it, and his footsteps shuffling back from the living room. He stood up, just as the old man opened the door.

"Hate to call you, Bill, but someone from the hotel . . ."

Dusty muttered a curse. "You've already told them I was here? Well, okay."

He thrust his way past Mr. Rhodes, and snatched up the phone. Then, forcing his voice to a semblance of politeness, he said, "Yes, sir. This is Bill Rhodes."

"How are you, fellow?"—it was Tug Trowbridge. "Sorry to wake you up, but I figured you and me had better have a little talk . . . Now, yeah."

NINE

Ten miles out of the city, the broad new highway was paralleled for perhaps a mile by an abandoned strip of blacktop pavement. It lay on the other side of the railroad tracks, gradually curving off through the hills and becoming lost in a wasteland of deserted farms. It was there, just over the crest of the first hill, that Dusty met Tug Trowbridge.

He parked his coupé behind the gangster's big black Cadillac. Tug beamed and extended a bottle of beer as Dusty slid into the seat next to him.

"Ain't this a scorcher, kid? Here, get a load of this inside of you and you'll feel better"

Dusty jerked his head nervously. "I don't drink, thanks. W-what did you—"

"Not even beer? Well"—Tug elevated the bottle and swallowed, gurglingly—"you could do a lot worse, kid. A guy's got to let off a little steam some way, and beer's about the safest thing I know of."

He belched, and tossed the bottle through the window. Reaching over the seat, he reached another bottle from a pail of ice. He pulled the cap with his teeth, took a long, thoughtful drink. He stared through the windshield absently, belching again.

"Yes, sir," he said. "A man can do a lot worse than drink beer."

"About last night," said Dusty. "Was that what—"

"Yeah," Tug said. "Last night, now there's an example. You stick to beer after this, fellow, and leave the babes alone. It'll save you a lot of trouble. Save everyone a lot of trouble."

Dusty's face flushed. "But it wasn't like that! It was like I told you! She called for some stationery, and then when I went in she—"

"So who cares," Tug shrugged, indifferently, "but that wasn't her story. And, kid, she seemed plenty legit to me. She talked it and she had the stuff to back it up. Newspaper clippings and letters and so on. It looked like she was just what she claimed to be—a high-class nightclub dancer. Came to town early figuring she might pick up an engagement during the races."

"But that doesn't mean—"

"Sure, I know. Maybe she'd just started on the make. Or maybe she just used the legit as a cover-up for the other. Maybe. But that little maybe could cause a hell of a lot of trouble. You put that maybe in there, and it's an entirely different deal from the one I figured on. Give some shakedown baby the heave-ho, that's nothing. She can't squawk or if she does squawk it don't do her no good. But a woman like this one—someone who can prove she's legitimate, or maybe make it impossible for you to prove that she ain't—well . . ."

He raised the bottle to his lips. Covertly, out of the corners of his shrewd animal's eyes, he studied Dusty's pale face. He grinned to himself, forcing his features into a thoughtful scowl.

"Not nice, huh, kid? I saw we'd caught a hot one right away, but of course it was too late to let go then. We had to go ahead, me and three of my boys, and I'm telling you, they don't like it much either. They got their necks stuck out to here—they have and you have and I have. And that little lady says just a few words, and all five are going to pop."

"P-pop?"

"Pop," Tug nodded solemnly. "Attempted rape. Kidnaping. They ain't the same thing as running through a traffic signal, kid, or spitting on the sidewalk. They particularly ain't the same thing down here in the south."

"But it's just her word—"

"Huh-uh. Not that her word wouldn't be plenty against us, a bellboy and three heavies, but there's a lot more than that. Think it over, Dusty. Probably a dozen people saw that little frammis this morning. It didn't mean anything to them at the time, but they saw it. And they'll talk just as soon as she does."

Think it over? Dusty's eyes were glazing. God, he didn't need to think it over. "Isn't there some way t-to to—?"

"Yes," said Tug, slowly. "There's a way. I'd sure hate to do it, and the boys don't like it either, but . . ."

His voice trailed off into silence. Dusty stared at him, not immediately understanding, and then his face went a shade paler.

"No!" he gasped. "No! You can't do that!"

"We-el"—Tug gave him another covert glance. "Like I say, I'd sure hate to. With some babes, it would almost be a pleasure, but a dame like her—real class and all kinds of looks and a shape that's out of this world, why . . ."

"You w-won't do it, will you? Promise you won't!"

"We-el . . . You know where you can lay your hands on ten thousand dollars?"

"Ten thous—Of course not!"

"Neither do I. But that's what it's got to be, Dusty. That or the other. For ten grand she keeps quiet. She puts it down in black and white that none of us laid a finger on her, and she left the hotel of her own free will."

He paused, again studying the bellboy, smiling again secretly. He went on, frowning earnestly. "When I say I ain't got it, I mean it, kid. It's strictly under your hat, see, but I'm broke. I'm a hell of a lot worse than broke."

"But"—Dusty shook his head, incredulously—"but how—"

"I can still flash a roll? Drive a big car? Pay heavy rent? Yeah, I can do it—for a couple more weeks. I've been slipping for a long time, Dusty, and now I'm right down at the bottom of the sack. I'm broke. I've got a hell of a big income-tax rap hanging over me. I've been stalling it for years, and now I can't stall any longer. I either pay up or else." He sighed, flung the emptied bottle out the window. "Of course, it makes it easy for me in a way. The spot I'm in, this dame could yell her head off and she couldn't make it much worse."

"B-but—"

"Sure," Tug nodded. "There's you and the boys to think about. And of course I don't like to just sit still and wait for old Uncle Whiskers to sock it to me. If I can't do anything better, I'd like to get a big enough roll to skip the country."

He lapsed into another silence, his big good-natured face long with concern. His big face that looked good-natured turned toward the window. There was a small mirror there, attached to the windscreen. It gave him a full view of Dusty's tortured features.

He sighed heavily, shifted the sound into an absently amused laugh. "Y'know it's a funny thing, kid—about this Hillis woman, I mean. You might think she'd be sore as hell at you, but she don't seem to be at all. In fact, I kind of got the idea that she liked you a lot. She's been pushed around and she figures she ought to be paid for it. But there's nothing personal in it, see? Why, I'll bet if you were in the chips—you'd have to be, of course, with a babe like that—I'll bet she'd come a running to you like—"

"I've got to know," said Dusty. "I've got to know the truth, Mr. Trowbridge. Is she—"

"Yeah? And why don't you just make it Tug, kid?"

"I've got to know, Tug. Is she—you haven't already killed her?"

"Huh!" Tug exclaimed. "Why, of course, we ain't, and we ain't going to if there's another way out. We got her hid nice and comfortable, a lot more comfortable than you and me are right now."

"Could I—could I see her?"

"Sure you can," Tug said evenly. "If you think I'm lying, just say so and I'll take you to her."

Dusty hesitated. Then, the implications of Tug's statement hit him full force, and he shook his head firmly. He had to believe the gangster. At least, he couldn't appear to doubt him. For if Tug had ordered her death to keep her quiet, and if he was forced to admit the fact ... well, he, Dusty, would also be quieted. Similarly. Permanently.

Tug would feel compelled to do it, and not merely to protect himself. The big man was desperate. He wanted something from Dusty and he intended to get it, and the woman was vital to his getting—a means of enforcing his demands. She had to be alive, then. He could not openly doubt that she was alive. To do so would be to make himself useless to Tug—a man with dangerous knowledge who refused to cooperate—and he would not live long.

Dusty thought it was that way, but he wasn't positive. He spoke cautiously, testing his theory:

"There's one thing I don't understand, Tug. You figure on jumping the country, anyway? Well, then, why not just let this woman go when you're ready to jump? Let her talk all she wants to. You won't be around to face the music."

"Well"—Tug shifted in the seat—"I, uh, couldn't hardly do that, kid. An income-tax rap is one thing. Kidnaping and abetting a rape is somethin' else."

"But you wouldn't be around. You don't intend to come back."

"Well, uh, like I said a moment ago, there's you and the boys to think about. We're all in this together, and you'd still be here, and—" He broke off, eyes glinting. "I say something funny, kid?"

"No"—Dusty shook his head. "I just wanted to know how things stood."

"Okay!" Tug snapped harshly. "Now you know. Now you got the picture. I got some plans and I ain't letting 'em be screwed up. I didn't figure you in 'em originally, but that's the way it's worked out. You're in and you're going to play. Or else!"

Furiously, he reached over the seat and snatched up another bottle of beer. The cap grated against his teeth, popped loose, and he spat it out and drank.

He coughed, leaning back in the seat, and the old joviality came back into his voice. A little strained, but nonetheless there.

"Aaahh, kid. This is no way for pals to talk to each other, and I've always been your pal, ain't I? Always friendly and easy to get along with, and tossing the dough around. I liked you, see? I felt like you were my kind of people and I know you felt the same way about me. Why, who did you come to this morning when you were in a real jam? Why, you came to me, didn't you, and I didn't hesitate a minute, did I? I had plenty big worries of my own, but I just said, Why, sure, Dusty. Just leave it to me and I'll take care of it. Ain't that right, now?"

"That's right," Dusty murmured.

"And I didn't know what I was getting into, did I? I didn't

have the slightest idea that it was going to work out so's I could put the squeeze—ask you to do me a favor. Help me out and put yourself on easy street at the same time. I didn't have any idea it was going to be that way. All I knew was—that you were a pal, and I was ready to knock myself out to give you a hand . . ."

His voice droned on earnestly . . . pals . . . favors . . . give you a hand . . . didn't know. And Dusty nodded earnestly. Fighting to keep his sudden excitement from showing in his face.

Suppose Tug *had* known. Suppose he had arranged the whole thing! It made sense, didn't it? It made sense to a degree that no other explanation could approach. It explained things that could be explained in no other way.

Bascom. Why had he allowed Marcia Hillis to register—a woman alone, arriving late at night? Why, because Tug had told him to and he had been afraid to refuse. And the ten-dollar room? Why, the answer to that was beautifully simply, too. There were only a few such rooms in the hotel, and one of them was on Tug's floor. Without arousing Dusty's suspicions, she had been put right where Tug wanted her—and wanted him—when she sprang the trap. The circumstance would practically impel his appeal to the gangster. His old pal, Tug, would be right there at hand, and he would run to him automatically.

The kidnaping. The "kidnaping." And he had been afraid that they wouldn't get away with it—justifiably afraid. For they wouldn't have got away with the real thing. They wouldn't even have attempted the real thing. It was all an act, part of the scheme to make him vulnerable to Tug's demands.

There were a few loose ends to the theory, but on the whole it made a very neat package. And relatively, at least, it was as comfortable as it was plausible. If Marcia Hillis was working with Tug, then naturally she was in no danger. If she worked with Tug, then she was attainable by him, Dusty. Not through money alone, of course. Despite the part she had played, or appeared to have played, he didn't believe that she could be influenced very far or very long by money alone. But certainly, with a woman like that, money would be an essential. She would expect it, take it for granted. And with Tug's help, by helping Tug with his scheme, whatever that scheme was . . .

"Just a minute, kid." Tug leaned over him, flipped open the door of the glove compartment. "I know you maybe think I'm giving you a snow job about that babe, so take a gander at this."

He drew it out of the compartment, a crumpled eight-by-ten oblong of glossy cardboard. He smoothed it out carelessly and handed it to the bellboy, and Dusty's breath sucked in with a gasp. It was her picture, a theatrical shot, with her name written along the bottom in white ink. She was posed against a background of artificial palms; she lay, smiling, along the sloping trunk of one. A wisp of some thinly leafed vine was between her thighs. Her hands, fingers spread in a revealing lattice, lay over her breasts. Otherwise she was nude.

"Well, kid"—Tug took the picture from his hands and crammed it back into the compartment—"she's just what I said, huh? I wasn't lying, was I?"

Dusty shook his head. So she was an entertainer, or had been one. That still didn't prove that she wasn't working with Tug.

"A lot of woman, huh, Dusty?" Tug smacked his lips. "You ever see anything like her in your life?"

"No. I mean not quite, I guess," Dusty said.

"But she ain't got a bit more on the ball than you, Dusty. For a man, you've got just as much as she has. All the looks and the class that she has, and then some."

"And you really think"—Dusty cleared his throat—"you really think that she would—that she might—"

"That she'd go for you? If you were in the chips? I'll tell you what I think, kid." Tug tapped him solemnly on the knee. "I'd guarantee it, know what I mean? Yes, sir, I'd guarantee she would."

Dusty hesitated. It was all wrong. He was all mixed up. Tug had aroused first one instinct, then another; played upon one after another. Self-preservation, avarice, fear for her, outright desire. He had offered too much, too eagerly; threatened too much. And the end result was confusion, or, more accurately, the canceling out of everything he had said.

She was in no danger, Dusty guessed. He guessed that he was in none—none that he could not escape from with a little fast thinking. At this point, he could still pull out with no harm to anyone but Tug. And, yet . . .

Well, he was only guessing, wasn't he? He might be figuring the thing wrong, and if he was she'd be lost to him. Dead. And if he was right, she would still be lost to him. He would have to go on as he was now, barely getting by from one day to the next. Trudging through a gray emptiness that grew emptier and grayer with every step.

He shivered inwardly; he couldn't stand it, even the thought of it. But could he—could he, on the other hand, accept the sinister alternative? Could he adopt a course which must certainly run counter to all the plans and preparations of years?

His voice faltered. "I don't know, Tug. It seems kind of crazy that I should even be thinking about ... well, what we've been talking about. You see, I've always wanted to be a doctor, my father and mother wanted me to be one. I was just working at the hotel—temporarily until—"

"Yeah?" Tug chuckled softly. "Who you trying to kid, kid? You're there at the hotel because the easy money's there, and you're an easy money guy. I know, see? I can spot 'em a mile off. Maybe you think different, but I know. You wouldn't go back to school if you was paid to."

"But I—"

"We've talked enough, Dusty. A lot longer than I figured on talking to you. But maybe I ought to tell you one thing more. Them boys of mine are pretty jumpy. They're pretty leery of you, kid. If they got the notion that you might jump the wrong way, I don't know as I could hold 'em in line."

Tug nodded at him grimly, and abruptly the doubts and confusion were dispelled from Dusty's mind. He didn't know Tug's hoods, as he knew Tug. He had never been friendly with them. To them he would just be a stumbling block, a guy who'd made trouble and might make more. And what they might do, *would* do, was reasonably easy to predict.

"... won't be around much longer, y'know, kid. They'll be on their own. So what's it going to be?"

What was it going to be? What could it be? The choice was not his.

"All right," he said. "All right, Tug. What do you want me to do?"

And Tug told him.

TEN

As the body has its limits to suffer, so is the mind limited to shock. One can be startled just so much, alarmed just so much, and then there can be no more. The wheel of emotions becomes stalled on dead-canter. And instead of turmoil there is calm.

So with Dusty. In little more than an hour a whole way of life had been jerked from beneath him and a new one proffered. He had been pushed to the outermost boundaries of shock; now he answered Tug quietly:

"It can't be done, Tug. Those deposit boxes are theft proof. It takes two keys for each one, the hotel's and the depositor's, and even if you could get them both..."

"Yeah? Go on, kid."

"There's a box for each room. It would take all night to unlock them all. And you wouldn't know whether they were worth robbing unless you did open them. I couldn't tell you. Practically all the deposits are made in the day time and—"

"Uh-huh, sure," Tug interrupted. "I know all that. Maybe I'd better lay it on the line for you, huh?"

"Maybe you'd better."

"The racing season starts the week after next. All the big bookies will drift in next week. They'll want to look over the track, study the early workouts, and so on. They'll be loaded with cash. There's no damned guess work about it, see? They'll have the dough, and with the hours they keep, they'll have to bank with the hotel. So we make 'em for their keys, say, six or seven of the biggest operators, and we hit the jackpot. We knock down a couple hundred grand, maybe a quarter of a million, in five minutes."

"Yes, but ..." Dusty licked his lips. "How do you mean, make 'em for their keys? You mean you'd—you'd—"

"Naah." Tug nudged him jovially. "Nothing like it, kid. I'll just throw a little party for 'em up in my suite; hell, they've been to plenty of my parties in the past. Then, me and the boys will give 'em a little surprise. Knock them out and hogtie them, y'know. Take 'em out of circulation for a while."

"Well..." Dusty hesitated. "But that still leaves the hotel keys. Bascom"—he paused again. "God, I can't do that, Tug! Bascom will be right there; and there's no way I could use the keys without—"

"Hold it. Hold it!" said Tug. "You ain't going to use them. Bascom is. All you're going to do is take the dough and lock it up in the checkroom. Put it in a satchel I'll give you and check it, just like it was a regular piece of baggage. I—"

"But Bascom! What about him?"

"—don't want it with me, see, in case of a foul-up. My boys might get a little excited, know what I mean? They might get to quarreling over the split. So you check it and tear up the stub—memorize the number first, of course—and I'll get in touch with you as soon as the heat dies down."

"Yes, but—"

"I'll split the take with you, kid. A full half for you and the other for me and the boys. You hang on to yours a few months, and then you get yourself fired, and—"

"I asked you about Bascom!" Dusty insisted. "Now, what about him?"

Tug's eyes shifted for a moment. He looked out into the brilliant sunlight, gaze narrowed musingly, and then he again looked at Dusty.

"All right, kid. I guess I'd better spread it all out. But you don't know from nothing, see? You don't know nothing about Bascom. He don't know that you and me got a deal."

"I understand."

"One of my connections tipped me off to Bascom three-four months ago. He's on the lam from a pen back east, crashed out with twenty years to serve of a thirty-year bank-robber rap. One word from me, and he'll be back doing time again."

"Well ... oh," said Dusty, and he nodded, remembering.

"They asked you about it, huh?" Tug grinned out of the corner of his mouth. "You know why I wrote that letter to the management, kid? Because of the way he was treating you. Yeah, I noticed it all right—I notice plenty. You did everything you could to get along with him, and all he could do was make it tough for you. I spoke to him, and he covered up while I was around. But I knew he hadn't stopped. So I figured I'd better give him a real jolt."

"Well," Dusty said, "that was, uh, certainly nice of you. But I still—"

"I know. I know just what you're going to say. You're going to say that Bascom can't play ball on this deal. If he does, he'll do his twenty years and maybe twenty more on top of it. But here's the angle, see? He plays, but it don't look like he does. He has a gun drawn on him and he loses his nerve, acts like a goddamned dope instead of—"

"He'll never get away with it." Dusty shook his head. "He just *can't*, Tug! A man on the outside of the cashier's cage couldn't cover a man on the inside with a gun. The window opening is too small. The cashier, the man on the inside, could just drop down to the floor or move a little to one side and he'd be out of range."

"He could if he thought fast enough. If he wasn't scared out of his pants."

"You can't make it look good," Dusty said doggedly. "They're bound to know that it was an inside job."

"Huh-uh. Maybe they think it is but they can't prove it. All they can prove is that Bascom ain't much of a hero, that he didn't use good judgment."

"I can't see it," Dusty frowned. "They'll never—I mean, I don't think they'll ever believe he was held up. Not from the outside. Now if there was a guy on the inside—one of the lobby porters, say—it would be different. He could be working in there and suddenly stick a gun in Bascom's ribs, and Bascom would have to come across. He couldn't get away, and—and—"

He swallowed, leaving the sentence unfinished. There was a long moment of silence, with Tug staring at him steadily, and then he found his voice again.

"Bascom. He's willing to take that kind of chance?"

"It's a chance," Tug shrugged. "If he don't take it, he doesn't have any chance at all. I see that he goes back to the pen."

"Well . . ."Dusty said. "And what about me? Where am I supposed to be while all this is going on?"

"Right there in the cashier's cage with him. Helping him with the work like you always are around two-thirty in the morning. You've got to be there, see? That money satchel will be too big to squeeze through the window, and there won't be time to chase all the way around the counter. You'll have to grab it and get rid of it fast."

"But that leaves me on the spot, too! If I'm right there—"

"How does it? You're just a bellboy; Bascom's your boss. You're supposed to try to stop him, risk getting yourself killed, if he's willing to open the boxes? Huh-uh, they couldn't expect it of you, kid. They'd think you was a damned fool if you tried it."

"Well," Dusty nodded, "maybe. I suppose you're right about that. But—well, what about the other? When I take the satchel and check it? You said that Bascom wasn't supposed to know anything about me, that I was in on the deal. But—"

"He don't. He won't. And you don't know anything, get me? Nothing about him, and nothing about what's coming off"

"But if I take the money right in front of him—"

"Kid," Tug sighed. "Dusty, boy. Jesus Christ, ain't there any goddamned little thing you can leave to me? You think I just dreamed up this caper five minutes ago?"

"No. But—"

"Bascom won't see you! When he gets back up near the window I grab him by the tie and slug him. Knock him unconscious. He'll hold still for it, see; it helps to make the thing look good. I knock him out cold, and he'll still be out when you get back from checking the dough and lock yourself into the cage again. So far as anyone knows you never left the cage."

"But if the satchel won't go through the window opening, he's bound to—"

"Goddammit, I—! It goes through when it's empty, don't it? It's got to, don't it? So on the return trip, I maybe take out part of the dough. Stuff it into my pocket or down the front of my shirt."

Glaring, his face mottled with irritation, Tug snatched another bottle from the pail. He almost slammed the cap against his teeth, jerked it with a grunt of pain. And drank. He did not lower the bottle until it was emptied.

"Sorry, kid"—he forced an apologetic laugh. "I don't blame you for wanting to know the score, of course. But, Jesus, every damned little thing! It kind of sounds like you thought I was a boob. Like maybe you didn't trust me."

"No," Dusty said hastily. "No, I don't feel that way. Its just—well, mixed up. There's so many things that might go wrong, and if anything does—"

"Nothing will." Tug dropped a friendly hand to his shoulder. "Let me tell you something, Dusty. It always seems that way when a guy's going on a caper. Always, particularly if it's his first one. He gets to thinking that everyone knows what he knows, that they see all the little holes he sees and that they're liable to reach through and grab him. But it ain't that way, y'understand! He's the guy with the answers, the only guy. The others—they don't see nothing or know nothing, or if they do it don't mean nothing to 'em."

Dusty nodded reluctantly. He hadn't said what he wanted to, he hadn't got to the heart of his concern, and he couldn't know. A gate had closed in his mind, blocking the words, cutting off the half-formed thought that lay behind them.

"Look at it this way, kid ... I'm not taking the dough with me, am I? You know I'm not just giving you a line about that?"

Yes—Dusty's lips moved wordlessly—he was quite sure of that. Positive of it.

"It'll be just like I said. You'll check the dough, and tear up the stub. You'll have to do it, see? The cops are going to talk to you, and they just accidentally might frisk you. Anyway, it just ain't a good thing to have around. There's too damned many things that could happen to it."

I know—Dusty's lips moved again. Memorize the number. Tear up the stub. Yes, that was the way it would have to be.

"Well, there you are, kid. There's only one way in the world I can get to that dough, get my share of it. And that's through you. So I can't let anything happen to you, can I? I've got to be sure that everything's going to go smooth, and that you'll come through without a rumble. I got to, see? I've got to be sure, and I am sure. Why, hell, I'd be crazy to pull the deal otherwise, now wouldn't I?"

Dusty nodded. He agreed with that, also. For his own sake, Tug would have to be positive of his safety. But, still ...

He couldn't say it. That tiny gate in his mind had closed tightly, imprisoning, with similar shoddy and hideous prisoners, the thought that he could not yet consciously accept.

"That's it, Dusty. That's all of it. You play it absolutely safe, and you get a cool hundred grand for your share. At least a hundred grand. Hell"—Tug nudged him, grinning. "I'll even take care of the babe's ten g's out of my end."

"Well," Dusty murmured. "I ... you, uh, don't need to do that. But, well, I was wondering about her, Tug. I mean, you said she was on the level, and—"

"So what? She's been around, she knows what the score is, she ain't some punk bobby-soxer with the mood in her eyes. Dames in her racket, kid—bouncing around in these nightclubs with everything showing but their appetite—they all belong to the same club. The let's-see-the-dough-honey-and-I'll-ask-you-no-questions."

Dusty laughed, a little unwillingly. Tug laughed with him, studying him, then continued, his voice confidentially low. "I'll tell you what, kid. If there ain't no hitch anywhere, like I'm sure there won't be, I'll put her in touch with you. Before we split the dough, yeah. We may have to wait quite a while for that, but there's no sense in you waiting for her. How'd you like that, huh? Connect with her right away, almost." He slapped the bellboy on the back, not waiting for an answer. "I'll fix it up for you, Dusty. You can count on it. Now about the dough, the split..."

"I was wondering about that," Dusty frowned. "You know, I can't carry any packages out of the hotel, Tug. I mean, they have to be opened and examined before they can be carried out. And—"

"Forget it," Tug interrupted. "I'll figure out something when the time comes."

"How will I—how will you get in touch with me?"

"I'll figure that out, too. It depends on how things are at the time, see? Just leave it to me, for Christ's sake—it's my headache, ain't it?—and stop knocking yourself out!"

His face had become flushed again, the irritation was back in his voice. Surlily, he hurled the emptied bottle through the window.

"Jesus, kid. I don't mean to blow my top at you, but—well, skip it. We're all set, right? We'll be running through it some more between now and next week, but we're all set. We've got an agreement."

"We're all set," Dusty said steadily—"We've got an agreement."

ELEVEN

Strangely, during the time intervening between his meeting with Tug and the morning of the robbery, he felt quite calm, quite at peace with himself. Only when he tried to examine his feelings—studied their nominal strangeness—was there any rift in the peace. And even then his qualms were faint and of brief duration. There was simply nothing for them to feed upon.

His handsome, olive-skinned face was as unfurrowed, as openly honest, as ever. The wide-set eyes remained clear and unworried. His voice, his manner, the manifold minutiae which comprised person-ality—they were all normal. For, for the first time in his memory, all his self-doubts were gone and he felt sure of himself. He was about to be made whole. He knew it, and the inner knowledge was reflected in the outer man.

Despite Tug's ambiguity, the robbery would be successful. He knew it and it was all he needed to know. More important, most important, he would have Marcia Hillis. Despite Tug's intentions, good or bad, he would have her. He felt it, knew it, and *it* was all he needed to know.

In his new-found sureness, he was unusually patient with Mr. Rhodes. He was quietly pleasant and polite to Bascom—a Bascom who had become drawn-faced, shifty-eyed, moodily silent unless he was forced to speak. It was easy to be patient now, easy to be pleasant and polite. Feeling as he did—unconquerable and unfearful—he could not be any other way.

The sureness grew. It remained with him, strong and unwavering, during the most acid of tests—his meeting with I. Kossmeyer, attorney at law.

The second day after his fateful talk with Tug Trowbridge, the day bell captain handed Dusty a note when he came on duty. It was from Kossmeyer, a curt scrawl on one of the attorney's letterheads. It said, simply, *Rhodes: Think would be advisable for you to drop into my office tomorrow morning.*

Dusty shredded the note, and its enclosing envelope, into a wastebasket. He did not call at Kossmeyer's office. He didn't like the little attorney, and he had—he told himself—better things to do with his time.

Two mornings later, as he was leaving the hotel, Kossmeyer met him at the service entrance.

"Want to talk to you, Rhodes," he said, brusquely. "What about some coffee?"

"Certainly," Dusty nodded. "Wherever you say, Mr. Kossmeyer."

They took a booth in a nearby restaurant. Dusty sipped at his coffee, set it down and looked up. And for the first time in days he felt a ruffling of his calm.

Not that he was afraid. He certainly wasn't afraid of this little pipsqueak of a man. But he was extremely irritated, almost angered. He stared across the table, his irritation mounting, a red flush spreading over his face.

The attorney's eyes had become preternaturally wide, brimmed with an exaggerated sincerity that made mock of the term. He had tightened the skin of his face, smoothing away its habitual wrinkles, leaving it bland and untroubled. His lips were curled with serenity— a preposterous caricature of it—and his chin was slightly outthrust, posed at an angle of quiet defiance. He was dignity distorted, bravery become knavery, sanctimoniousness masking sin. He was a mirror, jeering at the subject it reflected. Yet so muted were the jeers, so delicate the inaccuracies of delineation, that they evaded detection. True and false were blended together. The false was merely an extended shadow of the true.

Dusty's flush deepened. Unconsciously, he tried to alter his expression, and the attorney's face moved, following the change. Now he was wounded ("wounded" with quotes). Now he was losing his temper—in the manner of a Grade-C movie hero. And now—then— he was himself again. Neither friendly nor unfriendly, simply a man doing a job in the best and quickest way possible.

"You see, Rhodes? It doesn't mean a goddamned thing, does it? It's what you've got inside that counts."

"What do you want with me?" Dusty snapped. "Say it and get it over with."

"I've already got part of it over, showed you that you're not kidding anyone but yourself. Anyway, you're sure as hell not kidding me. Now that you understand that, you can stop trying. Stop covering up and come clean. Why did you sign your father's name to that petition?"

"Why? Why would I—"

"That's right. Why would you, why did you?" The attorney leaned forward, his shrewd face suddenly sympathetic and understanding. "It was just one of those things, wasn't it, son? You signed it without thinking, without any idea of what the consequences might be. It never occurred to you that with you and your dad having the same name—with your signatures so much alike . . . I imagine he taught you how to write, didn't he? Probably set down examples for you when you were a kid, and had you try to copy 'em."

Dusty hesitated. He wanted to explain, to make someone else believe and thus bolster his own belief. The words were in his mouth, almost, practically ready to emerge.

"Sure," Kossmeyer continued, earnestly. "That's the way it was— couldn't have been any other way. Hell, a signature that good, it takes practice; you had to have had it right back from the beginning. And it was perfectly natural that you would have it. You were your dad's junior, an only child to boot. That always makes a kid something special. The father identifies with him more closely—sort of tries to form him into his own pattern. It's a protective gesture, I suppose. By making his son part of him, he . . . Excuse me. Yeah?"

"It was that way," Dusty nodded, slowly. "It—he—was even more that way with me, I imagine, than if I'd been his own son. Yes . . . that's right. I was adopted. It was so long ago that I can hardly remember it, and I doubt that Dad knows that I know. So—"

"Sure, I'd never mention it. He and the wife couldn't have any kids of their own?"

"I guess not. Probably she could have; she was a lot younger than he was, and I think she . . . well, that she was physically okay."

"Mmm. A very beautiful woman, wasn't she? I seem to have heard that she was."

"Yes."

"I've been wondering: have you any idea why she married a guy so much older?"

"They met while he was lecturing at college. She was trying to work her way through, and he helped her a lot, I guess, and she felt like she couldn't . . ."

Dusty caught himself, with a start. How had they gotten to talking about her? How, and why, had he been led so far from the original subject?

He said shortly, "What's all that got to do with it?"

"What?" The attorney's eyebrows shot up. "Why, nothing that I know of. Just being curious. A set-up like that always makes me kind of wonder. It's none of my business, of course, so don't take it the wrong way, but—"

"Yes?"

"I wonder if she didn't marry him because she loved him. Do you suppose that could have been it?"

"Well," Dusty nodded, hesitantly, "I suppose she did. Naturally."

"She just didn't give a damn about surface appearance, don't you imagine? She knew a right guy when she saw him, and she latched onto him."

He stared at Dusty, gravely: a man discussing an interesting but impersonal problem. His bright bird's eye moved thoughtfully over the other's face. And narrowed imperceptibly.

"Now, getting back to this signature deal. You didn't forge your dad's name. It just came natural to you, and you didn't have to forge it. That's about the case, isn't it?"

"Well"—Dusty examined the insidiously objectionable statement, and was unable to object to it—"well, yes."

"And you just kind of accidentally left off the junior part. Without thinking of the consequences. Your dad was a public figure; everyone was certain to associate that signature with him. But that never occurred to you ... did it?"

"No, it didn't!" Dusty snapped. "I—look, I didn't even know what the petition was about. A woman on a street corner asked me to sign, so I signed. Like a lot of people did probably, just to be obliging."

"But you must have looked at it?"

"Certainly, I looked at it, but it didn't mean anything to me. You know how they phrase some of those things. You have to study them carefully to get at the meaning."

"Yeah," Kossmeyer nodded. "They get pretty cute sometimes. How was this one phrased?"

"Committee to Defend the Constitution—that was the heading.

Then it said, 'Recognizing the vital importance of an unhampered exchange of ideas, I, the undersigned, hereby—'"

His voice died on a strangled note.

Kossmeyer grinned at him wolfishly. "So you didn't know what it was all about, huh? It didn't mean a thing to you?"

"I—no! No, it didn't. I read it afterwards, after the paper came out with the story."

"Yeah? And what about that junior deal? Why didn't you tack it onto your name?"

"Because there wasn't room for it! If I'd known how important it was going to be, of course, I'd have—"

"You had room for all the rest. First name, middle name, last— the whole damned handle, all written out big and bold so that even a blind man couldn't miss it ... Don't try to horse-shit me, buster. You ain't even half-way smart enough."

"But you don't understand..." And he wanted him to. He wasn't afraid of Kossmeyer, but he did want him to understand. "I know it probably doesn't make much sense, but—"

"It makes plenty of sense." The attorney leaned forward grimly. "You've lived in this town all your life—you know how people think here, how they'd react to a thing like this Free Speech business. You grew up in a school-teacher's family, and you know what a teacher's problems are. How they can't even look crosseyed without some know-nothing bastard taking a pot-shot at 'em. You knew all that and you knew something else. You knew the old man was sick and that a blow like this one could easily kill him. And that's what you wanted, wasn't it? *You wanted him dead!*"

Dusty's mouth opened. It snapped shut again, and, quite calmly, he lighted a cigarette. He exhaled the smoke, staring back at Kossmeyer insolently.

"That's ridiculous. But as long as you seem to be so sure..."

"You know why. For the same reason I didn't come out to the house to see you. He's a swell guy, the kind this country needs a hell of a lot more of, and I didn't want to make things any harder for him. If he knew what kind of puréed, rotten son-of-a-bitch he'd given his name to—"

"That's about enough," Dusty snapped. "I'm leaving."

"You'd better not," Kossmeyer assured him. "You do and you'll be the sorriest son-of-a-bitch in sixteen states."

"What"—Dusty sank back down into the booth—"what do you mean?"

"I can't do anything about what's happened. All I can do is kind of let the case die quietly. But that's for the past, the present. The future, that's something else, buster. You won't be so lucky next time. You pull another stunt on him, and, by God, I'll stick you for it. If there isn't a law I can do it under, I'll get one passed!"

"You're crazy," Dusty said, coldly. "This whole thing's crazy. Why would I do anything to hurt him?"

"I've got a pretty good idea about that, too. A damned good idea. And I'm going to keep on digging until I can prove it. So don't try anything, get me? If you do"—Kossmeyer drew a finger across his throat—"zip! Curtains. It'll be the last goddamned thing you ever try."

He slid out of the booth, tossed a coin on the table and walked away. Dusty finished his cigarette, studying himself in the mirrored panels of the wall.

Nothing had changed. He was still as sure, inside and out, as when he had entered the restaurant. Kossmeyer had temporarily cracked his calm façade, but now the crevices were smoothly resealed.

The attorney had only been guessing, trying to frighten him. He realized that he could no longer get any money from Dusty—via his father—and the fact had enraged him. But there was nothing he could do.

He couldn't reveal the truth (rather, Dusty corrected himself, the seeming truth) about the petition. He couldn't possibly know what had motivated him, Dusty, to sign the petition. The motive—what *might* have been the motive—was gone. It had been buried, figuratively and literally, with her.

Confident and calm, he left the restaurant and drove home. As was frequently the case, Doctor Lane was just leaving the house when he arrived. The doctor had long since recovered from the exacted politeness of their one interview. Now, he was himself again, the self, at least, that he normally displayed to Dusty: irritable, brusque, virtually insulting.

How was Mr. Rhodes getting along? Well, he was getting along as well as could be expected, which was not, in Doctor Lane's opinion, very damned well.

"I've told you before, Rhodes," he said testily. "This is as much a morale problem as a physical one. Your father needs to feel wanted, that he's still of some importance. And no man can feel that way when he's forced to live and look like a tramp."

"He's not forced to," Dusty retorted. "I give him plenty of money to keep up his appearance. Anything he wants, within reason, I—"

"You do, eh? Within reason, eh?" The doctor gave him a cynical stare. "Well, you'd better start giving him a little more, get me? Be a little more reasonable. Do *something*, for God's sake! This is getting to be a disgrace."

He yanked the car door open, tossed his medicine kit upon the seat. With an irritated scowl, he started around to the opposite door, then, whirled and stamped back to the bellboy.

"Yes?" he said, his face thrust almost against Dusty's. "You said something to me, Rhodes?"

"I said," said Dusty, evenly, "that if you don't want to treat the case, I can call in another doctor."

"No"—Lane shook his head. "No," he said again, his voice muted to an icy purr. "I'll tell you what you can do, Rhodes. You can start taking better care of your father, or you can hire someone who will take care of him. Do I make myself clear? You can do it of your own free will, as a son should, or I'll take steps to compel you to." He hesitated, wet his lips, continued in a milder tone. After all, he'd been the Rhodes' family doctor for years. And he'd known this young man since he was a squirt in short pants. "Sure that, uh, nothing of that kind will be necessary," he went on. "I know your expenses have been pretty high, and it's hard for a man holding a full-time job to do much else. But, well, see what you can do about it, eh? Do the best you can."

Dusty promised that he certainly would. He was no more afraid of the doctor than he was of Kossmeyer, but there was no point in making an enemy of him. He needed friends; he was very apt to need them, at any rate. And—and the realization startled him—he had none. There were friends of the family, friends of his father. But there was none of his own. No one who could be depended upon to fight for him, stick up for him, if he got into trouble.

"I'll get busy on it right away," he promised. "I'm only sorry that you had to be bothered about such things, Doctor."

"Well. Well, that's all right," Lane said gruffly. "Know you've got the old man's welfare at heart—just a little thoughtless perhaps—or I wouldn't have said anything."

He drove away.

Entering the house, Dusty again sent Mr. Rhodes to the barber, again gathered up his clothes and called the laundry and cleaners. It would mean losing sleep today and still more tomorrow. But that would be the end of this particular difficulty. Kossmeyer was dropping his father's case. He would be making no more demands for money, and the old man would thus cease to filch from the household funds as he had been doing.

Dusty dialed the telephone, thinking of the attorney with sardonic amusement. That was always the way with these holier-than-thou guys, these guys who made such a show of standing on principles and to hell with the cost. They didn't care about money—oh, not at all!— but they never turned any down. They were too good to give you a decent word, to show a little understanding for you, but they weren't too good to take your money. If they couldn't get it in one way, they'd do it in another. Squeeze it out of someone close to you who was too trusting to see through them.

Kossmeyer must have known that Mr. Rhodes had no money of his own. He must have been aware that Dusty would not, or could not, have authorized the old man's steady and substantial expenditures. And yet—

Dusty frowned faintly, the smoothly satisfying chain of his thoughts temporarily unlinked. He didn't *know*, of course, that Kossmeyer had gotten any dough from his father. It would seem that he hadn't, in fact, since Mr. Rhodes had pestered him frequently to send the attorney a remittance. Then, well, then there was the way Kossmeyer had acted a few days ago: there in his office when the subject of fees had come up. He'd brushed it aside as something of no importance. In so many words, he'd offered to work for nothing. He'd been pretty sure, no doubt, that the offer would not be accepted, and, of course, a man as sharp as he was would know when to take it easy and when to put on the screws. But suppose ... suppose he had really meant it. Suppose he hadn't received those hundreds of dollars, as much as fifteen or twenty dollars a week for more than a year.

Well—Dusty shrugged and resumed his telephoning—suppose he hadn't? What difference did it make whether the old man had simply wasted the money, let it get away from him, or whether he had given it to Kossmeyer?

He hung up the phone, and leaned back on the lounge. Fretfully, he lighted a cigarette and leaned forward again.

... Hundreds of dollars, close to a thousand. And if Kossmeyer hadn't got it, who had? It didn't make any difference, of course— how could it?—but still it was damned puzzling. He couldn't push the riddle out of his mind.

Squandered? Wasted? Absently dribbled away or lost? The more he thought about it, the more preposterous the theory became. Mr. Rhodes had no vices, nothing he might have spent so much money on. Years of living on a modest salary had made him chronically frugal. He abhorred waste, and had demonstrated the fact frequently and recently. He was absent-minded, true, but not *that* absent-minded. On occasion, he might have forgotten his change from a purchase or lost a bill from his pocket. It was out of character, but he might have. But he would not have done so steadily, consistently, week after week.

There was only one explanation, then. Kossmeyer. The money had either gone to him, or it simply hadn't gone. And if it hadn't ...

Dusty crushed out his cigarette, and stood up. Stepping to the screen door, he looked up and down the street. He stood there in the door for a moment, hesitant, feeling a faint twinge of shame. Then, he turned away purposefully, and entered his father's room.

It was as neat as the old man was unneat. The bed was made. The floor appeared to have been recently swept. A handful of toilet articles was tidily arranged on the dresser. Books stood in orderly array upon their several shelves.

He examined them, the books first. Riffling their pages, shaking them, hastily replacing them on the shelves. Next, after another look up and down the street, came the bed. He jerked off the covers, went over the mattress swiftly but carefully. There was nothing. No smallest slit, nor any place where the ticking had been restitched. He re-did the. bed and moved to the dresser. In the bottom drawer he found a small steel file. He lifted it out, and raised the unlocked lid.

There was nothing here, either. Only old letters, old receipts, old and yellowed newspaper clippings. And a couple of old insurance policies. One, a thousand-dollar policy, carried a twenty-year-old date. The other—ten thousand dollars, double indemnity—was dated some five years ago. Both, of course, named his mother as beneficiary. Both, consequently, would have long since lapsed.

He returned the file to the drawer. That completed his search of the room.

The following morning, having sent his father to a picture show, he searched the rest of the house. His findings totaled a dime (under the bathtub) and three pennies (extricated from the cushions of the living-room furniture). That was all.

Well, he hadn't actually expected to turn up a horde. He'd been sure all along that Kossmeyer had got the money. He went to bed, more pleased than otherwise, glad that his opinion of the attorney had been positively confirmed.

TWELVE

He ate.

He slept.

He worked.

He conferred with Tug and his boys several times. He went to extraordinary pains to keep Mr. Rhodes presentable.

Eat, sleep, work: that was about the sum of his existence. It seemed that there should have been something more, but that was all.

The days, the nights, slipped by, blending uneventfully one with another. Almost abruptly the day came, *that* day.

Two-thirty in the morning of that day.

THIRTEEN

At midnight, politely but implacably, the Manton had begun urging its guests toward their rooms. Now, at two-thirty in the morning, with the coffee shop closed, the porters and elevator operator gone, the lobby was almost painfully quiet. It was as though no one had ever walked the sparkling marble floors, sat in the overstuffed chairs and divans. As though no one ever had or ever would. The cleanliness was so forbidding, the silence so sepulchral.

The silence was contagious; it pressed in on you, demanding silence. Up in the cashier's cage, Dusty unconsciously lowered his voice. Then, as Bascom squirmed on his stool, he raised it again.

Five-oh-five, Holloway. Food thirty-eight dollars, tips five, total forty-three. Bar twenty, tips three-fifty, total twenty-three fifty. Newsstand miscellaneous, twelve. C.O.D.'s fifty-two. Valet—"

"Let's see." Bascom held out his hand for the charge slips without turning around. "Hmmm. Living high, but he doesn't spend a nickel. Could be that he doesn't have it to spend."

"Could be," Dusty murmured.

"Well"—Bascom tossed the account to one side—"that's a headache for the day crew. Let's have the next one."

Dusty continued. Now and then he stole a look at the clerk. Bascom was strangely calm, matter-of-fact, tonight. Not friendly or unfriendly, simply a man carrying out a job that had to be done.

It was the way he should act, of course; everything had to go on as usual, right up until the time of the holdup. But Dusty wondered at his ability to do it. He, himself, was anything but calm. Now, here right at the last when he needed confidence most, it was suddenly draining away.

Dusty glanced at the lobby clock. Two-thirty sharp. What was holding them up? They—Tug and the two men who were in on the deal—should have started down the stairs at two-twenty. Ten minutes was more than enough time to get down to the lobby. So unless something had gone wrong . . .

Tug had warned him not to leave the cashier's cage after two-thirty. If there was a room call or an elevator signal at two-twenty-five, or even a minute or so later, fine. He was to take care of it, and get back to the cage as fast as he could. But after that, no. People couldn't expect prompt service at this hour of the morning. If they did comment on the fact later, nothing could be made of it. The robbery would have been going on, and—

But it wasn't going on! It was two-thirty-four, well, two-thirty-three, and nothing had happened. Suppose he got a room call, or the elevator night-bell rang, now. Suppose he stalled on it, and Tug and his boys didn't show up until three. How would he be able to explain that? And how could he cover up, meanwhile, with Bascom? Bascom wasn't supposed to know that he was in on the robbery. And Bascom certainly would suspect the truth, if he stalled indefinitely. A few minutes, yes: while they finished a transcript sheet or a series of charges. But a few minutes had already passed—it was already two thirty—and ... Where were they? *For God's sake, where were they?*

"Bill ..." Bascom spoke with his back still turned. "You made a bad mistake, Bill."

"W-what?" Dusty plunged out of fear and into terror.

"W-when? H-how do you—?"

"You've been making a lot of mistakes. You don't know what you're doing. Why don't you go home? I can say that you took sick, and call for another boy."

What was he talking about? The work or the other? Did he know or ...?

"Do it, Bill. Now. Before you make a really big mistake."

"I—*No!*" Dusty gasped. "I mean, I'm all right I—"

"You're all wrong. But if you leave now, you can still ..." Bascom paused, leaving the sentence unfinished. For from somewhere, up there on the echoing darkness of the mezzanine, a door had creaked open, and now there was the rapid *pad-pad* of feet upon thick carpeting. And then the clatter of those same feet descending the marble steps to the lobby.

They came down in a group, almost on each other's heels. One of them hurried up the lobby to the front door, another took up a position at the taxi entrance. And the third, Tug Trowbridge, stopped at the cashier's cage.

Something dropped to the desk from his hand, tinkled faintly. Six—no, seven tiny keys. The same hand grasped Bascom by the shirt front, hauled him up against the opening. The other thrust a gun into the clerk's chest.

"All right, kid," he snapped. "Get busy!"

"B-but—" Dusty stared at him, stupefied. This wasn't the way it was supposed to be. Tug had promised to keep him in the clear, with nothing to do but—

"Goddammit, move! Get the ledger and the other keys. Get them boxes out here!"

Dusty's head was swimming. He stammered, "B-but you s-said—"

"You heard what I said! Now, do it!"

He couldn't do it. He couldn't even move. Then his eyes moved from the gangster to Bascom, and he couldn't see him full-face, but what he saw was enough. Bascom was startled, too. For him also things were not going as they had been planned.

"You hear me, Dusty? I have to tell you one more goddamned time, and—"

And Dusty sprang into action.

He had left the platform. The plunge was over, and now there was nothing but the short easy swim to shore. This was as it should be. As he must have known it would be. He hadn't known, of course, or certainly he wouldn't have agreed to it. He'd had no idea of the real truth. But so long as it was this way...

He sank deeper and deeper into the water; its pressure was unbearable. And then he was on the bottom—absolute bottom. And amazingly the pressure was gone. Once he surrendered to it fully, ceased to resist, there was no more.

Sure, he'd known; and he knew what must certainly happen after this. And what the hell of it? All that mattered now was getting to shore . . . getting away with it.

Swiftly, he unlocked seven of the little vault doors, yanked out their long steel boxes. He placed them on the desk, to one side of Bascom, and Tug gave him a tightlipped grin of approval.

"Atta boy! Now, reach around him, kid—I got the bag under my coat—and . . . Swell. You're doing fine. Now stuff the dough into it, and—"

"What about a count on it?"

"Count!" Tug let out a surprised grunt, then chuckled softly. "A real pro, ain't he, Bask?" *Bascom was silent*. "A good idea, kid, but make it fast. Just riffle through it. Don't matter if you're a grand or two off."

Dusty nodded. He flipped back the lid of the first box, turned through the thick sheaf of bills. They were all hundreds and fifties, with a preponderance of the latter. Large enough to total high without bulk, small enough for easy negotiation.

"Twenty-seven thousand." He glanced at Tug. "Okay?"

"Yeah, yeah! For Christ's sake, Dusty!"

There was twenty-four thousand, five hundred in the next box. The third held thirty-eight thousand, fifty.

The fourth . . .

All together there was two hundred and thirty-two thousand. Approximately that much. Tug nodded impatiently as he repeated the figure.

"Yeah, hell. It's close enough anyway . . . Now, you remember the combo on that bag? One turn right from zero, back left to ten, right to forty, and then left to—"

"I know. All the way, ten, forty, thirty . . . What about your own box, here? Haven't you got—?"

Tug cursed shakily. "Jesus Christ! Forget it, will you? Just get the thing checked and get back here!"

Dusty snapped the bag shut, spun the knob of the combination lock. He unlocked the cage, and hurried down the long counter, snatching up the checkroom key from the bell captain's stand.

He emerged from behind the counter, turned into the alcove which bordered one side of the check stand. The baggage-receiving space opened onto that. He unlocked its long window, vaulted the brass-surfaced counter, and turned on the light switch.

Two cigar boxes were nailed to the wall immediately below the switch. Dusty took a rubber band from one, and an orange-colored oblong of pasteboard from another. He affixed a check to the bag, shredded its stub into a wastebasket, took a long look at the number as he slid the bag onto the shelf. *Four, nine, nine, four. Forty-nine, ninety-four.* Forty-nine and reverse. That would be easy to remember.

He switched off the light, vaulted back over the counter, relocked the window. Hurrying back down into the lobby, swift but sure of himself, unpanicked, he heard the ringing of the bell captain's phone. And yards away he saw the alarm on Tug's face, and the sudden uneasiness of the two men at the doors. Why, they were jumpy. *They* were, and he was not. He was grinning secretly, patronizingly, as he entered and locked the door of the cashier's cage.

Everything was all right. It was exactly eight minutes since Tug had thrust his gun into Bascom's ribs. How much better could they want it?

"That goddamned phone, Dusty! Maybe you ought to—"

"Huh-uh. The operator will figure I'm busy. She'll stop, and call back in a few minutes."

"You sure? She won't—" The ringing stopped, but Tug still looked anxious. "She won't call someone, tell 'em that she—"

Dusty shook his head. "What's the difference, anyway? It's all over, isn't it?"

"Well ... well, yeah," said Tug, almost wonderingly. 'I guess it just about is, kid."

"Bill!" Bascom spoke for the first time. "Listen to me, Bill! It doesn't matter about me, but you've got to prom—"

Tug's gun exploded. Bascom reeled backward, clutching his chest, and Tug fired again. And again. The clerk's body jerked. Slowly, it began to bend at the waist. It sagged down and down, and he was clawing at his chest, now, gasping and clawing—a terrible rattle in his throat. Then, his knees swayed and crumpled, and blood gushed from his mouth, and he pitched forward to the floor.

The rattling ceased. He lay silent, motionless.

"All right, kid"—Tug's gun swerved and pointed at Dusty. "Here's your story ..."

He spoke swiftly. He said, "Got it?" And then, "Now, just take it easy—we got to make this look good—but just take it easy and—"

And he fired again.

Dusty screamed. He staggered and went down, on top of Bascom's body.

FOURTEEN

Instinctively, he had tried to dodge the bullet, and the attempt came close to being fatal. Tug's aim was thrown off. The bullet went into Dusty's arm at an angle, and creased a furrow across his ribs. He was not seriously injured but he might have been. It looked as though Tug had tried to kill him.

So now he was a hero, above dispute and suspicion. A plucky young man who had tried to wrest a loaded gun from a murderer's grasp. The newspapers carried daily reports on his condition. The hotel, in addition to paying his hospital bills, had given him a check for three hundred dollars. Detectives had taken him back and forth through his story repeatedly, but they were respectful, apologetic, about it. They were at a dead end in the case, had been almost from the beginning. And they had to go through the motions of doing something.

A detective was with him today, the last of his nine days in the hospital. He had just happened to be in the neighborhood, he explained, rather abashedly. So if Dusty wouldn't mind, since he'd be going home tomorrow and they wouldn't be bothering him any more...

Dusty felt a little sorry for him. He said it was no bother at all. "I don't think I've overlooked or forgotten anything, but I might have."

"Well ... Now about the time, then. Were you and Bascom always in the cashier's cage at two-thirty?"

"Almost always. Of course, I might have a bell—a call—or Bascom might have to leave for a minute. But we'd almost always be there at that time."

"Why that particular time instead of some other?"

"It was the quietest part of the shift, for one thing. We weren't so apt to be interrupted. Also, there'd seldom be any room charges after that time. If we tried to do it before that, while the coffee shop was still open and a lot of people were still up—"

"Uh-huh, sure. But what about the tag end of your shift, say up between six and seven in the morning? You'd start getting more charges, then, wouldn't you?"

"A few. Bascom would put them on the room accounts as fast as they came."

"Why didn't you do them all at once? If you'd done that, held up your cashier work until there were other people around..." The detective broke off with a sheepish look. "How stupid can I get, huh? I ask you why you don't do something when you'd've been too busy to do it."

"That's right." Dusty smiled sympathetically. "I wouldn't have had time to help. Bascom would have been busy with people checking in and out."

"Yeah, sure," the detective nodded. "Now, what did you think when you saw Tug and his two thugs heading down the stairs? Didn't that strike you as pretty screwy? I know he was paying the hotel big money and he'd never caused any trouble before. But two-thirty in the morning—three guys hiking down nine flights of stairs at two-thirty in the morning—you must have—"

"It's like I told you," Dusty said. "I figured that the nightbell on the elevator must have gone out of order. They'd signaled and when I didn't come with the car they'd walked down."

"But what would they be doing up at that hour, anyway? I know you told me, but it just don't seem like—"

"I'm afraid it's about all I can tell you. We were used to seeing Tug up late. He usually came in late, with a couple of his men, and sometimes he came back downstairs with them when they left."

"Well"—the detective sighed and leaned back in his chair. Then, he straightened up suddenly. "Wait a minute! You say you figured the elevator bell was out of order. But if that had been the case he'd have called you, wouldn't he? When the elevator didn't come he'd have telephoned downstairs from his room?"

Dusty hesitated. It was a point that had been overlooked until now. "You're right," he said. "I should have thought of that. But I just wasn't suspicious of Tug like I might have been of some people, and there wasn't any time to think. I saw him and those fellows coming down the stairs. The next thing I knew, he'd grabbed Bascom and shoved a gun in his ribs. All I could think of was that I'd better do what he said or he'd kill Bascom."

"Uh-uh, sure." The detective sighed again. "Now what was it Tug said there at the last, just before he pulled the trigger on Bascom?"

"He said, Here's your share. Or maybe it was, Here's your cut."

"And that didn't register on you, either? It didn't occur to you that Bascom must have been working with Tug?"

"Look. Officer"—Dusty spread his hands. "Here's a man I've waited on for more than a year, a man who's always been friendly, a star guest of the hotel. And suddenly he holds us up, and shoots the man I'm working with. All within the space of a few minutes. You don't do much reasoning at a time like that. Maybe you would, but—"

"Okay, okay," the detective said hastily. "I didn't mean to sound like I was faulting you, Mr. Rhodes. You were a lot more clear-headed than most people would have been, showed a hell of a lot more guts. Me, I can't see myself making a grab for that gun."

"Well," Dusty smiled engagingly, "I probably wouldn't do it again either. I was just scared, I suppose, afraid I was going to get killed next."

"And you weren't far wrong at that." The detective shook his head, frowning. "That Bascom—y'know, I just can't figure him. Even if Tug had shot square with him, he must have known that he'd be on a spot. We'd investigate him, and find out about his record. The hotel had already got a letter about him—you know about that, I guess—and—"

"But they didn't pay much attention to it. Bascom had worked there for years, and he'd never given them any reason to suspect him. One anonymous letter wouldn't have counted much against a record like his."

"Yeah. Well, maybe not then. Maybe we wouldn't have checked on him. The way he thought the deal was going to be, it would have left him looking pretty good. Tug grabs him before he knows what's happening. He doesn't even touch the boxes himself. So maybe..."

His voice wandered on absently, aimlessly, a dull probe seeking the non-existent. And a sudden hunch sprang into Dusty's mind.

If his and Bascom's roles had been reversed, if he had been killed and if Bascom had quoted Tug as saying 'Here's your cut...'

Why not? A bellboy was about as low down the ladder as you could get, while a night clerk was a minor executive. His story would have been believed. He would have been the hero, and Dusty the dead villain ... Doubtless, Bascom had believed it would be that way. And, doubtless—perhaps—Had Tug planned it that way in the beginning?

It wasn't nice to think about. There was no sense in thinking about it, and there were much more pleasant things to dwell upon. Marcia Hillis, for example, and fifty per cent of two hundred and thirty-two thousand dollars.

"Well"—the detective stood up. "Guess I'd better be running along. If you should happen to think of anything, why ..."

"I don't know what it would be but I'll certainly let you know."

"Fine. Appreciate it." He turned dispiritedly toward the door, a big man with sagging shoulders and a tired gray face. "Oh, yeah," he paused. "Guess I didn't tell you, did I? We found those guys that were with Tug."

"Found them! W-what—?"

"Uh-huh. In the river. Tied together with bailing wire. Looks like they'd been there since the night of the hold up."

"W-well"—Dusty swallowed. "Why ... What do you suppose—?"

"Tug, of course. To beat them out of their split. Seems like they should have figured on it, and given it to him instead. But, well, that's the way things go."

He left.

Dusty walked over to the window, pulling his bathrobe around him. So Tug's boys had got it, too. Tug had double-crossed them, just as he had Bascom. And what about it, anyway? What difference did it make? Tug wouldn't double-cross *him*, because he damned well couldn't, and that was all that mattered.

He'd be out of the hospital tomorrow. In a few days, as soon as his shoulder limbered up a little more, he'd be back to work. Then, the split of the money—Tug would get in touch with him about that—and then ...

He turned away from the window. He sank down into an easy chair and leaned back, propping his feet up on the bed. The money. He still didn't know how Tug planned to collect his share. The gangster had impatiently pointed out that they'd have to wait and see, that circumstances following the robbery would dictate arrangements. And that was true, of course; it was just about the way it had to be.

But still—hadn't he been pretty offhand about it? Had he been concealing something on this point as he had on the other?

Well ... Dusty shrugged, dismissing the idea. That didn't matter either. Tug could only get to the money through him. There was no way that Tug could do him out of his share. That was the important thing, so to hell with details.

... A nurse brought his dinner on a tray. He ate leisurely and read the evening papers. There was a brief item about his leaving the hospital tomorrow. There was a long story about the discovery of the murdered gangsters. He laid the papers aside, yawning, and glanced at his wristwatch.

He had told his father not to visit him tonight, since it was his last night here, and he hoped to God that he wouldn't. Not that the old man hadn't looked presentable on his nightly visits, but—well, he'd just rather not scare him. His concern made Dusty uncomfortable. His presence was a reminder of a perplexing and seemingly insoluble problem. Dusty just couldn't think when his father was around. There was a stumbling block in his mind, an obscuring shadow over the pleasant picture of his thoughts.

Marcia Hillis was working with Tug. He had become more and more sure of that fact. He was also sure of his attraction for her—*strange how very sure he was of that*. And now that her work with Tug was done, now that he had money, it would only be a matter of time until they were together.

That was the way it would be. It was the way it *had* to be. It wasn't just wishful thinking—by God, it wasn't! He had lost her once, lost the only woman in the world. And, now, miraculously, she had reappeared, she had come back into the aching emptiness of his life. And this time, this time, he would not let her get away.

He would have her. It was unthinkable that he might not. In his mind, the possession was already accomplished; they were already together, he and Marcia Hillis, delighting in one another, delighting one another. And there was no room in the picture for his father. With his father, there was no picture.

How could he explain her to the old man? How could he explain the money? He wouldn't have to explain right away, of course. It would be months before he dared quit the hotel and move on to another city—another country. But the time would come. Or, rather, it would never come, as long as his father lived.

As long as he lived . . .

Dusty had no visitors that night. In the morning, the doctor gave him a final examination and a nurse brought his clothes. He took an elevator downstairs. Unused to exercise, he wobbled a little as he started across the lobby to the street. And a soft hand closed over his arm.

"Let me help you, Mr. Rhodes," said Marcia Hillis.

FIFTEEN

He wasn't surprised, merely startled for the moment. He had been expecting to see her, and her appearance there, as he was leaving the hospital, virtually explained the reason behind it. She wasn't quite through with her assignment with Tug. There was one more thing to be done. He knew what it was, and how it was to be done, almost before she said a word.

They took a cab to his house. She assisted him inside, was received with absent matter-of-factness by the old man. He was glad, he said, that Bill had hired her. They would need someone, with Bill just out of the hospital, and he himself wasn't much help he guessed.

"Now, nonsense, Dad!" Dusty was almost exuberant in his happiness. "You do a lot more than you should. I've been meaning to get someone in before this to make things easier for you."

"Well, now," Mr. Rhodes beamed. "I—that's certainly nice of you, son."

"You must have had a hard time while I was gone. So today you get a vacation. Go to a good show, get yourself a good meal; just take it easy and enjoy yourself."

He pressed a ten-dollar bill upon Mr. Rhodes. He saw him out the door, watched for a moment as he trudged down the walk toward the bus stop. That would take care of the old nuisance. It was worth ten times ten dollars to get rid of him for a while.

He was on the point of saying as much when he turned back around, but the look on Marcia's face stopped him. There was a tenderness in her eyes, a warmth in her expression, that he had never seen before.

"You know," she said softly, "I think I like you."

"Think?"

"Mmmm," she said, and laughed. "And I think I'd like some coffee, too. So if you'll introduce me to your kitchen, show me where you keep things..."

She made coffee, donning an apron he gave her. He watched her, dreamily, as she moved about the kitchen, drinking in every delicious detail of her. The hair, the compactly curving body, the clothes, the—

The clothes. He couldn't be sure of it, but she seemed to be dressed the same as she had been the last time he'd seen her.

She turned around suddenly, surprising him in his looking. She said, "Yes? Something on your mind, Dusty?" And he hastily shook his head.

"I was just wondering about your clothes. I mean, you'll be here for some time and ..."

"Oh," she shrugged. "Well, I'll pick my baggage up in a day or two. It wasn't convenient this morning."

She set the coffee on the table, and sat down across from him. Hand trembling a little, he lifted the cup. Reaction was setting in; he at last felt surprise—wonder at this incredibly wondrous happening. She was actually here! They were really together. And, of course, he had known that they would be, but now that they were ...

He had to put down the coffee cup. Fingers fumbling, he managed to light a cigarette and hold a match for hers. She smiled sympathetically, steadying his hand with her own.

"You don't have your strength back yet, Dusty. Why don't you lie down for a while?"

"I'm all right. We've got a lot to talk about, and—"

"You can lie down and talk. Come on, now, before you wear yourself out completely."

She guided him into his bedroom. He stretched out on the bed, and she sat down at his side.

"Well, Dusty ..." She smoothed the hair back from his forehead. "You didn't seem very surprised to see me today."

"I wasn't. I was pretty sure you must be working with Tug."

"You were? And how did that make you feel about me, Dusty, about being tricked into—?"

"It didn't change anything. I figured you were probably in the same boat I was in. You were on a spot, and you had to follow orders."

"Did you, Dusty?" She squeezed his hand. "I'm glad you understood. Some day I'll tell you how it was, but—"

"It doesn't matter. I—nothing mattered but you. Right from the first time I saw you."

The statement sounded awkwardly blunt, a little ridiculous. But she smiled gravely, obviously pleased.

"I'm glad, Dusty. Because, you see ... well, I rather felt the same way. It was the way you acted, I guess, as though you'd been waiting for me, expecting me. I felt like you were someone I'd known a long time ago, and—Oh, I don't know," she laughed. "Anyway, I don't suppose a girl should admit such things, should she?"

"Yes!" he exclaimed. "I mean—I don't mean you should—"

"I know what you mean, Dusty. I know."

She bent down, pressing her mouth against his. Then, as his arms went around her, she slid firmly out of his embrace.

"Not now, darling. I hope there will be more later—a great deal more. But, now, I don't know."

"But why?" He started to sit up, and she pushed him back down. "You said you liked me, felt the same way as I did. I'll have plenty of money, and—"

"The money isn't too important to me, Dusty. Not nearly as much, I'm afraid, as it is to you. I like it, yes, but I've never had a great deal and I've gotten along all right without it. I could keep right on getting along without it. I wonder if you could."

"But I—we won't have to!"

"Won't we? That money won't last forever, no more than ten years, say, if we're only mildly extravagant. What would you do when it's gone?"

"Well, I—" He shook his head impatiently. "What would anyone do? Marcia, I—"

"Not anyone. You. I'm quite a bit older than you are, Dusty. I won't be young ten years from now, but you will. How would you feel then—broke and saddled with a middle-aged woman? What would you do about it?"

"What?" he frowned. "I—look, Marcia. I want you to marry me, not just—"

"I hoped you did. But that still doesn't answer my question. What happens when my looks are gone, and the money's gone? Would there still be something left for you, something more important than money or appearances? I'd have to be sure of that, Dusty. I have to know you better than I do now."

"I ... I don't know what you mean," he said slowly. "I don't see what you're driving at."

"Murder, mainly. Murderers. If a man kills to get himself out of one unpleasant situation, he'll do it again."

She nodded calmly, staring down at him in the shade-drawn dimness, and a cold chill raced up Dusty's spine. He was suddenly conscious of the room's quiet, of their isolation here.

"B-but—" He gulped. "But I haven't killed anyone!"

"Not actually, perhaps, but technically. You knew Bascom was going to be killed!"

"But I didn't! Tug didn't tell me a thing about it. He told me—told me that no one would be hurt."

"And you believed him?"

"Why not? I didn't know anything about things like that. All I knew was that you were in trouble, that you might get killed if I didn't do what Tug told me to."

"That isn't what you said a moment ago. You said you knew I was working with Tug."

"Not at the time. Even afterwards, I wasn't positive. I—Who are you to talk, anyway? You got me into the deal. If it hadn't been for you, I—"

"Would it have made any difference, Dusty? You don't think you might have been in it anyway?"

"How could I have been? What do you mean? Dammit"—he sat up, scowling. "I could ask some questions myself. What about you knowing that Bascom was going to be killed? You quiz me about it when you must have known yourself that—"

"I didn't. If I had, I'd hardly be concerned about your being involved."

"Well, I didn't know either."

"I hope not, Dusty. I want to believe that you didn't. So let's not discuss it any more now, shall we not? Give me a little more time, tell me how we're going to get the money out of the hotel, and then—well, we'll see then."

"But, why? What's there to—?"

"Why not? We'll have to wait anyway. We've just met, supposedly. You'll have to go on working at the hotel."

"Yes, but—but, Marcia . . ."

He broke off, unable to say what he had intended to, to point out the incongruity of the situation. She was in this thing as deeply as he, she was closer to Tug apparently than he was. She'd been around—she damned well had to know what the score was. So why then all this squeamishness? Why all the fuss about Bascom's death?

It didn't add up. Even taking that older-than-you-are, what-about-the-future stuff at its face value it didn't fit together. So maybe they had to be careful for a while. Maybe it was logical for her to go slow on tying herself up permanently. But they were alone now, and she'd been around from way back. And yet he couldn't even give her a feel without—

"Oh," she said, and it was as though he had spoken the thought aloud. "I see, Dusty, and I don't blame you. I haven't been everything I should be, and—"

"Nuts, nonsense," he said quickly. "Now about the money. Come around to the hotel any time after I go on duty, a little after twelve, say. You want to get something out of a suitcase you've left in the checkroom—a lot of people do that—and—"

"I understand. I supposed you'd do it that way."

"Well, uh—that's all there is to it, then."

She nodded, went on looking at him. At last she said absently, "Perhaps we shouldn't wait. Perhaps it would be better now, since you feel as you do. Since it's so important—or unimportant."

"Now, wait a minute!" His face flushed. "I haven't said anything! My God, you can't blame me for wanting to—to—"

"I don't. Nor for thinking what you think."

She got up and left the room. He heard the front door close, and the snap of the lock, and then she was back again.

She toed off one shoe, then the other. Quite casually, she unfastened the snaps of her dress, slipped it up and over her head. The slip came next. Then—then the other things. All that remained.

And then she stretched out at his side. And waited.

He was too startled to move for a moment; it had all happened so swiftly. Then, his senses responded to the wonderful reality of her, and he moaned and . . .

She lay supine, docile, under his hungrily groping hands. They roamed over her body unhindered, nothing forbidden nor withheld. And her mouth received his in long, breathtaking kisses. It was almost too much, more ecstasy than he could bear. To have her at last, after all these years of hunger and hopelessness, to have this—the impossible dream come true—his for the taking.

He moaned again. He turned, pulling her body under his and then he opened his eyes. Looked into hers.

"What—what's the matter?" he said.

"You mean," she said, "you're not enjoying yourself?"

"Look. If you didn't want to, why—?"

"I thought I explained. To see how important this was to you— how much value or little value you placed on it."

"But that—that's crazy! What does it prove? For God's sake, Marcia, you can't—"

"To me, it proves a great deal. To you—well, I'm waiting to find out."

"B-but—" But it was impossible, unbearable! He couldn't stop now. Jesus, he couldn't! He *couldn't!* But if he didn't . . .

He bit his lip. Suddenly, he thrust himself up, dropped down panting at her side. And he lay there, eyes clenched, trembling from the terrible effort. It was all right now. He was exhausted, now, drained dry of strength—weak as he was disappointed.

Her arm went around his neck, pulling his head against her breast. She held it there, gently, stroking his hair.

"You'll be glad, darling," she whispered. "You'll see. You'll be so glad you waited."

"All right," he said. "I . . . all right."

"You don't hate me, do you, darling? Please don't. No matter what I—how I act. Because I won't be doing it to hurt you. I love you and I want you to love me, to keep on loving me, and if we don't get started off right . . ."

"All right," he repeated. "I said it was all right, didn't I?"

"And I said you'd be glad," she whispered. "And you will . . ."

SIXTEEN

Although there was still some soreness in his shoulder, he went back to work two days later. He wanted to get the pay-off made and over with. He wanted to—had to—get away from his father. For, that first day excepted, the old man had hardly left the house. And when he did leave on some errand, he was back within minutes.

He was always hovering around Marcia, offering to do things for her, inquiring about her comfort. He was always underfoot, butting into their conversations, making a thoroughgoing pest of himself. He stayed up at night until they retired. If they went to the kitchen to fix coffee, or out the porch for a breath of air, he tagged along. They couldn't get rid of him. Marcia, for her part, showed no desire to.

Once Dusty did manage to get her alone for a few minutes, and he made some sarcastic remark about the old man. She looked at him sharply.

"Why Dusty," she laughed, half-frowning. "What a thing to say about your own father! He's just been very lonely, that's all. Surely, you don't begrudge—"

"Oh, hell," he snapped. "I've been here right along, haven't I? Why would he be lonely?"

"Yes," she said. "Why would he be?"

He smoothed over the incident, told her laughingly that he guessed he was just jealous. And after that he went out of his way to be pleasant to Mr. Rhodes. But the effort told on his nerves. If he had to keep it up one more day, he felt—just one more day—he'd crack up.

She came out to his car with him the night he returned to work. It was dark, moonless. There was a threat of storm in the heavy, overheated air. She kissed him, remained within the circle of his arms for a moment.

"A little after twelve, then, darling?"

"Or later. Whenever Dad goes to sleep."

"I come to the side entrance in a taxi," she recited. "I have the taxi wait and come inside. If you're not there, I speak to the clerk and he'll have me wait until you return. I—He will, won't he, Dusty? He wouldn't offer to open the checkroom himself?"

"Not a chance. It would be beneath him, see, bellboy's work, and it would make me sore. He'd be cheating me out of a tip."

She nodded, still clinging to him. He bent his head a little and touched his lips to the sweet-smelling hair.

"About Tug, Marcia. I haven't asked before, and I don't want you to tell me if you'd—"

"It's a dangerous secret, darling; it could be one. There's nothing to be gained by your knowing, and everything to lose."

"Well"—he hesitated. "But is it safe for you? You know where Tug is. Once you give him the money, he might figure that—"

"I won't give it to him. I'm going to leave it in a certain place where he can get it. Don't worry, Dusty." She patted his cheek, lovingly. "Everything's going to be all right."

They kissed again, stood whispering together a moment longer. At last she stepped back, and he reached for the door of the car. A streak of heat lightning raced across the sky. He paused on the point of sliding into the seat.

"Your clothes," he said. "Want me to drive you in tomorrow, and pick them up?"

"Clothes? Oh, yes. Maybe that would be a good idea."

"Well. Anything else? Sure you can get all the dough in that bag of yours?"

He knew that she could. It was an outsize shoulder bag, and she would remove the contents before coming to the hotel. She nodded absently to the question but she continued to stand there at the curb, a small frown on her heart-shaped face.

He glanced at the radiant dial of the dashboard clock. Nine-fifteen, and he was supposed to be in uniform by ten tonight. They were taking his picture for the morning papers.

"I've got to run, Marcia. Is there something else—anything bothering you?"

"We-el . . . Oh, I guess not," she laughed ruefully. "I don't think I should mention it, anyway."

"Why not?"

"Because. It just isn't my place to suggest it. After all, it must have already occurred to you, and as long as you haven't said anything..."

"About what? What are you—Oh," he said slowly. "Well..." And his voice trailed off into an uncomfortable pause.

Actually, he had thought very little about it, how he was going to get his share of the money out of the hotel. A problem so simple required little thought. Unlike Tug, he had unlimited time. He could take months at the task, carrying it out in his wallet a few hundreds at a shift. It was the easiest way and the safest way. The Manton's bellboys made good money. No suspicion would attach to one with a mere few hundred in his possession.

He explained this to her, and she nodded her understanding. There was no sign of resentment or hurt in the upturned face. Still, however, his discomfort grew: he felt awkward, constrained to go on explaining. And the more he said—logical as it was—the worse it sounded.

It might be difficult to open the money satchel, take out Tug's share and transfer it to her bag. It could certainly be done, all right, but there might be difficulties. The safest and simplest thing to do would be to give her the satchel itself, with *all* the money.

And why not do it? Let her hold Tug's share *and* his.

Why not, unless...

She touched his arm gently. "I understand, darling. Now, run along and don't think anything more about it."

"It's not"—he hesitated—"I wouldn't want you to think I didn't trust you. It's just that I'd planned it the other way, and—"

"Of course" She urged him into the car, closed the door after him. "Why wouldn't you trust me? After all, you're practically trusting me with your life."

"Well ... well," he murmured, feebly. "I'll, uh, see you, then."

He drove to the hotel, downcast, feeling that he had acted like a suspicious fool. He decided—half-decided—to give her the satchel when she came that night. Why not? Either she was completely trustworthy or she was not to be trusted at all. If Tug's money could be trusted to her, then so could his own.

Or couldn't it? Why couldn't it be?

Frowning, he buttoned his uniform jacket, adjusted the wing tips of his shirt collar. *Why?* Well, there was one reason. One hideous, heart-wrenching reason. She might not be finished with Tug after the pay-off, nor he with her. She might be much more to Tug then she pretended to be. And if she was—well, she had pointed it out herself. A hundred and sixteen thousand dollars wouldn't last forever; it would be gone in a few years. But with two hundred and thirty-two thousand . . .

Furiously, Dusty pushed the terrible thought out of his mind. No! A thousand times no; she couldn't be Tug's woman. She was *his*. She liked to be, and she was. And just to prove it—to prove his complete faith in her—he would give her the satchel tonight.

Maybe. Probably. Surely. Unless he thought of some really *good* reason for not doing it.

He finished dressing and left the locker room. Tolliver, the superintendent of service, and Steelman, the manager, were waiting for him in the latter's office. Tolliver called to the two photographers in the reception room. They sauntered in and set up their equipment.

The first pose was of Dusty shaking hands with the manager, while Tolliver looked on beaming. Then he posed between the two men, each with a hand on his shoulder. Finally, he was photographed by himself, arms folded in the traditional manner of bellboys "standing post."

Repeatedly, he had to be reminded to smile. Toward the last, the photographers became quite sharp with him, and the two executives were showing signs of annoyance.

Dusty returned to the locker room for a brief, pre-work smoke. His lips twisted in silent mimicry, *Lets see a smile Rhodes—a SMILE DAMMIT—don't you know how to smile?* And scowling he hurled away the cigarette, and started up the steps. To hell with them. To hell with the hotel. She would take his dough out tonight with Tug's, and the sooner they fired him after that, the better. The money would be waiting for him when he got home in the morning—she and the money. And as soon as he figured out an angle on the old man, how to shake the old bastard without causing trouble . . .

That was the way it would be. It would—could—be that way if he was sure of her.

Preoccupied, now and then frowning unconsciously, he began the night's duties. A few minutes before midnight, he went behind the keyrack and manipulated a series of light switches.

"And just what," said a chilly voice at his elbow, "do you think you are doing?"

Dusty jumped, startled. It was Mr. Fillmore, the night clerk hired to replace Bascom. He had come from a smaller, second-rate hotel, and the Manton was a big step upward for him. Unsure of himself, fearful that his authority might be infringed upon, he made a point of appearing the opposite. He knew his job, by golly. He was in charge here, not some smart-alecky bellboy.

"I asked you what you were doing," he repeated. "Who told you to fool around with those lights?"

Dusty explained curtly; he had taken an immediate dislike to the clerk. "We always do this at midnight, dim the lobby and light up the—"

"But it's not midnight yet. Won't be for five minutes. You put those lights back on, understand? When I want them off, I'll tell you."

"I've got a better idea than that," said Dusty. "Do it yourself."

Turning on his heel, he left the desk area. He kept his back turned as the clerk emerged from behind the key-rack and spoke to him sharply across the counter.

"We may as well get this clear right now, Rhodes. The hotel appreciates what you did, and they've shown that appreciation, but you're still a bellboy. While you're at work you have no more rights or privileges than any other bellboy. It—uh—it has to be that way, understand? I'm sure that Mr. Tolliver or Mr. Steelman will bear me out. I hope—I'm certain, of course—that it will never be necessary for me to report—"

"Go ahead," Dusty grunted, still not looking around. "Go ahead and report me and see what they say."

"Well, uh—" Fillmore cleared his throat—"well, now, I wouldn't want to do that. Not at all. Sure we're going to get along fine, now that this little misunderstanding is cleared up, and ..."

He left the sentence unfinished, moving up the counter to the room-clerk section. He busied himself there, coldly furious, angry as only the self-fearful can be when character and circumstance conspire to make them ridiculous ... He'd been in the right, hadn't he? But that smart-aleck—he'd acted snooty from the minute he stepped on the floor tonight—had gotten gay with him. Crowded him into saying things that he hadn't meant to say. Well, maybe, certainly, he couldn't do anything about this. He'd look foolish if he tried. But just wait! Something else would come up. He'd put that young punk in his place yet!

There was a squeal of brakes at the side entrance. Instantly, Fillmore arose from his stool, stood briskly alert as a woman got out of the cab and came through the double doors to the lobby. She ascended the three steps from the foyer, paused for a moment in the muted glow of one of the huge chandeliers. Fillmore gaped, his fearful fussy old heart missing a beat. He'd never seen a woman who looked like that. She was so beautiful that it almost hurt to look at her. He hoped she didn't want a room. He'd have to turn her down, of course, a woman alone at this time of night, and he could see that she was a lady. As much a lady as she was beautiful.

Gratefully, he noted that the cab was waiting for her. (She didn't want a room, then.) Jealously, he watched as she started across the lobby and Rhodes stepped forward to meet her. Now there was presumption for you. There was sheer gall. Accosting a lady—asking if *he* could help her—instead of allowing her to proceed to the desk!

Fillmore's eyes glinted. He moved down the desk quickly, leaned over the counter.

"Yes, madam?" he called. "Can I be of service to you?" Rhodes whirled around, frowning. *That would show him, by golly!* The lady looked momentarily surprised, then smiled at him warmly.

"Could you, please? I left a bag here recently when I checked out of the hotel. I see that your checkroom's closed, but I wonder if—"

"Certainly. The boy will get it for you." Fillmore snapped his fingers. "Front, boy! Get the lady's bag out of the checkroom."

He slapped the key upon the counter. Rhodes snatched it up, tight-lipped, strode down the lobby and rounded the corner of the corridor to the checkroom window. The lady followed him after a gracious smile at Fillmore.

The clerk grinned to himself. He flicked an invisible speck of dust from his suit, silently crying down the small voice of his conscience. Petty? A show-off? Nonsense. This was a smart hotel—a real swell place. And its executives, and, by golly, he was an executive!, were supposed to conduct themselves accordingly. Maybe it wasn't absolutely necessary here at night, so much spit and polish, but he would never be criticized for it. It was a kind of bonus. He was giving more than was expected of him.

Fillmore's bony hands clenched and unclenched, exultantly. So perhaps he couldn't complain about Rhodes ... not unless he did something completely out of the way. But neither could Rhodes complain about him. He wouldn't get very far, by golly, if he tried. He could keep that smart-aleck on his toes all night long, make him toe the line. And Rhodes would have to take it or else. If he rebelled, refused to do as he was told—

Well, discipline, the chain of command, had to be maintained, didn't it? The management would have to uphold a clerk against a bellboy. They would have to do it or fire him, and how could you fire a man for being utterly correct?

So ...

Fillmore glanced up at the lobby clock. He straightened his shoulders, and his head reassumed its imperious tilt ... Three minutes, no, now it was four minutes. Four minutes to get a bag out of the checkroom, and he hadn't done it yet! Now that was fine service for you. That was certainly a fine way to run a hotel.

He waited until the big hand of the clock jerked again, marking off another minute. Then, easing open the door of the desk area, he moved silently down the lobby. Perhaps, he thought, Rhodes was sneaking a smoke, loitering along the baggage racks while the lady waited. Or perhaps ... perhaps he was trying to pull something funny. Trying to flirt with her. He was a good-looking punk—too darned good-looking to be trustworthy! Probably had the idea that he could crook a finger at a woman, and she'd come a-running.

Fillmore paused at the corner of the areaway, straining his ears to listen. He could hear them—what sounded like an argument—but he couldn't hear what they were saying. The bellboy's voice was strained. The lady's was softly insistent, faintly wheedling.

Fillmore hesitated, teetering in nervous indecision. Perhaps—well, it might be well to go a little slow. Rhodes was something rather special with the hotel management. He had risked his life in the hotel's interests, and if things came to a showdown—

But things wouldn't! He wasn't doing anything out of the way. After all, what was wrong with making an inquiry, intervening, where there was obviously some difficulty between a patron and an employee?

Fillmore patted his tie, threw back his shoulders and stepped around the corner.

"What's going on here?" he said briskly. "What's the trouble, Rhodes?"

Rhodes' face went white. *So he had been up to something!* The woman also seemed perturbed, but she managed a smile. She nodded at the bag, a kind of dispatch case, which the bellboy was holding.

"I've misplaced my baggage check," she said. "Can't I please get the bag without it?"

"Well, I—uh—" Fillmore hesitated.

"Please? My husband just returned to town tonight, and he's very anxious to have these papers. I know it's rather unusual, but I have been a guest here—this bellboy admits he remembers me and ..."

She looked at Fillmore winningly. He stared uncertainly at Rhodes. He'd had the same problem before at other hotels, and he'd known how to handle it. But at the Manton—well, it might be different here. Rhodes knew what the custom was better than he did.

"Well," he said. "I hardly—you do remember this lady, Rhodes?"

Rhodes hesitated. He said, his voice strangely tight, "I remember."

"And you can't—I'm not ordering you to, understand—you can't release a piece of baggage without a check? You don't do that under any circumstances?"

"No."

"Not even if the owner identifies the contents?"

"N-no. I mean, she—she—"

"Answer me! Speak up!" Fillmore was sure of himself again. His voice rang with authority. "That is the custom, isn't it? ... I'm sorry you were delayed, madam, but if you'll just identi—"

"But I already have! I satisfied the boy that it was my bag, but apparently"—she laughed a little wryly—"he wasn't satisfied with the tip I gave him."

"Oh, he wasn't, eh?" Fillmore's lips tightened grimly. "Give me that bag, Rhodes, do you hear me? Give it here instantly!"

Reaching across the counter, he snatched the bag from the bellboy's hand, presented it to the lady with a courteous bow. "I'm extremely sorry about this, madam. May I see you to your cab?"

Murmuring apologies, muttering sternly about the bellboy's conduct, he escorted her out into the lobby. At the steps to the side entrance, she interrupted, laying a hand on his arm.

"He won't lose his job because of this, will he? I'd feel dreadful if I thought he would."

"But, madam. The Manton cannot and will not tolerate discourtesy on the part of—"

"Oh, I'm sure he didn't mean to be discourteous. It was more thoughtlessness than anything else ... Promise?" She gave his arm a little squeeze. "Promise he won't be fired."

"Well," said Fillmore, and then, grandly, "Very well. I understand that he does need his place here. Has his father, a semi-invalid, depending on him."

"I know," said Marcia Hillis. "I mean, I thought he must be upset about something."

SEVENTEEN

Dusty never knew how he got through that night. It seemed endless, and each of the year-long moments was a nightmare of soul-sickening rage, of rage and hate and frustration—repressed, seething inside him, until the mental sickness became physical. He wanted to kill Fillmore, to choke him with his bare hands. He wanted to hide in a dark corner and vomit endlessly. He wanted ...

He wanted the unattainable. He wanted what he had always wanted—her. And now he was not going to have her. She was Tug's woman, obviously, irrefutably. Everything else had been pretence, all the caresses and the whisperings and the promises. All for Tug, nothing for him. They'd be together now, on their way out of the country together. They'd be laughing—she'd be laughing, as she told how she'd hoodwinked him. He'd been on the point of giving her the satchel. He couldn't bear to see her hurt, to have her think that he didn't trust her. *Goddam, oh, Goddam!* And he'd been just a little suspicious of her last-minute firmness, her insistence, but if she'd kept up the act a moment longer . . .

But it hadn't been necessary for her to keep it up. He hadn't had time to reach a decision. That goddamned stupid Fillmore had butted in, and there'd been nothing to do but let her have the bag. Jesus, what else could he do? Call her bluff? Say that she hadn't identified the contents, and risk Fillmore's taking over, calling the house dick maybe or the manager? He couldn't do that and she knew it, knew that he'd have to do just what he had done. Let her go, and keep his mouth shut. Let her take the money, and herself, to Tug. Tug's money, *his* money—the whole two hundred and thirty-two thousand.

And the terrible part about it was that he couldn't hate her. He tried to, but he couldn't. He wanted her as much—Christ, he wanted her more!—as he ever had.

Still sick and seething, he drove home that morning. A kind of vicious delight welled up in him as Mr. Rhodes met him at the door, mumbling worriedly about Miss Hillis' absence. He shoved past the old man. He turned and faced him, his pent-up fury spewing out at this easy and defenseless target.

"So she's left. What about it? What business is it of yours, anyway?"

"B-but—" Mr. Rhodes gave him a startled look. "But I—where could she have gone to? Why would she have left, gone away at night, without saying anything? Everything was all right when I went to bed. We'd sat up talking rather late, and then I helped her make down the lounge and—"

"I'll bet you did. It's a goddamned wonder you didn't try to go to bed with her. Christ knows, you haven't left her alone for a second since she's been here!"

"B-but—" The old man's mouth dropped open. "Son, you can't mean—"

"The hell I don't! That's probably why she left, because she couldn't stand the sight of you any more. She had all she could take, just about like I've had all I can take . . . Yes, you heard me right, by God! I'm sick of you, get me? Sick of looking at you, sick of listening to you, sick of—"

The phone rang. Raging, he let it ring on for a moment. And then he snatched up the receiver and almost yelled into the mouthpiece.

A muted chuckle came over the wire. "Something riling you, kid?" said Tug Trowbridge.

Dusty's hand jerked. His fingers went limp, and the receiver started to slide from his grasp.

"Now get this, kid," Tug went on swiftly. "I'll be by the side entrance there tonight, tomorrow morning rather, at one o'clock. Driving, yeah. I'll give three short taps on the horn, and—Dusty! You listening to me?"

"I'm l-lis—You can't!" Dusty stammered. "You—"

"Why not? I'll have this little collapsible bag you can slip under your jacket. You put mine in that, and bring it back out again, just like I'd given you a check on it. What—"

"But I—"

"Yeah?" Tug chuckled again. "Kind of surprised you, huh, thought it would be more complicated? Well, that's it. One o'clock tonight. Three taps on the horn."

"Wait!"

"Yeah? Snap into it, kid."

"I've got to see you," said Dusty. "Something's—I've got to see you!"

"Huh-uh. No, you don't. You just—"

"But I can't! I m-mean—" *He wouldn't dare tell Tug the whole truth. Tug had killed three men for that money, his share of it, and he would not believe the truth if he heard it. He would think that—*"I mean, that's what I've got to see you about."

Heavy silence for a moment. Then, softly, "You wouldn't be hungry, would you, kid? You wouldn't want it all ... and that ten grand reward besides?"

"No! My God, you know I wouldn't—that I couldn't do that."

"Yeah. Well, just so you know it, too, that you'd hang yourself if you tried it. They nab me and you're sunk, or you try putting the blocks to me and you're—"

"I'm not! It's—I can't explain now, but I've got to see you, *now*—"

"All right," Tug cut in, curtly. "I don't like it, but all right. Same place in about an hour."

The line went dead.

Dusty hung up the receiver, glanced at his father. The old man was slumped down into his chair, staring vacantly into nothingness. There was a stunned look on his face, a look of sickness that transcended sickness in his eyes. He was obviously unaware of the telephone conversation. It had meant nothing to him. Nothing, now, meant anything to him.

Dusty took a bill from his wallet, the first one his fingers touched, and flung it into his lap. A ten-spot, too damned much—anything was too damned much—but he had an idea that it wouldn't be much longer, now; with the props kicked out from under him, the old bastard might have sense enough to die. Meanwhile, it was worth any amount to crack the whip and see him cringe. To toss the bill at him as though it were a bone to a dog.

He waited a moment for the old man to speak—hoping for, wanting the opportunity to shut him up again. Then, as his father remained silent, he slammed out the door and headed for his rendezvous with Tug.

Things could be a lot worse, he thought. Yes, sir, they were not nearly as bad as they had seemed a while ago. He'd lost her, but at least she hadn't gone to Tug. She'd been working for herself, not Tug, and somehow that was not so hard to bear. He'd lost everything he wanted, but the loss had done something for him. It had pushed him to the point of losing, getting rid of, something he didn't want—someone who, he realized now, he had always hated. Yes, hated. Hated, hated, hated! Hated when he had touched her, the woman who was all woman. Hated—hated him—if he even came near her. Hated and wanted him to die. As he probably would die soon, now that he was completely stripped of reason to live.

And perhaps ... perhaps she was not lost yet: the she reborn in Marcia Hillis. Perhaps, with the ten thousand dollars in reward money, he could find her and ...

He turned off the highway, crossed over the railway tracks to the abandoned road on the other side. A car was parked just beyond the crest of the first hill. It was old and battered, but there was a look of sturdiness about it and the tires were new. The man behind the wheel was heavily bearded, dressed in faded overalls and jumper, and had an old straw work hat pulled low on his forehead. A sawed-off shotgun lay across his knees. He gestured with it impatiently as Dusty greeted him.

"So you wouldn't have known me. So forget it and start talking. What the hell did you have to see me about?"

EIGHTEEN

Tug cursed. He mopped his face with a blue bandanna handkerchief and went on cursing, pouring profanity through the polka-dot folds until he was strangling and breathless.

"Those bastards! Those stupid, blockheaded sons-of-bitches! Boy, I wish I hadn't already bumped 'em off! I'd like to do it all over again."

"Then you intended to kill her all along," Dusty said. "All that stuff you told me about how much she liked me and how you'd fix things up—"

"You kicking about it?" Tug turned on him fiercely. "You let her screw you for your share of the dough, and you're kicking?"

"I just want to get things straight. If you'd told me the truth in the first place . . ."

"Well, now you got it straight. We'd snatched her, hadn't we? Yeah, I know what you thought, but sure it was a snatch. So naturally she had to be bumped off. And if those stupid jerks had had any sense—" Tug broke off, choking, ripped out another string of curses. I should have known better'n to trust 'em with a dame like that. I should have known they'd try to keep her around a while, take her for a few tumbles before they knocked her off."

"But I don't understand. If she got away from them—"

"If? What the hell do you mean, if?"

"But why didn't they tell you?"

"Because they didn't know about it, goddammit! She made the break the night of the robbery, while we were all busy at the hotel. It had to 've happened, then. You can see that, can't you, for Christ's

sake? If she'd got away before then, there wouldn't have been any
hold-up. She'd have yelled to the coppers."

Dusty frowned. He stared out through the grimy windshield at the
sun-sparkled pavement. Back in the hillside underbrush a raincrow
cawed dryly. A gust of hot wind rolled over the abandoned fields,
rattling the yellowed, waist-high weeds.

"She knew all about me," Dusty said. "She knew where the money
was, that we hadn't settled on a way of splitting it up. So if she wasn't
working with you—"

"Goddammit, does it look like she was? She didn't know
nothing—it was just guesswork. She figured we couldn't decide on
how to divvy the dough until afterwards. I wouldn't know when
you'd be going back to work. I wouldn't know how soon I could get
in touch with you and—"

"She couldn't have guessed everything," Dusty said. "She couldn't
have guessed that the money would be in the checkroom. Someone
told her, that and everything else."

Tug shrugged irritably. "What's the difference? You got screwed,
that's the main thing, so that means I take a screwing, too. To hell
with her. What the hell difference does it make if—"

"I want to know," Dusty insisted. "I've got to know."

Tug hesitated, shrugged again. "All right. It don't make me look
real pretty, but—I guess I don't, anyhow, huh? And it's got no
connection with you. I've been playin' pretty rough, but I couldn't
cross you if I—"

"Who was she?"

"Bascom's daughter. She was a dancer like I said; that part was on
the level. Hillis was her stage name, and—"

"B-Bascom's—his—?"

"You want me to tell you or not? We ain't got all day. Every cop
in town is looking for me. Yeah, his daughter. I slapped the truth out
of her that morning. He'd had her check in there at the hotel. He'd
done everything he could to make you quit and it hadn't worked, so
she set you up for the push. She'd accuse you of attempted rape, see,
tell you she'd file charges if she ever saw you again. If you got
stubborn she'd actually call Bascom—her father, only you wouldn't
know that—and the way things would be stacked against you, you'd
have to quit. So . . . so that's the way it was, kid. Me and the boys put

the snatch on her. Bascom saw that I'd found out about him trying to cross me, and he figured she'd have a lot better chance of living if he got back on the track and stayed there. I kind of let him think that, see? He knew he was a goner himself, whatever happened, and all he could do now was—"

"Bascom," Dusty said slowly. "Why did he want me to quit? Why did he do all that, try so hard to—to—" He broke off, staring at Tug. Tug's eyes shifted uncomfortably. "Oh," he said. Then, "Well. . ."

Tug coughed and spat out the window. He shifted the shotgun slightly, mumbled something about, Christ, the goddamned heat.

"You were going to kill me," Dusty said. "Someone had to be killed and I was supposed to be it."

"What the hell?" Tug said, gruffly. "It was just business, kid, nothing personal. I really wanted it to be Bascom, right from the beginning, but—"

"Yes. He made a better fall guy, didn't he? But why did it have to be him or me? What difference would it have made if I'd quit or got fired and another bellboy had taken my place? You could still have gone right ahead and—"

"Huh-uh. It had to be someone that'd been there quite a while. Someone who knew the ropes and who'd have had time to pal up with me. Nope, if Bascom had got rid of you there wouldn't have been any hold-up. We'd have had to wait until the next racing season, and he knew I couldn't wait."

Dusty nodded. He had no more questions. None, at least, that Tug could answer. She'd spent two days there at the house, talking to him, probing him, watching him. And perhaps she'd been drawn to him, as she'd said; perhaps she'd felt pretty much the same about him as he felt about her. But there'd been some doubts in her mind. She hadn't been sure of his guilt, whether he'd been a willing and knowing accomplice to her father's murder, but neither had she been unsure. So—well, there was the answer: the clue to the exact amount of her sureness and unsureness. She had left him here practically penniless, to face Tug empty-handed with a story which might not be believed. She had been sufficiently sure-unsure to put him on a spot where he might have been killed, or—

Or? Dusty's pulse quickened suddenly . . . Tug. She'd have had no doubts about *his* part in the murder. Tug would have been the guy for her to get, and what better way was there—what other way, rather—than this one? She could only get to Tug through him. By making off with all the dough, she probably figured on—

Nuts. Nothing. It was all a pipedream. She'd wanted the money period. She'd got it period. That was all there was to it. That was as far as she'd thought. Like she'd pointed out, a hundred-odd grand wouldn't last long—only half as long as twice that much. So—

But maybe not! Jesus, maybe the pipedream was true! And there was nothing to lose by believing in it, nothing to lose regardless. Tug couldn't be told the truth. God, what he might do—would probably do—if he was told! Tug had to die, and—

Tug was watching him, studying him. Dusty lit a cigarette casually and thumbed the match out the window.

"Well?" he said.

"It ain't well," Tug grunted. "It ain't a goddamned bit well, but I guess I got to take it. Christ, if I'd known it was going to turn out this way, all that planning and sticking my neck out for a lousy fifty grand or so—"

"Fifty?" Dusty pretended surprise. "But she only got my half. Yours is still—"

"Who you kiddin'?" Tug glared at him savagely. "You'd just hand it all over and like it, huh? You wouldn't try to pick yourself up a few bucks—about ten thousand of 'em—some other way? Don't crap me, kid. Don't act stupid any more than you have already. You wouldn't play with me any longer'n it paid you, so I'm paying. I'm splitting with you right down the middle."

"Well," Dusty murmured. "I'll, uh, certainly appreciate—"

"Screw your appreciation. Forget it. Just don't pull anything funny, get me? Because maybe I'd get bumped off, but it wouldn't make you anything. They'd want to know why I was there, see, and they'd turn that place upside down to find out. And . . ."

And they wouldn't find anything. They might be suspicious, but they'd have no proof.

"All right," Tug concluded. "You better get going. I'll see you at one tomorrow morning just like I gave it to you over the phone."

"Suppose I can't be there right at one? I might get tied up on a call and—"

"Well, right around one then. Say five minutes of until five minutes after. I'll circle the block until I see you on the floor. And make sure you have my money."

Dusty nodded. He pushed open the door of the car and started to get out. Tug's voice, strangely strained and faltering, brought him to a halt.

"I—I always been nice to you, ain't I, kid? Always treated you like a friend, gave you plenty of dough without never makin' you feel cheap to take it?"

"Yes," Dusty agreed warmly. "You were always swell to me, Tug."

"Maybe it sounds like the old craperoo, now. But, well, I couldn't've gone through with the first deal. The boys thought I was nuts knockin' myself out to take you off the spot and put Bascom on it. It was risky as hell, y'know, and they gave me a pretty bad time about it. But I had to do it. I guess, kid—I know you probably won't believe me—but I guess there probably wouldn't have been any deal if you hadn't agreed to come in. I'd've just taken what dough I had and skipped."

Dusty murmured inaudibly, lowering his eyes to conceal their contempt. So this was the way a hard guy acted, this was the great Tug Trowbridge when the chips were down! Scared stiff, pleading. Whining about friendship.

"I ... it'll be all right, won't it, kid? You ain't—there ain't no reason why it wouldn't be all right?"

"How"—Dusty hesitated—"how do you mean?"

"I mean I won't be walkin' into a trap. You wouldn't—"

"I couldn't. You know that yourself."

"Yeah, but I been thinkin', kid. If that dame got away with *all* the money ..." Tug's hands came down on Dusty's shoulders. They gripped fiercely, then gently, humbly. "Just tell me the truth, Dusty. That's all the break I want. She didn't get it *all*, did she?"

Dusty shook his head. He said, "Of course not. Why would I give it all to her?"

"Don't be afraid to tell me, kid. If that's what happened, just tell me, for God's sake, an' ..."

"Afraid?" said Dusty, and now it was an effort to hide his disdain. "Why would I be afraid of you ... Tug?"

NINETEEN

Mr. Rhodes was in the kitchen when he reached home. His thin hair was damp from a recent shower, and his face was freshly shaved. He had done the little that he could to make himself presentable, someone not to be ashamed of, and now bustling about the cupboards and stove, he was demonstrating his usefulness, proving that here indeed, aged and ill or not, was an asset.

Dusty stood in the doorway watching him, grinning to himself. Contemptuously amused, his hatred challenged by what he saw. He had left Tug oddly exhilarated, elated and restive; he had been expecting an ordeal with the gangster and his nerves had been keyed for one. And there had been nothing to unkey them, no outlet for the building mass of nervous energy. Tug had been a virtual pushover, almost laughable there at the last. He was as bad as this old fool, still clutching at, fighting for, life—pleading for what he could no longer demand.

"Bill"—the old man kept up his brisk movements, spoke without turning around—"it was all my fault, this morning. You were tired and you've been under a lot of strain, and—well, anything you said, I know you didn't—"

"I meant it," said Dusty. "I meant every goddamned word of it."

"B-but—no! No, you didn't. Why would you—" A cup slid from Mr. Rhodes' hands, clattered and shattered against the sink.

Dusty laughed, jeered. His excitement was fresh water for the old seeds of hatred.

"Would you like to know a little secret, Dad? Would you like to know how your name got on that petition? Well, I'll tell you. I—"

"I—I—" Mr. Rhodes turned around at last. His eyes swept over Dusty, unseeing, blindly, and he moved dully toward the door. "I—I think I'd better lie down," he said. "I—I—"

"Oh, no you don't!" Dusty snapped. "I've been wanting to tell you for a long time, and now, by God, I'm—"

"I already know," the old man said absently. "Your mother—she and I, I think we both must have known right from the beginning, but we couldn't admit it. Now ... now, I think I'd better lie down ..."

He entered his bedroom and closed the door.

Later that day, when he had gone to bed, Dusty heard his father wandering around the house, moving back and forth through the rooms, aimlessly at first, then still aimlessly but with a kind of frantic desperation. He heard him leave the house, and, falling asleep, he did not hear him return. But when he left for the hotel that night, the old man was back in his room. Dusty listened at the door for a moment, to the blurred, muffled sounds that seeped through the panels.

It sounded like he was praying. Or singing. Kind of like he was praying and singing together. And occasionally there was something like a sob ... choked, strangling, rattling.

Dusty went on to the hotel.

At twenty minutes of one, he stepped into one of the lobby telephone booths and made a call to the police.

... They took no chances with Tug. They picked him up in their floodlights, from a mezzanine window of the hotel, from a second story window across the street. They shouted to him once. And perhaps he didn't understand the command, perhaps he was too startled to obey it, or perhaps—for he thrust the shotgun through the car window—he was starting to obey it. But the police did not deal in perhapses where Tug Trowbridge was concerned; they were resolving no doubts in his favor.

Five minutes after he drove up to the hotel, he was on his way to the morgue. Within the same five minutes, two detectives were searching the checkroom and two others were escorting Dusty to the police station, and still another two were speeding toward Dusty's house.

They found nothing there, of course; no trace of the loot from the robbery. Only the lifeless body of an old man, and a half-empty bottle of whiskey.

TWENTY

He had met most of the detectives before. They had talked to him at the hospital, visited him so often that they had become friendly, addressing him by his first name or nickname. But there was nothing friendly about them now. Curt and cold, they took turns at the questioning, asking the same questions over and over, making the same accusations over and over. Calling him you and bud and buster or, at best, Rhodes.

He sat on a hard chair under a brilliant light. Their voices lashed out from the shadows, impassive, relentless, untiring.

"Stop stalling . . ."

"We got you cold, bud . . ."

"Tell the truth and we'll make it easy on you . . . "

"Why did Tug want to see you? Come on, come on! you didn't have the loot stashed, why—"

"I told you!"

"Tell us again."

"He—all I know is what he said when he called me. Just before I called you. He said he was broke, and he wanted me to help him and—"

"Sure he was broke. He'd left the dough with you, and you wouldn't give him his cut."

"Why'd he come to you for money? What made him think you'd give him any?"

"Come on, come on!"

"I'm trying to tell you! He'd always been pretty nice to me, a lot of big tips, and I suppose he thought—"

"He was a pal of yours, wasn't he? You were like that. Ain't that right? AIN'T THAT RIGHT?"

"No! I mean he was nice to me, but—"

"Yeah. Cut you in on that robbery, didn't he? Made you his inside man, didn't he? Gave you the loot to stash, didn't he? Come on, why don't you admit it?"

"No! I didn't have anything to do with the robbery!"

"Why'd Tug want to see you then?"

"I told you why! I told you all I—"

"Tell us again . . ."

The door of the room burst open, and a man rushed in. "We found it, guys! We found the dough! Right where we thought it would be!"

"Swell. Attaboy!" The detectives congratulated him, turned back to Dusty. "Well, there you are, bud. Stalling won't get you anywhere, now."

"I'm not stalling! I just don't—"

"You heard what the man said. They found the dough there at the hotel."

"They couldn't have! I mean—"

"Yeah, we know. Because you didn't stash it there. Tug thought you did, but you'd sneaked it out."

"I d-didn't!"

"Leave him alone, you guys. Rhodes an' me understand each other . . . Now, look, kid (*whispering*), whyn't you and me make a little deal, huh? You just give me your word you'll take care of me, whatever you think's fair, and I'll make these jerks let you go. We can pick up the loot together, an' . . . What's the matter? Don't you trust me?"

"I don't know where it is! I didn't have anything to do with it! I—"

"Aaah, come on . . . Why did Tug want to see you, then?"

"I told you!"

"Tell us again."

. . . They gave up on him at seven that morning. Around ten o'clock, he was taken out of his cell and driven to the courthouse. The two detectives escorting him asked no questions, seemed almost indifferent to him. While he sat down on a bench outside the county attorney's office, they wandered away to the water cooler, stood there chaffing and joking with a couple of deputy sheriffs.

Dusty looked down at the floor dismally, listening to them, half listening. He raised his head, startled, then casually moved down to the end of the bench. The door to the county attorney's office was slightly ajar. He could hear two men talking inside. Arguing. One of them sounded irritable and stubborn; the other—the one who apparently was winning the argument—as placatory and resigned.

"Now, you know I'm right, Jack. We both know that kid is guilty as hell. He had to be, and the fact that the money has been returned—"

"Every nickel of it, by mail, Bob. And there's no clue to the sender. Under the circumstances, and regardless of our personal feelings, we have no case. Our only chance of sticking Rhodes was in tying him up with the money. Now that it's been returned . . ."

Dusty blinked. The money returned? It must be some kind of trap. This conversation was for his benefit; they meant him to hear it, so that—So that?

"He had an accomplice! When the accomplice saw Rhodes was in trouble, he—"

"But he wasn't in trouble at the time. The package was postmarked yesterday afternoon."

"He mailed it himself, then. That's it! Tug was turning on the heat, and . . . and, uh . . ."

"You see, Bob? You're talking in circles. If Rhodes had had the money, he could have paid off. Tug wouldn't have been turning on the heat, as you put it."

"But—but this just doesn't make sense, Jack. It leaves everything up in the air. Aside from the money, a man was murdered and—"

"You can't separate the one from the other, Bob. And who cares about that clerk, anyway? He was a crook, a fugitive from justice."

"Yes, but goddammit, Jack—"

"I know. There are a lot of loose ends. But they don't lead to Rhodes. They don't, and we can't make them."

"Well . . ."

"The hotel is satisfied. So is the insurance company. As long as they don't want to prosecute, why should we knock ourselves out? We can't win. Ten to one, the thing would never go to trial. He'd get a dismissal before—"

"Yeah. Well (grudgingly), all right. But I'm telling you something, Jack. Maybe we can't stick him on this, but I'm telling you. If that bastard ever pulls anything else—if he even looks like he's going to pull anything else—he's a dead pigeon! I'll hang him, by God, if I have to pull the rope myself!"

"Sure, ha, ha, and I'll help you. I feel the same way."

TWENTY-ONE

He no longer had a job. He did not have to be told that he could not
return to the Manton. And he did not care particularly—he felt dead,
inside, uncaring about everything. But the fact remained that he was
now without income, and practically broke. As for that reward on
Tug, well, he grimaced at his foolishness in ever expecting to collect
that reward. He had started to mention it to that county attorney, just
started to. And the guy had blown his top. He'd yelled for the other
guy to have him thrown back in the can, to throw him in and throw
the key away. And the other guy had jerked his head at the door, and
told him to beat it while he was still able to.

"You're a lucky boy, Rhodes, but don't lean on it too heavy. The
next time we pick you up . . ."

So Dusty had got out of there fast and, now, a dozen blocks away
from the courthouse, he was just slowing down. It was almost noon.
The humid heat poured over him stickily. His shirt was sweat-stuck
to his back, and he felt that he stank with the stench of the jail.

He walked two more blocks to the railroad station, and bathed in
one of the men's room showers. He got a shave in the station barber
shop, and, afterwards, coffee and toast in the grille. The food stuck in
his throat. He was hungry, but it seemed tasteless to him.

Leaving the grille, he moved out into the waiting room, stood
uncertainly in its vaulted dimness staring up at a bulletin board. Not
that he was going anywhere, of course. How could he? Where would
he want to go? He simply stood there, staring blindly, looking not
out but inward, puzzled and pitying himself much.

Bascom? Well, Bascom's life was forfeit anyway, wasn't it? Having
nothing to lose he could lose nothing. And his father, Mr. Rhodes—
well, he too had been a dead man already. Death had simply put an
end to futility. And as for Tug Trowbridge, a mass murderer, not
worth a second thought, deserving exactly what he had received. And
Marcia Hillis . . .

Why? Why, in the name of God, had she done it? What had she
hoped to gain by doing it? . . . He had a feeling that long, long ago,
he might have understood. But, then, naturally, back there in time,

there would have been nothing to understand. The situation would not have been posed then; he would have been incapable of bringing it about. Back there, so long ago, yet such a short time actually, he had been just another college student, and if he had been allowed to go on, if he had been given the little he was entitled to without being impelled to grab for it . . .

He left the railroad station, and walked quickly back toward the business section. He couldn't think about Marcia Hillis—face the riddle and reproach which she represented. He couldn't stop thinking about her.

Why? Why had he been singled out for this black failure, this bottomless disappointment? Why not, for example, some of those loud-mouthed clowns, the office holders and professional patriots, who had advanced themselves by ruining the old man? Mr. Rhodes had said that time, that history, would take care of them. But they had not been taken care of yet; they were still riding high. And he, he who was basically guilty of no more than compromise; he who, instead of fighting circumstance, had tried only to profit from it—

He was no better off than the old man. Alive, yes, but robbed of any reason to live.

. . . He got his car off the parking lot, drove it to a nearby sales lot. It was a good car; the dealer readily admitted its quality. But it seemed that there was just no demand for this particular make and model any more. The public, for mysterious and unreasonable reasons, just didn't want 'em at any price. Of course, if Dusty wanted to get rid of it *bad* enough . . . Dusty did. He accepted five hundred dollars without argument, and caught a bus homeward.

The money would just about take care of the old man's funeral, he supposed. Maybe he could get out of paying for it, but it would be troublesome, no doubt, and he'd had enough trouble for a while. Better get the old bas—better get him buried and forget him. Get it over with the fastest and least troublesome way possible. Probably it would have looked better if he'd gone by the funeral parlor this morning—but to hell with how it looked. He didn't have to care about looks. He was through pretending, and if people wanted to make something out of it, let 'em try.

He got off the bus, started past the little lunchroom-bar which his father had used to patronize. And inside he heard the creaking of stools, sensed the unfriendly eyes staring out at him. It was the same way when he passed the neighborhood grocery store, the barber shop and filling station, the open windows and doors of the dingy houses. Bums, loafers, white trash, scum floating from one day's tide to the next. And they were giving *him* the cold eye!

It couldn't be because he'd been in jail, a prime suspect in a quarter-million-dollar robbery. Jail was no novelty for the habitués of this neighborhood. So it must be because of the old man—they must think that ... It was unreasonable. They hadn't the slightest grounds for thinking that he had brought about Mr. Rhodes' death. But still, obviously, they did think that. Rather they knew that he had.

He began to walk faster. He was a little breathless when he reached the house, and he almost ran up the steps and into the living room. Relieved, and suddenly ashamed of the feeling, he sank down into a chair. He mopped his face, leaned back wearily with his eyes closed. The room seemed to echo with the beating of his heart, faster and louder, louder and faster, running a deafening race with his breathing, and suddenly frightened, he opened his eyes again. Now he was looking into his father's room—in at the bed. And something was ... something wasn't, of course, it was only a shadow, but—

He stood up. He backed out of the room, turned toward his own bedroom. And through the half-opened door, stretched out on the bed, he saw another shadow. He closed his eyes, reopened them. It was still there. A shadow, only, only an illusion born of the dimness and his imagination. But he backed away again. He entered the kitchen, and the shades were drawn high there and the sunlight streamed in. But somehow it was worse than the other rooms. He could see too clearly here, and the seeing was worse than the imagining ... The cupboards, recently rearranged so neatly. The sink, still half filled with dishwater. The shattered cup on the floor ...

But there was no place else to go. He was will-less to go elsewhere. He stood self-deserted, abandoned to a wilderness of the unbearable. For the wilderness would be everywhere now. It would always be everywhere.

Only she could have taken him out of it, filled the yawning emptiness, imparted meaning, and aroused desire. She could have

done that, but only she. Pursuing her, he had climbed deeper and
deeper into the pit, only to find nothing at the bottom but ... but the
bottom.

Blindly, he stumbled into a chair. He dropped down at the oilcloth-
covered table and buried his face in his arms.

He thought, "*Jesus, I can't stand it!*"

He sobbed out loud, "C-Christ, I can't stand it! I can't stand—"

The floor creaked behind him. He stiffened, choking back a sob,
too terrified to look around.

"I know ..." said Marcia Hillis, "but I'll help you, darling. We'll
stand it together."

TWENTY-TWO

They were on the lounge. His arms were around her and his face was
buried against her breast, and that, to have her again, was all that
mattered. He clung to her, wanting nothing more, only half-aware of
what she said.

"It's all right," he murmured, over and over. "It doesn't matter."

"You do understand, Dusty? It wouldn't have been any good the
other way. To start off like that, with stolen money ... I know what it
does to people. I know what it did to my mother, and my father—"

"It's all right," he said. "I don't care about the money."

"I wanted to ask you to return it. I was so afraid, for you, darling,
so terribly afraid of what Tug might do. But I hadn't had time to get
to know you, and I had to act quickly. And—and—"

"And you weren't quite sure, were you?" he said. "You felt that I
might have killed Bas—that I'd known your dad was going to be
killed."

"Well," she nodded reluctantly. "I didn't want to think that,
but ..."

"I don't blame you," he said. "You'd just about have to think that.
I was the inside man on the robbery, and how could I be unless I
knew that—knew everything that was going to happen? But Tug

didn't tell me, Marcia. He didn't have to explain anything to me. He threatened to kill you if I didn't do what I was told. That was all I knew, all I could think about. I was afraid to ask any questions, and—"

"I know, dear." She brushed her lips against his forehead. "It was too late to change plans then, but I knew—I was sure—that last night before I came to the hotel."

"Oh? How do you—"

"Your father. It was the first time we'd been alone together, you know, and all he could talk about was you. The sacrifices you'd made, everything you'd given up for him. How patient you were with him, how kind and generous. So ... so I knew, Dusty. I was sure. If you were like that, and I knew that you were, then you couldn't have ..."

"I—I didn't do much for him," Dusty said. "No more than I should have."

He was smiling to himself, exulting. Not, of course, because of his deception of her—he was sorry that that was necessary—but because of the broad triumph, the justification, which the deception repre-sented. He had been right, after all. The path into the pit had led not to emptiness but fullness.

"... heart failure, Dusty? The story in the morning paper was pretty vague."

"Heart failure induced by alcohol. That's what the police said. You see, the doctor didn't want him to know how sick he was, and as long as he'd never gone to any excesses, why ..." He explained, his voice muffled against the material of her dress. "It was my fault partly, I guess I knew he was feeling very depressed, and if I'd just bought him what he needed instead of giving him the money—"

"Don't! You mustn't feel that way, darling."

"Well ... If I'd had any idea at all that—"

"Of course. You don't need to tell me that." She kissed him again, murmured on soothingly, reassuringly ... When you loved someone you were sometimes too good for them for their own good. She knew how that was, how it had been with her father. "He thought a great deal of you, too, Dusty. He thought you were, well, not weak exactly, but a little too easy-going. But—"

Dusty nodded, humbly. He thought, *I'll have to get her out of this neighborhood fast. Get her away before any of these bastards talked to her.*

His arms tightened around her fiercely. Even the thought of losing her was terrifying. God, she couldn't find out the truth. He'd rather die than have her find out. He would die.

He held her, tighter and tighter, and still he could not get close enough to escape the fear. There was only one escape from that—there had never been but one escape from The Fear—and ... And she laughed, tenderly, and leaned back. She lay back on the lounge, pulling him with her.

"Yes, Dusty! Yes, darling!" she said, and her voice was eager. And, then, right at that long-waited-for moment, she suddenly frowned and pushed him away. "Dusty! Someone's stopped out in front."

"What? To hell with 'em," he said. "Just—"

"Don't! We can't!" She sat up firmly. "Who is it, Dusty?"

He released her reluctantly. He turned and looked through the curtains, cursed under his breath. It was a small black sedan. He didn't recognize the man behind the wheel, although he had a vaguely familiar look about him. But the man getting out of the car was Kossmeyer.

"My dad's lawyer." he grunted. "Now what the hell does he want?"

"Well..." She looked at him, a trace of a frown on her face. "He might want any number of things. After all, with your father dead..."

"Yeah. But, right now. Why the hell does he have to come now?"

The frown disappeared. Her eyes softened again with tenderness. And promise. And she kissed him swiftly. "I know, but it'll be all the better, darling. You'll see. I'll be waiting for you, waiting and ready, Dusty, and..."

She was gone, back into his bedroom. Frowning, he arose and went to the front door.

"Well," he said, curtly. "What do you want?"

"Maybe," said Kossmeyer, "I want to give you ten thousand dollars. Or maybe twenty thousand. Or maybe..."

He opened the screen and came in. He sat down and crossed his short legs, cocked an eyebrow expectantly at Dusty. Hesitantly, his pulse quickening, Dusty also sat down.

She hadn't closed the bedroom door. If Kossmeyer got nasty, she'd—But he could fix that, explain it. Kossmeyer had tried to take advantage of the old man. He'd put a stop to it, and the attorney had gotten sore at him.

"What do you mean?" he said. "Why should you want to give me ten or twenty thousand dollars?"

"We-el," Kossmeyer shrugged, "of course, I'm using the verb advisedly. I represent your dad's insurers, Rhodes. They're a client of mine."

"His insurers?" Dusty stared at him blankly. "What—?"

"Yeah, you know, the one he carried a policy with. Ten thousand dollars, double indemnity. We got kind of a little problem on it"— Kossmeyer raised his voice as Dusty started to interrupt. "Kind of a little problem. He died of heart failure, y'see, a natural cause. But the condition was brought on by, well, let's call it poison; that's what it actually was so far as he was concerned. In other words, the death could be construed as being an unnatural one, in which case, of course, the double indemnity clause would become applicable. Now—"

"Wait! Wait a minute!" Dusty raised his own voice. "You've made a mistake. Dad didn't have any insurance."

"He didn't, huh? You didn't know about it, huh?"

"Of course, he didn't!"

"Well," said Kossmeyer. "Well, let's see now." And he took a folded sheaf of papers from his pocket and smoothed them out against his knee. "According to our records, the records of the Great Southern and Midwest States Insurance Company, your father took out this policy approximately four years ago. You were entering college about that time, and I gather that he wanted to make sure of your education. Also, of course, he—"

Dusty laughed hoarsely, angrily. He said, "I'm telling you you're wrong. I remember when he took that policy out. My mother was the beneficiary, not me. Anyway—"

"Your mother was the beneficiary," Kossmeyer nodded equably. "Naturally, she'd give you such help as you needed, and she was able to give. And, naturally, in the event that her death preceded your father's, the insurance would simply become part of his estate. It wasn't necessary to name you the alternate beneficiary. When he died you'd inherit that estate . . . as, of course,"—the attorney looked up— "you were fully aware."

He waited. After a long moment, he said, "You don't seem very happy, Rhodes. You're the sole heir to a nice juicy wad, and you don't seem at all happy about it. It's kind of surprising, y'know. Certain recent events considered, I'd have said you were pretty hungry for dough."

"W-what—what do you mean by that?"

"Mean? Well, just that there's some other people around town that aren't very happy either. The hotel and their bonding company, and the county attorney. They kind of feel that they had their noses rubbed in it, know what I mean? They had to take it, but it left 'em pretty unhappy . . . But getting back to this insurance policy—"

"He didn't have one! It had lapsed! For God's sake, wouldn't I know if—if—" Dusty caught himself.

Kossmeyer grinned, and nodded again. "That's right, Rhodes. You'd know, all right. Your dad was pretty well along in years when he took that policy out, and he wasn't in the best of health. He had to pay a premium of almost one hundred and fifty dollars a month. And when he didn't have it to pay, when he had to depend on you . . ."

"I didn't pay it! I—"

"No. You gave him the money, and let him pay it. It had to be that way. The only money he had was what you gave him "

"But I tell you—Oh," Dusty said. "So . . . so that's what he did with it. I thought he was giving the money to you."

"Me? Why would I have dunned him, when I knew he didn't have it? The only payment I ever received was that one small retainer you gave me back at the start of the case."

"But that day I talked to you, you said—"

"I said that our expenses had been high. I didn't need to tell you that they hadn't been paid . . . What are you trying to hand me, Rhodes?" Kossmeyer grimaced cynically. "You knew where that money was going. Suppose he could have—from what I hear, I know damnned well you wouldn't have let him—but suppose he could have coaxed the dough out of you a few bucks at a time. Why would he want to anyway? What would be his purpose? The insurance was for your benefit. Why wouldn't he have told you about it?"

"I—I don't—"

But he did know, of course. The old man had been afraid to tell him. He hadn't wanted to admit his fear; probably, he had never admitted it consciously. But still the fear and distrust had been there: the knowledge that someone he loved—someone he had to love and be loved by—might be tempted to kill him.

And now?

Dusty brought a thoughtful frown to his face. Over his inner turmoil, he spread a shell of composure. Kossmeyer couldn't prove anything. He had said nothing yet that could not be explained on the grounds of personal malice. The thing now was to stop arguing with him, close the door on his insinuations. Otherwise . . .

He closed his mind on the alternative. She had heard nothing thus far that was even mildly damning. She would hear still less than that from now on.

"I wonder," he said, thoughtfully. "I wonder why Dad did that. I suppose . . . well, he probably thought I wouldn't let him make the sacrifices he had to if I'd known about it. He—"

"Sacrifices? With your dough?"

"It was as much his as mine. Anything I had was his, and—"

"It was, huh?" Kossmeyer's eyes glinted savagely. "Horseshit! I've talked to your neighbors around here! I've talked to the people you trade with. I've talked to your doctor. And I've got the same damned story out of every mother's son! That poor devil didn't have two dimes to rattle together. You never did a thing for him that you could get out of doing. It was a disgrace, by God, and the pitiful part about it was the way he stuck up for you—told everyone what a swell guy you were when a blind man could see that—"

"That's a lie! I don't care what anyone says, I—" Dusty paused, forced down the rising tide of panic. "I know what people probably say," he went on, "but it just isn't true. I gave him plenty of money, and I didn't pin him down as to how he spent it. I didn't know he was using it for those insurance premiums. I—why, my God, don't you see how the two things fit together? The one explains the other. The fact that he—that he went around like he did proves that he was using the money I gave him to pay for the insurance."

"Yeah? It don't prove anything like that to me!"

"But don't you see? If he'd used the money for himself, like I meant him to, he—he—"

He paused helplessly. He couldn't express the thought, present it as the pure truth that it was. But Kossmeyer must see it. Kossmeyer was an expert at separating truth from lies, and he must know that—that—Dusty gasped, his eyes widening in sudden and terrified understanding. He had chosen to play the game on the strict grounds of proof: to disregard the rules of right and wrong, truth and falsehood. Now Kossmeyer was playing the same way. Kossmeyer knew that he was guilty, of the old man's death and more. He *knew*, and as long as there were no rules to the game . . .

Kossmeyer. Just one little man, one small voice that could not be cried down. That was all, but in the world of bend-and-be-silent his littleness became large; he stood a Colossus, the little man, and the small voice was as thunder. Kossmeyer. He was retribution. He was justice, losing every game but the last one.

He said:

"At approximately nine o'clock last night, Rhodes, your father bought a fifth gallon of whiskey. You encouraged him to buy it, knowing full well that it would kill him . . . "

"No! I—"

"Where did he get the money then? He'd never had any such sum before. Never more than just enough for the barest necessities of life!"

"He did! He had plenty! I told you—"

". . . just barely enough. He returned to the house around nine-twenty—Yeah, I can prove all this. I been checking on you since I got the news flash early this morning and I can prove every goddamned bit of it!"

"But they're lying! They don't like me around here! They think that I—"

"You're telling me what they think?" Kossmeyer leaned forward grimly. "Save it. I heard enough already to make me sick . . . You left the house at approximately ten-fifteen. Aside from what anyone might say, you had to leave at about that time to get to the hotel and into your uniform by eleven. Between eleven and eleven-thirty, according to a sworn statement of the medical examiner, your father died. In other words, he was in very bad shape, near the point of death, when you left the house. Now"—the attorney suddenly smacked a fist in his palm—"now, Rhodes. Perhaps you can tell me this. You say you didn't want your father to die, and yet he was dying before you left for work. He might easily have been saved by prompt medical attention. So I ask you, Rhodes"—*smack*—"I demand to know,

Rhodes"—*smack, smack*—"why you did not intervene to save his life? Why, instead, you walked callously out of the house and left this helpless old man to die!"

Dusty licked his lips. He stared at Kossmeyer, staring beyond this moment and into the one that must certainly succeed it . . . *The courtroom. The coldly knowing eyes. The thundered question, Why, Rhodes? Why didn't you, Rhodes? And the smacking fist, the hammering fist, building a gallows.*

She was hearing all this. Unless he could say something, think of something, she would have to believe it . . .

"I—I didn't know," he said. "I didn't see him before I left."

"Oh." Kossmeyer appeared crestfallen. "Well! He was in his room, huh? He had his door closed and you didn't want to disturb him?"

"Y-yes! Yes, that's right."

"Uh-hah. I see. But if the door was closed, how did you know he was in the room?"

"Well, I—I could kind of hear him, you know."

"Yes? How do you mean you could hear him?"

"I—I mean, I—"

Kossmeyer was grinning again. Suddenly, briefly, Dusty's terror became cold fury.

"To hell with you! I haven't done anything! I don't have to answer your questions!"

"Sure, you don't," Kossmeyer said. "We can let the county attorney ask 'em. That's one of his boys I got out in the car."

"Well, I . . ." The county attorney. Kossmeyer and the county attorney. They'd had to take lies for truth, and now they would make truth into lies. He'd set the rules for the game, and now . . . "I spoke to him," he said. "I called goodnight to him!"

"Oh?" Kossmeyer was puzzled, he was astonished. "Then you weren't afraid of disturbing him? You knew he was awake?"

"Yes! I mean, well, I wasn't sure. I just called to him softly, and—and—"

"And he answered you? He said good night, son, or something of the kind? I'd say he must have. Otherwise, since you say you could hear him, he was audible to you through a closed door—otherwise, you'd have been alarmed. You'd have looked in on him."

"Well . . . ?"

Dusty started to shake his head. He changed the shake to a nod. "Y-yes. He answered me."

"What did he say?"

"W-what...? Well, just goodnight. Goodnight, Bill."

"Now, I wonder," said Kossmeyer. "Now, I wonder if you couldn't be mistaken. The man was right at death's doorstep. He was in the throes of alcoholic coma. And yet, when you addressed him, he replied to you. He responded in such a way that—"

"All right, then! I guess—maybe I didn't tell him good night! I didn't speak to him! I just heard him in there, I knew he was all right and—"

"But he wasn't all right!"

"Well I—I mean, it sounded like he was. I could hear him snoring—"

"You *could?*" Kossmeyer's astonishment was grotesque. "I know any number of doctors who will be very surprised at that statement. They'll tell you that anything resembling somnolence would have been impossible at the time in question. His physical suffering would have been too great, his mental state too chaotic..."

Was it true or not? Must it have been that way, and no other? He didn't know. Only Kossmeyer knew, and the game had no rules.

"I'll tell you what you heard, Rhodes. I'll show you..."

"N-No! Don't!"

"Yes," said Kossmeyer. "He'd been poisoned. He was in agony, out of his mind, and—"

His face sagged. Its lines became aged and gentle, and then they tightened, and the folds of skin swelled outward. He swallowed. His neck veins stood out like ropes. A thin stream of spittle streaked down from the twisted mouth, and he gasped and there was a rattle in his throat—a sound overlaid by other sounds. Mumbled, muttered, crazily jumbled yet hideously meaningful. And the gasping rattle, the rattle and the choking. The choking...

Dusty closed his eyes. The sounds stopped, and he opened them again. Kossmeyer was standing. He jerked his head toward the door.

"You made one mistake, Rhodes! One big mistake. You didn't figure on having to tangle with me."

"But I didn't! I m-mean, you know I didn't kill him! I didn't know about the whiskey or the insurance policy—"

"You'll have a chance to prove it. Come on!"

"Come—? W-where?"

Not that it mattered now. For he had heard it at last, the terrible sound he had been waiting to hear. The closing of a door. Softly but firmly. Finally.

Shutting him out of her life forever.

"Where?" said Kossmeyer. "Did you say where, Rhodes?"

Kossmeyer's legs were very close together; they seemed fastened together. And his hands were behind him, as though pinioned. His head sagged against his chest, drooped on a neck that was suddenly, apparently, an elongated rail of flesh. And gently, as a light breeze rustled the curtains, his body swayed.

He was hanging.

He was hanging.

In the quiet, summer-bright room, Dusty saw himself hanged.

AFTER DARK,
MY SWEET

ONE

I rode a streetcar to the edge of the city limits, then I started to walk, swinging the old thumb whenever I saw a car coming. I was dressed pretty good—white shirt, brown slacks and sport shoes. I'd had a shower at the railroad station and a hair-trim in a barber college, so all in all I looked okay. But no one would stop for me. There'd been a lot of hitchhike robberies in that section, and people just weren't taking chances. .

Around four in the afternoon, after I'd walked about ten miles, I came to this roadhouse. I went on past it a little ways, walking slower and slower, arguing with myself. I lost the argument—the part of me that was on-the-beam lost it—and I went back.

The bartender slopped a beer down in front of me. He scooped up the change I'd laid on the counter, sat down on his stool again, and picked up a newspaper. I said something about it was sure a hot day. He grunted without looking up. I said it was a nice pleasant little place he had there and that he certainly knew how to keep his beer cold. He grunted again.

I looked down at my beer, feeling the short hairs rising on the back of my neck. I guessed—I knew—that I should never have come in here. I should never go in any place where people might not be nice and polite to me. That's all they have to do, you know. Just be as nice to me as I am to them. I've been in four institutions, and my classification card always reads just about the same:

> *William ("Kid") Collins*: Blond, extremely handsome; very strong, agile. Mild criminal tendencies or none, according to environmental factors. Mild multiple neuroses (environmental); Psychosis, Korsakoff (no syndrome) induced by shock, aggravated by worry. Treatment: absolute rest, quiet, wholesome food and surroundings. Collins is amiable, polite, patient, but may be very dangerous if aroused . . .

I finished the beer, and ordered another one. I sauntered back to the restroom and washed my face in cold water. I wondered, staring at myself in the mirror, where I'd be this time tomorrow and why I was bothering to go anywhere since every place was just like the last one. I wondered why I hadn't stayed where I was—a week ago and a thousand miles from here—and whether it wouldn't be smart to go back. Of course, they hadn't been doing me much good there. They were too overcrowded, too under-staffed, too hard up for money. But they'd been pretty nice to me, and if I hadn't gotten so damned restless, and if they hadn't made it so easy to escape ... It was so easy, you know, you'd almost think they wanted you to do it.

I'd just walked off across the fields and into the forest. And when I came out to the highway on the other side, there was a guy fixing a tire on his car. He didn't see me. He never knew what hit him. I dragged him back into the trees, took the seventy bucks he was carrying and tramped on into town. I caught a freight across the state line, and I'd been traveling ever since ... No, I didn't really hurt the guy. I've gotten a little rougher and tougher down through the years, but I've very seldom really hurt anyone. I haven't had to.

I counted the money in my pocket, totting it up mentally with the change I'd left on the bar. Four bucks. A little less than four bucks. Maybe, I thought, maybe I ought to go back. The doctors had thought I was making a little progress. I couldn't see it myself, but ...

I guessed I wouldn't go back. I couldn't. The guy hadn't seen me slug him, but what with me skipping out about that time they probably knew I'd done it. And if I went back they'd pin it on me. They wouldn't do it otherwise. They probably wouldn't even report me missing. Unless a guy is a maniac or a kind of big shot—someone in the public eye, you know—he's very seldom reported. It's bad publicity for the institution, and anyway people usually aren't interested.

I left the rest room, and went back to the bar. There was a big station wagon parked in front of the door, and a woman was sitting on a stool near mine. She didn't look too good to me—not right then, she didn't. But that station wagon looked plenty good. I nodded to her politely and smiled in the mirror as I sat down.

"Rather a warm day," I said. "Really develops a person's thirst, doesn't it?"

She turned her head and looked at me. Taking her time about it. Looking me over very carefully from head to foot.

"Well, I'll tell you about that," she said. "If you're really interested in that, I'll give you my theory on the subject."

"Of course, I'm interested. I'd like to hear it."

"It's a pronoun," she said. "Also an adverb, conjunction and adjective."

She turned away, picking up her drink again. I picked up my beer my hand shaking a little.

"What a day," I said, kind of laughing to myself. "I was driving south with this friend of mine, Jack Billingsley—I guess you know the Billingsleys, big real estate family?—and our car stalled, and I walked back to a garage to get help. So I get back with the tow-truck, and darned if that crazy Jack isn't gone. I imagine what happened is—"

"—Jack got the car started himself," she said. "That's what happened. He started looking for you, and somehow you passed each other on the highway. Now he doesn't know where you are, and you don't know where he is."

She finished her drink, a double martini, and motioned to the bartender. He fixed her another one, giving me a long hard glare as he placed it in front of her.

"That darned crazy Jack," I said, laughing and shaking my head. "I wonder where in the world he can be. He ought to know I'd come in some place like this and wait for him."

"He probably had an accident," she said. "In fact, I think I read something about it."

"Huh? But you couldn't—"

"Uh-huh. He and a young lady called Jill. You read about it too, didn't you, Bert?"

"Yeah." The bartender kept on staring at me. "Yeah, I read about it. They're all wet, mister. They got their heads busted. I wouldn't wait around for 'em much longer, if I was you."

I played it dumb—kind of good-natured dumb. I said I certainly wasn't going to wait very much longer. "I think I'll have just one more beer, and if he hasn't shown up by then I'm going to go back to the city and catch a plane."

He slopped me out another beer. I started to drink it, my eyes beginning to burn, a hedged-in feeling creeping over me. They had my number, and hanging around wasn't going to make me a thing. But somehow I couldn't leave. I couldn't any more than I could have walked away from the Burlington Bearcat that night years ago. The Bearcat had been fouling me, too, giving it to me in the clinches, and calling me all kinds of dirty names. He'd kept it up—just like they were keeping it up. I couldn't walk away from him, just like I couldn't walk away from them, and I couldn't get him to stop, just like I couldn't get them to stop.

It came back with neonlike clarity. The lights were scorching my eyes. The resin dust, the beerish smell of ammonia, were strangling me. And above the roar of the crowd, I could hear that one wildly shrieking voice. "Stop him! Stop him! He's kicking his brains out! It's murder, MURDER!"

Now I raised my glass and took the rest of the beer at a gulp. I wished I could leave. I wished they'd lay off of me. And it didn't look like they would.

"Speaking of planes," she was saying. "I heard the funniest story about a man on a plane. Honestly, I just thought I'd die laughing when I—" She broke off, laughing, holding her handkerchief to her mouth.

"Why don't you tell it to him?" The bartender grinned, and jerked his head at me. "You'd like to hear a real funny story, wouldn't you, mister?"

"Why, yes. I always enjoy a good story."

"All right," she said, "this one will slay you. It seems there was an old man with a long grey beard, and he took the plane from Los Angeles to San Diego. The fare was fifteen dollars but he only had twelve, so they dropped him off at Oceanside."

I waited. She didn't say anything more. Finally, I said, "Yes, ma-am? I guess I don't get the point."

"Well, reach up on top of your head. Maybe you'll feel it."

They both grinned at me. The bartender jerked his thumb toward the door. "Okay, Mac. Disappear."

"But I haven't done anything, I've been acting all right. You've got no right to—"

"Beat it!" he snapped.

"I haven't asked you for anything," I said. "I came in here to wait

for a friend, and I'm clean and respectable-looking and polite. And—
and I'm an ex-serviceman and I've been to college—had a year and a
half of college and—and—"

The veins in my throat were swelling. Everything began to look
red and blurred and hazy.

I heard a voice, her voice, say, "Aah, take it easy, boy. Don't race
your motor, kid." And from what I could see of her through the
haze, she didn't look so bad. Now, she looked rather gentle and
pretty—like someone you'd like to have for a friend.

The bartender was reaching across the counter for me "Don't,
Bert! Leave the guy alone!" she said, and then she let out a scream.
Because he'd grabbed me by the shirt front, and when he did that I
grabbed him. I locked an arm around his neck and dragged him halfway across the counter. I slugged him so hard it made my wrist ache.

I let go of him. He slid down behind the counter, and I ran.

TWO

It's funny how wrong your first impressions of people can be. Me,
now, the first impression I'd had of her was that she wasn't much to
look at—just a female barfly with money. And she *did* hit the booze
too hard. Even I could see that. But I was all wrong about her looks.
She was young. I'm thirty-three and she couldn't have been any older.
She was pretty—beautiful, I should say—when she dolled herself up
a little. She'd led a hard life for a long time, and it told on her face.
But she had the looks, all right, the features and the figure. And
sometimes—well, quite a bit of the time—she could act just as nice as
she looked.

I'd only got down the road a few hundred yards when the station
wagon drew up beside me and she swung the door open. "Get in,"
she said, smiling. "It's all right. Bert isn't going to make any trouble
for you."

"Yeah? Well, he's not going to get the chance, lady. I just stopped
in there for a minute, and now I'm going on."

"I tell you it's all right. Bert's the last person in the world to holler for the cops. Anyway, we're not going back there. I'm taking you home with me."

"Home with you?" I said.

"It's not far from here." She patted the seat, smiling at me. "Come on, now. That's a good boy."

I got in rather uncertainly, wondering why she was acting so friendly now when she'd been so ornery a little while ago. She answered the question just as I started to ask it.

"I had a couple of reasons," she said. "For one thing, I didn't want Bert to know that I might be interested in you. The less a man like Bert knows about my business the better I like it."

"What else?"

"The other reason . . . well, I wanted to see what you would do; how nervy you were. Whether you were really the kind of guy I thought you might be."

I asked her what kind of guy that was exactly. She shrugged, a little impatiently.

"Oh, I don't know! Maybe . . . probably it doesn't make any difference, anyway."

The highway dipped down through a grove of trees with a narrow lane leading off to the south. She turned the car into the lane, and after about a quarter of a mile, just over the crest of a little hill, we came to her house.

It was a big white cottage standing in a clearing among several acres of trees. It looked like it might have been a nice place at one time. It still was fairly nice, but nothing like it could have been. The paint was peeling and dingy. Some of the front steps were caved in. Bricks from the chimney were scattered over the roof, and there were big rusted-out holes in some of the screens. The lawn didn't look like it had ever been cut. The grass was so high you could hardly see the sidewalks.

She sat looking out the window for a moment after we'd stopped. Then, she sighed and shook her head, murmuring something about work being the curse of the drinking classes.

"Well, here we are." She opened the door. "By the way, I'm Mrs. Anderson. Fay Anderson."

"I'm very happy to meet you, Mrs. Anderson."

"And I'm very happy to meet you. It's a unique privilege. I don't believe I've ever met a man before who didn't have a name."

"Oh, excuse me," I laughed. "I'm Bill Collins."

"No! Not *the* Bill Collins."

"Well, uh, I don't know. I guess maybe I am.'

"Well, don't you feel bad about it. It's your story so you stick with it."

She was changing again, getting back to the orneriness. She was on and off like that all the time, I found out—nice to you one minute—needling you the next. It all depended upon how she felt, and how she felt depended upon how much booze she had in her. With just the right amount—and that changed, too, from hour to hour—she was nice. But if she didn't have it, if she had a little too much or not quite enough, she got mean.

"Well, come on!" she snapped. "What are you waiting for, anyway? Do you want me to carry you piggy-back?"

I hesitated, kind of fumbling around for something to say. She swore under her breath.

"Are you worried, Mr. Collins? Are you afraid I'll rob you of your money and valuables?"

I laughed and said, no, of course not. "I was just wondering . . . well, what about your husband? You said you were—"

"He won't rob you either. They only let him out of his grave on national holidays."

She slammed out of the car and flounced away a few steps, then she kind of got control of herself, I guess, and she came back.

"I've got a big steak in the refrigerator. I've got some cold beer and just about everything else in the beverage line. I've got some pretty good suits that belonged to my husband, and— But let it go. Do whatever you want to. Just say the word and I'll drive you back to the highway."

I said I wasn't in any particular hurry to get back to the highway. "I was just wondering—I mean, what can I do for you?"

"How do I know?" Her voice went brittle again. "Probably nothing. What's the difference? Who are you to do anything for anyone?"

"Well, I guess I will come in for a little while."

We went in through the back door. She got busy in the kitchen fixing drinks, and I went on into the living room. Everything was kind of torn up and messy in there, like it was in the kitchen. The furniture was good—or rather it had been good—but there wasn't a whole lot of it. It looked incomplete, you know, like there might have been more at one time.

I kind of sauntered around, looking things over. I picked up some newspaper clippings from the sideboard and began to turn through them. They were all pictures of the same boy, a little seven-year-old youngster named Charles Vanderventer III. I tossed them back on the sideboard and sat down.

She came in with the drinks, bringing the bottle with her. While I was having one drink she had three.

"Bill Collins," she leaned back and looked at me. "Bill Collins. You know, I think I'll call you Collie."

"All right. A lot of people do call me Collie."

"That's because you look like one. Stupid and shaggy and with a big long nose to poke into other people's business. Just what was the idea in snooping around those clippings?"

"I wasn't snooping. They were just lying there so I picked them up and looked at them."

"Uh-huh. Oh, sure. Naturally."

"He's, uh, his family are friends of yours?" I was just making conversation; trying to steer her away from the orneriness. "You're related in some way?"

"He's my great-great grandson," she said. "One of the poorer branches of the family. I know you won't believe it, but they only have a paltry forty million dollars."

She poured another drink, filling her glass half full of whiskey. She leaned back again, face flushed, her narrowed black eyes sparkling with meanness.

"You're very fast with your mitts, Collie. Fast and efficient. Did you ever fight professionally?"

"A little. A long time ago I had a few fights."

"What happened? Stop a few too many with your head?"

"There's nothing wrong with my head," I said. "I got out of it before there was anything wrong."

"And when did you get out of jail? The last time, that is."

I tried to keep smiling. I said that, well, as a matter of fact I had

had a few brushes with the police. Just like any citizen would. Never anything serious. Just little misunderstandings and traffic tickets and so on.

"Oof!" She rolled her eyes. "Run for the hills, men!"

"I'll tell you something, Mrs. Anderson. I'd like to correct an erroneous impression you seem to have about me. I'm not at all stupid, Mrs. Anderson. I may sound like I am, but I'm really not."

"You'll have to swear to that, Collie. You give me your sworn statement, signed by two witnesses, and I'll take it under consideration."

"I'm not stupid. I don't like for people to treat me like I am. Most of my life I've been in—I've worked in places where it was hard to converse with anyone on an equal footing. It was hard to carry on an intelligent conversation, so I kind of lost the knack."

"Roger, Wilco. Collins coming in on the beam."

"I'm trying to explain something. Why don't you be polite and listen? I was saying that when you don't get to talk much, you get to where you sound kind of funny when you do talk. Kind of stilted and awkward, you know. You're not sure of yourself."

"Shut up!"

"But I—"

"Dammit, will you shut up? There's somebody coming!"

She jumped up and ran into the kitchen. I followed her. I watched as she opened the back door and stepped out onto the porch. It was getting dark now. The lights of a car swept over the trees and blinked out. The driver tapped out a shave-and-a-haircut on his horn.

Fay Anderson laughed and stayed down the steps.

"It's all right, Collie. It's just Uncle Bud."

"Uncle . . . Uncle Bud?"

"Fix yourself another drink. Fix three of them. We'll be in in a minute."

It wasn't a minute. It was a lot nearer, I'd say, to thirty minutes. And I couldn't hear their conversation, of course, but I had a strong hunch that I was the subject of it.

I fixed three drinks, and drank them.

THREE

His real name was Stoker, Garret Stoker. He wasn't her uncle and
I doubt that he was anyone's, but everyone called him Uncle Bud.
He was a man of about forty, I think. He had snowy, prematurely
grey hair, and warm friendly eyes, and a smile that made you feel
good every time he turned it on. I don't know how she'd gotten
acquainted with him, and probably she didn't either. Because that's
the kind of a guy he was, if you know what I mean. You meet guys
like Uncle Bud once—just over a drink or a cup of coffee—and you
feel like you've known them all your life. They make you feel that
way.

The first thing you know they're writing down your address and
telephone number, and the next thing you know they're dropping
around to see you or giving you a ring. Just being friendly, you
understand. Not because they want anything. Sooner or later, of
course, they want something; and when they do it's awfully hard to
say no to them. No matter what it is. Even when it's like something
this Uncle Bud wanted.

He wrung my hand, and said it was a great pleasure to meet me.
Then, still hanging onto my hand, giving it a little squeeze now and
then, he turned around to Fay.

"I just can't understand it, Fay. I still believe you're joking with
me. Why, I'd have bet money that there wasn't a man, woman or
child in the United States who hadn't heard of Kid Collins."

"Bet me some money," she said. "I'll give you seven to five."

"Well . . ." He laughed and released my hand. "Ain't this little lady
a case, Kid? Never serious for a moment. But she's true-blue,
understand, a real little pal, and the kidding's all in fun. She don't
mean a thing by it."

"Yes, sir, I understand."

"Let's see, now. When was that last fight of yours, the big one?
Wasn't it in, uh—?"

"It—it was in 1940. The Burlington Bearcat. He was—" My voice
trailed away. "I mean it wasn't a very big fight, sir."

"Sure sure. A preliminary bout. But it was still a mighty big fight.

Uh, it was in—I was arguing with a fellow about it the other day, and he claimed it was held in Newark. I said it was in, uh—"

"It was in Detroit,' I said.

"That's right. That's exactly right!" he exclaimed. "Detroit, 1940, a four-round prelim. What did I tell you Fay? Didn't I tell you I knew the Kid's record backwards and forwards?"

Fay groaned and slapped herself on the forehead. Uncle Bud winked at me, and I grinned and winked back at him.

I began to like him a lot.

Fay said that if we wanted any dinner, we could darned well fix it ourselves. So that's what we did. Uncle Bud pounded the steak and put it on to broil, and I peeled and sliced potatoes. He opened some cans of peas and apple sauce, and I made coffee and ice water.

"Well, Kid," he said, while we were waiting for the stuff to cook, "I'm glad you've decided to settle down for a while. Now, that you've found friends—people who admire you and really take an interest in you—"

"Settle down?" I blinked. "Settle down where?"

"Why right here—where else?" he said firmly. "Our little lady kind of needs someone to keep an eye on her, and there's a nice little apartment out over the garage. Yes, sir, you just move right in, Kid. Just take it easy for a few days. Get rested up and keep Fay out of trouble and I'll see what I can stir up for you. I got an idea that I might be able to put you next to something pretty good."

He nodded to me, giving the steak a turn.

I said, maybe he already had his eye on something he could put me next to.

"Sharp." He laughed. "I told Fay you were. I said, 'Now, Fay, maybe the guy's had a rough time, but if that's Kid Collins you've got with you, he's nobody's fool. He's nervy and he's sharp,' I said. 'He'll know a good angle when he sees one and he'll have what it takes to carry through on it. And you treat him right, and he'll treat you right.'"

"Look, sir. Look, Uncle Bud . . ."

"Yeah, Kid? Go right ahead and get it off your chest."

"Well, I appreciate your kindness, the compliments and all, but— but you don't really know anything about me. You couldn't. You're

just trying to be nice, and probably if you really knew the kind of guy
I was, you wouldn't feel like this."

"I'll tell you what I know, I know people, Kid. I know what they'll
do and what they won't. Or, put it another way, what they can do
and what they can't. I was a city detective here for years—maybe Fay
told you? Well, I was, and I was able to put a lot of bright boys next
to some pretty good things. Some of them had played an angle before,
but most of 'em hadn't. They'd never turned a trick—didn't think
they could—until I showed them the way."

"And you're not a detective, now?"

He glanced around sharply, frowning at me for the first time.
Then, he pursed his lips and went back to stirring the potatoes.

"We'll have to see," he said absently. "We'll have to get better
acquainted. I think you'd be just right—smart enough, but not
too . . ."

"Yes?" I said.

"Never mind, Kid." His smile came back. "There's no rush. It's
something we'll have to take our time on."

We ate dinner; he and I did, rather. Fay came to the table, but she
didn't really eat anything. She just sat there—mussing the food on
her plate, drinking and sniping at us every time we opened our
mouths.

"This damned house," she said, glaring at Uncle Bud. "I thought
you were going to turn it in for me right away. I thought you were
going to make me a nice little profit on it. You talked me into buying
the damned dump, and then you—"

"Now, Fay," he said, calmly. "You'll do all right on it. You'll make
out—one way or another."

"Oh, yeah?" Her eyes wavered. "And what about that lousy station
wagon? I tie up practically the last nickel I got in the thing, and
you—"

"Now, Fay. You know I got you a good deal on it. You know you
need a good car living out here."

"Who the hell wants to live out here?" She almost yelled it. "Who
the hell talked me into it?"

"You'll thank me for it. You just trust your old Uncle Bud, and
you'll be wearing diamonds."

He turned the conversation to me, asked me what I'd been doing since I quit fighting. I said I'd been in the army for a while right after I quit, and I'd just been knocking around since then.

"The army, huh? Get along all right?"

"Why, pretty good. I thought I did, anyway."

Fay laughed. Uncle Bud frowned and shook his head at her.

"I did the best I could," I said. "But they weren't very patient, and it kind of looked like they were trying to see how tough they could make things on me. So, well, I landed in the brig a few times, and finally they sent me to the hospital. And right after that they let me go."

"Mmm-hmm." He nodded thoughtfully. "You were, uh, all right then? Just, uh, just couldn't adjust to the military life. Well, that's not unusual. I understand that there were any number of men who had that kind of trouble."

Fay laughed again and Uncle Bud gave her another shake of his head.

"Sure," he said, softly. "I understand how it was, Kid. It's that way all through life, it seems like. People expecting a guy to get along with them, but they won't try to get along with him. Maybe he just needs a little help, just a little understanding, but ninety-nine times out of a hundred he won't get it."

I said I wouldn't want him to get the idea that there was anything wrong with me. There really wasn't much wrong with me, you know—not then, there wasn't—and I felt that I had to say it. Because if there's one thing that scares people, it's mental trouble.

You can be an ex-convict, even a murderer, say, and maybe it won't bother 'em a bit. They'll give you a job, take you into their homes, make friends with you. But if you've got any kind of mental trouble, or if you've ever had any, well, that's another story. They're afraid of you. They want no part of you.

Uncle Bud seemed to believe what I told him. The way he had me sized up, I guess, was as a guy who hadn't been too bright to begin with and had got just a shade punchy in the ring.

"Sure, you're okay, Kid. All you need is some dough, enough so's you can take life easy and not have to worry."

"Yeah. But . . . well, I guess I ought to tell you something else, too, Uncle Bud. I've—I've always tried to do the right thing. Never anything really bad or—"

"Oh, well." He spread his hands. "What do the words mean, Kid? What's good and what's bad? Now, I'd say it was bad for a nice guy like you to have to go on like he's been going. I'd say it would be good if you never had to worry about money for the rest of your life."

"Yeah, I guess it would be."

"Naturally. Naturally, you wouldn't want to hurt anyone. You wouldn't have to. It would just be a case of putting pressure on certain people—people that have more dough than they know what to do with—and making 'em come across. That would be all right, wouldn't it?"

I hesitated. "Well, it sounds—"

And Fay slammed her glass down on the table.

"It sounds rotten!" she yelled at Uncle Bud. "It sounds terrible, filthy, lousy! I don't know why I ever—I won't have any part of it, understand? You may talk Stupid here into it, b-but you can go ahead without me, and I w-won't—"

She stumbled to her feet, crying, and staggered out of the room. Uncle Bud raised his eyebrows at me.

"Poor little lady. But she'll snap out of it. Now, why don't you and I do these dishes, and then I'll run along."

We cleared up the dishes. I tried to talk to him while we were working, trying to get something more out of him about this proposition he had in mind. But he kept changing the subject, his voice getting shorter and shorter. And finally he turned on me, half-snarling, and told me to drop it.

"Forget it! I'll tell you whatever you need to know, when you need to know it!"

He glared at me, his eyes kind of glazed. And I was too startled to say anything back to him. I'd thought he was such an easy-going, good-natured guy, and now he looked like some sort of vicious, mean-tempered animal.

"I'll tell you something else, too." He tapped me on the chest. "I ain't just kidding about you sleeping in the garage. That's where you sleep, get me, and you sleep by yourself. You don't make no play for the little lady."

I nodded, feeling kind of hurt and embarrassed. I guessed I had stared at her quite a bit that evening, but I hadn't meant anything by it. I didn't have the slightest idea of trying to take advantage of her.

"Maybe I'd better clear out. If you think I'm that kind of guy, I wouldn't want to stick around."

"Aw, now, don't take it that way," he said soothingly. And suddenly he was his old self again. "You'll have to excuse me, Kid. Just forget I said anything. I've had a pretty hard day, and I spoke without thinking."

I walked out to the car with him. We shook hands, and he said not to worry about a thing, just to take it easy and he'd be out to see me the next day. He left then, and I went back into the house. And, of course, I didn't feel very easy. I couldn't help but worry.

I fixed myself a couple of drinks. They kind of eased me down a little, so I fixed another one. I sauntered over to the sideboard with it, and picked up the newspaper clippings again. I thumbed through them absently, wondering why they were there and why Fay'd had me come here—and suddenly I stopped wondering. Suddenly I knew why. I didn't know the how of it, the details, but I knew what it was all about.

I dropped the clippings, as though they'd all at once caught fire. I turned back around, and there she was, just coming out of the bedroom. She was pale and sick-looking, but she seemed fairly sober. She sat down and reached for the bottle, smiling at me in a kind of tired, taunting way.

"Well, Collie?" she said. "Well, my blushing boy, my beamish friend?"

"Well, what?"

"You really don't know?" She poured a big drink of whiskey. "You've been slapped in the face with a polecat and you still can't smell anything?"

I shrugged. She drained her glass, and reached for the bottle again.

"Sure, you know." She nodded. "This house and a crooked ex-cop and those pictures, and—and you. Even you could add that one up?'

"About that crooked ex-cop. About him ... and you. He sort of acts like—I mean he said a thing or two to me that—"

"Yes? Well, that's one thing you *don't* need to worry about. There's nothing between us. There isn't going to be anything."

"I don't think he looks at it that way. It's none of my business, of course."

"Right. So let's get back to something that is. Listen closely to Old Mother Anderson, and then get the hell out. Because I'm only laying it on the line for you once ... A chump is required, Collie. A Grade-A hundred-proof sucker. Someone with a barrel of nerve and a pint of brains. Does that description fit anyone of your acquaintance?"

"I wouldn't care to say. It might partly fit certain people I've met. Women who drink too much and talk while they're drinking."

"Boing!" She triggered a finger at her forehead. "But I'm my own chump, Collie. Strictly my own. Oh, I do an occasional benefit performance, but, by and large and on the whole, to coin a phrase—correction: two phrases—"

"I thought you were going to tell me something. You make a big production out of it, and then you don't say anything."

"I'll tell you something. This. All you need to know, Collie. If he thought you were half-way bright, Uncle Bud wouldn't want you. He's not too sharp himself—if he was he'd still be on the force—and he won't play with anyone who is."

"Including you?"

"Forget about me. I don't count—and you can sing that to any tune you like.'

"I guess I don't understand," I said. "You picked me up today. You brought me here to meet Uncle Bud. You do all that, and then, after I'm half-way in, you—"

"It's confusing, isn't it? Why not just say that I'm a cuh-razy, mixed-up neurotic. Or we might say that occasionally—just occasionally now—I feel a twinge of decency." She took a swig straight from the bottle, and the whiskey trickled down over her chin. "Get out, Collie. This little frammis has been cooking for months, and if you leave it'll go right on cooking until it boils away. Nothing will happen without you. No one else would be chump enough to touch it."

"Well," I said. "I guess ..." And then something happened inside my head, and I left the sentence unfinished. It was as though I'd been walking in my sleep and suddenly waked up.

Kidnaping? Me, a *kidnaper?* Why was I arguing with her? What in hell had come over me? I'd never done anything really bad. Just the things a man like me has to do to stay alive. Yet now, just since this afternoon, I was... I pushed myself to my feet, feeling dizzy and sick. Everything was kind of blurred for a minute. "That's my good boy, that's my Collie darling," I heard her say. "Just a minute, honey."

She hurried into her bedroom, and came back with her purse. She took out a small roll of bills, stripped off one of them and squeezed the rest into my hand.

"I'd ask you to stay tonight, Collie, if it wasn't for Uncle Bud. I don't want him talking you into this mess, and if he saw you before you got away—"

"I know. I'd better go now."

"Take the bottle with you. You look lonely, and a bottle can be a lot of company."

She stood on tiptoe and kissed me; and afterwards she leaned against me for a moment, her head against my chest. She made a mighty nice armful, all warmness and fullness and sweet-smelling softness. I brushed her thick black hair with my lips, and she sighed and shivered. And moved out of my arms.

"What about you? What's going to happen to you, Fay?"

"Nothing. The same thing that's been happening since my husband died."

"But I thought there was something, some organization or treatment that could help you."

"There is, but not for what ails me. They haven't found that yet. When you've leaned on someone all your life, been completely dependent upon him and never made a decision of your own. And when he's suddenly taken away— Oh, n-never mind, Collie. Just go and keep going."

She turned on the porchlight for me so I could find my way across the yard. Where the lane entered the trees, I turned around and waved.

The lights went off. If she waved back, I didn't see her. Everything was dark, and she and the house were gone. As though they had never existed. I felt kind of sad in a way, but at the same time I felt good.

I picked my way down the lane, taking a sip from the bottle now and then. A couple of times I stumbled and fell down, but it didn't bother me much. And it didn't seem dark, but light.

I'd been in the dark, a nightmare. I'd almost been trapped in one.

But now I'd waked up and got away, and it was light again. I'd seen my last of that place, I thought. It was gone away, vanished into the darkness. I'd never been there, and it had never been there.

But it was there. I hadn't seen the last of it.

FOUR

The truck driver took the bottle out of my hand, and poured a little of it in his coke. He passed it on to the other truck driver and the other one poured some in his coffee, and handed the bottle back to me.

The counterman watched us, frowning a little but not really sore. He'd taken a couple of drinks, too, and he was just worried, not sore.

"Don't flash the jug around so much, huh?" he said. "Some highway patrolman comes by here, he might make trouble."

"Aaah!" One of the truck drivers winked at him. "Why would anyone make trouble for Collie? Collie's just waiting for a streetcar."

"Not a streetcar. I'm waiting for this friend of mine, Jack Billingsley. You see—"

"Sure." The other truck driver grinned. "What kind of plane did you say he was flying?"

"I've told you several times now," I said. "It's an automobile. It—"

"Oh, yeah. A Rolls-Royce, wasn't it?"

"No, he's got a Rolls-Royce—two of them, in fact—but he wasn't driving one today. What he had today was a big Cadillac convertible. Some little thing went wrong with it, so I started walking back to a garage—"

"Maybe he had to stop to feed the horses . . ."

"Maybe the caboose ran off the track . . ."

"Maybe," I said, "a couple of wise guys would like to have their faces pushed in."

The lunchroom went dead silent. The truck drivers stopped grinning, and the counterman glanced uneasily toward the telephone. After a moment I forced a laugh.

"I'm only joking, of course. We're all here joking and drinking together, so I joked a little too. I didn't mean it any more than you meant the things you said to me."

One of the truck drivers laid some change on the counter. He and the other one got up, and kind of edged toward the door. I stood up too.

"How about a ride?" I said. "I've got a little money, and there's still some of the whiskey left."

"Sorry. Company says no riders."

"I can ride in the back. Just let me ride with you until daylight. Maybe not even until daylight. I'll probably see that darned crazy Jack Billingsley on the road."

The screen door slammed, then the truck doors. The motor roared, and they were gone. The counterman stared at me. I stared back at him. Finally his eyes wavered and he spoke sort of whining.

"Please, Mac. Clear out, will you, huh? You ain't never going to get no ride."

"I certainly won't get one out on the highway. No one'll stop for me at night."

"But that ain't my fault! You got no right hanging around here, getting me into trouble. What'll people think, for gosh sake? They come in here, an' you start jabbering away at 'em . . ."

"I'm sorry. I won't say another word to anyone. I'll just wait around quietly until it gets a little lighter."

He groaned and cursed under his breath. "Well, get away from the counter then! If you simply got to hang around, go an' set in that rear booth."

"Why, certainly. I'll be glad to."

I went back to the rear booth. I slid in as close as I could to the wall and put my head down on my arms. I was worn out, what with all I'd been through and not being in a bed for three days. But I couldn't relax, let alone sleep. My mind kept going back to Fay—how nice she'd been to me, and what was going to happen to her. I couldn't rest or relax.

I sat up and lighted a cigarette. I took a couple more drinks, and put my head down again. Finally I dozed. Or, I guess I should say, I passed out.

I came out of it frightened, not knowing where I was, not

remembering how I had got here. I jumped up almost before my eyes were open, and headed for the door.

The bottle slid out of my pocket. I made a grab for it, and it sort of jumped out of my hands. It bounced and rolled along the floor, and I stumbled after it, staggering and bumping into the other booths until I finally fell down in one.

There was a man in it, a customer, sitting on the bench opposite me. A young-oldish looking fellow, or maybe you could call him old-youngish looking. He glanced at the counterman and shook his head. Then he stooped down and picked up the bottle. He handed it to me, picking up the sandwich he'd been eating.

"Pretty good." He motioned with it casually. "Like to have me order you one?"

"No, thank you."

"I think you should. Have some coffee anyway."

I said, thank you; I guessed I'd wait to eat until my friend, Jack Billingsley, showed up. "That darned crazy Jack." I laughed. "We were on our way to California, driving at night, you know, because it's so much cooler. And . . ."

He went on eating, keeping his eyes on his plate. Then, suddenly he looked up. He listened, frowning, staring into my eyes and studying my face.

"All right . . ." He laid a hand on my arm gently. "No harm done. It's a nice harmless little story and shows a fine imagination, but it's not necessary with me. Where do you live?"

"Well . . ."

"I see. Been getting along all right?"

"About like always. Pretty good, I guess. Not really good, you know, but all right."

"How long since you were under commitment?"

I started to say a few days, but then I changed it real fast. I said it had been over a year. The name of the place I gave him was the one before the last one:

"Would you like to go back to it? Don't you think you should go back?"

"Well, I guess I should, kind of. I haven't been in trouble or anything, but— You're a doctor?"

"Yes. And I think you should go back, too. Unless, of course, you've got some friend or member of your family who can help you."

"I haven't."

"Well, let's see . . ." He rubbed his face. "Let's see, now. I wonder what you'd better—" He broke off scowling, looking sort of mad at himself. "I'll tell you—what's your name, Collins? Well, I'll tell you, Collins, you'd better take whatever money you can get together and go straight back."

"Yes, sir. I'll do that. I can probably hitchhike most of the way."

"I wish I could help you myself, but I just don't have the time and the money. I can only do so much, and I'm already—"

"I'll tell you what I might do," I broke in. "Maybe I could get a commitment in this state."

"A non-resident?" He laughed briefly. "Not that it would mean much if you were resident. Sometimes, Collins, sometimes I think they take them in the front door here and lead them right on out the back."

"Yes, sir. I guess it's pretty much that way everywhere."

"They can't get the money to operate on. There's money for highways and swimming pools and football stadiums. For everything but the most important things. And then people wonder. They wonder why, when some terrible tragedy takes place, that—"

"I'll be all right," I assured him. "You don't need to worry about me, Doctor."

"Well." He bit his lip. "Well, here. Let me give you my card, anyway. If you should remain in this section, and if there's any kind of emergency—even if it isn't an emergency, if you just want to talk to someone—why, be sure to call me."

I thanked him, and said I'd certainly do that. He slid out of the booth, walked over to the counter, and paid his check.

He started toward the door. Then he wheeled around abruptly and came back to the booth.

"You're sure you'll be all right, Collins? You'll lay off the booze, and, uh, behave yourself?"

"Yes, sir."

"Fine. Good boy. You go back there and stay this time. Stay no matter how long it takes."

"Yes, sir. That's just what I'm going to do, Doctor."

He kind of sighed and shook his head. "You are like hell! How can you? Why the hell should you? Come on!"

"What?" I said. "Come on?"

"And make it snappy, dammit. Before I have time to change my mind."

He lived in the city, the one I'd passed through that morning. He had a nice little brick cottage there, just inside the city limits, with his offices in the front and his living quarters in the rear. Except that I kept thinking about Fay Anderson—and worrying about her—the three days I spent there were just about the most pleasant I can remember.

There were plenty of books to read. There was a big lawn I could work on whenever I got restless, lots of food in the refrigerator, and a bedroom all of my own. I think I enjoyed that last more than anything else. Most places I'd been in—you know, "places"—I was always crowded. There'd maybe be a dozen of us in one little room. You looked around, and they'd be watching you. They looked around, and you'd be watching them. And you never got used to it.

The longer it went on, the more it bothered you. It would have been bad enough if you were all the same kind of guys and had the same degree of mental disturbance, but you just never were. Just when you thought you had a pretty good gang, they'd move in someone that was honest-to-gosh bad. A real wild-eyed guy—just anyone, it looked like, that could get around without a strait jacket. And before long you began to feel a little wild-eyed yourself. You couldn't rest. How can you rest when there's some lunatic in the same room with you?

There at Doc's house, in a big room all of my own, I really slept for the first time in years. I didn't have any medication after the first night. I didn't want any, and Doc said I didn't need any.

The third night—well, it was actually the fourth—he came in and sat down on the edge of my bed. He asked me how I was feeling, and I said I'd never felt better. He murmured that that was good, to get all the rest I could so I'd be in good shape for my trip.

"Of course," he said, not looking at me, "you'll probably be here several weeks yet. Perhaps several months. I sent the institution a wire three days ago, but these things take a lot of time."

"Yes," I agreed. "I don't know why they should, but I guess they do."

"I was going to ask you, Collie." He kept his eyes away from mine. "In case, they should refuse to send for you; if they don't feel able to, that is, because of the expense . . ."

"Yes, Doc?"

"How would you feel about staying on here with me? There's plenty you could do to earn your keep. Yard work and car repairs and so on. You'd be a big help to me, and I think I'd be of some help to you, and— Well, it would be a fine arrangement for both of us. What do you say, Collie? Would you like to do that?"

"I—I—Excuse me just a minute, Doc. I'll be right back."

I got up and went into the bathroom. I stayed in there with the door closed until I was sure I could control myself.

Good old Doc, I thought. He was a swell guy, but he was just about the world's worst liar. He'd had plenty of time to hear from the institutional authorities in that state where I'd been. I knew that he had heard from them, too, and that they had refused to send for me. I'd been almost sure that they would. They'll very seldom send for a guy unless he's a violent or criminal case.

Now since there was no one else to look after me, Doc was willing to take on the job himself. I washed my face, and ran a drink of water. Then I made myself smile, and went back into the bedroom again. I said that I'd be tickled to death to stay. I tried to look natural and sound natural, but I guess it wasn't a perfect try.

"I can afford it, Collie." He looked at me closely, and looked away again. "Why, I'd tell you so in a minute if I couldn't."

"Fine."

"It's all settled then? You'll stay?"

"As long as you can afford it."

"I can. I want you to and you must. You see, Collie, your judgment just isn't good. You're inherently decent with a lot of good, strong moral fibre, but that isn't enough. There'll come a time or a situation when it won't be enough. A man in your condition is readily influenced by others; broadly speaking, he has to depend on them. And you and I know they're not always dependable..."

He paused and lit his pipe. He took a few puffs on it, then went on again.

"Sometimes they're merely ignorant. Sometimes they're cruel or criminal. In any case, they're playing with dynamite. Actually, Collie, there'd be much less danger in your roaming around on your own if you were an out-and-out lunatic—one of the wild-eyed guys, to borrow your own expression. People could *see* the danger then. Now, well, what do they see, now? Why, they see an unusually handsome young man. A little eccentric perhaps, a little slow on the uptake occasionally, but in most respects normal. So they treat you as though you were normal, and the result sooner or later, is certain to be tragedy. For you, for others. You only need to look at almost any daily newspaper to see that I'm right."

"I don't know, Doc, I've been pretty good about steering clear of trouble. I've never hurt anyone or ever done anything really bad."

"What do you call really bad, Collie? And how do you take it when someone kids you or teases you? Never mind." He smiled and slapped me on the knee. "I'm sure you've done fine, hard as it was. And from now on you'll do even better. You stay here for a year or so, however long it takes, and..."

He left on his calls around ten the next morning. As soon as he was gone, I called the doctors' answering service and reported him out.

Then, I left too.

FIVE

Fay Anderson had given me about thirty dollars when I left her place, and I'd had around three of my own. But, now, I had a little less than five. I don't know what had happened to the rest of it, whether I'd jerked it out of my pocket and lost it or whether someone had gotten it away from me in that lunchroom. But that little bit, around five dollars, was all I had left.

It was almost worse than having nothing.

I couldn't really travel anywhere on it. It wasn't more than enough to live on a day or so. A few days before, five dollars would have looked pretty good to me. But I'd kind of changed since then. I didn't see how I could go back to living like I had—knocking around and getting knocked around. Sleeping in culverts and begging for hand-outs, and bumming rides to places I didn't actually care about going to.

As Uncle Bud said, that was bad. Really bad. When I thought about it, certain other things didn't look so bad at all.

I used fifteen cents of my money for a crosstown bus fare. I got off at the highway, the one that led past her place, and, well, for a while, I just loafed around there. I sat on the bus-stop bench, and I got an ice cream cone from a peddler, and I window-shopped the neighborhood stores. It was hard to decide what to do. I always have trouble making decisions, and this was a particularly hard one.

I paced back and forth in front of the store windows, arguing with myself, fumbling with that little bit of money I had in my pockets. I certainly didn't want to put Fay on the spot, more or less force her to go ahead with something she was against. On the other hand, she was already on a pretty bad spot, wasn't she? She couldn't go on like that, anymore than I could go on like this. And it would be good to see her again. So I could just stop by for a visit, couldn't I? I wouldn't need to stay.

It was when I was looking in a liquor store window that I finally made up my mind. There was a big curved-neck bottle inside—just wine, but it looked mighty fancy, and the price was only three ninety-eight. I figured it would make a nice present for her. I could take that out to her, and it would give me a reason for stopping by.

I bought it. Then, I stepped out on the highway and started thumbing. No one would stop for me, but finally a truck came by slow enough so I could hop on the tailgate.

It was pretty rough riding there, and the day was another scorcher. I kept jouncing up and down, and, of course, the wine did too. And I imagine it got a lot hotter than I did.

We came to the little lane that led up to her house. I swung off the truck, running, and that final jouncing was just a little bit more than the wine could take. The bottle exploded; it blew up right in my arms. There must have been a gallon of that sticky red wine, and I'll bet every drop of it went on me.

I hated to call on Fay looking that way, but I didn't have any choice. I had to get washed up and do something about my clothes, and her house was the only place I could.

It was early in the afternoon when I got there. She'd only been up a couple hours, so she hadn't had too much to drink. Quite a lot for the average person, I suppose, but not for Fay. It was just enough to put her in a good mood.

"Oh, Collie! You crazy, silly, sweet—" She threw her arms around me, laughing. "What in the world happened to you, baby?"

"Well, I just happened to be in the neighborhood. I thought I'd bring you a little present, a little wine."

"A barrel, darling? Were you rolling it across—" she laughed uproariously—"across the highway and through the trees to Grandma's house?"

She laughed and laughed, kind of crying along with it. She pushed me into a chair, and sat down on my lap. And I tried to tell her she'd get all messy, but she didn't even seem to hear me.

"I'm glad you came back, Collie," she whispered. "I wish you hadn't, I prayed that you wouldn't, Collie. But I'm glad."

"I'm glad, too. I didn't mean to, but it just seemed like I had to. After I met you and ... and everything, I just couldn't take that old concrete pasture any more."

"The—the what, Collie?"

"The concrete pasture. I mean, that's what it seems like to me. You keep going and going, and it's always the same everywhere. Wherever you've been, wherever you go, everywhere you look. Just greyness and hardness, as far as you can see."

"I know. I know what you mean." She shivered and kissed me. "But this other ... It seems like there should be some other way."

"I guess there probably is. There's probably lots of other ways. But no one's ever pointed them out to me, and I've never been able to find them for myself."

"Poor Collie. Have you had a hard time these last few days, darling? Where have you been?"

"Nowhere. Just fooling around."

I took a bath and put on some clothes she gave me. We had lunch, and then we talked some more.

At first she said we'd find another way out. There was bound to be another way and we'd find it. When Uncle Bud showed up we'd toss him out on his ear. But she was drinking while she was talking and she kept tossing the booze down. So it wasn't long before the good mood was gone, and she'd completely reversed herself.

"Collie, Collie, the wonder souphound. Why don't you dig us up some bones, boy? Dig us a cave to live in."

"You shouldn't say things like that, Fay. I know you don't mean it."

"There in the bar that day. You thought you were hooking into a soft touch, didn't you? You thought you could take me for everything I had. Well, you can so why don't you? Take the damned car and the damned house, and see what you can do with 'em! Of course, you'll have to pay off a couple of little mortgages first."

"Maybe I could," I said. "I mean, maybe if we had a little money, and I could get some kind of a job . . ."

"You jerk! You imbecile. What kind of job could you hold— hunting sand in the Sahara?"

A blinding pain stabbed through my forehead. I said that if that was the way she felt about me, I'd better clear out.

"Well, why the hell don't you?" she yelled. "Do it and stop talking about it!"

She staggered into the bedroom, slamming the door behind her. I got up and went out to the back porch. And, then, after a minute or two, I started down the lane toward the highway.

It was the best thing to do, I figured; the only thing to do. Because if she acted this way now, when she didn't know there was really anything wrong with me, how would she act if she knew the truth? A lot of normal people are scared to death of anyone with mental trouble. And with those booze-shot nerves of hers, she was a long ways from being normal. Probably she wouldn't say anything, do anything openly. She'd be too scared. But she wouldn't want any part of me—she wouldn't, and Uncle Bud wouldn't. And yet if I was tied up with them in a kidnaping, if I knew something about them that might send them to the chair . . .

Well, you see what I mean. They'd feel that they had to get rid of me. They might not like to do it—at least, Fay might not—but they'd think that they had to and they would.

Anyway, that's the way things looked to me just then.

I was almost to the highway when Uncle Bud's car turned into the lane. He came to a quick stop and leaned out. I gave him a grunt and a nod, and kept on going.

"Wait a minute, Kid!" He jumped out and caught me by the arm. "This is a way to treat a pal, Kid? I've been laying awake nights worrying about you and hoping you'd come back, and then the minute I see you—"

"I'm in a hurry." I cut him off. "I just stopped at the house to tell Fay good-bye, and now I'm on my way again"

"Naw. No, you're not, Kid!" he said firmly. "I ain't letting you pass up a deal as sweet as this. You hop right in the car, and whatever's bothering you, we'll— You ain't sore at me, are you? I didn't hurt your feelings with that little joke I made about sleeping by yourself?"

He looked up at me anxiously, his face all friendly concern. I said that it hadn't sounded like much of a joke to me.

"So I just wasn't thinking!" he said. "So—" he laughed uncomfortably—"so maybe it wasn't a joke. Maybe I don't like the idea of another guy making time with Fay when I've never been able to get to first base."

"Well, I wasn't trying anything like that."

"Sure, you weren't, But if you do try to, Kid—if you want to and she wants to—you'll never hear another peep out of me. I need you too much, know what I mean? I've been looking for a guy like you for months, and now that I've found you—"

"I think you'd better count me out. I—I don't seem to get along too well with Fay."

"Aah, sure you do!" He clapped me on the back. "She was needling you, huh? Well, don't you mind her at all, because she don't mean a thing in the world by it."

"But there's something else." I hesitated. "Something about me . . ."

"So you've had a little trouble." He shrugged. "Who the hell hasn't? Now pile into the car, and forget this stuff about clearing out."

I knew it was all wrong. He had to have me, so he was willing to forget about Fay for a while. But as soon as he was through with me—or if something made him decide that I wasn't any use to him . . .

It was all wrong any way you looked at it. Fay in the shape she was in. And me in my condition. And Uncle Bud feeling like he did about me. And the kidnaping itself. Kidnaping—the dirtiest kind of crime there is. Still, it was either this or nothing, the way things looked to me. It was either this, or the old concrete pasture. So I got into the car with him and went back to the house. I wanted to believe that things would turn out all right, so I went back. And inside of an hour I was back up on top of the world again.

Everything was fine. Everything was going to be finer. Uncle Bud knew it and he made me know it.

He didn't try to kid me that the job wouldn't be dangerous. But once it was pulled, we'd be safe and we were a cinch for the dough. We'd be able to duck the traps that kidnapers are usually caught in. We'd know about them in advance, whether the ransom bills were marked or registered, or whether there was a police stake-out at the payoff place. Uncle Bud still had all kinds of contacts inside of the department. He'd know every move that was being made, before it was made. So there might be traps, but they wouldn't catch anyone.

We'd get the money, a quarter of a million dollars, and we'd get away with it.

We didn't discuss the actual kidnaping that evening. Uncle Bud said we'd take that up after I got settled down a bit. I didn't argue with him. I was feeling good. Whatever there was to worry about— and I guessed there was probably plenty—I didn't want to face up to it just then.

Fay waked up. She got to feeling fairly good again, and the three of us went out to the garage apartment. We dusted it out, put clean sheets on the bed, and so on. Then we went back to the house, and after a while Fay began to razz me a little. But she was more funny about it than mean, so I didn't really mind.

Uncle Bud left around ten o'clock. Or, I should say, he started to. He was telling me good night, shaking hands with me, when he turned suddenly and looked out the window.

"Somebody's coming! Get that light off! Get out of sight, Kid! Fay..."

Fay hurried to the window and looked out. She stood there a moment, peering through the glass. I heard a car door slam.

"You'd better go into the bedroom, Collie. Take your glass with you. But it's all right for Uncle Bud to stay." She turned around. "It's only Bert."

"*Bert!*" Uncle Bud turned white. "You mean that character from the roadhouse? Hell, if he sees me..."

"What's the difference? He can't tie you in with anything."

"He's threatened to kill me! We were in on a deal together, and he thinks—" He broke off frantically, snatching up his glass. "Don't let on I'm here, understand? There ain't no one here but you!"

"But your car! What'll I tell him?"

"He doesn't know my car when he sees it! Tell him—tell him it broke down on the highway and the people pushed it in here for the night!"

I was already in her bedroom. He beat it in after me, leaving the door cracked open a little. He was really scared. I could hear him panting in the darkness, hear the nervous rattle of papers in his pockets. Whatever he'd pulled on Bert, it must have been pretty raw.

Bert only came in as far as the kitchen, so we couldn't hear everything that was said. But from what we could hear, it sounded like a purely social call. Fay was a good customer of his. She hadn't been into his place for several days, and he'd wanted to see if she was all right.

He left after a few minutes. Uncle Bud followed me out of the bedroom, wiping the sweat from his face.

"Boy," he said shakily. "Was that a close one!"

"Mmm," said Fay. "So it would seem. Just what kind of swindle did you work on him, anyway?"

"None. Nothing." Uncle Bud shook his head fretfully. "Bert's just plain unreasonable, know what I mean? You try to explain something to him, show him exactly why a proposition went wrong and it isn't your fault, and he won't even listen. He just holds his hand out, and tells you to come across."

Fay yawned and sat down again. She looked at me, that mean sparkle coming into her eyes.

"Well, Collie, what do you think of our head man, the genius who's going to lead us safely from rags to riches? A truly great mind, wouldn't you say? Of course, it may get him killed, but at least he did manage to swindle a barkeep."

Uncle Bud laughed and gave me a nudge. He said I wasn't to pay Fay any mind, because she was just the world's greatest little kidder. "But look, Fay," he added, "it ain't going to do for that character to be dropping by here. If it should happen later on, after we—"

"Forget it!" Fay snapped. "That was Bert's first visit here in months, and I'll see that it's his last. I've got a strong stomach, but one bird like you is about all I can take."

Uncle Bud laughed again. He was after something, you see, and he wasn't going to let himself be insulted until he'd got it. He left a few minutes later. Fay and I talked for a while longer, after he'd gone. Or, I should say, I tried to talk to her. Because I didn't have much luck at it. She'd slugged down four or five drinks in a row, so that killed any chance of really talking.

"Why do I ride Uncle Bud?" she said. "Well, why does one ride a jackass? Because it's the shortest distance between two points. *Quad erat demonstandum*, which translated into canine means—"

"Look, Fay, this is important. If you think he can't pull this off, or that he might try to pull something on me—"

"Will you stop interrupting? It means never look for bones in a bottle. You remember that, Collie. It's the secret of my success."

"Good night." I got up and started for the garage. I was just about to the back door when she called, "Collie," and followed me out to the kitchen.

"I don't know, honey," she said, putting her arms around me. "There's something insidious about the guy. He sort of takes you over, and makes you over, and it's hard not to like him. But the things he's pulled on people... And as for this present deal—a man who would dream up a thing like this, Collie, he's considerably less than upright. If it would make him anything, and if he thought he could get away with it, he'd double-cross anyone."

"But you don't see how he could? You just razz him to see him squirm, like you do me?"

"Something like that. When a person can't stand herself, Collie, when she loathes herself..."

"It'll be all right," I said. "Everything will be all right afterwards."

"Will it? Do you really think any good can come from it?"

"It's got to, Fay. It's got to come from somewhere."

We stood there close together, her arms tightly around me. She squirmed contentedly, and her robe opened a little. She had nothing on underneath. Fay bent her knees a little, sliding her warm flesh against me. She took a long shivery breath. The sweet softness of her breasts seemed suddenly to harden. Then, she waited. All I had to do was make one little move. And somehow I couldn't make it. With any other dame, yes. But not with her. She meant too much to me. This had to mean more than it could now.

After a moment Fay looked up at me, eyes twinkling, a soft smile on her face. "Well, Collie, is this part of your college training? Not to take advantage of a lady in her cups?"

"I—I don't know," I felt rather embarrassed and foolish. "I mean, well, I never really went to college. Just some night classes when I didn't have to work."

"So?" She stood on tiptoe and kissed me, gave me a pat on the cheek. "Well, it's an excellent argument for the midnight oil."

"Look, I don't want you to think I wouldn't like to—"

"Also for abstinence. Go to bed, my friend. Yes, I really want you to. We have a nice thing here, and let us not louse it up."

She kissed me again, and gave me a push toward the door. I went to bed.

SIX

Usually, during the past fifteen-odd years, I'd hated to see morning come. That's a psychotic symptom, you know, not wanting to awaken—hating to face things that are bound to be more than you can handle. It had gotten so that I was almost always sick in the morning. I'd start vomiting almost as soon as I opened my eyes. I'd gone on that way for years, for more than fifteen years, and I guess I'd just about forgotten there was any other way. But that morning I knew better.

That morning—the morning after *that* night—it was like all those years had never been.

I waked up early, not long after daylight, and the way I was feeling you couldn't have paid me to stay in bed. I lay real still for a minute, sort of holding myself in, feeling the energy build up. Then, I jumped up, and for about the next ten minutes you'd have thought I *was* crazy. I "skipped rope." I shadowboxed. I did a handspring up onto the bed and off the other side, and I wound up by walking into the bathroom on my hands.

I was breathing a little hard, but that was all right. It was good to have done something to breathe hard about. I shaved and showered, using the toilet articles Uncle Bud had bought me. I got dressed, and went over to the house.

Fay was still asleep, of course. She hardly ever got up much before noon. I fixed myself a big breakfast, keeping quiet about it so as not to disturb her, and after I'd eaten I went back outside.

I sat out on the back porch a while, looking at the waist-high grass of the lawn. It looked to me like it was just kind of begging for it, just daring me to move in and cut it down to size. So finally I dug an old scythe up out of the garage and went to work on it.

Well, though, it wasn't much of a scythe, and that grass was almost as tough as wire. After an hour of hard swinging, I'd hardly made a dent in it.

I straightened up, and rested my back. I walked up to the far corner of the garage, and sized the yard up from that angle. It looked to me like I'd better do my cutting in rows, starting here on the outside and working in toward the house. I could keep track of the job better that way. I wouldn't actually cut any more, but at least it would show up better.

I started swinging again, cutting a broad swath clear down to where the trees began. I was standing there resting in the shade, when I saw a car coming. I ducked down out of sight, wondering who it was because I could tell it wasn't Uncle Bud. Then, the sun struck against the license plate, lighting up the lettering. And I jumped up and ran.

I ran straight down the lane toward it. It stopped, and I hesitated a moment, panting, and then I opened the door and climbed in.

Doc Goldman took out his pipe. He tamped tobacco into the bowl and struck a match to it. Not looking at me. Just looking straight ahead through the windshield.

"I'm sorry, Doc," I explained. "I couldn't stay there with you. You know I couldn't. It—it just wouldn't have been right! I'd have been worried about it."

"But this didn't worry you, simply walking out on a friend? You thought that was all right?" He shook his head. "That's not very straight thinking, Collie. It's the kind of mixed-up, one-sided thinking that can get you into serious trouble."

"I'm not mixed up. It was just something that I had to do, so I did it."

"With a gallon of red wine, I suppose? And the rear end of a truck for transportation?" He laughed tiredly. "No, it wasn't too difficult tracing you, Collie. You're hardly what one would call nondescript. But with all that wine, I didn't expect you to get this far."

"That wasn't for me. It was a present. I bought it for the—for these people I'm working for."

"Here?" He motioned up the lane with his pipe. "Then, you lied to me when you said you didn't know anyone in this state?"

"No. I mean—well, I didn't really know them. I just met them that night, the night I met you. Kind of an elderly couple. We had a few drinks together, and—"

"Stop it, Collie! I've made a few discreet inquiries. I know who lives in this place."

I felt my face turning red. I wanted to tell him to go to hell; that it wasn't any of his business what I did. But he just wasn't the kind you could say things like that to. And I couldn't have done it anyway. He'd been too nice to me, and I knew he was trying to be my friend.

"She's a widow, isn't she, Collie?" he said. "She picked you up in a bar, just as, I suspect, any number of other women have—and for much the same reason. But being a nice guy, if a little naive, you didn't hang around. You knew it was the wrong thing to do, so you left. Then, yesterday, you changed your mind. You convinced yourself that wrong was right, so you came back and moved in."

"No! Not the way you mean it, Doc. I'm working here, really working. You can see that I am, and you can see there's plenty to be done." He glanced at the house and then skeptically at the patch of grass I had cut. "I'm not living with her," I explained hastily. "I've got a little apartment out there above the garage. Sure, I like her! I like her a lot, and she likes me. And she needs me. She—she drinks too much, and she needs someone to—"

"But, Collie! Collie, my friend." He laid a hand on my arm. "Don't you see—You *did* see the danger in such a situation a few days ago. You, by no means a well man, and a woman who also is not well, an alcoholic. The two of you together—a woman whose behavior is certain to be erratic and trying, at least at times, and a man who is apt to be upset by ordinary give-and-take."

"She needs me," I insisted. "Do you know what that means, to have someone really need you for the first time in your life?"

"I know. But, Collie, it still isn't right."

"It must be because when I woke up this morning, I was glad. I was glad to be alive, Doc, because I knew someone else would be glad. And people just aren't glad unless they need you. They may be nice and friendly, like you were, but if they don't need you, they can't really be glad. They can't really care whether you're alive or not. And when no one else cares, when it goes on that way year after year, Doc, and nobody cares . . ."

I stopped. I guess I'd said about everything there was to say. Doc cleared his throat uncomfortably.

"All right, Collie." He sighed. "I'll agree to your staying on here, but she'll have to be told about your condition." I gave him a scathing look and he added, "I can do it in a way so that she won't be alarmed."

"Not alarm her! You'll tell her that I'm on the loose from an insane asylum, that if I get crowded very hard I may haul off and start swinging. You'd tell her that—what the hell else could you tell her?—and you say she wouldn't be alarmed!"

"Now, Collie. I think I could pose the situation much better than that. Besides, it's for your own good, Collie. Yours and hers. I'd be violating my duty if I didn't do it."

The cords in my throat began to swell. I rubbed at my eyes, trying to brush away the red haze, and I said—I heard a voice saying, "Don't do it, Doc. If you do this to me, if you make me l-lose her, I'll—"

He turned full around in the seat. He put his hands up on the wheel where I could see them, watch them, and he simply sat there calmly. Looking into my face, and waiting.

The reddish haze went away. My throat relaxed. I leaned back in the seat, feeling limp and empty and kind of dull. But knowing what to do. I opened the door of the car, and started to get out. He drew me back. Looked at me worriedly.

"Collie . . ." He hesitated. "If you'd just understand . . ."

"I understand. I'll get my coat and leave with you."

"No, wait a minute." He stared at me thoughtfully. "You *are* looking good, Collie. You look a hundred percent better than you did when you left my place."

"I feel better. At least I did, until you showed up."

He winced and went on studying me. It seemed like an hour before he spoke again. "Are you covering up anything, Collie? I was thinking that if Mrs. Anderson was the type who picked up men in bars, she'd quite likely have some pretty shady acquaintances."

"She's not that type. She did it with me, but that doesn't make her the type."

He nodded slowly. "Well, all right, my friend. For the time being, until you're a little better settled at least, I won't see her."

"Gosh, Doc. I—gosh, I just don't know how to thank you!"

"Don't," he said, sort of embarrassed. "I'm not entitled to any thanks."

We talked for a few minutes more. Finally, we shook hands and he left, backing down the lane to the highway instead of coming up into the yard.

I went back to the grass-cutting, but I didn't work at it long. I was too weak. That strain I'd been under when I'd thought he was going to see Fay had taken too much out of me.

I stretched out in the grass, letting the sun beat down into my face, hoping I'd never have to go through a thing like that again. Doc Goldman, I thought—my friend, Doc, one of the squarest guys that ever lived. And for the moment I'd been on the point of killing him. I shivered, feeling cold despite the sunlight. Doc—I'd almost killed Doc. And I probably would kill him if . . .

But that "if" was never going to be. Because he'd promised not to see her.

It didn't hit me till later that he hadn't promised not to call her on the telephone . . .

SEVEN

It was three nights later. We were all sitting around the living room table, Fay and Uncle Bud and I, studying the city map and going over Uncle Bud's notes. There were a lot of them, the notes, I mean. As Fay had said, he'd been planning this thing, working on it for months. And there wasn't much about Charles Vanderventer III that he didn't know. As a matter of fact, I guess he knew quite a bit more than the boy's own folks did. Because if they'd known what we knew, and if they'd done anything about it, there couldn't have been any kidnaping.

I got to thinking about that part afterwards, when all the hullabaloo broke loose. When there was a four-state alarm out and thousands of police were called up for extra duty, and hundreds of suspects were rounded up and questioned. Just guessing, I'd say that it must have cost someone several million dollars. And of course there's no way of counting what it must have cost the parents—what they went through.

And it was all so senseless, you know. It would all have been so easy to avoid.

The more I thought about it, the more it seemed to me that Bill Collins and Charles Vanderventer III were pretty much in the same

boat. I know that sounds funny, but we were. Aside from Doc
Goldman, who really wasn't able to do anything, no one was
interested in either of us until the kidnaping. No one did anything to
stop it. They must have known that he was practically a cinch for
something like this, and they must have known that I—or someone
like me—was a cinch for it. But no one did anything about us. They
just let us rock along with a pat or a pinch now and then, but not
really giving a damn about us, it seemed like, as long as we kept out
of the way and were quiet.

But we were all in it then and plotting hard. I remember Uncle
Bud pouring himself a drink and raising his eyebrows at me.

"Well, Kid. I guess those are our two best bets, either the
playground or the picture show. You name it."

"Let's see," I said. "If it's the picture show, it would have to be
tomorrow?"

"Well, we could wait another week. It would have to be on a
Saturday. That's when they have the horse operas at this place, so
that's when he always goes."

"And the nurse leaves him alone there sometimes while she and
this chauffeur, Rogers, gad around?"

"She's done it, but not very much. We can't count on it. All we
can count on is that she'll leave him alone while she goes to the
women's rest room. A matter of fifteen or twenty minutes, maybe."

I hesitated. "She always stays that long?"

"I've timed her a dozen times, and it's never been less than that.
Once it was a half an hour. She doesn't care for cowboy pictures, I
guess, so she doesn't hurry."

"There's just one trouble with it. I couldn't already be in the show
in the uniform. Fay would have to be inside. Then when the nurse
left, she'd have to come out and tell me."

"I could do it." Fay shrugged. "And I'd just as soon do that as wait
in the car."

"Yeah," I said, "but it kind of leaves a time gap in there. Something
might happen between the time you came out and signaled me and I
got into the show."

Fay gave Uncle Bud one of her mean grins. She'd been tapering
down on the booze, doing a good job of it, and it was making her
pretty sharp.

"Smart boy, isn't he?" she said. "Just when you think he couldn't see holes in Swiss cheese, he spots one like that."

"I said he was smart." Uncle Bud frowned at her. "I said so right from the beginning."

"So you did. Yes you did say that."

"Well . . ." Uncle Bud twisted in his chair, sort of turning his back on her. "I still think it might be the best of the two bets. The chauffeur's come into the show before and picked him up. After all, the kid's used to doing what he's told."

"He'll do what he's told just as well at the playground," I said, "and we won't have the nurse to worry about."

"But you'll have to ask for him at the playground. He'll be mixed in with a lot of other kids, you know, and you'll probably have to go to the playground matron. All that takes time."

"I guess I'll take it," I said. "That show's right down in the middle of town. If there was any trouble, we'd never be able to get away."

Fay laughed. She poured a little whiskey into her glass, and shoved the bottle toward me. "To Collie boy. May his sense of smell ever sharpen. Will you drink to that, Uncle Bud?"

Uncle Bud gave her a hard look; then, he laughed too, and said he'd drink to anything.

"But watch this stuff, huh?" he added. "I know you've been cutting down, but you can't be boozed up or have a hangover on this job."

Fay gave him another mean smile. Then, she smiled at me in a different way. And I knew she meant to be sober *before* we pulled the job.

"Okay, then, Kid." Uncle Bud turned back to me. "We'll make it at the playground on Monday. Tomorrow's out, because of the show, and Sunday he stays at home. So make it Monday."

"Around three o'clock," I said.

"Around three—a few minutes before to play it safe. The chauffeur, this Rogers, takes the boy to the playground at one; and he never picks him up before three-thirty or four."

We went on talking, running through the details again. After a while, I buttoned up the uniform jacket and put on the big outsize sunglasses, and let Uncle Bud look me over.

He'd bought the stuff in another city. It was all exactly like the real chauffeur's.

"Uh-huh." He nodded for me to sit down. "Once we do that touch-up job on your hair, you'll pass fine. You're maybe a little taller than the other guy, but no one'll be measuring you."

"These glasses kind of bother me," I said. "They make my face sweat, so that I can't see good."

"Well, you won't have to do much seeing with 'em. You won't put them on until the last minute."

I picked up my drink, and took a swallow. I couldn't think of anything more to say, but I kept feeling that I should.

"Yeah, Kid?" He was studying me. "Feeling a little nervous? Something on your mind?"

I said I wasn't particularly nervous. I wasn't worried about anything I had to do. "I'm just—uh—"

"He's wondering about the money." Fay winked at me. "He feels lost without his pockets full of money."

"Well, he won't feel lost much longer," Uncle Bud said. "We'll have it inside of a week, Kid. A hundred grand for me. A hundred and fifty for you and Fay to split. That's fair enough, isn't it?"

"It's fair. I guess that's what bothers me—thinking about all that money. I mean, I just can't believe that we're really going to get it."

"We'll get it," said Fay. "We'll get our share, or someone else will get something else."

Uncle Bud lighted a cigarette and jabbed the match down into an ashtray. He took a couple of short, quick puffs, his hand jerky when he raised the cigarette to his mouth. "This ain't something to horse around with. The Kid's got something on his mind, he'd better unload it."

I said it wasn't anything really, just an idea that had come to me. "I was just wondering if maybe there wasn't some way we could make a haul without actually going through with the kidnaping. Just start to, you know—kind of fake it—and then you step in and rescue the boy, something like that."

"Yeah?" He stared at me, sort of startled. "Yeah?" He poured himself a drink, keeping his eyes on the glass. "Go on, Kid."

"Well, the family would probably give you a pretty good reward, and you could probably get your job back in the department. There wouldn't be nearly as much money to divide, of course, but Fay and I could get by on a lot less."

"But how could you work it out, Kid? Where's your convincer? How do I play the big hero when no one gets caught?"

I scratched my head.

Fay laughed. "Down, boy. That's a good Collie."

"It can't be done, Kid." Uncle Bud shrugged. "There's just no way."

"No," I said. "I guess it can't be."

"Nope. Not a chance. So we'll just go right ahead Monday, and by this time next week we'll be sitting pretty . . ."

EIGHT

I had a funny dream that night, a damned bothersome one, I should say. One of those dreams in which everything turns out to be just the opposite of what you thought it was. It began back with that first day when I went into Bert's roadhouse, and this guy Bert—according to the dream—was really a pretty good guy. He hadn't wanted to act like he had; he'd done it because he was told to. He was just following orders—and I guess you know who was giving them—and it was the same way with Uncle Bud.

Uncle Bud hadn't planned the kidnaping. Fay had. She was calling the shots all the way down the line. The drinking was an act; she didn't drink nearly as much as she appeared to. That business about being half-helpless and needing someone to lean on was an act. She was tough, scheming, rotten all the way through—according to the dream. To get what she wanted, she'd slept with Uncle Bud and Bert; that was the way she held them in line. But they didn't mean anything to her, and I didn't. And when she was through with us we'd wind up with a lot less than nothing.

It was all jumbled and mixed up, of course, as dreams always are. But that's the way it ran generally. It seemed to go on for hours, but when I waked up sweating, groaning out loud, I saw that it couldn't have. The alarm clock said a little after midnight, and I hadn't gone to bed until almost eleven.

I sat up in bed and lighted a cigarette. The dream went away, the
realness of it, and I stopped sweating and my pulse calmed down. I'd
had these nightmares before. The psychiatrists had explained some of
them to me, showed me that while they appeared to be different, they
were all basically the same dream. Back in the beginning, I'd usually
dreamed about getting beat up. I'd be in the ring with two or three
guys, and they'd all have me out-classed. Or maybe there'd only be
one, but the referee would be crooked. Or maybe the other fighter
would be a woman or an old man with a beard—someone, you know,
that I couldn't hit back at. Anyway, however it was, I'd get the hell
knocked out of me.

That was about the worst thing that could happen to a guy, you
see. I mean, it had seemed like the worst thing back in the beginning,
when I wasn't much more than a kid. As I got older, of course, I
began to see that there could be a lot worse things—like being sane—
and not being able to prove it. Or being crowded into a corner where
you might hurt someone. Or being around degenerates and perverts
so much that you got that way yourself. So I dreamed about those
things.

I'd always felt guilty about the Bearcat. Subconsciously, although
the feeling wasn't nearly as strong as it had been, I'd felt that I ought
to be punished. That was why I had the dreams, and that was why
I'd dreamed what I had about Fay. Losing her, having things shape
up so that I might lose her, was the thing I dreaded most. It was the
worst punishment I could get, so in the dream I got it.

I lay awake a while, thinking the thing through, making myself
see how foolish it was. I was just drifting off to sleep again, when a
light flickered through my window. And I jumped up and looked
out.

It was a moonlit night. Far down the lane, I got a glimpse of a car.
I couldn't see anything else, any people in or around it. Just a black
car, parked with its lights off. I put on my pants and shoes, slipped
quietly out of the apartment and down through the trees.

The car pulled away, started backing off toward the highway just
about the time I came even with it. But from the little I managed to
hear and see, I knew I'd gotten myself out of bed for nothing. It was
just a man and a woman, a guy and his girl friend. They'd driven in
here to do a little petting, and now they were on their way again.

It was as innocent as that, but coming right on top of the dream it bothered me a little bit. I couldn't help thinking that it *could* have been someone else; someone *could* park there and slip up to the house, and ten to one I wouldn't know about it.

I went back to bed. After a long time, I went to sleep. But even sleeping, I was still kind of bothered. I knew I shouldn't be, that there was nothing to be bothered about. But when a guy's whole life is wrapped up in just one thing or just one person, well, he doesn't really need anything to throw him.

Saturday, the next day, was kind of a bad day for me. Fay only took four or five drinks, but with the alcoholic fog pretty well gone from her mind she began to ask questions. She didn't appear suspicious, as though she thought I had something to hide. She simply wanted to know about me—as people do when they're deeply interested in a person. And I wanted her to feel that way. But you can see the spot I was in.

I couldn't tell her the truth. Even the half-way truth, glossing everything over, sounded like hell.

I'd been charged with murder after the fight with the Burlington Bearcat. Then, the charge had been reduced to second-degree manslaughter. I'd taken a plea to it, and the judge had made the sentence equal to the time I'd already spent in jail. I'd joined the army, and they'd bounced me out fast with a medical discharge. Since then, I'd gone from one institution to another, with a few cheap jobs in between. I didn't have the training for a good job. I couldn't give any references; and sooner or later my record always caught up with me.

That was the truth without going into a lot of details. What I told her was that I'd stopped fighting after I hurt a guy so bad that he never recovered from it. I said I'd been permanently banned from the ring after that, and anyway I didn't have the heart for it. But since I wasn't much good for anything else, I'd just sort of drifted.

That didn't satisfy her; I mean, she wanted to know more. But she saw I was getting upset, so finally she laid off. I went to bed early, completely worn out from the strain of all this. I slept well, and I waked up feeling pretty good.

I dressed and went over to the house. After breakfast, I went to work on the grass again. I'd just about shaken off the worrying. Like a guy will, I'd swung down through the bottom of the blues and come up on the other side. I wasn't entirely up, but I was coming up fast.

It was probably a couple hours after I went to work that I heard Fay stirring around in the kitchen. Then, maybe thirty minutes later, she came to the door and called to me.

I dropped the scythe and started across the yard. Wiping the sweat out of my eyes, mopping my face and arms with my handkerchief. I went up the steps and across the porch, opened the door, and went in. And—and then I just stood there, staring at her. Because I'd known she was beautiful, that she had the stuff to be, but I'd never thought Fay could be this beautiful. I didn't think that any woman could.

Her eyes were sparkling, crystal clear. Her hair had that soft, brushed-shiny look, and her face was rose-and-white softness that seemed to glow from the inside. She was wearing tan shorts, and a white off-the-shoulders blouse. She took a deep breath, smiling at me, and her breasts swelled. And I could see she was wearing nothing beneath the blouse.

"Well?" She tilted her head to one side, smiling. "How do I stack up as an advertisement for prohibition?"

"F-fine. You stack up period."

"Mmmm? Really think so? But you ought to make sure, shouldn't you?"

"Fay, Fay, honey—" I took a quick step forward, then I stopped, looking down at myself. "I guess with you so clean and pretty and everything, I ought to—"

I hesitated, kind of hoping she'd say it didn't matter. And I think she did start to say that. But this was something that meant a lot to her, as much probably as marriage would have meant, and in a sense it was marriage. It was something she wanted to be perfect, so, after a moment, she nodded.

"All right, Collie. It's a nice thing, as I recently remarked, so why louse it up?"

"I'll be right back," I said. "Just as soon as I wash up a bit."

"And you know where I'll be." She smiled. "I'll be ready. In fact, I think I may as well . . ."

Fay tugged suggestively at the blouse. Then she turned and went through the living room and into the bedroom.

I couldn't move for a second or two, and then I beat it out of there fast. I ran across the lawn, and up the stairs to my apartment. I turned the water on in the tub, and started shaving. I finished shaving, got in the tub, and scrubbed and soaked myself. Then, I put on all clean clothes and went back down the stairs again.

In all, I guess it had taken me about twenty-five minutes.

It couldn't have been any more than that. But in that little time— just that little time—everything changed for me.

I hadn't heard the car leave; I wouldn't have heard it with all the noise I was making in the tub. But it was gone and, of course, she was gone, too. I looked in the house, hoping against hope, hoping that it wasn't like I knew it was. But she was gone. Apparently, she'd gone dressed as she was, taking a coat with her maybe.

I sat down in the living room, and for a while I just sat, staring into space, staring at nothing, my mind a blank. Then, gradually I began to think again. And what I thought was that this was all so unnecessary, that it was one more piece of the pattern that had put me where I was.

Doc Goldman. Doc and the dozens of other doctors I'd come up against. They said that my thinking was one-sided, and, hell, compared with theirs, mine had more sides than a bar. They knew all about me—at least some of them did. But they knew me as something kind of isolated, something set off by itself and not really a part of the world. I was a case, not a person. What I thought or felt was of minor importance, if any. It was unreliable. I knew nothing, and they knew everything. And if I'd just hold still long enough, a year, two years, fifteen years, why, they'd fix me up in fine shape. Yes, sir, they'd take care of my case. Or if they didn't, it wouldn't matter. Because life would have passed me by.

I'd been listening to doctors for half my lifetime. But I couldn't remember one that had really listened to me, who'd actually given any thought to what I'd said. And why not? Tell me why not. I was the guy most concerned. I was the one guy who knew exactly what I was up against. I was the world's best authority on Kid Collins—not a case, but the *Kid himself*. I knew what he'd taken and how much he could take. And most of all, most important of all, I knew how people took him.

There wasn't any theory about it. There wasn't any of this business about how people ought to or should act. I *knew*, I'd learned by firsthand experience. and if anyone had listened to me, if Doc had listened . . .

Yeah, sure. I was in on a pretty rotten deal. But it had taken me more than fifteen years to get into it—more than fifteen years of holding still, of being the nothingness of a case. And . . . and Doc hadn't known about the deal. All he'd known was that I seemed to be getting along fine, that I had something to live for for almost the first time in my life. And still he hadn't listened to me. What I *knew* didn't matter, only what he *thought*.

I got the telephone directory, and looked up his number. I dialed it, and he answered immediately. I said, "Collie," and waited.

"Collie?" He hesitated. "Look, fellow, uh, where are you?"

"Right where I've always been."

"But—" He cleared his throat uncomfortably. "You remember, I didn't make any promises, Collie. I said we'd let it stand for the time being. And I only agreed not to see her. I didn't say that I wouldn't, uh, telephone."

"I know. You're a man of your word, Doc."

He was silent for a moment. When he spoke his voice sounded a little bewildered, kind of half-angry. "I didn't say a word that should have alarmed her, Collie. On the contrary, I was very careful to reassure her."

"Well, that makes her kind of crazy, doesn't it? She shouldn't have been alarmed, and she should have been reassured. But it turned out exactly the other way. She didn't react properly, did she, Doc? She's abnormal, isn't she?"

"Judging by her attitude, yes! She—"

"I know. I remember the time I had three spine taps in one month, and the time I had the electric-jolt treatment and the insulin-shock routine. There wasn't anything wrong with the treatment, you know. It wasn't the treatment's fault that I couldn't focus my eyes or stand up or remember my own name. That was mine; I just didn't react properly."

"Collie. Please listen to me."

"I remember a doctor at one of the places I was in, a guy that specialized in lobotomies. So he performed one of them right after another, and of course he was absolutely correct in doing it. But somehow the patients just wouldn't cooperate with him. They didn't react as they should have. He'd give 'em these swell prefrontals, just the prettiest jobs you ever saw. And these damned stubborn patients just wouldn't turn out right. I guess they probably liked being idiots, wouldn't you say? They liked being so stupid that they couldn't button their own pants or count the fingers on one hand. They liked—" I broke off, choking. "Let it go. Just let it go."

There was a pause and I could all but see him frowning. I could see the worry in his eyes. "I'm terribly sorry, Collie, but you must know that it was the only thing I could do. It's hardly my fault if Mrs. Anderson adopts an attitude that is completely unreasonable."

"That's the word all right, Doc. Now maybe you'll tell me what a reasonable attitude would be. She lives alone, remember, and her nerves are in pretty bad shape and she hasn't known me much more than a week. So tell me, Doc, just how should she have acted?"

"Well, I—I certainly don't think that she . . ." He paused. "Now, listen to me, Collie! I said I was sorry."

"You don't know, do you? You didn't know, but you know now. And you found out the easy way. Why didn't you do it to yourself, Doc? Why didn't you go to some of your normal people and tell 'em you were a mental case, and see how they acted?"

"Collie . . ." And now I could visualize the red flush on his face. "I did what I had to. I'm sorry that Mrs. Anderson took it as she did, and I'll be more than glad to— Is she with you, now?"

I laughed. I didn't say anything.

"You're at her house? Well, stay there and I'll come right out. I—you know I'm your friend, boy. I don't mean to throw anything up to you."

"I know. I'm glad I can remember."

"You'll stay there then—give me a chance to straighten this out?"

"I'm leaving here," I lied. "I'm hitting the trail again."

"No! No, Collie. If you don't feel that you can stay there, you must come back over here. We'll go ahead, just as we planned."

"I'm leaving, Doc. I'm hitting the trail, and don't try to pick that trail up. Because if you do . . . I might stop remembering."

I hung up the phone.

A minute later it started ringing again; it rang and rang, and then finally it stopped. And I went on sitting there, looking into nothingness. The tears streaming down my face.

NINE

I waited there at the house until around midnight. Then, I went out to the garage, stretched out on the bed and waited. At four in the morning, when I fell asleep, she still hadn't returned.

It was almost noon when I awakened and I was conscious of someone being in the room with me, I lay still, keeping my eyes slits, and looking out from beneath the lids.

It was Uncle Bud. He was seated near the bed, his hat pushed back on his smooth white hair. He was watching me, studying me rather. There was a thoughtful, calculating look on his too-friendly face; and I felt that I knew what he was thinking as well as he did.

So what if the Kid is a little off?—and it couldn't be more than a little. I can still use him. Use him, and then get rid of him ... with Fay's help. Because the way she feels about the Kid, now, she'd be even more anxious to wash him up than I am.

I waked up; I opened my eyes, I mean. I looked surprised, and Uncle Bud apologized for walking in on me. He'd just that moment come in, he said, and I told him, sure, it was okay.

I went into the bathroom and washed. When I came out, he had that warm, warm smile turned on. The friendliness and sympathy stuck right out at me.

"You know what happened, Kid? Fay had a pretty big load on when she showed up at my place, and I'm not sure I got things straight."

"I know what happened. I checked with my friend the doctor."

"A hell of a note! Yes, sir, a hell of a note." He shook his head sadly. "Two people hitting it off like you were, and then a thing like this has to happen. But she'll snap out of it, Kid. Just give her a little time to get used to the notion, and she'll come around."

"Sure, she will. It won't bother her a bit."

"Well—" He glanced at me sharply. "Well, no, of course it won't. But we better not rush it, huh, Kid? We better wait for her to lead. And, speaking of that, you just take it easy here and I'll bring you some breakfast."

Uncle Bud went over to the house and fixed me a tray, bacon and eggs and a big pot of coffee. Fay was really knocked out, he said, so sick and hungover she could hardly stand up. And that kind of put us on the spot, didn't it? It really fouled up the ball game, didn't it, Kid?

"It sure does. If we're going to pull it today, we ought to be leaving in a couple hours."

"Or less, Kid. Or less. I'd say to wait until tomorrow, but how do we know she'll be straightened out by then? Once she starts batting that jug, she's liable to be on it for a week."

"Yeah, that's right."

"Kid . . ." He hesitated. "What do you think, anyway? I'd take her place, go with you myself to take care of the boy. But I'm pretty well known in this town, and if someone should see us together . . ."

"Yes?" I said.

"Well, I don't think it would be a good idea. Maybe it wouldn't hurt anything, and maybe it would. The way I look at it, there's just no sense in taking chances."

I filled my coffee cup and lighted a cigarette. He waited, kind of fidgeting, wanting me to grab the ball and carry it. And I let him go right on waiting. I had to be absolutely sure, you see. It had to be his proposition.

"Well," he said, at last. "What d'ya say, Kid? What do you think? Me, now, I think you can swing it fine. You can do it just as well by yourself, as you could with Fay."

I took a swallow of coffee, hesitating; pretending to think it over. I screwed up my face thoughtfully, and slowly drained the cup. He watched every move. He leaned back in his chair, one arm thrown over the back, trying to appear easy and unanxious, but feeling so much the other way he just couldn't put it across.

Fay had called the turn on him all right. He was stupid—stupid and cheap. A little squeezing, and it cropped out all over him. It oozed out of him like sweat.

"Well," I said. "I'm pretty dumb myself. But if you think—"

"Yeah? Yeah, Kid?"

"If you think it'll be all right, why, okay."

"Swell! That's swell!" He jumped up beaming. "Now, if you're all through there, we'd better start getting you ready."

My hair is blond, almost yellow. Maybe I told you that? Well,

anyway, it is—it—was—and the real chauffeur's hair was black. So
that was where the dye touch-up came in.

I shaved, shaving extra close. When I was through, Uncle Bud
took the razor and shaved my neck. He stood back and looked me
over. He went over my face again, taking care of any little places I'd
missed, and then he went to work with the dye.

I looked pretty funny when I was through—the sides and back of
my hair black and the top of it yellow. The outsize sunglasses covered
my lashes and brows, so we let them go. I put on the uniform,
everything including the cap, glasses and gloves. Then, after Uncle
Bud had checked me over, I stripped off the cap, jacket, glasses and
gloves, and put on my hat. I was wearing a sports shirt. In the car, I'd
look just about like any other guy out for a ride.

Uncle Bud helped me carry the uniform stuff downstairs. We put
it down on the floor of the station wagon, behind the front seat, and I
got in. Uncle Bud wished me luck. He beamed at me—almost
laughing, he was so happy. And I almost laughed myself. I drove off,
wondering why it was always the stupid people who figured everyone
else to be stupid. Why they always think they can outsmart the other
guy. Because I wasn't supposed to be bright, of course, but even an
idiot could have seen through this stunt.

I'd never meant anything to him. Now that I didn't mean anything
to Fay either, and since I'd practically told him how he could cash in
and play it absolutely safe . . . Well, you see what he was going to do.
What *they* were going to do.

And it looked like a very sweet set-up for them. Everything
seemed to fit together perfectly. They could even use Doc Goldman
to back up their story.

Fay had felt sorry for me, and given me a job. Then, when Doc
had told her about my background, she'd fired me—giving me until
the following day, Monday, to clear out. She'd slept late that day, *this*
day, and when she waked up she found that I'd stolen her car. She
hadn't known quite what to do—being so innocent and unworldly,
you know. So she'd called Uncle Bud, and he remembered I'd done
some talking about the Vanderventer boy. He hadn't thought anything of it at the time, just supposed it was some wild talk. But if I
was an escaped lunatic and a car thief . . .

Well, maybe I didn't have it figured exactly right. But it was close enough. I was due to get killed. Uncle Bud was due—or thought he was—to be a hero.

Knowing what I did, I couldn't say why I was going ahead. Somehow, I didn't really think about the why of it. It just seemed like something I had to do—like I'd been set in a rut and had to follow it out to the end. I was hurt, of course; hurt and sore at the whole world. And probably that was why. But I don't know. All I knew was that I had to go ahead, and that I needed an angle to do it. Something that would pull them into the deal, and hold them in it.

It would drive them nuts, I thought. They figured on cashing in fast and easy, and it wasn't going to be that way. I'd make them go ahead. They'd have to play it right out to the end ... with an escaped lunatic for a partner. A lunatic who was suspicious of them, who knew they'd tried to kill him. And before it was all over, they'd probably be ten times crazier than they thought I was.

But I needed an angle. I had to have an angle.

TEN

That neighborhood was the finest in the city, just about the fanciest I'd ever seen anywhere. There were a few apartment houses, with pools and fountains in front and long wide walks leading up to them. But almost everything was estates. The houses sat far back from the street, so far and so hidden by trees that they could hardly be seen. Most of them, most of their yards rather, were enclosed by walls that cut them off from the street. I was parked at the corner of one of these walled places.

The playground was just across the street ahead of me. It covered a square block, and it had about everything you could name in the way of play equipment. Practically all of the kids that came here, of course, had as much or more at home. But this private park gave them something they didn't have at home—something that ordinary kids take for granted; a chance to play with other children. So I guess their folks felt it was necessary.

The grounds were enclosed by a high spiked-steel fence, with a gate on each side. Across one end, fronting on this street and a side street, was a brick clubhouse. I suppose you'd call it that. Anyway, it was a place where the kids could romp in bad weather, and with rest rooms and so on.

The gates weren't guarded; guess a guard for each one would have been pretty expensive. They weren't locked either, since the matron had twenty-five or thirty kids on her hands and she couldn't keep running back and forth to the gates.

She was a fairly young woman, dressed all in white like a nurse. She was kind of pretty, too, and also rather flustered—and—cross-looking. Because children like those, she could only crack down on them so hard. She could tell them what to do, but she couldn't really insist or get tough with them, if she wanted to keep her job. And it looked like she wasn't the only one who knew it. She'd been chasing after them, straightening out first one then the other, ever since I'd driven up. Now, finally, she had them all together in the middle of the playground, trying to get some kind of ring-around-a-rosy game started.

I took off my sunglasses and wiped them. I looked at the dashboard clock. It was five minutes after three. If he kept to his usual schedule, the real chauffeur would be showing up between three-thirty and four. So I had to be moving—if I was going to move. I had to, but I couldn't. I hadn't spotted my angle yet.

I put the glasses on again and looked back over at the playground. I looked just in time to see a kid, a little boy, give a girl a shove. She sat down hard on her bottom, squalling like she'd been killed. The matron shook her finger at the boy and squatted down in front of the little girl. She dusted her off and petted her, put her on her feet again. She straightened up and looked around for the boy. Then she sort of shrugged, and went back to the game. Maybe she thought he was still in the group, because with all those kids it would be easy to overlook one. Or maybe she thought he'd gone to the toilet. Anyway, she couldn't be bothered. And I mean she really couldn't be. She had maybe thirty kids to look after, so she couldn't devote her whole time to one of them.

But *I* could. Any guy who wanted to pick one off could do it. So I knew where the little boy was.

He'd gone off to the clubhouse, but he hadn't gone inside. Instead, he'd scooted through the patio, dropped down on his hands and knees on the other side, and started crawling along the row of sandboxes. He was headed straight for the gate. From the way he went about it, you could tell he'd done it plenty of times before.

I started the car, watching him as he reached out from behind a sandbox and eased the gate open a few inches. His hair was the same color as the Vanderventer boy's. They were about the same size, too, but I could see he was older. He must be at least nine, I guessed, and probably he was as old as ten.

He was my angle. He could be the angle—*if* he got out.

And he did.

He did it so fast that I almost missed it. One second he was snaked down behind the sandbox. The next second he was out the gate, running stooped along the concrete base of the fence. At the rear of the clubhouse, he straightened up casually and walked on down to about the middle of it. Then, he took a cigarette from the pocket of his little sawed-off pants and tapped it against his wrist a few times.

He took a lighter from another pocket, and lit it. He leaned against the building, one foot crossed over the other, puffing away like a little old man. I put the car into gear. I drove past the playground, the fenced part, and stopped at the rear of the clubhouse.

He flicked his fingers at me in a kind of wise-guy salute. "Hi, Rogers," he said, sauntering forward. "What do you know, for sure?"

I mumbled something, hello, or how are you, or something like that. Or maybe I didn't either. Because I was pretty mixed up to begin with, and the way he talked and acted, it didn't do anything to straighten me out.

"Okay?" He hesitated with his hand on the fender. Then he nodded at me through the windshield, went to the door, and climbed in. "How about a little ride, Rog? I want to talk to you about Charlie, and this will be my last chance."

I got the car started again. I started it with a jerk. He was doing exactly what I wanted him to do, doing everything for me. But, well, I just don't know. I just couldn't think.

"Don't remember me, do you, Rog?" He leaned back, propping his feet up on the dashboard. "Well, I guess you wouldn't. I've been on the Coast for six months—just here for a few days with

Grandma—and I have to go back to Paris tonight. That's the way the judge made it when my parents got divorced. Six months with Dad in the States and six months with Mom."

He lighted another cigarette, and held the package out to me. I shook my head, looking into the rear view mirror. There was a car or two behind me, but neither was Uncle Bud's. I wondered if I'd figured him and Fay wrong.

"Now, about Charlie," the boy said. "What's happened to him, anyway Rog? What kind of shoving around are those goofy parents of his giving him?"

"Shoving around?" I mumbled. "I, uh, I guess I don't know what you mean."

"Never mind. I know how they treat him, how they've always treated him. He's been sick for years, and he's getting sicker. And the worse he gets the toughei they make it for him. Making a man out of him, they call it. Teaching him responsibility... Boy, I wish I was a little bigger! I'd get me a club, and ..."

I saw them now, Fay and Uncle Bud. They were in his car. Fay was driving and they were coming up fast.

"Something wrong, Rogers?" The boy gave me a knowing look. "Want me to duck out of sight?"

"Just some friends of mine," I said. "And, no, I want you to sit right up. Just act like—"

"I get you. You were too early to pick Charlie up, so you're killing a little time with a pal."

I swung into the curb and stopped. Their car shot past us, skidded to a stop, and Uncle Bud jumped out. He started toward us at a run, his hand inside his coat. Then, he got a good look at the boy, and his mouth dropped open. And he stopped as suddenly as the car had.

I got out. I sauntered up to him, deliberately looking puzzled. "What's the matter?" I asked. "What are you two doing out this way?"

"I—we—" He shook his head helplessly, his eyes wavering. He'd planned on doing just one thing, and now he didn't know what the hell to do. "That b-boy," he said, at last. "Damn it all, Kid, you got the wrong boy!"

"Huh!" I let out a grunt. "But he looks—"

"Well, damn it to hell, he's not! A blind man could see he's not."

"I told you. I told you I couldn't see good with these glasses. But there's no use in getting sore. I'll just take him back and get the right one tomorrow."

"Just like that, huh? Hell, of all the dumb—"

"He won't say anything. I'll make him think it's some kind of game."

"Yeah, but—" Uncle Bud hesitated. "But it's so damned late! You're practically a cinch to run into the other chauffeur."

"I can make it," I explained, "and I'm sure the kid won't talk. He'll be afraid to, see? He slipped off from the playground, and he'll be—"

"Okay! All right!" He made up his mind suddenly. "But get moving, will you? Snap into it, and I'll see you out at the house."

Uncle Bud ran back to his car, pushing Fay back in just as she started to get out. They drove off with him at the wheel, and I went back to the station wagon.

"Well, Rogers..." The boy nodded at the dashboard clock. "I've got to be getting back to the playground."

"Right away," I agreed. I pulled the car around in a fast U-turn. "Now, about this little ride of ours. I'll appreciate it if you don't say anything about it."

"I won't," he promised, "and don't you say anything either. Just give me a minute to duck into the clubhouse. Then you can pick up Charlie, and no one'll know a thing."

I turned at the corner of the playground and parked at the side of the clubhouse. He opened the door kind of reluctantly. Sat, hesitating, half-in and half-out of the car. Then, he turned slowly around and stared thoughtfully into my face. And for a moment he looked every bit as old as he talked.

"Charlie's sick," he said. "Awful sick. I can't do anything about it, and anyway I've got to go back to Paris tonight."

"I'll see about him," I said hurriedly. "I'll look after him. Don't you worry."

"You better. You sure as heck better ... Rogers."

He slid out of the car, looked back in for a second. "Take it easy," he said. "His folks need a good jolt, but don't be too tough on 'em."

Then he was gone. So quickly that it was hard to believe that he had ever been there. I got out of the car right away, but by the time I reached the playground he was nowhere in sight.

I opened the gate. I went inside, leaving it off the latch. It was three-thirty—it *had been* three-thirty when I left the car. The real chauffeur was due at any time. But I had to go through with this deal, and it was now or never.

They were still out in the middle of the playground, the children and the matron. I stopped about twenty feet away, and after a moment she turned and saw me.

"Oh, hello, Rogers!" She said it in the half-haughty way people use when they think they're better than you are—and feel that they have to keep proving it. "You're early for a change, aren't you?"

I didn't say anything; just touched my fingers to my cap. She gave her head a little toss, and looked around at the children. "Charles, Charles Vanderventer," she called. "Oh, here you are! Run along with Rogers now."

He moved out of the group, a pale weak-looking kid. He looked at me uncertainly, and then he looked at her.

"Is that Rogers?" he said, puzzled.

"Is it— Oh, my goodness!" She took him by the shoulders and gave him a push. "Who else would it be?"

He started toward me, moving slowly. Feeling, knowing, that something was wrong, but afraid to say so. He followed reluctantly as I turned around and started toward the gate. I walked fast for a few steps, listening to him, listening to his footsteps. He kept that same slow pace, so I had to slow down, too. I couldn't let him get too far behind, and I couldn't hurry him. He was used to doing what he was told, but I couldn't lean on that too hard. If I tried to rush him, if he got scared enough . . .

"Oh, Rogers!" It was the matron. *"Rogers!"*

I paused, turned partly around.

"Charles has had a pretty trying day. Will you tell—will you please tell Mrs. Vanderventer that I suggest he stay at home tomorrow?"

I waved my hand. I started toward the gate again, and after a long moment I heard the boy following. Moving as slowly as he could. Barely dragging his feet.

My glasses were steaming over. I shifted them and they cleared for a moment, and then they seemed to fog up worse than ever. The gate was less than thirty feet away, but I could hardly see it. I glanced over my shoulder, and I could barely see the boy. Everything was blurred, a watery, hazy blur. Everything was kind of meaningless. I was a blind man, a man who had blinded himself to get something. And, now, whatever it was I'd wanted, was slipping away from me.

All at once my mind was a complete blank. I didn't know where I was. I didn't know how I had gotten here, or what I was doing or supposed to be doing. I was just there, here, walking across a children's playground. A guy in hot, funny-looking clothes, with a little boy tagging along behind him.

And how, why, what it was all about, I didn't know. I guessed it must be some kind of a gag. The only thing I could think of was that I'd blanked out there in Bert's roadhouse, and they'd dressed me up in these clothes and dumped me out here. It could have happened. I'd pulled blanks before when my mind got too tight, and people had done some funny things to me when I had.

I sort of laughed to myself, going along with the gag, thinking the joke would be on them when that crazy Jack Billingsley showed up. We'd been heading for the coast, see, me and that crazy Jack Billingsley. So the car had broken down, and I'd started back to the garage to get help, and somehow Jack had got it running again and . . .

I stumbled. I almost fell flat on my face. I yanked the glasses off and wiped them—cleaned them off good. And the bright sunlight struck into my eyes. And suddenly I knew where I was and why, and what I had to do.

I slapped the glasses back on. I whirled around, grabbed the boy by the hand and yanked him along with me. It was only a few steps to the gate, but there couldn't be any more of the foot-dragging. My nerves wouldn't take it. There wasn't time.

The boy whimpered a little when I grabbed him. Now he was hanging back, trying to, and I was afraid he might get up the nerve to yell. So I stooped and picked him up in my arms. That quieted him; paralyzed him with fear, I guess. I straightened up, and started through the gate.

And a big black limousine pulled in at the curb, and a chauffeur hopped out. He was dressed exactly as I was. He was the man I was supposed to be.

ELEVEN

He dusted at his trousers, like a man will when he first gets out of a car. He took his sunglasses off and wiped them, gave me a glance and a nod, and put them back on again.

I nodded back at him. I went through the gate and down the steps to the walk. He started toward me, still dusting at himself. We passed each other. He went up the steps and through the gate. I started down the walk.

I reached the corner of the clubhouse. I stepped behind it, glancing over my shoulder. The real chauffeur had stopped and was staring at me.

I don't know how it came about. Whether he got a glimpse of the boy's face, or whether it had just taken that long for the situation to sink in on him. Probably it was the last. A thing can be so completely startling that it doesn't startle.

Anyway, the man swung into action fast. He didn't even yell, which, of course, he should have. He came charging through the gate in a leap, and down the steps in another. And he came pounding up the walk after me, fists churning, his head ducked. All action and nothing else.

I backed away from him, getting further behind the clubhouse, still holding onto the boy. When he was right on top of me, I stuck my fist out. I gave him a straight arm with a fist at the end of it, and he piled right into it with his face.

His glasses exploded. I felt his nose flatten and crunch. He reeled, wobbled on his heels, and toppled forward. He was out like a light, hit harder than I could have hit him. And no one had seen it. That fancy clubhouse was in the way, and the estate walls were in the way.

They were walled off from the world, and the world was walled off from them.

I ducked around the corner. I put the boy flat on the floor of the car, climbing in over him, keeping a foot on him while I shucked out of the uniform stuff and put on the hat. Then, I wheeled the car around in a U-turn, crossed through the intersection, and headed for the highway.

The Vanderventer chauffeur was still lying where I had left him. As I turned the corner and the playground vanished from view, he was still sprawled behind the clubhouse. There'd been no cars passing by at the moment I gave it to him. But several had passed since then, and others were passing now. Yet no one stopped. They had other things to do, and it was none of their business if a man had fallen down.

I'd gone a couple of miles before I realized I had my foot on the boy. I lifted it off fast, and gave him a little pat. There was nothing to be afraid of, I told him. He'd just stay there and take it easy, and no one would hurt him.

He looked up at me, his big blue eyes filled with tears, his lips trembling and as pale as his face.

"All right. All—" He gulped. "I'll—I'll—"

He tried to tell me that he'd do what I'd said, but it got all tangled up in a sob. I told him not to try.

"Just rest, Charlie boy. Just be real nice and quiet, and everything will be fine. I won't hurt you. I won't let anyone else hurt you."

I went on talking to him, soothing him. I guess he must have believed what I said, because the sobbing stopped and a little color came back into his face.

I turned on the car radio, keeping the volume low.

There was nothing on the air yet about the kidnaping. I didn't think there would be, but I was curious to know when the news would break. How long it would take. Apparently the chauffeur was still knocked out, lying where I had left him. And no one had stopped to see why he was there. The matron? Well, I was kind of puzzled about her, too. Because she must have seen the two of us together, and she must have known that things weren't as they should be. But—well, there you were. That's the way it usually goes. People who might do something that needs doing are too busy to do it. The others don't give a damn.

Yes, the police department was on the job. Relatively speaking, that was just about the best patrolled area in the city. In this section there were regularly assigned squad cars covering a five-mile area. The way it worked out on paper, the cars were supposed to cover as much territory as a dozen men on foot. And they *could*, too—they could "cover" it all right. But the police in it couldn't do a hell of a lot more than that. They couldn't drive lickety-split all day and see everything they should see. The officers couldn't be looking into trouble while they were driving around. If there was trouble, they had to leave the car—and the radio—while they investigated. And if something popped, meanwhile, it had to wait until they got back.

That was the set-up. The same kind of "efficiency" arrangement you find in lots of cities. It saved money for the taxpayers, and it was good business—"running the department on a business-like basis." At least, it must have seemed that way then.

Ordinarily, it should have taken about half to three-quarters of an hour for the trip from the playground to the house, but I took the trouble to drive slowly so as not to attract attention from the police or anybody. It was a strain doing that, talking to the boy now and then, and listening to the radio, so I turned it off. I wanted more and more to open up the station wagon and get there as fast as I could, but I kept well within the speed limits. Then somehow—maybe because I was trying so hard—I managed to get lost. It was well over an hour and a half before I pulled up in the yard of the house.

Uncle Bud and Fay were at the kitchen door. Just standing there, white-faced and kind of dazed-looking, almost motionless. Inside the house, I could hear the radio blaring the news of the kidnaping. So it was out now. I took my time walking up to them, then I stopped just off the steps and listened.

Like all firsthand reports, it was confused. The facts of the kidnaping were more or less there, but the story was all garbled. They had no description of me, nothing beside the fact that I was "fairly tall and of medium build." They didn't know what kind of car I'd used.

Both the matron and the chauffeur were being questioned. All available police, including those off-duty, had been ordered to the area. The entire neighborhood had been blocked off, a search of every estate in the vicinity was underway, all servants—particularly uniformed-chauffeurs—were being "intensively grilled."

The boy's parents were "prostrated." The mayor had demanded "all-out action," the police commissioner was "pressing for an immediate solution of the case," and the chief of police had promised that "no stone would be left unturned."

The news had just broken, but everyone that was anyone was all ready with a statement. They were so ready with their predictions and promises and demands, you might have thought they'd been expecting something like this. But I don't guess they had, or if they had it hadn't bothered 'em much.

I went back to the car and around to the other door. I spoke to the boy, and then I lifted him out gently and started up the wall. He was sound asleep, exhausted with the excitement and strain. I was practically knocked out myself, but naturally everything had hit him a bit harder.

Fay and Uncle Bud moved out of the doorway; I'd have knocked them out of it if they hadn't moved. I brushed past them, carried the boy into the spare bedroom, and laid him down on the bed. I slipped off his shoes, partly unbuttoned his shirt. Then, I went back into the living room, pulling the door shut behind me.

Fay and Uncle Bud had snapped out of it a little. Enough, at least, to wobble back into the living room and fix themselves a drink. I fixed myself one, and sat down. Fay looked at me out of the corner of her eyes. She gave me a straighter look, her lips trembling as she tried to smile. I stared back at her, and she dropped her eyes and the smile went away.

Then it was Uncle Bud's turn. I went through the same thing with him. Staring through him, forcing the smile back into his face, making him look away. They both sat looking at the floor—almost holding their breaths, sort of poised on the edge of their chairs. They looked like they'd jump if I said boo, and I left them that way. It was the way I wanted them to feel.

I leaned back and sipped at my drink, listening to the radio. There was nothing new. Just the same hot air without anything behind it. I got up and fixed another drink. I switched the radio off, and sat back down.

"Well, what's the matter? I didn't surprise you, did I?"

Fay's head came up. Her breath went out in a deep, quavery sigh. "*Surprise* us!" she said. "Surprise us! Oh, Collie, how—why in the world did you do it?"

"Why not? It was what we planned on. It was what I was supposed to do."

"B-but—but not that way! Not after you'd made a mistake, and it was so late you were almost sure to-to—to—" Her voice broke, and she covered her face with her hands.

She rocked back and forth, kind of sobbing and laughing, smiling and frowning, all at the same time.

That seemed to bring Uncle Bud back to life. He let out a laugh, slapping his hand on his knee.

"Surprise?" He beamed at me. "And what a surprise, Kid! I got to hand it to you, boy. I bet there ain't another man in the country that could have pulled a stunt like that and got away with it!"

"There's plenty that could do it. All you'd have to do is get them sore. Pick yourself a guy that's a little bit off and then try to throw a curve under him, and he'd do it."

"Yeah?" He weaved around that one. "Well, I know what you mean, Kid. You hold the short end of the stick just so long, and then you start swinging it. You've had enough, see? People just don't want to get along with you, no matter how willing you are, so finally—"

"Shut up!"

"Huh? Now, look, Kid—"

"I said to shut up!"

"But—" He brushed the back of his hand against his mouth. "W-well, sure. Anything you say, Kid."

"You gave me a card when I first came here," I said. "You wrote your name and your address and telephone number on it in case I had to get in touch with you. It's in your own handwriting, remember. Not just a printed business card that I might have come by accidentally."

I paused, letting it sink in on him. He wet his lips uneasily.

"You wouldn't have found that card on me today," I went on. "You couldn't have got it back. I won't tell you where it is, but I'll tell you this: I've got a good friend or two around the country. Even a guy like me will pick up a few friends. And if anything should happen to me, the cops will get that card mighty fast and they'll be told where it came from."

I was lying, of course. Probably Uncle Bud had a good hunch that I was. But he wasn't very bright, and he didn't have much in the way of guts. And if his hunch was wrong, if I *wasn't* lying . . .

His eyes flickered as he tried to make up his mind. He brushed at his coat nervously, his fingers lingering at the ominous bulge under his handkerchief pocket. He wanted to do it; he wanted to so bad that he could taste it. But he couldn't quite talk himself into the job. It was a pretty screwy thing I'd told him; like something out of a cheap movie. But—well, I was a pretty screwy guy, wasn't I? I'd already outsmarted him once today, and with a stunt that made less than no sense at all. So if I'd done it once, why wouldn't I do it again? How the hell did he know what I might do?

"Collie," said Fay, breaking the silence. "What—what is *this*? What are you getting at?"

I didn't answer her, or even look at her. I sat watching Uncle Bud a moment longer, grinning at him. Then, I got up and walked over in front of him.

"Well, how about it? You've got a gun. You were all set to use it an hour or so ago. Why don't you do it, now?"

His mouth opened. His lips moved silently, helplessly. I caught him by the shirt front, and yanked him to his feet.

"Can't make up your mind, huh? You're scared, stupid and scared. Well, I'll give you a little help. Maybe if you get good and sore . . ."

I gave him a little jolt under the heart. Just a little tap with my fist. Uncle Bud grunted, his face went white, and I tapped him again. Around the heart, down in the kidneys, and up on the wishbone. I held him with one hand and fed him those little jolts with the other. And his face seem to turn from white to green, and his tongue slid out from his teeth.

I reached under his coat, grabbed his gun, and shoved it into my belt. Then, I dropped him down into his chair, and went back to the sofa.

Uncle Bud sat bent over, hugging himself. He wasn't really hurt bad, just temporarily paralyzed with pain. But I guess he thought he'd been about half-killed.

Fay frowned at me. Scared, but more puzzled it seemed than

anything else. "Collie!" she said sharply. "I want to know what this is all about!"

"You know, Fay. I told you right from the beginning. I told you I wasn't stupid, and I didn't like for people to treat me like I was."

"But, but what's that got to do with it?" She paused and went on in a lower voice. "Is it—does it have something to do with yesterday? I'm terribly sorry about that, darling. It just came as such a shock to me that I couldn't think; I didn't know what I was doing for a while. Then I ran off and started drinking and made such a mess of myself that I was ashamed to face you."

"Forget it. I know how you felt and what you felt. So don't bother to tell me."

"But..." She hesitated again. "Is it—I'm sorry I let you down today, Collie. But I just didn't see how I could go through with it. I wouldn't have been any good to you. The way I felt, I'd have been almost sure to spoil things."

"But you pulled yourself together. You felt well enough to leave right behind me. To be Johnny-on-the-spot after I'd pulled the job."

"Well." She nodded slowly. "Yes. Uncle Bud thought we ought to do that much to help, at least. If something went wrong—if there was trouble, we might be able to pull you out of it. I was still sick, but I was worried about leaving you to do everything. And Uncle Bud thought I—we—"

"That's right, Kid." It was Uncle Bud getting back to normal. "That's just the way it was. We were concerned for you, having to do everything yourself, and we figured we'd better kind of keep an eye on things."

I laughed. I didn't say anything, just laughed the one time and chopped it off short.

Fay's eyes flashed. "And it's a good thing we were there! If we hadn't been, you'd have taken the wrong boy."

"Yeah? It hasn't maybe occurred to you that I picked that boy up deliberately?"

"Deliberately! But, but why would you do that? What—now, look!" she said. "I'm getting fed up! What's he talking about, Uncle Bud?"

He looked at me uneasily. He cleared his throat, tried to work up a smile, and it looked like something on a corpse. Fay frowned. She asked him again what I was talking about.

It was a pretty good act. You'd have almost thought she didn't know.

"Answer me!" she said. "I swear, if this keeps up much longer, I'll, I'll—!"

"Now, now." He squirmed. "There ain't nothing to get excited about. The Kid's just kinda got the wrong slant on things, an'—and I don't blame him, y'understand. I don't hold the slightest grudge whatsoever. He's been under a big strain today."

'Will you stop stalling and tell me!" said Fay loudly.

"Well, uh, you remember what we were talking about the other night? About maybe not actually going through with the snatch— just faking it kind of, and then having me step in and collect a fat reward?"

Fay nodded. "But we couldn't do it. There was just no way we could. So what about that?"

"Well, uh, yeah, there was a way all right. Just one way to make it look good. And I guess that's kind of what the Kid's thinking about. Then maybe he thought I was jealous of you two or something. Of course, he's all wrong, but—but you see how it might look to him. You act like you're completely washed up with him. The Kid figures we're both plenty leery of having him around. So when he had to go by himself today, and then we show up, why—"

Fay's glass slid out of her hands. It bounced against the carpet, and then toppled onto its side; rocked back and forth, the ice tinkling.

She stooped and picked it up. She reached out and set the glass on the table. She wasn't looking at what she was doing—she was staring at me—and it fell to the floor again. Fay didn't seem to notice. There was an expression on her face I'd never seen before. A kind of waking-up expression. It was the way a blind person might look if he was suddenly able to see. If he really saw himself for the first time in his life.

"So that's what you think," she said. "That's what you think of me."

"Why not?" I said.

"Yes. Why not? If a person won't stop at kidnaping, why would he stop at murder? I don't think it makes much difference about yesterday, Collie. About what happened or didn't happen. It may have brought about this situation a little sooner, but with people like us—people who've become what we have—we were bound to arrive at it." She rubbed her eyes tiredly, and shook her head. "You were wrong about not being stupid, Collie. You are. I am. Uncle Bud also, to cite a self-evident fact."

"Now, now," said Uncle Bud. "What's the sense in all this glooming around? We had a little misunderstanding, but it's all over now. We're all square with the world again. We got what we wanted, and now we're all set to collect."

Fay laughed. "Collect. Yes, gentlemen and lady, now we can collect."

"I said so, didn't I?" Uncle Bud turned to me. "Now, I've been thinking, Kid. There's nothing in the news about the station wagon, but isn't there a chance that that first boy might peep? I know it don't look like he would. He wouldn't want to admit he'd sneaked off and gone for a ride with a stranger. And probably if he did admit it, that matron would swear he was lying. But the cops won't be passing up any bets on this one, so . . ."

Fay got up suddenly and went into her bedroom. I started to get up, too, just instinctively without thinking. Wanting to go after her, to ask her if something was wrong. And then I caught myself, and I settled back down again.

"I can ditch it over at my place, Kid. What do you think?"

"What? Oh, well, yeah. Maybe you'd better do that. I'm pretty sure the boy won't say anything, but someone else might have spotted it."

"Right. I'll take it with me then when I go and leave you my car. I can pick up another heap to get around in until we pull down our jackpot. Now—" He reached for the bottle, and poured his glass half-full. He was trying to be friendly and casual, but his hand shook. Underneath his big, easy smile, he was scared stiff. "Now, I figured I'd mail the ransom note tonight, if that's okay with you. They'll get it the first thing in the morning."

"Look," I said. "We've been all through this. You know what you have to do, and there's no point in asking me about it."

"Yeah, but . . ." He hesitated. "Well, I don't want you to get any more wrong ideas, Kid. I don't want to do anything that maybe you, uh—"

"I won't get any ideas without a damned good reason. Just don't give me any reason, and I won't get any ideas."

His smile warmed up, began to look a little more natural. "Now, you're talking, Kid. Hell, there's no use getting all up in the air and acting unfriendly, is there? We had a little misunderstanding—and I don't blame you a bit, see?—but now that we got it cleared up—"

"All right. Let's just cut it off there. I'm tired of kicking it around, and I'm tired period."

"Sure. Sure, Kid," he said hastily. "Now, what do you think about—?" He broke off, started another sentence. "I think I'd better have something of the boy's, Kid. A label out of his clothes, or maybe his handkerchief. Something to send with the ransom note, so they'll know it's just not some crank writing. A case like this, you know, there'll—"

I got up, cutting him off, and went into the bedroom. I eased the boy's handkerchief out of his pocket, saw that it was initialed, and took it back into the living room. Uncle Bud said it would do fine; it was just what he needed. And maybe he'd better be running along now.

I walked out to his car with him. He gave me the keys to it and got into the station wagon. But he still didn't leave. He kept rambling on, thinking of things to say.

"That uniform and stuff, Kid. Better get rid of it right away. Take it out and—"

"And bury it. I know. I'm going to."

"Better get to work on that hair right away, too. Scrub it out until there ain't a trace of the dye left in it."

I said I would. I knew everything I had to do, and I'd do it. But he still didn't leave. He still sat there, fidgeting with the car keys, making conversation. So, finally, I did the only thing I could do. He'd made a half a dozen starts at doing it, but he was afraid to carry through. So I took the lead. I shook hands with him.

And a minute or so later he drove off.

TWELVE

I buried the uniform and the things that went with it. I came back up from the trees, resumed the spade to the garage and went up to the apartment. I washed my hair out, flopping down on the bed for a while afterwards. But tired as I was I couldn't rest. I kept tossing around, trying to straighten my mind out. And I sure didn't feel much like laughing, but somehow I wanted to laugh.

Because I'd played one hell of a joke on myself.

Doc Goldman had called the turn on me, all right. My judgment was anything but good. Guys with my background—and maybe a lot of guys without it—can't think very far ahead. They knock themselves out getting something. They just have to have it, it seems like. And then it turns out to be something they don't want, and they don't know how to get rid of it.

I'd looked forward to making Fay and Uncle Bud squirm. Crowding them onto the ragged edge and keeping them there. But now I could see it wasn't going to work. They might crack up and be unable to do what they had to. They might feel I was just waiting for a chance to pay them off, that they had to get me before I got them.

I'd had to shake hands with Uncle Bud. I'd had to pull him off the spot I'd put him on, make him think that things were at least reasonably okay. And Fay, I'd have to do the same thing with her— if I could. Because the other wouldn't work. The other took more out of me than I had.

I couldn't beat them over the head without beating myself.

It was night, dark, when I finally thought things out. As good, I mean, as I could think them out. I got up and went downstairs, and I stood there in the yard a while, looking in through the back door of the house.

Fay and the boy were at the kitchen table. She was holding him on her lap, not eating anything herself. But it looked like he was eating quite a bit.

He finished after a few minutes. They left the kitchen, the boy holding on to her hand, and watching through the windows I saw her take him into the bedroom.

I went on inside. There was a lot of stuff left on the table—canned beans and boiled ham and half of a pie. So I warmed up the coffee, and started eating.

Fay came in, pulling the door shut behind her. I looked up and nodded.

"How's the boy doing? Did he eat his dinner all right?"

"Did he?" She shrugged. "Don't tell me you don't know."

I supposed she must have noticed me out in the yard. I said I'd just waited out there until the boy was through because I was afraid I might upset him.

"Uh-huh. Well, if that's all you were just doing, I'll just tell you that young Charles, heir apparent to the Vanderventer fortune, had a light repast consisting of one-half of a pie and approximately one pound of beans. Not to mention ham, bread, and perhaps another pound of beans by way of dessert."

"I see. I guess he must have been pretty hungry."

"Now, I'll just bet he was! It hadn't occurred to me, but I can see now that he must have been."

She'd brought a bottle in from the living room. A full one, so I guessed she must have finished the other one. Fay poured herself a drink, that mean little smile playing around her lips when she saw me frown.

"Yes, he must have been hungry," she continued. "And I must be thirsty. You have parted the clouds, Collie, and at last everything is clear to me."

"I want to say something. I've been thinking things over, and I think maybe I was wrong about today."

"Yes? You think so—*maybe*?"

"About you, not Uncle Bud. I know what he was planning to do, but you didn't have to be in on it. You'd've had to ride along with him after he'd done it, but you might not have known about it beforehand."

"Go on. I maybe didn't. I might not have." She nodded over her glass. "It's algebra isn't it? You multiply the two minuses, and it gives you a plus."

"Look, I— Did you or didn't you? Just tell me."

"Tell you? Oh, that's against the rules, Collie. When you have to ask another person for the answer, it doesn't count."

"Well . . . well, at least tell me this. About yesterday and you finding out about me. Could you—would it have been all right? I know how people feel about those things, but I was through the worst of it and if I could have just gone on . . ."

"Yes. So would I have cared to accompany you for the rest of the journey? Well—" Her eyes glinted. "Would I or wouldn't I? As I said before, my answer doesn't count."

I shoved my plate back. I poured coffee into my cup, slopping it over into the saucer.

Fay poured another drink of the whiskey.

"Aside from the rules, Collie, I can't answer you. The question is posed on circumstances that no longer exist. Before three this afternoon I could have answered it, and you would have believed me. You'd have had no reason not to. But after that, after your little set-to with Uncle Bud, and your flat accusation that I was—"

"All right!" I interrupted her. "Why do you have to keep harping on it? What would you have thought if you'd been in my place?"

"Exactly what you did, my friend. I implied as much at the time."

I got up suddenly and went to the door. I stood there, wanting to leave, feeling like I had to get away from her. And feeling and wanting just the opposite. Wanting, feeling—I didn't know just what. I didn't want her to think I was suspicious of her, but I didn't want her to think she could get away with a double-cross either. I didn't want to be afraid of her, or to have her afraid of me. I wanted . . .

I looked out into the yard, out at the raked-up piles of grass, withered heaps in the moonlight. And I knew that what I wanted, I wasn't going to get. It was gone. It couldn't be brought back to life any more than that mowed-down grass could.

"That door," Fay said. "If you go through it you'll find a walk and at the end of the walk there's a lane, and at the end of the lane there's a highway . . ."

"Yeah? That door is wide enough for two people."

"These two?"

"Look," I said. "I'm not sure I know what you want. You mean, just walk off and forget about the money? You're willing to forget the whole thing, if I am?"

"The money has nothing to do with the matter, Collie. After all, it was supposed to be purely a means to an end, wasn't it? Whether it would achieve that end—a happy partnership, we'll call it—depends largely on us."

"Well, sure, but—"

"So there's our door to life. Let's see if it's wide enough for both of us."

She got up and went into her bedroom. I listened to her moving around, wondering uneasily what she was up to. Because it should have been clear enough to me, but it wasn't.

It was almost twenty minutes before Fay came back, her face made up and her coat and hat on. She nodded to me, and started for the door. I was too startled to move for a second. Then, I jumped up and got in front of her.

"Wait a minute! Where are you going?"

"Going?" She smiled up at me. "Why, I'm going out."

"I said *where*? You've got nothing to see Uncle Bud about. You've got no business at Bert's place. So where else could you be going?"

Her smile drew in at the corners. She stepped back from me, just a step but it seemed to take her awfully far away, and held out her hand.

"I almost forgot. The car keys, Collie."

"But where—" I broke off. "Oh," I said. "You're . . . you're just going for a little ride? You want to get a breath of air?"

"The car keys, Collie."

I gave her the keys, sort of laying them in her hand without quite letting go. "What does this prove, Fay? You just get up without any warning and start to leave. I suppose it wouldn't have bothered you, if I'd done that?"

"Do you? Do you so suppose? Well, treasure the thought, my friend. Some wastrel who doesn't care about inflation may give you a penny for it."

She jerked the keys out of my hand, and left. Just before she started the car, I heard her laugh—angry and teasing. Or maybe disgusted and disappointed. I took a fast step toward the door, then I snatched up the whiskey bottle and went into the living room.

I sat down with my back to the windows. I made myself sit there, not moving or looking around until she'd driven away. But why I did it, I don't know. It didn't mean anything. Feeling like I did—wanting to stop her, worried about where she was going and what she might be doing—it meant just the opposite of what it should have meant.

We couldn't go through the door together. We couldn't walk together very far on the other side of the door. So she'd proved her point ... if that's what she'd meant to do. And how did I know that Fay had?

Maybe it had all been a build-up, a way of pointing me in one direction so she could move in another. Why not? Fay couldn't get me to clear out, and leave her and Uncle Bud or someone else with my share of the loot. So she'd picked up with another plan, another way of cutting me out of the deal. She'd know just how to go about it. Right from the beginning, she'd been able to get me so rattled and mixed up I didn't know what I was doing.

Sure, she'd sent me away that first time. But Fay must have known I'd come back. I didn't have any place else to go, and—

"Mister ..." It was the boy, standing in the bedroom door. "Mister, I'm sick. I got to—to—"

His tiny body swayed, doubled at the waist. He put his hands over his mouth, and there was a gurgling sound. Then I swept him up in my arms and ran with him to the bathroom.

I wasn't quite fast enough. He was vomiting before I could get him over the toilet stool. The stuff gushed out of his mouth, splashing over the bathroom floor. Just when I thought there couldn't be anything left in him, it started coming out the other way.

"Sorry." Gasping for breath, he tried to apologize. "I'll—I'll clean it up, mister."

"No, you won't," I said. "Never mind, sonny. You just cut loose as much as you want to."

I had him sitting on the stool at the time. I was down in front of him, mopping and wiping with a towel. And there was something in his expression that stabbed through me like a knife.

"Y-you're not—m-mad at me?" he said.

"Mad?" I chucked him under the chin. "Hell, no, sonny! Why should I be mad at a little boy for being sick?"

He looked at me doubtfully. Apparently, he'd been expecting a spanking, and he still couldn't believe that he wasn't going to get one.

"Honest?" he said skeptically. "You're really not mad?"

"Honest. I'm not mad, and no one else is going to get mad. Because if they do—if anyone even looks like they're going to say a cross word to you—I'll, well they'd better not, that's all!"

He was sick; terribly sick. But a smile slowly spread over his face, and I think it was the most beautiful smile I have ever seen.

Then his arms went around my neck, and he pressed his face against mine. And the words he whispered to me ... I guess they were the nicest I have ever heard.

"I like you, mister. I like you very much."

... It was around eleven o'clock when Fay got home. I'd dozed off in my chair, and I waked up when I heard the back door slam. There was another bang as she dropped a bag of groceries on the kitchen table. She came into the living room, threw her hat and coat into a chair, and sat down in another one.

She didn't look drunk; I mean, she didn't wobble or stagger. But you could see the booze in her eyes, see it in her tight twisted little smile.

"The rats are still in the harness," she said. "I'm saving the pumpkin to make a pie."

I didn't say anything. Right just then, I didn't trust myself to.

"That's pie without an e, Collie. You multiply it by the frammis, and it gives you Cinderella. Coach on, or would you like to try for the jackpot? If you win, you get a window to throw it out of."

"The boy's been sick, Fay. I've taken him to the bathroom a half a dozen times."

"My, my! Well, you just tell him he has to take you the next half dozen."

"Damn it, it's not funny! What the hell's the matter with you, anyway? I told you he's sick."

"And I heard you!" Her voice sharpened. "What do you want me to do about it, ring for Doctor Kildare?"

It told her she'd done too damned much already, stuffing a kid full of junk when he was already upset. "You must have known it would make him sick. You load him up on the worst stuff you could think of, beans and pie and—"

"Sure, I did!" she yelled. "I force-fed him, didn't I? I ran a hose down his throat and pumped it into him! I tried to kill him! Why the hell don't you say so?"

"Now, wait a minute. I didn't say—"

"Aah, shut up! Go file the point on your head. But just don't try to kid me. Don't tell me you hadn't thought of it."

I blinked. I didn't know what she was talking about. I'd been pretty mad when she first came in, pretty sore and worried, so I guess I'd talked kind of rough.

"You're not that stupid," said Fay. "Sure, you've thought of it. We've got him, haven't we? We collect just as much if he's dead, and we save ourselves a lot of trouble."

I shook my head. I just sat there shaking my head.

Fay grinned at me, her eyes narrowed. "Can't take it, huh? Well, in a case like that there'd seem to be only one logical alternative."

"You're drunk. You don't know what you're saying."

"Want to bet? Let's bet pumpkins. Yours looks pretty green from here, but I'm a sport."

She reached for the bottle on the table, and took a swig from it. She hefted it, studying me, two trickles of booze running down the corners of her mouth. Then, she shrugged and slammed it back on the table.

"To hell with it," she said. "To hell with you. I'm going to bed."

Fay pushed herself up from the chair, picked up her coat and hat. Wobbling a little now. That last jolt of whiskey had hit her hard.

"Midnight," she mumbled. "So it's the end of the ball. Li'l Cinderella's gotta crawl back under her cork. Well, what's layin' on your larynx, stupid?"

"Nothing had better happen to that boy," I said. "There'd sure better not anything happen to him."

"Yeah? Well, right back at you, brother rat. Paste it into your hat. Line that pumpkin with it."

"You heard me! You may be drunk, but you know what you're doing."

Her eyes flickered. Her face twisted suddenly, like maybe she was going to vomit. Then, she turned and staggered toward her bedroom door.

"Stupid," she mumbled. "S-s-stupid an' can't help it. H-he can't, but . . ."

Fay went through the door, kicking it shut with her foot.

I stayed where I was for a while afterwards. Thinking that the boy might need me to help him again, and just thinking in general. About myself, about Uncle Bud, about her. Thinking in circles, and not getting anywhere. That stuff she'd said about the boy, about it being better for us if he was dead. Maybe she was trying to chase me off with that talk, to scare me into leaving for my own good. Or maybe she was doing it for her—their—own good. Or maybe she really meant it. Or maybe she was just testing me out to see how I'd take it. And if they really planned on having him dead, and if I wouldn't go along with the plan . . .

Maybe. If. If and maybe.

How the hell was I going to know? How could you know what people would do if they'd go in on a deal like this one?

I made myself stop thinking about it. My head just wouldn't take it any more, all that chasing around and around. So I started thinking about the little boy. Not the one we had, Charles Vanderventer III, but the first one. That little kid who was heading for Paris tonight.

I wondered if he'd meant what he kind of seemed to mean. Whether, you know, he'd been wise to what I was doing and had deliberately let me get away with it.

I guessed he hadn't. It was hard to be sure—he was such a sharp, fast-talking youngster—but I guessed he hadn't. I mean, he just couldn't have! No kid would have felt like that, felt that another kid would be better off kidnaped.

I turned the radio on low. The newscaster was just winding up his last broadcast for the night:

". . . No further developments in the Vanderventer case at this time. And now a few words about that plane disaster I mentioned a moment ago. The deluxe trans-Atlantic airliner crashed at La Guardia Airport, shortly after eleven tonight, when two of its motors failed simultaneously during the takeoff. All of the crew and all but three of the passengers were killed. Among the fatalities was ten-year-old Jacques Flannagan, son of motion-picture actor, Howard Flannagan of Hollywood, and Margot Flannagan Wentworth D'Arcy Holmes of Paris and London. In accordance with their divorce agreement, the boy spent six months a year with each parent. He had left this city earlier tonight, following a brief visit with his grandmother . . ."

THIRTEEN

That next day.

Just about everything happened that day. Just about everything seemed to go wrong.

It was the day the boy almost died. It was the day Bert tried to kill Uncle Bud. It was the day I robbed Doc Goldman's office. It was the day Fay tried to—to what?

Everything happened. Everything went wrong. Everything got worse than it had been.

So maybe I'd better take it from the beginning. I'd better start with Fay shaking me awake. Yelling at me to get up, and me darting my hand under the pillow, and coming out with the automatic I'd taken off of Uncle Bud. I didn't mean to kill her, naturally—I hadn't got to that point then. It was just that I'd gone to bed late and gone to sleep a hell of a lot later, and when she—But let's go back to the beginning.

"Collie! Collie, *stop!*"

I heard her screaming from a long way off. Screaming my name, yelling for some guy named Collie to stop. And for a moment it meant nothing at all to me. It was just a voice, just a name; it was coming from just one more of the twisted, white faces that had swarmed around me all night long.

They meant nothing. The only thing that mattered was this thing that someone had put in my hand. Something hard and cold and heavy. I looked down at it while the screaming went on, not really looking because my eyes were open, but I couldn't see with them. I just knew I had it and that I must have it for a reason, and the only reason I could think of was—

"*Collie—don't!* D-DONT!"

"Huh? What?"

"The boy, Collie! H-he's—*put it down!*"

I saw that the face had a body. The two merged, then slid down the wall and into a chair. And my mind began to wake up. It moved up from the darkness slowly, patching up the past, trying to make the day something I would wake up to.

"Going to put the grass back," I mumbled. "Put everything back like it was. Wasn't very pretty, but ... but ..."

"Aaah, hell," she sobbed. "Aaah, damn it to hell."

My fingers loosened, and the gun dropped to the bed. I sat up, feeling the old sickness clutch at my stomach. I stared at her, rubbing the sleep out of my eyes. Hating her and myself and this whole world I'd had to come back to.

"What's the matter?" I said. "What's wrong with the boy? What did you do to him?"

"Do to him!" Fay's head jerked up. "Why, damn you, I—Aaah, what's the use? He's sick, that's what's the matter. He looks like he's dying. I just woke up a few minutes ago, and I went right in to see how he was and he—h-he— He can't seem to get awake, Collie!"

"All right. Get back over there with him. Just stay there until I get over. Don't bother him or try to feed him."

"Feed him! How the hell could I?"

"Go on. Get out!"

Fay got out. I threw on my clothes, shoved the gun into my hip pocket, and ran down the stairs. It was noon. The hot sunlight hit me like a club, stirring up my stomach all over again. I stopped and was sick. I ran on a few steps and then I vomited again. I stood panting, bent over, waiting a few moments. But that seemed to do it for the time being. The sickness was gone as much as it was going to go. I ran on into the house and into the boy's bedroom.

Fay was in there with him. I brushed her out of the way, and bent down by his bedside. I studied him, listened to his breathing. I turned on the light and went down on my knees, bringing myself closer to him while I looked and listened.

His skin was flushed, hot, but damp looking. His eyes were partly open—sort of slitted. They were glazed, but he blinked a little when I passed my hand in front of them. He hardly seemed to breathe at all. His breath had a faint sweetish smell, and there was the same smell to his body. His pulse was pretty slow, but the beat wasn't bad. I mean it seemed fairly steady.

"Well?" Fay frowned at me. "Damn it, say something! Do something!"

"Turn the radio on. Get the newscast."

"Turn the radio on!"

"There ought to be something about this," I said. "About the boy. I think I know what's the matter, but I want to make sure."

She turned it on. A minute or two later Uncle Bud arrived from town with an armload of newspapers, so we got the word both ways at once. And it was just what I'd thought. I was right about the boy, and I wished to God that I wasn't.

I covered him up good. Then, I got a spoon and a cup, and fed him a few sips of lukewarm water. That didn't seem to help much, but it was about all I could do. I turned the light off and went into the living room.

Fay was working on a water glass full of whiskey. Uncle Bud, who also had a drink, was settled back in a chair taking things easy. He'd been all pepped up when he arrived. The family had got the ransom note, and they'd asked the police to stay out of the deal—to "cooperate," as the newspapers put it. Just to keep hands off, and let them pay the ransom and get the boy back. And it looked like the police were going to let them have their way.

I sat down, looking from Fay to Uncle Bud. He wiped the pleased grin off his face, turned on a sympathetic frown.

"Diabetes," he said. "Now, that's bad, that is. Who'd've ever thought he'd have a thing like that?"

I could think of a couple of people who might have thought it. Who damned well ought to have known about it. Because, hell, Uncle Bud knew everything else about the kid, didn't he? He and Fay had been kicking the kidnaping around for months, and he'd been digging into the boy's and the family's background even before that. So why wouldn't he have found out about this?

But—well, maybe he hadn't. If the kid was taken care of properly, if he was kept on a strict diet and got the right amount of rest and exercise and so on, the disease wouldn't bother him much. He wouldn't need too much in the way of actual medical treatment. Then, maybe his family was touchy on the subject—like some people are touchy about anything in the way of sickness or weakness—and they'd tried to keep the trouble hushed up.

It could have been that way; the family keeping quiet, the boy not too bad off. Anyway, regardless of whether Fay and Uncle Bud had known or not, it didn't change anything. And there was no point in trying to pin them down.

"Yes, sir," said Uncle Bud. "Yes, sir, it's sure a shame, a nice little boy like that. I guess you know quite a bit about the stuff, huh, Kid?"

I nodded. "People in mental institutions have it the same as anyone else. They don't always get treated for it, but they have it."

"Yeah? Now, that's sure a shame. I don't suppose you—uh—you wouldn't have any ideas about what we ought to do?"

Fay laughed and choked on her drink. I said I had a pretty good idea of what we ought to do, but I didn't have the stuff to do it with.

"I've worked as an orderly in several places. They never have enough help, so when they find a patient that's intelligent, they—"

Fay let out another whoop. I looked at her, not saying anything. Just sitting and staring until she was all through laughing. She cut it off pretty fast. She raised her drink, holding it up in front of her face, and I went on staring a moment longer.

"The boy's in a diabetic coma," I explained. "It isn't a bad one, and I think he'll pull through it. I think he can be pulled through it. But if he is, if we get him through this, he's practically a cinch to slide into another one. And as weak and run down as he is . . ."

"Yeah," Uncle Bud frowned. "I guess all that starch and sugar was pretty bad for him, huh?"

"It's a wonder it didn't kill him."

"Well, maybe it will yet!" Fay snatched up the bottle, refilled the water glass. "Maybe I'll get him next time! Why, the h-hell don't you say what you mean?"

"Now, now." Uncle Bud shook his head. "So what do you drink, Kid?"

"He needs insulin. He'll die if he doesn't get it."

"Yeah? Well, let's see. I know a few places, drug stores where they ain't too particular if they know a guy. But to do it now, when it's in all the papers and the heat's on . . . It'd be asking for trouble, really begging for it. I'm out in front on this deal, and if the word leaked out . . ."

He was right. Even someone with a prescription would probably be checked on now.

"I just don't see what we can do, Kid. I don't hardly know what we could do if we had the stuff. I mean, you've been around people with the disease—worked with the doctors—but the papers and radio don't say how much of the insulin the boy's been getting."

"They couldn't. The dosage would vary according to his condition. I'd have to kind of feel around for what he needed, start off with the minimum dose and work up."

"Uh-huh. I see . . ."

He went on asking questions, sort of aimlessly it seemed to me. Not paying too much attention to the answers . . . He was all for helping the boy, y'know. He loved children, Uncle Bud did. But it looked to him like there was every chance of harming him rather than helping him. After all, I wasn't a doctor. I just naturally couldn't be sure of whether I was doing the right thing or not. And with the boy as bad off as he was, just one little wrong move would probably push him over the line.

"You see my point, Kid. And it ain't that I don't think you mean well."

"I see your point," I said. "I see yours, all right. But maybe you don't see mine. If there's no trouble, like we're all hoping, we don't need the boy alive. In fact, it's a lot less risky for us if he isn't alive. They have to take our word for it that we're going to return him. We get the money either way; and without him around as evidence— someone we might get caught with, and who'll be telling all he knows afterwards—we'd be a lot safer. But . . ."

I broke off for a moment. Because it was hard to talk this way, so cold-blooded and everything. But I figured it was the best way to talk. I didn't know what was in their minds, whether they were just putting on an act or whether they really didn't want the boy to die. But I knew that if they did want him dead, they'd see that he was. They'd arrange it somehow sometime. And the only way I could stop them was to prove that it just wouldn't be smart.

"Go on, Kid," Uncle Bud nodded. "Of course, I wouldn't want a nice little boy like that to die. But if we just can't help it, well, it's like you say. It would work out pretty nice for us."

"I didn't say that. I mean, I said it but I was just pointing out how you might look on it. Me, I don't look on it that way. That family has half of the money in the state. If they don't get the boy back, they'll probably spend every nickel of it running us down. But then—well, suppose things don't come off as smooth as we hope they will and we got caught. It would sure be a lot better for us if the boy was alive. Even if he wasn't, if we could just show that we'd done everything we could do for him, it would be a lot better."

Uncle Bud frowned, chewing his lip. He hesitated, nodded slowly. "Yeah." He sighed. "I guess you're right, Kid. We sure got to do what we can, even if it don't work out right. But how can we get that insulin?"

"Doc Goldman," I said impatiently. "He comes back to his office at two, and he's there until five. He doesn't take any office patients after that time. If someone could call him just before five, get him out on a fake call, I could have a good look around."

"I get it, I get you, Kid. There wouldn't be anyone there? You could get in and out all right?"

"Easy. He never locks the place up. I know right where he keeps everything. The chances are he'd never know that anyone had been there."

"Swell. Well, that settles that then." He got up and put his glass on the table. "Now, I'm going to be tied up right until about five. I got to keep right on top of this deal, you know, keep in touch with everything that's happening. So I'll just run along now, and you can come in later."

"Come in?" said Fay. "How's he going to get there? You think I'm going to be stuck out here without a car?"

"Why not?" I said. "What do you want with a car?"

"What do you think, stupid? I want to take the tires off and make myself a girdle!"

"But why—"

"She's right, Kid," Uncle Bud broke in hastily. "Everything's going to be jake, but still the little lady'll feel a lot easier with a car. I know I would. So you come in with me."

I guessed I probably would, too. Anyway, with Fay dead set on keeping the car, there was no use in arguing about it.

I ran over to the garage and got my coat and tie. He was waiting in his car for me when I came down, and we started for the city.

He'd dumped the station wagon with a salvage dealer pal of his, he said. A guy that bought hot cars and wrecked them for their parts. Of course, he went on casually, he hadn't been able to get any money for it—only a few bucks, that is. The guy was just trying to be friendly, y'know, just being a pal. So it wouldn't have been right to take money from him.

I grinned to myself. Kind of embarrassed for him, for Uncle Bud I mean. Kind of ashamed for him. Here he was, about to pull down a hundred thousand dollars, his share of the ransom, and he couldn't pass up the smallest chance to chisel someone. It was the way he was made. He'd rather chisel a dollar than earn a hundred.

"That's the way I am, Kid," he continued. "I play straight with my pals, and I like to have them play straight with me. Like take us for example. Now, we've had our little spats and misunderstandings maybe, but they don't amount to nothing. We all like and trust each other, we're pals, y'know. Everything's on the up and up with us, with no one holding out anything on another one."

He paused, studying me slyly out of the corner of his eyes. I didn't say anything, and he went on.

'Now, take that little yarn you told me, Kid. I was kind of hurt at the time, but I know you were just joking. Why, hell you wouldn't have passed that card I gave you to someone else! You'd be afraid the party might ask you some questions, try to cut himself in maybe. That's right, ain't it?" He laughed and nudged me with his elbow. "You were just having a little joke with your old Uncle Bud?"

I shrugged. I still didn't say anything.

"Well?" he said, his laugh trailing off. "What about it, Kid?"

"What about it?" I said.

"Well, uh, what I was saying, dammit. I said you wouldn't have done it, because you'd be afraid that—that—" He broke off abruptly, his face falling. "Oh," he said. "The guy ain't in a position to ask questions, huh? Or maybe you promised him a nice piece of change?"

I shrugged again. He was doing a lot better with the answers than I could.

"But that's not giving me a fair shake, Kid! Suppose something happens that's not my fault? I play it straight with you, but someone else pulls something and this guy cracks down on me!"

I still didn't say anything. He looked at me uncertainly.

"You wouldn't put me on a spot like that, Kid. You're a guy that likes to play fair, and you'd have seen it wasn't fair. You didn't do it ... did you?"

I smiled at him. He waited a moment, and then he grumbled

something under his breath. And for the rest of the ride he didn't
have much to say either.

It was two-thirty when he pulled up at a bar on the edge of the
business district. He said he'd pick me up there in a couple hours,
and I got out and went in.

It was a dingy, dimly lit place with a bar and lunch counter up
front and a few pool tables in the back. There were only a couple of
customers, and they drifted out while I was having a sandwich and
some beer. I bought another beer, picked up an afternoon newspaper
from the counter and went over to a booth.

There was a big picture of the boy on the front page. There were
pictures of his parents and the playground matron and the chauffeur;
practically everyone that could be tied into the case in any way. And
just about the whole paper was filled with news of the kidnaping. Or,
I should say, stories about it. Because they hadn't been able to dig up
much of anything new.

A ransom note had been received. The kidnapers had demanded a
quarter of a million dollars for the boy's return. How, where—and
when—the money was to be paid, "had not been revealed." The
details were a secret between the police and the family.

And, of course, Uncle Bud.

I went through the stories carefully, making sure that I didn't miss
anything. I took them apart word by word, and they still added up to
nothing. But for me it was a kind of uncomfortable nothing . . . The
cops wouldn't reveal the details about the ransom payment, but there
could be more than one reason for that. It could be that they just
didn't know any to reveal. Uncle Bud said that they did. He'd said
that the family had shown them the ransom note to make sure that
they wouldn't accidentally mix up in the case. Get in the way of the
pay-off, you know, and endanger the boy's life.

That sounded reasonable enough, because the boy wasn't to be
released until twenty-four hours after the money had been paid. The
cops might grab the guy at the pay-off, but it was likely to get the boy
killed if they did. So—so, it sounded reasonable. It was the way Uncle
Bud had planned things, the way he'd explained them to Fay and me,
and everything seemed to be going according to plan. So perhaps
everything was okay. But I was beginning to have some doubts.

It was Uncle Bud's job to pick up the money. It was his job to keep track of what the police knew. And if they didn't know how or where or when the ransom was to be paid—if they were "cooperating" because they had to, it made a nice setup for him. Or even if the cops did know, it was still just about as nice. If they weren't ready to cooperate yet, he'd just wait until they were.

And only he knew exactly when that would be. Only he knew how much time the Vanderventers had been given to come across. He'd told Fay and me it was seventy-two hours, but it could be less. He could collect the dough one night—tomorrow night, say—and be out of the country the next morning.

I got another beer, and brought it over to the booth. I wondered how, if he was planning a fast one, I could head him off... Demand to pick up the money myself? Uh-uh, I guessed not. He could send me into a police trap. Then, while I was getting bumped off, he could grab the money and skip. He wouldn't need to worry about that "friend" of mine then. That "friend" couldn't make him any more trouble than I could.

Fay? Should I wise her up, see if we could work out something together? Uh-uh, again. She might be in on Uncle Bud's scheme. She might have plans of her own. Anyway, and regardless of whether she was on the level with me or not, it wasn't safe to tell her anything. Not after she'd turned on me like she had. Not with her boozing like she was. She might do something crazy and dangerous, just for the hell of it.

I didn't know what I should do. Hell, I didn't even know whether I should even be thinking about doing anything. Everything was working out like we'd planned, wasn't it? The only thing that had really changed was me—my mind. I was getting so confused and mixed-up that nothing looked straight to me, and any little thing made me suspicious. Anything or nothing. If things went one way I didn't like them, and if they went another way I didn't like them. And—and it had to stop! If it didn't, if people didn't stop worrying me, coming at me from every direction, pushing and crowding and...

A band seemed to tighten around my head. I closed my eyes, and for a moment I just wasn't there. There was nothing but blackness with me floating away on it.

After a while the band got looser, and the blackness faded away. I gulped down the rest of the beer fast. And in a minute or two I was all right again. Or as right as I was going to be.

I lighted a cigarette. I heard the screen door slam, and I started to peer out of the booth. Then, I jerked my head back, and raised the newspaper up in front of my face. Because it was Uncle Bud, all right; he'd come right on the dot of four-thirty. But he had someone with him—Bert.

FOURTEEN

Uncle Bud was in front. Bert was walking right on his heels, kind of moving him along with his body. The bartender glanced at them casually and went back to polishing glasses. Uncle Bud was looking straight ahead, his face a white blur in the dimness; and Bert was looking straight at the back of Uncle Bud's neck.

They passed down the length of the bar. They went down the long lane at the side of the pool tables. They reached the rear of the place, and Uncle Bud stopped in front of the rest room door. Bert nudged him. He said something to him, gave him another nudge.

Uncle Bud opened the door. Bert shoved him through it and went in after him.

I was on my feet the moment the door closed. I carried my beer bottle over to the bar, took a step or two toward the front door, then turned around and headed back toward the rear.

Just short of the rest room, I turned and glanced behind me. The bartender was still at his glass-polishing. No one else had come in. I hurried on, walking on the balls of my feet and paused outside the rest room door.

Keeping an eye on the bartender. Listening.

"Cheatin' bastard!" Bert was saying. "Thought I'd never catch up with you, huh? Well, I'm the last guy you'll ever chisel! I'm gonna—"

"Naw, naw, B-Bert!" Uncle Bud gave a kind of stuttering gasp.

"You got to listen to me! You got to give me a little time! J-just give me—*No!*"

There was a *click*—a knife coming open. And a slow scuffing of feet as, I imagined, Bert moved toward him and Uncle Bud backed away.

"Naw, naw!" He gasped again. "A little time B-Bert, just give me a little time an' you'll get every penny! I swear it, B-B—"

I eased the door open a crack, saw that Bert's back was toward me. I pulled it open a little further, watching him, watching that long sharp knife in his hand.

"I'll give you somethin'!" The blade trembled and he grunted for emphasis. "I'll give you all the time in the world and the next one, too, you rotten, chiseling, no-account son-of-a-bitch!"

He brought the knife up suddenly. Uncle Bud sort of moaned and sobbed. Then I threw the door back and went in.

Bert didn't have time to turn around. I had one all set for him, a hard right hook, and he got it in the back of the neck.

The knife flew out of his hand. He pitched forward, striking his head on the stained iron urinal, then fell sprawling face-down to the floor.

Uncle Bud sagged against the wall, pawing the sweat from his white face. He looked down at Bert, straightened up suddenly and kicked him as hard as he could in the head.

"Going to give it to me, were you?" he spat. "Well, damn you, I'll—!" He aimed another kick. I shoved him back against the wall, then grabbed him by the arm and hustled him toward the door.

"Come on! Come on, dammit! We've got to get out of here!"

"B-but—" He tried to hang back. "He was going to kill me! You saw him, Kid. H-he was goin' to—" He took a deep shuddering breath, and the glaze went out of his eyes. "Yeah," he said. "Yeah, sure, Kid."

We got out of there. A few blocks away, we stopped at another bar and he put down a couple of fast drinks. He needed them. He had the shakes so bad that you could almost hear him rattle.

"Hell, Kid," he said, as we drove away from the place, "I never got such a scare in my life! I didn't dare turn my head to see if you were there. I was afraid maybe you'd stepped out for a few minutes."

"Yeah. Where'd he pick you up, anyway?"

"That's what I don't know! That's what gave me such a jolt! I'd parked my car and was just starting through the door of the joint, and there the murdering son-of-a-bitch was! Right behind me with that knife in my back. Hell, he seemed to come from nowhere! It was like he'd dropped down out of the sky!"

"Then he could have been tagging you around for quite a while."

"He could have been, but it doesn't seem likely. It looks like I'd have spotted him if he had. No, I figure he must have just been there in the neighborhood and he picked me up when I got out of the car." He shook his head, stared frowning through the windshield. "I hope it was that way, anyhow. I mean, that he just happened to bump into me accidentally. I'd sure hate to think that ..."

I nodded. I'd have hated to think it, too. I didn't care about Uncle Bud particularly, because a guy like he was—a guy that had taken everyone he could, that had caused all the misery he must have caused—was long overdue for the cemetery. But this would be a bad time for him to go there; and he'd be going there pretty fast if things were like they might be.

"I wonder," he said, worriedly. "I know a hell of a lot of people, and it could be that he's buddies with some of the same ones. He might have someone keeping an eye on me—several people, maybe— tipping him off every time they run into me anywhere. Why, hell, it could be and I wouldn't know it! All the people I've met, had dealings with, y'know, I don't always remember 'em myself!"

He was getting the shakes all over again. I told him there was probably nothing to worry about. After all, Bert had been gunning for him for quite a while, but he hadn't caught up with him until today.

"It was just an accident," I said. "He just happened to be in that neighborhood at the same time you were. If he had any help, he'd've tagged you before this."

"Well ..." He hesitated. "Well, maybe. It kind of looks that way, don't it? Of course, he may be just now deciding to crack down. It's been quite a while since I skinned him—since we had this little misunderstanding, I mean."

"What about that bar?" I said. "Are you in there every day?"

"Kind of on schedule, you mean? Uh-uh, not me, Kid. Not your old Uncle Bud." He winked at me, grinning. "I don't do things that

way. I move around. Even with living quarters, I don't keep any of
'em more than a few weeks."

"No one knew you were going to be there at the bar today? You
didn't mention it to anyone?"

"Uh-uh. Not a soul. Well, I may have mentioned it to Fay, but no
one else. Yeah, Kid," he pushed his hat back, began to relax, "I guess
it's like you say. It was just one of them things, just an accident."

I had a hunch that it wasn't—that someone had tipped Bert off,
and that someone would tip him off again. That they'd keep doing it
until Bert managed to nail him. But it was only a hunch; Uncle Bud
was jumpy enough already, and we still had things to do.

It was almost five o'clock when we stopped at a drug store a few
blocks from Doc Goldman's house. I sat down at the counter and
bought a coke, while he put in the phony call from a booth phone.

He came out of the booth, paused at my side a moment. "Okay,
Kid. He fell for it. I'll be back for you as soon as he leaves."

He drove off. About ten minutes later, when I was finishing my
second coke, he pulled up in front again.

He gave me a sharp-eyed look as I climbed into the car. "You look
pretty peaked, Kid. How you holding up with all this, anyway?"

"All right. I'm all right."

"Well, uh, isn't all this nervous strain and excitement pretty hard
on you? I know you're not really cra—I mean, you've just got a little
nervous trouble. But—"

"Don't count on it." I turned around in the seat and stared at him.
"Don't try to force me into it. Because if I do crack up, it won't be
nice for anyone around me."

"Aah, now, Kid." He looked hurt. "Ain't we pals? Didn't you save
my life today?"

"I'm all right. I'm going to go right on being all right, and no one
had better try to trim me or double-cross me."

"Sure. Sure, Kid," he said hastily. "I was just concerned for you
was all."

He let me out in front of Doc's place, and headed back to the drug
store to wait for me. I took a quick glance around, and started up the
walk.

The house was on the outskirts of the city—I guess I mentioned
that before. There were two vacant lots between his house and the

next one, and there were no houses at all on the other side of the
street. I could be seen, of course. The people in that nearest place
could see me if they happened to look that way. But if they did, I
guessed they wouldn't think anything of it. They'd be used to seeing
people come and go from Doc's house. I'd be just one more, another
patient.

I went up the steps and across the porch. Then I opened the door
and went in. That was the reception room there, the room the door
opened into. The living quarters were on through to the rear, and his
office and lab were on the right.

I looked around, and everything looked just as I remembered it.
The chairs sitting around the walls. The little table stacked with
magazines. The rug in the middle of the carpet to cover up a worn
spot. The dime-store ash trays. The—

I couldn't go any further for a minute. I just had to stand there
looking, feeling kind of good—safe and comforted—in one way, and
pretty lousy in another. It was like coming home and pulling some
dirty trick.

But I had to do it. I was doing it for the boy, not myself. So I
crossed the reception room, and opened the office door.

And bumped smack into Doc Goldman.

FIFTEEN

He had his hat on. He'd been coming through the door from the
other side, and he was just about as startled as I was. Which was
plenty, believe me.

I tried to speak, to smile, but my mouth seemed to be in a knot. I
didn't know what in the hell to do, and all I could think of was that
he'd caught me red-handed, right in the act of breaking in on him.

I backed up a step. I mumbled something, God only knows what,
and I was just about to turn and run.

But by then he was over his start.

"Collie! Collie, my friend!" He grabbed my hand and wrung it.

"I'm sorry I didn't hear you come in. I got a flat on my car right around the corner, and I just ran back to call a cab."

"Oh." I began to breathe easier. For a moment I'd thought that Uncle Bud had tried to trick me. "Well, if you're going out—"

"No, no. It'll take a few minutes for the cab to get here. How have you been anyway? Come on in the lab and let me get a look at you."

He herded me into the laboratory, made me lie down on the examination table. He went on talking, asking questions, as he took my pulse and rested his hand on my forehead.

I said that I was still living at Mrs. Anderson's. She'd got over the shock of finding out about me, and now things were just like they had been.

"Well, that's fine, wonderful. I know how it must have seemed to you at the time, Collie. I can't tell you how blue I felt after you'd called me."

"I'm sorry about that. I didn't mean any of that stuff I said."

"Of course, you didn't. Not that there wasn't a certain amount of truth in it. But you understand, now, don't you, Collie? You see that she had to be told?"

"She had to all right. But it would have been a lot better if I'd told her right in the beginning."

"Yes? Well, anyway, we've got it all over with now, haven't we? Now, if you'll just relax, just let yourself go limp . . ."

He dug his fingers into my biceps. He raised one of my arms and shook it, watching the movement of my hand. Then, he slid a light refractor onto his head and bent over me, pulling the lids back from my eyes.

"Uh-uh. Not that way, Collie. Look straight at me . . ."

He stared into first one eye, then the other. My eyes began to water and he let me rest them for a moment, and then he went on staring. At last, he straightened and took off the refractor. He stood frowning down at me, slapping the shiny metal disc against the palm of his hand.

"Not good, Collie. Not good at all. You're a lot more tense than you were the first night I met you."

"Yeah? I mean, I am? I feel fine."

"Like hell you do. What's bothering you? And don't tell me there isn't anything."

"Well, I—there isn't anything now, but there was. Mrs. Anderson took what you told her pretty hard. She's all right now, but I guess I'm still kind of upset."

"Kind of is hardly the phrase for it. And it doesn't quite add up for me, Collie. You were very far down in the dumps; the pendulum was right at its lowest point. Even without the situation ending reasonably happy—as you indicate it did—you should have been on the upswing by this time."

"Well, anyway it's like I told you. Everything is all right."

A horn honked in the street. His taxi. He hesitated, fidgeting.

"I guess I'll have to run, Collie, but—Can you wait here for me? I shouldn't be gone more than an hour."

"I don't know. I'd sure like to, but, well, Mrs. Anderson drove me into town tonight. There was some friends she had to see, and I guess I'll have to leave whenever she stops back by."

"You tell her to wait for you, Collie." He put his hat back on. "Tell her I'd like to see her, too. Will you do that?"

The horn honked again. I told him I didn't think she could wait; she'd probably be in a hurry.

"Well, wait by yourself then. I'll drive you home myself."

"I can't. I mean—well, I don't think I can. You see, I—I—"

"Yes?" he said. "Yes, Collie?" And then his expression changed, became kind of a no-expression, and he turned and started for the door. "I'll have to run now. You stay if you can, Collie."

He hurried out. The front door slammed, and a moment later I heard the cab drive off.

I eased a hand under my right hip. I turned carefully, grabbing the gun just as it fell to the table. The damned thing had slipped when I'd laid down. If Doc had shifted me around any, he'd've seen it.

I shoved it back into my pocket. I boosted myself off the table and went to work on the medicine chest. It was a tall steel cabinet with six big drawers and about a dozen little drawers inside of each of the six. They were all unlocked. The only thing Doc locked up was his narcotics, and they were in the office safe.

I took a two-c.c. syringe and a couple of hypodermic needles—two in case one got broken. I went on looking, working fast, jerking the drawers in and out, until I found the insulin. It was the regular type, but there were only two vials of it, two of those glass, 400-unit, 10-c.c. tear-drop tubes. I hesitated, staring down at the little crystal-clear tubes. Then I laid them on the table with the hypodermic syringe and the needles and went back to the cabinet. The drawer labels might be haywire. Doc had a pretty big practice and no one to help him. And sometimes he mixed things up.

I started at the top of the cabinet again, and worked down. Taking it slower this time, looking carefully through each drawer. I worked from the top to the bottom, not missing a bet. And then, well, that was it. There was just the twenty c.c.'s. There wasn't any more, and this would have to do. It didn't look like it, but it could be more than enough to get the boy out of it and keep him going awhile. Actually, I really didn't know. I didn't know a lot of things.

I got a paper towel from the sink and wrapped the stuff up. I left the house, worried about getting what seemed so little and worried about taking that little. Doc was sure to miss it—his entire supply. All I could hope was that he wouldn't need it any time soon.

Uncle Bud was waiting in front of the drug store. We started for the house, and I told him my doubts. It didn't seem to exactly break his heart.

"Might not be enough, huh? Well, that's sure a shame. But you did your best, Kid. We all did our best."

I looked straight ahead, not saying anything. He took his hand off the wheel and gave me a little pat on the back.

"Now, don't you take it to heart, Kid. It's too bad, sure, but these things always work out for the best. It's like we were saying this morning, you know. We sure don't want that nice little boy to die, but it might not be too bad for us if he did."

"Yeah, that's right, isn't it? I guess that kind of slipped my mind."

"Why, sure. So cheer up, huh?" He gave me a nudge. "This may be a good break. Of course, we'll hope this'll be enough."

"Well, we can't be sure that it won't be," I said. "It might just do it. It might keep him alive for another couple of days, anyway, maybe a lot longer. I don't know."

"Yeah? But you said—"

"I said he'd probably need more. In his condition, I'm not sure this'll even halfway put him back on his feet. But it could keep him alive until after we get the money."

"Well..." He shrugged. "So we got nothing to worry about either way, have we?"

I nodded, shook my head. And it looked to me like he'd said a lot in that last sentence. Fay might want the boy dead, or she might want him to live. I didn't know which. But Uncle Bud—he'd given himself away. He wanted to keep Fay and me satisfied, to keep us from doing anything that would upset the apple cart. Aside from that, he didn't care what happened to the boy. And there was just one reason why he didn't.

He was going to skip with the money. When the storm broke, he'd be a long way off.

Or, anyway, he thought he would.

SIXTEEN

The boy was conscious, but he was awfully weak. His kidneys had been moving all day, trying to get rid of the sugar that his system couldn't burn. He was too weak to even whisper. I asked him how he felt, and his lips moved a little but no words came out.

Uncle Bud had left. He just couldn't be around anything like this, he said; anyone getting a needle stuck in them. It made him sick to his stomach, and anyway he had things to do in town.

Using a fork, I lifted a needle from the pan of water boiling on the stove. Then I fitted it to the hypodermic syringe and jabbed it into the rubber-capped tip of one of the 10-c.c. vials. I pulled back the plunger carefully. The syringe held two c.c's, and I wasn't sure of the minimum dosage for a seven-year-old child, a mighty sick one at that. But I figured he needed a good jolt.

Still, giving him too much at one time could be bad—even fatal. I remembered from the mental hospitals that one cubic centimeter was equal to 80 units. The label on the tubes said this was 400-unit, regular insulin; I knew this had to do with the concentration, but— Well, I had to admit it. I was scared and confused, but I had to go through with it and hope for the best.

I lifted the boy's limp arm and Fay, who had been watching from the doorway, frowned. "That's not right, is it? I've always gotten shots in the left arm."

I shook my head, not answering her; concentrating on the boy. He gave a little jump when the needle went in. Fay jumped, too, standing right behind me, and of course that gave me a start. I gave him the full two centimeters, more than I'd meant to, but then I'd been startled. I took out the needle and waited. I watched his face carefully for a reaction, but there was none. So I refilled the syringe with another two c.c.'s, inserted the needle into his arm, and gave him more.

He jumped and she jumped and I jumped. I put the needle down, looked at the boy, and now there was a definite reaction. He shuddered suddenly, took a long, shivering breath. His face turned red, and he burst out all over with sweat. He really felt that one.

I was elated that he'd come out of it, overcome with doubts that I'd given him an overdose, and then suddenly confident that I knew what I was doing. It was like it should have been, like it often was as I remembered, and I knew just what to do about it. But I didn't get the chance. I'd just snatched up the bowl of thick sugar-water and started to spoon it down the boy, when Fay yelled and knocked it out of my hand.

"You don't know what you're doing! You're crazy! You—you—!"

I jumped up, and grabbed her by the shoulders. "But I know what *you're* doing! And now you're through doing it!" I shoved her out of the room. I ran her backwards through the doorway, and slammed her down hard in a chair. "Now, stay there! If you foul me up again, I'll—I'll—"

I raced into the kitchen, threw together another bowl of sugar and water. I ran back into the bedroom with it, mixing it on the way, and began feeding it to the boy.

It was all he needed. Something to cushion the shock of the insulin. I held him up with one arm, shoving the sugar into him as fast as I could move the spoon. His breathing eased, there were no more of those shuddering gasps. It leveled off, became even and effortless. The sweating stopped, and the red went out of his face.

I lowered him to the pillow. He looked up at me wide-eyed—still scared, naturally; frightened at being here and lonesome for his own home—but feeling a lot better. Feeling so much better than he had that he couldn't help smiling feebly.

I smiled back at him. His eyes drifted shut, and he fell asleep. I stayed there with him a while, watching to see if there was a delayed reaction. There wasn't any, though, so I turned off the light and went into the living room.

Fay was right where I had put her. I fixed myself a drink, and sat down. "He's all right. You can go in and look at him if you want to."

"I can, huh?" Fay looked grim.

"He's all right, and he's going to stay that way. I—it just makes good sense, Fay. You ought to see that. The better he is when he gets back to his folks, the better it'll be for us."

She grimaced. Her hand went out for the whiskey bottle and tilted it over her glass.

"When," she said dully. "You mean if, don't you?" Then, before I could answer her, "How long is that stuff you gave him going to last?"

"Long enough. I think it will, anyhow."

"Sure. You *think*. But you don't know, do you? All you know is that we've got him on our hands—a kid that's liable to go on us at any time. A kid that's got his picture in every paper in the country. We can't beat it with him, and we can't leave without him. We just have to sit here, hanging onto a keg of dynamite, and hope that lightning won't strike us."

"Have you got any better ideas?"

"Skip it. Forget it. I'll be screwy myself if I talk to you much longer."

I went out into the kitchen, and made a couple of sandwiches. I ate one of them and carried the other back into the living room.

She watched me as I began to eat, then laughed a kind of tired laugh. "Poor Collie. They may hang him, but he'll fill his stomach first."

"With food," I said pointedly.

"Mmm?" she frowned. Then, she laughed again. "Very good. Too damned good. It was things like that—that sort of thing that threw me off. You were so sharp sometimes that I didn't see how . . ."

"Yeah?"

"Never mind. That's the way it was. This is the way it is."

"I don't know what the doctor told you about me," I said. "Exactly what. But I'd like to know."

"Then I'll fill you in on the important points. He told me that with the right kind of environment and the right kind of associates you'd be all right. You were well on the road to recovery, and you'd soon be at the end of it. On the other hand—" She hesitated. "On the other hand . . ."

"Well?"

"Why bother with the rest of it? The unreasoning suspicion, the very-dangerous-if-aroused part. Let's just say that it's my fault, and I'm sorry. But that doesn't change anything. I can't let it change anything."

"Look, Fay. If I just knew what you wanted, if you'd just talk straight, maybe I could . . ."

"Ditto. Double ditto, you might say, since your background is considerably more ominous potentially than mine. No." She held up a hand. "Let's don't keep hashing it over. Because it gets a little messier each time, and I get a little sorrier for you. Just tell me one thing if you can. How long are you absolutely sure the boy will last without proper medical treatment?"

"I gave him proper treatment. Maybe you don't think so, but—"

"Now, don't go touchy on me, Collie! You know what I mean, so answer the question."

"Well, with the insulin I gave him and the way it took hold he's sure to be all right for another twenty-four hours."

"You sound so positive."

I had fooled her with my confident air so I ignored her remark. "He can eat something tomorrow and that'll help. A poached egg, maybe a little lean meat, and some milk."

She nodded, leaned back in her chair yawning. "Excuse me, it's not the whiskey, but the company. Why don't you take yourself off, doctor? I think they're calling for you in the annex."

I said I guessed I would turn in. I was pretty tired, and the boy should sleep soundly for the rest of the night. She looked at me absently, not saying anything, so I carried my plate out into the kitchen and left.

Quite a breeze had sprung up, and it was actually kind of cold.

But I left the front window of the apartment open. It faced on the driveway, and if she started the car or if anyone came up the lane I'd be sure to hear it. I—well, I just didn't know, you see. I didn't know why anyone might be coming up there, or why she might try to drive off. I didn't know what might happen or why, so I just had to try to look out for everything.

I undressed. I started to slide the gun under my pillow, but then I thought that might be something else to look out for. She knew I kept it there, so maybe I'd better put it some place else.

I looked around. Finally, I pulled the reading stand a little closer to the bed, laid the gun on top of it, and covered it with an opened magazine. That looked natural enough, like I'd been reading the magazine and laid it down open to hold my place. I could reach the gun as fast as if it was under my pillow.

I turned off the light, and went to bed.

I fell asleep right away. Thirty minutes later I waked up, still dead tired, but too tense to relax. I got a drink of water and smoked a couple cigarettes. Afterwards I dozed a little, and then came awake again. Restless and uneasy. My nerves drawn into a knot. My mind going around and around.

Uncle Bud. I knew what he was going to pull, so what was I going to do about it? How was I going to stop him? I knew I had to—even if didn't know why I had to—but I had no idea how to go about it.

He was there in my mind; there was a big picture of him there. Hat pushed back on his smooth grey head, an easy smile on his face, his eyes warm and friendly. I could see him as plain as day, hear his soft, restful voice. I concentrated and I could hear him talking about—about—I listened carefully, clearing my mind of everything but him, and the words came through at last—about the ransom pay-off.

He told me about it all over again, patiently, beaming at me. And all the time laughing to himself:

"Yeah, I know, Kid. That's the way it's usually done, and that's the way so many guys get knocked off. They go way to hell out in the country somewhere—and they fix it up so the money will be thrown out of a car or some deal like that. They think they're safe because there's no one else around, but that's just why they ain't safe. How do they know what's off

in the woods, or behind a hill? How do they know the whole damned area ain't been staked out? You see what I mean, Kid? They actually give the cops a setup. If there's no one around but one guy, that guy has to be it . . . So we won't do it that way. I won't. The way I'll work it—

The money would be left at the railroad station checkroom for a "Mr. Whitcomb." A messenger—ordered by telephone—would be sent to pick it up. It would be in a plain suitcase. There would be plenty of other people around in the station, coming and going from the checkroom. Carrying suitcases exactly like it. The cops would have a job keeping track of one of them; they'd be almost sure to give themselves away if they tried. If they did, though, if they did follow that plainclothes messenger, they wouldn't catch Uncle Bud.

He knew a stumblebum, a wino with a criminal record. The guy would do anything for a few bucks, no questions asked, and the suitcase would be delivered to him at this flophouse he lived in. If nothing happened after about an hour, Uncle Bud would pick it up. If something did happen—if the cops grabbed the guy—well, it was just too bad for him. He'd be caught with the evidence. He'd talk, of course, but he couldn't prove anything. Uncle Bud would just say that the guy was lying, and that would be that.

No, Uncle Bud wasn't taking any chances on anything. Chances were for the other guy—me. He'd already let me take them all, and now he was going to take all the money.

He was there in my mind, smiling and explaining—and laughing at me. All set to take the money—*my money* and laughing about it. Laughing, laughing, laughing, and there had to be some way, I had to find some way to stop him somehow . . .

I went to sleep.

. . . It was late when I waked up. Around noon. I saw what time it was, and I jumped out of bed fast. Kind of frightened, feeling that something was wrong, that someone must have pulled something on me all those hours I'd been asleep.

I looked under the magazine, and that was all right. The gun was right where I had left it. The door was all right, too, still closed tight like I'd left it with a chair hooked under the knob. I looked out the window, pulling on my pants.

ef4fffff

The car hadn't been moved. It stood in exactly the same spot as it had last night. There was no one coming up the lane, and everything seemed the way it should be. No! Someone was coming.

Fay. She was coming out of the house, carrying a coffee tray. She was coming toward the garage, and she was dressed as she had been a few mornings ago—the day that Doc Goldman had called her and everything had started going to pieces.

Bare legs, bare shoulders, ivory-colored in the sunlight. Tan shorts, curved to the curves of her thighs; and the thin white blouse, drawn tight, straining softly with the flesh beneath it.

She saw me staring at her, and smiled. She paused beneath the window, looked up smiling. And if last night's whiskey had left any marks on her, I sure didn't notice. She looked just as fresh and beautiful as she had that other morning.

Her eyes were as sparkling and crystal clear as I remembered. Her hair had that same soft, brushed-shiny look, and her face was the same rose-and-white softness.

Everything was the same. It was like that other morning all over again; as though it was still that morning and everything since then had been a bad dream.

"Well?" She smiled up at me. "Like to have some?"

I nodded. Or shook my head. Or something. I managed to mumble that I did.

"Some coffee, I mean?" she said.

And then she laughed and started toward the steps.

SEVENTEEN

I let her into the room, and set the tray down for her. I acted, tried to act, just like she did, friendly and joking and laughing. But I figured that there must be something wrong, that she just about had to be working up to some kind of trick. So I gave her a good chance—a chance that *looked* good—to spring it.

I excused myself and went into the bathroom. I turned on the

water in the sink, and then I tiptoed back to the door on my bare feet
and peered out through a crack.

Fay was still in her chair, several feet away from the bed. I watched
for a couple of minutes, thinking—and hoping that she wouldn't—
thinking that she'd look under the pillow for the gun; that she'd do
some more fast looking when she didn't find it there. Getting the gun
was just about the only thing she could be up to. And if she didn't try
for it, then what was she up to?

She didn't. She stayed there in the chair, one bare leg crossed over
the other; kind of humming to herself.

I washed and went back into the room. She poured two cups of
coffee, and handed me one. The boy seemed to be feeling fine, she
said. Very lively. He'd eaten two poached eggs and a glass of milk.

"He wanted to get up, but I wouldn't let him. I thought he should
stay in bed, don't you?"

I nodded. And I thought that maybe he was the reason for this.
With him feeling pretty good, why she wasn't so worried anymore;
she was feeling pretty good herself.

I frowned, not realizing that I did. Just thinking so hard, you
know. Thinking and hoping that things might really be like they
looked. She frowned, too, a sort of shamed expression crossing her
face, shamed and kind of doubtful. And then she smiled again.

"Yes, Collie? Yes, my pugilist Apollo?"

"Well—" I hesitated. "Well, I was just wondering—"

"And I. And I don't seem to be able to explain. I suppose—" She
paused and shrugged. "I suppose I said it all in the beginning. I'm
just a crazy, mixed-up neurotic—anyone who drinks as I do, for as
long as I have, is bound to be pretty shaky in the cerebrum. He—she,
I should say—was an unstable character to begin with, and the booze
makes her a lot worse than she was. It takes very little to throw her
out of kilter. Very little. And what I've taken in these past few days
has been somewhat more than a little. So—"

She put her coffee cup down. She glanced at me, took my cup, and
put it down with hers.

"So?" she said. "So Collie?"

I nodded that I understood. And I thought I did, pretty well.
Those institutions have a lot of alcoholic inmates. No one can be nicer

or smarter than they are when they've leveled off. And no one can be as downright ornery and crazy when they're in a bad way.

"Let's see." She tilted her head to one side. "Didn't we have a date a few mornings ago? Did we or not, Collie, do you remember?"

"Fay, I—I—"

"Words fail you, huh?" She laughed softly. "Well, let's hope it isn't symptomatic of any physical weakness. Now, if you'll just step into the bathroom . . ."

"The—the bathroom?" I stammered.

"That small room you were in a moment ago. The one with the concave furniture."

I got up and went into the bathroom. I heard her draw the shade, and I started to jerk the door open. Then I saw what she was doing, and I stayed where I was until she called to me.

Her shoes were on the floor beside a chair. Her blouse was on the chair, and so were the shorts. She was lying on the bed, her black hair spread out on the pillow.

She held out her arms to me.

. . . There are some things you can't fake, you can't pretend about, and that's one of them. A person wants you that way, or she doesn't, and you always know which. And I knew which it was with her. The want was there. There wasn't a second of pretence in that long hour we were together. So even if Fay had a reason—and, of course, she did—for allowing the want to take over, there wasn't any faking afterwards. That was genuine, if nothing else was.

Now, she was gone. She'd dressed and gone over to the house to see how the boy was. And I stayed there on the bed. Because she was coming back in a few minutes. She was just going to look in on the boy, she wanted to check to see if Uncle Bud had been calling, and then she'd be back. She'd be back there with me, any minute now. We'd be together again—Fay and I would be together. And this time, we'd talk things out.

I'd find out how she really felt about the boy. Whether she didn't really feel like I did, that if we could get him back to his family safe and sound nothing else would matter much. We wouldn't have to give ourselves up, although there was a good chance that the cops would catch up with us in time. We could just leave the boy here, say—or leave him some place where he'd be comfortable and safe. Then, we could beat it, and send back word where to find him. That would fix Uncle Bud, keeping him from getting money. If we did get caught, finally, things would sure go a lot easier on us. We'd done something pretty bad, but if we did our best to straighten it out . . .

Of course, it wouldn't be our best that way. What we ought to do was call the cops right now; give up without waiting to be caught. But I didn't think that I could go that far, and I was positive that she couldn't. A person that drinks a lot is always frightened. They may act just the opposite—tough and hard, like they don't give a damn for anything. But inside they're scared. They have too much imagination. Everything is magnified in their minds, made a hundred times worse than it actually is. And a thing like this, facing a kidnaping rap, was plenty scary without any magnifying.

So we'd just do the best we were capable of. If she felt like I did, if that was what she wanted. Like I'd told her, the boy was sure to be all right for a day. We could leave him here, or someplace else; then, beat it and tip off the cops where he was. We didn't have much money—I didn't have any and she couldn't have a great deal. But we'd get by some way, and the boy would be all right. Right now nothing else seemed to matter much.

I lighted a cigarette and lay down again. Wondering just how I could work around to the subject, hoping that she would bring it up first. Wishing I wasn't still suspicious of her, and that she wasn't of me. Because, of course, she was and I was. There hadn't been much between us but suspicion and distrust these last few days. It couldn't all be wiped away in an hour.

Even right now, I guessed, if she should make the proposition to me—suggest doing what I wanted to do—I'd be a little leery of it. I'd think she was just trying to test me out, find out what I was thinking so that she could make sure I didn't go through with it. And if I felt that uneasy about her, she was bound to feel the same way about me, only a hell of a lot more so.

I was a mental case. I was an escapee from an insane asylum, a psycho with a gun, an ex-pug who could do plenty without a gun if he took a notion. I was that—and she was the other, a kind of mental case herself. Unstable, always afraid inside. Trying to drown the fear in booze and always having it float to the top stronger than ever.

It would be hard for her to talk straight with me. Probably it would be just about impossible. She'd done just about all she could, I guess, toward breaking the ice. The rest would be up to me, and how I was going to go about it I didn't know. But I figured that it ought to be a lot easier after what had happened.

She must think a lot of me or she wouldn't have done it. Fay had to care, didn't she? Or did she?

She hadn't been faking, but maybe that didn't mean that she really cared. She'd been batting around on her own a long time. Drinking so much she didn't know what she was doing, or not giving a damn if she did know. Hanging out in joints like Bert's; getting on close terms with guys like Bert and Uncle Bud. A woman like that . . .

But Fay wasn't a woman like *that*. Like it seemed she might be. She wasn't cheap, shoddy, whatever else she was. She wasn't that, even if this was some kind of a trick. And I sure hoped that it wasn't for her sake, and mine. Because a guy like me, you sure never want to try to trick him.

For one thing, you probably won't get away with it. He's watching for it, he's thought of every angle you might try to play. You make just one little move toward one of them, and he's in there ahead of you. Moving in fast on you. He won't take any explanations. If you're smart, you won't try to give him any. You tricked him—tried to take advantage of him. That's all he sees. And about all you can do from then on is to keep out of his way. If you can. If he'll let you. For he'll never completely trust you again. He'll be watching you closer than ever, and if you take one little step in the wrong direction—or even look like you are—you'll never take another one.

I'd already had a fast one or two pulled on me. I was already damned watchful. I didn't want to be—I wanted to be able to trust Fay—but I just couldn't help it. So I sure hoped this wasn't some kind of a trick.

I heard the kitchen door slam. I pulled the shade back and glanced out the window. She was coming across the yard. She had a dress on, and she was walking pretty fast; and yet she seemed to be sort of dragging her feet, hanging back. As though she was working against herself, forcing herself forward.

I felt the tension coming back. I sat up and began putting on my clothes, shoving the gun into my hip pocket. I heard her coming up the stairs. I reached for my shoes, and started putting them on as she opened the door.

She came in. She looked at me, her face stiff, her eyes nervous and frightened. I straightened up and stared at her.

"What's up?"

"Collie, I—I—" She hesitated, took a deep breath. "I just talked with Uncle Bud, Collie."

"Yeah?"

"I—he thinks we'd better come over there right away! I c-called him, and that's what he said, Collie."

I nodded. I finished tying my shoelaces, and stood up. She backed away a step.

"Go on. Why does Uncle Bud think we'd better come over there right away? Don't you think maybe I'd better know?"

Her eyes wavered. Her face twitched as she tried to smile back at me. And then I guess she saw that I wasn't smiling, that it just looked like a smile. She backed away another step.

"You'd better watch out," I said. "You'll be out the door in a minute. You might fall over the banister and break your neck."

Fay looked over her shoulder quickly. She looked back at me, lips trembling, her face getting whiter than ever. I wondered how she'd ever gotten up the nerve to try this—even to get this far with the trick she was pulling. And knowing how frightened she was, I guess I should have liked and admired her for trying. But I didn't. What I felt toward her was anything but liking and admiration.

"Go on. You're not afraid to tell me, are you, Fay? After all, two people as close as us; sweethearts, I guess you'd call us—they shouldn't be afraid of each other."

A touch of red came into her face. She took another deep breath, hesitated, and then at last she got it out.

"The boy, C-Collie. He's run away!"

EIGHTEEN

I nodded and gave her a smile—a smile that wasn't one. I said that, well, there wasn't anything to get too excited about. The shape the boy was in, he couldn't have gone very far. He was probably over in the house, hiding somewhere.

"N-no!" Fay shook her head. "I looked before I called Uncle Bud."

"Well, let me look. We'll look together. Stay nice and close together, you know, so that if one of us sees something he can point it out to the other."

"B-but—"

"That's what we'll do. And we'll do it right now."

I took her by the arm, pushed her through the door. We went down the steps, across the yard, and into the house. We started going through the rooms, with me talking and kind of joking, and Fay stammering and answering me in almost a whisper.

"Well, his clothes are gone. It sure looks like he dressed himself and ran off."

"Collie. We've got to—"

"Yes, sir. That's just the way it looks. And it looks like he probably did it when you were over there with me. When we were both pretty busy, with the shades pulled, and we weren't paying much attention to anything for about an hour. That's when it happened—it looks like."

I grinned at her. I let go of her arm suddenly, let go with a jerk that jerked her shoulder.

"We've got to leave, Collie! He's had plenty of time to get to the highway."

"He wouldn't get that far. I'm sure of it, and so is Uncle Bud. Otherwise, he wouldn't be coming anywhere near here."

"B-but—"

"Uncle Bud thinks the same thing that I do, that he's passed out somewhere right around here. He's got to that place, some nice secluded spot where no one can see him, and that's as far as he'll go. That's what Uncle Bud thinks—and I got a hunch it's what you think."

"No! Aaah, no, Collie! I wouldn't—"

"I told you. I told you that boy had to stay alive, and I told you why he had to stay alive. Now, where is he? Where did you leave him?"

"I—I—" She shook her head. "Is that what you think of me? D-do you really think I'd do that to him?"

And for a moment I wavered. For a moment, I could almost see why she'd done it—and why she'd done it in this way. Fay was afraid. She wasn't sure of what I wanted to do, so she'd tried to take the decision out of my hands. She'd hidden the boy, left him where he'd be safe until she could get word to the cops. Then, she'd told me he'd run away, so that we'd have to run. It was the only thing she could do, as she looked at it. It was practically the same thing that I'd been thinking about doing.

So . . . so I had it all figured out, almost. We were on the same side of the fence. We both wanted the boy to get back to his parents. That's the way I figured, the way I thought it was. But with a thing like this—a guy like me—figuring and thinking weren't enough. I needed Fay to tell me—just to come right out with the truth without any tricks or hedging around. It was all she'd've had to do . . . and she didn't do it.

She was too frightened, too anxious. And when a person's that way, they almost always do the wrong thing. And what she did was the worst thing she could possibly have done.

She'd just hit me with one trick. Now, while I was still rocking from it, fighting to hang onto myself because I thought so much of her—now, she hit me with another one.

"Collie. . ." She forced herself to smile. "Let's be nice, hmm? Let's—l-let's lie down a while, get all nice and calm so we can talk a-and . . ."

Fay came toward me, holding onto the smile; forcing herself every inch of the way. Her hand went up to the shoulder of her dress, tugged at it shakily, and slowly slid it down. She hesitated then, pleading mutely with her eyes. Blushing, shamed despite the fear. Then, she took hold of the other shoulder, and slid it down. And waited.

"Sh-shall we, Collie?" She was almost against me.

"What do you think?" I sneered and swung with my open hand.

Fay screamed and staggered backwards, doubled over and clutching at her breasts. She bumped into a chair, and screamed again.
Then, she fell down on the sofa, sat there moaning, rocking back and
forth.

"That was just a sample. Try something like that again, and I'll
really clobber you!"

"*Y-you!*" Fay gasped. "You—you—" The rocking stopped. She
raised her head slowly, and looked up at me. "I want you to know,
I want you to remember I warned you. I'm going to kill you for
that!"

"Maybe. Maybe you will. But right now you're going to do
something else. Fast and no maybe!"

She didn't argue about it. Fay pulled her dress back up and led the
way down through the trees. We came to the culvert that ran under
the lane. She nodded and stood back, and I got down and lifted him
out.

I didn't know whether he was just unconscious from the exertion,
or whether he'd been slugged. But there was a big bruise on the right
side of his forehead. I looked down at it, at him, so little and so limp
in my arms. And then I looked at her. And if I'd had my hands free
just then—well, it was a good thing for her that I didn't have.

We went back to the house and I put the boy down on the sofa.
Fay stood watching, kind of defiantly, as I sponged his face and
forehead with cold water.

He came to and whispered that he felt, "F-fine," when I asked
him. I guessed that he wasn't really hurt, just weak and frightened by
so many things he couldn't understand. Most of the "bruise" turned
out to be dirt. He had a little knot there on his forehead, but the
biggest part of it—what I'd thought was bruise—washed off.

"Well . . ." Fay sloshed whiskey into a glass; gulped it. "I guess I
missed that time, didn't I? I didn't hit him hard enough."

"What happened? Did you fall down with him?"

"Did I?" She reached for the bottle again. "You've got all the
answers. You tell me whether I did or not."

"I guess you probably did."

"You do, huh? You'd actually give me a break? Well shove it,
bright boy! I hit him, get me? I slugged him as hard as I could with
a big rock. And if I'd had more time I'd've beat his brains out!"

I told her to quiet down; she'd disturb the boy. Fay yelled that she didn't give a damn if she did disturb him.

"Why the hell should I? Didn't I try to kill him? Well, didn't I, you rotten, mean, hateful, son-of-a-bitch? Sure, I did! That's the kind of a dame I am! I meant to kill him! I tried to! *I did, I did, I did . . .*"

And I knew that she hadn't—I knew it in my heart—but still it was easy to believe that she had. Fay looked twenty years older, haggard and vicious, her eyes glaring crazily. She was all crazy meanness and viciousness, drained dry of everything else. And it was easy to believe she'd do anything.

I told her to shut up. She yelled all the louder, backing away as I moved toward her.

She'd never said anything dirty before—sharp and ornery, maybe, but never dirty. But now she cut loose; and the names she called me, the things she said. Well, I've heard some rough talk but never anything as bad as that. Some of the words, but never all at one time. No one had ever called me one of them without losing some teeth.

The red haze gathered in front of me. I had to get rid of it, let off steam some way, because if I didn't I'd kill her. So I started yelling myself. I shouted back at her, cursing, calling her names. I yelled and she yelled, and how long it went on I don't know. Everything was a screaming red haze, yells and filth and redness, and how long it lasted I don't know.

But it was long enough.

Long enough for him to stop his car in the drive. To come up the walk and onto the back porch.

Whether he knocked I don't know—we wouldn't have known with the noise we were making. Probably he did knock, then just walked right on in like doctors do.

We heard the screen door slam, and that brought us up short. The room went completely silent. But by then, he was right on top of us. He'd heard it all. And, of course, he'd seen the boy.

He sauntered forward, casually; winked at me and smiled at Fay. "Mrs. Anderson, isn't it? I'm Doctor Goldman."

"H-how—" Her mouth twisted. "How do you do, doctor?"

"I just dropped in for a moment. I'm due at the office now, but I happened to be out this way and ..." His voice trailed off, and he nodded toward the boy. "Your son? Collie didn't tell me you had any children."

"It's her nephew," I said. "He's just visiting here for a couple of days."

"I see. Fine looking boy. A little under the weather, is he?"

He strolled over to the sofa and sat down. Still acting casual. Acting as though he hadn't heard the racket we were making, as though he didn't know exactly who the boy was.

"Not feeling too well, eh, sonny? Never mind. You don't need to talk. Let's see if I don't have something to ..." He opened his medicine kit, snapped it shut again. "No, I guess not. I remember I was looking for some this morning before I left the office."

He bent over the boy a minute or two longer. Afraid to look around, I guess. Nerving himself for what he was going to do. Then he stood up carelessly and picked up the kit.

"He could do with a B-1 shot," he said. "You might mention it to his mother. I'd give him one, but I haven't any with me."

"A-all right." Fay shot a glance at me. "Thank you, doctor."

"Don't mention it. Just sorry I couldn't do something for him."

He smiled and nodded to us—or, to be more exact, to the space between us. Then, he moved toward the doorway, looking at the floor just ahead of him, making a big business out of buttoning his coat.

He paused, looking down. He went a couple of steps further, and came to another stop. I watched him silently, then crossed in front of him.

Outside, the wind rustled the dead grass, and the curtains swirled away from the windows. They fell back softly, flattening against the screens. And in the kitchen the clock ticked off the seconds.

Fay's breath went out in a sigh. Doc looked up. His eyes wavered at first, then they steadied and held mine.

"How did it happen, Collie? How could you have done it?"

I shook my head. I didn't really know how it had happened. It seemed simple enough, taken step by step, but I couldn't explain now. And explaining wouldn't change anything.

"Get out of the way," he ordered. "Do you hear me, Collie? Stand out of the doorway at once!"

I shook my head again. Waiting for him to make the first move. Wishing he'd get it over with, so that I could do what I had to.

"You don't know what you're doing, Collie. I'm sure Mrs. Anderson can't realize what she's doing. Someone has duped you into this; they're using you for their own criminal purposes."

"It doesn't make any difference, Doc. You're not going anywhere. We're leaving and you're going to stay."

"No, Collie! You can't—" He bit his lip, looked at Fay. "Can't I appeal to you, Mrs. Anderson? Can't you understand, make him understand?"

"Fay," I said, "we're leaving. Get together anything you want to take and go on out to the car."

I stared into his eyes, waiting and watching. Fay circled around behind him and went into her bedroom.

There was another gust of wind. The grass rustled again and the curtains swirled. And in the kitchen the clock ticked off the seconds.

"Well," Doc said. "Well." He shrugged. "I suppose, if that's the way it has to be . . ."

He turned. Then, he whirled suddenly, hurled the medicine kit and dived for the door. I ducked and swung all in one motion. I pulled the punch, but it landed right on the button.

Doc's head snapped back. His knees buckled, and I had to catch him to keep him from falling. I picked him up and carried him into the bedroom.

. . . His answering service knew that he'd come here. They phoned, just as I finished binding and gagging him with his own adhesive tape. I told them he wouldn't get back to the office today. He was tied up on an emergency, and they were to check here again in the morning.

Fay was already waiting in the car. I put the boy down on the floor in the rear, got in with him, and we drove off fast. Down the lane and into the highway. Headed for Uncle Bud's place.

Rushing toward the end.

NINETEEN

Uncle Bud kept on the move, switching from one place to another. But I guess that every place he lived would always be just about like the others. It would have the same features.

It would be a dump because he was tight with his money; because he seldom stayed at home if he had any place else to go. It would be fairly close in, a place he could circulate from easily. It would be a place you'd probably never find by yourself, one he'd have to tell you how to find.

This one—the place we went to that day when everything began rushing toward the end—was in the city's old business district. Or on the edge of it, I should say. Fifty years ago it had been the main part of town, but then the railroad station had been moved and the highways built around the city instead of passing through it. That had put it on the downgrade, and now it was about as far down as it could go.

Flop houses. Two-bit hotels. Cheap bars and greasy-spoon restaurants. That was about all you saw there now, and you didn't see any of them after the first few blocks. After that there were just empty buildings, or vacant lots where the buildings had been torn down, until you came to a bridge, a kind of a viaduct. It crossed the abandoned railroad right-of-way and opened into the abandoned highway. Right at the foot of it was an old garage building—well-built and still in pretty good shape—with living quarters on the second floor. And that was where Uncle Bud lived.

I drove the car into the garage part. Uncle Bud was waiting for us, and he led the way upstairs. He wasn't at all upset about what had happened. It didn't change the picture at all, he said. Not that much, Kid; no, sir, not even that much. Everything was working out fine and dandy, and we'd all be wearing diamonds in another day or two.

Fay went into the bedroom with the boy. Uncle Bud nudged me, whispered that I didn't want to be too hard on the little lady. She was just jumpy, like little ladies got sometimes, and it was up to me and him to keep our heads, now, wasn't it?

"I'm going to. That's just what I'm going to do, Uncle Bud."

"Atta boy! You're my kind of people, Kid. Now, you just sit tight here, and I'll get you fixed up right."

I looked him over as he left. I gave him another good once-over when he came back and started piling groceries, beer, and whiskey on the table. And I saw that he wasn't packing a gun. Things were working out real nice for him, he thought, and there was nothing he needed a gun for.

"Well, Kid." He motioned toward the table. "See anything I overlooked? Anything you think of, just name it."

"You've got plenty. We're not going to need all that."

"Well, you can't never tell now. I want you and Fay to be comfortable, and you may have to hole up here quite a while."

I grinned to myself. I said I was sure we'd have plenty of everything.

"Yeah?" He gave me a sharp look. "But they'll find that doctor in the morning, won't they? You won't be able to do no chasing around after that."

"That's right," I said.

"Well, uh, well," he said hastily, "what I meant was, you might want something and I wouldn't be around to get it for you."

"Sure. But we'll have plenty. You don't have to worry about that at all."

He hesitated, started to say something else. Then, he gave up on it—chalked it up, I guess, to some more of my screwy talk—and uncorked a bottle of whiskey. We poured drinks. He went on with the gabbing, talking about how fine everything was. And I nodded and grinned and told him he was sure right.

The fun was going to be over pretty soon. Pretty soon, now, I was going to set him back on his heels. So I let him enjoy himself while he could.

Fay came out of the bedroom and fixed the boy an egg and some milk. I watched from the doorway as she tried to feed it to him, and it was just no go. He just didn't have the strength or the stomach for it.

She brought the plate and the glass back into the kitchen. Uncle Bud pulled his everything-is-fine line on her, and she stood and looked at him until he was all through. Until the words kind of died in his throat. Then, she filled a glass with whiskey and sat down in a corner with it.

Evening came on. Uncle Bud got busy with the food, made a plate of lunch-meat sandwiches and opened up some potato salad and a few cans of stuff.

I ate a pretty good meal. Fay took a sandwich and more whiskey. Uncle Bud didn't eat anything.

"I'll just grab me a bite later," he said, taking a big swallow of his drink. "I ain't real hungry now, so I'll just get something when I go into town."

I didn't say anything. He took another drink, fidgeting a little.

"I still got to keep right on top of this deal, y'know, Kid. This is the most important time. We're due to pull down the money in less than twenty-four hours. And if the cops got any fast ones cooking— they might try to pull something right at the last minute, you know— why, it's up to me to find out about it."

I waited, still keeping silent. Looking at him, and saying nothing. He filled up his glass again.

"Yeah," he mumbled. "Yes, sir, I sure got to keep a close eye on everything from now until the wind-up. You, uh, I guess you and Fay can get along here all right by yourselves, huh?"

I smiled at him. Just smiled. He glanced nervously at Fay, and she gave him a dead-eyed stare.

"I guess it all works out pretty good. We can't very well all of us stay here, so it's just as well that I'll be away. I, uh—" Uncle Bud paused, fumbling with the buttons of his coat. "You're sure you don't need anything now? You'll be all right until tomorrow night? Well, I'll just run along then"

And I spoke at last. I told him to stay right where he was for a moment, and Fay and I and the boy would go with him.

He laughed. He put on his hat and started to get up. And then it registered on him, what I'd said, and he sank back down in his chair.

"G-go with me?" he stammered. "W-what—what for?"

"For the same reason you're going," I said. "To get the money."

His mouth dropped open. A guilty, red flush spread over his face. "K-Kid, I, I—it ain't the right time yet. You know it ain't, Kid! It's not supposed to be until tomorrow night!"

"Yeah? How do I know that?"

"Why—why, because! It's what we planned right from the beginning! I gave the family seventy-two hours."

"Seventy-two hours from when? From the time I took the boy? From the time the ransom note was mailed? From the time the family got it, or the night of the day they got it or when?"

"Well, it—it was—"

"Forget it. It doesn't mean anything. It doesn't change anything. Maybe you didn't plan on running out on us in the beginning, but you'd never pass up a setup like the one you've got now. Fay and me tied down here—the cops looking for us after tomorrow morning. You on the loose." I shook my head, nodded to Fay. "Get the boy ready. We're leaving."

She got up and went into the bedroom. Not saying a word. Ignoring him when he told her to wait, to talk the Kid out of this crazy notion. Fay shut the door. He stared at it helplessly.

"All right, Kid. The money ain't there, but if you won't take my word for it, I'll prove it to you. It's all wrong, sending the messenger now—showing our hand in advance—but if that's the way you got to have it—"

"It's not the way," I said. "We're going to pick the money up ourselves."

TWENTY

That one really threw him. Uncle Bud looked like he was about to faint.

"*No!*" he said. "No, you can't mean it, Kid. Take that boy into the railroad station? W-why, hell, we probably wouldn't much more'n get him out of the car before he was spotted."

"All right. We'll leave him in the car then. Just you and I and Fay will go in."

"Leave him? Damn it, that's even worse! He might start stirring around. Someone might look in and see him."

"That's right." I nodded. "And no one's going to do anything to him to make sure that he doesn't stir around."

"Well, then? You can see yourself that your idea won't work, Kid."

"Fay doesn't trust me. I don't trust her. And we don't trust you. But I can fix that part—you. We'll park near the station, where I can see you go in and come out. If you aren't back in fifteen minutes, I'll tip the cops off to you."

"But—Kid! Kid." Uncle Bud mopped his face. "That—it just ain't right! Suppose the money really isn't there?"

"It is. We both know it is. So get it. Get it by yourself, or Fay and I will go with you and get it."

"But you can't! You can't leave the boy in the car like that."

"So that brings us right back where we started from, doesn't it? You get it, and don't take more than fifteen minutes to do it."

"B-but—"

His mouth worked helplessly. He looked down at the floor, shaking his head, wagging it back and forth, until I thought it was going to fall off. And, then, at last he looked up again, there was a kind of greenish cast to his face, but a red flush was spreading beneath it. Uncle Bud was sick—really sick, he was scared so bad. But along with it he was ashamed.

"Kid, I guess I got to tell you something. This deal—I—there wasn't much risk the way I had it figured. With the messenger picking up the money, you know, and that wino to take the fall if there was one. I—well, I didn't have to know if there was a police stake-out at the pay-off place. I mean, if there was it wouldn't catch me. I wouldn't lose nothing but the dough. I—I—" He licked his lips.

"Go on."

"Well, uh, about the money. About maybe it's being marked or the serials registered. There wasn't any risk there either, the way I figured. Hell, all those small bills—the biggest ones twenties—they just couldn't trace 'em. There's too many in circulation, and by the time they traced 'em back to a guy, why—well, I didn't believe they could. I didn't think the family would play around to begin with, they'd be so anxious about the boy. And if they or the cops did try anything funny, it wouldn't get them anywhere. So . . . so." He paused, glanced at me pleadingly. "You see what I mean, Kid? You see what I'm driving at?"

I nodded. I saw it, and I felt sorry for him. But not as sorry as he wanted me to feel, not after what he'd done to me. Except for him, I wouldn't be in this spot. I wouldn't have hurt Doc, the only man who'd ever done anything for me. And the little boy wouldn't be dying. And Fay and I—things might have been a lot different between us. You couldn't judge by the way things were now. We'd both been pretty mixed up, easy to swing one way or another, and we might have swung the right way instead of this one. We might have. It could have worked out that way.

If Uncle Bud had left us alone.

"I've been lying to you, Kid. I don't have no pipelines into the department. Most of the guys I know, they don't even speak to me any more. They see me comin' they turn the other way. I guess I can't blame them much, but anyway that's the way it is. I don't know what they're doing or what they've done. I figured I could get by safe enough without knowing. If there was any kind of jam, it would be someone else that got stuck, and—and naturally, I didn't want no one else to get into trouble."

"Let it go at that. You don't know anything. You're not sure that the guy who goes for the money won't be walking into a police trap."

"That's right, Kid."

"Well, you'll know pretty soon," I said. "You're going to find out awfully fast."

... We sat there for another half-hour or so, and he was talking every minute of it. Begging, pleading with me, actually crying a little toward the last. The words poured out of his mouth, and they didn't mean a thing to me. I didn't even hear them. They were just a noise, just a lot of noises coming from a sickish-white face. I didn't mind them particularly. I didn't care whether Uncle Bud made them or whether he didn't. Other people had never meant anything to him. What they said meant nothing to him. And now it was his turn. Now, he was meaningless, and what he said was meaningless.

I was all those other people, all the people in the world, and I couldn't see him and I couldn't hear him.

He stopped talking, at last. He'd talked himself kind of hoarse. I finished my drink, and set the glass on the table.

"Anything else? If you're all through, we'll shove off."

"Sh-shove off? But, Kid, I just—"

"All right. There's no hurry. You talk as long as you want to, and then we'll leave."

His eyes watered. His lips trembled, and he managed to get his mouth open, but no words came out. I grinned at him. I asked him again if there was anything he wanted to say.

Uncle Bud looked at me dully, hesitated, and made one last try. "I know quite a few people around that station, Kid. Guys that ain't got much use for me. If one of 'em should get in touch with Bert—"

"Go on. Make it nice and scary."

"It could happen, Kid! He always comes into town for dinner, and if he had the word spread around to look out for me— And you know he has! You know he's been tipped off!"

"Uh-uh. I don't know it, and neither do you."

"Don't make me do it, Kid!" His eyes filled with tears again. "Please don't make me do it. If one of those guys should call Bert, he could be there in five minutes."

"Only five minutes?" I grinned. "You don't think he could make it in three?"

"I'm beggin' you, Kid! I got a bad feeling about this. If the cops don't get me, why—"

"Shut up! Get up and start moving. I'm sick of looking at you."

TWENTY-ONE

I rode in the back with the boy. Fay drove, and Uncle Bud sat in the front with her. There wasn't a half-dozen words passed between us on the way into town. About three blocks from the railroad station, I had Fay stop the car and Uncle Bud got out.

It was about seven-thirty, the quiet part of the evening. The day rush was over, and it was too early for the dinner and theatre crowds.

Uncle Bud trudged down the street, practically by himself. He turned around near the end of the block and looked back at us.

He crossed the intersection and looked back again. He hesitated, sort of teetering—too scared to go ahead, knowing it was go ahead or else. Then he went on, walking fairly fast. Anxious, I guess, to get the job and the suspense over with.

I got behind the wheel and made the boy lie on the floor in back. Then I followed Uncle Bud down the street, letting the car creep along, letting him stay well ahead of me.

The railroad station occupied a block on the other side of the street. I stopped in the middle of the block just below it and shut off the motor. I watched as Uncle Bud went up the broad marble steps and disappeared through the entrance.

I scooted down a little in the seat and peered up at the clock in the station tower. It was twenty minutes of. He had until five of eight to get back with the money. If he wasn't back by then . . .

I kind of hoped that he wouldn't be. Because I'd meant just what I'd said about calling the cops, and that would wind everything up just that much faster. And that was all I wanted now. Just to get it over with, to have the end come. Because it was bound to be bad; no good, no happiness, could come out of this now, so the quicker it was over the better.

I'd have ended it myself if I could have. But somehow I couldn't, and I guess it wasn't so strange that I couldn't. There's something inside of every man that keeps him going long after he has any reason to. He's no good to life and life is no good to him, and he knows it will always be that way. But still he can't quit. Something keeps prodding him, whispering to him—making him hope in the face of hopelessness. Making him believe there's a reason to stay in there and pitch, and that if he fights long enough he'll stumble onto it.

It's that way with everyone, or almost everyone, I guess. It's hardly ever been any other way with me. For years, for as far back as I could remember, I'd kept going when going didn't seem to make any sense. And I had to keep on now. If any quitting was done, it had to be done for me.

Uncle Bud had been gone a little more than five minutes. It was five minutes, I mean, since he'd entered the station. I looked down from the clock to the tall doors of the building, and I saw a man hurry through one of them and pause at the top of the steps. He had something in his hand—a flashlight. He flashed it three times, and the light was red.

It didn't mean anything to me for a minute. I just thought, still, there's a guy with a red flashlight, so what about it? Then, Fay sat up with a gasp, turned toward me, her face blurred white in the semi-darkness. "Collie! L-look!" she said and pointed. But I was already looking, for the street had suddenly come to life.

A police car had pulled into each side of the intersection ahead of us. Two other cars had stopped at the next intersection, shutting off the side streets. And in the block beyond, a car was out in the middle of the intersection, and a cop was directing traffic off of the street.

"Collie!" Fay whispered. "Collie! W-what are they doing?"

"It's a stake-out. They tagged him as soon as he got the money, but they're afraid to take him in a crowd. I guess that's the reason."

"Well do somethin'! L-let's get out of here! Aah, Collie, I—I—"

I kind of frowned, jerked my arm away from her hand. This was what I wanted, you see, the end. And it seemed like she should want it, too; that she should damned well get it, regardless of what she wanted. Because Fay wasn't fit to live, because she'd be better off dead or locked up for life. And I started to tell her that. And then—

When a man stops caring what happens, all the strain is lifted from him. Suspicion and worry and fear—all the things that twist his thinking out of focus—are brushed aside. And he can see people as they are, at last. Exactly as they are—as I saw Fay then.

Weak and frightened. Self-pitying, maybe. But good, too. Basically as good as a woman could be, and hating herself for not being better. She'd planned to call the cops, telling them the boy was in the culvert, after we'd made our escape. I *knew* that now. I knew that if it came to a showdown, she'd protect him with her life. I *knew* it, and suddenly I wanted Fay to live.

Suddenly, it made sense for Fay to live; it was the only way my having lived would make any sense. It was why I had lived, it seemed like. It was why I had been made like I was. To show her something, to prove something—to do something for her that she could not do for herself. And, then, to protect her so that she could go on. So that she would have the reason for living that I'd never had.

I turned on the switch key. Then, I glanced over my shoulder, hesitated, and turned it off again. Because it was too late, of course. The whole area had been blocked off at the same time. The street behind us was blocked, and a motorcycle cop was bearing right down on us.

I barely had time to check that the boy was down flat, when he drew up at the side of the car, bracing his feet on the pavement. I looked out the window, smiling at him, and he turned the flashlight into my face. He held it on me for a moment, then switched it over to Fay, then brought it back to me again.

"Something wrong?" I said, hoping he wouldn't see the boy on the floor in back. "Aren't we supposed to park here, officer?"

He grunted as he held the light on my face.

"What's all the excitement about?" I said. "Why all the police cars? My wife and I were just sitting here and—"

"Why?" He snapped off the light. "What business you got here? Who you waitin' for?"

He was an older man, maybe fifty. He was kind of heavy-set, like motor cops get, and he had a fat, hard-looking face.

"We're waiting for a friend of mine, Jack Billingsley. He's coming in from the East about eight-thirty, coming in on the train, and we were waiting for him."

"What's your name? This your car? Let's see the papers on it," he said all in one breath.

I gave him my right name, William Collins. "This is our car, all right, but we left the house in kind of a hurry tonight and I'm not sure that—" I glanced at Fay. "I guess you've got the papers with you, haven't you, honey? In your purse, maybe?"

She got her purse open, fumbled it open. She began pawing through it, moving the stuff it was filled with this way and that. The cop scowled suspiciously and bent close to me.

"I've seen you some place before. What'd you say your name was?"

"Collins. We're waiting for a friend of mine, Jack Billingsley. He's due on the train soon."

"I've seen you. Ever been in any trouble? What do you do for a living? How about them papers, lady?"

"No, I haven't been in any trouble. You must have me mixed up with someone else. I'm retired now, but I used to—"

"I ain't got you mixed up. I've seen you. Let's see your driver's license."

He glanced over into the back of the car. I thought of the boy and I reached for the gun in my pocket, but he jerked his eyes back to me. Then he turned the flashlight into my face again.

And suddenly he grabbed me by the arm.

"Hold it!" The light filled my eyes, blinding me. "What'd you say your name was?"

"Collins."

"Yeah. Yeah, why sure, it is!" He laughed and let go of my arm. "Kid Collins, why, sure. It was on the West Coast. I won twenty-five bucks on you."

He shook hands, leaned in and shook hands with Fay. "You say you're retired now, Kid? Livin' here in town, are you? Didn't mean to give you and your wife a bad time, but it's been so long ago and you being right here where all this is happening . . ."

"What's going on?" I said innocently. "Some kind of trouble?"

"You said it." He glanced over his shoulder. "Let's see. Don't believe you'd better try to pull out now, but maybe . . . Back it up a ways, Kid. Get back there around the middle of the block."

I started the car and put it in reverse. He backed up with me, kind of pushing himself along with his feet. And I had to watch where I was going, of course, and keep an eye on him, too. So that was why I missed what went on.

I didn't see Uncle Bud come out of the station. Uncle Bud with the suitcase, and Bert right on his heels. I didn't see him try to break and run from Bert. I was looking behind me until I heard the shot, and by the time I got turned around it was all just about over.

Uncle Bud was sprawled on the steps. Bert had grabbed up the suitcase and was heading back toward the station entrance. And he's got just about two steps when the cops inside cut loose on him—the detectives who had been waiting in there.

He screamed. I heard the one scream above the blast of their guns. Then, he toppled over backwards, still hanging onto the suitcase, went tumbling and rolling down the steps until his body struck the sidewalk.

"Well, that's it." The cop nodded to me. "Guess you'll have to pick

up your friend a little later, Kid. This place is going to be pretty hot
for a while."

"Yeah. It kind of looks like it would all right."

"Just make you a U-turn right here, and I'll signal for the boys to
let you through."

I turned around in the street, and drove back to the intersection.
He signaled, the cops let me through, and I kept on going.

TWENTY-TWO

I drove almost until dawn, just driving aimlessly, just riding—going
on—until it was time to stop going. I didn't know when that time
would be, but I figured it couldn't be very far off. And I knew I'd
know it when it did come. Things would work out a certain way,
so that I could stop living and Fay could go on. It would all work
out in time, just a little more time, and meanwhile I had to keep
going.

Finally, a little before daylight, I turned off the highway and into
an old trail. It was so overgrown with weeds and grass you could
hardly see it, and it faded off into a sort of jungle of underbrush. But
I ploughed the car on through it. And after a few hundred yards, the
ground sloped downwards to a creek. It was practically dried up, just
a little trickle of water between two high banks, so I turned the car
into it and stopped. I had to. With a trail that no one would ever spot
and with this archway of trees overhead it was just what I needed.
Exactly the right place to wait while things were working out a
certain way. And now that I'd gotten to it, the car had run out of
gas.

Fay had brought a full quart of whiskey with her from Uncle
Bud's place. She'd started slugging it down as soon as we'd got out of
that police trap, and now she had passed out.

I corked the bottle and sat it down on the floor. I looked back at
the boy. He was asleep. Really asleep and not just unconscious. I
tucked the blanket around him a little better and went to sleep myself.

It was safe enough with Fay passed out. She'd be that way for hours, and I'd be sleeping pretty lightly.

I waked up around noon when the boy started stirring. I got out quietly, lifted him out, and laid him down on the ground. I scooped up some water in a rusty can and gave him a drink. Then, I let him go to the toilet, washed his face and hands for him, and put him back in the car. There was nothing else I could do for him, and he wanted to get back in. Just that little exertion had worn him out.

I got back in the car myself. There was still a good pint of whiskey in the bottle, a little more than a pint I mean, and that would be more than enough for Fay. So I took one pretty good drink of it and corked the bottle back up again.

It was the middle of the afternoon before Fay waked up. She took a drink and left the car for a few minutes. When she returned she looked at the boy, tried to talk to him—to ask him how he was, and so on. And then she got back into the seat with me and picked up the bottle.

"Well? What do we do now, stupid?"

I shrugged. "How do I know. You tell me if you've got any ideas."

"Hell!" She shook her head dully. "Hell! What a mess! The whole damned country looking for us. No money and no car and a kid that's as good as dead, and——" Her voice broke, and she took another big drink. "What a mess! What a combination! Everything else, and a lunatic to boot."

"I'm not crazy. I'm just——"

"No, you're not! You're just mean and rotten and no good! I could feel sorry for you if you were really crazy, but—— Aah, forget it. Turn on the radio."

I turned it on. We sat listening all through the afternoon, and it was all pretty much the same thing. A lot of words built around a few facts. Or, I should say, what they thought were facts.

Bert and Uncle Bud had died before they could talk. The playground matron "believed" that Bert was the kidnaper, and the cops "believed" that he and Uncle Bud were the principals in the crime. Fay and I were kind of small fry, supposedly. Just a couple of stooges.

Then a familiar voice came over the radio—Doc Goldman's.

Doc Goldman wasn't sure that Fay was actually in on the deal. It was possible, he thought, that she might have been acting under coercion. As for me, well, I wasn't completely responsible for what I did. I knew what I was doing, so I could be held legally responsible. But I *had* tried to save the boy's life—I'd risked discovery and capture to steal that insulin. And it was just possible that I'd been forced to take part in the crime along with Fay. I could have been, even though I'd slugged him and tied him up. That was a natural reaction for a guy like me who thought he was in danger. Any time I got in a tight spot, I'd just about have to turn violent.

It was a pretty thin theory, of course; about me being coerced. I mean. There were all kinds of holes in it that I couldn't fill, and I sure wasn't going to try. Still, it *sounded* hopeful, taken along with some of the facts. And what Doc and the cops thought about Fay sounded a hell of a lot better. All she needed now was something to kind of top off their theories. To sew them all up tight and leave her in the clear.

Doc talked quite a while—about us and to us. He kept urging us to come in, if we had the boy. *If.* We couldn't get away. We'd have to give up sooner or later. So if the boy was alive, if Bert or Uncle Bud hadn't killed him, if he was with us . . .

The car battery was going dead. Doc's voice grew fainter and fainter, and finally it faded out entirely. And now it was night again.

I heard Fay take a drink. I heard her as she took another one, a long one, and dropped the bottle out of the side of the car. She'd be feeling pretty steady by this time. Her nerve would be built up, and that hard, ugly streak would be cropping out. She'd be up to anything in this mood.

And they didn't know that we had the boy. That motorcycle cop had said that we didn't, and the cops who'd let us through the street block said the same thing. Maybe they really believed they'd looked in the car, or maybe they were just trying to get themselves out of a jam. But, anyway, no one knew the truth.

Fay struck a match to a cigarette. It glowed in the darkness, lighting up her face as she took a long deep puff. "Well, we know what we have to do. Let's get it over with."

I nodded. I said, yeah, we might as well.

"One thing, Collie..." She hesitated, some of the sharpness going out of her voice. "You've done some pretty inexcusable things, but I know you weren't responsible. You thought you had to protect the boy from me. Whatever I said, I'm sorry."

"Forget it, Fay. It's all my fault. I thought it was smart to keep the boy alive, but I guess it's just about the dumbest thing I ever did."

"Well, regardless of who was at fault, I—*What*?" Her head snapped around. "Why, C-Collie, what do you mean by that?"

"You don't get it? You call me stupid. and you don't see what I mean?"

"N-no. No, I don't see!"

"Aw, you've got to! Bert's stuck with the actual kidnaping, isn't he? He and Uncle Bud could be blamed for practically everything that I did, couldn't they? And you—"

"Collie!" she said sharply. "What are you getting at?"

"And you," I went on, "you've got it just about perfect. It looks a hundred per cent better for you than it does for me. You were a woman living alone. Bert and Uncle Bud threatened you, and you were scared to death of me so you went along with us."

"I asked you, Collie. I asked you what you were getting at."

"You really don't get it?" I laughed. "Well, I guess you probably wouldn't at that. You're sitting pretty already, and it won't hurt you if the kid talks. But it'll hurt me plenty. So—so there's your answer, all spelled out for you. He's not going to do any talking."

Fay stared at me, silent and motionless for a moment. Then, still staring at me, she raised her hand and let the cigarette butt drop out the window. Slowly she shook her head.

"You don't mean that. You can't mean it. Y-you—you've been through more than even a normal person could take, and you're excited and frightened. You don't mean it, do you, darling. I know my Collie, and I know he'll—"

I laughed, cutting her off. "I really had you fooled, didn't I? Well, I guess I should, all the practice I've had. I started in almost fifteen years ago—I was up for a murder rap, see, and it was the only thing I could think of. So I went into the act, and it got me out from under. And then I went into the Army, and it got me out of that. It looked like such a sweet deal that I started working the act full time."

"What act?" she said. "W-what are you saying?"

"The crazy stuff." I laughed again. "Hell, it's better than a pension. I could just roam around doing what I pleased—acting stupid, and cracking down when people fell for it. Then, whenever I got tired, I'd just turn in at some institution for a while. Those places are pretty swell, you know; just like a high class country club. A swell private room and anything you want to eat. Hell, you never tasted anything like it! And you ought to see how people knock themselves out to wait on you. Why, I was in one place where they had a nurse for each patient. Real pretty ones, to keep you cheered up and feeling good . . ."

I made it as strong as I knew how. Laughing and kidding about it. Rubbing it in on her hard. And at first Fay cut in a time or two, and then she just sat and listened. And, gradually, I felt the change in her. I could feel the last bit of uncertainty giving way to coldness and hatred and disgust.

"I don't know why people never get wise," I said. "You do all sorts of things to give yourself away—to prove, you know, that you're plenty good at looking out for yourself. But somehow they never seem to catch on. They go right on falling for the act and feeling sorry for you."

I snickered and lighted a cigarette. I held the match for a moment, while I took the gun from my pocket and checked the chamber. "Well, I guess I'll get it over with."

As I expected, she made a wild grab for the gun. I jerked it back and thrust it forward suddenly. Fay screamed as she had that time back at the house.

"I won't kill you. I'll just mark you up real good, like you'd been through a struggle. I was trying to keep you from killing the boy, see, and the gun went off accidentally."

"D-don't," she sobbed. "Do anything you want to me, but don't kill him."

"Now, there's a good idea. It's better than just bumping off the brat and leaving him here. After all, it was Uncle Bud's gun and you knew him a long time before I did."

I turned in the seat and opened the door. I slid the gun back onto my hip, but not into the pocket. I let it slip past the pocket—as though I'd missed and didn't know it—and down onto the seat. Then I got out, my back turned to her.

There was one shattering explosion, and I pitched forward against the creek bank.

Everything was silent for a moment. Then, I heard Fay scramble out of the car and take the boy out. Stagger away with him, her footsteps growing fainter and fainter ... and then vanishing entirely. And I stayed where I was, unable to turn, my face pressed into the dirt. And that was the way it should be, I guessed, right where it had always been. And this—this, what had happened, was, as it had to be. She'd had to hate me. Fay had to go on hating me, thinking what she did about me, as long as she lived. And ... and that ... that was the way it would be, too.

But I wished she'd stayed a little while longer. Just a riffle, the minute or two more that I was going to stay. And if she'd wanted to talk mean or call me dirty names, it would have been all right, because it was just her way, you know. Fay just ... if she'd just—

"... *You silly looking goof! You couldn't sell cyanide in a suicide colony!*"

"*I'm just waiting for a friend. Maybe you know him—Jack Billingsley? Big real-estate family. We were driving to California, and ...*"

"*California, huh? Well, New York here I come!*"

"*The car broke down and I went for help, and I guess that darned crazy Jack Billingsley ...*"

"*Jerk! Stupid! Souphound! Bark for me. Roll over and do some tricks ...*"

... I grinned, because she didn't really mean a thing by it, you know. I barked, I guess it sounded like a bark maybe; and my body jerked, rolled a little. And then I stopped.

I just kind of stopped all over.

NOTHING MORE
THAN MURDER

ONE

WANTED: *Unencumbered woman for general work in out-of-town home. Forty to forty-five; able to wear size 14 uniform. Excellent wages, hours. Box No.—*

"I'll let you write in the box number," I told the girl behind the counter. "Have to let you do something to earn your money."

She smiled, kind of like an elevator boy smiles when you ask him if he has lots of ups and downs. "Yes, sir. What is your name, please?"

"Well," I said, "I'm going to pay for the ad now."

"Yes, sir," she said, just as much as to say you're damned right you're going to pay now. "We have to have your name and address, sir."

I told her I was placing the ad for a friend, "Mrs. J. J. Williamson, room four-nineteen, Crystal Arms Hotel," and she wrote it down on a printed slip of paper and stabbed it over a spike with a lot of others.

"That runs one word over three lines. If you like, I think I can eliminate a—"

"I want it printed like it stands," I said. "How much?"

"For three days it will be two dollars and forty-four cents."

I had a dollar and ninety-six cents in my overcoat pocket—exactly enough if Elizabeth had figured things right. I pulled it out and laid it on the counter, and fumbled around in my pants pocket for some change.

I found a quarter, two nickels, and a few pennies. I dropped them into my coat as soon as I saw they weren't enough, and reached again. The girl stared at my hands—the gloves—her eyebrows up a little.

I came out with a half dollar and slid it across to her.

"There," I said, "that makes it."

"Just a minute, sir. You have two cents change coming."

I waved my hand at her to keep it. I didn't want to try to pick up those pennies with my gloves on, and something told me she'd make me pick them up. I wanted to get out of there.

She hollered something just as the door closed, but I didn't turn around. I hit the street and I kept right on walking without looking back.

I guess I must have gone a dozen blocks, just walking along blind, before I realized I was being a chump. I stopped and lighted a cigarette, and saw no one was following me. It began to drift in on me that there really wasn't any reason why anyone should. I felt like kicking myself for letting Elizabeth plan the thing.

She'd insisted on my wearing gloves, which, I could see now, was a hell of a phony touch. She'd had me print out the ad in advance on a piece of dime-store paper, and that looked funny, too, when you put it with the other.

And then she'd figured out the exact price of the ad—only it wasn't the exact price.

I went on down the street toward film row, wondering why, since she always fouled me up, I ever bothered to listen to Elizabeth. Wondering whether I was actually as big a chump as she always said I was.

I wish now that I'd kept on wondering instead of plowing on ahead. But I didn't, and I don't think it proves I wasn't smart because I didn't.

TWO

When Elizabeth and I were married there was another show in Stoneville. It wasn't much of a house—five hundred chairs, and a couple of Powers projectors that should have been in a museum, and a wildcat sound system.

But it was a show and it pulled a lot of business from us, particularly on Friday and Saturday, the horse-opera nights. Not only that, it almost doubled the price of the product we bought.

In a town of seventy-five hundred people, you hadn't ought to pay more than thirty or thirty-five bucks for the best feature out. And you don't have to if you've got the only house. Where there's more than one, well, brother, there's a situation the boys on film row love.

If you don't want to buy from them, they'll just take their product across the street. And the guy across the street will snap it up in the hopes of freezing you out and buying at his own price the next year.

The fellow that owned the other house was named Bower. He's not around any more, don't know what ever did become of him. About the time his lease came up for renewal, I went to his landlord and offered to take over, paying all operating-expenses and giving him fifty per cent of the net.

Of course he took me up. Bower couldn't afford to make a proposition like that. Neither could I.

I gave Bower a hundred and fifty dollars for his equipment, which was a good price even if he didn't think so. Motion picture equipment is worth just about as much as the spot you have it in. It's tricky stuff to move; it's made to be put in a place and left there.

Well, Bower had about the same amount of stinker product under contract that I had. Part of it he'd bought because he couldn't help himself—we had block-booking in those days—and part because it would squeeze me.

Ordinarily, if he played it at all, he'd have balanced it up with good strong shorts. But there was a lot of it he couldn't have played on a triple bill with two strong supporting features.

What I did was to take his stinkers and mine and shoot 'em into the house, one after another. And I picked out shorts that were companion pieces, if you know what I mean. Inside of two months the house wasn't grossing five dollars a day.

The landlord was—he still is, for that matter—old Andy Taylor. Andy got his start writing insurance around our neck of the woods almost fifty years ago, and now he owns about half the county in fee and has the rest under mortgage. You could hear him crying in the next county when he saw what he was up against. But there wasn't a thing he could do.

He had the choice of taking twenty-five a month or fifty per cent of nothing, so you know what he took. I left the house standing dark, just like it is now.

No one but a sucker would think of trying to open a third house under the circumstances, and he wouldn't have anything to play in it if he did. I buy all the major studio product and everything that's playable from the indies. Our house is on seven changes a week, and we actually change four or five times. The rest of the stuff we pay for and send back.

Our film bill only runs about thirty per cent more on the week than it used to, and our gross is about ninety per cent more. Of course, we've got to pay rent on the other house, and the extra express and insurance charges plus paper—advertising matter—runs into dough. But we've done all right. Plenty all right. We've got the most modern, most completely equipped small-city house in the state, and there's just one guy responsible.

Me.

I only book a month at a time. But booking with me for a month is equal to booking with the average exhibitor for three months; and the boys on the row don't exactly throw rocks at me.

I like to never have got away from the Playgrand exchange.

The minute I stepped in the door they rushed me back to the manager's office, and he just pushed his work aside and reached for the drinks.

They had some shorts in that he wanted my opinion on, so after a while we went back into the screening-room, which is just like a little theater, and checked them over. They were good stuff, some of the brightest, snappiest shorts I'd seen in a long time. Even with all I had on my mind I enjoyed them.

I've known the manager of Utopian since the days when he was on the road, and it was pretty hard to get away from there, too. And we got to talking baseball over at Colfax; and at Wolf I had to sit in on another screening and have another couple drinks.

I almost didn't book anything at Superior.

They had a complete new setup from booker to manager, and none of them knew straight up. They didn't even know who *I* was. I gave the booker three feature dates and five shorts, and I explained about six times that that was all I had open for the month. But he wouldn't give up. He reached over and took my date book right out of my hands.

"Why, here," he said. "We've made a mistake, haven't we? We've got an open date next Sunday."

"I've got something planned for that," I said.

"Now, let's see," he said. "What can we give you there? What do you say to—"

"That date's taken," I said.

"We'll fix that, get the other pic set out for you. You don't want an inferior picture in a Sunday spot when we can give you—"

Well, I don't mind seeing a man try to do his job, and all the row guys are pretty fast talkers. I'm a shade fast myself. I've never poked my tongue in my eyes, yet, though, and it's not because I close them when I talk.

I was about to tell him off in a nice way when the manager came out. He came up behind me and kind of worked his hand over my back like he was giving me a massage.

"Getting along all right?" he said. "Everything going to suit you, Mr. Barclay?"

I could feel myself turning red. "My name's not Barclay," I said.

"Oh," he said, stepping back a little, "I thought you were from Barclay Operating Company at—"

"I'm Joe Wilmot," I said. "I've operated Barclay for the past ten years. The property's in my wife's name. Okay?"

He let out with a silly laugh, trying to pass it over, and made a grab for my hand.

"Mighty glad you came in, Joe. Anything we can do here for you, just say the word."

"You can't do a goddam thing for me," I said. "I won't pull out the dates I've given you because I'm in a hurry. But it'll be a hell of a long time before I give you any more."

"Now, Joe. Let's go back in the office and—"

"Go to hell," I said.

He and the booker both followed me to the door. I slammed it in their faces.

Every film row I've been around there's at least one place like Chance Independent Releases, and one guy like Happy Chance. Not exactly, but you know what I mean.

They get ahold of maybe three or four features a year that you can throw in a middle-of-the-week spot, and a sex picture or two, and a

few serials, and some stag-party shorts. They own the prints on the
sex and stag stuff, and handle the other on commission for studios
that don't have their own exchanges. Hap seemed to get by better
than some of them, but Hap would. I've known him for more than
twelve years, since he was working the booth in a grind-house, and I
was driving film truck. And if he ever missed skinning anyone, I
don't know when it was. He'd even skinned the Panzpalace chain;
and when you skin a guy like Sol Panzer, who's run a ninety-three-
house string up from a nickelodeon, you've got to be good.

  I don't know why I liked Hap. Maybe it was the attraction of
opposites as they say in books.

  "Glad you dropped in, laddie," he said, after we'd sat down and
the drinks were poured. "Been thinking about popping out to see you.
How are things with the Barclay?"

  "What's the use of kicking?" I said. "You wouldn't believe me."

  "No, seriously. You must be coining it. How many changes are
you on, anyway?"

  I grinned at him over my glass. "All I need, Hap."

  "Some chap was telling me the other day you were on more
changes than any house in the state."

  "I could be; I've got the product. I don't often make more than
four a week though."

  "Playing shutout with the rest?"

  "That wouldn't be legal," I said. "They call that acting in restraint
of trade."

  "Uh-hah," he drawled. "Certainly. I should know you wouldn't be
involved in anything like that."

  "The town's wide open to anyone that wants to come in," I said.
"I'll run all the good pix in the Barclay and all the stinkers in the
Bower, and split the rest with the competition."

  "Uh-*Hah!*" Hap let out a chuckle. "What's your house worth there,
laddie, if you don't mind my asking?"

  "Well, let's see. Ten times the annual return—between seventy-
five and a hundred grand."

  "It wouldn't possibly be worth a million, would it?"

  "Not without a Sunday-night audience. We've got some good-
looking gals out there."

  "Just so, just so," he said.

"What's on your mind? Got a buyer for me?"

"We-ell—" He hesitated, frowning, plucking at the sleeve of his tweed suit. Hap goes for the English stuff right on down the line. And it doesn't suit him so bad—or so good. He sat there all diked out and talking like a duke; and he turned his head a little and spit, and rubbed it into the carpet with one of his saddle-soaped shoes.

I wanted to laugh, but I knew I hadn't better. Hap isn't a good guy to have sore at you.

"Well, how about it?" I said.

"I guess not, laddie." He sighed and shook his head. "The proposition isn't quite big enough."

He looked at me a minute or two longer, and I thought he was going to say something more. But he didn't, and I didn't prod him. It wouldn't have done any good, and I thought I could see his angle, anyway.

"By the way," I said, "what'd you ever do with that sixteen-reeler? What do you call it—'Jeopardy of the Jungle'?"

Hap shrugged. "Oh, that goddam thing! Why, it hasn't been out of the can in months, laddie. It—" He broke off and gave me a sharp look. "Oh, you mean 'Jeopardy of the Jungle'!" he said. "It's going like wildfire. It's booked practically solid for the next three months."

I did laugh then. This was business, and I could.

"There aren't that many penitentiaries in the country," I said.

"Word of honor, Joe. The way it's been pulling 'em in even surprises me. You know I didn't care for it myself, even if it did have Gable and Bergman—"

"Yeah. A ten-frame shot of them sitting in the Stork Club. And what it has to do with the picture nobody knows."

"—but you can't argue with the b.o., Joe. The box office doesn't lie. Did you see last month's grosses in the *Herald*? The Empire grossed seven grand on 'Jep' the first—"

"I saw it," I said. "The only other attraction was Tommy Dorsey's orchestra."

"Let me show you something, Joe! Let me get out the *Herald*. I can show you small-city grosses for two days during the fall—"

"What two? Thanksgiving and Labor Day?"

"Okay," he said, "so it stinks."

"You know it does."

"But you want it."

"Well—"I said. And then I swallowed, and it was just like I'd forgotten how to talk.

A puzzled grin spread over Happy's face.

"Yeah," he said, "you want it. But why? You've already got more stuff than you can use. Tell Hap why you want it, laddie."

"Hell," I said, "use your head, Hap. This is the end of the season. We always get down toward the bottom of the pot at this time of year."

"Uh-hah. Mmm."

"Ordinarily I do have more product than I can play, but I've already let it go back. I don't have to have 'Jep.' I just thought I saw a nice spot for it next Sunday."

"'Jep' on *Sunday?*"

"Okay," I said, "I'm dumb. I was holding the spot for Superior, but they got me sore and I walked out."

He looked disappointed but not as much as I'd like to have seen him. There were still traces of that puzzled grin.

We settled on a price, and I got up to leave; and I stepped into it again right up to my neck.

"Aren't you forgetting something, old man?"

"You mean you want your rental now?" I said. "I don't play that way; I pay on delivery. You know that, Hap."

He shook his head.

"Well, what do you mean?"

"Paper," he said, as though he were talking to someone else. "First he books a stinker for Sunday, and then he starts to leave without so much as a one-sheet. Why would Joe Wilmot forget to buy paper?"

"I'll be damned," I said. "I guess that Superior crowd did get me upset."

"Uh-hah," he said. "Mmm."

I was so rattled that I let him sell me twice as much paper as I usually use. A dozen three-sheets, eighteen ones, and two twenty-fours. That and fifty window cards and the stuff for my lobby display.

I was shivering as I walked back to the hotel. Even thinking about Carol couldn't warm me up.

THREE

It was a Saturday morning, a little over a year ago, when I first saw Carol. We had a kids' matinee coming up at eleven o'clock and I was in the projection booth screening some stuff. I'd just made a change-over, and was putting a roll of film on the rewind.

Elizabeth waited for me to look around, but she finally saw I wasn't going to.

"This is Carol Farmer, Joe," she said. "She's going to stay with us."

"That's fine," I said, keeping my eye on the film.

"Our ladies' aid group is helping Carol attend business college," Elizabeth went on, "and she needed some place to cut down on expenses. I think we can use her very handily around the house, don't you?"

I still didn't look around. "Why not?"

"Thank you, dear," said Elizabeth, opening the door. "Come along, Carol. Mr. Wilmot has given you his approval."

I knew that she was laughing. She'd only brought Carol there to show me up. She didn't need my approval for anything.

Well, though, I passed old Doc Barrow, who runs the business college, on the street that afternoon; and he thanked me for being so generous in taking Carol in. I began to feel a little better, and kind of ashamed of the way I'd acted. Not on Elizabeth's account but Carol's.

She was about twenty-five and she'd spent most of her life on a two-by-four farm down in the sand flats, raising a bunch of brothers and sisters that ran off as soon as they got big enough to be any help. Her father was serving a five-year stretch for stealing hogs. Her mother was dead. Now, she was starting out to try to make something of herself.

We were changing programs the next day, and it was after midnight when I got home. But Carol was still up. She was sitting out at the kitchen table with a lot of books spread in front of her, and you could tell they didn't mean a thing to her. Not as much even as they would have to me.

She jumped up, all scared and trembling, like I'd caught her stealing. Her face got red, then white, and she snatched up a dish towel and began scrubbing at the table.

"Take it easy, kid," I said. "You're not on twenty-four-hour duty around here."

She didn't say anything; I don't guess she could. She stood watching me a minute, then she snatched up her books and sort of scuttled over to a corner and sat down on a stool.

She pretended to be studying, but I knew she wasn't. I knew it because I knew how she felt—because I'd felt the same way. I knew what it meant to be nothing and to want to be something. And to be scared out of your pants that someone is going to knock you down— not because of what you've done but because you can't strike back. Because they want to see you squirm, or they have a headache, or they don't like the way your hair is parted.

I opened the refrigerator door and took a look inside. It was full, as usual, with the leftover junk that passes for food with Elizabeth. Little plates of salad, bowls of consommé, sauce dishes of fruit, and nonfattening desserts. But way back in the rear I spotted a baked ham and a chocolate cake.

I took them over to the table, along with some bread and butter and a bottle of milk.

"You ain't—you're not supposed to eat that, Mr. Wilmot."

"Huh?" I almost dropped the carving-knife.

"Huh-uh. I mean, no, sir. Mrs. Wilmot said that was for tomorrow."

"Well," I said, "ain't that just dandy?"

"Yes, sir. There's some soup on the stove. That's what I-we—what we're supposed to have tonight."

I didn't argue about it. I just went over to the cupboard and got two plates, and I filled one of them so full it needed sideboards.

"Now, come over here," I said, "and eat this. Eat every damned bit of it. If there's any holler I'll say I did it."

Christ, I wish you could have seen her! She must have been empty all the way down. She didn't hog the food. She just sat and ate steadily, like she was going at a big job that needed doing. And she didn't mind my watching her. She seemed to know that I'd been the same way myself.

When she'd finished I told her to take her books and go to bed; and she said, "Yes, sir," and took off.

It made me a little uncomfortable for anyone to be so obedient, and yet I can't say I didn't like it, either. And it wasn't because I ever thought about telling her to do anything, well, anything bad. I just couldn't see the gal that way. I couldn't see her at all, if you know what I mean. If there was ever a woman that you wouldn't look at twice she was it. Probably she still is.

Because the more I think about it, the more I'm convinced that I'm seeing something that no one else can. And it took me three months before I could see it.

It was a Sunday afternoon. Elizabeth had taken her car and gone visiting, and I was lying down. We don't operate the house on Sunday afternoon. Local sentiment's against it.

There was a knock on my door, and I said, "Come in, Carol," and she came in.

"I just wanted to show you the new suit Mrs. Wilmot gave me," she said.

I sat up. "It looks very nice, Carol."

I don't know which I wanted to do most, laugh or cry.

She was a little bit cockeyed—maybe I didn't tell you? Well. And she was more than a little pigeon-toed. The suit wasn't new. It was a worn-out rag Elizabeth had given her to make over, and she'd botched it from top to bottom. And she had on a pair of Elizabeth's old shoes that didn't fit her half as well as mine would.

The blouse was too tight for her breasts, or her breasts were too big for the blouse, however you want to put it. They were too big for anything but an outsize. A good deep breath and she'd have had to start dodging.

I felt the tears coming into my eyes, and yet I wanted to laugh, too. She looked like hell. She looked like a sack of bran that couldn't decide which way it was going to fall.

And then the curtain rose or however you want to put it, and everything was changed.

And what I began to think about wasn't laughing or crying.

That tiny bit of cockeyedness gave her a cute, mad look, and the way she toed in sort of spread her buttocks and made a little valley under her skirt, and—and it don't—doesn't—make sense but there was something about it that made me think of the Twenty-Third Psalm.

I'd thought she looked awkward and top-heavy, and, hell, I could see now that she didn't at all. Her breasts weren't too big. Jesus, her breasts!

She looked cute-mad and funny-sweet. She looked like she'd started somewhere and been mussed up along the way.

She was a honey. She was sugar and pie. She was a bitch.

I said, "Come here, Carol," and she came there.

And then I was kissing her like I'd been waiting all my life to do just that, and she was the same way with me.

I don't know how long it was before I looked up and saw Elizabeth in the doorway.

FOUR

I always stop at the Crystal Arms when I'm in the city. They know I pay for what I get, and no questions, and whenever they can do me a favor they don't hold back.

There wasn't anything in my room box but a few complimentary theater tickets. I gave them to the bell captain and took the elevator upstairs. The heat was just being turned on full, and the room was a little chilly. I dragged a chair up to the radiator and sat down with my coat and hat on.

I wasn't worried. Not too much. I guess I just had a touch of the blues. I had everything in the world to look forward to, and I had the blues. I got out part of a pint I had in my Gladstone, and sat down again.

The lights were coming on, blobbing through the misty night haze that hung over the city. Over in the yards a freight gave out with a highball. I took a drink and closed my eyes. I tried to imagine it was fifteen years ago, and I was on the freight, and I was looking at the city for the first time. And I thought, *Hell, if you had to be blue why not then instead of now?*

When I saw it was getting really dark I pulled myself together and changed my socks and shirt. I took the stairs down a couple of floors, and knocked on Carol's door. The ventilator was open, and I could hear her splashing around in the tub.

"House dick," I said. "Open up."

She came to the door holding a big bath towel in front of her. When she saw it was really me—I—she dropped the towel and stood back for me to come in. She locked the door and walked over to the bed and lay down.

"That's all right," I said, sitting down by her. "You can put something on if you want to."

"Do you want me to?"

"I don't want you to catch cold," I said.

She said she wouldn't.

I gave her a drink out of the part of a pint, and lighted a cigarette for both of us. She sat up on one elbow and coughed and choked until I had to slap her on the back. I remembered then that I'd never seen her smoke before and that that was the first drink I'd ever given her.

"Is that the first time you smoked a cigarette?" I asked.

"Yes, Joe."

"And that's your first drink of liquor? What'd you take it for?"

"You gave it to me."

"Hell," I said, "you didn't have to take it."

There was a little finger of hair hanging down the middle of her forehead. She looked at it, turning her eyes in to be more cockeyed, and blew upward over her nose. The wisp of hair rose and settled down on her forehead again. I laughed and patted her on the bottom. I put my head down against her breast and squeezed. She freed one of her hands . . .

We had supper in her room—club sandwiches, waffle potatoes, apple pie with cheese, and coffee. I stood in the closet when the waiter delivered it. She'd never seen waffle potatoes before. She kept turning them around in her fingers, and nibbling the squares off a little at a time.

"Did everything go all right today?" she said finally.

"Pretty good."

"Why are you worried, then? Did something happen at the newspaper office?"

"Nothing much," I said; and I told her about it. "It's a good joke on Elizabeth. She's always acted like we didn't have good sense, and—"

"Maybe we don't have."

"Huh?" I said. "What do you mean, Carol?"

She'd never spoken up much before, and it surprised me; and I guess I sounded pretty abrupt. She dropped her eyes.

"I'm afraid, Joe. I'm afraid Elizabeth's trying to get us into trouble."

"Why, that's crazy!" I said. "We're all in this together. She couldn't make trouble for us without making it for herself."

"Yes, she—I mean, I think she could," said Carol. "You and me have to do everything. We run all the risks."

"Well, but look," I said. "I admit I got pretty much up in the air at the time. But what's actually the worst that could have happened there at the newspaper office? All they could have done was to refuse to take the ad, isn't that right?"

She shook her head as though she hadn't heard me. "Anyway, she's trying to get me in trouble. Why did she have to have me register here as Mrs. J. J. Williamson?"

"Why not? We had to agree on some name so we could reach you in case of emergency. You had to have some name to receive answers to the ad."

"But not *that* one, Joe. I got to thinking about it today; it's the same initials as yours. It kind of sounds like yours."

"Well—well," I said. I laughed, not very hard. "It's just a coincidence. What harm could it do, anyhow?"

She didn't answer me. She just shook her head again.

"If anyone made any boners it was me," I said, and I started telling her about Hap Chance. "It looked suspicious, see? With all the product I've got, why should I want sixteen reels of junk from him?"

Carol shrugged. "You explained it to him."

"Yeah, but it didn't look so good, particularly with me forgetting to buy paper."

"Well."

"It made it look like I didn't intend to play the picture. I almost might as well have told him I wanted that sixteen-reeler because of its length. Because it would make twice as hot a fire as—"

It wasn't true. The slip couldn't have meant anything like that to Hap, and Carol knew it. She saw I was just trying to divert her from Elizabeth.

We'd turned off all the lights except the one in the bathroom, and I was holding her on my lap in a big chair in front of the window. She began to breathe very deeply. I turned her face away from my chest, and I saw that she was crying.

"Don't do that," I said. "Please, Carol."

"Y-you're in love with her," she said. "She treats you like a dog, an'—and you go right on loving her."

"The hell I do!"

"Y-you do. And it's not fair! I'd do anything in the world for you, anything, Joe! And she hates you. And—a-and it doesn't make any difference. Y-you k-keep right on—"

"But, damnit, I don't!"

"You do, too!"

It would have gone on all night, but I didn't let it.

As the guy said on his wedding night, it was no time for talking.

FIVE

It was the next afternoon, and I was feeling pretty low.

Coming out of the city I'd passed a guy walking, a tired shabby-looking guy that looked like he needed a good night's sleep and a square meal; and I started to stop for him. And then, just when he was about to catch up with me, I stepped on the gas and drove off.

It was a mean thing to do and I hadn't intended doing it. What I meant to do was carry him down the road as far as he was going, and give him some food and change. Instead of that, I'd torn off when he almost had his hand on the door.

All of a sudden it came over me why I'd had so many blue spells lately. It was because I felt like I didn't amount to much any more. It was because I didn't feel that I was as good as other people—that I shouldn't put myself with people who wouldn't do what I was doing.

Subconsciously, I'd been afraid that hitchhiker might sense something, like maybe he'd pass up the car or ask to be let out after he got in. Subconsciously, I'd felt like he ought to.

I wondered again, like I had a thousand times, how the hell it all started.

One time, years ago, I sat in on one of Elizabeth's literary club meetings when they were discussing some lady poet. This poetry, this stuff this lady wrote, wasn't like real poetry. It wasn't like anything, in fact. It was just a lot of words strung together about God knows what all, and they'd say the same things over and over.

Well, though, it seemed like the stuff did make sense, once you understood what this lady was trying to do. She was writing about everything all at one time. She was writing about one thing, of course, more than the others, but she was throwing in everything that was connected with it; and she didn't pretend to know what was most important. She just laid it out for you and you took your choice.

I'll have to do the same thing.

Offhand, you'd say it began with Elizabeth catching Carol and me together that Sunday afternoon. But if there was a murder every time a husband or wife got caught like that there wouldn't be any people left. So—

It might have begun with the time I closed up Bower's house, and moved part of his equipment up to our garage. Or the time, right after we were married, when Elizabeth and I each took out twelve thousand five hundred dollars' insurance on the other. Or the time when I was delivering film for the exchanges, and it was raining, and I drove her up to her house in the company truck.

It may have started with Carol's old man being pinched for stealing hogs. Or the pushing around I took in reform school. Or at the orphanage—although it wasn't so bad there. The head matron was an old Irishwoman, weighing about three hundred pounds and so cross-eyed she scared me stiff the first time I saw her. But an angel couldn't have been any better.

But—Well, I'll tell things the best way I can.

One night I lost my key ring and couldn't lock up the show.

Elizabeth wasn't in the house and she carried her keys with her, so I went out to the garage, upstairs, where she was checking some film.

"You don't need to do that," I said. "I can look that over in the morning before we open up."

"I'm quite capable of doing it."

"I didn't say you weren't."

"Thank you," she said. "I'm glad you feel I'm still of some value."

"Okay, be stubborn," I said. I took the keys and started to leave. "Where's the new cord for that motor?"

She looked blank.

I told her I'd bought a new cord and laid it by her breakfast plate that morning. "I thought you'd have sense enough to know what it was for. That cord's got a short in it."

"Why, how gallant of you, Joe!" she said. But she was scared.

I got the new cord and changed it, and threw the old one in the trash bucket. But the next time I was out there I saw that she'd dug it out and put it on one of the metal shelves.

And now that I think of it, it might have begun with her mother. The old lady never threw anything away. For months after she died, Elizabeth and I were throwing out balls of string and packages of wrapping-paper and other junk.

I don't know. It's hard to know what to put down and what to leave out.

There was a lot of stuff on the radio and in the newsreels and newspapers. People getting run over, blown up, drowned, smothered, starved, lynched. Mercy killings, hangings, electrocutions, suicides. People who didn't want to live. People who deserved killing. People who were better off dead.

I don't suppose it was any different from usual, any different from what it always has been and always will be. But coming then, right at that time, it kind of tied in.

Day after day and night after night, there was a row. With one breath Elizabeth would tell us to get out; with the next she was threatening what she'd do if we tried.

"What the hell do you want?" I'd yell. "Do you want a divorce?"

"Be publicly displaced by a frump like that? I think not."

"Then I'll clear out. Carol and I."

"What with? And how would I run the show?"

"We'll sell the show."

"We can't. We couldn't get a fraction of its value from an outsider. I'm willing to give you credit, Joe. You're at least half the business."

That was true. A showman would know that. Anyone that was a showman wouldn't want to buy.

"I think I get you," I said. "You want me to give up any claim I've got on the business. Then you could peddle out at any old price and still have a nice wad."

She raised her eyebrows. "Such language, Joe! What would your parents think?"

"Goddam you!"

"How much, Joe? What will you give me to leave you in undisputed possession of the field?"

"You know damned well I haven't any money."

"So you haven't. Mmm."

There was more talk. Carol and me talking by ourselves. Elizabeth and me talking. The three of us talking together. Nagging and lashing out, and getting madder and edgier. And the stuff in the newspapers, and the newsreels, and on the radio. There were some Canadian travel folders, and a farmer's wife over in the next county who stumbled into a tubful of hot lard and was burned unrecognizably. There were the premiums on those insurance policies falling due. Twelve thousand five hundred dollars—double indemnity.

Then there was Elizabeth saying, "Well, Joe. I've finally hit upon a nice round sum."

And me, kind of shaking inside because I knew what the sum was, and trying to sound like I was kidding. "Yeah, I suppose you want about twenty-five thousand bucks."

There must have been something else, but I can't think of it now.

SIX

Our house, the show, I mean, is just four doors off of Main Street. On the corner, on our side and fronting on Main, is a dime store. On the opposite corner, catercornered from us, is the Farmers' Bank. Down the street a block is the City Hotel, and next door to it is the bus station and a garage.

I'm not taking credit for picking the location, but I couldn't have picked a better one if I'd done it. Any time you can get close to a bank, a hotel, a garage, a bus station, and a dime store—above all, a dime store—you've got something.

The average person might think a Main Street location would be better, but it wouldn't. It's too hard to park on Main.

I sat in the car a minute after I parked, feeling kind of good and proud like I always do when I look at the house. It's not as big as some city houses, but there's nothing to come up to it in a town of our size. And it's my baby. I built it all out of nothing.

We've got a copper-and-glass marquee that you couldn't duplicate for five grand, although naturally I didn't pay that. I had the job done by an out-of-town firm, and it just so happened that they couldn't get the work okayed by our local building inspectors. You know what I mean. So I settled for five hundred, and that, plus a few bucks for the inspectors, was all the marquee cost me.

The lobby is fifteen feet deep, spreading out fan shape from the double doors, with a marble-and-glass box office in the center. There's a one-sheet board on each side of the box office, glassed in with gold frame. The lobby walls have a four-foot marble base. The upper half is glass panels for display matter, with mirrors spotted in every three feet.

There's a carpet running from each door to the street.

That carpet would cost fifteen dollars a yard, but I got it for nothing. I was the first showman in this territory to lay a carpet through his lobby. I sold the equipment house on the idea, showed them how it would be opening up a big new market, so they put it in for me. Of course, I let them take a picture of me in front of the house, and I gave them a testimonial and an estimate on the number of miles that had been walked on the carpet without it showing any wear.

The house doesn't have a balcony. The ceiling's too low. I don't mean we're cramped. We're twenty feet at the entrance, which is four feet higher than the average show ceiling. But it's not high enough for a balcony.

We've only got a ninety-five-foot shot from the projection booth to the screen, and the floor can't drop much more than an inch to the foot. I'd have to double the pitch for a balcony, and even now it hurts people's necks to sit in the front row.

We get along pretty well without a balcony, anyway. I've got four rows of seats on tiers at the back of the house, extending up to the projection booth. Not full rows, of course, on account of the entrance and exit and the aisle down the middle from the booth door. It's more like loges.

When I put them in my customer liability insurance jumped a hundred dollars a year, because you can't tell when some boob might fall and break his neck. But the extra seating-space is worth it.

Jimmie Nedry, my projectionist, was just making a change-over when I went into the booth. He started the idle projector and put a hand on the sound control. At just the right instant he jerked the string that opens one port and closes the other. He pulled the switch on the first projector, lifted out the reel of film and put it on the rewind. There wasn't a break of even a fraction of an instant. You'd have thought the picture all came in one reel.

"Well, Jimmie," I said, "how's it going?"

He didn't say anything for a minute, but I knew he was nerving himself up to it. I feel sorry for Jimmie. Any way I can I try to help him out. I've got his oldest girl ushering for me, and I use his boys as much as possible in putting out paper.

"Look, Mr. Wilmot," he blurted out suddenly. "Grace and me were talking last night, and we was wondering if you couldn't put her on selling tickets. She could sit down that way, and people wouldn't see that she was—couldn't see much of her. And—"

"I'd like to have Grace," I said. "But you know how I'm tied up. I just about have to use women from the Legion auxiliary. If it wasn't for that I'd jump at the chance to take Grace."

"We got to have a little more money, Mr. Wilmot. If you could use the boys some on the door, or taking care of the—"

"I've got to spread that work around for the high school team. I'm doing all I can for you, Jimmie," I said.

"Well," he said. And he hesitated again. "I got to have some more money."

"There's no way I can give it to you," I pointed out. "You're classified as a relief operator. The union only allows me to work you twenty-four hours a week."

"You mean that's what you pay me for," he snapped. "I'm actually workin' about sixty!"

"That's all I can pay you for," I said. And it was true. The unions really keep an eye on social security records. "If you don't want the job perhaps you'd better quit."

"Yeah?" he grunted. "Where the hell would I get another one?"

"As a projectionist?"

"That's my line. It's the only thing I've ever done."

"Well, that makes it tough," I said. "If you had a couple grand for transfer and initiation fees, you might get into another local. But the chances are all against it."

He gave me a sore look, started to say something, then turned back to the machines. I went back downstairs and outside.

I was standing out near the curb, just lighting a cigarette, when a big black roadster pulled up and Mike Blair got out. He was the last man in the world I wanted to see. He's a business agent for the projectionists' union, and I'd seen more than enough of him six years before when this town was in his territory.

We shook hands, neither of us putting much pressure into it, and I asked him where he was headed. He pushed his hat back on his head, taking his time about answering and giving me a mean grin.

He took the cigar out of his mouth, looked at it, and put it back in again.

"I'm already there, Joe. This town's back in my district."

"Yeah?" I said. "I mean—it is?"

"Nice, huh?" He waggled the cigar in the corner of his mouth. "In fact, it's been back in my district for three days. I was over here last night, looking the old burg over, and the night before."

"Well," I said, "it's funny I didn't see you."

"It'd been a hell of a lot funnier if you had. Don't kid me, Joe. I like you in a nasty sort of way, but I don't like to be kidded. You were out of town."

"I couldn't help it. I—"

"I don't give a damn about that. You remember what I told you at the time I left here? What I told you a dozen other times?"

"Well—"

"I'll tell you again for the last time. You're an indie. You can run your own projectors and use a card man for reliefs, and we'll carry you on the fair list. You do that or else. You do it or put two men in the booth. Full time."

"Now, look, Blair," I said, "let's be reasonable about this. You—"

"We ain't got time to reason, Joe. Jimmie Nedry's already run over his twenty-four hours."

"But how can I run the projectors and the house too? Just show me how, Blair, and I'll—"

"Maybe you can't. I'll send you down another operator, and you keep out of the booth. How's that?"

He knew how it was without asking. Two full-time operators would cost me a hundred and eighty bucks a week.

"Look," I said. "Where did you get that two men to the booth and ninety-dollar scale to begin with? I'll tell you. Panzpalace framed it for you to freeze out city competition. They could carry four men at a hundred and fifty if they had to, but the indies couldn't, so you guys threw in with them. I—"

"Look who's talking," he said. "Well?"

"I can't pay it," I said. "Goddamn', you know I can't."

"Get up in the booth, then, and stay there. All but twenty-four hours of the week."

"I can't do that, either."

He grinned, nodded, and walked off. I had to follow him out to his car.

"You're going to pull the house?"

"You know I am, Joe."

"After all I've done for union labor in this town, you're going to—going to—" I couldn't go on. The look on his face stopped me.

"Why, you chiseling son of a bitch," he said softly. "You got the nerve to talk about what you've done for union labor. You get them to practically put you up a new house for nothing, and—"

"I paid scale all the way through the job."

"Sure you did. With coupon books. And the coupons weren't even good for full admissions; just a ten-cent discount. The boys put in an eight-hour day for you, and got out and sold tickets at night. That's what it amounted to. They built you a new house and then kept it packed for you."

"They all got their money. I didn't hear any of them kicking about it."

"Okay, Joe," he said. "It's none of my business, anyway. But this other is. You're off the fair list starting tomorrow."

Maybe you don't know what it means to have a house struck in a town like ours. It means you settle fast or go broke. There'd be spotters from every local watching out front. Any time a union man or a member of his family bought a ticket, it would mean a twenty-five buck fine for him. Consequently, in a place where everyone knows everyone else, there wouldn't be any bought.

"All right," I said. "But I'd like to ask you a couple of questions, Blair."

"As many as you like, Joe."

"When did your men take out cards in the bricklayers' union?"

"Huh?" He blinked. "What do you mean?"

"I'm talking about the job your boys did in the house over at Fairfield last week."

"Oh, that!" He forced a laugh. "Why that wasn't a bricklayer's job. All it amounted to was putting a few bricks under the projectors. Leveling them up. They had to make a longer shot, see, and—"

"It was brick work, wasn't it?"

"But the bricklayers couldn't have done it. The operators had to!"

"Then you should have had bystanders in from the bricklayers," I said. "You know what I think, Blair? I think the bricklayers are going to file a complaint against you with the state federation. I think that brick work at Fairfield is going to have to be torn out and done over by the proper local."

He stopped grinning, and his face fell a little. "You get around, don't you, Joe?"

"More than you'd think," I said. "More than you do, apparently. Did you know that the projectionists at View Point installed over fifty seats in the house there?"

"Sure I know about it," he snapped. "There wasn't enough carpenters to do the job so the projectionists finished it up."

"Why didn't the carpenters work overtime?"

"Because the chairs had to be in for the night show!"

"I get you," I said. "Rules are rules until they start pinching you. Then you throw them out the window."

He stood at the side of his car, thinking, bobbling the cigar around in his mouth. The bricklayers and carpenters are our two biggest locals; they're usually the biggest locals in any district. If they took a notion to—and Blair knew they would after I got through needling 'em—they could make him wish he'd never been born.

"Okay, Joe," he said, finally. "Maybe I was a little hasty."

"I thought you'd see it my way," I said. "No hard feelings?"

"All kinds of 'em." He looked down at my hand and shook his head. "I'm not through with you, Joe. Some day I'm going to hang one on you that you can't squirm out of."

SEVEN

Our house, our residence, sits out on the edge of town, almost a hundred yards from the highway. It's all that's left of the old Barclay homestead, just the house and a couple acres of ground and the outbuildings.

It was a little after midnight when I got there. I parked the car in the yard, in back of Elizabeth's, locked it up, and went in the kitchen door. The coffee percolator was going, and there was some cheese and pickles and other stuff sitting out on the table. I went through the door to the dining-room and started up the stairs.

"Oh, there you are, darling!" called Elizabeth.

She was sitting in the living-room with a book in her lap, and the light turned low.

"Wasn't it nice of me to wait up for you?" she said. "I've even fixed a lunch. I know you must be famished."

She had on a little gingham house dress, and she was smiling, and for a minute I was crazy enough to think she wasn't giving me a rib. Then I thought of all the times in the past she'd picked me up just to slap me down; and I went on upstairs without speaking.

I washed, combed my hair, and went back down again.

"All right," I said, "spit it out. What's up?"

"Don't you want something to eat, Joe?"

"I've ate—eaten," I said.

"Did you ate—eat—with Carol?"

"Pour it on me," I said. "I'm used to it. Hell, how could I eat with Carol? I left the city this morning."

"I hope you weren't foolish enough to register in together, Joe."

"No, we didn't. I don't know just when Carol registered. Just after the bus got there, I guess."

She sat staring at me, not speaking; her head thrown back, her eyes half closed. I told her about the bonehead she'd pulled on the price of the ad; and she only shook her head a little, as if nothing I could say would be of any importance.

After a long time she said, kind of talking to herself, "No, it's true. It *is* true."

"What's true?"

She held out her hand. "Let me see your date book, Joe."

I tossed it to her. It fell on the floor and she picked it up. She turned the pages to the month's bookings.

"I see Playgrand has been consulting you again," she said. "I hope you received a suitable fee?"

"Those are good shorts," I said. "After all, we've got to buy from someone, don't we?"

"Now, what did we do at Utopian?" she said. "Did we give him a third of our feature bookings because he's an old friend of ours? Or were we just a teenyweeny bit—ah—intoxicated?"

"All right," I said. "I do give my friends the breaks. What's the difference as long as it don't lose us any money? You never saw me lose money helping a friend, did you?"

"No, Joe, I never did. And you never lost any in striking back at any enemy. But tell me. What did they say to you at Superior? Didn't they know you were the great Joe Wilmot—sole proprietor of his wife's property?"

"They didn't say anything. That was all the dates I had open."

"Really?"

"Yeah, rahlly," I said. "And I wouldn't push that wife's-property business too far. All you had when I met you was a run-down store building and a couple of hundred seats that weren't worth the chewing-gum that was stuck on them."

She shook her head, smiling that set, funny smile.

"It's weird, isn't it? Positively fantastic."

"Goddamn'," I said, "if there's something there you don't like, say so. We can change it easy enough."

"But I do like it, Joe! I like—I wasn't criticizing. I was only evaluating. Weighing things, I suppose you'd say."

"I don't know what you're talking about," I said. "And that's only half the story."

"Stupid," she said. "Yes, actually stupid. That with everything else. Vain, vindictive, lying, dishonest, a philanderer. And stupid. And yet—"

"You've left out a couple," I said. "Repulsive and nauseating."

She nodded. "Yes, Joe. I left them out."

She seemed to be waiting for me to say something, sitting there smiling at me, her hands caressing the arms of the chair.

"You're slipping," I said. "I'm going to eat something and go to bed."

"Joe!"

I turned in the doorway. She was standing. It looked like she had started to follow me.

"Well, what?" I said.

"Nothing, Joe. I guess—nothing."

I went on into the kitchen.

I fixed a sandwich and a cup of coffee. When I'd got away with about half of it the lights blinked, went dim, and came on full again.

It didn't register on me for a second. Then it was as if something was holding me back when I tried to move.

It seemed like I was about to see something; I mean I could almost see what it was. And it scared me so badly my stomach rolled and my scalp crawled. I came alive and stumbled to the door. I half fell down the back steps and ran for the garage. I raced up the outside stairs and threw myself against the door.

The room was lined with sheet metal. Floors, ceiling, walls. The projectors and sound tables I'd got from Bower were stashed in a corner. In the center of the room was the metal film table, with a reel at each end and a quarter-horse motor at one.

There was a metal stool in front of the table, and Elizabeth was seated on it, bent over. Her face wasn't six inches from the film that was traveling in front of her.

Two full reels were lying on the table next to the motor. They were partly unwound, and their ends dangled down into the open film can. There were seven more reels in it. It was a full-length feature, seven in the can, two on the table, and one in the rewind. A can with a two-reel travelogue and one with a one-reel cartoon were under the table. Close to Elizabeth's feet. They were standing open, too.

The film was wet. As it passed through the reel it sent a fine spray over the motor. The spray formed a trickle that ran down the pear-shaped back of the motor.

The cord sparked.

The trickle of water seemed to catch fire.

There was a flash as if someone had tossed a barrel of yellow paint into the room.

I struck out with my hand, and something seemed to grab it and push my arm back into my shoulder. A streak of lightning shot across the table. There were a couple of pinwheels of fire at each end. Then, a loud *pop* and darkness; and the sound of the broken film whipping against the table.

And Elizabeth crying.

I found the cord and jerked it loose. I fumbled along the wall until I found the circuit breaker, and the lights came on again.

I turned them off and opened the door. I picked up Elizabeth and carried her back to the house and into the kitchen. I put my foot up on a chair, and pulled her over my knee, and whaled the tar out of her.

She stopped crying and laughing, and really began to cry.

Some way she got turned around and put her arms around my neck.

EIGHT

You wouldn't think we'd have been hungry, but we were. We ate some sandwiches and coffee; and afterward she made me go upstairs to the bathroom with her to get my hand fixed up.

It wasn't a bad burn; it just looked bad. But she insisted on doping it all up, so I let her.

"What'd you want to do a crazy thing like that for?" I asked. I'd asked her about umpteen times already.

"You know why," she said.

"No, I don't, either."

"Well, you do," she said. Like a little girl. And she did look like one then. Her skin was always so clear you could almost see through it, and now it was rosy and flushed.

She acted like she was afraid to look at me; bashful, you know. She'd duck her head and look the other way. Her hair was like silk as she bent over my hand. Black silk, with a finger-wide streak of white through the center.

"You're awfully pretty," I said, all of a sudden.

"I'll bet I'm black and blue."

"Let's see if you are."

"Now, Joe—don't—"

But she didn't pull away.

I put a kiss on my hand and patted her.

"Feel better now?"

"Uh-huh. And now you're going to bed."

"We've got some talking to do first," I said.

"All right," she said. "But just a little. I know you're worn out."

I didn't know why she blushed; why she didn't want to talk. Not right then, I didn't. I should have, sure, but you know how it is. You don't think about water when you're not thirsty.

She sat on the edge of the bed while I undressed and lay down.

"Now, what's it all about?" I said.

"I don't know, Joe. It just seemed at the moment that it was the only thing to do."

"We don't have to go through with this business," I said. "Maybe we can think of something else."

"Do we have to think of something else, Joe?"

"What—how do you mean?"

She was leaning back on one elbow, her legs drawn up under her. She lifted her eyes and gave me a long, slow look. She didn't answer.

"Well—well, maybe we don't have to," I said. "Gosh, Elizabeth, I don't know—I don't know what to do or what not to do. I never have known."

"I know I'm terribly difficult," she said. "No, I mean it. But I do hope you understand my intentions were good."

"Oh, sure," I said. "I understand."

"I'm afraid you don't," she said and laughed, "but we'll not argue about it. It's no longer important now. I hope it will never become important again."

"Tell me something," I said. "About what we were going to do. Did you feel like I did—like you wouldn't want to have other people around you any more? Like you'd be ashamed, not for yourself but for them?"

"Well—"

"I guess I'm not sure of what I mean myself," I said. "It wasn't the idea of breaking the law or not going to heaven. I didn't really see how we were doing anything very wrong. If it was someone you knew it would be different. If it was someone that was, well, respectable and a valued citizen and all that, it would be different. But when it's not—Well, if you can sacrifice—If three people can have happiness and go ahead and amount to something just by someone—someone that doesn't stand a show of being anyone or doing anything—getting out of the way, why—"

"I'll tell you why you felt as you did," said Elizabeth. "It was too simple."

"No, that wasn't—"I hesitated. "I don't think I get you, Elizabeth."

"We're strong people, Joe. Stronger at least than many. Without being too flattering we can say that we have good minds, good bodies, a good financial position."

"Not good enough."

"There's room for improvement," said Elizabeth. "There usually is. And there comes a time when the improvement seems imperative. So what do we superior people do? How do we exercise our fine talents in the emergency? We don't. We don't use them at all. We do something that the first man could have done much better. Something that anyone could do. We—we push over someone who is more trusting or less strong than we are."

'Well," I said, "it was the only thing we could think of."

"Yes, Joe. It was the only thing we could think of. "

I frowned, and I suppose she thought I was getting mad.

"You go to sleep now, dear," she said. "We'll talk more later."

She got up and pulled down the shades, and turned off the light. She came back and bent over me, her face flushed, looking more like a little girl than ever.

"Think you can sleep, Joe?" she said.

And before I could answer, she lay down by my side and pulled my head against her breast.

We lay there for a long time. Long enough to give me every chance in the world. And I could feel her growing stiffer and older by the minute.

She didn't get mad.

She just acted sorry and sort of resigned. She moved away from me, and stood up.

"When was it, Joe?"

"I don't know what you're talking about," I said.

"Was it before you came here—to me?"

"Hell," I said, "you knew how it was all along. You've known about it for months."

"I didn't *know* until now, Joe. But that isn't the point. I'd have sworn this would be one time when, as you'd put it, you'd pass up a bet. If it wasn't, well, then there'll never be such a time. You've got nothing to share with me. There's nothing I can do for you."

As she started for the door I said, "Well, what do you want to do? Do you still want to go through with it?"

"By all means," she said. "I've changed my mind about its being too simple for us."

I let her go. I'd gone a little goofy when I thought she was in danger. But I should have known we couldn't patch things up. I still wasn't hot for the killing—who would be?—but if that was the only way to lead a happy, decent life, why . . .

NINE

If you're like I am you've probably spotted a thousand couples during your lifetime that made you wonder why and how the hell they ever got together. And if you're like I used to be you probably lay it to liquor or shotguns.

Not that I can tell you why I married Elizabeth or she married me. Not exactly. But I can tell you this. We both knew exactly what we were getting, barring a few points, and we went right ahead and made the grab anyway.

And looking back it all seems perfectly natural.

That first rainy night when I drove her home in the film truck she got out, fumbled in her purse, and handed me fifty cents.

"No, I want you to take that, Joe," she said, when I sort of began to stutter. "It would have cost me much more than that to take a cab."

"But—but look here, Miss Barclay—"

"Good night, Joe. Be careful of the flower beds when you drive out."

I told her what she could do with her flower beds and four-bit pieces. I told her she could walk in mud up to her ears before I gave her another ride. I—

But I was ten miles down the road when I did it. At the time I couldn't think of any more to say than I can now when she ties me into knots. Not as much, maybe, because I hadn't had any practice.

My next run-in with her was a Sunday, about two weeks later. I was still sore, or thought I was; but when she motioned me over to the box office I went running, like a dog running for a bone.

"Come around to the door," she said, "you're in the way of the patrons there." And I went around. Then, she said, "I want you to do an errand for me, Joe. "And I said, "Well—well, thank you."

"A whole row of seats has broken down," she went on. "I want you to go over to the Methodist Church and pick up thirty of their folding chairs. I've already called about them."

I gulped and got started so fast I didn't really understand what she'd told me. I heard it, you know, but I didn't understand it. And when I did, or thought I did, I still couldn't believe it.

I got the chairs after some pretty chilly looks from the parson, and took them back and set them up. By that time I was so late on the route that a couple of hours more wouldn't make any difference, so I found a little engine trouble, and I'd just got it fixed when the show closed for the night. So I drove her home again.

She didn't hand me fifty cents that night. She said something about not having any change—I knew she had a five-pound sack full—and that she'd pay me some other time.

"I'll settle cheap," I said, bracing myself. "Tell me—I mean, can I ask you a question?"

"Certainly you may."

"Were those chairs you got tonight—were they some you'd loaned to the church?"

"No. I thought I mentioned they were theirs."

"You mean,' I said, "you borrowed thirty chairs from a church for a picture show on Sunday night?"

She frowned a little, then her face cleared. "You mean they might have been using them? Oh, but I knew they wouldn't be. That church never has anything approaching a crowd on Sunday night."

"Well," I said, "well, that makes everything just dandy."

I found out later that her old man, her grandfather rather, had donated the sites for most of the churches in town, so I guess she felt like they owed her a few favors and they apparently felt the same way.

Jesus, what a hell of a way to collect! It was like asking to sleep with a man's wife because he owed you five dollars.

After that, after I really began to notice things, to do something besides set the film cans in the lobby and beat it, I saw her head for one jam after another. And instead of pointing my nose the other way, I'd jump in and try to give her a straight steer.

She had trouble spelled all over her. She'd always have it. And I knew it, and I didn't want it any different—then.

You don't buy a twenty-three-jewel watch and hope to turn it into an alarm clock. I didn't have any idea of ever changing her.

The funniest deal came up one night over some color film.

She was using Simplex projectors with nine hundred-watt Mazdas, and the way the stuff came out on the screen was pretty God-awful. Most of the time you could tell the men from the women characters but they all looked like they'd been brawling in a jelly closet.

"I'm going to make them give me a rebate on this," she told me. "I've never seen such a thing in my life!"

"You won't get any rebate," I said. "This print is brand new; that's the trouble with it. What little color stuff you've played in the past has been old and those Mazdas would shoot through it. But there's more and more color coming in, and you'll probably be getting a lot of new prints."

"Oh?" she began to look a little sick. "What should I do, Joe?"

"Get rid of the lamps and put in carbon arcs. They'll cut through anything."

"Are they—pretty expensive?"

"Well, it's going to cost you something to convert, sure," I said. "But you should be able to squeeze around that. Talk it over with your power-and-light man here. Show him how the arcs will burn more juice and it's to his advantage for you to have them. If you handle it right you might be able to get him to put them in for you."

She brightened up and said she'd try it.

Two weeks later she was still using lamps, and from what little I could get out of her I knew she'd keep right on using them as far as the manager of the power-and-light company was concerned.

Well, I picked a light night on the route, drove to beat hell for sixteen hours straight, and got back into Stoneville early the next morning. I brushed up a little bit and paid a call on the power company.

Not that I'd expected him to be, but the manager wasn't an imbecile or a boor or a grafter. He was just a pretty pleasant citizen who'd spent a lot of time learning his business. And he wasn't going to let anyone tell him where to get off, even if he had been trotting around town with his tail sticking out at a time when she had six dresses for every day in the week.

I don't know what I said to him. Nothing in particular, I guess. We sat around and talked for thirty minutes or so and went out and had coffee together, and that was all there was to it. Two days later the arcs went in.

I could tell you some more things along the same line, but there wouldn't be too much point to it. The time's better used, probably, in mentioning that she'd found out plenty about me. About all there was to find out.

Her mother was pretty feeble, and I used to inquire about her. So sooner or later, of course, we had to inquire about mine—about my folks. And that brought up the orphanage, and one thing led to another. At first I told her I'd picked up the projectionist trade when I was in the orphanage. But then I remembered telling her I'd skipped out of the joint when I was fourteen, and, rather than look like a liar, I told her the truth.

"Was the reform—the industrial school very bad, Joe?"

"I thought it was at the time," I said. "But after I saw a few—"

I told her about the jails.

I told her how it was when you really got down to the bottom of the pot, how you'd get seventy-two hours on vagrancy as soon as you hit a town, how they'd float you back on the road again before you could get a job or even a good meal in your belly.

"I'm never going to go back to stuff like that," I said. "They'll have to kill me first."

"Or?"

"Yeah," I said. "It'll be 'or' before they get me down again."

I didn't have to tell her why I was sticking to what looked like a pretty cheap job, because I knew she knew. Maybe she didn't know any more about business and public relations than a two-year-old. But she could see an angle a mile off, particularly where it concerned me. Most of the time it was like we were looking out the same window.

There were around fifty customers on my route. They bought product on everything from a two-day to a week's option. I mean it was their right to keep it for a week if they wanted to, which didn't mean that they always would. They just bought a long option to play safe.

Well, suppose they decided to keep it four days or less, then turned it back to me for pick-up. I take it on down the road a ways and give another house a run on it for half price. The house is able to make one more change on the week than it's been making and I pick up a ten spot or so.

I had to be careful. Bicycling film is a penitentiary offence. But a guy that's actually hauling the product—a guy that knows just who is buying from where—can get away with it. The exchanges can't afford to check the small towns. They've maybe got a damned good idea they're being roped, but unless it gets too bad they let it go.

I never let it get too bad.

Well, there's not a lot more to tell.

Stoneville wasn't important enough as a show town then for the union to bother with, and Elizabeth had a punk boy working in the booth. One of those sharp lads who has to think ten or fifteen minutes before he can decide which end of the match to strike.

His best trick was to get the reel in backward or out of sequence, but he had a lot of others. Missing changeovers. Forgetting to turn the sound on. Hitting the arcs before the film was rolling.

It was the last one that finally got me.

By this time I'd rearranged my route so that Stoneville was my last stop instead of the first one; and I'd stay there overnight before going back to the city—Sure, at a hotel. Where do you think?

Anyway, I was sitting in the house that night when I finally got just as much of that punk as I could take. He'd already run one reel backward. He'd missed two change-overs, and he'd turned the sound on full and forgot about it. That's more boners than a good projectionist will pull in a lifetime, but the punk wasn't through yet. Right after the second miss, he caught the film on fire.

If you've gone to many picture shows, particularly back in the early days of the business, you've seen it happen once or twice. The film will hit the screen like a still. Then it looks like someone is punching a live cigar butt through it from the back.

That's caused by not having the film rolling while the arcs are on. Because those arcs are just like a blast furnace, and nothing burns as easily or faster than film.

Projectors are fixed so that nothing but the film in the frame can burn. But not everyone knows that, and even if they did—what the hell? No one's going to thank you for not roasting them. No one's going to pay dough to sit in a dark house while some boob splices film.

I climbed up into the booth without saying a word, and the punk didn't ask me anything. I just took the splicing-knife and the glue pot away from him, tied the film back together, and started the projector rolling again. Then I walked over to him and stood up close. He wasn't home talent. Any trouble that was made would have to come from him.

"Which way do you want to go out of here?" I said. "Walking or sliding?"

Before he could say what he was getting ready to—that I couldn't fire him and that if Elizabeth paid him better dough he'd do a better job—I slapped him. I gave him the old cop trick. A slap for taking up my time, a slap for not answering questions, a slap because he couldn't answer 'em, a slap because it hurt my hand, a slap because he was such a sickening-looking son of a bitch with the blood running out of him. And a dozen good hard ones on general principles.

I shoved fifteen bucks at him, his week's pay, told him to go out the exit and keep going, and tossed his coat and hat after him. That's the last I saw of him from that day to this.

When the box office closed and Elizabeth came up, I was still sore enough to tell her what I'd done. The details.

"Do you think that was necessary, Joe?" Her eyebrows went up.

"What the hell can he do?" I said. "He's too scared to sue, and he doesn't have any friends or family here."

"Joe," she said. "Ah, Joe."

I drove her home and sat in the kitchen while she made coffee and sandwiches. She'd hardly spoken a word since we'd left the show, and she didn't say much more until the food was ready. Then she sat down across from me, studying, her chin in her hand.

"How much money have you, Joe?" she said at last.

I told her I had a little over two grand, around twenty-one fifty.

"Well, I haven't any," she said. "No more than my operating capital. On top of that I can't go on much longer without at least a little new equipment, and on top of that there's a fifteen-hundred-dollar past-due mortgage on this house."

"I'll lend you the money," I said. "You can have anything I've got. I'll get you a decent projectionist, too."

"For fifteen a week, Joe?" She shook her head. "And I couldn't take a loan from you. I'd never be able to pay it back."

"Well—" I hesitated.

"I'm a good ten years older than you are, Joe."

"So what?" I said. "Look—are we talking about the same thing? Well, then put it this way. I'll run your machines until we can train some local kid to do a halfway decent job. I'll get a couple weeks' vacation and do it. And you can have the money as a gift or you can take it as a loan. Hell, you can't ever tell when your luck will change. But as far as—"

"Joe, I don't—"

"—but I'm not buying any women," I said. "Not you, anyhow."

She looked at me and her eyes kept getting bigger and blacker, and there were tears in them and yet there was a smile, too, a smile that was like nothing I'd ever seen before or ever got again—from her or anyone else.

"You're good, Joe," she said. "I hope you'll always hold on to that thought. You are good."

"Aw, hell," I said. "You've got me mixed up with someone else. I'm just a bum."

She shook her head ever so little, and her eyes got deeper and blacker; and she took a deep breath like a swimmer going under water.

"Isn't it a pity, Joe, that you won't buy me—when you're the only person I could possibly sell to?"

I've only got a little more to say about us, our marriage, and probably it isn't necessary.

What smells good in the store may stink in the stew pot. You can't blame a train for running on tracks. Ten years is a hell of a long time.

So, to get back to the present . . .

TEN

When I went downstairs around ten the next morning, Elizabeth was
in the living-room and old Andy Taylor was with her. I shook hands
and asked Elizabeth why she hadn't called me.

"I wouldn't let her," said Andy. "Just stopped by for a little visit;
nothing important. Have a good trip to the city?"

"So-so," I said.

"How'd you hurt your hand?"

"I cut it on a bottle I was opening," I said. "It's nothing serious."

He's a sharp old buzzard. A buzzard is just what he looks like,
now that I come to think of it. He's got reddish-grey hair that's
always hanging out from under his hat because he's too stingy to get
it cut, and his nose is like a beak. I've never really seen his eyes they're
so far back in his head. And I've never seen him in anything but an
old broadcloth suit that you could beat from now until doomsday and
not get the dust out of. He's somewhere past sixty. He lives in back
of one of his buildings.

"Where's that hired girl of yours?" he shot out suddenly.

"What?" I said. "You mean Carol? Why, I guess she's—"

"I let her have a few days off," said Elizabeth. "The child's not
been anywhere or got to do anything since she's been here."

"Saw her down to the bus station. Wondered where she was
goin'."

I laughed and lit a cigarette. "Don't tell me you didn't find out."

"Meanin' to, but it kind of slipped my mind." He grinned. He
knows that everyone knows how he is, and he doesn't care. He's rich
enough that he doesn't have to.

"Believe I'll take one of your cigarettes," he said.

I gave him one. Elizabeth excused herself and went out.

Andy sat puffing on his cigarette, puffing on it until I thought he
was going to suck it down his throat. He didn't talk while he smoked.
Just kept puffing until there wasn't anything left to puff.

"Well, what's on your mind, Andy?" I said, when he had dropped
the butt on an ash tray. "Want some passes to the show? I'll leave
them for you at the box office."

"Thank you, Joe," he said.

"I guess my customer liability falls due this month," I said. "I can give you a check now if you want it."

"Ain't no hurry, Joe. No hurry at all."

I started getting fidgety. Waiting isn't my long suit, and, anyway, I knew what he had on his mind. He'd never given up prodding me about it since it had happened.

"Don't want to rent me another show for a percentage of the gross, do you?" I asked.

"Well, no. Can't say as I do."

"Okay," I said, "I'm here listening. You can talk when you're ready."

"You did give me a raw deal, Joe. Now, you'll admit that, won't you?"

"Oh, sure," I said. "Just the kind you'd like to give me."

"No, I wouldn't, Joe. I'm pretty tight, maybe, but I never crooked anyone out of a penny yet."

"I didn't crook you. I outsmarted you."

"I wouldn't brag about it, Joe. It don't take much brains to outsmart a man who trusts you. There's another name for that."

"Hell," I said, "you brought it up. What do you want to do about it, anyway?"

"I'll leave it to you, Joe. Twenty-five dollars a month don't even pay taxes on that building. What do you think you ought to do?"

"Well, I told you before, Andy. I'll let you out of the lease if you want to remodel the building—change it into something besides a show house."

"Huh!" he grunted. "An' what would that cost?"

"Plenty," I said. "Enough so you couldn't ever afford to convert back into a show again, no matter what kind of deal was put up to you."

"That's your last word, Joe? You've made up your mind not to do anything?"

"Not a goddam thing." I nodded. "You ought to know that by this time. You don't need money, so I don't feel sorry for you. And there's no way I can be forced to pay you more than twenty-five a month."

"How about yourself, Joe?"

"How do you mean?"

"Don't you think you ought to do the right thing for your own sake?"

"You mean so my conscience won't hurt?" I laughed. "Don't kid me, Andy."

"No, that ain't what I mean." He scowled and got up. "But I don't reckon there's any use talking to you. You mark my word, Joe Wilmot. You better change your ways or—or—"

He turned and stamped out without finishing.

I went into the kitchen and poured a cup of coffee.

Elizabeth was having some coffee, too, and I tried to strike up a conversation with her. Because, after all, we *had* been married for ten years and we didn't have much time left to spend together.

But she wasn't having any, and I didn't care much.

There wasn't anything girlish about her this morning. She looked plain damned old.

I drove into town yawning, wishing that the whole business was over so I could relax and get some rest.

I fished my mail out of the box office and read it in my car. It was the usual stuff. Confirmation of bookings, advertisements, a copy of the *Motion Picture Herald*. I put the other stuff in my pocket and opened the *Herald*.

There was a story in it I was following. Some exhibitor out in the western part of the state had filed suit against the major exchanges to compel them to supply him with pictures. That was two years ago and they were still hearing evidence in the case. My personal opinion was that he'd better turn his house into a shooting-gallery.

You just can't win against the exchanges. They've got too many loopholes on their side. Take substitutions, for example.

Every once in a while I'll get a picture I didn't book in place of the one I did. It has to be that way in a business where a highly perishable product has maybe a hundred other buyers.

It happens pretty seldom with me because I stand in well, and I'm an important exhibitor. But if I didn't and wasn't—well, see what I mean? I *could* get substitutes five times out of five. My advertising money would be wasted. My customers would never know for sure what I was showing.

In any small-city house a large part of the patronage comes from the farmers and surrounding villages. I can stand out in front of my house and count people from half a dozen smaller towns. And it's because I get the pictures ahead of the smaller places.

It's no more than fair because I've got a bigger and better house and I can pay more than the small town—*and* the exchanges are willing to give me preferred booking. If they weren't I'd probably have to close up. I'd hate to try to operate with every wide place in the road around me getting pictures before I did. Almost as bad as I'd hate to show in court why I was entitled to pull trade away from another showman.

Jimmie Nedry showed up around eleven, and we went inside. It was Thursday, and our Friday's product should have been in for screening. But it wasn't. I called home, and it hadn't been dropped off there, either.

I put in a call to the city, and got Jiggs Larrimore on the wire. Jiggs is manager of one of the little exchanges. I don't particularly need him, and he needs me bad.

"I guess there's been a little mix-up, Joe," he said. "I'll tell you what you'd better do. You just hold over the picture you've been playing, and we'll take care of anything extra you have to pay on the option."

"Yeah?" I said. "Now I'll tell you what you'd better do. You'd better get that picture here to me and get it here pronto."

"Now, look, Joe—"

"It's for my Friday-Saturday show. You know I've got to have a Western on Friday and Saturday. The yokels won't go for anything else."

"But it's too late to—"

"Huh-uh. No, it isn't, Jiggs," I said. "Craig City's got that picture advertised for today. They've been advertising it here in my home-town paper. You pull their print over to me, Jiggs. It doesn't make any difference in a town that big whether they play horse-opera on the week-end or not."

"Well, now"—I could hear him gulp—"I don't believe we can do that, Joe."

"Why not? Because it's one of Sol Panzer's houses?"

"Well. After all—"

"Look," I said. "How many of those Panzpalace houses are you in? Sol gives you a spot whenever he feels like it, and that ain't often. I buy the block. You pull that pic over here, Jiggs. You get it here quick. If you don't I'll set out every one of your dates and sell you a roll of tickets besides."

Jiggs sighed. "I hear you talking, Joe. Here it comes."

I hung up, and turned to Jimmie Nedry. "I guess that'll show Mr. Big Time Panzer something," I said. "He'll do a little thinking before he runs any more ads in this town."

"Yeah," said Jimmie. "So what?"

I let it pass, and went on outside. I knew Jimmie was feeling low about his money troubles, and I'd thought it would cheer him up to hear Jiggs Larrimore catch hell. That's one reason I'd cracked down on Jiggs. But Jimmie didn't react like he should have. He couldn't think about anything but his own worries.

The thought flashed through my mind for a second that maybe there was something more to that picture mix-up than Solly Panzer's trying to pull a fast one on me. And crazy as the idea was it made me shiver to think about it.

It was just one of those things that happen. It couldn't be anything else. I had the Barclay in a spot that no one could touch and everyone knew it.

Just the same, though, I couldn't help thinking, *Wouldn't that be hell? Wouldn't it just be sweet to mix yourself in a murder and then find out that it hadn't got you anything?*

ELEVEN

I worked my way around the square, shaking hands and slapping backs, and talking about crops and kids until I got to Sim's Pool Hall. Then I went inside and drank a bottle of beer and bought one for Sim. There were a lot of young bucks in there, and it wasn't long before most of them were around me. I'd picked up some new stories on film row. After we'd all had a few laughs and they'd bought me a beer or two I moved on again. Well, I did buy a package of mints, first.

About a block down the street I ran into Reverend Connors, the Christian Church minister. I bought a couple of tickets he was selling to a pie sociable, and wrote him out a pass to the show. I knew he wouldn't use it, and no one else could since I'd put his name on it.

"I'll tell you what, Reverend," I said. "If the church ladies would like to set up a table for their stuff in the lobby of the show I'd be glad to have them."

"Bless you, Brother Wilmot!" he said. "They'll be delighted to hear that."

He went away real pleased. I was sort of pleased myself. It would help to draw a crowd, and wherever there's a crowd there's business.

A half hour or so later I ran into Jeffery Higginbotham, the high school principal. He and I don't ever get familiar but we understand each other. He was kind of worried—on my account. The junior class was giving a play next month. They'd picked a Saturday night date to give it. What did I think?

Naturally, I thought it was a hell of a note, but I didn't say so.

"Why, that's swell," I said. "I'll let you have the show to put it on in."

"But we couldn't do that," he said. "You couldn't lose your night's business for us, Mr. Wilmot."

"I couldn't afford to, but I would," I said, "if it wasn't for sentiment among the town businessmen. You know, a picture show draws a lot of business to a town. I'm afraid they wouldn't like it if I didn't run on a Saturday night."

"No, I don't suppose they would" he said. "But—"

"Now, here's my idea," I said. 'I'll turn the show over to you after midnight. The kids will love that. You know—having a regular midnight show, big-city style. And you'll catch a lot of customers you'd miss otherwise. A lot of people that come for the picture will stay to see the play."

"That's good reasoning," he said, and his eyes twinkled. "And a lot of people who intend to see the play will come early to see the picture. Or had you thought of that?"

"It never entered my mind," I said.

We both laughed, and I moved on again. I got back to the show at two o'clock when the matinee was starting.

Mrs. Artie Fletcher, my cashier—yes, and president of the Legion auxiliary—was talking over the telephone with her back half turned to the window. I've got a sign on that phone saying *No Personal Calls Please,* and I've given her more than one hint about using it. But it don't bother her any. I guess she thinks the rules don't apply to auxiliary women.

I guess they don't, either.

Several people had to wait around for tickets.

My doorman is Harry Clinkscales, the captain of the high school football team. If I could buy him for what he's worth and sell him for what he thinks he is I'd retire tomorrow. He's not even honest like you'd ordinarily expect a big overgrown pie-faced dumbbell to be. I know he knocks down on the popcorn machine, and if I didn't keep close watch on him he'd pass in a dozen females a day.

I wouldn't mind if it was just a few.

The day went fast. It was five o'clock before I knew it. I ate supper at the Palace Restaurant, had some pie and coffee at Mike's Barbecue, and bought some cigarettes at the City Drug.

I suppose that sounds pretty narrow and scheming, that trade-spreading stunt and some of the others I've told you about. But when everyone else is the same what choice have you got?

Bower—the guy that used to own the other house—couldn't be bothered about stuff like that. But look what happened to him. Elizabeth couldn't be bothered, either, and look at the shape she was in when I first met her.

I didn't tell you, I guess, but Elizabeth went into the show business in the first place because she knew she wasn't a mixer and she thought it was one business where she wouldn't have to be. People would just lay their money down quietly, and pass inside, and that would finish the transaction.

She thought!

At six o'clock I gave Jimmie Nedry a two-hour relief. After that, I went back outside.

Sheriff Rufe Waters and his deputy, Randy Cobb, sauntered up and stood beside me at the curb.

"Good show, Joe?" Rufe said.

"Fair," I said.

"Ain't got an empty seat or two you ain't using?" said Randy.

"Sure, I have," I said, and I gave the doorman the nod. "You boys go on in."

It wasn't more than fifteen minutes before Web Clay, our county attorney, showed up with his wife; and I had to pass them in, too. And before the evening was over I must have walked in a dozen.

Hell, I don't know how people get that way. I don't know what they're thinking about. Sure, I've got empty seats. That's the only kind I can sell. What if I walked into a bank and asked 'em if they had some four-bit pieces they weren't using.

It's the same proposition.

The Literary Club brought an author here once, and I was sold a ticket so I went to hear him. He was a big gawky guy named Thomas or Thompson or something like that, and I guess he'd put a few under his belt because he sure pulled all the stops.

He spent most of his time talking about people who asked him for free books and seemed to think he ought to be tickled to death to give 'em away. He said that sarcasm was wasted on such people and that the homicide laws ought to be amended to take care of them. Well, there wasn't a person in the house that hadn't hit me for an Annie Oakley at one time or another. But do you know what? Instead of getting mad or ashamed, they sat there and clapped their hands off. They didn't seem to realize that they were the kind of people this author was talking about.

Well . . .

At ten-thirty, Mrs. Artie Fletcher closed her window so fast she almost took off a customer's fingers; and Harry Clinkscales tore off without even pulling the switch on the popcorn machine.

I took a look inside. Jimmie Nedry was just making one of his perfect change-overs, and his daughter Lottie, my usher, was brushing up the aisles. I went back outside again. I didn't need to worry about those two. They'd be on the job as long as there was a customer in the house, and everything would be in good shape when they left.

I went into the box office, checked the receipts, and locked them in the floor safe. Just before midnight while I was taking a last turn through the house, Jimmie's two boys came in with what was left of the display matter. They'd been on the run all day, and they were shaking and so out of breath they could hardly talk. They hurried right on home with Lottie to get supper ready before Jimmie got there.

All of a sudden it hit me that the only people who were dependable and hard working were those that didn't amount to anything. It wasn't fair, but it was that way. And I wondered why it was.

I wondered why, when there was so damned many of 'em, they didn't get together and run things themselves. And I made up my mind if they ever did get an organization—a going organization, that is—they could count me in!

TWELVE

Elizabeth woke me up early Saturday morning.

"The film truck just came, Joe," she said. "It's here."

"'Jeopardy of the Jungle'?"

"Yes. You'd better get up right away. We've got a lot to do."

I said okay, and she left the room. I didn't want to get up. I wanted to stay right there and leave everything that was going to happen a good long way in the future. And I couldn't. I couldn't because, while I didn't want to go through with it, I didn't want *not* to, either. That sounds crazy but it's the only way I know to put it.

Just a few days before, any little thing was enough to make me throw the brakes on. Like, for instance, passing up that hitchhiker. But now I knew nothing could stop me. I hadn't liked the scheme, but neither had I fought it. I'd just rocked along with it, getting a little more used to it every minute, and now it was doing the rocking.

I couldn't back out.

I didn't want to back out.

Coming out of the bathroom, I glanced into Elizabeth's room. A hat with a heavy veil was laying-lying—on a chair near the bed. Next to it was a little overnight bag. The hat was an old one and would never be missed in case anyone should get funny ideas and start checking up. The few odds and ends she was taking in the bag would never be missed, either.

I went downstairs, swallowed some coffee, and went out to the garage.

I'd got a travelogue, a newsreel, and a cartoon along with 'Jeopardy.' In all there were twenty-three reels of film.

"I was just thinking," I said. "Carol may not be able to get anyone. Perhaps we ought to wait until—"

"How are you going to wait?" Elizabeth asked. "You've got to go into the city."

"I don't have to," I said.

"Yes, you do, Joe. The farther you're away from things the better off it'll be. If Carol shouldn't get anyone there's no harm done. I'll straighten things up and we'll try again in a few weeks."

"But someone might look in and—"

"Don't be silly. I'll keep the door locked."

We ran the reels through the rewind to shake the water off of them. It was turned on full speed, since we weren't checking the film, and it didn't take long.

I unreeled fifteen or twenty feet of the cartoon, and Elizabeth knitted it back and forth through the other film. We shoved the pile underneath the rewind table.

I pulled the good cord loose from its connections, and hooked the motor up with the old one. I threw a few loops around it with the cartoon and pulled the rest of the reel under the table.

I stood back and looked things over.

The film was touching the bare copper of the cord in a couple of places. I shifted it back and forth until it was just right. Carol wouldn't need more than a minute. But she'd sure as hell need that.

Elizabeth was sitting on the stool. She looked even paler than usual.

"You didn't need to help with this," I said. "I could have done it."

She got up. "You're all through now? You're not going to leave that other cord on the floor are you?"

"Why not? It's the best way of getting rid of it."

"Yes," she said. And I wasn't just imagining that she was paler then.

She went out the door ahead of me. I put the padlock on it, and gave her the key.

That's the way it was. We'd done it so often in our minds that I guess it would have seemed stranger not doing it than doing it.

I went up to my room, threw a few things into my grip, and came back downstairs. Elizabeth got up from a chair in the living-room and took a step toward me. I took one toward her.

"Well, Joe?" she said.

"Well," I said. "I guess this is it. I guess we won't be seeing each other any more. That is, if Carol gets the—her party."

"She'll get her, all right," said Elizabeth. "I've never had any doubt about that."

"Well, good-by," I said. "I'll always remember you, Elizabeth."

"You'd better, Joe."

"I'll—What do you mean?"

"Twenty-five thousand dollars."

"That's what we agreed on," I said. "Where's the argument?"

I hoped she wouldn't say anything more. It's hell to want to sock your wife the last time you're seeing her.

"I want to make myself clear, Joe. If your memory should fail you there will be exceedingly unpleasant consequences."

"Hell," I said, "what do you think I am, anyway?"

"Exactly what I always did."

I walked out.

Ordinarily, if I'd wanted to go into the city I wouldn't have bothered to make excuses to anyone. I'd have just gone. But now it was different. I had to have a good reason for going, and there was only one I could think of.

I beat Jimmie Nedry to the show by about thirty minutes, and went up to the projection booth. By the time he got there I'd taken the parts cabinet off the wall and had everything in it spread out on the rewind table.

He didn't say anything at first, just gave me that sullen, hopeless look he'd been pulling lately, and stripped out of his coat, shirt, and undershirt. Those carbon arcs really heat up the booth. I went on pawing, though, and finally he asked me what I was looking for.

"I'm looking for the spare photoelectric cells for our sound heads," I said. "It doesn't look like we have any."

"We've got 'em," he grunted.

"Well, I don't believe we have, Jimmie," I said. "I thought I'd make a check on our parts last night when you were on your relief, and I couldn't find them then. And I've taken everything out this morning, and—"

"They got to be there," he said. "Let me look." He began sorting through the stuff impatiently, half sore. He wound up by picking up each part separately and putting it back in the cabinet. His face had fallen about a foot.

"I—I just can't believe it, Mr. Wilmot. We had some spares up there, well, I know it couldn't have been more than two or three days ago."

"You haven't used any since?"

"Of course I ain't! If I had I'd have told you so you could reorder."

"Hmmm," I said. "Did you actually see the cells or just the little carton they come in?"

"Well—"

"That's it," I said. "At one time or another we've replaced the cells in the machines and put the empty cartons back in the cabinet. I'm not saying you did it. I may have myself."

"But what became of the cartons?"

"They must have dropped down and got swept out. No one would pay any attention to them as long as they were empty."

"Yeah, but—"

"I'm not blaming you, Jimmie. The thing is to get some more. We don't want to be playing silent over Sunday."

"No," he nodded, "that would be bad. You'll bring some cells back when you go into the city?"

"I wasn't planning on going into the city," I said, "but I'll have to now. It's too late for the express to reach us, and the stores will be closed tomorrow."

"Yeah—I see." He rubbed his chin, giving me a puzzled, funny look. "When'll you be back?"

"Just as soon as I get the cells. Probably early tomorrow morning."

"You—you won't have to stay over for anything else?"

"Why should I?"

"Nothin'," he mumbled, turning around to the projectors. "I was just wondering."

A hundred miles up the road I stopped at a restaurant for a bite to eat, and called Carol from a booth phone.

She must have been waiting right by the phone because she answered right away.

"I'm coming in," I said. "Will I get to see you?"

She said, "No. I'm leaving right away."

That was right. It was what she was supposed to say.

"Get your baggage taken care of?"

"Not all of it," she said. "I'll send for the rest later."

That was right, too.

"Did you get in touch with that party you spoke about?"

"Yes. And she's going to be very helpful."

"Well, have a good trip," I said. "And be careful."

"I will be. You be careful," she said.

We said good-by and hung up.

THIRTEEN

The car was running pretty hot by the time I got to the city, and I had good reason to take it to a garage. I told them I wanted the radiator back-flushed, a grease job, and an oil change. They were rushed, since it was Saturday, and they wouldn't promise to get the work done before nine that night. I groused a little about it, but I left the car.

Of course, if I'd started back home right away I couldn't have got there ahead of Carol. But I didn't want to be on the road when things popped. I wanted to be able to prove where I was.

I bought two photoelectric cells at the theatrical equipment house, and dropped them into the first trash can I passed. It was just like throwing twelve bucks away, but it couldn't be helped. I'd left the two I'd lifted from the show in the car, and there was no way I could explain the extras. And, anyway, what was twelve bucks?

I could prove that I'd had to come into the city, and that I'd actually bought the cells. Twelve dollars was pretty cheap for that.

I ate dinner at a restaurant on film row, and walked around awhile, restless, not knowing what to do with myself. All the exchanges except Hap Chance's had been closed since noon, and I wasn't sure that I wanted to kill any time with him. On the other hand, a sharpie like that might be just the kind to use for an alibi.

I stopped across the street from his place, trying to decide whether to drop in on him, and he looked out and saw me. He got up, dimmed the lights and drew the shades. I was thinking, *What the hell?* when he opened the door and motioned.

I crossed the street. "What's up, Hap?" I said.

"Pop in, laddie," he said, "I'll tell you in a sec."

He closed the door and locked it, and we went back to his desk. He brought out the whisky and a couple of glasses, and we both had a drink. He poured a second for himself.

"Well, Hap?" I said.

"I've got some information for you, old man. I wouldn't care to have anyone know it came from me."

"All right," I said. "Under the hat."

"You recall our conversation of a few days ago?"

"Yes."

"What did you make of it?"

"Why," I said, "I hadn't thought much about it. I supposed, maybe, you had a buyer for a house and you thought you might make a deal for mine."

"Nothing else?"

"No."

He frowned slightly, shaking his head. "I suppose not. I didn't give you a great deal to go on. Still, there at the last, when you forgot to buy paper on 'Jep—'"

"I don't claim a perfect memory. What's on your mind, Hap?"

"You're broke, laddie."

"What?" I said.

"I say you're stony. I'd have told you the other night, but I wasn't too sure about my facts. At any rate, I don't know that there's anything you could have done about it."

"You haven't told me anything yet," I said. "What do you mean I'm broke?"

"Sol Panzer's moving in on you."

I laughed. "Nuts, Hap."

"All right, laddie."

"The town's too small for Panzpalace. It isn't a fourth big enough."

"It's big enough," said Hap. "It's big enough if Sol says it is. Think it over. In ten years you've built a fine house with a fine business out of nothing. Sol can point to that if he needs to justify himself, which he won't. Panzer owns control of Panzpalace. He's always made money for the stockholders. Now—"

"I don't give a damn about that," I said. "Panzpalace doesn't build anything less than a million-dollar house, and a million-dollar house just won't pay off there."

"You mean you can't sell enough admissions?"

"Certainly that's what I mean. How else could you make it pay?"

"Oh, laddie"—Hap made a clicking noise with his tongue—"what hour yesterday were you born? You can make it pay by cutting your overhead, rather, by shifting the costs. You can't do it because you don't have any place to shift them to. But Sol has ninety-three other houses. He can make a house earn just as much or just as little as he wants it to."

"Yeah, but—but why does he want to do it?"

"I dropped you a hint about that the other night. I asked you if there was a chance that your house would be worth a million— meaning, of course, would anyone be jailed for paying you that much for it. I thought we might peddle it to him."

"Did you try?"

"No use. Merely wishful thinking on my part. There's a lot of loose change when you start breaking up a million dollars, but you have to break it to get it. Sol has to build. I saw that as soon as I'd taken time to study the matter."

I began to tremble inside. I mopped my face.

"You're not lying to me, Hap?"

"Really, old man—But I can't blame you for being disturbed. If you're looking for confirmation, drop around to the exchanges and try to buy for next season. I think you'll find that they'll stall you."

"Jesus!" I said.

"Or have they already?"

"I see it was a stall, now," I said. "I didn't think anything of it at the time. It's such a relief not to have them trying to load you that I—"

Hap clicked his tongue again, trying to look sympathetic. I saw his angle. Sol hadn't needed his stuff to shut me out. The other exchanges were enough. Now, since it wasn't costing him anything, Hap was palling up to me, hoping that it would hurt Panzer in some way.

"I can't tell you how sorry I am, old man. I was just wondering—"

"Yeah?" I said.

"Perhaps you could force Sol to drive a deal with you. You can probably pick up a dozen pix or so from the little fellows, and of course you can count on my line-up. Every last picture I've got. Why—"

"What the hell are you talking about?" I said. "If there was any way I could run on your stuff it wouldn't be open. And you wouldn't be sitting there offering it to me."

"Please, laddie. Not so loud."

"Nuts," I said. "Panzer tried to play without you and you found out about it. You don't care whether he finds out you told me. You hope he will. It'll teach him to call you in the next time he cuts a pie."

Hap sighed. "We should have been partners. Great minds, et cetera. You know what I thought when I first saw you tonight?"

"I don't particularly give a damn."

"Don't be rude, Joseph. I might slap the unholy God out of you."

"All right," I said. "What did you think?"

"Well, I thought you *had* caught my hint after all; that that was why you were in town."

"I don't get you," I said. "I had to come in to buy some photoelectric cells."

"Perfect," he beamed. "But let's not be coy with one another. You know my attitude toward insurance companies. Feel it's more or less a civic duty to rook 'em."

"Now, wait a minute," I said. "I—I—"

"I thought, here's old Joe, virtually on the point of losing his shirt, and here's this unwholesome insurance policy, just lying around and collecting dust and doing no one the slightest good. And I put myself in your place, laddie. I thought, now what would a keen chap like old Joseph do?"

"B-But—"

"You do have insurance on the show?"

"Certainly, I have. But, goddam it—"

"Don't be vehement, laddie. I'm on your side."

"Yeah," I said. "Yeah, but—but—" My voice rose and he frowned and started to call me down. And then his eyes narrowed, and he just sat there watching me. It wasn't necessary to tell me to shut up. I couldn't say anything. I couldn't move.

You see? He had the whole thing wrong, and yet he was in the right. He was right enough to pin my ears back and keep them pinned, if he wanted to. And he would want to. He'd play it for all it was worth.

But, bad as that was, it wasn't what really got me. What got me, what made me feel like I was going crazy, was the realization that the woman was going to die for nothing. Her death wasn't going to mean a thing. It was just murder, nothing more than murder, with none of us better off than if she had lived.

And now there wasn't any way I could stop it. I knew those bus schedules backward and forward; and I knew it was too late.

There's nothing quite so silent as film row on Saturday night. The Playgrand exchange was half a dozen doors up the street, but when their phones began ringing they sounded like they were in the next room.

They stopped ringing in Playgrand and began in Utopian. And then they rang in Colfax and Wolfe. And finally—

Hap was watching me like a hawk. He spit on the carpet without ever taking his eyes off me, and picked up his phone.

"Yes," he said. "Righto, operator. Put 'em on ... Mr. Wilmot? Why, yes. I believe I can reach him. Was there some message you—"

"Give me that phone," I said, and grabbed for it.

He planted his foot in my stomach, and I doubled up with the wind knocked out of me.

"What?" he said. "Why, that's terrible! I can't tell you how sorry I—Certainly, I will! Certainly. As a matter of fact, he's just stepped into the office. I'll break the news to him gently."

He hung up the receiver, poured a glassful of whisky, and handed it to me.

"Brace yourself, old man. There's been a terrible accident. Your wife—"

There was a grin on his face a foot wide.

FOURTEEN

All Stoneville is grieving over the death of Elizabeth Barclay Wilmot, wife of Joseph J. Wilmot, local theater magnate, who passed away in a fire at the Wilmot estate Saturday night. Cause of the fire has not been determined, but it is suspected that rats gnawing at the wiring may have been responsible. The fire broke out about nine o'clock, shortly after Mrs. Wilmot had returned from Wheat City where she had gone to pick up Miss Carol Farmer, a household employee. Miss Farmer, who was on her way back to Stoneville from a vacation, had missed her bus while dining in Wheat City, and had called Mrs. Wilmot to come after her. Upon reaching the Wilmot residence here, Miss Farmer went into the house and Mrs. Wilmot repaired to the upstairs of the garage, which was equipped as a film-inspecting room. When the fire burst into being a few minutes later, Miss Farmer notified the Stoneville fire department which promptly and efficiently answered the call. But little if anything could be done to defeat the holocaust. While the inspection room itself was fire-proof, the heat was so intense that the supports and exterior walls of the building ignited and crumbled. Mrs. Wilmot was pinned beneath a work bench. Mr. Wilmot, who was out of town on business, was notified of the tragedy by telephone. Suffering from shock and grief, he was accompanied home by Mr. Harbert A. Chance, film company executive. Mr. Chance, an old friend of Mr. Wilmot's, will remain in Stoneville temporarily to assist in the conduct of the latter's affairs. Mr. Wilmot has been

*convalescing in the Stoneville Sanitarium, suffering from shock and grief,
but is expected to ...*

I read a story one time about a fellow that was accidentally slipped
into a big job; president of a company or something like that. He
looked like the guy that actually was president, see, and when this
guy ran off or fell in a mudhole or something and wasn't ever seen
again, why this one hooked his place. He didn't know beans about
the business, and all he planned on doing was to stick around long
enough to snap a few rubber checks and maybe get the other guy's
gal alone in the parlor for a while. But once he got inside, the graft
looked so good that he decided to stay for a real milking. He was
scared out of his pants, naturally, because he didn't know any more
about the setup than a hog does about ice skates. But he ran a bluff,
and damned if he didn't make good on it.

His work was just cut out for him, see what I mean? The
stenographers would bring him letters to sign, and he'd just sign 'em.
And when he got any letters, his vice-presidents or some of his
secretaries would take charge of them. And when people showed up
for conferences all he had to do was keep his eyes and ears open, and
he could see what he had to do. He didn't have to move. He *got*
moved. As I remember the yarn, he wound up by getting made
president of a lot of other companies and marrying the other guy's
gal, and no one ever knew the difference.

Well, when I read that I thought it was strictly off the cob. And I
knew it'd be just my luck to have the thing made into a movie and
I'd have to see it. But if you asked me now I'd say it wasn't corn. If I
hadn't been worried about Hap Chance, and being broke, I wouldn't
have done much worrying. Up to a certain point.

I didn't have to explain the accident—if you want to call it that.
There were several stories going around that were better than any I
could dream up. I didn't have to pretend I was suffering from shock
and grief. They told me I was.

A delegation brought me some mourning clothes Tuesday afternoon, and Sheriff Rufe Waters and County Attorney Web Clay and a
couple of fellows from the chamber of commerce drove me over to
the mortuary in a limousine. Rufe and Webb took me into the chapel

to look at the casket—but not inside it—and then they took me right out again.

I didn't hear much of the services because someone thought I was looking peaked, and they took me into the rest room. They gave me a couple of drinks to brace me up, and made me lie down on the lounge. And after the services were over they got me up again.

I rode out to the cemetery with Rufe and Web and one of the Legion boys and a fellow from the Farmers' Union. Rufe is the wheel horse for the Democratic party and Web is the same for the Republicans. If I'd been picking a foursome to ride with from the standpoint of keeping all sides happy, I couldn't have done better. And I hadn't had to do it. It was done for me.

It started to rain a little on the edge of town, just a few drops, but by the time we passed our—my—place it was misting pretty hard. I looked up the lane toward the garage, and of course there wasn't any. Just part of the framework and a pile of timber and metal and ashes. But there was a guy chasing around, trying to cover things up with pieces of canvas.

I asked who he was.

"That's the investigator from the insurance company," said Rufe. "Looks like he'd have enough decency to lay off during the ceremony."

"I've got my eye on him," said Web. "I'm just hoping he gets out of line a little. He can't come into my county and tell me how to run things."

I wanted to ask him what the trouble was, but I decided it wouldn't be appropriate. Or smart. The longer I could stay in the background and let my friends do my arguing the better off I was.

I guess almost the whole county was at the cemetery. There wasn't room for half the people inside, and they were parked along the grade for almost a mile on either side of the gates.

They all stood up when we passed, stood along the side of the road or on their running-boards or wagon beds, with their heads bowed. It gave you an awfully funny feeling. It made you feel almost like it was Judgment Day; like they'd all been pulled up out of everywhere for the trumpet's blast before they could move. It was kind of scary.

I remember one woman in particular. She was standing up in a wagon box with a big fat squawling baby in each arm. They looked damned near as big as she was; and she'd started to feed them, I guess, because she had her blouse open and what babies go for was hanging out on each side. It wasn't hanging right, though, and the kids were as mad as all hell, twisting and screaming and grabbing at it, and trying to raise their heads up. But she just stood there with her head bowed like everyone else.

We drove through the cemetery gates, and got out. Web and Rufe stood by me at the grave.

The minister began his oratory, a lot of mumbo jumbo about being washed in the blood of the lamb and people being better off dead than they were alive; and all the time, by God, acting like it was deep stuff. And the different bands began to play "Nearer My God To Thee," and they couldn't play with themselves, let alone with each other. And the church choirs kept racing ahead and falling behind. And—but it wasn't funny. I've never felt more like bawling in my life.

There are some things so bad and so careless that you wish to God they didn't pretend to be good-intentioned so you could put in a holler without making a heel of yourself. I've felt pretty much the same way looking at newsreels of ceremonies at the tomb of the Unknown Soldier. The bands playing and the people singing, all in their own way, the right way; and the generals, the statesmen, and the club ladies all speaking a little piece for themselves. And they all mean so goddam well—I guess—and no one is responsible any more than I was responsible for her.

I bawled; there beside the grave with the rain coming down harder and harder. I felt just as bad as if I'd known the woman.

I could hardly see a thing I was crying so hard. I saw Carol for a second on the other side of the grave, and then everything got blurry again.

Web and Rufe led me away. We went back to the car and they put me inside while they waited outside, one at each door.

It came over me all of a sudden that I was a prisoner; that the reason they were with me was to watch me. I leaned forward to get out of the car, and Web Clay eased me back.

I tried it again. I knocked his hand out of the way. "You let me out of here!" I yelled. "I can't stand any more! Take me away from here!"

"Maybe we'd better, Web," said Rufe. "Joe's been under an awful strain."

Web said, yes, I had, and went and got the other two fellows. We drove away.

Web rode with his arm around me, almost with my head pulled down against his chest; and Rufe made me take a new silk handkerchief to blow my nose on. They took me into the house.

"What you need, Joe, is a good stiff drink," said Web. "Rufe, you got anything in the car?"

"I've got something," I said, straightening up a little. "I guess we all need a little something."

We went up to my room and had a few good stiff drinks, and swapped a little talk. Rufe and Web got friendlier than I'd ever seen them. While we were up there, Carol and some of the town ladies were busy downstairs fixing coffee and laying out sandwiches and cake. When the crowd began to come in from the funeral, the boys took me downstairs again.

I was sat down and stood up and made to eat cake and sandwiches and coffee, and when the people began to file past me in a line on the way out, they—the ones that were taking care of me—even did my talking.

"Yes, yes. That's very kind of you, neighbor—"

"Joe appreciates that very much—"

"Joe thanks you very much—"

I guess they would have even shook—shaken—hands for me if they could have.

By this time it was dark, practically everyone was gone except the ladies who were staying to help Carol. I went upstairs and had a few more drinks and tried not to think. It was raining to beat hell now, and the wind was coming up. I heard Rufe and Web pulling out for town, and pretty soon another car left behind theirs. The insurance man's.

There seemed to be a draft coming from somewhere. I thought maybe someone had left a window open. I took another stiff drink and looked through the upstairs room by room. There wasn't any window open. I went downstairs again.

All the ladies had left except Mrs. Reverend Whitcomb. She was staying that night to keep the proprieties. She fussed around me for almost an hour, trying to do things for me that I didn't want done. When she'd worn us both out she hobbled into the downstairs bedroom and closed the door. I'd think she weighed around two-eighty. And she wasn't much taller than a quart of beer. She'd been going through doors sideways for so long that she kind of waltzed when she walked.

When she got into bed one of the slats popped like a gun going off. Then, there was a rasping, grating sound, like a bale of wire being dragged across a tin roof, and the whole house shook.

"Are you all right, Mrs. Whitcomb?" I called.

She was silent, or not exactly silent, either; I could hear her panting for breath.

"Quite all right, Brother Wilmot," she said finally.

I hesitated. "Are you sure there's nothing I can do for you?"

I knew damned well the bed had broken down.

"Oh, no, Brother Wilmot. I'm just dandy. Now you run along."

Carol was still busy in the kitchen. I went upstairs, took another drink and went to bed.

I didn't hear her when she came up the stairs. She opened the door and came in without turning the light on; and in one of the dim flashes of lightning from the storm I saw her pulling her dress off over her head.

"You shouldn't do that, Carol," I whispered.

"It's all right," she whispered back. "I peeked in at Mrs. Reverend Whitcomb. She's sleeping down inside the bedstead. The mattress and springs fell through with her."

I grinned. I even laughed a little, quietly. It's funny how you still laugh.

"You'd better go on, anyway, Carol," I said. "I've got a chill, a pretty bad cold. You're liable to catch it."

"I won't face you," she said.

I was lying with my knees drawn up, my hands under the pillow; taking up most of the bed.

She got in with her back to me; pushed back gently until my knees came down. She pulled one of my arms under her and the other over her, and folded them over her breasts; and she held them there with her own arms.

"Now, you'll be warm," she said. And pretty soon: "You were just afraid, that's what made you cold. You don't need to be afraid, Joe."

I didn't say anything, thinking, and she spoke again.

"Do you love me?"

"Sure I love you."

"You've got to, Joe. You just got to. Maybe you don't want to now, but it's too late to change. You got to love me."

"Hell," I said, "what are you talking about? I love you or I wouldn't have done it, would I?"

She didn't answer right away, but I could feel her getting ready. I knew, almost to a word, what she was going to say. Because we weren't the same people any more. If you won't stop at murder you won't stop at lying or cheating or anything else.

"I don't know, Joe. Maybe—maybe you were afraid of me, of what I might do. You and Elizabeth. Maybe your business wasn't so good, and you thought—well—"

"Carol! For God's sake—"

"I'm not saying it was that way. I'm—don't be mad at me, Joe! I've had to—most everything I've had to do and I've got to talk! I want to talk so you can tell me I'm wrong!"

"Well, you're wrong," I said.

And I thought, *Jesus, what a break, what if I'd told her about Hap and Panzer and the show being washed up?* And I thought, *I'll have to get things straightened out. She's just dumb enough to—*

"You mustn't try to see Elizabeth, Joe. You won't, will you?"

"Of course I won't. Why should I?"

"You mustn't. You're mine now. You're all I've got."

"All right," I said.

"You won't try to see her or write to her or anything? Promise me, Joe. Please, Joe."

"For Pete's sake! All right, I promise!"

"You'll let me send the insurance money to her to the General Delivery address like we agreed?"

"Yes. When I get it."

We went on talking, whispering in the darkness, with the lightning staggering dully through the windows and the rain scratching against the shingles and splashing into the gutter. Everything had gone all right, she said. The woman didn't have any friends or relatives. They'd had separate seats on the bus. She was practically the same size and coloring as Elizabeth.

Carol had told her that they were going on from Wheat City by car—that they'd have to wait until a friend from out in the country brought it in to them. And the woman may have thought it was funny, but she didn't say anything.

They met Elizabeth on a side street, and Elizabeth got out and kept right on going. And Carol and the woman drove home, and Carol took her up to the garage to show her her quarters—

"Don't tell me any more," I said. "I don't want to hear about it."

"All right," said Carol.

"I'm sorry," I said. "I meant, I don't want you to talk about it. I know how hard it was on you."

There wasn't much said after that.

After a while Carol got up and locked the door and set the alarm clock.

FIFTEEN

Appleton, the man from the insurance company, was already outside the next morning when I went downstairs. I walked over by the place where the garage had been and introduced myself.

He was a big fellow, not much over thirty, and he had a rather joking manner of speaking. When I came up he was bending over a sort of suitcase he had on the running-board of his coupé. One that opened at the top with a lot of vials and bottles and envelopes, and little racks and clips to hold them.

"I'm afraid there's not much to work on," I said, looking around.

"Oh, I've got everything I need already," he said. "I cleaned up the last of it yesterday evening. Just making a final check this morning."

"Did you—find anything to help you?" I asked.

"Don't know yet." He grinned. "I've got it all, though, up at the hotel. I've signed enough receipts for your county attorney to fill a bushel basket."

"I'm glad you've had co-operation," I said. "If there's anything I can do let me know."

"Swell," he said, "just pass the word along to the C.A. and the sheriff and their cohorts that the quicker I'm satisfied the quicker you'll get your dough."

"I'm not in any particular hurry to get the money," I said.

"Oh, hell," he said, "we're all in a hurry to get the money. What's your opinion on the origin of the fire?"

"I don't know," I said. "According to the paper, rats—"

He threw back his head and laughed. "I'll bet that tied you in knots didn't it? Would rats be in a metal-lined room? Wouldn't your wife have known if there were rats? And would she have put herself within a hundred yards of them?"

"I've not had any experiences with fires," I said. "What's your idea?"

"I've got a couple. One is that it was incendiary." He grinned, watching my face. "The other, that it was an accident."

"Well—"

"Pretty good, huh? All I've got to do is get rid of one of 'em, and I can hand you a check or have you slapped in the jug."

And before I could say anything, he laughed and clapped me on the back to show that he was joking.

"I'm sorry, Mr. Wilmot," he said. "I know how you must feel at a time like this, and I don't mean to be flippant. I see so much tragedy that I'm a little hardened to it. Don't pay any attention to me."

"That's all right," I said.

"I'll be frank with you, Joe—Mr. Wilmot—"

"Joe's okay."

"I'm kind of puzzled, Joe. Now, you didn't have any knob-and-tube wiring in here? It was all in conduit, right?"

"Sure. Just like it is in my show."

"What about the cord on the rewind motor?"

"It was all right. So far as I know."

He shook his head reproachfully. "You mean to say you're not sure?"

"Well, of course I'm sure," I said. "Mrs. Wilmot would have been sure, anyway. She'd been doing this for almost ten years. If there was anything wrong with the cord she'd have known it."

"It looks like she would have, Joe, "he nodded. "She didn't smoke, I understand?"

"No, she didn't."

"Well, there you are," said Appleton. "Apparently there wasn't any cause for the fire. And yet there was a fire. You see why I'm puzzled, Joe?"

"Yeah," I said. "I see."

"How long did you say Mrs. Wilmot had been doing this sort of work?"

"Ten years or so. Almost ever since we were married."

"Why did she do it? Don't get me wrong. We're not denying liability."

"I suppose she did it because she wanted to."

"Just like that, huh?" He laughed.

"Yes."

"You screen your stuff before you play it, don't you? Running it through the rewind here didn't save any time or money."

"I wouldn't say that. Every once in a while she'd run across a reel that was wound backward or needed splicing, and—"

"But not very often. Not often enough to justify so much time and expense. It strikes me that this setup would have been more of a nuisance than anything else."

Well, it was. I couldn't deny it.

"Tell me. Did she do any other work connected with the show?"

"Yes. She did quite a bit. Worked on the books now and then. Made out the deposit slips. Things like that."

"Why?"

"Why?" I said. But I knew what he meant.

"Sure. From what I've learned of you, Joe, you didn't need that kind of help. You're a first-rate businessman. I happen to know that Mrs. Wilmot was anything but an expert businesswoman."

"I don't see what that has to do with the fire."

"Maybe it hasn't got anything to do with it." He was still grinning, but his eyes were hard. "For twenty-five thousand bucks I could even ask foolish questions."

"I think I see what you're driving at," I said slowly. "You're implying that my wife was butting in where she wasn't wanted and that I resented it."

"Well, Joe?"

I nodded. Something seemed to nod my head. And when I spoke it was as though someone were whispering the words to me. The right words.

"It's probably pretty hard for you to understand," I said. "You see, Mrs. Wilmot was quite a bit older than I was. We didn't have any children. I think she felt from the beginning that she wasn't pulling her weight in the partnership—"

He cleared his throat, sort of embarrassed like. I went on.

"Her work didn't help me," I said—I heard myself saying. "It was a nuisance. I've spent hours undoing some of the things she did; and I used to get impatient and bawl her out. But I guess I was always ashamed afterward. She was trying to make up for things—for the things she couldn't give me and felt that she should—

"I wish she was back here, now. She could turn the show into a bathhouse and I'd never say a word. Anyway—well, that's the way it was. She did butt in, and I resented it. But we understood each other in spite of everything. That's all I've got to say."

Appleton blew his nose. "I think—I—I understand the situation, Joe. I'm sorry if I put the wrong interpretation on it."

"You've got your job to do," I said.

"I'll be frank with you. We don't like the looks of these fires where everything is so completely destroyed. Now, this Farmer girl—" He lowered his voice. "She was the last person to see Mrs. Wilmot alive. How did they get along together?"

"Why, all right, I believe," I said. "I can tell you this much. If Elizabeth hadn't wanted her here, she wouldn't have stayed one minute."

He nodded again. "That jibes with my information."

"If I had the slightest idea that Carol—"

"Now, don't let me put ideas into your head," he said quickly. "I'm just groping in the dark."

I glanced at my watch.

"I've got to be getting into town pretty quick," I said. "I suppose you'll be around for a while?"

"Oh, sure. You'll be seeing a lot of me before we get this thing settled."

I knew he meant just what he said, nothing more. I'd sold myself to him as much as I could be sold under the circumstances. He'd swallowed everything I'd said about Elizabeth.

Carol was fixing some breakfast when I went into the house. I sat down at the kitchen table and waited, and I think I said something about the coffee smelling good. She didn't answer me or turn around. Pretty soon I saw her hand go up to her face.

I swore under my breath, and got up. The back door was closed and the shades were drawn. I went over and stood beside her.

"Now what?" I said.

"N-nothing."

"Come on, spit it out!"

I guess I sounded pretty harsh, but I was nervous. I had things to make me nervous. She whirled, her eyes flashing.

"I heard what you said to him!"

"What I said to him?"

"Yes. About Elizabeth!"

I couldn't figure out what she meant for a minute. Then I said, "Well, for God's sake, what did you think I should say to him? That I hated her guts and was damned glad she was gone? That would have sounded good, wouldn't it?"

"N-no—You didn't really mean it, did you?"

"Of course I didn't mean it."

She wiped her eyes and tried to smile. I sat down on a chair and pulled her onto my lap.

"Look, Carol," I said, "you're going to have to get over this suspiciousness and jealousy. If you don't it'll crop up at the wrong time, and that'll be just too bad. Don't you see? If people thought there was anything between you and me it would give you a motive for Elizabeth's—for this woman's—death."

"I know," she said. "I'll behave, Joe."

"You've got to, Carol," I said. "If they ever get the idea that you or I wanted Elizabeth out of the way, they'll do an autopsy on that—on the remains. They'll do one to end all autopsies. They won't know what to look for so they'll look for everything. And they'll find out it wasn't Elizabeth."

"But—well, there wasn't anything left—"

"Oh, yes, there was. The teeth were left, and that's all they'd need. The teeth would show that it wasn't Elizabeth."

She didn't know about things like that. She sat looking at me, making sure I wasn't kidding.

"Maybe—You don't suppose they've already—"

"Not a chance," I said. "If they had we wouldn't be sitting here. Oh, sure, they've had an inquest. Decided she died by reason of fire and so on. But that's all they've done, and we mustn't give them any reason to do any more than that. You'd better clear out of here tomorrow, at the latest."

"No!" She threw her arms around my neck. "Please don't make me, Joe!"

"But you've got to, Carol. We planned it that way. It don't look right for us to be staying here together."

"No! I don't care how we planned. It's different now."

"You'll be all right. You can get you a little job of some kind here in town and go ahead to school. In six or seven months, when all this blows over, we can start seeing each other and—"

"But what if something should happen that I ought to know about? You wouldn't be able to let me know until—until it was too late."

"It'd be too late from the start," I said. "This isn't something we can run out on if things get hot. Anyway, if anything went wrong you'd know it as soon as I would."

"No, I wouldn't, Joe."

"Why the hell wouldn't you?"

"Elizabeth was your wife, and I was the last one to be seen with her. And you were out of town when it happened. They'd talk to you before they did anything."

"Well," I said, "what of it? You're not going to be at the north pole. If talking to you would do any good after things had gone that far, I could reach you easily enough."

She sat not looking at me. "They can't prove anything against you, Joe," she said in a funny voice. "Not what they can with me. If—if I took the blame—"

"Oh," I said slowly. "I see."

"Please, Joe—"

"Why don't you say what you mean?" I said. "You think if I got the chance I'd throw everything on you. Is that it?"

I shoved her to her feet and got up, but before I could move away she had her arms around me. She began crying again, and her breasts shivered against me, and I patted her and finally held her close.

"You shouldn't feel that way, Carol," I said. "We've got to trust each other."

"I d-do, Joe!" she said. "I trust you and love you so much that— and that wasn't the reason I wanted to stay! I—I just want to be near you. It doesn't seem like I'm living when I'm not with you."

Well, hell. I was pretty sure she meant it, but even if she didn't it sounded good. A woman can't make a man sore talking like that.

"Well," I said, "we'll talk about it again. I guess it will be all right if you stay around a few days. Maybe something will turn up by that time."

"That Mr. Chance. How long is he going to be in town?"

"I don't know," I said, wishing to God that I did. "I've got a lot of stuff to catch up on. He may be around helping me for quite a while."

"If he stayed here, too, it'd be all right for me to stay, wouldn't it?"

I didn't know how to get around that one. If I'd had my way Hap would be staying at the bottom of some good deep well.

"We'll see," I said.

SIXTEEN

I told Carol I wasn't hungry yet and left the house without eating breakfast. If there was ever a time in my life that I needed to keep my mind clear this was it, so I got away before I could be caught up in another argument.

I stopped at the Elite Cafe and ordered ham an'; and while I was eating Web Clay came in for a cigar. He saw me and came back to my booth. He'd already eaten but I got him to take a cup of coffee.

"Web," I said, after we'd talked for a while, "what do you think about the fire? About Elizabeth's death?"

"I don't think you need to ask me that, Joe," he said. "She was an irreplaceable loss to the entire community. I grieved with you."

"I appreciate that, Web," I said. "What I'm asking is, do you think Elizabeth could have been murdered and that the fire was used to cover up the crime?"

A slow flush spread over his face. He lit his cigar and dropped the match into his coffee cup.

"You don't think my investigation of the case was sufficiently thorough?"

"Now, Web—"

"You're a friend, Joe. I knew—I believed—that you trusted me, and I wanted to spare you all the pain that I could. Now, I'll tell you something; something that only Rufe and I have known up to now. Before that fire was cold, before that whippersnapper Appleton got here, I had a man here from the state bureau of criminal investigation. He went over the ground thoroughly, and found nothing of an incendiary character. It was his theory that the fire must have been started by rats."

"But—"

"I know. We don't see how it could have been. But if it wasn't for the impossible and improbable we wouldn't have any accidents. Do you recall reading, a few years back, about the hardware clerk who was killed while unpacking a shipment of rifles? The gun had never been out of the packing-case, but it was loaded. It *couldn't* have happened at the factory. The chief inspector had examined it and sealed the breach with his tag. It *couldn't* have happened at the store because it had never been out of the box. But it *did* happen, Joe."

"I remember the case," I said. "Well, suppose, then, that the fire was an accident—and I've felt like you that it must have been. But—"

"The two things go together, Joe. Elizabeth's death was undoubtedly caused by the fire. It's true that the post mortem, such as it was, was not very revealing. The body—excuse me, Joe—was pinned beneath the remains of that metal table and other wreckage. But we were able to ascertain that the fire and nothing but the fire caused her death. That's all we need to know."

"I see," I said.

"She actually died of the fire, Joe. Therefore, in the absence of any incendiary materials or mechanism, we know that her death was an accident."

"Yeah—yes," I said.

He spread his hands. "Well, you see, Joe? I didn't take the case as lightly as you seemed to think I did. I didn't go around with a lot of fuss and bluster—"

"Now, Web," I said. "I wasn't criticizing."

"That's all right. I know this man Appleton has got you all stirred up. We may as well talk the thing out now that we've started. When I say that the fire caused Elizabeth's death I'm not overlooking the possibility that she could have been stunned and left to die in the fire. You were going to ask me about that, weren't you?"

"Well," I said, "it did occur to me that—"

"But where is your motive, Joe? You've got to have a motive, haven't you? Now, you—excuse me—profited by the death. But you weren't there, and, as I've said, there was no trace of a delayed-mechanism device tallow or anything of that kind. And there always is some trace where anything of the kind has been used. Could she have been the victim of robbery or assault by some person unknown? We know that she couldn't. There wasn't time for it. The fire broke out almost as soon as she got home.

"Then there's—what's her name?—Carol Farmer. She was the last to see Elizabeth alive, and she was on the grounds. But what do we find there? Why, she and Elizabeth were on the best of terms. Elizabeth had taken her in and given her work. She'd just treated her to a holiday. She'd driven all the way to Wheat City to bring her home.

"We're friends, Joe, but I've always put duty ahead of friendship. I even considered the possibility—ha, ha—the impossibility, I should say, that you were attracted to Miss Farmer. Ha, ha. I'd hate to go before a jury with a theory of that kind. One look at her, and they'd lock me up. They'd send for a strait jacket—ha, ha, ha!"

I laughed right along with him. I think I've already said that no one saw in Carol what I saw. It suited me fine if they never did.

He went on talking while I ate, working himself into a good humor. As we were leaving the place we ran into Rufe Waters. Appleton had been in to needle him about something or other, and he was hopping mad. He was threatening to punch him in the nose if he came near him again.

I told Web and Rufe so-long, and drove over to the show. I parked in front of Bower's old house, feeling fairly good. Appleton was getting nowhere fast. In a few days he'd probably decide to pay off and clear out.

I got out of the car and started across the street. Then something nailed to the box office of Bower's old place caught my eye, and I turned around and went up on the sidewalk. It was one of Andy Taylor's signs. It said:

FOR RENT
Taylor Inv. & Ins.

I was standing there staring at it, not knowing whether to laugh or get sore, when Andy came up. I guess he must have been standing a few doors down the street, waiting for me.

"What's the idea, Andy?" I said. "You know you can't rent this building. I've got it under lease."

"But not the right kind of lease, Joe." He waggled his head. "That twenty-five a month don't hardly pay my taxes."

"I can't help that. I—"

"How's your hand?"

"What?" I said. "Why, it's all right."

"Looks like a pretty bad burn. How'd you get it?"

"Oh, hell," I said, without thinking. "When you're working around motion-picture equipment you're liable to—"

"Got it over to the show, huh?"

"Where else would I get it? Now, dammit, Andy get that sign—"

"You could have got it up to your house. Out there in the garage. There could have been something wrong with the machinery out there. Somethin' that you let go without fixing an' that started the fire."

"And wouldn't that tickle you pink?" I said. But my heart began to beat faster.

"You didn't get that burn at the show, Joe."

"The hell I didn't!"

"Huh-uh. I saw you that night when you were hangin' out around the front of the Barclay, and you didn't have nothing wrong with your hand. But you did the next morning when I talked with you up at your house. Reckon you remember, all right. You told me then that you'd cut it on a bottle."

"Well," I said, "maybe I—" But what was the use lying about it? With my hand unwrapped anyone could see that it was a burn.

"Still want to take the sign down, Joe?"

I hesitated and shook my head. "To tell the truth, I don't care either way. If anyone wants to try to compete with the Barclay in this rattrap they can hop to it'."

"I'll take it down."

"Suit yourself," I said.

"I'll take it down. I just wanted to see how you felt about things." He pulled the sign loose from its tacks and crumpled it, grinning. "I reckon you and me had better have a good long talk, Joe. Private."

"I'm busy," I said. "I've got a lot of business to catch up with."

"It ain't as important as mine. Think it over, Joe."

He let out a mean cackle and shuffled off down the street. And I let him go. I didn't give him the horse laugh or tell him to go to hell, as I should have. I couldn't. If you're a poker player you know what I mean.

You're holding, say, kings full in a big pot and everyone has laid down but you and one other guy, a guy with a big stack. And he gives your chips the once-over, counting 'em, and antes for exactly that amount. Well? You'd bet your right arm he couldn't beat your full house, but they're not taking right arms; just chips. And if you're wrong you're out of the game. So you lay down, and the other guy wins—with a pair of deuces.

I crossed over to the show and went up to the projection booth. Jimmie Nedry wasn't there and neither was Hap, and the booth was messy as hell. There was even a reel of film left in the right projector. I ran it out, rewound it, and put it in the film cabinet. Then I went back downstairs and looked up and down the street for Jimmie. Show business gets you that way. No matter what else you got on your mind, you can't forget the show.

Jimmie lived in a little dump over across the tracks, and he didn't have a telephone. I was wondering whether I should drive over and see what was up when he and Blair came around the corner in Blair's car. Blair pulled in a little toward the curb, and I went out to them.

"My deepest sympathy, Joe," he said. "I hope you received our floral offering."

"Yes, I did," I said. "Thanks very much, Blair."

"I was planning on bringing Jimmie and his wife to the obsequies, but they didn't feel that they should attend."

"Why? Why didn't you, Jimmie?" I said. "The show was closed. You didn't need an invitation."

"We didn't because we didn't have any decent clothes to wear, that's why!" Jimmie snarled.

"Well," I said, "I know you wanted to, anyway. It's the spirit that counts in these things."

Blair threw back his head and laughed.

"Good old Joe," he said. "Always right in there pitching, aren't you?"

"Somebody's got to," I said. "Are you coming in pretty soon, Jimmie? It's only about an hour until show time."

He shook his head without looking at me. "I'm takin' a couple weeks off."

"Huh?" I said.

"That's right, Joe." Blair leaned around him, grinning. "Mr. Chance is giving Jimmie a vacation—at full pay. Don't tell me you didn't know about it?"

"I didn't, but it's all right."

"Mr. Chance a partner of yours now?"

"Whatever he does is all right," I said. "He's been kind enough to take care of things for me. He'll probably have to stay on for a while longer."

"Well,"—Blair stroked his chin—"technically he doesn't have the owner's right to operate the projectors. But we'll play along with you. Under the circumstances."

"Thanks," I said.

"Don't mention it, Joe. You don't owe me a thing."

He laughed again, and Jimmie kind of smirked, and they drove off.

I headed for Hap's hotel, boiling.

He was in his room, dressing, when I went up. He had on his pants and shoes, and he came to the door taking the pins out of one of those fancy twenty-dollar shirts.

"Goddam you, Hap," I said. "What's the idea of giving Jimmie two weeks off? What do you think you've got on me, anyway? I suppose you think I'm going to pay him."

"Entirely unnecessary, old man. I paid him myself—out of the receipts."

"I asked you what the idea was!"

"Just a sec," he said. "I'll open the windows. They can hear us in the next block then as well as this one."

I sat down and lowered my voice. "All right. Spill it."

"Why, it's quite simple, laddie. I intend to stay around for a time, and staying requires some justification. Ergo, young James gets a rest; a rest which, even from my conservative viewpoint, seems long overdue. "

"Generous, aren't you?" I said.

"Oh, now, but why shouldn't I be with your money?" He raised his eyebrows. "As a matter of fact, however, I'm quite taken with Jamie boy. He's the sort I've often found it profitable to cultivate. You know? The humble downtrodden worm with big ears?"

"If you intend to pump him about me," I said, "you won't get much."

"Probably not, probably not," he said. "You always were frightfully clever. And it isn't really necessary, is it? Still—"

"What do you want, Hap?"

"Ah, now that's being sensible." He sat down on the edge of the bed, and poked an arm into his shirt. "Shall we say about five thousand dollars?"

"What for? Why should I give you five grand?"

"Well, to put it euphemistically, we'll say it's for the replacement of sixteen reels of priceless film."

"Priceless? That crap!"

"Or we can say it's to keep me from doing my unpleasant duty. Unpleasant, that is, from the standpoint of losing five thousand. Aside from that, I really don't care whether you swing or not."

He lit a cigarette and held the match, watching a fly crawl across the scarf of the reading-table. Suddenly, his hand went out and he stabbed it through with a pin. He held it into the flame, turning it while it sputtered and frizzled. He dropped it onto the floor and smeared it with his foot.

"Dashed funny thing, fire, isn't it?"

"Hap," I said. "Hap, suppose I had known that Sol Panzer was moving in on me, that I was broke. If I was trying to—if I was taking a quick way out, I'd have fired the show. I carry sixty thousand straight on it plus one-fifty a week operation loss."

"Uh-*hah*." He nodded. "Exactly the thought that occurred to me until I'd inspected your house. A splendid piece of construction, laddie. Utterly fireproof."

"But—but I didn't—"

"But me not buts, old man. Simply earmark five of the twenty-five thousand now due you as indemnity for your late spouse for yours truly. And please hurry it along. I'm purchasing a new car."

"I can't—there's no way I can hurry it," I said.

"No? I suppose not. Well, it shouldn't be long at any rate."

"Yeah, but—"

He looked at me sharply. "You haven't bungled things, have you?"

"No. I didn't mean that. Everything's jake."

"If I thought you were going to be turned up anyway—"He paused, frowning. "You know I have a very large conscience. I'm not at all sure that five thousand will be sufficient to salve it."

"Yeah," I said, "I know."

I'd been bluffed again. If I'd told him to go to hell in the beginning—But I couldn't tell him. Not any more than I could have told Andy Taylor to take his sign down. Now, as long as I had anything to get they'd never let up on me. And if either one of them got the idea that I might get the murder pinned on me, they'd step right in and give me a shove.

A person would be nuts to hold back evidence in a murder case unless he stood to clean up by it. There's such a thing as being an accessory. Besides, the insurance company would probably come through pretty heavy for information that would save twenty-five grand.

Hap finished dressing and we went downstairs together. I told him that I was running into the city.

"Oh?" he said. "You wouldn't be taking a powder on me, would you?"

"Do I look stupid!" I said. "Why should I?"

"No," he said, "I suppose you wouldn't. You want to check on my news about Panzer. Is that it?"

"I want to see if I can do something about it."

"Such as?"

"I don't know," I said. "But I've got to make an effort. I've got a hundred-thousand-dollar property here. I can't just sit back and let it slide without lifting a hand."

He stood studying me a moment, then nodded and opened the door of the car. He even took me by the elbow and made as if to help me in.

"Well, the best of luck to you, laddie, and Godspeed and all that rot."

"So long," I said.

"I have tremendous faith in you, old man. As well as a certain mercenary interest—you know?"

I drove off without answering. I knew, all right. He'd want a good heavy cut on anything I was able to pull. The more I had the more he and Andy would demand.

I eased up on the gas just outside of town, and started looking for a crossroads to turn around on There wasn't a damned bit of use driving into the city. There wasn't any way I could stop Panzer and even if there was what would it get me? It would all go for blackmail.

As I say, I almost stopped and turned around. And then I stepped on the gas and went on toward the city. But fast.

Carol? Well, sure, she wasn't to be overlooked and I hadn't. But as long as I could keep her from knowing I was skinned clean until afterward it would be all right. As long as she was sure I wasn't going to run out on her, she really wouldn't give a whoop about the money.

Believe it or not, it was Elizabeth who had slipped my mind. With Hap and Andy both tackling me in the space of an hour, Elizabeth had slipped into the background. And, anyway, it wouldn't have made much difference if she hadn't. Elizabeth was supposed to be dead. I couldn't tell Hap or Andy that the twenty-five grand had to go to her.

It would have to, though. What was it she'd said? *"There will be exceedingly unpleasant consequences if your memory should fail you—"*

She'd have to get it all, right up to the last penny.

Keeping Hap and Andy quiet wouldn't mean a thing, otherwise.

I had to go on. I had to keep the Barclay valuable so that I'd have something to trade for Hap's and Andy's silence.

With the best luck in the world I couldn't wind up with anything. With a little bad luck—just a little—well—

It wasn't right. It was crazy. All this trouble over a woman I didn't know—hadn't ever even seen; a woman, who, when you got right down to cases, didn't amount to a damn.

SEVENTEEN

I woke up the next morning about six o'clock and just lay in bed, not knowing what to do, until after nine. In the back of my mind, I guess, I was trying to kid myself that Hap had been stringing me about Panzer. Or that, maybe, he'd had the wrong dope. And I hated to get up and find out the truth.

Finally, a little after nine, I got up, caught some breakfast and a barbershop shave, and headed for the row. I hadn't brought any toilet articles with me. I'd been afraid to bring any luggage on account of Carol. I was wondering now what kind of story I'd hand her when I got back.

Everyone on the row had heard about the fire, and I wasted about an hour shaking hands and receiving sympathy before I could get to the Utopian exchange. Of course there was more of the same stuff there. But the manager saw it was bothering me and he cut it short by taking me back into his office.

Maybe I told you he was an old friend of mine? I'd known him since the days when he was peddling film and I was hauling it.

We had a couple of drinks and talked a little. After a few minutes, he took out his watch and glanced at it.

"Well, Joe," he said, "what brings you into town? What's on your mind?"

"Not much of anything, Al," I said. "I just wanted to get away from things for a day or two."

"I see. I understand." He shuffled some papers on his desk. "Well, I'm glad you dropped in."

"I was just wondering," I said, "if you had anything on next season's product yet. Of course, I know you've always got a good line-up, but if you had anything unusual I'd kind of like to know. I've been figuring on enlarging the house a little."

He sat there, smiling and nodding. "I believe I have got a few press sheets, Joe. Yeah, here's something. Take at look at those. Something, huh? I'm not going to run down our competitors, but you can see for yourself that—that—"

His eyes met mine, and the sheets slid out of his hand. He cleared his throat, and looked away.

"You've got a nice house, Joe. It always struck me as being just about the right size."

"Thanks," I said.

I'd known it was coming, but it didn't make it any easier to take. I knew it was kid stuff, foolish, to argue. But I couldn't help myself.

"It always seemed to me, Al," I said, "that I was a white man to deal with. I don't give nothing away, but I don't ask for noth— anything. If I'm not profitable to deal with, that's a different matter. But it always seemed to me like I was."

"Oh, hell, Joe," he said. "I'm in the business so I've got to talk price, but I don't think you've actually skinned us six times in ten years. I wouldn't say that to everyone, but I'll say it to you. You're a hundred percenter in my books."

"Well, that's the way I feel," I said. "You've maybe skinned me a few times on superspecials, and you've got a damned bad habit of accidentally shipping me stuff I don't want on the same invoice with stuff that I do, so that I have to take all or nothing. But when I look back upon our whole friendship it's been pretty pleasant. It's something I hate to see broken up. I mean if it was going to be broken up."

"I'm glad you said that, Joe. I like to keep things on a friendly basis. After all, what are we arguing about? It's just a hypothetical case."

"Sure," I said. "Oh, sure. But take even a hypothetical case, Al; it's kind of hard for me to understand. I mean, I think I get it but I'm not sure. The town isn't going to get a whole lot bigger, if any, and film rentals are based on population. A can of film is a can of film. If you push it too far back on the shelf it begins to stink. Twenty-five per cent more, and I could reach it. Fifty, and I'm still not crazy. They'll let me go around if I wear a muzzle. But higher than that—well, they call in the health department."

"They've called it in before, Joe."

"You know what I mean," I said.

"It's hard to understand, all right," he said. "Personally, I don't try to. I just sit back and take orders. By the way, have you seen 'Light o' Dawn' yet? We booked it into the Panzpalace here in town last week."

"I played it," I said. "Don't you remember how you jacked me from twenty-five to thirty bucks for it?"

He didn't seem to hear me.

"We booked it into Panzpalace at fifty per cent of the gross. It pulled seventeen grand the first five days."

I got up and held out my hand. "Well, good-bye," I said. "I've got to go buy a bottle of liniment."

"Goddamit, Joe," he said, "I like you. If there's ever anything I can do for you—personally, that is—you know where to come."

"I don't think there's anything you can do, Al."

"Well—" He let me get to the door. "Come back a minute, Joe."

I went back and sat down.

"Joe, I feel like a heel about this."

"What for?" I said. "It's just a hypothetical case."

"Oh, can that crap. The cat's out of the bag. I feel terrible about it, Joe. It's a hell of a note to hit a man with a thing like this right after he's lost his wife."

"I won't argue with you there," I said. "It looks like if Sol had to build another house he could have picked some spot besides Stoneville."

"No, he couldn't, Joe." Al shook his head. "You've got the best show town in the state. You've got a draw there of a town three times its size. It's the only place where he could possibly justify the building of another Panzpalace."

"It's going to be one then? One of his regular articles?"

"It has to be, Joe. You've got a pretty nice house there yourself. Sol couldn't build enough house for three or four hundred grand, even a half million, to freeze you out."

"I don't know that I get you," I said.

"Sure, you do. You mentioned it yourself a few minutes ago. If you had to, you could pay three or four times as much for product as you are now and keep running. But you couldn't pay six or seven times as much. Neither could Sol with less than a million-buck house. I mean, he couldn't justify rentals like that."

"I see," I said. "But actually he won't pay you any more than I do, if he pays that much. He'll shave you down somewhere else in the chain."

Al shrugged. "I showed you the answer to that, Joe. Panzpalace controls every important house in the state—the big city houses that play product on percentage instead of at a flat rate. As long as he doesn't ask us to do anything out-and-out illegal we've got to play with him."

"I'll make you a little bet," I said. "I'll bet inside of ten-fifteen years Panzer has shaved you enough, you and the other exchanges, to pay for that house."

"Maybe. I just work here."

"You're cutting your own throats, Al!"

"Better worry about yourself, Joe. What are your plans?"

"I—I haven't thought too far ahead," I said.

"Why don't you go and see Sol? Maybe you could work out something. I happen to know he likes you."

"Yeah," I said, "he must."

"He does, Joe." Al leaned forward. "Look. Those big boys don't look on things like you and I do. The way Sol sees it, it don't make no difference if there's a Barclay in Stoneville or not. Relatively, you know. It's unimportant. But if he don't put in this Panzpalace—and like I say he's got to put it in Stoneville—he sees himself as losing several million dollars."

I let that sink in, and, if there'd been a laugh left in me, it would have come out.

"I see," I said. "It's easy for a man to figure that way. You lose track of the fact that something that doesn't mean a thing to you may mean a hell of a lot to the guy that has it."

"That's it exactly."

"But how does he figure several million dollars?"

"Well, Sol has a reputation as a money-maker, doesn't he? When he puts up a new house the public looks on it as another mint."

"They're not far wrong at that," I said. "I see. Panzpalace stock will take a jump."

"It will, but don't get any ideas, Joe. This is Sol's surprise and only he knows exactly when he's going to pull it. He'll drive the stock down first. If you got in anywhere besides the basement you'd lose your shirt."

"Not bad," I said.

"But that's only part of the picture, Joe." Al held up a finger. "A Panzpalace house will use around ten thousand dollars worth of paper and display matter a year. If you and I bought it, it'd mean a flat outlay of ten grand, but Sol uses the same paper over and over. And he owns his own paper company. It's not a big outfit; has a capitalization of about a quarter of a million. But—"

But that was all to the good. Dumping ten thousand bucks' profit into a company that size meant a four-percent increase in dividends.

"Then there's his film-express company. It'll take a jump in profits with practically no increase in overhead. And his equipment companies, Joe. You know what show-house equipment is; high-profit, slow-moving stuff. A big order suddenly dumped in on those companies—"

My head began to swim. I'd thought I was halfway smart but beside Panzer I wasn't anything. He'd mop up in a dozen different ways, and the mopping up would be legitimate. His companies *would* be worth more. He'd have an actual operating loss in Stoneville, but it wouldn't ever show, and the house wouldn't cost him anything in the long run. He could show that he was increasing Panzpalace assets by a million bucks. That would stop any squawks.

Of course, someone was going to lose. The money had to come

from somewhere. Suckers would be shaken out. The film companies would have to pinch a little, and there'd be wage cuts and layoffs. The—But what the hell of it? Sol would mop up and he'd be in the clear.

That's business.

Al leaned back in his chair. "By the way, Joe, who tipped you off?"

"No one," I said. "I just had a premonition."

"I read the papers, Joe. Hap Chance seems to be your bosom friend all of a sudden. Well, all I got to say is I wouldn't want to be in his shoes. This is one time he's got out beyond his depth. I suppose he thought this was just a little petty chiseling that he should be taken in on."

I didn't answer him. I didn't want to talk about Hap. If he was washed up on the row—and Sol could wash him up if he wanted to take the trouble—he'd bear down that much harder on me.

"When's Sol moving in, Al?"

"Only Sol knows that."

"Where's he going to build?"

"Well—"He hesitated. "Maybe I've been talking too much. But you can figure it out for yourself. Where would you build if you were in his place?"

"That's simple," I said. "You couldn't pick a better show lot than the one I've got, and people are accustomed to going in that direction. But—but—"

I choked up. I could feel my face turning purple. Al looked down at his desk nervously.

"Now, Joe. You couldn't expect him to talk it over with you."

"Goddam it'," I said. "I'll make him wish he had! Maybe I won't sell! Maybe I got some ideas on making money, myself! Maybe—"

"You won't have any income, Joe. How long do you think you can play holdout?"

"A hell of a lot longer than Sol thinks! I don't give a goddam if I starve, I'll—I'll—" I choked up again. I wouldn't get a chance to starve. I wouldn't even have time to get real hungry before Hap or Andy or Elizabeth or—"You see, Joe? It wouldn't be smart, would it?" "No," I said, "it wouldn't be smart." I got up and walked out.

EIGHTEEN

I've probably given you the idea that Elizabeth didn't have much tact or, at least, that she didn't go out of her way to use it. And that's true and it was the cause of a lot of our trouble. But now that I think about it, it seems like the thing that caused the most hell was that I never knew quite how she was going to react to a given situation.

I don't mean that I'd want any woman to be all cut and dried in her actions, or that I ever expected anyone to use me as a pattern. But I do say you've got to have some—well, some standard of conduct or you don't have anything at all. You've got to know whether what you're going to do will make a person happy or sore. You've got to know whether a person is actually happy when they—he—she looks like and says she is or at least you've got to know that she isn't. And if that sounds mixed up I am and I was, right from the day we were married.

We closed the show up for two weeks for our honeymoon, since it wasn't making a damned thing anyway; and, seeing that it was summer, we went to a resort up in the eastern part of the state. It was just a small place—but nothing cheap by a long shot—and everyone had you sized up the minute you walked in. Everyone knew that Elizabeth and I were just married, and everyone was doing a little under-the-breath kidding about it. And I thought that Elizabeth was taking it perfectly all right—as why the hell shouldn't she have?

But when the waiter brought our dinner up that night she suddenly blew the lid off of things. One minute he was chuckling and just being pleasant as waiters will; and the next minute he was out the door so fast his jacket tails were flying. I don't exactly remember what it was Elizabeth said to him. But I knew it was the wrong thing. And before I knew what was happening she was telephoning the manager and reporting this boy for insulting us.

"For Christ's sake," I said, when I finally got my breath, "what did you do that for, Elizabeth?"

"I'm sorry, Joe," she said. "I should have let you do it."

"Do what? Why should I have done anything?"

"Oh?" Her mouth tightened, then relaxed. "I know you've been thinking about business matters, dear. But if you'd noticed—"

"I tell you what I have noticed," I said. "I've noticed you standing right out in the middle of Stoneville, gabbing and laughing with some washwoman and her ragged-assed pickaninnies until—"

"Don't use words like that, Joe!"

"All right, then, they were just ragged, but—"

Well, how can you argue with a person like that? Someone that's absolutely determined to miss the entire point of a conversation?

I said, "Well, hell, let's forget it and go to bed." And we went, and there wasn't any more argument the rest of that night. But I still felt bad about getting this boy in trouble and maybe letting ourselves in for a lot of rotten service. And, like she always knew, Elizabeth knew that I was bothered.

When we went down to breakfast the next morning, the waiter captain gave us a funny look and led us over to a table in the middle of the dining-room. And then he snapped his fingers, and this same boy we'd had the night before came running over.

"George wants to apologize for his conduct," the captain said. "I'm sure you'll have no more trouble with him."

"Sure, not," I said. "Just give us a menu and skip it. We'll get along all right."

I almost jerked the menus out of the waiter's hands, and shoved one at Elizabeth; and I got behind the other one fast. But it wasn't any go. Elizabeth wasn't ready to drop it until I looked like a complete damned fool.

"Why, sure, everything's okay," she said, letting out with a big laugh. "George and I are pals, aren't we, George?" And right in front of everyone she reached out and grabbed his hand and shook it.

We ate breakfast. I guess.

We got out of there and went for a long, fast walk. Elizabeth didn't say anything and neither did I. It wasn't until noon, after we'd eaten at a little hamburger joint in the town, that we got to speaking to each other again. And then it wasn't so good.

I did all I could, God knows. I admitted she'd played me for a chump, and tried to laugh it off. But right in the middle of my trying to make a joke of it she busted out bawling, and then she ran back to the hotel by herself.

I guess this waiter George must have been a pretty good boy because I had to pay the captain fifty bucks to fire him. That made things a little more comfortable; and after a day or two—a night or two, I should say—Elizabeth and I were beginning to feel that marriage wasn't such a bad deal after all.

We were a little edgy with each other, but, generally, I'd say that that feeling lasted on through our honeymoon and for several months afterward. It wasn't until I put Bower out of business that we had another real blowup.

"But you just couldn't have done it, Joe!" she said. "The Bowers are one of the oldest families in town, and they've always been good friends of ours. You can't deliberately ruin people like that."

"I'm not ruining them," I said. "If Bower wants to start another show it's all right with me."

"You know he can't start another one!"

"Well, that's his fault, then," I said. "I've got to protect our investment. It's up to him to look after his. What could be fairer than that?"

She sat and stared at me for a long time, and I began to get nervous. There wasn't any reason why I should have, but I couldn't help myself.

"Well, what's wrong?" I said.

"What do you think, Joe?"

"I don't think anything," I said. "All I know is that I work my can off trying to put us on a good spot and you can't do anything but find fault with me. Whose side are you on, anyhow? Mine or Bower's?"

"Do I have to take sides against people who've never done me any harm?"

"Look," I said. "This is business, Elizabeth. You just can't—"

"Never mind, Joe. I think I understand."

The smile she gave me wouldn't have fooled me later on, but it did at the time. And when she said of course she was on my side, where else would a wife be? I was completely taken in.

I went ahead and told her about the other things I had planned. How I could get the work done on a new house for nothing. How I could get the marquee and other stuff for next to nothing. How I could use them to get credit to pay the bills that couldn't be ducked. How we could run the house union at less expense than it cost to scab.

I must have shot off my mouth for an hour. And then, since everything seemed to be going so well, and we hadn't been married very long—

We went up to the bedroom, and that—it—was the craziest goddam thing that ever happened to me. Action? Sure; as much as you'd get on a roller coaster. Affection? The only twenty-dollar girl I ever had gave me a lot less. Heat? Like a furnace. It was lovely and wonderful, and so goddam phony I felt myself gagging right into her mouth.

I jumped up and began jerking on my clothes.

"All right," I yelled, "have it your way! I'll let everything slide, and you can have your goddam rattrap back as it stands and I'll clear out!"

"But I don't want you to clear out, Joe." She got up and stood in front of me. "I happen to love you."

"Damned if you don't," I said. "Just leave me alone. I won't bother you again."

"And I want you to bother me, too. Perhaps I'm a little disappointed in—in things, but—"

"You're disappointed?" I said. "What the hell do you think I am?"

She didn't answer that one, and I went ahead flinging on my clothes, trying not to look at her.

I finished dressing and started for the door, and she got in front of me.

"Well?" I said.

"Is this better, Joe?" she said. Then, cr-aack! She slapped me. "Do you like that better?"

And before I could come to my senses, before I could get over someone who was supposed to be a lady acting like a four-bit floozy, she'd shoved me out the door and locked it.

Well, I built the show. I did the other things I've told you about. And every once in a while, during those first few years, I thought we were going to be able to straighten things out and get along like married people should.

I thought so the strongest when she got pregnant, but then she miscarried and it was worse than ever. It was like I mentioned a while back. I never knew what she was going to do. I was never sure whether her actions and words meant one thing or whether they meant another.

About all I could ever be sure of was that she hated my guts, and that she hated them most right when she claimed to be loving me the loudest.

The funny part about it all was that with all her high-toned sneering, she wasn't too good to profit by the corners I cut. She insisted on keeping the show in her name, and she made almost as big a job of running it as I did. Not that anything she ever did was a damned bit of help, but she kept her hand in and held in there right on up to the end.

No, I don't think she was ever afraid of my skipping out if I wasn't tied down. And I don't think the main idea was to humiliate me, although that may have been part of it. I think—no, I don't, either. If I really thought that, then nothing would make sense.

I don't think I mentioned that she fired Carol that afternoon she caught her in my room. Well, she did, and I let her. It didn't look like I had much grounds for argument, and I figured I'd see Carol later and slip her some money and fix it up.

Carol packed up her things, or started to. Before she could finish Elizabeth called her down to the living-room.

"I'm partly to blame for this," she said to us. "Perhaps, by bringing Carol into this house, I'm entirely to blame. At any rate, I'm ready to assume some of the responsibility for it. Carol, exactly what are your feelings toward Mr. Wilmot?"

"None of your business," said Carol.

"And yours toward Carol, Joe?"

"There's no use in me saying anything," I said. "You've already got your mind made up."

"I see. Well, in preference to having this affair carried on around the countryside, I think Carol had best stay here. Go and unpack your things, Carol."

Carol looked at me, and I nodded. After she'd left the room Elizabeth stood up.

"I'm going to give you a little time to decide exactly what you want to do, Joe. And when you do reach a decision I expect you to stick by it. Do you understand?"

"Maybe I've already decided," I said.

"And?"

"Let's say I'm about as sick of you as you are of me."

"All right," she said. "Now, the little matter remains of what to do about it."

From where I sit now I'd say she thought she had me; that she knew there wasn't anything I could do and that I'd have to backwater on the deal. Looking back I'd say that she wasn't really thinking about the insurance when she agreed to settle for twenty-five grand. It was just her way of saying that she wouldn't trade at all.

I don't mean that she wanted me herself, because everything that she'd ever done or said pointed to the fact that she didn't. But she wasn't going to let Carol have me, either. Not Carol. She didn't hate Carol, exactly, she didn't think enough of her even to do that. It was Carol who did the hating and she did a good job of it. But—

But that's beside the point.

The insurance did get mentioned, and there was just one way we could cash in on it. And when I laid the plan out, little by little, Elizabeth went for it. It surprised me, but she did. She even took full charge of the plans, pushing them along faster than I would have myself.

Carol thought it was all a gag, that Elizabeth was just trying to land her and me in trouble. But I didn't and don't think so. Elizabeth didn't need to pretend anything. She was in the saddle. And there was no way she could have made trouble for us without involving herself.

Why did she try to burn herself up there toward the last? The answer to that is, she didn't. It just looked that way. She knew every trick to that rewind motor. She knew just how much she could play around with that short-circuited cord without being in danger. I didn't move as fast as she thought I would and consequently she almost had herself a funeral party. But, anyway, it was a good trick and it almost worked.

If it hadn't been for Carol, for what had happened between us—
And, yes, I guess Carol had been doing a little thinking, too, which
was why things turned out as they did.

Carol could so some pretty straight thinking even if she didn't
always come up with the straight answers. Word for word, I can still
remember what she said that first night we talked about the murder.

"Why do you want to do it?" she said, staring hard at Elizabeth.
"That's the part I don't get."

Elizabeth shrugged. "It seems that some move is indicated."

"By Joe and me, maybe. You don't need to stick your neck out."

"Well—shall we say I'm trying to be co-operative?"

"Don't make me laugh!"

"I wish I could," Elizabeth said. "Almost anything would be an
improvement over your normal expression. However! I need a
minimum of twenty-five thousand dollars to leave, and—"

"You've got a lot more than twenty-five thousand without leaving."

Elizabeth sighed and shrugged, as much as to say Carol was
making a damned fool of herself. "There's not much more for me to
say, is there? Think whatever you like."

"I am," said Carol, real slow. "And I—I don't understand—"

NINETEEN

I felt sick driving home from the city after leaving Al, kind of like I
was catching the flu. The outside of my body was warm enough,
maybe a little too warm, but inside I was cold. Shivering.

But sick or just scared sick, however you want to put it, I couldn't
help but admire the way Sol Panzer had laid his plans. They added
up to a knot behind my ear, but I still had to admire them. By God,
they were perfect.

Or do you get it?

A stunt like Sol was pulling takes a lot of preparation and a lot of
dough. He had to have his stocks rigged for the jump; he had to be
able to show that he wasn't bluffing. Just an announcement to the

newspapers of what he intended doing wouldn't be enough. The papers wouldn't go for it and neither would the suckers. The architect's plans would have to be drawn and the construction contracts signed, and money earmarked for the building. And, of course, the film exchanges would have to be lined up.

Up to that point, there was almost no chance of a leak, of someone's taking the edge off his surprise. Sol was dealing with people he controlled. He could make it worth their while to stay mum, and make 'em wish they'd never been born if they didn't. The outsiders might *think* he was up to something, but they wouldn't know what it was. Their one chance of finding out would be when he bought a location. So?

So, he hadn't bought any. He hadn't risked having an option or a lease or a sale traced back to him. He didn't need to. I had the location he wanted, and when he got ready he'd step in and take it off my hands. I'd have about ten minutes to make up my mind. I could take a few grand and get out, or take nothing or next to it later on. I might cause him a little trouble, but it wouldn't make me anything. I'd take what he offered, whatever it was. I'd have to.

If I was still around . . .

I got into Stoneville a little after dark and drove around the square a few times, trying to make up my mind what to do. I was afraid to go home; I didn't know what I was going to say to Carol. I was afraid to go to the show; I didn't know what I could say to Hap. Finally, I parked across from the house, in front of Bower's old place, to give myself a little time to think; and I hadn't much more than shut my motor off before Andy Taylor was there, poking his head in the window.

"Been looking for you, Joe," he said. "Figured it was about time you an' me had a little talk."

"What about?" I said.

"I reckon you know."

"What do you think you've got on me, Andy?"

"I don't know, Joe. I ain't got the slightest idea. But I know I got somethin'."

"All right," I said. "I'll see you in a day or two. I'm sick and worn out right now. I think I'm coming down with the flu."

'Don't wait too long, Joe." He cackled. "I might talk to someone else."

He showed signs of needling me some more, so I mumbled something about business and walked across the street to the show.

Mrs. Artie Fletcher was in the box office, filing and buffing her fingernails and looking like she'd stab anyone that bothered her. You know, efficient and attractive like a cashier ought to look. Harry Clinkscales, my half-witted doorman, was doing his best, too, to run people off. He kept tossing grains of popcorn into the air and catching them in his mouth, stumbling around the lobby with his head thrown back and his mouth open about a foot. I wished to God a light bug would drop down it.

When he saw me he stopped and wiped his greasy hands on his uniform. My uniform.

"That's a good act, Harry," I said. "What'll you take to put it on inside?"

He grinned like an ape. "There was a guy here to see you a little while ago, Mr. Wilmot."

"A gentleman, Harry?"

"Yes sir."

"What was his name?"

"Dunno. He didn't tell me."

"Well, that was pretty dumb of him, wasn't it?" I said. "What did he say when you asked him?"

Harry got kind of red in the face. "I think I know who he was, Mr. Wilmot. I think it was that guy—that gentleman from the insurance company."

"Oh," I said.

"He said he'd stop back later on in the evening."

"Good," I said; and I went on in and up to the projection booth.

Hap had just put on a new reel and was leaning back against the rewind table, watching the picture through the port. The booth speaker was roaring; the sound was too loud. It gets that way early in the evening when there aren't enough people in the house to provide the right kind of acoustics.

Hap turned down the control a little, and wiped the sweat from his face and arms with a dirty towel.

"This is a veritable blast furnace, laddie. Why is it you didn't air-condition the booth when you did the rest of the house?"

"Why should I?" I said. "I don't sell any seats up here."

"Uh-*hah*," he said, narrowing his eyes at me. "Right to the mark, as usual, eh? Well, what luck in the city?"

"Nothing," I said. "None. I didn't get to see Panzer."

"Ah? You had your eyes closed?"

"No. He was out of town."

He took a step toward me, and I moved out of the way. He pulled a reel out of the film cabinet, slipped it into the off-projector, and flipped the switch on the arc.

"You're a bloody liar, old man. You're a blasted stinking, filthy liar."

"For Christ's sake, Hap," I said. "Give me a little time! This thing hit me out of a clear sky. What the hell, anyway? I've got the insurance money coming."

"Have you, now? I wonder."

"I will if you—if—"

"Maybe it won't be left to me."

"How do you mean?"

"Your now-vacationing projectionist and I have been having some nice long talks. Got quite pally young Nedry and I have."

"If you don't stop trying to pump him," I said, "he will suspect something. Leave him alone, Hap. He doesn't know anything."

"I wish I were confident of that. He's dropped several sinister hints. He's intimated that he isn't going to be around very long, that he's got certain information which, transmitted to Blair—who's been after your scalp a long time, I understand—will get him a transfer to one of the city houses."

I laughed. I'd been wondering why Jimmie and Blair were running around together.

"Blair's letting his wishbone get in the way of his brain," I said, "and Jimmie is just hungry enough to string him along. He'll be right here as long as I want him."

"Oh? Are you—"

"I don't blame Jimmie for trying. Those city locals only have their charters open about an hour out of the year, and only the insiders know when that is. If some floater does get the word, all they have to do is give him an examination no one could pass or put the initiation fee out of his reach."

"I know all that, laddie."

"Well, Blair isn't going to go to all the expense and trouble of fixing things up unless Jimmie gives him some real dirt, and Jimmie can't because he doesn't have any. He's demanding the transfer before he talks."

"I don't know. It looks like Jimmie would have to know something. Suppose Blair gives him the transfer? What's his story going to be?"

"He won't need any. He can tell Blair to go laugh up a rope. He'd be in then, and out of Blair's jurisdiction."

"Well, I hope you're right, laddie. I sincerely hope so. For my sake."

"I'm right," I said. "By the way, don't you want me to give you a relief?"

"Oh, no. Nedry'll be along in a few minutes. He gives me a relief twice a day."

"Oh," I said. "Well, that's pretty nice of him."

"Isn't it, though?"

"Well, good night," I said.

"Cheerio! And remember—on your toes. I'm not waiting around here forever."

He started the off-projector, slid the port on the other one, and began unthreading the run-reel of film. I took a good long look at the back of his head and went downstairs again.

It wasn't much different from three thousand other nights. People strolling by, walking up to the box office or stopping to look at the lobby cards, asking how I was and being asked how they were. Now and then a car would pass by slow, and there'd be a light tap on the horn; and I'd turn around and wave and be waved at. A couple of bobby soxers stood up near the popcorn machine, giggling and talking to Harry, and watching me out of the corner of their eyes. Overhead, up above the marquee, the thirty-foot sign went on and off, spelled and flashed, painting the street and the cars green and red. Without looking, without even noticing, I knew when it went B-A-R-C-L-A-Y, then BARCLAY, then *BARCLAY*.

I remembered all the arguments Elizabeth and I had had about that sign. How I'd hated it at first, yeah, how I'd hated her, not because I wanted my own name up there but because she didn't; because she wasn't as proud of Wilmot as she was of Barclay. And what did it matter? What did it really matter, anyway? Everyone knew who'd built the house. People always know those things. And Elizabeth was the last of the Barclays, and it was the oldest family in the county.

When people haven't got anything but a name you can't blame them for leaning on it. And maybe—just maybe—that wasn't her reason. Maybe it was her way, as she'd put it, of being responsible. Of backing me up before the whole damned world.

Oh, hell . . .

I'd got hot up in the booth, and now I was beginning to chill. I passed a word or two with Mrs. Fletcher, and crossed the street to my car.

I got in and rolled up the windows, and lighted a cigarette. I let my head lie back against the seat and tried to rest. Maybe I dozed a little, but I don't think so. I think I was just so wrapped up in worrying about Carol and Elizabeth and Hap Chance and Andy and Sol Panzer and wondering what I was going to do that I was deaf and blind to everyone else.

I don't know how long Appleton stood outside the car looking in at me. But finally I rolled my head and there he was.

I kind of jumped, and then I opened the door and let him in.

TWENTY

"Gloating over the scene of your victory?" he said.

I didn't get what he meant.

"The show here," he said. "I understand you put your competitor out of business."

"Oh, yeah," I said. "No. I was just sitting here. Figuring on whether I wanted to eat a bite before I went home."

"By the way, I went to your show yesterday."

"I meant to give you some passes," I said. "I don't think I have any with me, but—"

"Forget it, Joe. It all goes on the expense account. But I wanted to ask you about those loges. Do you think they're safe?"

"I pay extra coverage for them," I said.

"Well." He laughed. "That makes everything all right, then. As long as you're covered."

I knew I'd made a dumb remark and that he was digging me, but I didn't particularly give a damn. My nerves were on edge. I was too sick and worried to think.

"I took a look at your exits, too, Joe. You know our state fire laws require two rear exits in a picture show."

"I've got two," I said.

"You've got a double door closing on the same jamb."

"It's good enough for the fire commissioner."

"Oh? Well, if it's good enough for him, who are we to quibble?"

He laughed again and nudged me, and I wanted to sock him. A guy can't be on his toes all the time.

"How are you getting along with your investigation?" I said. "About wound up?"

"Well—hardly," he said. "Those things take a lot of time, you know."

"I guess I don't know," I said. "The thing seems simple enough to me. The legal authorities are satisfied. I've been paying in premiums for ten years; and you've had plenty of time to find out if there was anything wrong. It looks to me like I'm entitled to a settlement or a damned good explanation."

He didn't get a bit sore. At least, he didn't show it.

"Well, that's the way it looks to you," he said. "Now I'll tell you how it looks to us. We don't have anything more to gain from you. You won't be carrying insurance on your wife, naturally, and the chances are that you'll drop your own. We don't want to pay you. We won't if we can get out of it."

"Thanks," I said. "I'm glad to know what kind of an outfit I'm dealing with."

"Don't quote me, Joe—don't mind my calling you Joe, do you? I'd hate to have to call you a liar."

"You may have a chance," I said. "I don't want anything I'm not entitled to, but—"

"Oh, sure you do. We all do. That's like saying you don't want anything more out of a thing than what you put into it. Where's the percentage in a deal like that? But you were threatening to sue us?"

"No, I wasn't threatening," I said. "I wouldn't want to sue unless—"

"And I don't think you will, Joe. You're too smart. There isn't a court in the land that wouldn't allow us from three months to a year to make our investigation. The chances are I'll have my report ready long before that. We haven't refused to pay the claim. We won't unless we have reason to."

I began to get hold of myself.

"Skip it," I said. "There's no hurry. I guess I was just sore because you knocked the house. I know those loges and exits aren't right, but I can't do everything at once. I haven't had a lot to work with."

"Sure. That's all right, Joe."

"But I'm kind of curious. Would you mind telling me something?"

"My life story if you want it."

"Maybe I'm stepping out of line and if I am, just say so. But— well, just what is there to investigate? I mean it all looks pretty much cut and dried to me. The fire wiped out everything and—"

"Not everything, Joe."

"Well. You know what I mean."

"But you don't know what I mean. The most important clue to any disaster is the man who profits by it. Don't take that the wrong way. I'm not implying anything."

"How do you work on a clue like me?"

"Well, I don't slip around, dropping sly hints and giving people the wink. Nothing so crude as that, Joe. It's more a matter of moving around, observing and listening, gathering impressions, figuring out whether you're the kind of guy that would—"

"I suppose you try to put yourself in the—the other fellow's place, too."

"No. No, I don't, Joe." Rolling down the window, he threw out the butt of his cigarette and lighted another one. "In the first place that requires a preconceived notion of what the other fellow is; I'm making up my mind about him before I ever go to work on him. What kind of an investigation is that?"

"I've never thought about it that way," I said. "You hear the expression used so often, putting yourself in the other fellow's place—"

"It's bad business all the way around, Joe. If you put yourself in the other man's place often enough you're very likely to get stuck there. Some of your worst criminals began their careers as officers of the law. There's probably a higher incidence of insanity among psychiatrists than any other group. I remember a case I worked on several years ago—"

He paused and gave me a glance as much as to ask if he was boring me. I told him to go on. He was an easy guy to listen to, and I didn't want to go home.

"It was a murder, Joe. Just about the messiest job I've ever seen. A woman was literally clawed, clawed and chewed to death. Obviously, the murderer was a degenerate or a lunatic; we needed an expert on morbid psychology to get to the bottom of the crime. One of the best men in the country lived right there in the neighborhood, so, with the permission of the authorities, we called him in.

"Well, the police threw out the well-known dragnet, pulled in all the twist-brains they could lay hands on, and this guy went to work. And, Joe, by God, it was enough to make your flesh crawl to watch him. He'd sit there in a cell with some bird that you and I wouldn't touch with a ten-foot pole—the sort of bird that does things a lot of newspapers won't print—and he'd pal right up to him. He'd talk to him like a long lost brother. He'd find out what special sort of craziness this guy went in for, and for the time being he'd be the same way. If you closed your eyes and listened, you wouldn't know which one was doing the talking. And, yet, he was one of the most likable guys I've ever known. He talked my language, too. We seemed to click.

"We got to where we saw quite a bit of each other outside the line of business. He'd drop in on me a night or two a week, or I'd run in on him. We'd have a few drinks and a bite to eat, and bat the breeze around. And, gradually, without knowing I was doing it, I began to get his guard down. He started tipping his hand."

Appleton shook his head, started fumbling for another cigarette. I gave him one, and held a match.

"For God's sake," I said. "Let's hear the rest of it."

"He had a big German shepherd, Joe; a big brute that was a hell of a lot more wolf than it was dog. And I began to notice—he and that dog were a lot alike. Sometimes he'd snap at a sandwich or a piece of food just like the dog. Sometimes there'd be a trace of growl in his voice, or he'd scratch the back of his head with that stiff, rapid stroke a dog uses. Sometimes they even looked alike.

"The payoff came one night when he started to play with the dog. It started off as a romp, but before it was over they were down on the floor together, snapping and slashing and clawing, yeah, and barking. Both of 'em. And when I got the cops in they turned on us—the two dogs. Wolves. I don't need to tell you who our murderer was."

I shivered. He gave a short laugh.

"Not nice, huh, Joe?"

"I think I'm coming down with a cold," I said. "I've been having chills all evening."

"Well, I'll shove off and let you go. How about dinner some night this week?"

"Sure," I said. "But don't rush off. Tell me some more about this guy."

"What about him?"

"Well, why did he choose to be a dog? It doesn't seem to make sense. I can understand how a guy who worked with crooks all the time might turn out to be a crook, but—"

"He was a man of innate and extraordinarily fine sensibilities, Joe. And a man has to identify himself with something. He has to be able to picture himself as being some certain thing. If he can't, he's helpless. There's no motivation, no guide for his acting and thinking."

"Yeah," I said. "That's right, isn't it?"

"This man couldn't identify himself with the human race. He appeared to be able to do it with extreme ease, but actually he was losing a little of his character and personality with every contact. In the end, there wasn't anything left; nothing but the idea that humanity was pretty rotten. So—"

"I see," I said.

I shivered again, and he reached for the door.

"You ought to be in bed, Joe. I've got to be going anyway. I've got another case to handle. Going to be on the jump for the next few days."

"Where's the fire this time?"

He shook his head. "It's not in my line, but as long as I'm here I'm taking a crack at it. It's a disappearance case. Some dame is supposed to have come out here from the city a few days ago, and she hasn't been heard of since."

"The hell!" I said. "What do you know about that?" And he gave me a funny look.

"You don't need to be polite, Joe; I'm not interested in it, either. We get a hundred like it every year."

"But—but where could she disappear to in a town this size?"

"She couldn't; I'll turn her up in a few days. She's a houseworker; came out here to take a job. That narrows it down a lot. There aren't many people here who hire household help."

"No," I said. "Uh—how did you know she disappeared, anyway? Who reported it?"

"Her former landlady. She didn't have any relatives, it seems, and she owed this landlady a hell of a big bill. So, as a gesture of good faith, she switched a little paid-up policy she had—actually it would just about take care of her burial expenses when she died—to her landlady. That is, she named her as beneficiary until such time as she could clear up her debt. Well, she left the city in a hurry and was supposed to send for her baggage, and she hasn't done it. Naturally, the landlady is sure—she hopes—that something has happened to her, and she comes down on us."

"Y-Y-you're pretty sure y-you can f-f-find—"

"How can I help it? Say, you have got a chill, haven't you?"

My teeth were clattering too hard to answer. I nodded, and he said good night and got out. Up on the curb he hollered at me not to forget our dinner date; and I nodded again.

I backed the car out into the street, made a U-turn, and headed for home. As I started to angle around the square, I glanced into the rearview mirror. He was still standing where I had left him. Up on the curb, with his hat thrust back and his hands on his hips.

Watching me.

TWENTY-ONE

I must have been off my nut by the time I got home. I had to be to do what I did. I ran up the steps almost before the car had stopped rolling. I pushed the door open, half fell inside, and stood leaning against it.

"Elizabeth," I panted. "Elizabeth—"

And, of course, it wasn't Elizabeth. But even when I realized that, I couldn't come to my senses. It only made me worse.

I started to say that I was sorry, that Elizabeth's name had just slipped out; but I felt so ugly and scared, I guess, that it acted on her. And when it did she wasn't something I cared about hurting. She got me in the same way Elizabeth had used to.

It was all I could do to keep from slugging her.

"You—you muddle-headed bitch. Goddam—damn you! Didn't know where she was going, huh? Everything was all right, huh? Now they got us they got us *they got us!* They—"

I don't know what I said, the words were coming so fast and so mixed up, but somehow Carol got the sense of it.

"She didn't, Joe! She didn't know. I swear that she didn't!"

"Huh? How—"

"She was too anxious for the job to ask questions, and I slid over it. I told her I was hiring her for a friend. I told her I'd give her the exact address after we got here. I slid over it that way. She didn't know a thing until we got on the bus!"

"She called from somewhere! Or maybe she wrote! Her landlady—"

"I tell you, she didn't, Joe! She *did not!* I was with her every minute."

"But Appleton—"

"Don't you see, Joe? It's someone else. It's another woman. It must be."

"Oh," I said. "Oh—"

My knees were about to give way under me. I wobbled over to the lounge and sat down.

"You're sure about everything, Carol? Elizabeth got away all right?"

"Yes."

"And the woman? No one saw you, heard you, when—"

"No," said Carol. "We were all alone. We—she knew what was coming, right at the last, but there wasn't anything she could do. No one would hear her. I was stronger than she was. She didn't even try to fight. She—"

"Carol," I said. "For God's sake. You don't need to draw me a picture."

"I was just trying to tell you, Joe. Everything's all right. There's nothing to be afraid of."

The funny, intent look went out of her eyes. She turned them in toward the bridge of her nose and pursed out her lower lip. And then she blew upward at the little wisp of hair that had fallen over her forehead.

That got me, just like it always had. All at once we were right back where we'd been that Sunday afternoon when she'd come into my room in her made-over clothes, and I'd felt so damned sorry for her I didn't know whether to laugh or cry.

"Come here, Carol," I said; and she came there, over to the lounge.

I gave her a grin and squeezed her hand, and after a minute she slid close to me.

"I'm sorry," I said. "That Appleton guy got me rattled. You know how you'd feel if you had a piece of news like that thrown at you."

"Yes," she said. "I'd know."

"I meant to tell you I was going into the city but I didn't have a chance. I had to leave in a hurry."

"Did you?"

"Yes, I did."

"Why?"

"Business. I could tell you, but you wouldn't understand."

"Oh."

"All right, 'oh,' then," I said. "It's the truth. God, Carol, I'm out in front in this deal! I can't stop and explain every time I turn around. I've got to do what I think's best."

"I know."

"Well, then?"

She hesitated, then turned and looked squarely at me. Or as squarely as she could with those eyes of hers.

"Will you answer me one question, Joe?"

"Certainly, I will."

"And tell the truth? Wait a minute, Joe! I didn't mean to insult you. But I've just got to know."

"All right, shoot," I said.

"Is there something wrong at the show?"

I shook my head. I couldn't find my voice right then. "You're not—that's the truth, Joe?"

"Of course, it's the truth. What are you driving at? What could be wrong?"

"I don't know," she said. "But there is something wrong. There's something wrong somewhere, and you're afraid to tell me about it. That's what—w-what I c-can't stand. Your being afraid of me."

"Aw, hell," I said, trying to put my arm around her. "Why would I be afraid of you?"

"It's no good asking each other questions, Joe." She brushed at her eyes. "What we need is answers. We're in this together, but we're pulling different ways. You don't trust me."

"It don't—doesn't—look like you trusted me a hell of a lot, either."

"I love you, Joe. Sometimes you love a person so much you can't trust them. It's for their own good that you don't."

"Well," I said. "I don't know what you want me to say."

"I—I guess there isn't much to say."

I jumped to my feet and headed for the kitchen. And I didn't stop or look around when she called me. Things had been coming at me too fast; I didn't have anything left to fight with. I had to do something quick or I knew I'd be yelling the truth at her. *You're goddam right I'm afraid! You'd think I pulled you into this to get Elizabeth and me out of a hole! You think I'd sell anyone out! You—*

I got the cupboard door open and reached down the whisky bottle. I raised it, turning around, and she was standing in the doorway watching me.

The whisky never reached my mouth. I couldn't get it that high. It trickled out on my shirt front, and then the bottle dropped from my hand to the floor. And I followed it.

Instantly she was at my side, lifting me. And sick and dizzy as I was, the one thought that filled my mind was how much strength she had. I weigh around two hundred, but she hoisted me up and got me over to the table as easily as if I'd been a child.

"Joe, darling—What do you want me to do, Joe?"

"I'm sick." I kept repeating it. "I'm sick, Carol."

"Do you want me to get a doctor?"

"No!" No, I didn't want a doctor. He might give me something to knock me out, and I'd start raving.

"I'm just awfully tired and weak," I said. "Running around too much. Not eating. Got a chill—"

She put a hand to my forehead. "You've got a fever, too. "

"I'd better go to bed," I said. "I get in bed and I'll be all right."

"All right, Joe."

She started to lift me again, but I held back. "We can't go on staying here alone, Carol. We'll have to have someone come in."

"Do you want me to call Mr. Chance?"

"Jesus, no! I mean I may be in bed several days. We want someone who can be around all the time. Get Mrs. Reverend Whitcomb. Take the car and go after her. She'll do anything to get a few square meals."

She got up slowly, kind of hanging back. "Couldn't I just call her, Joe?"

"How would she get over here? The Whitcombs don't have a car. Now, go on and go after her before it gets any later."

"But—but I don't drive very well. I don't like to drive after dark."

"You drive good enough. You drove all the way home from Wheat City after dark, didn't you?"

"All right," she said. "I'll go right away."

After she'd gone, I went on sitting at the table for a few minutes, thinking or trying to; something tickling my mind. Something important. But the idea wouldn't come. I was too tired.

I don't know what time it was when she and Mrs. Whitcomb got back. I was already in bed and asleep.

Back in reform school, once, some big-shot lawyer talked to us at chapel, and he made the statement that nature hated a crime. "Nature abhors a crime," was the way he put it.

At the time, it struck me as being just some more of the grapefruit they were always squeezing out to us. It seemed to me that for a guy that had nature against him, he was doing pretty well. But now, twenty-five years later almost, I was beginning to see what he meant.

We'd planned everything perfectly. By all the laws of logic nothing could go wrong. And, yet—well, why say it?

On top of everything else I was afraid I was losing my nut.

I woke up early the next morning and tiptoed into the bathroom. I got a drink of water at the sink, and stood staring out the window. And there was the garage, just as big as day. Yeah, it was there. The old barn with the cupola that had been made over into a garage. I saw it just as I had seen it for ten years. I don't know. Maybe the eye holds images that don't go away, that don't ever really go away. Maybe the average guy is so stuck on himself that everything he sees becomes important, and he won't give it up, not to himself, until he's past seeing and past remembering.

I don't know.

All I know is that I almost let out a yell that they could have heard over in the next county.

I had to put my hand over my mouth to hold it back. I got back into bed, shivering, and finally dozed off again. But it wasn't good sleep. Not sound, I mean. I kept dreaming that Elizabeth was in the room with me. And it was like I was looking back or ahead on something that had happened.

She was climbing up on a chair to get something down from the ceiling—I don't know the hell what—and anyone could see that the chair was made out of straw and wasn't going to hold her up. But she kept climbing up on it and I'd run and catch her, and then she'd throw herself back in my arms and kiss me.

Then, there was a little guy that kept coming to the door and trying to get in. And there wasn't a damned bit of sense in her being afraid of him, because he was so damned little and funny-looking. But anyway he kept coming and I'd go to the door and tell him to get the hell out, and he'd beat it for a minute or two. And then I'd go back over to the bed and pull the covers off of Elizabeth, but instead of doing what I should have done I'd stand there and laugh. Because, dammit, I know it's crazy, but she'd turned into a statue. She had and she hadn't. We had to do it first or she would be, but if we didn't she was. And—

And then it was our wedding anniversary, it seemed like, and she was reminding me how, wherever we were, we'd promised that we'd always get together on our anniversary. And even dreaming, I knew it really was our anniversary, and I kind of remembered that we'd said that, that we'd promised like, I suppose, every couple does when they're first married.

She kneeled down at my side and put her hand on my forehead. She leaned forward and kissed me on the mouth.

And I woke up, and it was Carol.

"How are you feeling?" she whispered.

I blinked my eyes.

"All right," I said.

"Your fever seems to have broken."

"Yeah," I said, "I'm all right. Just weak."

"What would you like for breakfast?"

I told her just a little toast and coffee would do. "Better bring up some whisky, too. I'm chilling."

She was back in ten minutes or so with a tray. I sat up and made out like I was going to eat.

"You'd better run along, Carol. It won't look good for you to spend too much time up here."

"I—there's something I want to say to you, Joe."

"Well?"

"But I've got to know something first. I've got to know the truth. Do—do you really love me?"

"Oh, Jesus Christ!" I slammed down my coffee cup. "If you've got anything to tell me, spit it out! If you haven't, leave me alone for a while. We're not supposed to be together and I'm sick, and I've got a thousand and one things to think about. I'm sorry, but—"

"That's all right, Joe. I'm going."

"I do love you, Carol," I said. "You know that."

But she was already gone.

I took a bite or two from the toast, and put the rest in a bureau drawer under some shirts. I drank the coffee down halfway, and filled up the cup with whisky. After a second cup of the stuff, I felt pretty fair. I could have got up as well as not. But I stayed where I was. I wasn't ready to face people yet. Andy Taylor and Appleton and Happy Chance. Maybe I'd never be, but I sure wasn't now.

Around noon of the third day, right after I'd got through taking a bath, I heard a car coming up the lane from the road. I looked out the window to see who it was, but it was already up and in front of the house by then.

A minute or so later Carol tapped on the door, and I told her to come in.

"There's a man here to see you, Joe. He said to tell you it was Sol."

"Oh," I said. "Tell him to come up."

"Who is he, Joe? Is there—"

"Tell him to come up," I repeated.

She got that hard, stubborn look on her face like she used to get around Elizabeth. But finally she turned and went back downstairs, taking her time about it.

TWENTY-TWO

Sol Panzer looked more like a jockey than the owner of a ninety-house chain. He was maybe five feet tall, and he might have weighed a hundred and ten with his clothes wet. I guess he had something wrong with his vocal cords, because his voice matched up with the rest of him. It was thin and soft; not much more than a whisper.

If Carol tried to listen, and I figured she would, she wouldn't hear much.

He stood by the door a moment, looking at me out of the big horn-rimmed glasses he wore. Then he moved over to the bed like greased lightning, grabbed my hand and shook it, and dropped into a chair right in front of me.

"Joe," he said, speaking in his fast half-whisper. "I'm sorry to see you sick. I was sorry about Mrs. Wilmot. I hope you got our flowers. This is a nice place you have here."

"Thanks," I said. "Stick around and maybe you can buy it cheap."

"I'm sorry, Joe." He began to slow down. "It's nothing personal."

"That's all right. Have a drink."

"No, no. I never drink during business hours."

"If this is business," I said, "maybe we'd better get down to it."

"Cold turkey?"

"Without the stuffing."

"Well—a dollar and other valuable considerations."

"Remember me?" I said. "I own the place. How many valuable considerations?"

"Say, about five thousand."

I let out a grunt. "Five thousand wouldn't pay for my projectors and sound heads."

"Probably not, Joe."

"Then there's my chairs," I said. "Fifteen hundred of 'em with a factory list of eighteen seventy-five."

"You bought cheap. They'll run you twenty-two fifty, now."

"I've got a thousand yards of six-bucks-a-yard carpeting. I've got four grand in air conditioning. I've got—"

"Joe."

"Oh, all right," I said. "You don't want the stuff."

"I couldn't buy it if I did want it, Joe. I got friends in the theatrical supply line. Close friends, y'know. What would they think if I didn't patronize 'em? They'd be hurt, Joe. You know they would."

"Yeah," I said, "I guess they would."

I'd known how it was going to be. But I couldn't fight, and when a man can't fight the best thing he can do is stall.

"Well, Joe?"

"Well," I said. "Twenty-five grand isn't a bad price for the location. I'll take it."

"I don't speak very loud, Joe. Maybe you didn't hear me say five."

"Twenty."

"Five. But don't be afraid to beg, Joe. My way of refusing is very polite."

I took another drink and lighted a cigarette. I looked down at the floor, pretending to study. Stalling.

"I don't know, Sol," I said. "Doesn't it strike you that this is a pretty hard thing to do to a friend?"

"A friend, Joe?" He looked puzzled. "I hardly know you when I see you."

"Make it an enemy, then," I said. "You're obligated to come into this town. I don't know how much you're already in on the deal, but it must be plenty. You've got to come in, and I'm sitting on the spot you want."

"Yes, Joe?"

"Well, maybe you'd better take it from there."

He nodded and leaned back in his chair. "You got bills outstanding, Joe. You got insurance to pay, you got taxes to pay. You got a little bank loan, maybe two of 'em. Not much. None of it amounts to much—if you're running. But let your house go dark and see how big all them little things are. See how fast people start coming down on you. Then—"

"Oh, hell," I said. "I'm—"

"I'm not through, Joe. I could wait you out two-three months, but I won't have to. I'm going to crack down if you even look like you want to be stubborn. I'm going to get you for that marquee you swindled me on."

"You?" I said.

"Me. I was interested in that company. I still am. I started watching you when you beat me on that deal. I figured you were a man worth watching. I figured I could make a lot more by letting the five grand ride than cracking down on you. Funny, ain't it? If you'd played square with me I never would have started looking into Stoneville. I wouldn't have noticed the kind of business you were building up."

"Hell, Sol," I said, "you shouldn't hold a grudge over that. I didn't know it was your company."

His eyes closed for a second behind the big horn rims. "Joe," he said. Then he shook his head and sighed. "I don't hold any grudge, Joe. I'm just showing you what's going to happen if you try to hold me up. I'll sue you for that marquee; the actual price of it plus interest plus general losses due to having my product unjustly condemned. Do I make myself clear? I'm moving in. I'll either buy your lot or I'll take it."

"But five grand, Sol," I said. "That's no dough at all. You can do better than that. You know damned well you'll give the lot a book value of thirty or forty thousand."

"But it was my idea, Joe." He shrugged. "You can't expect to cash in on my ideas, can you?"

"What'll I do with my equipment? It's no good without a house to put it in."

"So I've heard. You gave your former competitor a hundred and fifty dollars for his stuff, didn't you?" He shrugged again, smiling out of the corner of his mouth. "Don't cry on me, Joe. On you tears don't look good. And don't stall me. That marquee deal ain't the only thing I've got on you. I can pile up stuff to the doors of the Barclay if I take a notion. You got the most remarkable record of chiseling I ever laid eyes on."

"I'm not trying to stall," I said. "I'm just trying to think. It seems like everything has come down on me at once. Being sick, and losing my wife, and now—"

"I know, Joe." His face softened a little. "But I'm not moving in tomorrow. You can run until the end of the season."

"You want an agreement to buy at the end of that time?"

"That's it."

"All right," I said. And I took the biggest, almost the biggest gamble I've ever taken in my life. "Give me your check for five thousand and we'll close the deal." If he'd taken me up on it, I'd have been washed up. But I had a pretty good idea he wouldn't, and he didn't. You see? Why should he have made a special trip out from the city to bully me into selling something he could take?

"If you want it that way, Joe," he said slowly. "But for your own good I'd advise you to hold off. You've got to run until the end of the season. Selling now would ruin your credit."

"It wouldn't help it any," I agreed. "But I supposed—"

"I just wanted to reach an understanding with you. I'm not afraid of your trying to sell to someone else. No one's going to buy a big show property without a lot of investigation. I can muff any deal you try to make."

"I know," I said. "That's the deal, then. Five grand at the end of the season for the lot. I keep everything else."

"Providing you move it."

"That's understood."

He stood up and held out his hand. "We'll let the option slide, then, as long as we understand each other."

"You're the doctor, Sol," I said.

I walked him to the door, closed it, and poured myself another drink. I swallowed it just as I started to laugh, and for a minute or two I thought I was going to strangle. When Carol came in I was staggering around, sputtering and laughing like a hyena with the whooping cough.

She slapped me on the back and got a drink of water down me. Finally I began to get my breath back.

"You're drunk, Joe," she frowned. "You shouldn't get drunk at a time like this."

"Baby," I said. "I was never more sober in my life.'

"Who was that man? What did he want?"

"That was Sol Panzer," I said. "Sol is the s-smartest—" I had to stop for a second, "showman in the business. He wanted to buy the Barclay."

"Oh?" She stiffened a little. "How much will he give you for it?"

"Nothing, baby. Nothing. And do you know why? Because he doesn't want it."

"But you just said—"

I didn't say anything for a minute. I just put my arms around her and squeezed until her breasts flattened against me, until the veins in them swelled and began to throb. Then I said, "Leave it to me, kid. Just a little longer. Leave it to me, and we'll pull out of this town with two hundred grand. Will you do that?"

I felt her nod, slow, unwilling. Eager.

"Yes, Joe. Yes!" she said. And: "Mrs. Whitcomb—she's taking a nap, Joe—"

Once, right at the last, like you will, you know, I looked into her face. Then, I closed my eyes and kept them closed.

TWENTY-THREE

Hap Chance called during the afternoon. I had Carol tell him I was sleeping. Andy Taylor called, too; and I had her tell him I'd see him that night. She called Appleton for me and made a date for dinner. She was curious, of course, but she didn't ask questions. I'd taken care of that for a while, at least.

I drove down to the hotel about six. Appleton was waiting for me in the lobby. We shook hands and found a table in the dining-room.

"Well, Joe," he said, looking me up and down, "your rest seems to have done you a lot of good."

"I needed one," I said. "I guess I've been going around in a daze ever since the accident. I got to the point where I couldn't go on any longer."

"That's the way it goes," he nodded, glancing at the menu. "By the way, what's this talk about you having a competitor in here?"

The glass of water I was holding almost slipped out of my hands.

"Where did you hear anything like that?"

"Oh, it wasn't anything definite. Just a rumor."

"There's a rumor for every inch of film in show business," I said. "Your statement was that there was talk going around. I want to know where it's coming from."

I could see that he didn't really know anything. There's always gossip in any good spot where one man has control. Someone will start talking about how much the showman must be making, and how there ought to be another show there. And, before you know it, the story gets twisted to where there is another house coming in.

"I've got a hundred-thousand-dollar investment here," I said. "If there's a rumor going around I want to know what there is to it, and who's spreading it."

"It wasn't anything, Joe. Just some wishful thinking, I guess. Let's forget it."

"I can't afford that kind of talk," I said.

For once he was on the defensive. "Let's forget it," he mumbled. "If I hear anything more, I'll put the damper on it."

He didn't have much to say during the meal. As soon as we had finished we went up to his room.

"Well, here we are, Joe," he said, grinning again. "The secret lair of Operator 31."

It was one of the sample rooms that salesmen use. Two of the big sample tables were fixed up for kind of a laboratory. He even had a little weight scale, and a centrifuge like they've got down to the creamery, only smaller. One of the tables was covered with stuff from the fire—little envelopes of ashes, pieces of wood, wire, and metal.

I looked away. There was a picture of a woman and a little boy on the dresser. The boy was about four, I imagine.

"Is that your boy?" I asked. "He looks a lot like you."

"That's him," he nodded. "Think he looks like me, huh? Not everyone can see the resemblance."

"Why, he's the spit and image," I said. "How old is he, about six?"

"Four. He wasn't quite four when that picture was taken."

"Well, he's certainly big for his age," I said. "I'd have taken him to be six, anyway."

Appleton nodded, his smile a mile wide. "Yes, sir, he's a real boy. You ought to see him out playing ball with me when I'm at home. He's the craziest kid about baseball I ever saw, and he can really play, too. I mean, Joe, he's got baseball sense. He—"

He kind of shook himself, and gave me a wink.

"Damn you, Joe!"

"What's the matter?"

"Let it go. What do you know that's new since I saw you last?"

"Nothing much. I don't know whether I told you last time that I'd talked with the county attorney. He's still confident that the fire was an accident."

Appleton wagged his head. "I'm inclined to agree with him, Joe. At any rate I'd probably say the same thing if I were a public servant."

"Now what do you mean by that?" I said.

"It's a public servant's job to serve the public, Joe. The living public."

"I guess that's a dirty crack," I said.

"Not at all. I'm not hinting that Mr. Clay is dishonest. He's in office. Mrs. Wilmot is dead. You're one of the city's most prominent citizens. Why should he go out of his way to prove something which, in all probability, didn't happen?"

"Well," I said, "I'm glad to hear you say that."

"You don't owe me a nickel, Joe."

"I got to thinking while I was sick," I said. "It seems like I must have made a chump of myself the first time I talked to you. Maybe the next time, too, but that time particularly."

"You're referring to what I said about the fire being incendiary?"

"That's it. I don't know why—"

"I'll tell you why. I didn't intend for it to register on you. I thought it was better for it to come over you gradually. Frankly, if you had gone around offering rewards for the murderer and evidence of your own innocence I'd have been exceedingly suspicious of you."

"Now, what am I supposed to say to that?" I said.

"Anything you like, Joe. The bars are down tonight. That's why I had you come up here."

"Okay. What do you think about things?"

"As I've said before, that it was an accident in all likelihood. Of course, you and Mrs. Wilmot didn't get along, but—"

"Who says we didn't?"

"You do. Everything about you says so. Everything I've learned about her says the same thing. But the fact that you were opposites doesn't mean that you would kill her. In fact, I'm confident that you loved her very much."

"Well, thanks," I said.

"It's none of my business, but would you mind telling me something? How did two people like you ever happen to get married?"

I laughed in spite of myself. It was such a hell of a crude thing to ask that instead of getting sore I felt sorry for him for doing it.

"I'll tell you why," I said, looking straight at him. "Every time she opened her mouth she put her foot in it. She was about to go on the rocks. I got sort of used to helping her out, and finally—well—"

"Mmm," he nodded. "That one, eh?"

"What do you mean?"

"Not a thing, Joe. Just thinking out loud. Mind if I ask another question?"

"Go right ahead."

"Well, this Farmer girl—Mrs. Wilmot strikes me as having been a well-educated, extremely fastidious person. How did she happen to take anyone like la Farmer into her home?"

It was something I'd always wondered about myself and I didn't need to fake looking puzzled.

"There you got me," I said. "Elizabeth was pretty tight about money, and I thought at first that she might be trying to get a little cheap household help. But she wasn't tight that way, you know. She wouldn't have done something that went against her grain to save dough."

"I see."

"Anyway, we didn't need any help. There was just the two of us and I always ate out most of the time. On top of that, Elizabeth had her own way of doing things and nothing else would suit. It was more trouble showing Carol how to do things than it would have been to do 'em herself."

"Perhaps she just felt sorry for the gal."

"She didn't show it much. If I hadn't—well, if I hadn't prodded her now and then, Carol would have been pretty hard up for spending money and clothes and everything else."

"Oh? Weren't you a little out of practice at that sort of thing—charitable enterprise, I mean?"

"I don't think I like that," I said. "I'm in a tough business. I don't think I've been any tougher than I've had to be."

"Want to call it an evening, Joe?"

"Not unless you do. Go ahead. I can take it."

"Well, I was going to say, if this Farmer girl was a baby doll the thing would be a lot more complicated—or simple. A little thing like murder doesn't stop a woman from getting a man she really wants—particularly if she thinks she's going to get to help him spend a sum like twenty-five thousand. But Farmer has nothing minus in my catalogue. I just can't picture you making a play for her."

"Thanks," I said.

"So the girl is out, and you're out on that angle. Of course, you get your wife's property in addition to the twenty-five grand. But for all practical purposes you already had the property, and you didn't need the money. Not bad enough to kill for it. You have a good income, a good business. You loved your wife. You weren't chasing a dame. If it wasn't for certain events in your early life—"

"So you've found out about that," I said. "That's a hell of a thing to do! Drag up something a man did when he was a kid, and smear him—"

He shook his head. "Keep your shirt on. We're not smearing anyone, and we didn't drag it up. You did. The company doesn't issue policies of this size without some investigation."

"Hell," I said. "I was fourteen years old; I didn't know my tail from straight up. I'd never been away from the orphanage before. I didn't know what a seal on a freight car meant. I just wanted to get out of the snow. Tampering with interstate commerce! Hell, did they think I was going to walk off with a sack of cement? That's all there was in the car."

"It was a bum rap, all right."

"Bum rap?" I laughed. "You're telling me! Seven years of sappings and kickings and doing work that would break a man's back. Seven years, from fourteen until I was twenty-one—'until I learned a proper regard for the property of others'! It's things like that—that—"

I broke off, remembering.

"Go ahead and say it, Joe," said Appleton. "It's things like that that makes criminals."

"Okay," I said, "you're doing the talking."

"Do I look like a criminal?" He leaned back grinning, his hands clasped behind his head.

"What's that got to do with it?"

"I was in, too. Exactly the same number of years that you were."

"The hell!" I said.

"That's right. Borrowed a car for a joy ride, and the cops caught me. My old man wasn't very fond of me anyhow, so I went right on over the road. No, things like that don't need to mean any more than we let 'em."

"But you said your company—"

"It's a fact they have to consider, certainly. It's tough, but that's the way it is." He sat brushing at his knee, looking down. "I'm sorry, Joe. I know pretty well how you feel. Can't you think of some logical explanation—some explanation that would be acceptable to the company—for the fire?"

"No, I can't."

"The motor was in good condition? There wasn't any possibility of a short?"

"Not a chance. If there had been any I'd have had it repaired."

"Sure. Naturally."

"It isn't the money so much," I said. "I'd just like to get things settled."

"Sure you would." He nodded sympathetically studying me. "I'll tell you something, Joe, if you'll keep your mouth shut. I've been stringing you along a little. I've recommended payment on this case. I'm just waiting to mail my report."

"Waiting?"

"Orders." He smiled out of the corner of his mouth. "You're running in hard luck, Joe. You remember that missing dame I told you about?"

"Yes."

"Well, there's the rub. I've got to turn her up, and as long as I'm here and it isn't costing them anything extra the company's having me keep your case open. At least they think they are. As far as I'm concerned it's already closed. As soon as I find this woman I'll put a date on the report and shoot it in."

"Well," I said, "that's something." I wished I had been outside so that I could have taken a deep breath. Or let out a yell. Just of pure relief.

I didn't care if I never got the money. I was going to have plenty without it.

We talked until midnight about show business, and the war, and things in general. Finally I figured it was time for me to go.

We shook hands. "Got any leads on the woman yet?" I said.

"Oh, one or two, Joe. I'm expecting a break in the case any minute."

"Well, luck to you," I said.

"And to you, Joe. And, Joe—"

"Yeah?" I said. He'd opened the door and I was standing halfway out in the hall.

"Do yourself a favor. Do a little deep thinking about some of the stuff we've discussed here tonight. It may make you feel bad for a time, but you'll profit by it in the long run. It'll make it a hell of a lot easier for you to get along with yourself."

"You're not telling me much," I said.

"It's something you'll have to see, Joe. Good night, and take it easy."

"I'll do that," I said.

TWENTY-FOUR

The front of the building was dark, but I could see a faint light in the back. I tapped on the window and rattled the doorknob. And in a couple of minutes Andy Taylor came shuffling around from behind the screen that separates his so-called office from his living-quarters.

I don't know whether he'd been in bed or not. He still had his clothes on, but I'd always had the idea he slept with them on most of the time.

"Kinda took your time about gettin' here, didn't you?" he said. "Come on in."

I followed him back to the rear of the building, and he put the coal-oil lamp he'd been carrying down on a packing-box. He didn't have any real furniture. Just a cot and some boxes and a little monkey stove. I sat down on the cot.

"So you decided to take me up," he said. "Well, well."

He moved a dirty pie plate and a coffee cup off of one of the boxes and sat down across from me. The light from the lamp made his beard seem redder than usual. He looked like the devil with a hat on.

"Not so fast," I said. "Take you up on what?"

"I don't know, Joe. I don't know."

"I got a burn on my hand," I said, "that's all. Anyone that works around electricity as much as I do is bound to get burned."

"Sure they are."

"Well?" I said.

"You were willing to cancel the lease on the Bower."

"I was willing to do that, anyway. I've been thinking for a long time that I hadn't treated you right on that lease."

"Yeah. I bet you did."

He rubbed his chin, looking straight into the flame from the lamp. For a minute I was afraid that I'd been too independent, that he wasn't going to walk into the trap.

Then he laughed, just with his mouth, and I knew everything was all right.

All he needed was a little steering.

"All right, Joe," he said. "I ain't got a thing on you. Not a thing. Why don't you just get up and walk out of here?"

"Okay," I said. "I will."

I got up slow, brushing at my clothes, and turned toward the door. He watched me, the grin on his wrinkled old face getting wider and wider.

"O' course," he said. "You know I'm going to tell Appleton about that burn."

"What for?" I said. "Why do you want to do that, Andy?"

"What do you care? As long as it don't mean nothing."

I shrugged and took a step toward the door. Then I let my face fall and I sank back down on the cot.

I heaved a sigh. "Okay, Andy. You win."

He nodded, his eyes puzzled. "Thought I would," he said. "Wonder why, though?"

I didn't say anything.

"That motor was in good condition. Elizabeth wouldn't have been foolin' around with it if it wasn't. Not Elizabeth."

"No," I said.

"And we know the fire wasn't set. There's proof positive of that."

"No," I said, "it wasn't set."

"And you were in the city when it happened."

"That's right. I was in the city."

"But there was something wrong, mighty wrong. So wrong that you're willin' to give me—how much are you willin' to give me, Joe?"

"What do you want?"

"Make me an offer."

"Well, I'm short of cash right now. But I could give you part of the money from the insurance."

"Not part, Joe. All."

"But, Jesus," I said. "All right, goddamit. All!"

He cackled and shook his head. "Huh-uh, Joe. I wouldn't touch that money. How would it look for me to plank twenty-five thousand in the bank after a deal like this? Huh-uh! I just wanted to get some idea of what it was worth to you for me to keep quiet. Some basis for tradin'."

"Well, now you've got it."

"Yeah, now I've got it. And you know what I'm goin' to do with it, Joe? Somethin' I've been wanting to do for years."

"Spit it out," I said. "For God's sake, you know I've got to come across. What is it you want?"

"Nothing more than what you owe me, Joe. I had a good thing once, and you ruined it for me. Now I'm handin' you back the ruins and takin' your good thing."

I looked blank. "What the hell are you driving at?"

"I'm makin' you a swap, Joe. I'm going to give you the Bower for the Barclay."

You know, it was a funny thing. It was what I'd expected and wanted. It was what I'd been edging him toward from the start. But now that he'd fallen for it I didn't have to pretend to be sore or surprised.

It burned me up just as much as when I'd heard about Panzer moving in. It's funny; maybe I can't explain. But that show—that show—

No, I can't explain.

I came to my senses after a minute, but I kept on cursing and arguing awhile to make it look good.

"That's not reasonable, Andy," I said. "The Barclay's a first-class house. The Bower's just a rattrap."

"It wasn't always a rattrap. Maybe you can build it back up again."

"Like hell. I see myself building the Bower up with the Barclay as competition."

"Oh, I ain't no hog, Joe. I won't shut you out. Probably wouldn't know how even if I wanted to."

"Why not do this, Andy," I said. "We'll be partners. I'll run the business, and we'll—"

He let out another cackle.

"Oh, no, we won't, Joe! I've had a little experience running things on shares with you. The first thing I knowed I'd be out in the cold."

"But how's it going to look," I said, "to make a trade like that? I ain't got any reputation for being crazy. People will know there's something screwy about the deal."

"Now, you're smarter'n that, Joe." He shook his head. "They won't

know a thing more'n we tell 'em—and I reckon neither you or I is
going to talk. We'll make it a trade, plus other valuable considerations.
Just like ninety-nine per cent of all real estate deals is made."

"But Appleton—"

"Appleton'll be gone from here when I take over. Like I said, Joe,
I ain't operatin' no kind of business with you. You go ahead and
operate the Barclay until the end of the season. I'll take it then."

"Andy, can't we—"

"Yes or no, Joe?"

"Oh, hell," I said. "Yes!"

He went up to the front and brought back some legal forms and
his rickety old typewriter, and we finished the business then and
there. We drew up a contract agreement to a transfer of deeds at the
end of the season, and he gave me a check for a dollar and I gave him
one, each carrying a notation as to what it was for.

That made the deal airtight, even without witnesses. There was no
way either of us could back out.

I offered to shake hands as I was leaving, but he didn't seem to
notice. I let it pass. He'd feel a lot less like shaking hands when the
end of the season came.

It was about one in the morning, now. I debated going home and
decided against it. It would save arguing and explaining, and, anyway,
there wasn't much time for sleep. I wanted to be in the city when the
business offices opened in the morning.

I went over to the show, got the clock out of the projection booth,
and set the alarm for two hours away. I sat down in one of the loges,
put the clock under the seat, and leaned back. The next thing I knew
I was back as far as my memory went.

With my mother, or the woman I guess was my mother. I was
living it all over again.

The big hand of the clock was pointing to twelve and the little one
to six, and she was coming up the stairs, slow—slowly—like she
always came; like she wasn't sure where the top was. Then a key
scratched against the lock, and finally it turned, and the door opened.
And she tottered over to the bed and lay down and began to snore.

She'd brought something in a sack with her, and she was half lying

on it, and I had to squeeze and tug to get it. It was a piece of jelly roll
and a hamburger, all squashed together, and I hogged it down. After
that I felt through her pockets until I found the crisp green pieces of
paper she always brought me; and I hid them in the bureau drawer
with the others.

Then it was morning, and she was gone again. I filled my tin cup
with cornflakes and canned milk, and ate it. And I played with the
green pieces of paper and looked out the window; and I ate a little
more of the cornflakes and milk.

The big hand of the clock pointed to twelve and the little one to
six. It pointed to them, and passed them. I laughed about it, holding
my hand over my mouth so no one would hear me.

I was still laughing when I went to sleep.

She was gone in the morning, but she was always gone in the
morning. I ate some of the cornflakes and milk, and played with the
green pieces of paper and looked out the window. And the big hand
of the clock pointed to twelve and the little one to six, and—and—

It was like a dream inside of a dream. I was chewing the wrapper
inside the cornflakes box, and the tip of my tongue was cut where I'd
tried to stick it through the little hole in the milk can, and the water
pitcher was red from my licking. I wasn't looking out the window
any more. I was on the bed. I had been on the bed for a very long
time, and the green pieces of paper were scattered all around me.

Then, and then, it was another room, and a big fat woman with
crossed eyes was holding me in her arms and rocking me.

"Mommy? Sure, now, an' we'll get you a whole raft of 'em! I'll be
your mommy meself."

"My money! I got to have my money!"

"An' ain't I the one to know it, now? Bring his bundle in, Mike—
That mess of whisky labels . . ."

The alarm clock went off, and I woke up. I went into the men's
lavatory and washed and headed for the city.

TWENTY-FIVE

Sol Panzer didn't make nearly as much fuss as you might have thought he would. He was on the spot and we both knew it, and he wasn't the kind to cry.

I was in his office at nine. By eleven, it was all over and I was on my way home.

I got into Stoneville about dusk, stopped at the show and ran up to the booth. Hap wasn't there. Jimmie Nedry was running the machines.

"How's it going, Jimmie?" I said. "Giving Mr Chance a relief?"

"I guess so," he said, not looking at me.

"How soon will he be back, do you know?"

"He ain't coming back," Jimmie said. "He's taking the night off."

"Oh," I said. "Well, I appreciate your working for him, Jimmie."

"Don't mention it."

He got kind of red in the face and moved over between the projectors. I could understand his being embarrassed. Unless he was a lot dumber than I thought he was, he probably knew that I knew what he'd been up to.

I told him good night, just like we were the best pals in the world, and drove over to Hap's hotel. He wasn't there, either. I went on home.

There was a big new black coupé standing in the yard. Hap's, of course. I was plenty glad I'd swung that deal with Panzer. Hap had finished waiting.

He was flopped down on the living-room lounge, a glass and a bottle of whisky at his side; and he had his shoes up on one of Elizabeth's crocheted pillows. The ash tray was full and running over. There was a big circle of ashes and butts on the carpet.

I looked at the mess, and then looked at him. He sat up slowly, grinning.

"Well, laddie," he said. "I get the impression that you've pulled a plum from the pudding—or, shall we say, a phoenix from the fire? Have a drink and tell me about it."

I forced a smile. "Sure, Hap. Where's Carol?"

"In her chambers, I believe. She doesn't seem to be frightfully keen for my company."

"I wonder why?" I said.

I went into the kitchen and brought back a glass and an old newspaper. I spread the paper under the ash tray and set the bottle on it after I'd poured our drinks.

"Clever," Hap nodded. "Too bad you're not married. But give me the news, laddie, I'm all ears."

"You want it right from the beginning?"

"Oh, absolutely."

"Well, right from the start," I said, "I heard that Sol wanted my lot. As soon as I learned that he was moving in, I heard that he was going to take me over. At the exchanges. From you. Everywhere I went. Then, yesterday, just to clinch matters, he drove out here to see me and offered five grand for the lot. He told me he'd give me five to clear out at the end of the season, or I could be stubborn and he'd run me out."

I paused to sip my drink. Hap began to frown.

"He can do it, laddie. Little Sol can take your shirt and charge you interest for wearing it."

"Sure he could."

"So this is the old build-up, eh? The easy letdown. All you've got is a measly five grand."

"Nothing like it," I said. "I didn't sell. Sol doesn't want my lot."

"You said he offered you five yards for it?"

"That's right."

"But he doesn't want it?"

"Of course, he doesn't."

Chance leaned back on the lounge again. He tapped his forehead. "Feeble, laddie. Humor me."

"What would Panzer want with my lot?"

"What would he want with it? Well, fantastic as the idea seems I suppose he'd erect a house on it. There's nothing like the site of an old show for a new one. People are used to the location, and—"

"And," I said, "it's one hundred and three feet from the sidewalk to the alley. No matter how you work it, you can't get much more than a ninety-foot shot from the projection booth to the screen."

Hap blinked. "Lord lummie!" he whispered. "Comes the dawn—

But wait a minute! Maybe he intends to pitch his floor in reverse and put the projectors below the screen."

"That still wouldn't give him enough room. Not for a million bucks' worth of house. A million that's got to look like two million."

"But, laddie"—Hap waved his hands—"it's fantastic!"

"Call it anything you want, that's the way it is. There's width and to spare, but not depth. You see how it was, Hap? Sol was using the old magician's trick of misdirection. When I was told that he wanted my lot, over and over, I and everyone else assumed that he did. It never occurred to me to question the fact. Or if I had any idea that it was a little screwy, I brushed it aside. Sol knew what he was doing. He had to know.

"But he got a little too anxious. Too anxious in one way and not enough in another. When he thought that I was convinced, when he believed I was ready to take the five grand, he agreed to let the deal hang fire. I knew, then, that he didn't want my lot. He was misdirecting me. He was doing it because he didn't have the lot sewed up that he did want."

"Careless. I can't believe it of Sol."

"Careless, nothing. Where would he be most likely to tip his hand that he was coming into Stoneville? Why, when he bought his lot. So he was saving that until the last, until he was ready to jump."

"I still say it was careless. Suppose someone jumped in ahead of him—like, I gather, you've done?'

"No one could. What he wanted was the Bower lot, and I had the place leased. I was playing shutout with it. As soon as I went broke, of course, I'd give up my lease and Sol could buy."

Hap shook his head. "Marvelous, laddie. Positively brilliant. And that's the only place in town that Sol could move in on?"

"The only one. That's the only block without an alley; the lots run straight on through. The Bower lot is kind of bottle-shaped. It squares off and spreads out after a few feet."

"And there's no other lot in that block?"

"Two—but the bank and the hotel are sitting on them."

"Terrific! One more question, old bean. How did you happen to acquire this juicy bit of real estate?"

"You know, Hap. I traded something for it that's going to be worthless."

"Uh-hah, your show. That's what I supposed. But there's one little point I'm not quite clear on. Our friend Taylor doesn't know that your house is going to be worthless. He regards it as a little gold mine. Why wasn't he suspicious when you swapped it for his prize white elephant?"

I'd stepped into one again; he knew now that I was walking a pretty ragged rope.

He laughed softly.

"This is much better than I thought, laddie—or worse. Y'know, I think I'll raise my sights on you. I really think I shall."

"What's the Taylor deal got to do with you?" I said. "You don't know anything, Hap."

"Haven't I said so all along? I know enough to sound the alarm. The firemen, speaking metaphorically, will do the rest." He tapped a yawn back with his hand. "Odd how this subject of fires keeps cropping up, isn't it?"

"What do you want?"

"Well, what kind of holdup are you pulling on little Solly? Honor bright, now. I'd be very hurt to catch you in a falsehood."

"I've got a check for fifty grand in my pocket."

"Uh-hah. A very neat evasion. Perhaps I'd better ask Sol about it and explain my interest in the matter."

"I get a hundred and fifty more," I said, "when he moves in."

"You see?" Hap shrugged. "You can tell the truth when you have to." He sat up and reached for the whisky bottle. "Shall we drink on it—partner?"

"Yeah," I said.

"Partner?"

"Partner," I said.

He poured us a drink and we touched glasses; and I couldn't help thinking how nice it would be to drop a little arsenic in his. Then, I saw a shadow in the hall and I knew Carol was listening, and I thought—Well, never mind. Sometimes you get an idea in your head, and it's pretty hard to get it out.

Hap swished the liquor around in his glass, studying me. "Y'know," he said, "you're really a very lucky man, Joe."

"Sure," I said. "Sure, I am."

"Oh, but you are. If I hadn't become interested in the success of your little plan—which necessarily involves your own safety—I probably would have stood aside and let Fate take her course with you. A very unpleasant course."

"Now what?" I said. "What are you trying to pull now?"

"Take yourself back to the morn of the tragedy, old man. You stop by the show and visit the projection booth, and, lo and behold, you discover that your supply of photoelectric cells is exhausted. It comes as a complete surprise to you. You hadn't planned on going to the city, but now you must. *Ergo*, you provide yourself with an alibi for being out of town."

"Well?"

"But you had your suitcase in your car. Jimmie Nedry saw it when he passed by on his way to work. So you must have planned on going to the city before you ever noticed the alleged absence of those cells."

"So what?" I said. "Maybe I was—"

"—taking some clothes to the cleaners? Not good enough, laddie. That could be checked on. And that isn't the clincher, at any rate. It wasn't the first time you'd hopped Jimmie about missing equipment; and he'd taken certain precautions. He's ready to swear that the cells you supposedly bought in town bore the same serial numbers as those that were missing from the show. In other words, old chap, your alibi is a phony."

"He—he told you all this?"

"Mmm. Got quite fond of me, did Nedry. And in the morning, when Blair swings his transfer, he's going to tell him."

He grinned at me over his glass, and I began to see red. What the hell! This was my deal. I'd taken the risk and done all the thinking, and here was another guy with his hand out!

"Let the little bastard talk," I said. "Let him go to hell. He's lying! He got the numbers of those cells wrong. He—"

"Huh-ah. But even if he had it wouldn't make any difference. You still couldn't afford to have him tell that story."

"He can tell anything he pleases! By God, I'm—"

Hap's hand shot out. He caught his fingers in my collar and jerked and twisted.

For a minute I thought my neck was broken.

"That's how a rope feels, laddie. Just a little like that. But don't fret. If you crumb this deal, I'll settle with you myself."

My throat felt like I'd swallowed a cantaloupe. "How—h-how much do you think—"

"Nothing. Not a red."

"Nothing?"

"No money. It wouldn't do any good. Your projectionist has one of the most alarming cases of honesty I've ever seen. He's even conscience-stricken at having used his information to pry a better job out of Blair."

"But he hasn't told him yet?"

"He hasn't. And he won't."

"I see," I said. And he nodded and looked at his wrist watch.

"Well, I really must be shoving along. I told them at the hotel that I'd be checking out tonight. Told several people, in fact. Must be getting back to the city."

"I hate to see you leave," I said.

"It's trying, isn't it? But the best of friends, you know, and all that rot—Oh yes—"

"Yeah?"

"It's terribly lonely when friend Nedry gets off work. Been thinking it might be awfully awkward for you if he should be slugged by footpads or some such thing. Perhaps you'd best be at home here around eleven-thirty. Miss Farmer can alibi for you."

"Okay, Hap," I said.

"On second thought, I incline to the belief that some doubt might be cast on the Farmer veracity. Call your telephone operator at eleven-thirty. Ask her the time. They still give it here, don't they?"

"Yes."

"Cheerio, then."

"Cheer—so long," I said.

TWENTY-SIX

There was a chocolate cake in the refrigerator and part of a baked ham. But I passed them up and opened a can of soup. I wasn't particularly hungry, and I'd been eating too much recently. Just this morning I'd noticed that I was getting a little paunchy.

I heard Carol come through the door, and I could feel her standing behind me. I went on eating and pretty soon she walked around into my line of vision. And it was all I could do not to burst out laughing.

She had a new kind of hairdo, and a plain black dress, and she was trying to stick her nose in the air and hold her chin down at the same time. Sure, Elizabeth. Or Carol's idea of Elizabeth.

I ducked my head over my soup.

"You look mighty pretty, Carol," I said, as soon as I could say anything.

"Do you like me better this way?"

I wasn't sure of the answer to that one. "You always look good to me. How about some soup?"

"I've already ate—eaten."

"Coffee?"

"No. You go ahead."

I went ahead, taking my time about it, doing some thinking. This was the second or third time she'd listened in on my conversations. She was nervous and scared, of course, but, hell, I was a little uneasy myself, and I didn't pop out at her every time she opened a door.

I wondered if it was always going to be like this. I wondered if I could never go any place or do anything without having her breathing down my neck.

Without worrying about her getting worried.

I shoved my plate back and lighted a cigarette. "I guess you know," I said, "that there's been some trouble."

She nodded. "Yes. I know now."

"I'm glad you heard," I said. "I intended to tell you as soon as I could see my way out. Didn't want to worry you unless I had to."

"You—you weren't afraid to tell me, Joe?"

"Now, why do you say a thing like that?"

"I—I couldn't stand it if you were afraid of me, Joe! I know how you feel—how you got to feel. I'm different now! When you kill someone it changes you. But—"

"I was afraid," I said, "but not that way. You'd stuck your neck out. It looked like it might not get you anything. You might have thought that we—I—had known it wouldn't get you anything. That I'd put you on a spot, and was going to walk off and leave you."

"And try to go to Elizabeth?" she snapped.

"You see?" I said. "Now get that idea out of your head, Carol. I had Elizabeth and I didn't want her. She had me, and she didn't want me. I figure she brought you here with the idea that I'd fall for you."

"Oh, no, she didn't!"

"She had some reason for doing it, and it sure wasn't charity."

"She wanted me around to make herself look good! I'm a woman myself and I know. That's why I hated her so much! Don't you suppose if she'd wanted to get rid of you she'd have got someone that didn't look like—like—"

"Carol," I said, and I got up and put my arm around her and gave her a hug.

The dame *was* nuts if she thought that about Elizabeth. Elizabeth didn't need anyone around to make her look good.

"Well, it's the truth," Carol said.

"No, it's not," I said, leading her into the living-room. "And you're getting yourself all upset over nothing. All that matters is that we'll be in the clear after tonight, and we'll have plenty of money. Let's not spoil it."

"Promise you won't try to see her, Joe."

"Of course, I won't," I said. "Do you think I'd run a risk like that?"

"You'll give me her—the money and let me send it to her?"

"I told you I would. Now forget it."

She wiped her eyes and smiled, sort of trembly; and I fixed us a drink. I thought for a minute the arguments and explanations were over, but of course they weren't.

I was beginning to see that they weren't ever going to be over. I wondered how Elizabeth felt about it all now.

"How long will it be before everything is settled, Joe?"

"Two or three months, anyway."

"Can I stay here until—"

"No," I said. "You know you can't, Carol."

"Just until that insurance man leaves, Joe! Just let me stay that long. He—he scares me. I don't want to be away from you as long as he's around."

"Well," I said, "we'll see."

I meant to get her out of the house in the next day or two if I had to pitch her out a window.

Rain began to patter on the roof. It started in easy, and got harder and harder. Inside of a half hour it was a regular downpour. There was a hell of a crash of lightning somewhere near by, and Carol shuddered and snuggled close to me. I reached back to the wall and turned on the furnace.

"Joe."

"Yeah," I said.

"It's kind of nice being this way, ain't—isn't it? Being able to do just what we please around the house."

"I'll say."

"Elizabeth would say it was too early for the furnace."

"Yeah, she sure would." It sounded pretty half-hearted, so I had to say something else. "If you wanted to see someone that was really tight you should have seen her old lady. We cleaned out her room after she died, and she had darned near a whole closet full of dry bread—just scraps, you know."

Carol snickered. "She must have been crazy."

"I guess she was along toward the last. You could hardly blame her, though, with a husband that spent all his life writing a history of the county."

"What'd he do that for?"

"God knows," I said.

Carol snuggled closer. The room began to get warm. The wind rose and fell, throwing the rain against the roof in long steady swishes; and she seemed to breathe in time with it.

My knees began to ache from her weight, but I didn't move. I didn't want to talk any more about Elizabeth or her folks or anything. Everything was all right now. I'd told her about a hundred times that

I loved her and didn't love Elizabeth. A man can't spend his life hashing over the past.

I dozed for a few minutes, what seemed like a few minutes. When I woke up, the clock had just finished striking.

I jerked out my watch. Eleven-thirty. I shoved Carol off of me, waking her up, and stumbled out to the hall. My legs had gone to sleep and I could hardly walk.

The phone rang just as I was gripping the receiver.

I answered it automatically.

"Joe?"

"Yes."

"I've got to talk with you, Joe. How soon can you come down?"

"Why," I said, "what's wrong?"

"I'm at my office. You'll be right down?"

"Well—It's kind of a bad night."

No answer.

"Well, sure," I said. "I'll be right down."

I hung up.

Carol was still sitting on the lounge, her face whiter than anything I ever hope or want to see. Her lips moved, but no sound came out of them.

"Web Clay," I said; and, as if she didn't know: "Our county attorney."

TWENTY-SEVEN

She swallowed a couple of times and finally found her voice.

"W-what does he want?"

"I don't know."

"Mr. Chance?"

"Goddamn'," I said. "I told you I didn't know!"

Hap wasn't supposed to call; he was going right on into the city. But I didn't think it could be about him. Hap was too smooth an operator to be taken in by any of the Stoneville clowns. If there'd been a chance of being caught he wouldn't have taken it.

But even if they had got him, what could he say? What could Jimmie Nedry say, for that matter? Enough to start the ball rolling, sure, but the ball hadn't had time to roll yet. Even Web Clay wasn't dumb enough to tip his hand to me until he had a lot more to go on than he would have.

I went over to the hall tree and took down my hat and coat. And . . .

And she didn't say anything and I didn't hear her move. But her hand went past mine and grabbed her coat.

I jumped, startled. Before I knew what I was doing, I whirled and slammed her against the wall. It hurt her. It hurt and I was damned glad of it.

She bounced forward, trying to dodge around me; and I caught her by the wrists and we struggled. And then we stopped, posed like a couple of wrestlers in a picture. Ashamed. Scared stiff.

"Sorry if I hurt you, baby," I said. "You kind of startled me."

"It's all right, Joe." She tried to smile back at me. "I just want to go with you."

"You know you can't. How would it look, Carol?"

"I've got to, Joe!"

"You can't!"

"No one knows there's anything between—"

"You're damned right they don't," I said, "and they're not going to, either. What would you be doing up at this time of night? Why would you be traipsing along with me?"

"You don't understand, Joe. I—I—"

"I understand all right," I said. "You're afraid I'll spill something. You want to get in on the ground floor when the talking starts."

It was a bad break but I couldn't hold it back. I'd held myself in as long as I could. Anyway, she might as well know that I was onto her. We knew where we stood now.

"Do—do you really think that, Joe?"

"What do you expect me to think? You're certainly not worried about me chasing off after Elizabeth."

"No. I'm not worried about that."

"Spit it out, then, if you've got anything to say."

"You'd better go on, Joe."

"You'll stay here?"

"Where else would I go? Yes, I'll stay here."

I shrugged on my coat and pushed past her. She spoke again, just as I was opening the door.

"Joe—"

"Now what?"

"I just wanted to tell you, Joe. Everything's going to be all right. You don't have anything to be afraid of."

"Not any more than you have," I said. "Not as much. Don't forget it."

I got the car started, and went slipping and skidding down the lane to the highway. At the intersection I jerked the wheel toward the right, toward town. I had to jerk it. Something had almost made me turn the other way.

People in Stoneville go to bed pretty early, even when there isn't a storm to keep them off the streets. I toured around a dozen blocks without passing anyone or without seeing any lights except those in the courthouse. There were a few cars parked out, but none of them was Hap's. I began to breathe easier. He must have done the job and got away.

There was just one way to make sure, of course. That was to drive by Jimmie Nedry's house and see if he was there. But I didn't have any reason for doing that, any excuse I mean, and there wasn't time.

It was almost a half hour, now, since Web had called me. Regardless of what had happened, he'd start wondering if I didn't show up soon.

I drove back to the courthouse, parked, and ran up the walk to the building. I went up the stairs and down the hall, not hurrying but not taking my time, either, just businesslike. I put the right kind of expression on my face—puzzled and a little put out—and then I opened Web's door and went in.

Web was sitting behind his desk, looking about as uncomfortable as I felt. Sheriff Rufe Waters was standing, leaning against the wall. He acted like he didn't want any part of what was going on.

I sat down in front of Web, slapped the rain from my hat, and waited. He made a job of clearing his throat.

"Well, Joe," he said at last. "I suppose you're wondering why I asked you to come down here."

"You can't blame me for that," I said.

Rufe laughed and muttered something under his breath, and Web gave him an angry look.

"Rufe thinks I'm playing the fool," he said. "But I'm running this office, and I've got to do what I think is best. I wouldn't have had you come down here, Joe, if I hadn't figured I had to."

"So?" I said.

"Well, I just wanted to know, Joe—I wondered if you thought, perhaps—"

Rufe Waters laughed again.

"I'll tell you, Joe. He thinks it wasn't Mrs. Wilmot that got killed in the fire."

TWENTY-EIGHT

I tried to keep from jumping. Then I remembered that I should, that anyone would be startled by a statement of that kind; and I gave a good healthy start.

I leaned forward, frowning, interested.

"Web must have some reason for thinking that," I said. "What is it, Web?"

He wiped his face, relieved that I wasn't sore. "Has Appleton said anything to you about a woman he was looking for? A woman that came out here on the day of the fire and disappeared?"

"Why, yes," I said, "I believe he did make some mention of it."

"Well, that's it. He prowled the town from one end to the other looking for her, and then he called us in and we checked with everyone that hires household help. Everyone but you, and, of course, Elizabeth."

"Yes," I said. "Go on, Web."

"Well, Joe, we figure—Appleton and I figure—that that woman must have gone to your place."

"She didn't," I said. "Elizabeth didn't say anything about hiring anyone."

"But that doesn't mean she didn't do it!" Web laughed apologetically. "No offence. I just mean she wouldn't have been a Barclay if she hadn't been a wee bit highhanded. All the Barclays were."

"You're right about that," I said. "But—"

"You were in the city, Joe. You didn't go home after you left in the morning. So the woman could have been there, and you wouldn't have known a thing about it."

I shook my head, stalling; waiting to be convinced. I could see where the conversation was leading, but there wasn't anything to do but follow it. It was a crazy way for things to turn out, to be tripped up by a dame that didn't belong in the plot at all. But there it was.

And I couldn't help Carol. All I could do was save myself.

"I don't think Elizabeth would have done that," I said. "But give me the rest of it."

"Here's the way we see it," said Web. "Mrs. Wilmot put an ad in one of the city papers and hired this woman. She hired her, and the Farmer girl didn't know about it until Mrs. Wilmot picked her up that night in Wheat City. Probably Elizabeth was a little bit curt, and Carol got sore. You couldn't blame her much. Here she was coming back from a vacation with all her money spent more'n likely, and she finds herself out of a job.

"It's thirty miles from here to Wheat City. We figure that somewhere between here and there, Elizabeth was killed and her body hid. We figure that Carol drove on home by herself, killed the other woman to keep from giving her play away, and then put her in the garage and set it on fire."

"I—I can't believe that Carol would do anything like that, Web."

"Oh, she could have." Rufe Waters spoke up. "All them Farmers are a dead-hard lot. I wouldn't put a killin' or two past any member of that family. But the rest of it's all bunk. I mean about this other woman, and all."

Web glared at him. "What's bunk about it? It all fits in, don't it?"

"I ain't going to argue," said Rufe. "I'll go along with you so far as to say that the girl might have had an argument with Mrs. Wilmot and killed her, but that's as far as I will go."

"I can't believe it," I said again. "Carol and Elizabeth got along fine—at least, while I was around."

"Well," drawled Web, "what getting-along is to a man isn't the same as it is to a woman. A man doesn't really know when womenfolks are at outs and when they're not."

"But if Elizabeth hadn't wanted her around—"

"—she'd have fired her," said Web. "And I'm claiming that's just what she did do! She went right ahead without asking or telling anyone and canned her."

Rufe scratched his head thoughtfully. Web had made a point with him.

"It's a little too pat," I said. "Carol had been with us for almost a year. If Elizabeth had wanted to fire her, it looks like she'd have done it long ago."

"Maybe the trouble just came up lately. Maybe Elizabeth couldn't find anyone to take her place. Maybe she was waiting until Carol was out of town. That's common sense, isn't it?"

"Well," I hesitated, "it sounds reasonable."

"I tell you, Joe; it just had to be something like that. The more you think about, the more you see I'm right. I'm not saying that the girl just hauled off and deliberately started killing. Probably it was kind of an accident to begin with. She was mad. She flung out at Elizabeth and killed her before she knew what she was doing. Then she had to go on and do the rest to protect herself."

He stared at me, waiting, and I nodded my head a couple of times. "I don't know, Web. The way you put it—'

"It's a cinch that fire didn't start itself," said Rufe Waters.

"No, it didn't," said Web. "The girl had to do it, Joe. She was the only one that could have."

I could have said, "How can you be so damned sure that the woman stayed here? How do you know she's not in some other burg right now, throwing herself a whing-ding?"

But what I said was, "Maybe you're right."

"It's not just my idea," Web went on. "This insurance fellow, Appleton, really thought of it. Didn't he ask you anything about how things stood between Carol and Mrs. Wilmot?"

"Yes, he did."

"Well, he—we hadn't really started putting two and two together, then. We thought it was just a matter of a little work to turn this missing woman up. When we couldn't find her he started putting two and two together, and we figured it like I just told you. He heard from his company tonight, and they think he's on the right track. They're willing to back him up in anything he does. That's why I got you down here."

"I see," I said.

"Appleton's going to ask that the bod—that the remains be exhumed and examined in the morning. He's going to demand a *real* post mortem. If it don't show it was Elizabeth that was killed in the fire, he's going to put a murder charge against Carol Farmer. I don't like to have him running things on me like that. I figure if there's any murders to be solved we people here in the county ought to solve 'em ourselves."

"Especially with election coming up," nodded Rufe.

"That's got nothing to do with it!" Web glared at him. "Now, here's what I thought we'd better do, Joe. There's no use in Rufe or me trying to talk to that girl. She'd just freeze up on us, like the rest of that ornery Farmer gang. So I want you to talk to her. Tell her—"

"*Me* talk to her?" I said.

"Yes, you, Joe."

"Well, gosh," I said. "I—"

"You know how to gentle people along, get on the best side of 'em. You can get her to talk when no one else could get to first base. You know. Sympathize with her, but show her she hasn't got a chance to beat the case. I know it's asking a lot, but—"

"I don't think it is." I looked from Web to Rufe, jutting my jaw out. "If things are like you think they are, it's my duty to help to get to the bottom of 'em!"

"I knew you'd see it that way, Joe."

"The only reason I'd hesitate at all is because of the possibility that I might gum things up. If the girl is guilty, I want to be sure she pays the penalty. What'll I do if she tries to skip out, or—"

"Just a minute," said Rufe.

He crossed the room, opened the connecting door to his offices, and went inside. He came back with a Colt automatic in his hand.

He twirled it, caught it by the barrel, and handed it to me butt first.

"You take that, Joe."

"Well," I said, shying away. "I don't know as *that's* necessary."

"Take it, Joe," said Web. "That girl may have a gun herself for all you or we know. She might come at you with a knife. She might try to knock you out with a club and make a run for it. You can't take any chances. You take the gun, and if you have to use it, don't hesitate."

I held back a few minutes longer. But finally they talked me into taking it.

TWENTY-NINE

Driving home in the rain, with my guts kind of knotting and unknotting, I thought about Elizabeth and how goddam unfair it was that I had to do all the dirty work on a deal she'd really started.

I hadn't hired Carol. I never would have brought her into the house. Maybe I wasn't too satisfied with married life, but it never occurred to me to do anything about it. It was Elizabeth who had brought her in. It was just one more stupid thing she'd done that I had to be the fall guy for.

About a year after she'd had her miscarriage I went home one afternoon and some dame was in the living-room with Elizabeth. I stuck my head in the door to say hello, and she and this woman both looked kind of embarrassed. And then Elizabeth laughed and told me to come in.

"This is Mrs. Fahrney, Joe," she said. "Mrs. Fahrney is connected with the children's protective society."

"Oh?" I said, wondering if she had a kick on some of the shows I'd been playing. "That must be very interesting work."

"Well—it is," said the dame, glancing at Elizabeth.

And Elizabeth laughed again.

"We may as well tell him," she said. "He'll have to sign the papers, anyway."

"The papers?" I said.

"I was keeping it for a surprise, dear. We're going to have a son. The sweetest little boy baby you ever—"

"Wait a minute," I said. "You mean you want to adopt someone else's kid?"

"Not someone else's, Joe. Ours. Perhaps I should have told you sooner, but—"

"I guess you should have, too," I said. "I guess you might have saved this lady a trip out here if you had. Any time I have any kids of my own I guarantee I'll feed 'em and take care of 'em and do everything else I'm supposed to. But I'm not spending my dough and my time on other people's brats. I don't want any part of 'em."

Elizabeth sat biting her lip, looking down at the floor. This woman got up and walked over to her.

"I'm sorry, Mrs. Wilmot," she said. "I'll run along now."

"Oh, wait a minute," I said. "I didn't mean all that. If she wants to adopt this—boy, it's all right with me."

"But it isn't all right with me," she said, looking straight through me. "Good-by, Mrs. Wilmot."

And she sailed out the door without giving me a chance to reason with her.

I tried to explain to Elizabeth how I felt. A kid is always a hell of a big expense and we just couldn't spare the dough from the show. And, anyway, how could you tell what you were getting into when you take a kid out of an orphans' home?

All Elizabeth would say was, "I understand," and she didn't understand at all.

Well, no one can say I'm not human, and I was kind of ashamed of the way I'd acted. I suppose she did get lonesome around the place by herself, and when she got a cat I didn't say a word. I don't like cats. They demand too much attention. If you're trying to read or eat or no matter what you're trying to do a cat will butt right in on you. Short of killing them, there's no way of keeping them from rubbing against your legs or jumping into your lap or just bothering you in general.

I didn't say a word, though. When it got to where it bothered me too much I'd just go to my room and lock the door.

I guess it finally got on Elizabeth's nerves, too, because she gave it away to someone. I never asked who and she didn't say. I was just satisfied that it was gone.

About six months later she bought a dog—a tan-and-white collie pup. And I didn't say anything about that, either, but I never knew a minute's comfort at home until she got rid of it. I can't stand dogs. I mean, I can't. And if you'd been on the bum as much as I have, you'd know why.

Well, so that brings us up to Carol. And I know what you're thinking—it's what I thought at first—but it's not the case. She didn't take Carol as a substitute for the cat or dog. She didn't treat her half as good as she'd treated either one of them.

I've already told you how she didn't even give her a decent feed the first night she was there. That's just a sample of the way she acted toward her. And it didn't get me anywhere when I jumped her about it.

"Really, Joe, you amaze me," she said, sort of smiling down her nose. "How can you possibly be interested in the welfare of a girl like that? I'm already willing to admit it was a mistake to bring her here."

"Well, she's here," I said, "and she's going to stay. And we're going to treat her decent, too."

"Are we? '

"All right, don't, then," I said. "But if you won't do anything for her yourself, don't stand in my way."

"I won't," she said, still smiling. "That's a promise. I won't stand in your way at all." And that was the way it ended.

All that was ever done for Carol was done by me. I hadn't lied to Appleton about that. But it was Elizabeth that brought her into the house in the first place. I don't know why, unless it was just another one of her ways of getting my goat, and I don't know that it matters.

All I know is that Carol coming there is what started all the trouble, and that it was left to me to clean it up.

There was one thing that still puzzled me and always had—the money. The way Elizabeth had argued about a split. The way she'd kept telling me I'd be sorry if I tried to get out of sending her the insurance dough.

The people who really care about money are those who lack

something without it, and Elizabeth had always felt just as complete and respectable and important without a dollar as she had with a pocketful. She'd been saving and thrifty, sure, but that was more habit than anything else. She'd proved a hundred times over that money didn't mean a thing to her.

When she'd first begun to make an issue of it I thought she was just trying to put a spoke in my wheel, to make it harder to settle the problem between her and Carol and me. And right up until the last, I guess, I was expecting her to say, "All right, have your Carol and everything else. I'd scrub floors before I'd take a penny from you."

That would have been Elizabeth's way of doing things, and maybe I would have taken her up on it and maybe I wouldn't have. The point is that she did just the opposite—something that just didn't fit in with her character. And now when it mattered least of all, I couldn't get it out of my mind.

I remembered how insistent Carol had been on sending Elizabeth the money herself, and the answer to that one popped into my head and made me shiver. She hadn't intended sending it. She'd have burned it up first. She hated her enough to do that, to risk getting us all in trouble just to take one final punch at Elizabeth.

It had to be the answer, because I never wrote even a business letter if I could get out of it and I sure wouldn't have written Elizabeth after we were all washed up. It was a standing joke around the house, my not writing to anyone. At least it had been a joke back in the beginning, back during the first year that Elizabeth and I were married.

We were awfully cramped for dough that year. We had good prospects and I knew we'd pull out in the long run, but I was trying to do too many things at once and we ran short. It got so bad that I even considered closing down for a while and going back to driving film truck. But right at the time when things looked darkest this old uncle of Elizabeth's died back East, and everything was jake. He left her twenty-five hundred dollars, enough to clear up the mortgage on the Barclay home with a thousand left over.

Well, I took her down to the train when she started back to collect, and while we were waiting on the platform she asked me to send her a dollar.

"Send you a dollar?" I laughed. "What's the idea? Here, I'll give you—"

"No, I want you to send it to me, Joe. I know that's the only way I'll hear from you."

"Oh, now," I said. "I don't think I'm that bad. I'll drop you a card."

"Oh, but you are that bad," she said. "Send me the dollar or you'll be sorry when I come back."

She was kidding, you know, like newly married people will. But I thought if it meant that much to her I'd play along. And that was the cause of two of the worst weeks I've ever spent in my life.

I am careful about money; a businessman has got to be. I'd double-checked the hotel address where Elizabeth was supposed to be staying, and I put a five-day return on the envelope when I mailed it. And then, through some kind of mix-up, it came back to me, and the envelope was stamped *Not known here.*

Scared? Worried? Brother!

I didn't know where else to write. I knew she was supposed to be at the address I had. And of course, she thought I'd broken my promise so she didn't write me either. She finally broke down and sent me a wire, and I sent her one, and—and that was the end of it.

But until I heard from her I was imagining all sorts of things. I'd about halfway decided that she must be dead . . .

THIRTY

I used to know a drunk years ago, a booker at one of the film exchanges in the city. He was one of those God-awful, noisy, messy drunks; the worst of the worst kind. And do you know something? That guy couldn't stand the sight of another drunk. It wasn't any pretence. He actually hated 'em. He'd walk six blocks to keep from passing one on the street.

I was thinking about him, and wondering why I was thinking about him, as I turned into the lane toward home. Then, as I drove into the yard, another funny thing popped into my mind—the tag line on an old joke. *It's not the original cost but the upkeep.*

There it is. Make anything you want to out of it.

After I'd shut off the motor I sat in the car for a moment, pulling myself together; thinking—trying to think—what a hell of a mess Carol had got me into by going to work for us. Then, I rubbed the gun in my pocket, wiped the sweat off my hand, and got out.

I went up the steps.

I crossed the porch and opened the door.

As far as I could see, there from the hall, everything was just like I had left it. The shades were drawn. The furnace was still ticking away, throwing out warm waves of heat. The lights were . . .

"Carol," I called. "Carol!"

And every light in the place went out.

I stood where I was, paralyzed; too shocked to move. And the air from the furnace didn't seem warm any more. It got colder and colder. It brushed against my face like the draft from an icebox. Somehow I got my foot behind me and kicked the door shut. As an afterthought, I turned the key in the lock and put it in my pocket.

I called her one more time. "Carol!"

There wasn't any answer.

It wasn't the storm, then. She'd pulled the switch. She'd done it without even waiting to see what Web had wanted, or what I was going to do about it. And she'd been nagging me about not trusting her!

I was sore and relieved at the same time. It made things easier.

I started to strike a match, but caught myself. She'd see me first; and she hadn't turned out those lights for the fun of it. She was sure I'd put her on the spot. Or, maybe, she'd guessed that I could never feel safe as long as she was alive. Anyway, she was playing for keeps.

I don't know whether I've described the layout of our house or not. There's a hall extending from the front door to the kitchen. On the left, as you go in, is the living-room. The dining-room is across from it, on the right.

I went down the hall on tiptoe to the living-room, and eased the drapes apart. My eyes were getting used to the dark, and I could see a little. Not much, but a little. The outlines of the furniture; shadowy blotches on the wall where pictures hung.

The living-room looked empty, and I decided it must be. The master light switch was in the kitchen. She hadn't had time to move far from it.

I tried to figure out which way she'd go. Up the hall toward me, or through the door into the dining-room? Or would she still be there in the kitchen?

I started down the hall. And stopped.

A door had creaked. The door connecting the dining-room and kitchen. She was coming around that way. Getting behind me.

I pivoted and crept back to the dining-room. I slid through the portiers, holding my breath.

The door creaked again as it was opened wider. Now I could see a black oblong as it was opened all the way.

I could see a shadow, a crouched blur upon the black.

I touched the trigger of the automatic.

The explosion was almost deafening, but I heard her scamper back into the kitchen. I heard one of the chairs go over. I eased forward again, not seeing too well because of the flash of light from the shot. At the door into the kitchen I dropped down on my hands and knees and started to crawl across the threshold.

It was a minute or two before I saw her, her shadow against the far wall. I waited until I was sure, until I saw it edging toward the spot where the hall door would be. Then, slowly, I began rising to my feet.

I was too slow for her. In a split second the door banged open. Crashed shut.

I stood up, panting, sweat pouring from my face. I felt my way along the wall to the switch box.

The cover was open, as I'd known it would be, and the switch was pulled. I pushed it back into place, blinking my eyes as the lights went on. I locked the back door and put the key in my pocket. I waited, looking upward.

Listening.

At last I heard it. The squeak of a bedspring. I started to tiptoe out of the kitchen, then stopped again. She'd have to come out of her room. It wouldn't look right to break the door down.

I began to whistle to myself, as I thought it over. And then I started to whistle louder, loud enough for her to hear me and just as if I didn't have a care in the world.

I tramped up the stairs, and knocked on the door of her bedroom.

"Carol!" I called. "Are you asleep?"

There was no answer, but the bed creaked again. In my mind I could see her sitting there, huddled as far back as she could get. Staring at the door.

I let out an embarrassed laugh. "Did you hear all that racket I was making? The light switch dropped down and shut off the current. I thought there was a prowler in the house." I laughed again. "Guess I'd be shooting yet if my gun hadn't jammed."

I could own a gun. She couldn't be sure that I didn't.

I heard—I thought I heard—a faint sigh of relief. A scared, doubtful sigh.

"Get dressed, Carol. We've got to get out of here. Right away, tonight."

There wasn't any kind of sound this time; nothing I could identify. But she seemed to be asking a question.

"Do you hear me, Carol?" I knocked again. "We've got to beat it. They've found out about the woman you hired. They haven't got the straight of things, but they know enough. They're going to open the grave in the morning. As soon as they find out it wasn't Elizabeth, we'll be sunk. They'll run Elizabeth down, and she'll squawk, to save her own neck. The whole thing will be pinned on us." I banged harder on the door.

"Come on! We can be a long ways from here by daylight. Open the door and I'll help you pack!"

She didn't answer. It dawned on me that she probably couldn't. She was too frightened, too scared of what her voice might tell me.

But she had got up. She was standing. And now she was coming to the door.

Afraid, yes. Scared as hell. But more scared not to.

I raised and leveled the gun. My hand was shaking, and I gripped my wrist with my other hand and steadied it.

The key grated and clicked in the lock. The doorknob turned.

Then the door flew open, and just as it did I squeezed the trigger.

There was one long, stuttering explosion. And then it was all over.

And through the smoke I saw Appleton grinning at me.

THIRTY-ONE

"Thanks a lot. I think that establishes an intention to kill, even though you were shooting blanks." His grin broadened, seeming to contract his eyes. "Not that we needed it after your interesting revelations. You're a hard man, Joe. We thought you'd give the gal some kind of explanation before you started shooting."

"I—I—" I said. "The sheriff gave me that gun. I—I thought she was going to kill me, and—"

"Oh, come now, Joe." He shook his head. "Who do you think was playing that game of tag with you—trying to get you to open up? Why do you think Waters gave you a gun loaded with blanks? What do you think happened to your buddy, Chance?"

I swallowed. Hard. "You got—Hap?"

"Uh-huh. Caught him right in the act of slugging Jimmie Nedry. He was quite co-operative, but his information wasn't very helpful. He put the finger on you, but it didn't mean anything to us. Not any more than what Andy Taylor had to tell."

"Cut it out!" I laughed in his face. I was caught, but that didn't mean I was a sucker. "If Andy had told you anything—"

"Of course, he did, Joe. Think a minute. What could you possibly offer a man in Taylor's position that would reimburse him for the risk of a long prison sentence? Don't put yourself in his place. It doesn't work. Taylor told us when you offered to cancel the lease on the Bower. Nedry told us about the stunt with the photoelectric cells; Nedry and Blair. But that still didn't give us enough. You could have had a change of heart with Taylor. Nedry and Blair were sore at you."

He paused, one eyebrow raised, and I nodded.

"Go on. Give it all to me."

"You already know it, Joe. Most of it, anyway. I was sure that you'd loved your wife. I knew that if the fire had been set you couldn't have done it since you were out of town. That gave us one, or, rather, two possibilities to work on. If a crime had been committed Carol was involved in it. And if you were really covering up for her—and we couldn't be sure that you were—then you were in on it, too, and—"

His voice trailed off, and he paused again. And it seemed as if he was trying not to look at me.

"Maybe you'd better sit down, Joe."

"What the hell for?" I said. "I can take it. I can hand it out and I can t-take it. You figured that we must have—must have brought in another woman. You made up that story about looking for one to see how I'd take it. That's it, ain't—isn't it? There wasn't any other woman, was there?"

"No, Joe, there wasn't. When I first gave you the yarn I thought it had struck home. But later on, that night in my hotel room, I wasn't sure. In fact, I'd have been willing to bet that you were on the level. If you hadn't made that one-sided swap with Andy Taylor—"

"Jesus!" I laughed. "Jesus Christ! I gave you the cards myself. If I'd just sat tight you'd never have known about—that it wasn't Elizabeth."

He shook his head. "You don't understand, Joe. Waters and Clay were your friends. They didn't want to tell you something that might hurt your feelings. That was in the beginning. Later on, when this Nedry and Taylor business developed, they agreed to keep quiet. They were safe enough regardless of how the thing turned out. You couldn't blame them for not mentioning a routine measure, particularly since I'd instigated it."

"You're talking a lot," I said. "You're talking a lot and you're not s-saying—you're not saying—"

"Better accept it, Joe. Face it and get it over with."

"I—I don't know what—"

"You must know. Otherwise we'd have arrested you right in the beginning. I don't know why she did it. I don't know why she came back here and walked into the trap she'd helped to set. That's something for you to figure out if you haven't already got it figured. All I can tell you is this, Joe. We identified the body days ago, and"— his voice dropped—"Carol came back from the city alone."

His hand shot out as I staggered. I threw it off.

"Carol—Where is she?"

"Look on the bed, Joe."

He stood aside.

I looked.

The heft of the scissors stood out from her breast like an unclasped pin. That was all I could see of her. The scissors, and her breast arched up to meet it.

"She left a note, Joe. A confession. She was going to take all the blame on herself. I put the screws on her, and she told me she'd talk to the county attorney. I let her come up here to get ready, and—"

He broke off, watching me.

"If she'd told me," I said. "If she'd told me—"

"Yes, Joe? If she'd told you she'd killed the woman you loved?"

I looked from the bed to him. I looked back at the bed. I took a step forward.

"Would it, Joe? Would it have been all right?"

I didn't answer him. I couldn't. I didn't know the answer until I reached the bed. And then I knew, but there weren't any words left in me.

It wasn't the way she looked, but the way I did. Because all I'd ever seen in her was myself, the little of myself that was pitying and compassionate and unselfish or whatever you want to call it. And, now, in the ending, even that little was gone. And all that was left was what I could see here, in her eyes. Dead eyes, turning in slightly.

I shivered and tried to look away.

I thought, *They can't hang me. I'm already dead. I've been dead a long, long time.*

GLOSSARY OF
EXHIBITOR TERMS

B.O.
   box office (receipts)

DARK
   not in operation; a dark house

GRIND-HOUSE
   a show which operates 24 hours daily

INDIE
   an independent exhibitor or exchange

ONE-SHEET (THREE-SHEET etc.)
   posters. Largest dimension is the 24-billboard size

PAPER
   advertising matter

PRODUCT
   pictures

SOUND HEADS
   the part of the projector which picks up the sound from the film.
See below.

SOUND TABLE
   a now-obsolete device, similar to a phonograph, used in transcribing
sound. Dialogue and musical accompaniment of early "talkies" were

recorded on discs which were synchronized (perhaps!) with the film by the projectionist. An imperfect and expensive arrangement, it was supplanted by the recording of sound on the film proper and the use of sound heads.

A HELL OF
A WOMAN

ONE

I'd gotten out of my car and was running for the porch when I saw her. She was peering through the curtains of the door, and a flash of lightning lit up the dark glass for an instant, framing her face like a picture. And it wasn't a pretty picture, by any means; she was about as far from being a raving beauty as I was. But something about it kind of got me. I tripped over a crack, and almost went sprawling. When I looked up again she was gone, and the curtains were motionless.

I limped on up the steps, set my sample case down and rang the bell. I stepped back from the door and waited, working up a big smile, taking a gander around the yard.

It was a big old-fashioned dwelling, a half-mile or so beyond the state university campus and the only house in that block. Judging by its appearance and location, I guessed that it had probably been a farmhouse at one time.

I punched the bell again. I held my finger on it, listening to its dimly shrill clatter inside the house. I pulled the screen open and began pounding on the door. You did things like that when you worked for Pay-E-Zee Stores. You got used to people who hid when they saw you coming.

The door flew open while I was still beating on it. I took one look at this dame and moved back fast. It wasn't the young one, the haunted-looking babe I'd seen peering through the curtains. This was an old biddy with a beak like a hawk and close-set, mean little eyes. She was about seventy—I don't know how anyone could have got that ugly in less than seventy years—but she looked plenty hale and hearty. She was carrying a heavy cane, and I got the impression that she was all ready to use it. On me.

"Sorry to disturb you," I said, quickly. "I'm Mr. Dillon, Pay-E-Zee Stores. I wonder if—"

"Go 'way," she snarled. "Get out of here! We don't buy from peddlers."

"You don't understand," I said. "Of course, we would like to open an account for you, but what I really stopped by for was some information. I understand you had a Pete Hendrickson working here for you. Did some yard work and so on. I wonder if you could tell me where I can find him."

She hesitated, squinting at me craftily. "He owes you some money, huh?" she said. "You want to find him an' make him pay."

"Not at all," I lied. "It's the other way around, in fact. We accidentally collected too much from him, and we want to—"

"I bet you do!" She let out with an ugly cackle. "I just bet you collected too much from that drunken, lazy bum! No one never got nothing from Pete Hendrickson but a lot of sass and excuses."

I grinned and shrugged. Usually, you had to do it the other way, because it's damned seldom that even a man's worst enemies will tip him off to a bill collector. But once in a while you find someone real low down, someone who just naturally likes to see a guy get it in the neck. And that's the way it was with this old witch.

"Mean and lazy," she said. "Wouldn't do nothing and wanted two prices for doing it. Sneaks off an' gets hisself another job when he's supposed to be workin' for me. I told him he'd be sorry . . ."

She gave me Pete's address, also the name of his employer. It was a greenhouse out on Lake Drive, only a few blocks from where I was now, and he'd been working there about ten days. He hadn't made a payday yet, but he was just about due.

"He came whinin' and beggin' around here last night," she said. "Tryin' to borrow a few dollars until he could get his wages. I guess you know what I told him!"

"I can imagine," I said. "Now, as long as I'm here, I'd like to show you some very special items which—"

"Huh uh! No, sir-ee!" She started to close the door.

"Just let me show them to you," I said, and I stooped down and flipped the sample case open. I laid the stuff out in the lid, talking fast, watching her face for an expression of interest. "What about this spread? Make you a very nice price on that. Or this toilet set? We're practically giving it away, lady. Well, some stockings? A shawl? Gloves? House slippers? If I don't have your size here, I can—"

"Huh-uh. Nope." She wagged her head firmly. "I got no money for such fol-de-rol, mister."

"You don't need any," I said. "Hardly any. Just a very small payment now on any or all of these items, and you can set your own terms on the balance. Take as long to pay as you like."

"I'll bet," she cackled. "Just like Pete Hendrickson, huh? You better go on, mister."

"What about the other lady?" I said. "That other young lady? I'm sure there's something here she'd like to have."

"Huh!" she grunted. "And how do you figger *she'd* pay for anything?"

"I figured she'd probably use money," I said. "But maybe she's got something better."

I was just being snotty, understand. I didn't like her and I'd gotten everything out of her that I was going to get. So why be polite?

I started repacking the stuff, jamming it in any old which way because that junk was hard to hurt. Then, she spoke again, and there was a sly wheedling note to her voice that brought my head up with a start.

"You like that niece o' mine, mister? You think she's pretty?"

"Why, yes," I said. "I thought she was a very attractive young lady."

"She minds good, too, mister. I tell her to do somethin' and she does it. No matter what."

I said that was swell or fine, or something of the kind. Whatever a guy does say in a situation like that. She pointed down at the sample case.

"That chest of silverware, mister. How much you gettin' on that?"

I opened the chest and showed it to her. I said I really hadn't intended to sell it; it was such a bargain I was saving it for myself. "Service for eight, lady, and every piece of it solid heavy-Sterling plate. We usually get seventy-five dollars for it, but we're closing out these last few sets at thirty-two ninety-five."

She nodded, grinning at me slyly. "You think my niece ... You think she could pay for it, mister? You could fix it up some way so's she could pay for it?"

"Why, I'm sure of it," I said. "I'll have to talk with her first, of course, but—"

"You let me talk to her first," she said. "You wait here."

She went away, leaving the door open. I lighted a cigarette, and

waited. And, no, I'll swear to it on a stack of Bibles, I didn't have any
idea of what the old gal was up to. I knew she was pretty low down,
but I'd never known many people who weren't. I thought she was
acting pretty goofy, but most of Pay-E-Zee's customers were goofs.
People with good sense didn't trade with outfits like ours.

I waited, wincing a little when there was a sudden flash of
lightning, wondering how many more goddamned days it was going
to go on raining. It had been raining for almost three weeks straight,
now, and what it had done to my job was murder. Sales way to hell
down, collections way to hell off. You just can't do good door-to-door
work in rainy weather—you can't get the people to open up. And
with accounts like mine, a lot of day laborers and the like, it didn't
do much good when they did open up. They'd been laid off on
account of the weather. You could cuss them and threaten them, but
you just couldn't get what they didn't have.

I was getting fifty a week salary, just about enough to run my car.
My earnings had to come from commissions, and I hadn't been
pulling down any. Oh I was making something, sure, but not nearly
enough to get by on. I'd kept going by doctoring my accounts,
pocketing part of the collections and altering the account-cards
accordingly. Right now I was in the hole for better than three
hundred dollars, and if someone should squawk before I could square
up . . .

I swore under my breath, flipping my cigarette into the yard. I
turned back to the door, and there she was—the girl.

She was in her early twenties, I believe, although I'm not the best
judge of ages when it comes to women. She had a mass of wavy
blonde hair, kind of chopped off rather than bobbed, and her eyes
were dark; and maybe they weren't the biggest eyes I'd ever seen on
a gal, but in that thin white face they seemed to be.

She was wearing a white wrap-around, the sort of get-up you see
on waitresses and lady barbers. The neck of it came down in a deep
V, and you could see she had plenty of what it takes in that area. But
below that, huh-uh. Out around the ag college—I had an account or
two out there—the guys would have said she was poor for beef, fine
for milk.

She pushed the screen door open. I picked up the sample case, and
went in.

She hadn't spoken to me yet, and she didn't now. She'd turned and was walking down the hall almost before I got inside. Walking with her shoulders kind of slumped, as though she were tipping forward. I followed her, thinking maybe she didn't have much there in the rear but there wasn't anything wrong with the shape of it.

We went through the living room, the dining room, the kitchen. Her in the lead, me walking pretty fast to keep up with her. There was no sign of the old woman. The only sound came from our footsteps and the occasional clashes of thunder.

I began to get an uneasy, sickish feeling in the pit of my stomach. If I hadn't needed to make a sale so badly, I'd have walked out.

There was a door leading off the kitchen. She went through it and I followed her—kind of edging around her, keeping my eyes on her. Wanting to say something and not knowing what the hell it would be.

It was a small bedroom; a room with a bed in it, rather, and a washstand with an old-fashioned bowl and pitcher. The shades were drawn, but quite a bit of light seeped in around their edges.

She closed the door and turned her back; started fumbling with the belt of the wrap-around. And I got the pitch then, of course, but it was too damned late. Too late to stop her.

The dress fell to the floor. She had nothing on underneath it. She turned back around.

I didn't want to look. I felt sick and sore and ashamed—and, me, I don't get ashamed easy. But I just couldn't help myself. I had to look, even if I never looked at anything else again.

There was a welt across her like a hot iron might make. Or a stick. Or a cane ... And there was a drop of blood ...

She stood, head bowed, waiting. Her teeth were clenched tightly, but I could see the trembling of her chin.

I said, "God. God, honey..." And I stooped and picked up the wrap-around. Because I wanted her—I guess I'd wanted her right from the moment I'd seen her at the door, a picture lit up by lightning. But I wouldn't have taken her this way if I'd been paid to.

So I started to get this doohickey back around her, but the way things worked out I didn't quite get the job done. Not right at the moment, anyway. I was fumbling with the damned thing, telling her not to cry, she was a baby girl and a sweet child and I wouldn't hurt her for the world. And finally she looked up into my face, and I guess she must have liked what she saw there as well as I liked what I saw in her.

She leaned into me, snuggled up against me with her head buried against my chest. She put her arms around me, and I put mine around her. We stood there together, holding on to each other for dear life; me patting her on the head and telling her there wasn't a goddamned thing to cry about. Telling her she was a baby girl and a honey child and old Dolly Dillon was going to take care of her.

It seems funny as hell, now that I look back on it. Strange, I mean. Me—a guy like me—in a bedroom with an armful of naked woman, and not even thinking about her being naked. Just thinking about her without thinking about her nakedness.

That's the way it was, though. Exactly the way it was. I'll swear to it on a stack of Bibles.

TWO

I got her soothed down, finally. I helped her back into the dress and we sat down on the edge of the bed, talking in whispers.

Her first name was Mona, her last was the same as her aunt's, Farrell. So far as she knew, that is. All she had to go on was what the old bitch told her. She couldn't remember living with anyone else. She didn't have any other relatives that she knew of.

"Why don't you clear out?" I said. "She couldn't stop you. She'd get in plenty of trouble if she tried to. "

"I. . ." She shook her head, vaguely. "I wouldn't know what to do, Dolly. Where to go. I—I just wouldn't know."

"Hell, do anything," I said. "There's plenty of things you could do. Slinging hash. Ushering in a movie. Sales clerking. Housework, if you couldn't find anything else."

"I know, but—but—"

"But what? You can swing it, honey. Don't tell her you're leaving if you don't want to. Just pull out and don't come back. You get out now and then, don't you? She doesn't keep you inside all the time?"

No—yes, she nodded. She got out quite a bit. Downtown and around the neighborhood to shop for the old woman.

"Well, then?" I said.

"I c-couldn't, Dolly . . ."

I sighed. I guessed she couldn't either. She was too beat-down, completely lacking in confidence. If there was someone to take her away from here, keep her going until she was built up a little . . .

She was looking at me apologetically. Humbly. Begging me with her eyes. I looked down at the floor.

What the hell did she expect me to do, anyway? I was already doing a damned sight more than I should.

"Well," I said, "you'll be all right for the present. I'll leave the silverware here for you. The old girl won't know that—that—she'll lay off of you for a while."

"D-Dolly . . ."

"Maybe you'd better make it Frank," I said, trying to steer her away from the important thing. "Dolly"—I laughed at myself. "Now, ain't that a hell of a handle for a big ugly guy like me to have?"

"You're not ugly," she said. "You're pret . . . Is that why they call you that? Because you're so—so—?"

"Yeah," I said. "I'm a real pretty guy, I am. Pretty damned tough and ornery, and pretty apt to stay that way."

"You're nice," she said. "I never met anyone who was nice before."

I told her the world was full of nice people. I'd have hated to try to prove it to her, but I said it, anyway. "You'll get along swell, once you're away from here. So why don't you give yourself a break, honey? Let me give you one? I can tell the cops what—"

"*No!*" She gripped my arm so hard I almost jumped. "No, Dolly! You've got to promise."

"But, baby," I said. "That's all bushwa, she's handed you. They won't do anything to you. She's the one that—"

"No! They wouldn't believe me! She'd say I was lying and she'd make me say it, and a-afterwards—afterwards when she got me alone . . ."

Her voice trailed off into terrified silence. I put my arm back around her.

"All right, honey," I said. "I'll think of something else. You just sit tight, and . . ." I paused, remembering how quick the old woman had come out with her offer. "Have you had to do anything like this before, Mona? Has she made you?"

She didn't speak, but her head moved up and down. A faint flush spread under the delicate white of her face.

"Just people stopping by, like I did?"

Again a reluctant nod. "M-mostly . . ."

That was good, if you know what I mean. Her aunt would pull that on the wrong guy—the right one, rather—and she'd be in the jug, but fast.

"Well, she won't do it any more," I said. "No, I won't give you away. So far as she'll know everything went off per schedule. That's the angle, see? I'll be coming back with plenty of other nice things, and I don't want you bothered."

She raised her head again, and her eyes searched my face. "Will you, Dolly? W-will you come back?"

"Didn't I say so?" I said. "I'll be back, and I'll get you away from here just as soon as I do. It's going to take a little working out, know what I mean? It's kind of complicated the way I'm set up. You see— well, I'm a married man."

She nodded. I was married. So what? It didn't mean anything to her. I guess it wouldn't mean anything, after what she'd been through.

"Yeah." I went on. "Been married for years. And this job I got, it keeps me humping to make a living."

That didn't register, either. All she knew was that I had a hell of a lot more than she had.

It made me a little sore, the way she was acting, but yet I kind of liked it. She was so damned trusting, so sure that I'd work things out no matter how tough they were. I hadn't had many people believe in me like that. Many? Hell, any.

She smiled at me, shyly, the first time she'd really smiled since I'd met her. She took my hand and moved it over her breast.

"Do you . . . want to, Dolly? I wouldn't mind with you."

"Maybe next time," I said. "Right now, I think I'd better be shoving off."

The smile faded. She started to ask me if I minded about the others. I said why would I mind for God's sake, and I gave her a kiss that made her gasp.

Because I did want her, and I wasn't coming back. And when a girl offers you that—all that she has to offer—you ought to be damned careful how you turn it down.

I took the silver chest out of my case, and put it on the dresser. I gave her another kiss, told her not to worry about a thing, and left.

The old hag, her aunt, was in the hallway, grinning and rubbing her hands together. I wanted to bat her in her goddamned rotten puss, but of course I didn't.

"You got something there, lady," I told her. "Take good care of it, because I'm going to be back for more."

She cackled and smirked. "Bring me a nice coat, huh, mister? You got some nice winter coats?"

"I got more coats than you can stack in a barn," I said. "Nothing second-hand, get me, and I'm not trading for anything second-hand. I come by here and find someone else in the sack, it's no deal."

"You leave it to me, mister," she said eagerly. "When'll you be back?"

"Tomorrow," I said. "Or maybe the next day. I'm liable to drop by any old time, so don't try any doubling-up on me if you want that coat."

She promised she wouldn't.

I opened the door, and ran back down the walk to my car.

It was still pouring down rain. It looked like it was going to rain forever. And I owed the company another thirty-three dollars. Thirty-two ninety-five to be exact.

"You're doing swell, Dolly," I told myself. "Yes, sir, Dillon, you're doing all right... You think this Staples character is stupid? You think that's how he got the job of checking on characters like you? You think he ain't the meanest, toughest son-of-a-bitch in the Pay-E-Zee chain?"

Goddamn, I thought. Double goddamn and a carton of hells.

Then, I shoved my car into gear and got going. It was only four-thirty. I had plenty of time to get out to the greenhouse and see Pete Hendrickson before he knocked off for the day.

And if Pete wasn't a real good boy...

Suddenly, I grinned to myself. Grinned and scowled at the same time . . . He'd gotten to that poor damned girl, Mona; I'd have bet money on it. The old woman would have tried to pay him off that way, and Pete wouldn't have turned it down. He'd let his bills go to hell—let me chase all over town hunting for him—and do *that* to her. And even if he hadn't he was still no good.

And I needed every nickel of what he owed us.

I parked in front of the greenhouse, in front of the office, that is. I reached into the pocket of the car, took out a sheaf of papers and thumbed through them rapidly.

I found his sales contract—a contract that was also an assignment of wages. You had to look for it a little because of the fine print, but it was there all right. All legal and air-tight.

I took it into the office, and presented it to Pete's boss. He paid off like a slot machine. Thirty-eight bucks and not a word of argument. He counted it out to me, and then I recounted it, and while I was still standing there he told a clerk to go and get Pete.

I finished the count fast, and beat it.

Wage assignments and garnishees—employers just naturally don't like the things. They don't like to be bothered with them, and they don't like employees who cause them to be bothered. Pete was going to get the gate. I figured I'd better be some place else when he did.

I drove down the street a few blocks to a beer joint. I ordered a pitcher of beer, carried it back to a rear booth and took down half of it at a gulp. Then, I spread a blank contract out on the table, and made out a cash sale to Mona Farrell for thirty-two ninety-five.

That was one thing off my mind. That took care of the silver, with five bucks left over. Now, if this rain would only stop and I could get in a few good weeks in a row . . .

I began to feel a little better. Not quite so damned blue and hopeless. I ordered another pitcher of beer, sipping it slowly this time. I thought what a sweet kid that Mona was, and I wondered why I couldn't have married her instead of a goddamned bag like Joyce.

That Joyce. Now, there was a number for you. Kid Sloppybutt. Princess Lead-in-the-Tail, Queen of the Cigarette Girls and a free pinch with every pack. I'd thought she was hot stuff, but it hadn't been recently, brother. I may have been stupid to begin with, but I wised up fast. Joyce—a lazy, selfish dirty slob like Joyce for a wife.

Why couldn't it have been Mona?

Why was it that every time I thought I was getting a break it went sour on me?

I glanced at the clock. Ten minutes of six. I stepped to the telephone, and dialed the store.

Staples sounded just the same as usual. Smooth, oily, soft-voiced. I told him I was chasing a skip through the sticks, and I thought I'd wait until morning to check in.

"Quite all right, Frank," he said. "How's it going anyway? Any lead yet on Hendrickson?"

"Nothing yet," I lied, "but I've had a fairly good day. I made a cash sale on that silver special."

"Good boy," he said. "Now, if you can just get a line on Hendrickson."

His voice lingered over the name. Underlined it. He was more than five miles away, but I felt like he was right there. Grinning at me, watching me, waiting for me to trap myself.

"What about it, Frank?" he said. "What about that thirty-eight dollars Hendrickson owes us?"

THREE

"What the hell you think I've been doing?" I said. "I haven't been sitting around on my can in some nice dry office all day. Give me a little time, for God's sake."

The phone was silent for a moment. Then he laughed softly.

"Not too much time, Frank," he said. "Why not put in a little extra effort, eh, as long as you're working over? Use that shrewd brain of yours. I can't tell you how delighted I'd be if you could bring that Hendrickson money in the morning."

"Well, that makes two of us," I said. "I'll do the best I can."

I said goodnight, and hung up the receiver. I drank the rest of my beer, not enjoying it very much.

Had he been giving me a hint, a warning? Why was he bearing

down so hard on this one account? Hendrickson was a dead beat, sure, but practically all of our customers were. They seldom paid unless they were made to. They traded with us because they couldn't get credit anywhere else. Why, with at least a hundred other skips and no-pays to pick on, had Staples jumped me about this one?

I didn't like it. It might be the beginning of the end, the first step toward the jailhouse. Because if he caught me tapping one account, he'd figure I'd tapped the others. He'd check on all the others.

Of course, he'd done things like this before. Kind of like this. You'd knock yourself out and have a pretty good day maybe, and instead of a pat on the head you'd get what I'd got tonight. You know. Maybe you've worked for guys like that. They just slide over what you've done, and needle you about something else. The first damned thing that pops into their minds. That has to be done, too, and what the hell are you waiting on?

So ... so that must be it, I decided. I hoped that was it. You couldn't satisfy Staples. The more you did the more you had to do.

I went up to the bar and paid my check. I walked to the door and looked out into the rain. Turning up my coat collar. Getting ready to make a run for my car.

Night was setting in early, but it wasn't quite dark yet. I could see pretty good, and I saw him down near the end of the building. A big husky guy in work clothes, standing back under the eaves of the building.

I couldn't get to my car without passing him.

I guessed I'd stopped a little too close to that greenhouse.

I went back to the bar, and ordered a quart of beer to take out. Gripping it by the neck, I sauntered out the door.

Maybe he didn't see me right away. Or maybe he was just trying to work his nerve up. Anyway, I was almost parallel with him before he moved out from under the eaves and placed himself in front of me.

I stopped and backed up a step or two.

"Why, Pete," I said. "How's it going, boy?"

"You sonabitch, Dillon," he said. "You get my chob, hah? You get chob, now I get you!"

"Oh, now, Pete," I said. "You brought it on yourself, fellow. We trust you and try to treat you nice, and you—"

"You lie! Chunk you sell me. Suit no good—like paper it vears! In chail you should be, chunk seller, t'ief, robber! A fine chob I get, and because I no pay for chunk, you—you—I fix you, Dillon!"

He lowered his head, clubbed his big hands into fists. I moved back another step, tightened my grip on the bottle. I was carrying it back behind my thigh. He hadn't seen it yet.

"Jail, huh?" I said. "You've hit a few jails yourself, haven't you, Pete? You keep on fooling around with me and you'll land in another one."

It was just a guess, but it stopped him for a moment. You couldn't go very far wrong in guessing that a Pay-E-Zee customer had made the clink.

"So!" he sputtered. "In chail I haf been, and my time I serve. Dot has nodding to do mit dis. You—"

"What about a sentence for rape?" I said. "Spit it out, goddamn you! Tell me you didn't do it! Tell me you didn't have that poor, sick, starved-to-death kid!"

I moved in on him, not giving him a chance to deny it. I knew damned well that he had and it made me half-crazy to think about it. "Come on, you ugly, overgrown son-of-a-bitch," I said. "Come on and get it!"

And he came on with a rush.

I sidestepped, swinging the bottle like a bat. My feet slipped in the mud. I caught him squarely across the bridge of the nose, and he went down sprawling. But his right fist got me as he went by. It landed, skidding, just below my heart. And if I hadn't bounced back against the building I'd have gone down with him.

I was doubled up for a moment, feeling like I'd never breathe again. Then, I got pulled together a little, and I staggered over to where he was.

He wasn't completely out, but there wasn't any more fight in him. There was no sense in socking him again or giving him a kick in the head. I grabbed him by the collar and dragged him over against the side of the building. I propped him up so that he was kind of out of the rain and wouldn't get run over. And then I knocked the beer open on a rock and pushed it into his hand.

It wasn't the kind of treatment he'd expected. Or was used to. He looked up at me like a beaten dog. On an impulse—or maybe it was a hunch—I took five ones from my pocket and dropped them into his lap.

"I'm sorry about the job," I said. "Maybe I can turn up another one for you ... Like to have me do that? Let you know if I hear of anything?"

He nodded slowly, brushing the blood away from his nose. "I like, yess. B-but—but *vy*, Dillon? Mis-ter Dillon. Vy you do dis en' den you do—"

"No choice," I shrugged. "The company says get the money, I have to get it. You say you want to fight, I fight. When I have my own way, well, you can see for yourself. I treat you like a long-lost brother. Give you dough out of my own pocket, try to find another job for you."

He took a drink of the beer; took another one. He belched and shook his head.

"Iss badt," he said. "Vy you do it. Mis-ter Dillon? Soch a nice man, vy you vork for bad peoples?"

I told him he had me there: I guessed I was just such a nice guy that people took advantage of me. Then, I told him to take it easy, and headed for home.

My ribs ached like hell, and I couldn't get Staples off my mind. But in spite of the pain and the worry, I laughed out loud ... What a character! If people kept on telling I was a nice guy, I might start believing them. And yet—well, what was so damned funny about that? What the hell was there to laugh about?

I'd never hurt anyone if I could get out of it. I'd given plenty of people breaks when I didn't have to. Like today for example; just take today, now. Pretty good, huh? You're damn well right it was! How many other guys would have passed up Mona, and given a hand to a guy who'd tried to murder 'em?

Pete had the right dope. It wasn't me, but the job. And I didn't know how to get out of it, any more than I knew how I'd got into it. I—

Did you ever think much about jobs? I mean, some of the jobs people land in? You see a guy giving haircuts to dogs, or maybe going along the curb with a shovel, scooping up horse manure. And you think, now why is the silly bastard doing that? He looks fairly bright, about as bright as anyone else. Why the hell does he do that for a living?

You kind of grin and look down your nose at him. You think he's nuts, know what I mean, or he doesn't have any ambition. And then you take a good look at yourself, and you stop wondering about the other guy . . . You've got all your hands and feet. Your health is okay, and you make a nice appearance, and ambition—man! you've got it. You're young, I guess you'd call thirty young, and you're strong. You don't have much education, but you've got more than plenty of other people who go to the top. And yet with all that—with all you've had to do with—this is as far as you've got. And something tells you, you're not going much farther if any.

And there's nothing to be done about it now, of course, but you can't stop hoping. You can't stop wondering . . .

. . . Maybe you had too much ambition. Maybe that was the trouble. You couldn't see yourself spending forty years moving up from office boy to president. So you signed on with a circulation crew; you worked the magazines from one coast to another. And then you ran across a nice little brush deal—it sounded nice, anyway. And you worked that until you found something better, something that looked better. And you moved from that something to another something. Coffee-and-tea premiums, dinnerware, penny-a-day insurance, photo coupons, cemetery lots, hosiery, extract, and God knows what all. You begged for the charities. You bought the old gold. You went back to the magazines and the brushes and the coffee and tea. You made good money, a couple of hundred a week sometimes. But when you averaged it up, the good weeks with the bad, it wasn't so good. Fifty or sixty a week, well, maybe seventy. More than you could make, probably, behind a gas pump or a soda fountain. But you had to knock yourself out to do it, and you were just standing still. You were still there at the starting place. And you weren't a kid any more.

So you come to this town, and you see this ad. Man for outside sales and collections. Good deal for hard worker. And you think maybe this is it. This sounds like a right job; this looks like a right town. So you take the job, and you settle down in the town. And, of

JIM THOMPSON

course, neither one of 'em is right, they're just like all the others. The job stinks. The town stinks. You stink. And there's not a goddamned thing you can do about it.

All you can do is go on like those other guys go on.

The guy giving haircuts to dogs, and the guy sweeping up horse manure. Hating it. Hating yourself. And hoping.

FOUR

We lived in a little four-room dump on the edge of the business district. It wasn't any choice neighborhood, know what I mean? We had a wrecking yard on one side of us and a railroad spur on the other. But it was choice enough for us. We were as well off there as we would be anywhere. A palace or a shack, it always worked out to the same difference. If it wasn't a dump to begin with, it damned soon got to be.

All it took was for us to move in.

I went inside, taking off my coat and hat. I laid them down on my sample case—at least it was clean—and took a look around. The floor hadn't been swept. The ash trays were loaded with butts. Last night's newspapers were scattered all over. The ... hell, nothing was as it should be. Nothing but dirt and disorder wherever you looked.

The kitchen sink was filled with dirty dishes; there were soiled sticky pans all over the stove. She'd just got through eating, it looked like, and of course she'd left the butter and everything else sitting out. So now the roaches were having themselves a meal. Those roaches really had a happy home with us. They got a hell of a lot more to eat than I did.

I looked in the bedroom. It looked like a cyclone had struck it. A cyclone and a dust storm.

I kicked the bathroom door open, and went in.

It was one of her good days, I guess. Here it was only seven o'clock at night and she'd actually got some clothes on. Not many; just a garter belt and some shoes and stockings. But that was damned good for her.

She drew a lipstick over her mouth, squinting at me in the medicine cabinet mirror.

"Well," she drawled, "if it isn't the king! And just as polite as ever, too."

"Okay," I said. "You can hop back into your nightgown. I've seen you before, and I still say there's better ones on sidewalks."

"Oh-yeah?" Her eyes flashed. "You rotten bastard! When I think of all the good guys I passed up to marry you, I—"

"Passed them up?" I said. "You mean lined 'em up, don't you?"

"You're a goddamned liar! I n-never—" She dropped the lipstick into the sink, and whirled around facing me. "Dolly," she said. "Oh, Dolly, hon! What's the matter with us?"

"Us? What do you mean, us?" I said. "I'm out knocking myself out every day. I work my can off, and what the hell do I get for it? Not a goddamn thing, that's what. Not even a decent meal or a clean bed, or even a place where I can sit down without a lot of cockroaches swarming all over me."

"I—" She bit her lip. "I know, Dolly. But they just keep coming back, those insects, no matter what I do. And I can just work from morning until night and this place always looks the same. And, well, I guess I just get tired, Dolly. There doesn't seem to be any sense to it. There's nothing here to work with. The sink keeps stopping up, and there's big cracks in the floor and—"

"So what about the other places we've lived? I guess you kept them all clean and pretty?"

"We've never lived in a really nice place, Dolly. Any place where I had a chance. It's always been some dump like this one."

"You mean they got to be dumps," I said. "After you lazed and loafed around and let everything go to hell. You just don't give a damn, that's all. Why, dammit, you should have seen what my mother had to work with—how nice she kept the place we lived in. Seven kids in an east side coldwater tenement, and everything was as shiny and spotless—"

"All right!" she yelled. "But I'm not your mother! I'm not some other woman! I'm me, get me? Me, me!"

"And you're bragging about it?" I said.

Her mouth opened and closed. She gave me a long slow look, and turned back to the mirror.

"Okay," I said. "Okay. You're a princess charming, and I'm a heel. I know you don't have it easy. I know it would be a lot better if I made more money, and I wish to God I could. But I can't and I can't help it. So why not make the best of things as they are?"

"I'm through talking," she said. "I might have known it was no use."

"Goddammit," I said, "I'm apologizing. I've been out in the rain all day while you were lying in the sack, and I come home to a goddamned pig pen and I'm sick and tired and worried, and—"

"Sing 'em," she said. "Sing 'em, king."

"I said I was sorry!" I said. "I apologize. Now, what about chasing your pets out of the grub and fixing me some supper?"

"Fix your own damned supper. You wouldn't like anything I fixed."

She laid down the lipstick and picked up an eyebrow pencil. A crazy, blinding pain speared through my forehead.

"Joyce," I said. "I said I was sorry, Joyce. I'm asking you to please fix me some supper, Joyce. Please, understand? Please!"

"Keep on asking," she said. "It's a pleasure to refuse."

She went on making with the eyebrow pencil. You'd have thought I wasn't there.

"Baby," I said, "I'm telling you. I'm kidding you not. You better drag tail into that kitchen while it's still fastened onto you. You screw around with me a little more and you'll have to carry it in a satchel."

"Now, aren't you sweet?" she said.

"I'm warning you, Joyce. I'm giving you one last chance."

"All hail the king." She made a noise with her lips. "Here's a kiss for you, king."

"And here's one for you," I said.

I brought it up from the belt, the sweetest left hook you ever saw in your life. She spun around on her heels and flopped backwards, right into the tub full of dirty bath water. And, Jesus, did it make a mess out of her.

I leaned against the door, laughing. She scrambled out of the tub, dripping with that dirty soapy scum, and reached for a towel. I hadn't really hurt her, you know. Why hell, if I'd wanted to give her a full hook I'd taken her head off.

She began drying herself, not saying anything at first, and I kind of stopped laughing. Then, she said something that was funny as hell, and yet it was kind of sad. She said it sort of thoughtful and soft-voiced, as though it was the most important thing in the world.

"That was my last good pair of stockings, Dolly. You ruined my only pair of stockings."

"Aah, hell," I said. "I'll give you another pair. I've got some in my sample case."

"I can't wear those. They never fit around the heel. I guess I'll just have to go barelegged."

"Go?" I said.

"I'm leaving. Now. Tonight. I don't want anything from you. I can pawn my watch and my ring—get enough to get by on until I land a job. All I want is to get away from here."

I told her all right, if she wanted to be stupid: those number fives of hers weren't nailed to the floor. "But I think you ought to mull it over a little first. You ought to stick around, anyway, until you run across a job. You know there's no nightclubs in a burg like this."

"I'll find something. There's no law that says I have to stay in this town."

"Why the hell didn't you get a job before this?" I said. "If you'd ever contributed anything, tried to help out a little—"

"Why should I? Why should I want to? I should get out and work for a guy that couldn't even say a nice word in church?" Her voice rose and went down again. "All right, Dolly, I said it all a while ago. I'm me, not someone else. Maybe I should have done a lot of things and maybe you should have, but we didn't and we wouldn't if we had it to do over again. Now, if you'll excuse me ... let me get cleaned up a little ..."

"Why so damned modest all of a sudden?" I said. "We're still married."

"We won't be any longer that I can help it. Will you please leave, now, Dolly?"

I shrugged and started out the door. "Okay," I said. "I'm going downtown and get some chow. Good luck and my best regards to the boys on the vice squad."

"D-Dolly . . . is that all you can say at a time like this?"

"What do you want me to say? Peter, Peter, Pumpkin Eater?"

"D-don't you . . . Would you like to kiss me good-bye?"

I jerked my head at the mirror. "That?" I said. "Three guesses, toots, and the secret word is still no."

I went on out, turning my back like a damned fool; and the next thing I knew a scrubbing brush socked me in the skull. It hurt like hell, and the dirty names she was yelling at me didn't exactly help it. But I didn't sock her any more, or even curse back at her. I'd said enough, I guessed. I'd done enough.

I loaded my sample case into the car, and took off for town.

I killed a couple hours, eating and doctoring my account cards, and went back home.

She was gone but her memory lingered on, if you know what I mean. She'd left me something to remember her by. The bedroom windows were pushed up to the top, and the bed was soaked with rain. My clothes—well, I just didn't have any clothes.

She'd poured ink all over my shirts. She'd taken a pair of scissors and cut big holes in my suit, the only other suit I had. My neckties and handkerchiefs were snipped to pieces. All my socks and underwear were stuffed into the toilet.

A real swell kid, didn't I tell you? A regular little doll. I'd have to do something nice for her if I ever ran into her again.

I went to work, straightening things out the best I could, and it must have been two in the morning before I got through and stretched out on the lounge.

Worn out, burned up, wondering. I just couldn't get it, you know. Why, if she didn't like a guy and didn't want to get along with him, had she gone to so damned much trouble to get him?

I'd met her in Houston about three years ago. I was crew manager on a magazine deal, and she was pushing cigarettes in this dive; and I used to drop in for a ball every night or so. Well, she started playing for me right from the beginning. The way she hung over my table you'd have thought she was the cloth. I couldn't lift a drink without seeing her through the bottom of the glass. So—so one thing led to another, and I began taking her home from work. What's a guy going to do, anyway, when a chick keeps throwing herself at him? I left her at her door a few nights, and then she let me come inside.

And she had one of the nicest little efficiency apartments you ever saw. I guess they had maid service in this joint, and with just herself to look after she got by pretty good. Not that I made any inspection of the place. I had my mind on something else. So I said, howsa about it, honey, and—*boing!* She hauled off and slapped me in the kisser. I jumped up and started to leave. She started crying. She said I wouldn't think she was a nice girl if she did; I wouldn't want to marry her and I'd throw it up to her afterwards. And I said, Aw, now, honey. What kind of a guy do you—

No, now wait a minute! I think I'm getting this thing all fouled up. I believe it was Doris who acted that way, the gal I was married to before Joyce. Yeah it must have been Doris—or was it Ellen? Well, it doesn't make much difference; they were all alike. They all turned out the same way. So, as I was saying: I said, What kind of a guy do you think I am? And she said ... they said ... I think you're nice. I—

... I went to sleep.

FIVE

Pay-E-Zee had seventy-five stores across the country. I'll tell you about this one, the one I worked for, and you'll know about them all.

It was on a side street, a twelve-foot-front place between a shine parlor and a fruit stand. It had two small show windows, with about a hundred items in each one. Men's suits, women's dresses, work clothes, bathrobes, wristwatches, dresser sets, novelties—more stuff than I can name. Why it was there, I don't know, because it wasn't once in a month of Saturdays that we got a customer off the street. Practically all the selling was done on the outside by me and five other guys.

We did a volume of about fifteen grand a month, with collections running about seventy-five per cent. And, yeah, that's low all right, but our mark-up wasn't. With a mark-up of three hundred per cent you can take a big loss on collections. You'll still do better on a fifteen-g volume than most stores do on fifty.

I was a little late getting in that morning, and the other collector-salesmen were already gone. A heavyset guy—a "just looking" customer—was thumbing through the rack of men's jackets. Staples was in the office at the rear, a space separated from the rest of the store by a wall-to-wall counter.

Pay-E-Zee didn't have the usual office employees. Just the credit men-managers like Staples. I laid out my collection cards and cash on the counter and he checked one against the other.

He was a little guy of about fifty, gray-haired, paunchy, sort of baby-mouthed. Back in the days when he was ringing doorbells, they'd called him The Weeper. He'd get on some poor bastard's doorstep or maybe call on him on the job, and then he'd howl and cry and carry on until they could hear him in the next county. He wasn't up to the rough stuff, so he'd pull that. And they'd have to come across to get rid of him.

He talked kind of sissified, not with a lisp, exactly, although you kept expecting one. He finished the check, and smiled at me pleasantly. He removed his glasses, polished them slowly and put them back on again.

"Frank," he said. "I'm disappointed in you. Very, very disappointed."

"Yeah?" I said. "What's the beef now?"

"Such clumsiness, Frank. Such preposterous ineptness. We did things much better in my day. Why in the world didn't you steal from the profit and loss file—the inactive p. and l.'s? If you were at all clever, you might have got away with it for years."

He shook his head sadly, looking like he was about to cry.

I forced a laugh. "Steal? What the hell you handing me, Staples?"

"Oh, Frank, please!" He held up a hand. "You're making this very painful. Pete Hendrickson's employer called me yesterday; his ex-employer, I should say. It seems that he wasn't very favorably impressed with our way of doing business, and he felt constrained to tell me so."

"So what?" I said.

"Frank . . ."

"All right," I said. "I borrowed thirty-eight bucks. I'll have it back for you by the end of the week."

"I see. And what about the rest of it?"

"What rest?" I said. "Who you trying to crap, anyway?"

But I knew it was no use. He sighed and shook his head, looking at me sorrowfully.

"I've only had time to spot check your accounts, Frank, but I've already found a dozen—uh—defalcations. Why not get it off your chest, my boy? Give me the total amount of the shortage. I'll find out, anyway."

"I couldn't help it," I said. "It was the rain. It's cleared up now, and if you'll just give me a few weeks—"

"How much, Frank?"

"I've got it all written down." I took out my notebook and showed him. "You can see for yourself I was going to pay it back. Hell, if I didn't intend to pay it back I wouldn't have written it down, would I?"

"We-el, yes." He pursed his lips. "Yes, I think you would have. I know I would have. It looks much better in such unpleasant eventualities as the present one."

"Now, wait a minute," I said. "I—"

"Three hundred and forty-five dollars, eh? Why don't you just dig it up, like a good boy, and we'll consider the matter closed."

"I'll write you a check," I said. "For God's sake, Staples, if I had any money or if I'd been able to beg or borrow any, I wouldn't have taken this."

"Mmm. I suppose so. What about your car?"

"Who's got a car? Talk to the finance company."

"Furniture?"

"Nothing. I rent furnished. I'm telling you, Staples, I don't have it and there's no way I can get it. All I can do is—"

"I see," he said. "Well, that's certainly too bad, isn't it? Very depressing. The company isn't at all vindictive in these matters, but ... I suppose you're familiar with the law of this state? Anything over fifty dollars is grand larceny."

"Look," I said. "What's that going to make you? What the hell good is it going to do to have me slapped in jail? God, if you'll just—"

"Well, it might do quite a bit of good," he said. "A man faced with a long prison sentence often thinks of resources he's previously overlooked. That's been our experience."

"But I can't! I won't!" I said. "There's no one that will help me. I haven't seen any of my relatives in years and they're all poor as hell anyway. I don't have any close friends or—"

"What about your wife?"

"I'm telling you," I said. "There's just one way I can get that dough. Give me six weeks. Give me a month. Three weeks. I'll work seven days a week, sixteen hours a day until—You've got to, Staples! Just a few weeks, a—"

"Oh, I couldn't do that, Frank!" He shook his head firmly. "I'd love to, but I honestly couldn't . . . Officer!"

"For God's sake—*Officer?*"

It was the guy I'd thought was a "just looking" customer. He sauntered up behind me, a toothpick bobbling in the corner of his mouth, and gripped me by the elbow.

"Okay, Buster," he said. "Let's go bye bye."

Staples beamed at him. He smiled at me. "I can't bear to say good-bye, Frank. Shall we just make it au *revior?*"

SIX

It may sound funny, but it was the first time in my life I'd been in jail. That's the God's truth, and I'm kidding you not. I'd crisscrossed the country, been in every state in the union at one time or another; and some of the deals I'd worked were as raw as a tackfactory whore. But I'd never made the can. Guys all around me did. Guys working right across the street from me. But never me. I guess I just don't look like a guy who'd get out of line. I may talk and act that way, but I don't look it. And I don't, if you know what I mean, really feel it.

It was about ten o'clock in the morning by the time they got me booked and locked up. I looked around the tank, the bullpen, and I'm not snobbish or anything, you understand, but I went over in a corner and sat down by myself. I just couldn't take it, somehow. I couldn't believe that I was part of this, that I was in the same boat with these other guys and a lot worse off maybe. Me, old Dolly Dillon, in the jug on a grand larceny rap? It was crazy. I felt like I was dreaming.

I knew better, but all that day I kept thinking that Staples would soften up. He'd realize that I couldn't raise anything in here, and he'd withdraw the charge and let me work the debt off. I kept thinking that, hoping it, and I figured out just the proposition I'd make him. My rent was paid for the month, and I was paid up with the finance company. So I'd say, Okay, Staples, here's what I'll do with you. You buy me a few meal tickets and pay for my gas and oil, and everything over that . . .

I remembered that the store owed me money. Two—two-and-a-half day's wages if they'd allow a half for this morning. So, hell, there was twenty-five dollars right there. All I actually owed was, well, call it three hundred in round numbers. That wasn't any money, for God's sake! I could make it up in no time, now that Joyce had pulled out.

I knew Staples would get me out. I mean, I *knew* it.

And I guess you know he didn't.

The next day came and passed. And I began to think about other angles, other ways I'd get out. They were all as hopeless as the Staples deal, but I dreamed up one after another. Maybe some crew would hit town, and they'd know what I could do, and they'd all take up a collection—they'd find out where I was some way—and . . . Or maybe I had a big bonus coming from one of the companies I'd worked for and the check was just now catching up with me. Or maybe one of my kinfolks back east had passed on and I was down for the insurance. Or maybe Doris would pop up with a roll. Or Ellen. Or— or someone. Someone had to, dammit! Something had to happen.

No one did, nothing did. And it was hard to take, brother, but it finally sank in on me that that was the way it was going to be. I was stuck. I couldn't kid myself any longer.

I thought about Mona, how she was really the cause of the whole trouble. If I hadn't used Pete Hendrickson's money to pay for that silverware, Staples wouldn't have caught up with me. I called myself all kinds of a damned fool, and I cussed her a little, too, I guess. But

I didn't really have my heart in it. I knew I'd have done the same thing all over again, and I wasn't sore at her that much. How could you be sore at a sweet, helpless kid like that?

I sat off by myself in a corner of the bullpen, thinking about her and getting a nice warm feeling. She'd come right to me that day. Put her arms around me and laid her head against my chest. She'd stood there naked and shivering. And she'd hugged me tighter and tighter until I seemed to be part of her.

She was out of this world, that little girl. Not one of these goddamned tramps like I was always latching onto. You could really go places with a kid like that. You'd do anything in the world for her because you knew she'd do anything in the world for you, and you could just naturally go to town.

I wondered what she'd think when I didn't come back. I wondered what would happen to her. I closed my eyes, and I could almost see it happening: The guys coming there to the door and the old woman propositioning them, and Mona . . . Mona there in the bedroom . . .

I opened my eyes fast. I forced my mind away from her, and started thinking about that house.

I'd had a feeling about it from the moment I set foot inside the door; that it wasn't as it should be, you know. I couldn't figure out what it was at the time, and I'd had plenty of other things to think about afterwards.

But now it finally came to me. There weren't any pictures in the place; pictures of people, I mean.

I guess I've probably been in ten thousand of those old houses, places occupied by old people. And everyone of 'em's got a flock of pictures on the walls. Guys with beards and gates-ajar collars. Women in high-necked dresses with leg-of-mutton sleeves. Boys in Buster Brown suits, and girls in middies and bloomers. Grandpa Jones, Uncle Bill and Aunt Hattie. Cousin Susie's kids . . . All those old houses are like that. They've all got those pictures. But this one didn't have a damned one.

I kept turning it over in my mind, and finally I thought, So what? What's it to you, anyway? I got kind of sore at myself, you know, thinking about a thing like that in the spot I was in. So I forgot about it, went back to worrying about myself, and it was days before I thought of it again. And by that time—

I don't know. You'll have to decide for yourself. Maybe any time would have been too late.

Maybe it would have turned out the same way, anyway ... I went to jail on Wednesday morning. I was scheduled for arraignment Friday afternoon. The turnkey came around at two that day, and took me to the showers. I bathed and shaved while he stood and watched, and then he gave me my clothes.

I got dressed. He led me up a long corridor, through a lot of gates, to the receiving room. He gave my name to the cop behind the desk. The cop opened a drawer, thumbed through a bunch of envelopes and tossed one on the counter.

"Open it up," he said. "Anything's missing, you say so now."

I opened it up. My wallet was in it and my car keys and a check to the police parking lot.

"Okay?" he said. "Well, put your John Hancock on this."

I signed a receipt. I thought this was a screwy way to do things, put a guy through all this just to go before a judge. But like I say, I'd never been in jail, and I figured they ought to know what they were doing.

I put the stuff in my pocket. The door to the street was open, and I thought, man oh man, what wouldn't I give to be out there.

The turnkey had gone back behind the counter. He was over at the water cooler, rinsing his mouth out and spitting into a big brass gaboon. He seemed to have forgotten all about me. I stood and waited.

Finally, the desk cop looked up at me. "You like this place, Mac?"

"I guess I got to like it," I said.

"Beat it," he said. "What the hell you waiting on? You got all your junk, ain't you?"

"Yes, sir," I said. "Thank you kindly, sir!" And I went out of that damned place so fast, I bet I didn't even cast a shadow.

I was sure it was a mistake, see? They had me mixed up with some other guy. I didn't see how it could be any other way.

I got my car off the parking lot. I came off of it like a bat out of hell, and I must have gone four or five blocks before I came to my senses and slowed down.

This wasn't going to get it. How far did I think I'd go with a finance-company car and a little over two bucks? Maybe the cops had pulled a boner, and maybe Staples had decided to give me a break. Either way I couldn't lose by seeing him. If this was on the level, swell. If not, that was swell too. At least I could beat his rotten tail off before I went back to jail.

I parked a few doors below the store. I sidled up to the window, and glanced through the door.

He was about halfway down the aisle, counting stock, it looked like. His back to me.

I jerked the door open fast. and went in. He started, and whirled around.

He came toward me, swiftly, hand extended.

"My dear boy! I'm so glad they released you promptly. I asked them not to take a moment longer than was necessary. I made it very urgent, Frank."

"Well, okay," I said. "I'm not kicking, understand. But you ask me, three days isn't very damned prompt."

"But, Frank." He spread his hands. "It wasn't three days. It was hardly an hour ago that your wife repaid the money."

SEVEN

My wife? A wife I didn't really have, now, had ponied up the dough? Hell, she couldn't have. She wouldn't have if she could.

Staples looked at me expectantly. "You mean to say you didn't know? She didn't tell you she was arranging your release?"

There was a purring, pleased note to his voice. I didn't know what the situation was, or what he might make out of it. But a guy like that, you don't share your troubles with him.

"Well," I said, "I knew she was *trying* to get it, but I didn't think she could. I guess it's like you say. You never know what you can do until you have to do."

"Mmm." He nodded, studying my face. "I was wondering. You know, any number of people called the store here for you; accounts who'd bought from sample pending your delivery. I explained the situation to them, about your shortage, and—"

"Swell," I said. "Why didn't you advertise it in the papers?"

"Now, Frank. I was only trying to help you. You can be very ingratiating, when you choose to, and I thought some of your clients might like to help you out in your hour of need."

I shook my head at him. The guy was off his goddamned rocker. "Sure, they would," I said. "This is Saks Fifth Avenue. I got a bunch of millionaire clients. I don't practically have to club 'em over the head to get a one-buck payment."

"Well," he smiled, sheepishly, "I suppose it was a rather forlorn hope. But ... what I started to say was that I don't believe your wife was among those who called about you."

"So?" I said.

"Nothing," he said, hastily. "Naturally, you'd have called her from the jail. It just struck me as rather curious, your wife not calling and then sending the money in with another woman. I thought that, possibly—uh—"

I shrugged. It struck *him* as curious!

"I'll come clean with you," I said. "I didn't call my wife. I called all these scrubwomen and dishwashers I got for customers and I said they either laid it on the line, or I was through with them."

"Really, Frank!" He gave me a slap on the arm. "As a matter of fact, this woman—the girl—who brought the money in wasn't at all unattractive. Rather dowdy and weatherworn, but not bad withal."

"That must have been Frances Smith," I said. "The neighbor's girl. Joyce probably got herself a job, so she sent Frances with the money."

I lit a cigarette, casually, and dropped the match on the floor. That eager, foxy look went out of his eyes.

"Well, Frank. As long as you're here—"

"As long as I'm here," I said, "I'll take the dough I've got coming."

"Now, Frank," he pouted. "You mean you're angry with me? You're going to quit?"

"Well," I said. "I just supposed that—"

"Not at all. I'm sure you'll be extremely scrupulous from now on; just about have to, you know. You can go back to work right now, if you like."

I said I was pretty pooped; thought I'd better wait until Monday. He let me have twenty bucks against my pay, and I drove home.

The place smelled like a sewer. It stank with mildew and rotting food. I cleaned out the refrigerator, piling the stuff onto the junk on the table. Then, I just bundled it all up in the tablecloth, dishes and pans and everything, and threw the whole mess out into the garbage.

I opened all the windows, and hung the bedding on the line. There was still plenty to be done; there always would be in that place. But I let it go at that. I was feeling sort of limp, what with all the worry and nerve strain I'd been through. Almost too tired to wonder who had bailed me out or why she'd done it.

Maybe it would turn out to be a mistake after all.

It got dark. I put the windows back down, and drew the shades. I hadn't eaten much of anything while I was in jail; I couldn't eat that slop. So now I was pretty hungry. But there wasn't a damned thing in the cupboard but coffee and half a pint of whiskey. I took the whiskey into the lounge and had myself a slug.

I leaned back, and put my feet up. I sipped and smoked, thinking about the way I'd been last night and how much better this was; thinking how a guy never knew when he was really well off, and maybe I hadn't done so bad for myself after all.

I began to relax. I started wondering again

Now, who in the hell did I know . . .

Who in the name of God could have . . .

Someone was coming up the walk. Running, almost. Up the walk and the steps and across the porch. I jumped up and threw the door open.

"Mona!" I said. "Mona, child. What is the—?"

She half fell into my arms. Sobbing, out of breath. I kicked the door shut and carried her over to the lounge.

"Baby," I said. "It's all right, baby. Old Dolly's got you, and—"

"Oh, Dolly, Dolly!" She rocked back and forth, hugging me. "I was s-so afraid, so afraid you might not be here and . . . Don't let her get me, Dolly! Take me away! Help me to get away. I've got money, enough for both of us, Dolly! P-please, please, please—"

"Wait! Wait a minute!" I said, and I shook her by the shoulders. "Slow down, now. I'll do anything I can, honey, but I've got to know—"

"Take it, Dolly! You can have it all, but just take me with you."

She jabbed her hands into the pockets of her faded, old coat. She pulled them out again and money tumbled into my lap, crumpled wads of fives and tens and twenties.

"P-please, Dolly! Will you? Take the money and take me—"

"Sure," I said. "You bet I will. But we got to get a few things straight first. You took this money from your aunt?"

"Y-yes. This and the other, the money I gave to the man at the store. I d-didn't know what to think when you didn't come back. I knew something awful must have happened to you. You'd promised to come back, and I knew you wouldn't have broken your promise if you could help it. Anyone as g-good and nice as you were w-wouldn't—"

Her voice faltered. I patted her hand, uncomfortably.

"Yeah, sure," I said. "I just couldn't help it, see what I mean?"

"S-so I looked your number up in the phone book, and I called here. I called and called. And f-finally, today, I called the store, and the man said . . ."

The rest of it came out with a rush:

Staples had given her the lowdown on me. She knew where the old woman kept her money. She'd tapped it for enough to get out, plus what she had here. Now, with what looked like five or six hundred dollars—and me just out from under one larceny rap—we were supposed to take off together. Live happily ever after, and so on.

And I wanted to—I wanted her; and I was grateful as hell. But, hell, how could I?

She was looking at me, pleading with her eyes. "D-don't you want to, Dolly? Was that why you said you were married—b-because you didn't really like me? I called and called here, and no one—"

"No, I wasn't lying to you," I said. "My wife left me. She doesn't figure in the deal any more, so that part's swell. But . . ."

"She'll kill me when she finds out, Dolly! She'll know I took it, and—" She began to cry again, a low helpless sobbing that cut through me like a knife. "It's a-all right, Dolly. I d-don't mean to m-make you feel bad. I g-guess I should have known that you c-couldn't really l-like—"

"Baby," I said. "Listen to me, honey. Like isn't the word for the way I feel about you. I love you, understand? You've got to believe that. That's why we've got to go slow on this, because if we do it the wrong way—what you're suggesting—we'll never be together. They'll have us both in jail."

"But—"

"Listen to me. Let me ask the questions, and you answer 'em ... You're supposed to be out shopping tonight? Okay, the store was closed and you had to go on to another one. That takes care of that. Now, how about this dough your aunt had hidden. She doesn't know that you knew about it, does she?"

"N-no. But—"

"Just answer the questions. Where did she keep it? How did you happen to find out about it?"

"Down in the cellar. Behind some old boards and boxes. I was down there one day, cleaning out the furnace, and she didn't know I was there. She pulled the boards and boxes away, and there was a hole in the wall and the money was in it. In sort of a little suitcase. She took it out and counted it, mumbling and cursing—acting like she was half-crazy, a-and—she scared me to death, Dolly! I was afraid s-she might see me and—"

"Yeah, sure," I said. "The old miser act, huh? Did you ever see her down there again? When was the last time?"

"That was. It was the only time, about three months ago. The stairs are awfully steep, and I always go whenever there's anything to—"

"Uh-huh, sure. Well, don't you see, honey? It's all right. Anyway, it's all right for the present. Why, hell, it might be a year before she misses the dough."

She saw what I was leading up to, and she started getting frantic all over again. It might not be a year. Or even a day. The old gal might be checking over the dough right this moment, and—

"Stop it!" I said. "Get me, baby? I said to stop, and that's what I mean ... Your aunt doesn't know you took the money. She isn't going to know it. I go back on the job Monday. I'll have the three hundred-odd you got for me within a month or so. You'll put it back in that satchel, and you'll put this back tonight and—"

"*No!* I—"

"Yes! Don't you see, honey? We haven't got any choice. If you didn't go home tonight, the old gal would look for her dough right away. It's the first thing she'd think of. She'd know you'd taken it, and the police would pick you up in no time ... You don't want that, do you? You see I'm right, don't you?"

"Y-yes." She nodded reluctantly. "Y-you—you really do love me, Dolly?"

"I wish I had time for a demonstration," I said, and I wasn't just woofing. "But you've been gone pretty long as it is. I'll drive you back over there, drop you off at the shopping center, and we'll get together in a day or two. Have a hell of a time for ourselves."

I stuffed the money back into her pockets, petting and kidding her until she was smiling. She was still pretty nervous and scared, but she thought she could swing it all right. She had the downstairs bedroom. The old woman slept upstairs, and once she went up for the night she stayed up.

"It's a cinch," I said. "You won't have a bit of trouble, baby. Now, let's have one big kiss and then we'll be on our way."

We had it. I headed the car across town. She rode with her head on my shoulder, hardly saying a word; pretty well at peace with the world. And that was the way I wanted her, of course, but me, I wasn't feeling so good.

Mona didn't know how often her aunt counted her money. She'd only caught her at it the one time, but there were probably plenty of other times she didn't know about. The old woman could be doing it right along, you know, when she sent Mona out to shop. It figured that she would, a dame that liked dough as well as she did. And if she did it before I got that three-forty-five back ...

It wouldn't take her five minutes to beat the truth out of Mona. Staples would have to return the money, and I'd be returned to jail. On a double rap, probably: the store's charges and a charge of getting Mona to steal.

I wondered if maybe I wasn't playing this the wrong way.

I couldn't think of any other.

Of course, if the old woman had had any real dough, it would be different. If she'd had thousands instead of hundreds—enough to do something with, you know, enough so's you wouldn't mind sticking your neck out—well, I'd have known exactly what to do, then. She was a rotten, worthless old bitch. She had something coming to her, and I was just the boy to deliver it. And—and, hell! There didn't have to be much risk. Some, sure, but not much. Because Pete Hendrickson had something coming to him, too; and if he wasn't built to be a fall guy I'd never seen one.

Yes, sir, I knew just how I'd use Pete. A plan popped into my mind almost without me thinking. But for a few hundred—huh-uh. Or even a few thousand. When and if I ever pulled anything like that, I'd be playing for the jackpot. One big haul, and then Mona and—

Suddenly, I thought of something.

"Baby," I said. "Mona, honey. Does your aunt have some other money around the house? I mean, if she hardly ever digs into this cache in the basement—"

"Well," she hesitated, "I guess she must have; she keeps it in her room, probably. I don't know because the door's always locked, and she's never let me go in there."

"Uh-hmm," I said. "She must have quite a bit, wouldn't you say? After all, she's got the day to day expenses of the two of you, and—"

"They're not very much, Dolly. We eat mostly rice and beans, and things that are cheap. I have to shop all around—buy stuff that the stores are about to throw out. We don't spend hardly anything."

"Yeah, but still . . ."

"D-dolly . . ." She drew closer to me. "I didn't w-want to tell you, but—I've had to do that—you know—a lot. I've had to do it for a long time. She's m-made me, and that's where . . ."

Jesus! It made me sick to think about it. Hustling this kid, making her hustle since she'd really been a kid . . .

"Never you mind, honey," I said. "You won't have to do it any more, so you just don't think about it. I don't."

We were almost there, almost to the stores where I was supposed to let her out. She started getting the shakes again.

"Do I have to, Dolly? C-can't we just take the money, and—"

I shook my head. "No, baby, we can't. I mean, we really can't. We'd have to travel—we'd have to do plenty of traveling. We'd have to have money to live on. We just couldn't make it on this. It just ain't enough, know what I mean?"

"Well . . ." She sat up on the seat, turned and looked at me eagerly. "I could get the rest, Dolly. There's a lot more, and I could get it, too."

"Huh! But you said—"

But she hadn't said that. I'd just assumed that she'd cleaned out all the old girl's cash. It was what I'd have done, if I'd been in a taking mood, and I supposed she had, too.

So there was more—a lot. But maybe there wasn't. What did a lot mean to a kid like this?

My hands were shaking on the wheel. I gripped it tighter, fighting to keep the excitement out of my voice.

"Now, let's just keep calm, baby," I said. "Old Dolly's in the saddle, and there's nothing to get up in the air about. N-now—now, how much is there? Tell papa, baby. What do you m-mean when you say a—"

"Well . . ." She chewed her lip, frowning. "I'd have to count off for what I gave the man at the store, and this that I—"

"For God's sake!" I said. "Don't stop to do arithmetic problems! Spit it out! Just give it to me in round numbers."

She gave it to me.

My hands jerked on the wheel. I almost ran up on the curb.

"M-Mona," I said. "Baby, child. Sweet thing. Say that again."

"A hundred—will it be enough, Dolly? A hundred thousand dollars?"

EIGHT

I sat and stared at her, kind of stunned, and she looked at me, anxious eyed, her breasts rising and falling. We were like that for a minute or two, her staring at me hopefully and me too shocked-stupid to say anything. And then her face went dead again, and she said I'd better take her on home.

"It's all right, Dolly. I'm not afraid any more. She'll k-kill me, and then it'll all be over with and—"

"Hush your mouth, honey child," I said. "*She* isn't going to kill anyone. *She* isn't, get me?"

"But she will! She'll find out and—"

"Huh-uh. That ain't the way it's going to be, at all. Now, tell me something, baby. Where did an old bag like that get a hundred thousand dollars?"

"Well," she hesitated, "I'm not sure, but . . ."

She couldn't remember much of anything about her early life. But the old lady had let drop a few things, and piecing it all together she had a pretty good idea about the source of that hundred grand. At least, it sounded good to me.

I started up the car again and drove on toward her place. Thinking. Wondering just how to put the proposition up to her. Or whether I really wanted to put it up to her.

"One more thing, honey. I think this is going to be all right—I mean, it could be all right. I think I can work it out so's you and I can go off together, and—and—" I couldn't get the words out: what I really wanted to say. I swallowed and made another try, coming in at it from an angle. "This Pete Hendrickson character; remember him, honey? Now, just suppose that Pete—"

She shivered and turned her head. You know. Sick, shamed, scared, just at the mention of Pete's name.

I gave her a little love pat, and called her a honey lamb.

"I'm sorry, baby. We won't talk about Pete any more, about any of those dirty bastards your aunt made you—well, never mind. What I was going to say was—was—suppose someone broke into your house and—"

"No," she said. "No, Dolly."

"But, baby. If—"

"No," she said again. "You're too nice. You've done too much. I couldn't let you do it."

I swallowed, feeling like I ought to be disappointed. Because this was the first crack I'd ever had at the big dough, and I figured it'd just about be the last. But I reckon that I was actually pretty relieved. I was glad that it wasn't going to happen.

"Well, all right," I said. "I just thought that—"

"She's got a gun. You might get hurt, or even killed," she said.

And I was back in business again.

We'd come to the shopping center where I was supposed to let her out. I pulled in at the curb, and stopped.

"The old gal's counting on me coming back to your house.

Remember, honey? I told her I'd be back. So if I should drop around late some night and ..."

I laid it on the line for her. Not the whole stunt, because I didn't have it all figured out yet, but the main thing. What was going to have to happen to the old woman.

"You don't have to mix into it yourself, baby. All you have to do is have the dough ready for me to grab and call the cops after I've left."

"And then ..." The shine came back into her eyes, the deadness went out of her face. "And we could go away together, then, Dolly? We could be together after that?"

"In a week or so, sure. Just as soon as things cool off a little."

"Do it tonight, Dolly," she said. "Kill her tonight."

... Well, of course, doing it that night was out of the question. A deal like this, it was going to take some planning; there was Pete Hendrickson to be got ahold of and worked on. I told her we'd have to wait: probably I could swing it Monday. Meanwhile, she was to beat it on back to the house, and pretend like everything was hunky-dory.

"But what if she finds out I took that money, Dolly? If she finds out before Monday—"

"She won't," I said, making her believe it. Making myself believe it. "Beat it on home, now, and I'll talk to you again tomorrow night. I'll meet you right here around eight o'clock."

She hung back, scared as hell to face the old dame, just wanting to hang on to me. But I sweet-talked her, kind of getting hard-boiled at the same time, and finally she took off.

I watched her until she rounded the corner. Then, I made a u-turn in the street and headed for home.

Now that it was all settled—if, of course, I could suck Pete in—I began to get cold feet. Or, maybe, I should say, I started to go cold on the deal. I wasn't really scared; hell, there wasn't anything to be scared about; and I sure wanted that little Mona and I sure wanted that hundred grand. But I just couldn't see myself doing what I'd have to do.

"Why, you're crazy, man!" I thought. "YOU'RE going to kill someone? YOU'RE going to kill a couple of people? Not you, fella. It just ain't in you."

I got about half way home, and then I jerked the wheel to the

right and headed for town. I'd hardly eaten anything for the last
three-four days. Maybe that was what was making me so shaky and
nervous. Maybe things would look different to me with a good meal
under my belt.

I toured around the business section for a few minutes, trying to
think of something I wanted to eat and some decent place to eat in. I
finally wound up at the same old joint I usually ate in—a little
combination bar and grill around the corner from the store.

I sat down in a booth, and the waitress shoved a menu in front of
me. There wasn't anything on it that sounded good, and anyway, one
look at her and my stomach had turned flipflops. I don't know why
it is, by God, but I can tell you how it is. Every goddamned restaurant
I go to, it's always the same way . . . They'll have some old bag on the
payroll—I figure they keep her locked up in the mop closet until they
see me coming. And they'll doll her up in the dirtiest goddamned
apron they can find and smear that crappy red polish all over her
fingernails, and everything about her is smeary and sloppy and smelly.
And she's the dame that always waits on me.

I'm not kidding, brother. It's that way wherever I go.

I told her to bring me a shot and a bottle of beer, I'd settle on
something to eat later. But she was one of these salesmen, you know.
She hung around, recommending "good things," the day's specials
and so on pointing 'em out with those goddamned red claws. So I put
up with it just as long as I could, and then I gave her the old eye and
told her off.

"Maybe you didn't hear me, sister," I said. "Maybe I better have
the manager bring me that shot and the beer."

"B-but—" She looked like I'd hit her in the face, and it was just
about as red as if I had. "I'm sorry, sir. I was j-just trying to—"

"And I'm trying to get a drink," I said. "Now, do I get it or not?"

I got it fast. But the next round I ordered, another girl brought it
to me. Not that it made any difference because she was just as bad as
the first one, they all were; they always are. They may be okay up
until then, but the minute I step in through the door of a place it's
let's get sloppy, girls, here comes Dolly. The poor bastard ain't got
enough trouble, so let's make him sick at his stomach.

I know how they do. They can't kid me a damned bit.

Well, anyway. I finished the first set-up and started on the second. I was sitting there sipping beer thinking and trying not to think, when a shadow fell across the table.

"Ah, Frank"—Staples' lisping, oily voice. "So you are here, aren't you?"

I gave a little jump, and he grinned and sat down across from me. I asked him what he meant by that so-I-was-here stuff.

"A little bet I had with myself. I—Oh, thank you, miss. A bowl of your delicious soup, if you please, and a tall glass of milk ... As I was saying, Frank. I worked rather late at the store tonight, a special inventory, and afterwards I found myself in the mood for a pre-bedtime snack. But I do so hate to eat alone, you know; I'd almost rather do without. And just on the offchance that I might encounter some dear friend, I—Not you, of course. I had no idea that you would be eating out tonight..."

"This looks like I'm eating?" I said. "The wife had some girl friends in tonight so I got out of her way."

"How thoughtful of you. And how thoughtless of her; to entertain on your first night at home ... Are you and the little woman getting along all right, Frank? You haven't quarreled?"

"Sorry to disappoint you," I said. "Now what's the pitch on this bet you made with yourself?"

"Oh, yes." He spooned soup into his pussy-cat mouth. "As I say, I was hoping to find someone to break bread with, and just on the offchance that you or one of the boys might be here, I glanced through the window..."

He grinned, waiting for me to feed him the straight line. I let him wait, taking another slug of beer, and his lips pulled down in a little pout.

"I couldn't see you from the street, Frank. And yet I knew you were here. Aren't you interested in knowing how?"

I was curious about it. But I shrugged and said it made me no difference.

His eyes glinted spitefully. "The atmosphere of the place, Frank. The look on the faces of those poor girls. Tell me, if you don't like the food and the service here why don't you go some place else?"

"What's the use?" I said. "They're all alike."

"Oh? But—" He studied me puzzledly; then, his head moved in a nod, and he smiled in a way I didn't understand. "Yes," he said, "yes, I suppose they are all alike if . . ."

"Yeah?"

"Nothing. This is quite cozy, Frank; it's always such a joy to talk to you . . . I trust you're fully readjusted after your recent ordeal? You harbor no ill-will toward me?"

"A swell guy like you?" I said. "How could I?"

"I'm so glad. Incidentally, inasmuch as we are such good friends . . ."

"Fire away."

"How in the name of heaven did you get so deeply in the hole? After all, the other collectors also had the rain to contend with, and they didn't appropriate more than three hundred dollars in company funds."

"Well," I said. "Well, you see, Staples . . ."

"Yes, Frank?"

I couldn't tell him. I wouldn't have told him even if I could have found the right words, because it just wouldn't have been smart. But I couldn't find the right words.

"Are you fed up, Frank? Is that it? Feel like your best effort gains you no more than your worst, that existence itself has become pointless?"

Well, like I say, I couldn't tell him; but he hadn't missed it very far. I couldn't get out and hit the old ball any more because I just didn't give a damn any more. And I guess there's nothing that can make a guy give a damn if he doesn't feel like it.

"How about it, Frank?" His lisp was gone. "You may as well tell me now, if that's the case."

"Hell," I said. "You talk like a man in a paper hat. What's the difference anyway?"

He didn't bother to answer me. Just waited. The difference was that if I couldn't earn my dough, I'd probably go back to stealing it. And I might skip out with a wad before he could nail me.

"I don't get you," I said, stalling for time. "If you were worried, why didn't you jump me about it this afternoon instead of—"

"I'm not the jumping kind, Frank. I always think things through, put all the various pieces together, before I act. Now, what happened to that money?"

A month or so later on I could have told him to go to hell; that, sure I was fed up with the damned stinking job and who wouldn't be, and so what the hell about it? But it wasn't a month or so later, and until it was—until everything had cooled off and it was safe to skip with Mona—I had to have a reason for staying in this crummy burg. I had to hang onto the job.

"... you understand, dear boy." He was quizzing me again. "I'm not merely being nosy. If it's simply something shady or unwise, if, for example, you spent it on a woman or took a little flyer on the ponies ..."

I looked up, meeting his eyes at last. He'd rung the bell with that last bit. He'd shown me how to get off the hook, and he'd also opened the way for me to ask him some questions.

"You remember that sales letter I showed you a while back? From that oil company down in Oklahoma?"

"Letter?" He shrugged. "I think you've showed me at least a dozen. For a man with some pretensions to sophistication, you seem to have landed on a truly amazing number of sucker lists. But—" He broke off, staring at me. "Oh, *no!*" he said. "No, Frank! You didn't send *that* outfit any money."

"Yeah," I looked sheepish. "I guess I did, Stape."

'But I distinctly told you—"

"Yeah, I know," I said, "but look at all the other things you told me. About the chances you missed when you were running a store down there years ago, and—"

"But my dear Frank! That was entirely different. I had a chance to buy land—leases. The real thing, not merely wild promises on paper."

"Well, I'll know better next time," I said. "You could have got in on the ground floor, huh, Stape?"

It was his favorite topic, the one thing he'd really talk to you about instead of jabbing you with the needle. Once you got him on the subject of oil and this town where he'd managed his first store, he was a different guy entirely.

"... you never saw anything like it, Frank. Nominally, it was the sorriest land in the world. Rocky, eroded, worn out. Then, the boom came and these poor farmers—people who actually hadn't had enough to eat a few months before—were suddenly rich beyond their wildest dreams. Why, I personally know of one little eighty-acre plot that went for a million and a half dollars, and—"

I whistled, wonderingly, cutting in on him; sliding in one of the questions I wanted to ask. "I don't suppose they all cashed in that heavy though, did they? I mean, some of 'em probably sold out too early or—"

"That's right. That's right, Frank. It just seemed too good to be true, you know. In a great many instances, the first lease hound that came along and shook forty or fifty or a hundred grand under a farmer's nose—"

"Cash?" I whistled again. "You mean they actually swung that much *cash* at 'em?"

"Oh, yes, and even much larger sums. The psychological effect, you know; and then these people were poorly educated and inclined to be suspicious of banks. Cash they understood. A check—well, that to them was nothing more than a piece of paper."

"What about the people like that, anyway?" I said. "I'll bet a lot of them didn't know what the hell to do with the money after they got it."

"True. Oh, so true, Frank. You or I, now—if I were ever able to get my hands on any substantial sum..." He broke off, sighing, and dipped into the soup again. "Yes, Frank. It was an experience that might have permanently embittered a man of a less philosophical turn of mind. Here was poor little me, filled with appreciation for the finer things in life yet lacking the money to achieve them. And here were these loutish creatures with scads of money and no appreciation whatsoever. Why, in case after case, they wouldn't even buy themselves the necessities of life. They simply went on living as they always had, and hoarded their tens of thousands."

I grinned. "I'll bet that really did burn you, Stape. You right in the middle of all that cabbage, and not being able to latch onto it."

"Oh, I tried, Frank," he nodded, seriously. "I tried, oh, so terribly hard. But I'm afraid I was a little green and callow in those days. A trifle clumsy. The only result of my efforts was a sudden transfer to another store."

I had another round of drinks while he was finishing his snack. Then he left for his hotel, and I started for home. I still hadn't eaten anything, but I was feeling pretty good. The talk with Staples had warmed me back up on the deal.

No, I didn't really know anything. All I had to go on was the few things that Mona remembered, or thought she remembered, and the little that she'd picked up from the old woman's remarks. But all in all, and taken with what Staples had told me, it seemed to add up.

They'd lived down south at one time—Mona and the old woman and some other people she couldn't remember: her own folks, I figured. It must have been the south or southwest, because it was warmer and things stayed green longer—*she remembered, or thought she did*. And there'd been towers—oilfield derricks—and ... And that was about all, as much as she could tell me. Why they'd come up here to settle down, I didn't know; so there was kind of a hole in the picture there. But I didn't see that it was too important, and the rest was solid enough.

Oil had been struck on their farm down south. The old woman had sold out for a hundred grand. Or maybe she'd got even more, and was just hoarding the hundred grand. Low down white trash. Too miserly to let go of a buck, and not knowing what the hell to buy with it if she did let go. Sitting on a hundred thousand, and hustling her own niece for bean money.

Yeah, it figured.

I wanted it to be that way, so that's the way it was.

NINE

I picked up a few groceries the next morning, and had a real meal for a change. French toast with bacon, hashed brown potatoes, fruit cocktail and coffee. I ate and ate, grinning to myself, thinking by God they might *think* they could starve old Dolly to death but they had another goddamned think coming. To hell with those damned sloppy waitresses. To hell with that damned bitchy Joyce, and Doris, and

Ellen and ... and all those other tramps. Old Dolly could take care of
himself until he got someone decent to do the job. And, brother, that
happy hour was not far away.

I refilled my coffee cup, and lighted a cigarette. I sat back in my
chair, relaxing. Pete Hendrickson was the next step. I'd look him up
today on the quiet—naturally it wouldn't do to be seen with him—
and ...

I choked, and banged down my cup.

Pete.

I didn't know where the guy lived.

The last address I'd had on him was the one he'd skipped from,
you know, before he went to work at that greenhouse. And where
the hell he might be living now, God only knew. He might not even
have an address since he lost his job. He could be bunking in a boxcar
somewhere or sleeping under a culvert.

I jumped up cursing, paced back and forth across the living room.
I thought, *by God, I might have known it! I knock my brains out to
shape up a sweet deal and someone screws it up for me!*

I don't know how long I paced around, cursing and ranting, before
I finally got a grip on myself. Then, I got out the phone book, looked
up the number of the greenhouse and dialed it.

I got the foreman on the wire.

I said, "Please, sor, iss Olaf Hendrickson speaking. Iss very
important dot I speak to my brudder, Pete."

"Not here any more," he said. "Sorry."

"Perhaps you vould tell me vere—"

"Nope, nope," he said, curtly, before I could ask him the question.
"Don't give out information like that. Not sure, anyway."

"Please, sor," I said. "Iss—"

"Sorry." He banged up the receiver.

Well, I'm a funny guy, though. People try to screw me up, to keep
me from doing what I got to do, I go at it all the harder.

I looked at the clock. I shaved and brushed my teeth and gandered
the clock again. Eleven-fifteen. Just about right. I got in my car, and
headed for the other side of town.

It was pretty close to noon when I got to this beer parlor, the one
just down the street from the greenhouse. I picked up the name and
address as I drove by, and stopped at a drugstore in the next block. I

waited in my car until the noon whistles blew. Then, I got out and stood looking down the street.

My hunch had been right. Workmen were coming out of the greenhouse and making a beeline for the beer parlor. I gave them a few minutes to get inside and get settled. I went into the drugstore, then, and called the place from a booth telephone.

The phone rang and rang. Finally, someone snatched it off the hook, the proprietor or a bartender or maybe even a customer, and hollered hello.

"There's a fellow there named Pete Hendrickson," I said. "One of the boys from the greenhouse. Will you call him to the phone, please?"

He didn't answer me; just turned away from the phone and shouted, "Pete—Pete Hendrickson! Any of you guys named Hendrickson?"

Someone shouted something back, and someone else laughed; and this guy spoke into the phone again. "He ain't here, mister. Ain't at the greenhouse no longer, either."

"Gosh," I said. "I've just got to talk to him. I wonder if there's anyone around who could tell me where—"

"Hang on," he said, pretty short, like I was giving him a hard time. "ANY OF YOU GUYS KNOW WHERE..."

They didn't. Or if they did, they weren't saying.

"Sorry, mister," this guy said. "Any other little thing I can do for you?"

I told him yeah. "Go take a flying jump at yourself, you snotty bastard." And I slammed up as he started to cuss.

Well, that had been my best bet but it wasn't my only one. Characters like Pete Hendrickson were my meat. I knew just what they'd do, just where they'd go. Sure, it'd taken me weeks to run him down before; and I could work out in the open then instead of slipping around like I had to now. But that had been different. I hadn't been looking for him for myself. This time it was for me—for me and Mona and a hundred grand—and by God I'd find him.

I drove into town, and parked at the foot of skid row.

I got out and started walking.

I must have walked fifteen miles that afternoon. Past the employment agencies with the bums hanging around in the front. Past the flop houses with their fly-specked windows and stinking lobbies. Past the greasy spoons. Past the pool halls and wine joints and cheap beer parlors.

Hell, it was Saturday afternoon wasn't it? And even if he had a home, a guy like Pete wouldn't stay in on Saturday afternoon. He'd be down here where he could stretch a few dimes into a party. Where he could guzzle and scoff and have enough left over for a flop.

So I walked and walked, just strolling from place to place, going around and around and around. And Saturday afternoon went away, and it was Saturday night.

I was too jumpy to eat—not that I could have got anything to eat, anyhow. I found a bar that wasn't too completely crummy looking, and threw down a few double shots. Then I started walking again.

He had to be here, someplace. Son-of-a-bitch, he just *had* to! If he wasn't around here, then he must have left town and—

I gritted my teeth together. *No! NO! He couldn't do that to me. They couldn't do that to me.*

Saturday night.

Eight o'clock Saturday night. Still no Pete ... and it was almost time to meet Mona.

I bought a pint of whiz, and went back to my car. I yanked the cap with my teeth, making them ache to beat hell and liking the ache. I threw down a slug—two or three slugs. I dropped the jug down on the seat, and stepped on the starter.

High? Man, I was higher than a kite; but not from the old gravy. It was the kind of high you get on when you got to do something and can't. When you've got to have the answers and you don't know any.

What was I going to do now? What was I going to tell Mona? I'd told her I was going to fix it, and I'd reached the point where I could almost feel that hundred grand ...

I fingered the cap off the bottle and took another long drink ... Tell her? Tell her nothing. If I could dig up Pete tomorrow or the next day, fine. If not—and I'd better not hang around town much longer after that—well, she'd have a few days of hope before she found out the truth. And me, I wouldn't have had anything more than I was entitled to.

It was the only thing to do, as I saw it. Brush her off on the questions. Play it close to the vest. Make her happy and grateful, and then—You know. Nothing wrong with that, was there? I wasn't taking anything that she wasn't perfectly willing to give me.

"Nothing wrong," I said—and I said it out loud. "Dolly Dillon says there's nothing wrong with it—the rotten son-of-a-bitch!"

So, anyway, I admitted it; and I was mad enough at myself to bite nails. But I knew I was going to go right ahead, just the same.

She was waiting in the shadows of a tree a few doors down from the super-market. She climbed into the car, laying a little sack of groceries up behind the seat, and I stepped on the gas. The jerk threw her against me. She moved away, looking a little frightened; her voice trembling.

"W-where are we going, Dolly? I've been away from the house quite a while, and—"

"I won't keep you long," I said. "What's the matter? You act like you're not glad to see me."

"Oh, no, Dolly! I mean, I am glad. But—Is everything all right? W-we ... you're still going to do it?"

"Didn't I say so?" I said.

"Monday? N-no later than Monday, Dolly? I'm scared to death she'll—"

"I told you, didn't I?" I said. "You want me to put it in writing?"

I drove across a railroad spur, turned down a dirt road and parked. There weren't any streetlights over that way, and there wasn't any traffic. I put my arms around her, and pulled her against me.

I kissed her, and ran a hand over her. And what happened then was so wild and wonderful that—well, I don't know how to say it. I guess a hop-eater's dream might be something like that.

I've been around, see? I'm not one of these old country boys that can work up a boil around a lingerie counter. I've known the twenty-dollar gals and the nicey-nice babes who were just out for kicks. But I'd never known anything like that before.

Then, it was all over—it was, as far as I was concerned. But that didn't seem to mean nothing to her. I said, "Baby ..." and then I said, "My God, honey ..." and finally I said, "What the hell is this?"

I shoved her away, and got back on my own side of the seat. That seemed to break the spell, as they say in story books.

"I'm s-sorry." She bit her lip, trying not to look at me, looking ashamed. "I j-just love you so much that—that—"

But how about a babe like this? Maybe I had the wrong angle on things. Maybe the old woman was just selling something to keep it from going for free.

That thought went in and out of my mind fast. It didn't even have time to say hello before I'd booted it out in the cold and slammed the door. Because even a damned fool could see that this kid was a doll, just as sweet and innocent as they come. And naturally with everything I was doing for her—with everything she *thought I* was doing for her—she wanted to do something special for me.

That was the way I wanted it, the way it should be. After all the tramps I'd been tied up with, it was about time I met someone who was grateful and loving and appreciative.

I told her she was swell, and everything was swell. I just hadn't wanted to hold her up tonight when she was already late. "About this gun your aunt has," I said, starting the car. "Where does she keep it?"

"Upstairs. In her room . . . Dolly—"

"She keeps the key to the room with her? Swell. Now you get your clothes straightened out, and I'll drive you back to the shopping center."

"Dolly"—she started brushing at her clothes—"What—how are you going to do it, Dolly? I mean, I ought to know if—"

"Huh-uh," I said. "You don't need to know a thing. If you had it on your mind you might accidentally give it away, so just forget about it."

"B-but—"

"You hear? Forget it," I said. "All you have to do is be at home Monday night between eight-thirty and nine."

"Eight-thirty or nine?"

"Or ten. Somewhere along there," I said.

"You asked—you started to ask about Pete Hendrickson last night. What does he—?"

"Nothing," I said, and it didn't look like I was lying about that. Pete wasn't going to have anything to do with it. I wasn't going to. And I sure felt sorry for her, but what could I do? "Now leave it lay, will you?" I said. "You keep asking questions I'm liable to think you don't trust me."

"I'm sorry. I just wondered what—"

"Here's where you get out," I said, and I handed her the groceries.

"Now, hurry on home and don't worry about a thing. Everything's going to be fine."

She opened the door of the car and started to get out. She turned back around worriedly, apologetically, her lips parted for another try.

I leaned forward and kissed her, gave her a little punch. "Beat it," I said. "You hear me, honey? I want to see you move."

She smiled. She beat it. I drove away.

I made a few more tours of skid row, and it was still no soap. It looked like Pete must have jumped town. I got a bite to eat and bought another pint, and drove home; figuring, well, hell, maybe that's the way it's supposed to be.

I think I told you earlier that this shack of ours was on a railroad siding, that there was the tracks on one side and a wrecking yard on the other? Anyway, I meant to tell you. So I drove home that night, and there was a string of cars shuttled onto the siding: an empty box and a gondola and a couple of flats. And I thought, oh, oh, no damned sleep in the morning. They'll be in here humping those cars at six a.m.; and—

I gulped. I stood staring at the open door of the box car, and I sort of froze in my tracks.

It was dark on that street. Ours was the only house in the block. I'd already locked up the car and I knew I'd never have time to get my hands on a wrench or something to slug with before this guy could get to me. Because he'd already started toward me. He'd swung down out of the door of the box, a hell of a big guy, and was coming across the yard. And I couldn't see what he looked like, of course. But I reckoned he wasn't up to any good or he wouldn't have been . . .

He stopped about six steps away from me.

"Dillon?" he said. "Iss Dillon, yess?"

And I sagged back against the car.

"P-Pete," I said weakly. "Pete Hendrickson."

TEN

He'd taken the five I gave him the night before and jungled up with some 'boes down on Salt Creek. They'd all got on a hell of a wine binge and he hadn't woke up until tonight, needing a drink like a baby needs its mother. A drink and some chow and an inside flop. And there was just one guy he could think of who might hold still for a bite. I had been "so nice" to him. The "fife dollars" I had given him, and I had spoken of a "chob," so . . .

He cleared his throat, uncomfortably, misunderstanding my silence. "I did not go to your door, Dillon. Your vife—you have a vife, yess?—I was afraid of alarming; so late at night to see a bum like me at the door. So I vait in the box until I hear your car, and—"

His voice trailed away.

I snapped out of the jolt he'd given me.

"I'm glad you came by," I said. "I've been wanting to see you. Come on inside and—"

"Better I had not. Such a bum I look, and your vife vould not like. If you could chust—vell, a dollar or two—chust until I find vork . . ."

"Huh-uh," I said, and took him by the arm. "You need a lot more than that, Pete. Come on in, and I'll tell you about it, and, no, don't worry about the wife. She's away on a little trip."

I got him inside. I saw that the shades were drawn, and I turned on the light, and gave him the opened pint.

He killed it at a gulp, shuddered, sighed. I passed him the fresh pint and gave him a cigarette.

He took another drink, drew a long drag on the cigarette. He leaned back in his chair, sighing.

"Ahhhhh," he said, just like that. "Ahhhhh. My life you have safed, Dillon."

"Maybe not your life," I said. "Just about forty years of it. I think that's the stretch in this state for raping a minor."

It didn't register on him for a moment. He'd been stuck in the basement, and now he was riding the express car up; and it wasn't stopping for signals.

He took another swig from the jug. He wiped his mouth, and said

I was a nice man. He said I was a "chentleman" and a fine friend. And then he said, *"Vot!* Rape?" And leaned forward in his chair.

"You heard me," I said. "Old lady Farrell's niece. Mona."

"B-b-but," he said. "B-b-but—"

"Yeah?"

"A lie it iss! I—I—" He swallowed and his eyes shifted away from mine. "With the girl I was, yess. Vy not? I vork, and dot is some of my pay. She does not object, it iss agreeable with her and—"

"It was, huh?" I said. "Maybe she took it away from you, huh?"

And I thought, oh, you dirty bastard! You dirty lying bastard! You just wait.

"Vell"—he started to smirk, then straightened his face when he saw the look I was giving him. "Vell, no. I haf told you how it vas. I vork, she iss the pay."

"And she's a minor. A child in the eyes of the law."

"But she iss not! She could not be! And anyway, I did not force—"

"The old woman says she's a minor," I said. "She says you threatened to kill her and the girl, and then you took it."

"B-but—but—"

He lifted the bottle again. He stared at me, his eyes crafty.

"I t'ink maybe you—maybe you not tell truth, Dillon."

"All right," I said.

"Vy—vy vould she do such a thing? I am not the first; many others there have been. And—and how you know, anyvay?"

"Let it go," I said. "I felt like I'd given you kind of a raw deal getting you fired, and I wanted to make up for it. But as long as you think I'm lying, let it go."

I stood up and took out my wallet. I got out a couple of ones, letting him see them, and then I shoved them back and took out a five. I held it out to him.

"And take the bottle along with you, too," I said. "You'd better have a good one before they pick you up."

"B-but—" He drew back from the money. "I did not mean to offend. It iss chust—"

"Just for your own satisfaction," I said, "why don't you call the old gal up? There's the phone. Ask her if she isn't going to send you over the road just as soon as she can arrange it."

"B-but if I did dot—"

"But it isn't true, remember? I'm lying to you."

His face was turning gray. He took such a slug out of the pint that he almost killed it.

"Dillon," he said. "How—vot—vot *iss?*"

I sat down in front of him. I looked him in the eye and began to talk.

So maybe he wasn't the first one with Mona, I said. But could he prove it? And could he prove that she wasn't a minor, and that she and the old woman had agreed to the deal? It would be his word against theirs. And *he* had a police record and a bad rep for drinking.

Why was the old gal doing this to him? Well, she was a pure mean bitch and low down as all hell *(he nodded)*, and she was sore at him, remember? They'd had a knock-down dragout brawl before he'd quit working for her *(he nodded again)*, and she was plenty burned up about it. She was out for blood, that baby, and she meant to stick him.

Pete shook his head dully. A thin thread of slobber oozed down from the corner of his mouth, and he brushed it away.

"Vy?" he said. "I do not doubt you, Dillon, but vy does she tell—"

"Because she thought I was on her side, see?" I lied. "I went there trying to trace you down for the store, and you know it was just business with me; I wasn't sore at you at all, and I proved it to you. But, anyway, she figures I am, and I play along with her, so just as I'm leaving, she says to come back and let her know if you're still there at the greenhouse. She's got an idea how we can make it plenty tough on you.

"Well, like I say, I wasn't sore at you at all. I'm really your good friend and I proved it, didn't I? *(He hesitated, nodded firmly.)* So I go back and tell her you've quit the greenhouse, and then I ask her what the score is. I want to find out, see, so I can tip you off.

"I guess maybe she got a little suspicious of me about then because all she'll say is never mind; the cops will be able to find you and when they do it'll be just too bad. But I kept on hanging around, pretending like I'm burned up with you, too, and anxious to help her, and finally she tells me what she has in mind . . ."

I coughed and turned my head. Man, it was all I could do to keep from busting out laughing! . . . That slobber running down his chin again; and his eyes—glazed and bugged out like marbles. He was one scared bastard, and I'm crapping you negative.

"Well, I was afraid to try to talk her out of it," I went on. "She'd have seen I was really your friend, see, and she'd probably have called the cops right away. So I said swell, I was all for it, but maybe she wouldn't be able to make it stick. Maybe it would be better if I looked you up and brought you there. You know; had a few drinks with you and then suggested that we go over there for a party. We'd frame you—I told her—see? We'd call the cops in, and . . ."

Yeah, it was pretty wild, but he was a pretty dumb guy. Didn't have much education, anyway. And I guess he'd been pushed around plenty by the cops. He stared at me, his lips too stiff to move, his face turning green under the gray. And I coughed and turned my head again.

"V-vot . . . I haf some time, Dillon? I can get out of town before—"

"How far would you get?" I said. "The cops have your mug and prints. They put out a flier on you, and they pick you up in no time."

"B-but vot—"

"I'm telling you," I said. "She gave me until Monday night, so Monday night we go over there. I'll go in first and tell her you'll be along in a few minutes, and then you slip up on the porch and I start talking to her. I tell her I'm sticking my neck out a mile, so how about a roll with the gal for my trouble. And she'll go for it, see; she practically propositioned me already. So then I say I've got to be sure she won't try to stick me some time. She'll have to give me something in writing to show that she and the gal consented to the deal. That the kid's over twenty-one and she's done it before and—Well, what's the matter?"

He'd been frowning a little. I gave him a hard look, and he cleared his throat apologetically.

"It . . . a little strange, it sounds. You t'ink she vould do such?"

"Sure, she will. It's a cinch."

"Den vy iss it necessary for me to be dere?"

"Why?" I said. And for a minute I couldn't think of anything else to say. "Why, dammit, I don't need to explain that to you, do I?"

"If you vould not mind, please. So mixed up I am, I cannot—"

"Why, it's because she's liable to hang back, know what I mean? She's liable to think I'm trying to pull a fast one on her. So I step to the door and say, well, here you are now. I want that statement. I want it right then or the deal don't go no further. I'll tip you off and tell the cops it's a frame, and she'll be in heap big trouble."

He nodded, his face clearing. He hesitated.

"Vould you—You do not t'ink perhaps you could go to the police now and—?"

"I thought of that," I said, "but I'm afraid it wouldn't work. They'd probably lock you up while they were trying to get to the bottom of things, and maybe they wouldn't stick you on a rape rap but you'd still be in for a long jolt. It's a pretty messy deal, you know, anyway you look at it. Even if it wasn't rape—"

"It vas not! I svear it, Dillon!"

"—it still looks bad. You can't make it look any other way. There are at least a couple of charges they could stick you on, and they'd damned well give you the maximum on each."

He sighed; nodded again.

"You are right, my good friend. So, if you are villing to do me dis great favor ..."

"I owe it to you," I said. "I got you fired, and now I'm trying to square things. Anyway, it's a pleasure to put a crimp in that old bitch's tail."

He told me I was a nice man and a "chentleman," again. He looked at the bottle, set it down on the end table, and stood up. "So much you haf done, I am ashamed to ask—"

"Sit down," I said. "You're going to stay here. Stay right here until this is all over with."

"B-but"—he sat down again; he didn't need any urging at all—"It iss too much."

"Nuts," I said. "I'm glad to have some company. Now how about some bacon and eggs?"

His eyes filled up; I thought, by God, he was going to start blubbering. "My good friend," he said. "My fine friend." And he brushed his nose on his sleeve.

"There's just one thing," I said. "You'll have to stay under cover, understand? Keep inside the house and don't let anyone know you're around here. It wouldn't look good, know what I mean, if the old gal decided to get tough and we had to go to the police. They'd figure that we were buddies, see? Get the idea that one of us was lying and the other was swearing to it."

A HELL OF A WOMAN

"So," he said. "I vill do as you say."

I fixed him some grub.

I went out and got more whiskey.

I made him go to bed in the bedroom, and I took the lounge.

I fell asleep fast, but along about three in the morning I woke up, feeling kind of cramped and like something was hugging me.

Something was. The bedclothes. I was all tucked in like a two-year-old.

I started to lug the stuff back in to him; and then I remembered Mona, that sweet child, and the way he'd taken advantage of her. So I just took what blankets I wanted, and dropped the rest on the floor.

Let the son-of-a-bitch freeze. He'd be plenty hot in the place he was going to.

ELEVEN

The next day was Sunday, and it was just about the damnedest longest day I ever spent in my life.

Pete was pretty well leveled off of his binge. His mind was about as clear as it ever got to be, and he was over his first scare. So he starts to worrying, wondering, firing the questions at me. And frankly my mind wasn't very clear. Everything was kind of mashed together inside, like I'd been crawling through a rat hole.

I started feeding him whiskey right away. I got out my collection cards and pretended like I was working. But I couldn't hedge him off. They kept coming, the "vys" and the "vots" and the "hows" until, man, I was almost ready to murder him right there.

"I told you" (I told him). "Goddammit, Pete, how many times do I have to explain it? I get this business in writing from her, and then she's screwed. You could whip her with a wet rope and she wouldn't dare let out a peep."

"But"—he kept shaking his head—"but so strange, it seems. Like a movie almost. It iss hard to believe that she vill—"

"Well, she will! Wait and see if she doesn't."

"Still"—he kept on shaking his goddamned head—"it iss hard to ... it iss so strange. For her to be so angry with me over somet'ing dat—For her to tell you of her plans, and for you to—"

"All right," I said. "I'm lying. I made it all up. Why the hell would I lie to you, for Christ's sake."

"Pleass! My good friend, my dear friend. I did not mean—"

"What do you mean?"

"Vel. I vas chust wondering. I merely wished to ask vy ..."

No, I don't think he was actually suspicious; he was too well sold on me and him being swell friends. It was more as though he was afraid I was going off half-cocked: like maybe the old woman had been tossing some bull and I'd got the wind up over nothing. Or maybe I was setting a bear trap to catch a skunk: making such a big deal out of it that we were liable to get screwed up in the machinery.

Anyway, he kept on and on, fussing and quizzing and worrying out loud, until by God! I had just all I could take and I couldn't take any more. It was about an hour or so after dinner when it happened. I'd gone out to the delicatessen and bought enough damned grub to feed a horse; thinking, you know, that a good scoff would keep him quiet for a while. But all through the meal he was making with the talk—talking with his goddamned big mouth full—and afterwards he had to help with the dishes; I mean he insisted on it. And the talk kept on, on and on and on until ...

The words began to dance through my mind. *Vy, vot, vy-vot—* faster and faster and yet somehow slow—*vy-vot, VY-VOT. VYVOTVY VYVOT ... Why, what, why-what, whywhat. Why? WHY? WHY? ...*

All of a sudden something seemed to snap inside of my head. It was just like I *wasn't* any more, like I'd just shriveled up and disappeared. And in my place there was nothing but a deep hole, a deep black hole, with a light shining down from the top.

The light began to move downward. It rushed downward with a swishing, screaming sound. It reached the bottom of the pit, and shot back upward again. And then I came back from wherever I had been; and Pete and I were standing in the front room. And I was talking to him.

Very quietly.

"You're right," I said. "The whole thing's a damned lie. She isn't out to get you; I'm out to get her. She's got a pile of dough, see, a hundred thousand dollars, and no one else knows about it. I figured on bumping her off and grabbing it, and making it look like you—"

"Please"—he patted my shoulder awkwardly. "Ogscuse, my good friend. I am vorried and I talk too much, but now I vill say no more."

"I'm telling you," I said. "I'm laying it on the line for you. Now get the hell on out of here, and forget the whole deal."

He put both hands on my shoulders and pushed me down into a chair. He gave me another little pat looking sad and apologetic. "Soch a bum, I am. So much you do for me, and not'ing I do but chatter like a skvirell. Vell! No more. Now you vill rest, and the dishes I vill finish."

"I don't want you to," I said. "All I want you to do is—"

"And I vill not do it," he said firmly. "Only the dishes I vill do, and keep my so-big mouth shut."

Well I'd told him. And even if I'd been able to go on telling him— and I couldn't—he wouldn't have listened. He finished the dishes. He mopped up the kitchen, and scrubbed the oil cloth on the table. He came back into the living room, and he poured a very small drink for himself and a big one for me.

He kept his word. There were no more questions. But I could see he was busting with them, that he was itching inside like he'd swallowed a poison ivy bush. And seeing him that way, it was ten times worse than if he'd actually talked.

I poured him a big drink. I made him take three or four big slugs, but it didn't seem to help much. I tried to get his mind off of what he was thinking about—what I was thinking about.

I got out a deck of cards and a box of matches, for chips, and we played a few hands of draw. We switched from poker to cooncan, and then on to monte and faro, and then on to a lot of wild games like baseball and spit-in-the-ocean.

The cards seemed to help some. They were a long time in doing it, but finally they did. He began to hum, to kind of mumble-sing. The first thing I knew I was doing it with him. We grinned and came in on the chorus together. It was *Pie in the Sky*, as I recollect. And by the time we got to the end we'd dropped the cards, and were laughing like fools.

"Dillon"—he wiped his eyes—"soch a pleasure. Good friends, good viskey, a good song. I do not belieff I haf heard that song since—"

"I'll bet I can tell you," I said. "Up in the northwest, wasn't it? Were you ever up around Washington and Oregon?"

"Vas I! Vy in 1945—"

"Nineteen forty-five!" I said. "Why, hell, I was there myself that year. Running a pots and pans crew . . ."

Well, I guess it wasn't so strange, because guys like us would just naturally get around a lot; we wouldn't do the same kind of work but we'd land in a lot of the same places. It seemed funny, though; strange, I mean. And when I could make myself forget—the other— it seemed kind of good.

We sang one song after another. Keeping our voices down, of course. We sang and drank and talked, and I guess we got pretty tight before the evening was over. I guess I got even tighter than he did. The day had been endless, you know; it had taken everything I had out of me. So now I filled up on the music and the talk and the drink, and I got tight as a fiddle.

"What's it all about, Pete?" I said. "What the hell are we looking for, anyway?"

"Looking, Dillon?"

"Yeah. Chasing from one place to another when we know they're all alike. Moving from job to job, when we know they're all alike. That there isn't a goddamned one of 'em that doesn't stink."

"Vell"—he scratched his head. "I do not t'ink ve are looking, Dillon. I t'ink radder ve are trying not to look."

"Yeah?"

"Yess. At somet'ing ve alvays find whereffer ve go . . . No, no more. And no more for you, my friend. Vork you must do tomorrow, so now you shall haf coffee."

"Don't want any coffee," I said. "Want another drink. Wanta talk. Wanta—"

"Coffee," he said, firmly, getting up. "And then bed."

He went out into the kitchen. I heard the water tap go on, and then there was a lot of sloshing. Sloshing and sloshing and sloshing. I listened to it. My head began to ache again, and all the good feeling went out of me.

I got up and staggered to the kitchen door. I stood staring at him, and the blood pounded through my brain.

"Why?" I said. "What the hell kind of slop-gut are you?"

"Vot?" He whirled around startled. "I do not under—"

"Why didn't you do it in the first place?" I said. "You knew it had to be done. Everything was swell and you had to screw it up. Why? An-answer me, you dirty son-of-a-bitch! Why ... w-why didn't you wash out that coffee pot ...?"

I began to bawl.

I started to slide down the door jamb, and he picked me up in his arms and carried me into the bedroom ...

... That Monday, the next day, was a toughie. I wasn't bothered about him any more, except for worrying that he might show himself outside the house, because after the way he'd acted he had it coming to him. But there were plenty of other things on my mind. I couldn't concentrate on my work, and this was one day I had to concentrate. Staples had his eye on me. If I sloughed off very much I'd be out of a job, and that job I had to have. For a while.

So I had the job to think about, to make a good showing on. And I had all this other stuff, the hundred grand and Mona, and what I was going to have to do to get 'em. And the whole shidderee was all jumbled up inside me. And I couldn't make any headway on any of it.

I couldn't collect; I couldn't sell. I mean, sure, I collected and sold some but nothing like I should have. As for the other, well, the more I thought about that—and I couldn't stop thinking about it—the more mixed up I got.

You see? You've probably seen it. If there was ever a bastard that was going off half-cocked, I was it. I didn't know the layout of the house. I didn't know how long it would take Mona to get that dough out of the basement, or which room was her aunt's, or whether she'd let me into the place at night, or—or a goddamned thing. Worst of all, I hadn't laid the deal out for Mona. I hadn't rehearsed her in how she was supposed to act afterwards; what she was suppose to say and the story she was supposed to tell the cops and so on. I hadn't done it because I hadn't really planned on going through with the deal. I'd figured that Pete had skipped town, and I couldn't go through with it. So there it was. There I was. I hadn't asked Mona half the questions that I should have, and I'd told her practically nothing that she needed to know. And now it was too late. I didn't dare call her. There was no way I could see her. Maybe I could catch her outside the house if I hung around that neighborhood long enough. But that wouldn't look good: people might remember seeing me later. And anyway I didn't have the time.

Wait? Put it off a night or two until I got a chance to talk to her? I couldn't do that. There was that story I'd given Pete; and then the old woman might discover that the till had been tapped.

So there it was, like I say. I was fumbling before I even got started. I hadn't really made a move yet, and I'd already bollixed the frammis. Anyway, I hadn't done what I should have.

I got to thinking about that while I was whipping the dead-beats. Or trying to whip 'em, I should say. I thought, well, Dolly, you ain't changed a bit, have you? You haven't learned a goddamned thing, you stupid bastard. You couldn't learn a prayer at a revival meeting. You see something you want, and that's all you got eyes for. You ain't watching the road at all, and the first thing you know you're up to your tail in mud . . .

Well, though, that wasn't so. It maybe looked that way, but it wasn't the way it really was. There's just some guys that get the breaks, and some that don't. And me, I guess you know the kind I am.

I got through the day somehow, and along toward quitting time my mind began to clear. I began to figure I hadn't done so badly after all. The money was there—wasn't it?—and I had Pete sold—didn't I?—and Mona would do what I told her to—wouldn't she? Everything important I'd taken care of fine; and all that was left was just a few little details. Of course, it would have been better if I could have explained things to Mona. But it didn't really matter. I'd done all right, and everything was going to be all right. It had to be, know what I mean? Take the most hard luck guy in the world, and he's bound to get a break once in a while.

I worked until after six, trying to make a showing. The other guys had already checked in and left when I went in; and Staples was back behind the cash wicket, fidgeting and waiting for me.

He looked through my sales contracts—the new ones and the ad-buys. He checked through my collection cards, and counted my cash.

"A little light, Frank," he purred, looking up at me at last. "Quite-some-much light. I trust you can bulk it out with a good story?"

"What the hell?" I said. "I've been off work for almost a week. It takes a few days to get back into the swing of things."

"No." He shook his head. "No, it doesn't, Frank. It takes exactly one day. Today. Do I make myself clear?"

"So all right," I said. "I'll do much better tomorrow."

"You will indeed. Much better. Otherwise, I am very much afraid that—"

I shrugged and told him to stop making a production out of it. If I didn't do okay tomorrow, he could beef then. So he let it go at that and we said goodnight, and I started for home.

I would do all right the next day. If I couldn't do it legit, I'd feed a little of that hundred grand into the accounts. Just a few bills, enough to make myself look good. I could afford it, with that much dough, and it would save me knocking myself out.

I got home. Pete was pretty uneasy from being cooped up all day; all set for another quiz program, it looked like. So I told him I had to take a bath and he was to fix the grub I'd brought home. And that got him off my neck for an hour.

We ate around seven-thirty. By eight, we were finished. I told him I had a little work on my accounts to do, and he was to wash the dishes. So that took care of him until eight-thirty.

He came out into the living room, then, and I folded up the collection cards I'd been playing with. I told him to get his hat and coat on, and he did—looking like he was about ready to pop. Then I gave him one of the two big drinks I had poured. And as soon as he got it down, I poured us another.

"Dillon, good friend. Dere is somet'ing—"

"Drink your drink," I said. "Hurry! We're running late."

"But—"

But he drank his drink, and I drank mine. I switched off the lights, took his elbow and started him toward the door in the darkness.

"It iss only a small t'ing, Dillon. Unimportant but it hass been running through my mind. Since last night, ven ve vere—"

"You hear me?" I said. "I said we were late. Now, come on."

He came along, but that question, whatever it was, was still bothering him. And all the way across town he was kind of mumbling and muttering to himself. I guess I told you that the house was out beyond the university, the only one in that block? Well, it was, anyway; sitting off by itself. But I still didn't take any chances. I speeded up a little at the end of the adjoining block, then cut my lights and motor and coasted the rest of the way.

I opened the door. I told Pete to stay in the car until I called him.

"Oh?" He turned and looked at me. "But I t'ought—"

"I know," I said, "but she might hear you come up on the porch. Figure that something screwy was going on, and it would blow the whole deal."

I left him sitting in the car, mumbling and muttering. I was about half way up the walk when I thought what if someone should come by, a prowl car, and ask him what the hell he was doing. But ... well, I couldn't help it. It wasn't good, but it wasn't good to have him come up on the porch either like I'd told him to last night. That wasn't good and this wasn't—and maybe nothing could be that I would dream up. But goddammit, I just hadn't had much time to think, and I was a hard luck bastard to begin with, and ...

I knocked on the door, and, man, it just sounded like an echo from my heart. The old pump was beating that hard. After a long time—a dozen years, it seemed like—the old woman tipped the shade back and peered out at me.

There was only a dim light on in the hall where she was standing. But it was apparently enough for her to recognize me. She opened the door and unlatched the screen, and I went inside.

Her face fell a little when she saw I wasn't carrying anything. Then she jerked her head toward the door, and started grinning again. Rubbing her hands together.

"You bring my coat? You got it in your car, hah?"

I didn't say anything, do anything. I was like a mechanical man with the batteries run down. I wanted to boff hell out of the old bitch, and I just couldn't move.

"You bring it in, mister. That's why you came, ain't it? You bring in the coat, and then..." She winked and jerked her head toward the rear of the house. "She's already in bed, mister, and you just br—"

She just shouldn't have said that. Honest to God, I'd planned it and I'd already come three-fourths of the way. But if she hadn't've said that, I don't think I could have gone any further.

She brought it on herself when she said that. She asked for it.

And she got it.

I left-hooked her, I right-crossed her. I gave her just the two haymakers, left and right. Fast. Batting her one way, then the other. Batting her back before she could fall. And then I let her go down, back against the foot of the stairs; and her neck looked about four inches longer. And her head was swinging on it like a pumpkin on a vine.

Kill her? What the hell do you think it did?

Mona had been standing behind the living room drapes. Now, she came out, and she took just one look at the old woman and then she looked away again.

And she threw her arms around me, shivering.

I kissed her on top of the head, gave her a little squeeze. I pushed her out of the hall, into the living room.

"D-Dolly. What are we g-going to—"

"I'll tell you," I said. "I'll tell you exactly what to do. Now, which room is your aunt's?"

"A-at the head of the stairs. On the right. Oh, Dolly, I'm—"

"Save it," I said. "For God's sake save it! Where'll she have her key? Where's her key?"

"I d-don't—maybe in h-her—"

I ran out in the hall, and frisked the old woman. I found a key in her pocket and took it back into the living-room.

"Is this it? Now, what about the gun? In her room? Goddammit, answer me!"

She nodded, stammered that the gun was in the old gal's room. She gulped and tried to smile, tried to get ahold of herself.

"I'm s-sorry, Dolly. I'll do whatever—"

"Swell," I said. "Sure, you will, and everything's going to be fine." I smiled back at her—did the best I could at smiling, anyway. "You go get the money, now—how long will it take you? Can you get it in five minutes?"

She said she could, she thought she could. She'd do it just as fast as she could. "But what are you—"

"Never mind, goddammit!" I said. "Just go get it, and leave the rest to me. Move, for God's sake!"

She moved. She turned and went off at a run.

I went back out into the hall, slung the old woman over my shoulder and carried her up the stairs.

I got to the top, and dropped her on the landing. I unlocked the door to her room, and went inside.

There was a chair, a bed, an old dropleaf writing desk. Nothing else. No books. *No pictures. And with an old house like this, an old woman like that, there should have been pictures...*

I opened the dropleaf of the desk, scared sick that there wouldn't be any gun or that it wouldn't be loaded. And I thought, man oh, man, how stupid can you get? You could have checked on *that*, anyway. You've gone too far to back out, and if that gun isn't ... But it was there; a big old forty-five, of all things. Just about the last gun you'd expect an old woman to have. And it was loaded.

And there was some money, too: a little roll of bills in one of the desk drawers.

I took the money and shoved the gun into my belt. I jerked the drawers out and dropped them on the floor, and I knocked over the chair as I went back into the hall.

I walked down the stairs a few steps. I reached back up and got the old woman by an arm, and pulled her down head first.

I left her lying about half way down. I went on down the rest of the way, scattering the bills on the steps. I switched off the light, opened the door and called to Pete. Then, I went back up the stairs a little way and waited.

I was sweating like a chippie in church. It wouldn't work; it *couldn't* work. It was like some of those stupid jobs you read about in the newspapers. Guys tackling some big deal and doing everything bassackwards, tripping over their own feet in a hundred places until it's almost like a comedy. I'd read some of those stories, laughing out loud and shaking my head, thinking, what a jerk! The damned fool ought to have known, he ought to have seen: if he'd done any thinking at all, he'd—

The door opened. Closed. I heard him breathing heavily, nervously; and then his whisper in the darkness:

"Dillon? Vot—"

"Everything's swell." I spoke softly. "She's up in her room now writing the statement. I'm going up to check it over."

"Oh?" I could almost see the frown on his face. "Den vy am I—"

"I want you to look at it before we leave. It's okay. She won't know you're here until I get my hands on it."

"Vell," he said, hesitating, trying to unravel things. And then he gave it up and chuckled. I was his pal, I was the brain man. I was taking care of him, just like I'd been taking care of him. And he was a simple guy; and there was this other thing on his mind:

"... all day I haf been trying to remember, Dillon. Soch a crazy thing. How does it go, dot song ve vere singing: der vun about der bastard king of England?"

"*Song!*" I gasped. "*Song!*" Is that what—" I brought my voice down. "Turn on the light, Pete. I accidentally brushed the switch with my sleeve when—when—" *When what?* "You'll have to turn around. It's there on your right, back near the door."

I saw the black shadow that was his body revolve in the darkness. I heard his fingers tracing their way along the wallpaper. Then, the chuckle again, almost childish:

"... soch a foolish t'ing at a time like dis. No attention you should pay me. Later, perhaps, ven—"

"No," I said. "This is a good time. Here's the way it goes, Pete:
'*Cats on the rooftops, cats on the tiles,*
'*Cats with their bottoms wreathed in smiles ...*'"

The light went on. His back was to me like it had to be.

I got him six times through the head and neck. He pitched forward, and that was the end of him.

I made sure of it. I checked him before I left. His face was pretty much of a mess, but it looked like he'd died happy. It looked like he was grinning.

TWELVE

Through Thick and Thin: The True Story of a Man's Fight Against
High Odds and Low Women ... by Knarf Nollid

I was born in New York City one score and ten years ago, of poor
but honest parents, and from my earliest recollections I was out
working and trying to make something of myself and be somebody.
But from my earliest recollections someone was always trying to give
me a hard time. Like this time when I was running errands for a
delicatessen and, hell, I wouldn't have stolen a damned dime from
anyone: I was only about eight years old and just wasn't smart
enough. So this old bag shortchanges me on an order, and the delly
owner says I took the dough myself. Well, anyone could have seen
she was a goddamned bag, dirty dishes and clothes strung all over her
apartment, living like a hog. And later on she pulls the same stunt on
some other delivery boys around there, and everyone gets wise to her
and they know I didn't take the money. Meanwhile, though, this
delly owner has canned me and told my old man I was a thief, and
the old man beats me black and blue.

So a hell of a lot of good it does me.

That is one thing I can't figure out. Why your own parents will
take some outsider's word for something before they will yours. But I
realize that this incident is of no importance, so I will get on with my
tale. I simply wished to demonstrate how right from the beginning
people were giving me a bad time.

Well, it went on and on, and I will not trouble you with a full
recital of it all. Because all the crap I caught, it's pretty hard to believe,
and you'd probably think I was a damned liar.

So finally I'm in my second year of high school, and people have
been giving me trouble all the way, trying to hold me back, and I'm
pretty big not to be any further along. Anyway, there's this English
teacher, and she's pretty young; not a hell of a lot older than I was, I
guess. And she keeps giving me the eye and putting her hand on my
shoulder when she shows me how to do something. And I figure,
well, you know. So one day when she keeps me after class—it's the

last class of the day and we're all alone—one day when she's leaning over me and kind of rubbing up against me, why I give her a feel. I thought she wanted it, you know, so I did it. But dear reader it was a trap.

Well, I suppose it was an invaluable lesson, and one that profited me greatly in the future. That little bitch taught me something I never forgot, viz: the prettier and the sweeter they act toward you, the less you can trust 'em. They're just leading you on, see, to get you in trouble. And maybe you don't see it right at the time, but, brother, you will.

But it was sure a lesson purchased at great cost. I get the chilly drizzles right now when I think about it.

She yells and slaps my face, and some of the men teachers come running in, and I try to explain how it was, what I thought, and that just makes it worse.

They call the principal, and they all start knocking me at once. It's their fault, see, that I'm not any further along. But they claim it's me. They give out with a lot of craperoo about how I won't study, I haven't really got my mind on school, and I'm uncooperative and antagonistic toward the other kids. And they make it sound like I'm public enemy number one or something; and it all started because this babe gave me a play, and I foolishly picked her up on it.

Well, to make a long story short, I got expelled and thus through no fault of my own, my formal education was terminated at a tender age. But to hell with 'em all, I say. People that act as dirty as that, they're not worth soiling my mind thinking about, and I don't.

You are aware by now that I am one hard working bastard with plenty of experience in many fields. But incredible as it seems, my earnest efforts and ability were never appreciated. The rookings I got right from the time I left home and took to the road are something to challenge the imagination. You'd have to see it to believe it, by God!

There was the manager of this circulation crew I first went out with. A crook from way back, and, man, what a crap artist. He gives me the old bull about traveling to California and back in new cars and making seventy-five bucks a week. And me, I'm just an innocent kid, unwise in the ways of the world, so I swallow it like candy. I sign on with the crew, there's about eight of us in this ten-year-old

Dodge, and it seems like our first stop on our way to California is
Newark, N.J. and—

You ever do the door-to-door in Newark? Well, don't do it. They
get all the crews coming out of New York, see. These circulation
outfits and so on, they shake the crews down in Jersey, and it's not
really a fair test because the goddamned place is worked to death, but
that's the way it is.

They shook out two of the guys in Newark, and another one
before we're out of the state. Then, the rest of us go on westward, the
crew manager and us four men. Well, I really knocked myself out. I
made the doors and I made the sales. But it don't do me no good. It's
like it's always been with me: working hard and being honest, and
getting nothing for it. The crew manager, this bull artist, would do
the call backs on my orders, and on about two-thirds of 'em he'd give
me a can't-confirm. He'd look me right in the eye and say the lady
had changed her mind or her husband wouldn't let her go through
with the buy. And then he'd write the orders up as his own and take
the commission.

Well, we got into Illinois, and I'm practically dead of doughnut
poisoning by that time. I've been working my can off, and all the time
I have to eat in dumps, taking a lot of guff from the hired help just
because I'm a kid and I can't tip or anything. So just about then I
began to get wise. I made a few call-backs myself, and then I jumped
this crap artist. I wasn't mean about it or anything. Just asked him
how about shaking it out fair from now on. And that shows how
little I knew of the ways of life. The son-of-a-bitch slugged me with
a water pitcher, and then he kicked the hell out of me. And then he
fired me off the crew. And I wanted to fight or argue about it or
something, but somehow I just couldn't. Getting slugged and kicked
when I'd been trying to be nice—well, I couldn't do anything for a
while. Just hole up in my room and think.

Well, pretty soon I joined up with another crew, and inside of a
month I was manager of it. Me, just a kid, managing a crew, so I
guess you can see I had what it took. But there were a couple of these
punks that were always kicking, hinting maybe that I was crapping
them on the can't-confirms. So finally I got 'em alone in my room,
and beat the sap out of them. And then I gave 'em the gate. But they
still weren't satisfied. It wasn't enough that I had to go out and dig

up a couple of more men. They wrote to the home office, and the next thing I know I'm yanked off the crew and I can't ever work for that company again.

It went on and on like that, every damn thing I tried. I work into a nice premium deal, and the superintendent robs me on territory. I buy gold, and the refinery gives me the cob; even the big buyers do it, by God. They try to kid me that my eighteen-karat is fourteen and that the fourteen is ten, and so on. And I'll bet I was skinned out of thousands of dollars before I saw I was struggling against hopeless odds, and moved into another racket.

It was that way with everything I did, the aluminum ware, the pots and pans, the premiums, the magazines: everything. One way or another, I'd get the blocks put to me; so I will mercifully spare you the sordid details. I often thought, I kept thinking, that if I had some little helpmeet to dwell with, the unequal struggle would not be so unequal. But I didn't have any more luck that way than I did in the others. Tramps, that's all I got. Three goddamned tramps in a row ... or maybe it was four or five, but it doesn't matter. It was like they were all the same person.

Finally, I was working in this small city in the middle-west. Outside collection-sales. It could have been pleasant and remunerative, but my boss was just about the most no-good son-of-a-bitch I ever worked for. Character named Staples. He just wasn't satisfied unless he was giving me a hard time, and when I go home at night, exhausted with the struggles against unequal odds, it's more of the same. Because the babe I'm married to then, she's out of this world, what I mean. The queen of the tramps, and a plenty tough bitch to boot.

To get ahead of myself a little, she starts giving me a hard time one night, talking dirty to me and using bad language. So like I always do, I try to be reasonable and show her the error of her ways. I say it is not the best time to talk when a man just comes home from work, and perhaps we will both be in a better mood after we have a bite to eat. I say, will she please fix us a bite, and I will cheerfully help her. Well, for answer she gives me some more of the dirty talk. And when I try to pet her and soothe her down, gently but firmly, she somehow slips and falls into the bathtub.

I helped her out and apologized, although I hadn't done a

goddamned thing. "I'm very sorry, Joyce," I said. "Now, you just take it easy and I'll fix us a nice dinner..." That's the way I talked to her, but you know how much good it does trying to be nice to a tramp. She almost called my skull in with a scrubbing brush. Then, when I leave the house to calm myself, she ruins all my clothes and pulls out. I guess she saw that she couldn't get anything more out of me, and it was time to latch onto another sucker.

Meanwhile, to go back and take events in their proper order, I have met one of the sweetest, finest little girls in the world. Her name is Mona, and she lives with a mean old bitch of an aunt. The old woman's holding her prisoner, practically, working her tail off and making her do a lot of dirty things. She, this little girl, asks me to rescue her and let her be my helpmeet, and then we can live happily forever after. And touched by her plea, I agree to do so. I agree even before I know about all this dough the old woman had stashed away, which—when you come to think about it—is rightfully Mona's, because the old bitch has given her a hard time every day for years. And if a little girl ever had a hundred grand coming, she did.

Well, I go over to the house that night, and, hell, I wouldn't have laid a finger on that old woman. But she keeps egging me on, talking dirty and giving me a bad time. So there just wasn't any other way out.

Well, just about then, maybe a few minutes later, this fellow Pete Hendrickson came in. I think maybe he was a Nazi or maybe a Communist—one of 'em that slipped over here during the war. But, anyway, he was a no-good bastard; he admitted being a bum, himself. And he would have given me a hard time, too. So there was only one thing to do about him.

Well, I'd done it to him; and I was wearing gloves, but I wiped the gun off good and put it in the old woman's hand. And just as I'd finished, this Mona shows up with the money.

And she sees this Nazi or Communist or whatever he was, and she goes all to pieces. Acts like I was a criminal or something. Acted like I hadn't done it all for her.

Well, she pulled herself together when she saw how jarred I was, the notion I was getting. She said it was just a shock, seeing him there when she hadn't expected to, that she just didn't like to have it happen to anyone unless it was her aunt. And she was sorry and so on, and she'd do whatever I asked.

So I'm a pretty understanding guy, and I kind of liked her for feeling that way. *If* she did actually feel that way. So everything was jake between us again.

I told her what she was supposed to do, what to say to the cops. I told her it would be a leadpipe cinch, and in a couple of weeks we could get together. Then, I kissed her and left, taking the money with me.

It—the money, I mean—was in a black leather bag something like a file-briefcase or a doctor's medicine kit. It was packed tight and it was heavy, about sixty or seventy pounds. And all the way home I was wondering where in the hell I could keep it. I was afraid to hide it in the house. That was a pretty bad neighborhood, and it would be just my luck to have some son-of-a-bitch break in and lift it. I finally decided to carry it with me, at least for a while. I could bury it down in the bottom of my sample case—throw out some of the samples if I had to—and keep it with me all day long.

I got home, and took it into the house. I set my sample case up on the coffee table, opened the lid and tried fitting the bag inside. I kind of fiddled around with it, trying it this way and that way. I was sort of delaying the pleasure, I guess, letting my anticipation build up. And I guess probably I was a little afraid. Because with a hard luck guy like me, damned near anything can happen. That little satchel might turn out to be filled with bricks or magazines. Or some kind of booby trap that would blow my head off when . . .

I opened it. It bulged open the second I pressed the catch, and I made myself look inside. And I sort of moaned, nickered like a colt going for its mother.

It was there, all right. Packs and packs of paperbanded bills. Fives, tens, and twenties. I dipped my hands down into it, and brought them up again. And it was all money—no false packages, no junk: I didn't have to count it. Hell, I could almost count it in my head . . . a hundred grand.

A hundred grand!

And Mona. I'd rescued her from her wicked aunt and meted out justice to this guy who had molested her, and I'd recovered this money which was rightfully hers. And soon we would shake the dust of this old land from our feet, depart this scene of my many tragic disappointments, and we would go to some sunny clime like Mexico. And, man, what a happy life we'd lead. Me and that sweet child, that honey babe, and a hundred thousand dollars.

Or practically a hundred thousand. I'd probably have to feed a few hundred into my accounts to keep Staples happy.

I dipped down into the money again, squeezing and rubbing it between my fingers, hating to let go of it. It was old, of course, but still clean and crisp. And, yeah, hell—you think I haven't been around?—it was the real thing. I make no pretence of being a great mental genius, but there is one thing I cannot be fooled on, dear reader. The green goods. I cannot be deceived about counterfeit. You get stuck a few times like I have, when you are an innocent, trusting kid, and have to make it up out of your own pocket. And you learn to spot the goddamned stuff a hundred yards away.

I took six bills, thirty dollars, from a packet of fives and stuffed them into my wallet. That would give me a good day at the store, and keep this unappreciative character, Staples, who was always giving me a hard time, from giving me a hard time.

I dropped the rest of the pack back into the satchel, and started to fasten the catch. And I was a happy man, dear reader. I had won out in the unequal struggle, with every son-of-a-bitch in the country, even my own father, giving me a bad time. I had forged onward and upward against unequal odds, my lips bloody but unbowed. And from now on it would be me and Mona and all this dough, living a dream life in some sunny clime—Mexico or Canada or somewhere— the rest of the goddamned world could go to hell.

But though I seldom complain, you have doubtless read between the lines and you know that I am one hard luck bastard. So, now, right as I stood on the doorstep of Dreams Come True, my whole world crumpled beneath me. I had all this dough and I had Mona— or I soon would have her—and then I looked up, and (TO BE CONTINUED).

... She was in her nightgown. She was all prettied up like I hadn't seen her since I don't know when; and she wasn't more than a dozen feet away. Standing in the entrance to the little hall that led back to the bedroom.

Smiling at me, but sort of watchful. Kind of smile-frowning.

Joyce.

My wife.

THIRTEEN

I didn't think she'd seen the money. I wasn't sure but the lid of the sample case was up, you know, and it wasn't likely that she would have.

I let it drop casually—the lid, I mean—and locked it. I said, "What the hell are you doing here?"

"I—" Her eyes flashed, but she held onto the smile—"I still had my key, Dolly."

"So you had a key," I said. "So suppose you had a nickel. You got to make a telephone call with it?"

"Please, Dolly. Don't make it any harder for me than it is."

"And you never made anything hard for me, did you?" I said. "You didn't do your goddamned best to wreck this house before you left. You didn't screw up every goddamned stitch of clothes I had. You didn't—"

"I know. I'm sorry, Dolly. But I've thought things over, and if you'll just listen to me—"

"Listen, hell," I said. "Listening to dames like you is what's put me where I am today." And then I shrugged and said, "All right, spill it. I'm listening."

I'd decided I'd better. Because maybe she *had* seen that dough, and anyway this was no time to get into a brawl. I had to live nice and quiet for the next few weeks. My nerves wouldn't take anything else, and anything else—anything that might draw attention to me—just wasn't safe.

She hesitated, looking at me, a little suspicious I guess of the sudden change. I said, "Well, come on. Give. Sit down and I'll get us a drink."

"I don't think I want a drink." She shook her head. "You've been drinking quite a bit, haven't you, Dolly? There's all kinds of bottles around and it looks like you slept in the bed with your shoes on. And—"

I was staring at her. Not saying anything, just staring. She cut off with the nagging fast, stretched her smile.

"Just listen to me, will you? I'm not back in the house an hour, and already I'm—you get us a drink, honey. Please."

I got a bottle out of the cupboard, and a couple of glasses. I came back into the living room; and she was sitting in the same chair Pete had sat in. And, well, it gave me an awfully funny feeling.

I poured the drinks and handed her one. My hands shook, and I patted the lounge at my side. "Why so unsociable? Why not sit over here?"

"We-el. You really want me to?"

"What the hell? Sure."

"Well—" She sat down on the lounge kind of crossways to me. "Well, here I am."

"Yeah," I said. "There you are, all right."

"I—I guess it would be too much to hope ... I guess I shouldn't ask if you're glad to see me."

I let myself frown a little; thoughtful, you know. I took a sip of my drink, lighted a cigarette and passed her one.

"Well, it's kind of a funny deal," I said. "A guy's wife wrecks damned near everything he has, and then she takes off for a week— almost a week—and he thinks it's all over. He doesn't know where the hell she's been, what she's been doing with herself. She shows back up without any warning, and for all he knows—"

"I've been in Kansas City, Dolly. I'd started back to Houston; I was going to get my old job back—"

"Where'd you get the money?"

"From the owner of the club. I called him collect after I left here that night, and he wired me two hundred to get back on."

"Oh."

"No, Dolly. Please don't act like that, honey. You know I wouldn't—couldn't. You know there's never been anyone but you."

"I didn't say anything," I said. "So you stopped off in K.C., huh?"

"Yes, I had a four-hour layover there between trains, and then I was going on. But..." She paused a moment, looking down into her glass. "I don't know quite how to put it, honey. Maybe it was getting off by myself for a while, being able to stand outside of things and look at them. I could see the whole picture that way, Dolly, the good and the bad, and it began to look a lot different to me. I began to wonder why things had turned out as they had. I wasn't sure that I should come back, but I felt that I should at least think about it. So ... so that's what I did. I took a room in Kansas City, and I really thought. For the first time in months, I suppose. It was quiet and peaceful, and there wasn't something to get me upset the minute I—"

"Like me, for example?"

"I've been more to blame than you, Dolly. Entirely to blame, I guess. I was responsible for the way I acted."

"Well," I said, "I'm not throwing anything up to you, understand, but as long as you mention the subject yourself I . . ." I turned and looked at her, feeling the blood push up into my face. "What the hell you mean, you were responsible?"

"Please, honey. I'm here to help you. I love you and I'm your wife, and it's a wife's place to stick by her husband."

I poured myself another drink, the neck of the bottle rattling against the glass. I threw it down at a gulp, and it calmed me down a little bit, but only on the outside. It didn't change the way I felt.

"You think I'm crazy, is that it?" I said. "Well, it wouldn't be any goddamned wonder if I was. I've been knocking myself out for people almost from the time I began to walk, and all I got for it was a royal screwing. It's like it was a plot, almost. The whole goddamned world sitting up nights to figure out how to give me a hard time. Every bastard and son-of-a-bitch in the world working together to—to—"

I stopped. It was all true, by God, but somehow saying it out loud, saying it just then, it didn't sound so good.

"Well, anyway," I said. "You've got to admit I've had plenty of hard luck."

"Of course you have, dear. So have a lot of other people."

"A lot of other people, hell! You name me just one person that's got the rooking I've got. In his work and his home life and—"

I stopped myself again.

She slid over on the lounge, put one of her hands over mine. "You do see it, don't you, honey? And now that you understand and I understand, we can stop it before—We can do something about it."

I'd do something about it, all right. She may have thought she'd had a tough time before, but she hadn't seen anything yet. I'd have her run out of here inside of a week, long before Mona and I were due to get together.

"There's . . . I don't want to upset you, honey, but there's something I want to ask."

"Yeah?" I said. "Well, go ahead."

"Maybe I'd better not. Not tonight. I'm sure you wouldn't—uh—"

"Come on. Spit it out."

"Well. About the money. I—*Dolly!*"

I let go of her wrist, grinned and gave it a little pat. It had been a dumb thing to do, to cut her off before she had a chance to say whatever she was going to. But I just hadn't been able to help myself.

"'Scuse, please," I said. "I guess seeing you in that nightgown I kind of lost my head. Now what about the money?"

"We-el . . . nothing. Do you really like the gown, honey?"

"Love it. What about the money?"

She hesitated. Then, she smiled and shook her head. "Nothing, honey. No, really, it's nothing. I was just going to say that—uh—well, I had quite a bit of money left from cashing in my ticket and all. And—uh—of course, I'll have to pay it back, but we could use if for a while and . . ."

She went on smiling at me, smiling into my eyes. And, of course, she was a goddamned liar like every other woman I'd ever known. But I couldn't be sure she was lying now.

"Well," I said, "I won't say I couldn't use a little extra money."

"I'll give it to you in the morning," she said. "Be sure and remind me of it."

"Those deadbeats have really been giving me a time," I said. "The rotten bastards, you'd think they were trying to see how hard—Well, skip it. I must be beginning to sound like one long gripe."

"It's all right, darling. Don't ever be afraid to talk to me."

"Well, anyway," I said. "I caught up with a flock of 'em tonight.

Pulled in a nice little wad of dough. Ought to make Staples act half way decent toward me for a change."

"Wonderful," she said. "I'm so glad for you, honey." And it seemed to me that her smile became a lot more real; the watchfulness went out of her.

She turned down another drink. I poured one for myself, and sat sipping it, thinking; and then I happened to look at her out of the corner of my eyes. And she was looking at me the same way, her head cocked to one side.

I laughed and she laughed. I set down my drink, and pulled her over on my lap.

I kissed her. Or, I guess you could say, she kissed me. She put her hands back of my head, and pulled my face down to hers. And I thought we weren't ever coming up for air, but you don't hear me kicking. She was a lot of woman, that Joyce. She had the face and she had the build. It wasn't hard to forget, for a little while, that she was just plain no-good and never would be.

She pulled away at last and lay back, smiling up at me, wiggling and breathing pretty hard as I made with the hands.

"Mmmm," she said, half closing her eyes. "Oh, Dolly, we are going to be happy, aren't we?"

"Hell," I said. "I'm happy right now."

"Do you really like my nightgown, honey? Tell me the truth, now."

"Huh-uh," I said. "I don't like it."

"Oh? Why, honey, I spent almost one whole afternoon picking it out, and I was just sure—"

"It covers you up," I said. "I don't like anything that covers you up."

She laughed and said, "Oh, you!" and gave me a little pinch. She pulled my head down again, and whispered in my ear. "I'll tell you something, honey. It's a new kind of gown. It . . . comes off . . . "

Well.

Well, afterwards—after she'd gone to sleep—I got up to get a drink of water. And on the way back to the bedroom, I locked the sample case and put the key in my pocket.

I got back into bed. I turned on my side, and closed my eyes. And it was as though a guard had been taken away from a gate, or a door suddenly thrown open, letting in a hundred images that I hadn't looked at until then—that I hadn't really looked at. Letting them all rush in at me at once. The old woman and Pete. The way she'd looked, the way he'd looked. Her head swinging like a pumpkin, her body sprawled on the stairs. His face—his face and neck, the way he'd chuckled when he asked me . . .

I screamed. I flung myself up in bed, rocking and screaming. Because, Jesus, I hadn't wanted to do it, and I wouldn't ever have done it again. But now it was done, and there wasn't any way I could undo it. And, God, I'd be caught sure as hell. I'd just blundered my way through, and probably I'd done a hundred things that the cops could trace me on. Or if they weren't bright enough to catch up with me, Mona would probably do the job for them. She'd get scared and talk to save her own neck, and—

"Jesus!" I rocked back and forth, screaming and crying. "Oh, God Almighty. My God, God, God . . ."

And then there was someone else saying, "My God. Oh, my God, darling . . ." And Joyce was holding onto me, her body rocking with mine.

"I'm s-sorry," I said. "I—I—God, I'm sorry! I didn't mean it! I'm—"

"Lie down," she said. "Lie down, and mother will hold her boy. Mother's never going to go away and leave her boy again. She's going to stay right here and hold him close like this, and nothing can hurt him then; there's nothing to be afraid of. He's with mother, and he's safe, and mother will understand whatever . . . w-whatever . . ."

I got hold of myself, partly. I said, "I must have been having a nightmare. I—"

"There, there," she said. "It's all right. Everything's going to be all right, darling. He's going to lie down now, and . . . there. There, there."

She pulled me back down. She moved her pillow up a little bit and moved mine down a little.

"There," she said. "No, baby; around this way. Tha-at's my boy! Now, down a little, just a little more . . . and then closer, darling. Very close to mother . . ."

And she drew me close.

And slid the gown down off her shoulders.

FOURTEEN

Well, even a punching bag gets a rest once in a while. And now and then, usually right after I've been torn all to pieces, I get a little relief. Things will actually begin to look pretty good to me. I've been down as far as I can go, you see, so I start going back up again—kind of soaring. And man, when you catch me that way I'm a hard guy to stop.

Joyce was up ahead of me the next morning. By the time I'd dressed she had breakfast waiting—and a good one, no kidding. And she didn't say a word about the night before. I'd been sort of worried about that; worried and kind of ashamed. But she didn't let out a peep about it, or let on like there'd been a thing out of the way. So that day was started off right, right from the beginning.

She kept a little of the money from her trip for groceries, and gave me the rest. She gave me a love pat now and then while she was waiting on me; and I got a big hug and a kiss when I was ready to leave.

"Notice anything?" she said, smiling up at me. "I've got a house dress on and my hair is combed and my face is made up, and ... Did you notice?"

I started to say, so what: you want me to shoot off some skyrockets? But it just wasn't that kind of morning, so I said, "You're darned right I noticed. You look swell, baby."

"You'll be right home tonight?"

"Well, sure," I said. "Why not? Why wouldn't I come right home?"

"I just wanted to know. So that I could have dinner ready."

"Something on your mind?" I said. "Anything bothering you?"

Her face fell a litle: at the tone of my voice, I figured. Then, she stood on tiptoe and kissed me again; and she said, laughing, "Yes. You. I've got you on my mind. Now, run along so I can get some work done."

I started for town. On the way in, I stopped and bought a newspaper. And I had a hard moment or two before I found the story, and made myself read it.

It was okay. It was swell. The case was so open-and-shut that it hadn't even made the front pages. It was back on page three, and there was only about half a column of it:

Mona had been in bed asleep, and had been awakened "by the sounds of struggle." At first "too terrified to investigate," she had finally forced herself to "when the sound of several shots was followed by a prolonged silence ... Mrs. Farrell's niece identified Hendrickson as a one-time odd-jobs man in her aunt's employ. He had quit, swearing vengeance, she said, after a dispute over his wages. As police reconstructed the case, Hendrickson returned to the house last night— drinking and surly—and demanded payment of the disputed sum. Angered by the elderly woman's refusal, he gave her a near-fatal beating, robbed her and started to flee. Mrs. Farrell managed to follow him to the head of the stairs and shoot him. She then fell and broke her neck, although, it is believed, she would have died anyway as a result of the beating ...

"Police revealed that Hendrickson had a record of several arrests for drunkenness, disorderly conduct and battery. He recently completed a six months' jail sentence for assaulting an officer who was taking him into custody."

That was just about it, all that's important. Mona had recited her story just as I'd given it to her. And thank God, there weren't any pictures. If they'd gotten her picture and she hadn't kept her face covered—like she was crying, you know, like I'd told her to—I'd've had some questions to answer. Staples would have recognized her as the same girl who bailed me out of jail, and he'd've been mighty curious about it. He'd've wanted to know what I was to her and she to me, and just where was I last night at the time of the killings. And if I couldn't answer his questions—

But there weren't any pictures. The case was too open-and-shut. The people involved just weren't important enough.

I stopped at the store, and checked in and out. I went to work, trying to figure out some place where I might stash that dough. It was pretty awkward to lug around with me; heavy, and the samples didn't cover it too well. Lift up a few and there it was. Someone might accidentally spot it before I could stop 'em. Joyce might want some panties or stockings out of the case, and—well, any way you looked at it, it wasn't good to have it with me.

I thought about it all morning as I drove around. I fretted and fumed, trying to think of something, getting pretty sore at myself because I couldn't. But I couldn't, and that was that. I thought of a couple places, but they weren't any good. They were worse—or they seemed worse—than keeping the dough with me.

Check it at the railroad station? Well, you know how that is. Those guys are always banging stuff around, breaking stuff open accidentally-on-purpose. Or they give your baggage out to someone else. Or they get screwed up on the claim check, and you have to identify the contents ... You know. You read about it all the time.

A safety deposit box? Well, that would be just as bad, or more so. I'd have to give references to rent one—and maybe I could give Staples, huh? And, anyway, characters like me, we aren't supposed to have anything worth locking up.

I had to keep it with me. It was the only thing I knew to do. I'd just have to take the stuff out of the case that I was going to show people (and I wasn't going to show very damned much; I wasn't going to do very damned much work at all). As for Joyce, well, I could handle her. She was on her good behavior now, afraid of getting me sore, and I wouldn't need to give her any explanations or act apologetic. I'd just tell her to go down to the store if she wanted anything: I was tired of getting my samples screwed up. I'd keep the sample case locked, and tell her to keep the hell away from it. And if she didn't like it, she could lump it.

I framed the words in my mind, just how I'd tell her off if she started nosing around. And, then, I got to thinking about last night ... and I decided it wouldn't be necessary to talk to her that way. I'd say—well—I'd say, "Now, honey. I'm not even going to let your pretty fingers touch that junk. You just tell old Dolly what you want, and he'll bring you home something good."

It would be better to say something like that. It was just good sense, you know. Hell, you can still be polite to people even if you don't give a damn about 'em.

I knocked off work about one o'clock, and checked over my take. I had twenty-eight dollars—pretty good for a morning, but nothing at all for a day, of course. But with that other thirty, the six fives I'd taken from the hundred grand, it would make me a plenty good day.

I stopped in a bar. I ordered a pre-wrapped sandwich—those

bastards could eat their own slop!—and a bottle of ale; and took it over to the booth. I ate and drank. I got another ale, and spread out my collection cards.

They were really honeys, these accounts we had. They made the first payment, and then you fought 'em for the rest. Catch those characters coming in or sending in the dough. You either fought 'em for it, or you didn't get it. And you didn't always get it then.

I picked out six past-dues, six accounts that owed us five bucks each. I marked them up on the cards, shifted the thirty from my wallet to the company cash bag, and, well, that was it.

It was about two o'clock by now. I moved on to another bar, buying a late paper on the way.

They'd cut the story down to about three paragraphs in this one. There was nothing new in it, or, rather nothing that mattered. The house and the furniture were just about the sum total of the old woman's estate. And it seemed like she was so far behind in her taxes that the property would just about cover 'em. She hadn't left any will. Mona was her only known survivor. And so on. Nothing that mattered. Everything was still okay.

I ordered my second double shot, and another ale for a chaser.

It was kind of funny about those taxes, the old woman not paying 'em. All that dough, and she'd let the taxes pile up until the county was on the point of taking over. But—well, maybe it wasn't so funny either. So strange, I mean. A lot of people don't pay taxes until the gun's right on them. And she'd been just as stingy and tight-fisted about everything else. Living on beans and junk. Making Mona lay for everyone that came along. She was just a miser, and there's no accounting for misers. The only money she'd spent that she could have got out of was that little bit of yard work she'd hired Pete to do. And—I guessed—she probably hadn't laid out much cash then. If any. Pete had taken it out in trade . . . got his pay from Mona.

Mona. She was a plenty sweet child, and I was in love with her. But I'd fallen in love before, thinking I was getting something special; and how had it turned out? How did I know it wouldn't turn out the same way with her?

I hadn't thought much about it until last night; hadn't had any real doubts about her. I'd been just a little bothered the way she'd cut loose with me. But except for last night I'd've been ready to skip it.

When you put the two together, the way she'd acted with me and the way she'd blown her top over Pete, and when you got to thinking about all those other guys . . .

Well, I wasn't putting up with any more tramps. I mean, I'd had enough goddamned tramps to last me a lifetime! I was sure that she wasn't one—pretty sure—but if I ever got the notion that she was, brother, look out!

What the hell could she do about it, anyway? What if I told her right now that she'd been on a buggy ride and this was where she got off? Why she couldn't do anything, that's what. I could keep the money and tell her to go to hell—well, maybe I'd give her a few bills—and there wasn't a damned thing she could do about it.

And it wouldn't bother me that much.

If there's anything I can't stand, it's a goddamned tramp.

Joyce, now. Well, I've talked pretty rough about Joyce, and she *was* as lazy and sloppy and ornery as they come. But there was always one thing I was sure of—pretty sure—damned sure—regardless of what I said. She didn't play around. She never had, and she wouldn't know how to begin. It just wasn't in her, see?

If she'd been as square about other things as she'd been about that; if she kept up this act she'd been putting on since she'd been back . . .

If it was an act. I figured it just about had to be, because a leopard don't change her spots. But it was a damned good one, as good as the real thing, so what the hell was the difference?

Joyce. Yeah, Joyce had her points all right. And now that I wouldn't have to knock myself out to make a living, now that I could feel like I amounted to something and we could have nice things, and—But that was the trouble. The money. How could I explain to her about the money? What kind of story could I hand her?

I guessed I couldn't explain; anyway, I couldn't think of a good story offhand. And there wasn't any hurry about it. I wasn't supposed to see Mona for a couple of weeks, and I could probably think of a lot of things between now and then.

Well . . . I drank another round and left the place. I got some black coffee, and started driving again. Just around, just killing time. It was four o'clock. More than two hours before I could check in at the store, and get home to Joyce.

Joyce. Mona. Joyce? Mona?

What the hell? I thought, and I tried to push it out of my mind. Mona was a good kid. Anyone could see that she was; and she'd carried through on this deal like a little brick. Doing what she was told. Helping to murder her own aunt for her dough—

Well. Well, she was on the square, all right. She'd damned well better be. Because I knew Joyce was, and if I could just think up the right kind of story to account for that hundred grand . . .

I drove around until after six, making myself look good. Then I checked in at the store, bustling in like I'd been on the run all day; and Staples' eyebrows went up a little when he saw what I had for him.

"Not bad, Frank," he said, counting the money. "Oh, not half bad. Perhaps by the end of the week you'll be doing a decent day's work again."

"Gee, thanks," I said. "You better watch that, Stape. You keep patting me on the back like that and you're liable to break your wrist."

He grinned down his nose. We said goodnight and I started to leave, and he called me back. "By the way, I see that a couple of your customers came to a violent end last night. One of your customers, I should say, and the relative of one."

"Yeah," I said, "I read about that. Too damned bad they don't all get bumped off."

"Oh, now, Frank. What would we do for customers?"

"I mean it," I said. "If every one of the rotten bastards dropped dead of the bleeding piles, it would tickle me pink."

"It really would, wouldn't it?" he nodded. "But this Farrell case. There's an angle of it which struck me as being rather curious."

"Yeah?" I said. "I mean, it did?"

"Mmm. Uh-hah. Mrs. Farrell was apparently a virtual pauper, yet her niece—her dependent—spends thirty-three dollars for a chest of silverware."

He stood looking at me, eyebrows cocked, waiting for me to say something.

I swallowed, and it sounded, by God, like Niagara Falls.

"Well?" I said. "What about it?"

"Frank! Honestly! And I've always looked upon you as my best man—in a hideous sort of way, of course ... You actually don't see anything contradictory in the situation?"

"Well, I'll tell you," I said.

"Yes? Yes, Frank?"

"I'll tell you the way I feel, Stape. These bastards we got on our books, I don't try to figure them out. It's no use, know what I mean? You can't expect 'em to make any sense. If they weren't nutty as a pecan orchard they wouldn't be trading with us."

"We-el"—he hesitated—"yes. I can't say that I disagree with you. You'd attribute this, then, to merely another of the mental aberrations peculiar to our clientele? Spending their last dollar on—"

"Like I say," I said, "I don't think about 'em at all. Don't even try to figure them out. All I'm interested in is have they got the money, and can I get it away from 'em."

"Hear, hear!" He clapped his hands together "Spoken like a true Pay-E-Zee man. Well, toodle-oo, dear boy, and pleasant dreams."

I started for the door again.

He called to me again.

"For God's sake!" I said, whirling around. "What the hell you want now, Stape? It ain't enough I knock myself out all day. I got to stand around here half the goddamned night talking to you."

"Why, Frank," he pouted. "I do believe you're annoyed with me! Is there something about this case that—uh—Did I say something that disturbed you?"

I told him sure he disturbed me. He bothered hell out of me. Hanging onto me this time of night when I wanted to get home and get my shoes off, and get some grub under my belt. "I've been working all day, know what I mean? I haven't been sitting around on my butt reading newspapers."

"I see," he nodded. "You feel a slight twinge of conscience. Mrs. Farrell tipped you off to Pete's whereabouts—didn't she?—and he no doubt guessed as much and—"

"So why should that bother me?" I said. "It all turned out all right. They both got killed."

He frowned, staring at me; turning a little pale. Then, he laughed, unwillingly, shaking his head.

"Oh, Frank," he said. "What will I ever do with you?"

"Keep me standing around here a while longer," I said, "and you won't have to do anything. I'll keel over from hunger."

"Unthinkable! . . . 'Night, Frank."

"'Night, Stape," I said. And I headed for home.

He didn't know anything—didn't even guess anything. He was just staying in character, that was all, and I'd been stupid to get upset about it. Hell, hadn't he done the same thing a hundred times before? Picked at me; tried to rattle me; nosed around like a skunk in a garbage dump. Not because there was anything to act that way about, you understand. Just because he was the boss and you had to hold still for it, and being on the make himself he figured everyone else was.

Yeah, I should have counted on it tonight. He figured I'd had a hard day, and you could almost always count on it after a hard day.

So . . .

So there wasn't anything to get up in the air about. Not a damned thing at all; and everything was jake. But still I was glad to get home. I was glad to have Joyce's arms around me, holding me tight; to hear her whisper that I was her boy—mother's boy—and she would never leave me again.

She held me, reaching up to stroke my head; and finally we sat down at the table side by side. It was all ready, the dinner I mean. She'd put it on the table when she heard my car. It was good and it was hot; and we sat next to each other, squeezing hands now and then. And I hadn't had much appetite before—hadn't thought I could eat a bite—but I really stowed it away.

She poured the coffee. I lighted two cigarettes, and gave her one.

"You asked me something last night," I said. "Now I'd like to tell you the answer."

"I'm glad, Dolly. I was hoping you would."

"You asked me if I was glad you'd come back. All I've got to say is you're damned right I am."

"Oh?" She hesitated. Then she leaned forward and kissed me. "I'm glad that you're glad, Dolly. It's wonderful to be back."

She cleared away the dishes, and I helped her. She didn't want me to, but I did, anyway. I wiped while she washed them; and then we moved into the living room. The light was turned down low. She curled up next to me on the lounge, her legs pulled up under her, her head resting against my shoulder.

It was pretty nice, mighty peaceful and pleasant. I felt like if it could just be this way forever, I wouldn't ask a damned thing more.

"Dolly," she said, and right at the same time I said "Joyce." We spoke together, and then we laughed, and she said, "Go ahead, honey. What were you going to say?"

"Oh, nothing much," I said. "Probably nothing will come of it."

"Of what?"

"Well, it's a chance to make some real dough, a pile of it. Anyway, it looks like a good chance. One of the fellows down at the store, one of the collectors, well, his brother-in-law is manager of a big gambling house out in Las Vegas. And the owners of the place haven't been treating him right, see? He's made 'em rich, and now they're about to kick him out. So he wrote his brother-in-law, this collector down at the store, and told him that if he could get up some money, he— this manager—would place it with a shill, and let the shill win and— and—"

She hadn't said a word, hadn't changed her position. But all of a sudden the room seemed to have gotten cold, and her shoulder felt stiff against mine.

"Well," I said, "I guess maybe that isn't such a good idea. Might get in trouble on a deal like that. But there's another proposition I run across, and—"

"Dolly," she said. "I have to know. Where did you get that money?"

FIFTEEN

I leaned forward and stamped out my cigarette in an ash tray. I stayed leaned forward while I lighted another one, and then I sat back again, and I yawned.

"Man, am I tired! You about ready to turn in, honey?"

"Dolly ..."

"What?" I said. "Oh, the money! I thought I told you about that. I caught a few old accounts at home last night, people that really owed us a wad, and—"

"I saw it, Dolly. I don't know how much there was, but I know there was a lot. A whole bag full."

I turned around and stared at her. I gave her the hard eye, trying to stare her down, and she didn't flinch. There was a little frown on her forehead, but it wasn't unfriendly. She didn't look tough or like she might get tough. If she'd been that way, I'd've known what to do. But the way it was, I didn't. I couldn't've slugged her if I'd been paid to.

I couldn't do anything.

The silence must have gone on for five minutes. Finally, she reached out and took one of my hands in hers. And spoke.

"I came back to you, Dolly. It wasn't easy after everything that had happened between us, but I felt that I had to. I loved you and I wanted to help you."

"Well," I said, "you don't hear me kicking, do you?"

"Do you remember last night, honey? Don't you think that after that—d-don't you know that I love you and you can trust me, and that all I want is to help you?"

"I tell you," I said. "I'll bet we get waked up pretty early in the morning. I notice they've got a couple of cars of gravel switched onto the siding out here, and they'll probably be hooking onto 'em—"

She stood up, smoothed down her house dress. She looked down at me, frowning slightly; gave me a little nod like a teacher dismissing a kid.

"All right, Dolly. I guess there's nothing more I can say. Perhaps it's my fault for leaving you, going off in a tantrum when I should have known that you were—that a man who acted as you did was— wasn't himself and might ... Oh, Dolly! *Dolly!* What have you d-done...?"

She threw her hands over her face and sat down on the lounge again, crying. Sobbing helplessly. And she seemed so alone, as lost and scared as I'd been last night.

"Joyce," I said. "Please, baby. What the hell? What are you acting that way for?"

"Y-you ... you know why. A-all that money—I hoped you'd tell me, that there'd be some innocent explanation. I d-didn't know what it c-could be, but I hoped. And now I know that you can't explain. Y-you're afraid, and—"

"Aw, now, wait a minute," I said. "Wait just a minute, baby."

I tried to pull her onto my lap. She moved her shoulders, shaking off my hands.

I waited a minute, looking at her, listening to her. Feeling myself come apart inside. Then, I tried again, and that time I made it.

"I wanted to tell you about it," I said. "But I wasn't sure I was going to get to keep it, see, so I thought I'd better hold off a few days. Otherwise you'd be counting on it, and then you'd be disappointed."

"I d-don't . . ." She pulled her head away from my chest and looked at me. "What—how do you mean—?"

"I found that money."

"Oh, Dolly!" She started to cry again. "Please. Not any more, I j-just can't stand it if you lie to me any—"

"I'm not lying. I know it sounds crazy as hell, I could hardly believe it myself. But it's true."

"B-but it—"

"I'm telling you. I'll tell you if you give me a chance. You want me to tell you or not?"

She sniffled, and looked at me again. I thought she was never going to stop looking, but finally she nodded.

"A-all right, Dolly. But p-please don't—if it isn't true, d-don't—"

"Well," I said. "I can't guarantee that you'll believe me. I've been afraid that no one would believe me, and that's what makes it so hard to know what to do."

"I w-want to believe you, honey. There's nothing I want more."

"Well, it happened last night. One of my accounts—a skip named Estill—I got a tip that he was living out on West Agnew Street. So I beat it out there, and the house was empty. If he'd ever lived in the place, he wasn't any more. Well, I got my flash out of the car and went inside, and—"

"Went inside?" She frowned. "Why?"

"Why?" I said. "Well, you'd know if you'd ever done any collecting, honey; if you'd ever worked for an outfit like Pay-E-Zee. We always go in if we can get in. You might pick up a telephone number off the wall, you know, or maybe there's been an old letter left behind. Something that will give you a lead on the skip."

"Oh," she said; and her frown faded and some of the doubt went out of her eyes. "Go on, honey."

"So I went in, and I looked around from room to room and I couldn't find a thing. Not a scrap of paper, or an address or nothing. It looked like—well, it almost looked like someone had gone to a lot of trouble to see that nothing was left behind. Like everything had been washed and scrubbed before they left. It was very screwy, know what I mean? It got me curious. So I kept on looking, and finally I found this—this little satchel, pushed way back on the shelf on one of the bedroom closets. I opened it up and looked inside, and I'm telling you, honey, it really threw me for a loop..."

I paused to light a cigarette. I offered her one—giving her a quick size-up—and I took a long deep breath. She'd swallowed it all, so far. It was a pretty good yarn, and she was anxious to swallow it.

"What did you say this man's name was, honey? This man you were tracing when—"

"Estill, Robert Estill. I've got his card right here in my pocket if you want to look at it."

She said, oh, no; but she hesitated a second first. So I took the card out and showed it to her. It was on the level—actually his card— which was a hell of a lot more than I could say for him. We'd got two payments out of him, and then he'd done the disappearing act.

"I can show you the empty house, too," I said—and I could have shown one to her. "It's at 1825 West Agnew, and I can drive you out there right now."

"N-no, that's not necessary. I—How much money is there, Dolly?"

I started to lie, to tell her there was five or ten grand or some such figure. Because she might ride along with that where she might not with more. And once she'd started riding, the rest would be fairly simple. I could say—well, I could pretend like I'd invested part of the dough. Or gambled with it. Or—or done something to make myself a pile.

But she wasn't completely sold, yet. Not so sold, anyway, that it wouldn't be awfully easy to unsell her. If she asked to look at the money, to count it—

I told her the truth.

She jumped and almost fell off my lap.

"Dolly! Oh, my goodness, honey! A h-hundred thous—It must have been stolen! Or it could be kidnap money, or—"

"It's not marked," I said. "I know that. I checked it over, but good!"

"It's bound to be something like that! It just has to be. You've got to take it to the police, Dolly!"

"And suppose there is something shady about it—like there probably is? Where does that leave me, a guy like me—a floater with no friends or background? I'll tell you what would happen. If they couldn't beat me into signing some kind of confession, they'd just lock me up and keep me until they could dig up the right answers."

"But if you took the money in, that should prove that—"

"I tell you, they'd never believe me! They'd think I just got scared and was trying to do a cover-up. That's what makes it so hard, why I've been so worried. I won't say that I don't want to keep it, but what difference would it make if I didn't? The story sounds screwy. I can hardly believe it myself, and I don't reckon you believe it and—"

I shoved her off my lap suddenly. I went into the kitchen and reached a pint out of the cupboard, and I took a long stiff slug from the bottle.

I'd thought of something right while I was talking to her, something about the money. And it had rattled me like lightning on a tin roof. The dough wasn't marked, I knew that. But suppose there was something actually shady about it, that it actually hadn't belonged to the old woman? Suppose the cops or the FBI were on the lookout for certain serial numbers . . .

I shivered. Then I remembered . . . and I sighed with relief. Mona had bailed me out of jail with part of the money four days ago. If the stuff was hot, I'd have known about it by now.

I put the bottle back in the cupboard. I turned back around, and Joyce was there and she threw her arms around me.

"I believe you, Dolly," she said, her voice sort of desperate. "I believe every word of it."

"Well, gosh," I said, "I'll be frank with you, honey. I wouldn't blame you much if you didn't."

"W-what are you going to do, Dolly? We can't keep it."

"Well I don't know," I said. "I mean, what else can we do? I won't say that I don't want to keep it, but even if—"

"No! Oh, no, honey. There must be some way to—to—"

"How? You name some way where I won't have to go to jail, and probably get loused up for the rest of my life. "

"We-el. Well, couldn't you go out to that neighborhood and make some inquiries? Find out—"

"Huh-uh! Attract a lot of attention to myself, and maybe have someone call the cops? Not me. I was out there after dark and no one saw me. I'm in the clear so far and that's where I'm staying."

"But we just c-can't—"

"So tell me what we can do," I said. "Just tell me and I'll do it. You don't want me to go to jail, do you?"

"N-no. Oh, no, dear."

"If I thought it would do any good," I said, "I would. But all I can see is getting fouled up. It wouldn't help anyone. That much money, if it was stolen it must have been insured and the insurance money's already been paid over. No one's out anything but the insurance companies, and you know those birds. They already got half the money in the world. Got it from gypping people— foreclosing on farms and giving everybody a hard time. I see no reason why I should stick my neck out for some thieving insurance company."

She was silent. Thinking.

I stooped down and kissed her on top of the head.

"You and me, Joyce," I said. "We never really had a chance, honey. It was always one goddamned dump after another, never having a nickel to spare ... Hell, I tell you. You may try hard—you may patch things up temporarily—but you go on living like that, and sooner or later ..."

Her arms tightened. She whispered, "Oh, Dolly. Oh, I love you so much, honey."

"A hundred thousand," I said softly, "and it belongs to us just as much as it belongs to anyone. A hundred thousand ... A decent house. A place with lots of windows so that the sunlight could stream in, and ... and decent furniture instead of junk. And a good car for a change. And no worries. Not being half out of your mind all the time, wondering how the hell to make both ends meet. And—"

"And—?" she whispered.

"Well, sure," I said. "Why not? I'm all in favor of kids, if people can take care of 'em."

She sighed and hugged me closer.

"I knew you'd feel that way, honey. You were always so good about so many things, I don't know why I ever thought that—that—"

Her voice trailed off.

I waited, stroking her hair.

"I don't know, Dolly. I want to—I want to so much—"

"Why don't you look at it," I said. "Feel it. Count it. Let's count it together, honey, figure out how we can spend it. Like to do that, huh?"

"Well—" She hesitated. "No! No, I'd better not. It's hard enough' to think straight as it is. Let's—let's just not talk about it any more. Let's . . . let's . . ."

So we didn't talk about it any more.

I picked her up in my arms, and carried her into the bedroom.

SIXTEEN

I had a good night.

I got off to a good start the next morning. Joyce was pretty thoughtful and a shade pale around the gills, as the saying is, but that was the way it should be. She was a swell kid—always been on the level and all—and naturally something that wasn't strictly kosher would give her a jolt.

I bought a paper on the way into town. I had to turn through it twice before I found the story about—well, you know—and it wasn't really about that, then. It was just mentioned in passing in connection with a little squib about the old woman's estate.

The county was filing a suit for the back taxes. Mona had been served with a thirty-day eviction notice.

I threw the paper away. I drove on to the store, thinking that the poor kid really wasn't getting any breaks. If the property had been clear, she might have got a nice piece of change for it. Enough to live on a couple years and make a new start somewhere. But it just wasn't in the cards; she was just the original hard luck kid. Of course, I'd give her a few bills—I wouldn't let her be put out on the street with no clothes and not a dime to her name. But it would have been a lot better if she'd had some real dough.

I wondered if she had any money to eat on, and I thought for a minute of slipping a few bills in an envelope and sending it to her. I felt sorry for the kid and I really wanted to help her, you know. But I finally decided against it. The police might be keeping an eye on the place. With all I had to lose, I wasn't taking any chances.

She'd get by all right. The way she was used to living, she probably wouldn't feel right if she had enough to eat.

Staples usually opened the store at eight-thirty, a half hour before I and the other outside men went to work. But he hadn't done it that morning. It was a few minutes before nine when I got there, and the place was still closed up tight. And the other guys were waiting out front for him to show.

I got out of my car and joined them. We waited around, smoking and talking, wondering if the son-of-a-bitch had got run over by a truck and hoping to hell that he had. But there was no such luck, of course. At nine-thirty, he showed up.

He unlocked, and we followed him inside. It didn't seem to be done deliberately, but somehow the other guys were all checked out ahead of me, and I was left alone with him. He began checking me out, kidding and laughing. I felt myself getting uneasy.

He just wasn't himself, know what I mean? He was in too damned good a humor. Well, sure, he was always ribbing and making with the fast talk, but it wasn't because he was Mr. Gayheart, scattering pearls of joy and so on. It was about as genuine as a dime-store diamond. He couldn't work you over with a ballbat, like he wanted to, so he swung the old needle. Making like it was a joke in case you got sore.

This morning, though, it was different. The son-of-a-bitch was really tickled pink about something.

I picked up my cards, and asked him what the big joke was.

"I'll bet I know," I said. "You tripped a blind man on your way to work."

"Ah, Frank," he giggled, giving me a pussy-cat tap on the wrist. "Always putting others in your place. As a matter of fact, I paid a call on an old friend. Someone I hadn't seen in almost twenty years."

"No kidding," I said. "You mean you go out to this nut house— they got you inside—and then they let you go?"

He giggled again, made another pass at my wrist. "You're getting warm, dear boy. Strange how our minds seem to run in the same sewer. The friend I visited, the acquaintance I should say, *was* in a public institution."

"Jail, huh? I knew it," I said. "Well, it's a good thing you've got a stand-in with the local cops."

"A stand-in I've gone to some pains to develop, Frank. It proves very useful in a position such as mine. But, no—you're still a little wide of the mark. It wasn't actually jail. More of a corollary establishment, I should say."

"Yeah?"

"Mmmm. An adjunct to the jail ... But I see that I'm boring you, and I've already delayed you unpardonably. Away with you, good friend! On to the assault on the heels, and may their Achilles heel be bared to you."

"I don't dig this," I said. "This party you visited—he was in some kind of trouble?"

"No—ha, ha—I wouldn't say that, Frank. At least, the party made no complaint to me."

"Well, hell, then. What—"

"No—"He held up a hand. "No, I won't let you, Frank. You're just being polite, pretending an interest in my poor conversation, and I can't allow it. Do run along, now, I insist on it. And—oh, yes ..."

"I know," I said. "I know. You want me to knock 'em dead again."

"Knock them—? Oh, well put! Oh very well put," and he grinned.

I turned my back on him and walked out.

My stomach was all tight and funny feeling. It seemed to be narrowed, drawn down at the bottom, like I'd swallowed something heavy. And there was a sickish feeling in my throat, and hot-icy needles were jabbing through my head.

I got in my car, so shaky that I could hardly turn the switch key. I backed away from the curb and started driving, aimlessly, sort of blind. Finally, I pulled up at a bar, and parked myself in a rear booth.

The drink helped. The drinks helped. I began to calm down.

He couldn't know anything. The cops didn't, so how could he; and what the hell? Somehow he'd spotted that I was a little uneasy. He'd seen it and started working on it, trying to needle out the answer. He was swinging every which way, throwing out the scatter shots in the hope that one of them would hit something.

This frammis this morning, now; it just about had to be a dammed lie, when you started studying it. An ordinary guy would have come right out and admitted that he overslept or got stuck in an elevator, or something of the kind. But Staples wasn't an ordinary guy—a decent one, I mean. He'd lie just for the hell of it. Climb a tree to lie when he could stand on the ground and tell the truth. So, since he wanted to needle me anyway, he'd come up with this story about visiting an old friend.

A friend that wasn't anywhere, know what I mean? No place I could pin down. No place that I could check on if I took a notion. The party was in jail, but he wasn't—and so on. A big mystery. A lot of double talk.

If he just hadn't been so damned tickled, so pleased with himself ... but that would be part of the act, another scatter shot. Or maybe he had actually screwed someone, and it had put him in a good humor. He'd been boasting around about how he was going to make one of the maids at his hotel. He'd been working on it for weeks, hinting that he was going to get her fired, then turning the other way, sweetening her up with little presents from the store. So maybe he'd finally connected.

Anyway ...

Anyway, he didn't know anything.

DAMMIT, HE DIDN'T KNOW ANYTHING!

But I sure didn't feel like working. I couldn't whip the deadbeats today. If I tackled 'em the way I felt, they'd probably wind up collecting from me.

What I wanted to do was go home. Not do anything, you know, but just be there; stay there all day close to Joyce. But, hell, it was out of the question. She was already plenty bothered about the money, so upset that she hadn't even wanted me to leave it there in the house with her. She was about ready to go along with keeping it, instead of going to the police, but she still didn't like it. And if I laid off today she'd realize that there was a lot more not to like than she knew about.

I had four or five drinks in that bar, stretching them out until around noon. Then, I went back to my car and started driving again.

I drove to the outskirts of town, and turned off on a dirt road. I parked. I leaned over the seat, and opened my sample case.

I took twelve of the five-dollar bills this time. Enough to add up to a full day's work. I fingered them hesitating, thinking, and then I put six of them back and took three tens instead.

That was more like it. Twelve fives and nothing else might look a little funny.

I put the bills in my cash bag.

I spread the collection cards out on my clip-board, and doctored them.

Then ... well, that was all. There was nothing left to do, and I had almost five hours to do it in.

A picture show? Hell, who wanted to go to a picture show ... sit there in the dark ... alone. I could have enjoyed reading, because I'm quite a reader, see. But I couldn't sit out on the street and do it, and there's never a damned thing worth reading in these libraries. No good confession stories or movie magazines, or anything interesting.

I started driving again.

I guess there's nothing that'll get you down so fast as driving when you've got no place to go.

I kept thinking how nice it would be to go home—knowing it was out of the question—and I began to get pretty sore. What the hell, anyway? A guy's sick and worried and he can't even go to his own home, talk to his own wife. It was a pretty damned sorry state of affairs, if you asked me. A man knocks himself out—puts himself on the spot on account of her—and she keeps right on giving him a hard time. Banging his ears and worrying him, as if he didn't have enough to worry about already.

Mona wouldn't act like that. That little Mona, now, there was a real sweet kid, a real honey. She'd had to do a few things that she shouldn't have done, so maybe she wasn't high-class like Joyce ... like Joyce pretended to be. But—

Huh-uh: about Joyce. Joyce wasn't much good at pretending; she'd told me off plenty of times in the past. The way she acted was the way she felt, and no put-on about it. But—Mona was okay, too, and I needed to see her, I needed to be with someone, talk to someone.

Someone—almost anyone—that was on my side.

I drove across town to that center where she sometimes shopped. I went into the little bar there, next to the drugstore, and sat down near the door.

It was one of those places: the kind that makes you wonder how the hell they stay in business. Because this joint, it sure didn't have any. An old codger nursing a dime beer. Some painted-up dame getting high on sherry, and counting her change every two minutes ... That's all there was.

I had a couple of double Scotches. I told the bartender to pick himself up a buck tip, and I thought he was going to drop dead.

He set a bowl of peanuts in front of me. He dropped a handful of slugs into the jukebox. I told him the light up front was pretty bright and would he mind turning it off. Or, rather, I started to tell him. He had it turned off before I could finish the sentence.

"Okay? Anything else, sir?"

"I'll let you know," I said. And he took the hint and left me alone.

I turned a little sidewise on my stool. I sat looking up front, one elbow on the bar, drinking and thinking. And the time loafed by.

I bought another drink, and the bartender bought me one. I took a swallow or two from it, glanced at my watch. It was a few minutes after three. Probably she wouldn't be by. You never can see people when you really want to, so probably I wouldn't get to see her.

I got up and went back to the john. I came out ... and there she was, just going by. I just got a glimpse of her. I sauntered up to the door, like I wanted to get a breath of air.

She went into the super-market. I waited a couple of minutes, and then I went back to my stool. I stood by it, sipping my drink and watching the door out of the corner of my eye.

The jukebox had run out of slugs. The dame and the old codger had left. It was quiet in there and kind of echo-y, and I heard her—

heard those fast footsteps of hers—before I saw her. I got to the door, just as she was passing. And, yeah, I let her pass.

I wanted to talk to her, but there was something I wanted worse. Something I wanted to know. So I let her go right on by, and stood in the door watching.

I watched her until she rounded the corner, two blocks away. I watched her and the cars on the street, the people, and then she was out of sight; and I felt a hell of a lot better. She wasn't being tailed. The police weren't keeping an eye on her. She was in the clear, which meant I was. So that jerk, Staples, could take his goddamned needle and . . .

I went back to my stool, kind of sorry that I hadn't got to talk to her—because she was a swell kid, you know—but glad that I'd handled it this way. Now, I was *sure*, and now I didn't need to talk to her. I was feeling okay, and I had the biggest part of the day licked.

I motioned to the bartender. He made with the whiz and the soda. I took out a cigarette, and he lit it for me, smirking and giving me the wink.

"Quite a dish, huh, sir? A really well-stacked babe."

"What?" I said. "What babe?"

"You didn't notice her, the one that just went by? Pretty little girl with so much above the belt she can hardly see over it?"

"Oh, her," I said. "Yeah, I believe I did notice her. Went by when I was getting some air, didn't she?"

"That's the one. Lives around here someplace, I guess. A real hot customer from all I hear."

"No kidding?" I said. "I thought she looked like a pretty nice girl."

"Well, you know the saying, mister. The nicer they look, the lower down they are. I—"

He caught my eye, and broke off. He began scrubbing the counter with the bar-towel, his smirk drawing in around the edges.

"Of course, I don't really know anything," he said. "All I've got to go on is what some of the fellows around here have said. Could be a lot of lies, and probably is."

I took another swallow of my drink. I said, well, I didn't know about that. "The way I figure, where there's so much smoke there's got to be fire."

"Well . . ." His smirk started to spread again.

"She didn't get them breastworks from chinning herself. I wonder how a guy would go about getting some?"

"Well, they tell me it's pretty simple. From what I hear—and I got no reason to doubt it—all you got to do is give her the old proposition."

"Yeah? Just like that, huh?"

"So they tell me. They tell me it's just a matter of howsabout it, toots, and you can get out the coal shovel."

He nodded, giving me another wink.

I picked up my change—every damned penny of it—and left.

I drove around a while, got myself some coffee and ate a handful of mints. It was that time, by then, so I went to the store and checked in. There was no hurrahing or needling from Staples. He had a dinner date, I guess, or maybe he'd decided that there wasn't anything he could nose out. Anyway, he checked me out fast, and I went home.

Everything was about like it had been the night before. A good dinner; Joyce being sweet and nice despite the way she was worried about the money. I couldn't think of much to say to her talk, so I just let her ramble on. At one time I got to frowning, unconsciously, staring around the living room and frowning. I wasn't really thinking about it at all, you know, but she thought I was.

"I'm sorry, darling," she apologized. "I've been meaning to clean house from top to bottom, but I've been so—well, never mind. I'll get busy on it the first thing in the morning. You won't know the place when you get home."

"Oh, hell," I said. "Let it go. It looks okay to me."

"No," she said, "I'm going to do it. It'll help to take my mind off of . . . of . . ." She didn't finish.

The next day was Thursday. Like the other days since Joyce had come back, it started off good. Breakfast was ready and waiting for me. Joyce was swell. There was no mention of the mur—of the case—in the morning papers.

I thought, well, everything else is so good, that goddamned Staples will probably give me a hard time. But I was dead wrong about it. I was the first guy he checked out, and he didn't waste any time about it.

I went back around the corner, and climbed into my car. I backed away from the curb, and—

I don't know where she'd been hiding, waiting. Back in some doorway, I guess. But suddenly there she was—Mona was—piling into the car with me. Stammering scared. So scared that I could hardly understand her.

"S-something's w-wrong, D-Dolly! Th-th-the p-police are f-f-following me . . ."

SEVENTEEN

The police! Great God, the police were after her and she'd led them right to me!

My foot slipped off the clutch, and the car leaped forward. I jammed my foot down on the gas. Inside of two blocks I was doing seventy, right through the early morning traffic, and God, I don't know how I kept from being pinched or from smashing into someone. Then, I began to think again, and I slapped on the brakes. But I didn't stop.

The hell the police were following her! I knew damned well they weren't. But I wanted to get her away from the store neighborhood. If Staples saw us together, it would be just as bad as if the police were on our tail.

"Now, what's this all about?" I said, finally, heading the car toward the country. "I know the police aren't watching you. *I know*, see."

I told her about the afternoon before, how I'd wanted to see her but I wasn't the kind of guy to give way to my emotions. The important thing was to take care of her, make sure that everything was okay. So I'd taken time off from my job, gone to all kinds of trouble, and done it.

"B-but they don't do it in the daytime, Dolly. J-just at n-night. Tuesday night and last night. I was afraid to call you or g-go to your house, and I knew you wouldn't be there during the day, s-so . . ."

Well, that was a break. It would have been a hell of a note if she'd come busting in on me and Joyce.

"Never mind," I said, pretty damned disgusted with her. "Never mind the trimmings. You say the police have been watching you. How do you know they were police?"

"W-well, I—" She hesitated. "I d-don't know, but I supposed—"

"Tell me what happened. Start with Tuesday night."

"Well, I—I was just going out for a walk, Dolly. That house . . . I get so scared in it now. I've hardly been able to sleep s-since—"

"Never mind, dammit. Just tell me what happened."

"This car. It was p-parked up at the next corner. Right where they—whoever was in it—could watch the house. And just before I got to it they turned the lights on me. I went on by and they started up—I m-mean, the car started up. It turned around in the street and began to follow me. I walked five or six blocks and it followed me until I turned the corner to go home."

"Well?" I said.

"Well—" She looked at me, looking like I was supposed to turn flipflops or something. "Well, I went for a walk again last night, and the same car was there. It was over on the other side of the street and they didn't turn the lights on, a-and—and I started walking pretty fast, so I didn't hear it when it started up. But I'd only gone a block when—"

"Yeah, sure," I said. "Oh, sure. And it followed you back to the corner again?"

"Yes. Well, no, not quite. You see, there were quite a few cars passing and—"

"I see," I said. And, boy, did I want to paste her. Scaring hell out of me; coming down around the store where Staples might have seen her. "Are you even sure that it was the same car? What kind of car was it, anyway?"

"I—I d-don't know. I don't know much about cars. I—I think it was the same as this one."

"You do, huh?" I said. "And do you know how many cars there are like this one on the road? Well, I'll tell you. Just about eight million!"

"Then you don't th-think—?"

I shook my head. I couldn't trust myself to speak. She saw how I felt, apparently, and she shut up, too.

Stupid. How stupid could you get, anyway? It wasn't enough that she was a tramp, she had to be stupid on top of it.

There were a lot of college guys out in that section of town. One of 'em—or some guy—had tried to pick her up. He sees a swell-looking kid out by herself at night, so he follows her, thinking she'll give him a tumble. And all he'd have to do was say how about it, toots, and she'd probably have jumped into his car. But he didn't know that, so...

Well, anyway, that's what had happened. Something of the kind. It had given her a hell of a jolt, naturally, being scared and having a guilty conscience and having to stay in that house where everything had happened. But still she shouldn't have acted like this. This was a hell of a stupid way to act.

I drove along toward the country, calming down. I began to feel sorry for her, to think that I couldn't really blame her for losing her head. It might have jarred anyone that was in the spot she was in. Even me, I might have been jarred myself. And I'm a guy that's used to taking it.

I started talking again, dropping in a sweet word now and then. I explained to her what had happened—that there wasn't a thing in the world to be scared about. She couldn't believe it at first. She'd been knocked for such a loop that she couldn't see the truth when it was pointed out to her. And proved to her. But I went on talking, and finally she did.

We were in the country by then. I turned off the highway, and parked. She leaned toward me a little, smiling kind of timidly. I put my arms around her. The coat she had on was worn thin, and all she had on underneath was one of those wraparounds. I could feel her, the warmth and the softness.

"Well?" I put my mouth to her ear and whispered. "Howsabout it, toots?"

"W-what? Oh," she said, and she blushed. "You mean here—in the d-daytime."

"What the hell?" I said. "You know the score. You ought to know it, anyway."

She didn't say anything, but something happened to her eyes. They went sick, so sick, as sick as a sick dog's. And I moved my hands away from where they had been, and just hugged her tight around the shoulders.

"I'm sorry," I said. "I talk pretty rough, you know, and I just wasn't thinking how it sounded."

"I-it's—it's all right, Dolly."

"Forget I said it, huh? Because I didn't mean a thing; just a manner of speaking. Hell, I knew all about you—everything there was to know in the beginning, didn't I? And it didn't make a damned bit of difference, did it?"

"I n-never wanted to, Dolly. With you, yes. Everything was different and I wanted to give you everything that I—"

"Sure. Don't you suppose I know that?" I smiled at her, gave her a big hug—and for a moment I forgot all about Joyce. "You're the sweetest, nicest girl in the world, and we're going to have a swell life together. We'll hang around town two or three weeks longer—just to make sure—and then we'll pull out. And there won't be any past, baby, just the future, and . . ."

She snuggled up against me. After a while, I ran out of words, so I just held her and patted her. I kept it up for, well, maybe fifteen or twenty minutes. Then, a string of cars started to go by, and we had to move apart.

"Dolly. I hate to—I don't like to bother you, but—"

"You *couldn't* bother me," I said. "You just tell old Dolly about it, and if he can fix it up he will."

"Well, could I see you tonight? Just for a little while. I get so s-scared in that house! If I could see you for just a little while b-before I went to bed . . ."

There was still some of the sickness and hurt in her eyes. Not a whole lot, but it wouldn't take much to make it into a lot. I couldn't have her think I was slapping her down again.

"Well, I'd sure like to," I said, "but it might not be too smart, see? If someone should spot me over there around your place—"

"Let me come over to yours, then! P-please, Dolly. Just for a few minutes and I won't ask you again until—until it's all over."

Well . . .

Well?

"You weren't—you meant that about the police? You're sure they're not watching me? You're not afraid to have me—"

I said sure I was sure; I wouldn't snow her about a thing like that. "You see it's this way, honey. Here's the rub. My boss, this character Staples—the guy you took the bail money to—well, he drops out a lot in the evening. To talk about the work, you know. And if he saw you there, it would blow things higher than a kite. He was pretty suspicious about that dough, anyway. I wasn't supposed to have any, see, and you're sure not supposed have any. We're not supposed to mean a thing to each other. So if he found out—"

She was nodding almost impatiently. She understood about Staples. But that still didn't take me off the hook.

"I could come later, Dolly. Any time—midnight. He wouldn't be there that late."

"Well, yeah, sure," I said. "But—uh—"

"Oh," she said, dully.

"Now, wait a minute," I said. "I'm trying to explain, honey. You see, well, it's kind of hard to put into words, but—uh—uh—"

"I understand," she said.

I couldn't have her feeling that way. It made me squirm, and it just wasn't safe. Not now. Not at this stage of the game, anyway, when she was still so shaky that she could hardly cast a shadow.

"Why don't we do this?" I said. "Suppose you come over around nine o'clock, and I'll meet you outside. I'll say—in case someone's there—I'll say that I want to get some cigarettes, and I'll meet you down the block there from the wrecking yard. On the corner there by the drug store."

"Well . . . If you're sure you want to."

"I'd love to. I just wanted to play it safe, see, that's all. Hell, baby, there's nothing I like better than being with you."

I made her believe it. I said I'd been worried about her being without dough, and I started to reach back to my sample case. And, then, I caught myself, and took out my wallet. I didn't want her to know I had the loot with me. The way she'd been feeling, just a little doubtful about me, she might decide to ask for a cut.

I gave her five bucks of my own money. We talked a little longer, and then I drove her to the bus stop and let her out.

I didn't feel like working that day, either, but I put in a few hours, just to pass the time. I took in around twenty dollars, padding it out with forty from the satchel. The rest of the day, I just fooled around; and at six I checked in.

Staples was okay. I mean, he didn't give me the needle. I was out of the store in ten minutes, and on my way home.

The gravel cars had been pulled off the siding, and three gondolas of coal were there tonight. One of the cars was sticking half way out into the street, and it was a close squeeze getting the car past it. I finally made it and I parked and went into the house.

I called out to Joyce. Her voice came back to me faintly from the bedroom. I glanced into the dinette.

Dinner was ready. It was on the table, but there was only one place setting. Mine.

I set down the sample case, took off my hat and coat. I hesitated, and then I went back to the bedroom. I paused in the doorway— it didn't seem like I could go any further—and stood looking in at her.

She was in bed with the covers pulled pretty well over her, but I could see she had on her nightgown. She was facing the wall, her back to me, and she didn't turn around.

"Y-you"—I cleared my throat—"You sick or something, honey?"

She didn't answer for a moment. Then, she said, her voice muffled, "I don't feel too well. Go and eat your dinner while it's hot, Dolly."

"Well, hell," I said. "Where are you sick, anyway? What's the matter?"

"Eat your dinner," she said—pretty crisply. "We can talk afterward."

"Well, okay," I said. "Maybe I'd better."

I didn't have much of an appetite for some reason, but I ate. I ate slow, taking my time, and I drank three cups of coffee afterwards. And when I couldn't hold any more coffee, I started smoking, lighting one cigarette after another.

She called to me.

I called back, "Yeah, I'll be there in a minute, honey."

I finished my cigarette. I got up and went down the hall toward the bedroom. And I got there. And I couldn't make myself go in. I said, "B-be . . . be with you in a minute, baby," and I went into the bathroom and closed the door.

I looked around in there, and it was like I'd never seen the place before. No, nothing had been changed, nothing had been done to it, but something had happened to me. Everything seemed strange, twisted out of shape. I was lost in a strange world, and there was nothing familiar to hang onto.

Nothing. No one. No one I could talk to, explain things to.

I sat down on the edge of the tub, and lighted a cigarette. I crushed it out in the sink without thinking; and then I got up and crumbled the butt into shreds and washed the shreds down the drain. I washed the sink out real good until there wasn't a spot or a stain left on it.

I sat down on the toilet, and lighted another cigarette.

I stayed there in the bathroom. It was a strange world, but it was even stranger outside. I could sit here and explain to myself, and hell, it was clear as daylight. But I couldn't explain to her.

She called to me.

I yelled that I'd be out in a minute ... and I stayed where I was.

She called again; I yelled again. She came to the door—finally—and knocked. And I yelled, for Christ's sake, what's the hurry, anyway? And she turned the knob and came in.

She'd been crying; so much and so long that she was cried out. And now her face was drawn, streaked with tears. But her eyes were clear, and her voice was steady.

"I want to know, Dolly. I intend to know, so don't try to lie to me. Where did you get that money?"

EIGHTEEN

Through Thick and Thin: The True Story of a Man's Fight Against High Odds and Low Women ... by Knarf Nollid

Well, dear reader, in looking over my last installment I discovered that I have made a small error or two in fact. This was no fault of mine because, although I seldom complain, you have doubtless discovered that I am one hard luck son-of-a-bitch, and people keep pouring it on me until I don't know my tail from a t-bone. So this was the case in this case. There was so much happening at once that I got slightly balled up in my facts.

The truth is this—the truth about this girl, Mona, I was telling you about. This old woman she was living with, she wasn't actually her aunt at all. She was a kidnapper, see, and she'd kidnapped this poor girl from her wealthy parents while she was still no more than a tot—so naturally she didn't remember anything about them—and this one hundred thousand dollars was ransom money. The old woman was afraid to spend it because, well, hell, how do I know? Oh, yeah. She was afraid to spend it because at first she had to lay low until the heat was off, and after a while everyone got to believing that she didn't have a dime to her name and she *couldn't* spend it. It would have looked funny as hell, know what I mean? So that was the way it happened, or something like that. She couldn't bring herself to throw the dough away, but she couldn't spend it either. It was some sort of screwy deal like that, and however it was, it isn't really important. The important thing is that the money really belonged to Mona, since her wealthy parents had been dead many years of broken hearts. And since I had saved her from a fate worse than death, it wasn't any more than right that she should kind of let me take care of it for her. Or maybe even keep it all. Because if she was actually a tramp, like rumor said, I sure as hell wasn't going to have her tagging around with me.

Well, I was going to explain these true events to my wife, Joyce, when she returned unexpectedly and caught me with the dough. But I just couldn't think fast enough, I guess, so I stalled and a day or so later I told her I'd found the money. It sounded more logical than the truth, and anyway I hadn't been able to figure out the truth yet. Hell, how could I, the way things were popping at me right and left? This character Staples was giving me a hard time. Mona was giving me a hard time: worrying me about whether she was a tramp or not, and getting scared and making me scared. And, Joyce, well, I was glad she'd come back, because it looked like she'd turned over a new leaf and all was about to be well between us. But you can see how it was just one more goddamned thing to mix me up.

So I hadn't got around to tell her the truth yet. There wasn't any real incentive to, you know, as long as she believed that I'd found the money. Then the day came when she gave the house a good cleaning—and believe me it could stand it! and when I get home that night, all knocked out after a rugged day of toil, she starts giving me a hard time. She hardly lets me finish my dinner before she starts yapping at me—wants me to come back in the bedroom and do some talking. So I rush through my meal and step in the bathroom for a minute—for God's sake, what's the world coming to when a guy can't go to the bathroom? But it seems like even this humble privilege is not to be mine.

I hardly have the door closed before she's calling to me. And I know something's plenty wrong, see, and all I want is time enough to figure out a good story. It's for her own sake, understand? Because if she decides I'm lying about the money, it leaves her in a pretty bad spot. She'll want me to go to the police or she'll go herself and I just can't allow that. Even though the money is rightfully mine. The cops won't believe the truth any more than she does, so ... so, well you can see the situation.

I'm a pretty easy-going guy, and never hurt anyone in my life if I could get out of it. But if she tried to pin me down, give me a hard time when I already had more than I could stand, it would be just too bad for her.

So I stalled in the bathroom, wondering what the hell she'd found out and how the hell I could squirm out of it. But she just wouldn't have it that way; she wouldn't let me protect her. She had to bust into the bathroom on me, and ask where did I get the money. I told her. I said hell, honey, I already told you where I got it. And she said, you lied, Dolly. I must have known it right from the beginning, but I wanted so much to believe that—that—

"Where were you on Monday night, Dolly?"

"Monday night?" I said. "Oh, the night you came home. Why, I was out collecting, baby. I caught up with some long-time skips, and they paid off like—"

"They did not pay off. Because you weren't collecting."

"Now, wait just a minute," I said. "I told you about it at the time, told you exactly where I'd been. You saw the money I took in, and—"

"I saw you take some money out of that little bag and put it in your wallet. That was all you had, Dolly, except for a dollar or two. I could see that it was the next morning when you took the money I'd brought back from my trip."

I shrugged. I gave her the cold eye. Hell, what if I hadn't told her the whole truth? Was that any reason for her to break into the bathroom and accuse me of lying, and act like I'd committed a crime or something?

I will leave you to be the judge, dear reader.

All I will say is that, if you insist on putting yourself on a spot, pushing a man who has already been pushed too far, you have got to take the consequences.

"How well did you know Pete Hendrickson, Dolly?"

"Pete?" I said. "Pete Hendrickson? I never heard of him in my life."

"He was killed Monday night. He and a woman named Farrell."

"Yeah?" I said. "Oh, yeah. Seems like I remember reading something about it."

"You didn't know him personally?"

"Know him?" I laughed. "Why would I know a character like that?"

"You didn't know him?"

"I'm telling you," I said

"Then why was he in this house? Why did he sleep here?"

I gave her a look like I thought she was crazy. I wanted to protect her, see, and believe me I was doing everything I could. "Why, my God, honey," I said. "That's the screwiest thing I ever heard of! What ever gave you the idea that—?"

"This," she said. "I cleaned house today, and I found this. Down on the floor behind the bed."

She opened her hand, and held it out: a little blue and white card. Pete Hendrickson's social security card.

The stupid, sloppy bastard had slept with his clothes on that one night, and he'd let this slip out of his pocket. Just to give me a hard time later, sure. And—and what did it matter, anyhow? Look at the way he'd treated Mona; and besides that he was a Nazi or a Communist or—

"Why did you lie about it, Dolly? Why did you tell me you didn't know him?"

"Well, hell," I said, "I know a lot of people. I just didn't see that it made any difference."

"Were any of those other people here while I was away?"

"You think I'm running a hotel?" I said. "No, there wasn't anyone else here, and the only reason he was here was because I felt sorry for him and—uh—"

"Then he was with you Monday night, wasn't he? Monday evening before the murd—before it happened. There'd been someone with you; I could tell it the minute I stepped into the house. Two people had been here, drinking and smoking ... and if there wasn't anyone else ..."

"Baby," I said. "You're making a lot out of nothing. So what if he was here, what if it works out that I wasn't collecting that night? Don't you—"

"I want to know," she said. "That's what I want to know. Why you lied if it didn't matter."

"Don't you trust me?" I said. "Don't you love me? My God, maybe I did get a little mixed up and forget a few things, but—"

She moved away from me, shrugging my hands off her shoulders. "Why, Dolly? And where? Where were you Monday night, and where did you get that money?"

"Leave me alone," I said. "Goddammit, leave me alone!"

I didn't like to talk to her that way, understand, but why did she have to give me a hard time? And all over nothing.

"I'm waiting, Dolly."

"I already told you," I said. "I mean, maybe it wasn't the truth exactly. But that doesn't mean I did anything wrong. I am—m-my God, you act like you thought I'd killed those two people. Beat the old woman to death and shot Pete and ... Where you going? Where do you think you're going?"

"Oh, Dolly," she said. "H-how—what have you—"

I tried to tell her, then, what had happened. How things really were. How they could have been. And how did she know it wasn't true? How did she know that the old woman wasn't a kidnapper and that this money didn't belong to Mona's wealthy parents who had died years ago of broken hearts and ...

And she wouldn't even listen to me. She was tugging at the doorknob, staring at me with her eyes getting wider and wider like I was a goddamned maniac or something.

I made a grab for her, just trying to make her listen to reason you know. And for a moment I thought she was going to scream—yeah,

call for help against her own husband—but she didn't. All she did
was say—nothing. Nothing I remember. Not anything important.

It was an accident, of course. Hell, you know me, dear reader, and
you are aware that I wouldn't hurt a goddamned fly if I could get out
of it. I was just trying to grab her, to hold onto her while I made her
listen to reason. But I grabbed pretty hard, I guess—sort of swung—
and an unkind Fate decreed that the small understanding between us
should end otherwise than happy . . . TO BE CONTINUED
(MAYBE).

*. . . She said, "N-no, Dolly. Oh, n-no. I had to come back. I wanted to,
anyway, but I had to. I was going to tell you as soon as everything was
settled—"*

"Everything's settled," I said. "It's damned good and settled."

*". . . don't know what you're doing! You can't, Dolly! N-no, please,
NO! I'm pregnant!"*

*It was too late to stop. Anyway, how could I have stopped, even if it
hadn't been too late?*

*I hooked her, and she went down in the bathtub. I bent over the tub,
and . . . And when I finally stripped off the nightgown and lifted her out,
she didn't look like Joyce any more. Or anyone.*

*I carried her out the back door. I tossed her body up on the top of one
of the coal cars, and climbed up after it. I dug down in the coal with my
hands, scooping out a long shallow hole, and I buried her in that. Buried
them.*

NINETEEN

It was enough for one night. It was too much for a million nights,
and I came back into the house feeling pretty good and relaxed. You
understand. Nothing else could happen now, because everything had
already happened. The worst. They couldn't throw anything more at
me after this. They couldn't ever give me a bad time again.

It was too much, but now it was all over and they couldn't—

I came back into the house. I washed and cleaned up, thinking, thinking—just thinking—but not worrying.

They couldn't identify her. That train would be three days getting into Kansas City, and it stopped a half a dozen places between here and there. They wouldn't know where it had happened, when she'd been put onto the coal car, who she was. All I had to do was get rid of her clothes when I cleared out of here—and I'd be clearing out damned fast.

Because too much had already happened, and now nothing else could.

Mona could stay here with me tonight. Why not? The deal was on ice—nothing to worry about—and she was one swell kid. And I needed someone to be with me. I've always needed someone to be with me, and tonight—

So she'd stay here tonight, and in the morning I'd quit the store. Pick an argument with Staples and then tell him to go to hell, and walk out. And then Mona and I would take off, just the two of us and that good old hundred grand. It would be okay. There wasn't a hole in it any place, not on my side or hers. The county had ordered her to clear out of the house. No one could make anything out of it if she got out a little ahead of time.

We'd take off together, Joy—Mona—and me, and from then on, from now on . . . Nothing more could happen.

I finished cleaning myself up and cleaning up the bathroom. I went out into the living room and had a good stiff drink. It seemed like it should have been awfully late, but it was only a little after eight-thirty. Almost twenty-five minutes before I was to meet Mona—before someone would be here with me.

I poured another stiff drink. I drank it, and I got to thinking it couldn't have happened—so much, so quickly—and if it couldn't, why it hadn't. And maybe I ought to take her back a little drink, since she wasn't feeling well. And I poured it out for her.

And drank it.

There was a knock on the door. I gave a little jump and then I went to answer it; and, no, I didn't hesitate. Because there couldn't be anything more now, nothing ever again, and there was nothing to be afraid of.

I opened the door. Staples said, "Good evening, Frank," and I didn't answer—I couldn't answer—and he walked in past me.

"Well, Frank. You don't appear at all pleased to see me. Aren't you going to ask me to sit down?"

I shook my head. I said, "No. What the hell do you want, Stape?"

He sat down, crossing his fat little legs. "What do I want, Frank? We-el, let's say I'll be quite happy with pot luck. I'll take whatever you have."

TWENTY

He couldn't mean what I thought he probably did. He couldn't know anything, and too much had already happened and ... I sagged down in a chair across from his. It was the chair Pete had sat in, and he was in the place I had sat in when I was talking to Pete. I was in Pete's place, and he was in mine.

I started shaking my head. I didn't know what to say or do so I just shook my head.

"Yes," he said. "Oh, yes, Frank. Yes, indeed."

"No-no! I won't—" I broke off, made my voice steady. "What do you want? What are you talking about, anyway?"

And he laughed softly.

"Oh, Frank. You've been so clumsy, so obvious; such a thorough botch from the very beginning ... Must we go into the tiresome details, or can't you see it for yourself?"

"I don't know what you're talking about," I said. "You h-hear? I don't—"

"Well," he sighed, "if we must, we must. I'll begin at the beginning and spell it out very slowly. Item ..."

He held up a hand, then folded one of the chubby little fingers back into his palm. "Item one, Frank. On the day before your arrest for stealing company funds, you collected some thirty-eight dollars from the late Pete Hendrickson. On the same day you made a cash sale—or, rather, you turned in a cash-sale contract—in the amount of thirty-three dollars to one Mona Farrell. In the morning, then, on these two accounts, you should have checked in about seventy-one dollars. And frantic as you were to stave off arrest, you certainly would have turned it in, if you had had it. But you didn't; all you had was the money for the silverware. You used Pete's money, or most of it, to buy the girl a present."

"Now, wait a minute," I said. "That doesn't mean—you can't prove—"

"Prove?" His lips pursed thoughtfully. "Well, perhaps not, if we take it out of context, which, happily, I am not forced to do. At any rate, and at the moment, we are not discussing proof. I am merely pointing out your initial error, delving down to the center strand of that very ugly rope which you have hung around your neck.

"You gave the girl a thirty-three dollar present, and perhaps that is meaningless of itself. One more manifestation of a distorted personality. But it is not meaningless—it is not, my dear boy—when this same girl arrives at the store, and bails you out to the tune of more than three hundred dollars ... Or are you going to tell me that it wasn't the same girl?"

There was no use in denying it. I knew now who'd been watching her, who'd turned the car lights on her.

"All right," I said. "So I know her, I like her and she likes me. What of it? My wife skipped out and—"

"Please!" He held up his hand again. "I'm not at all interested in your morals. Nor in you personally, for that matter. Only in the money you obtained from what must be the two clumsiest murders on record."

He waited, waiting for me to deny it. And it wasn't any use, of course, but I did. "Money?" I said. "Murders? I don't know what you're—"

"Money. Murders," he nodded. "And, please, Frank, you're trying my patience. I don't know how you got next to the girl or how you managed to frame Pete, but I know that you did. The girl tipped you off to the fact that the old woman had a substantial sum of money. You—skipping over the gory details—you got it, and you still have it. Except for those amounts which you checked in as collections."

"Now, wait a—"

"Which you checked in as collections," he said firmly. "Would you like me to show it to you? I've laid it aside just in case you became stubborn. Approximately a dozen bills, supposedly collected from an assorted group of people but with their serial numbers in sequence. You got it, Frank, and you got a very substantial sum. Nothing less would have tempted you to take such a terrible risk, and Ma Farraday was just the woman to have had a hefty chunk of cash."

"But—Ma Farraday?" I said.

"Mmmm. Do you recall my telling you that I'd been to visit an old friend? That was Ma—better known locally as Mrs. Farrell. I went to see her in the morgue after my suspicions about you became aroused. Once I recognized her, I was certain that—but I see you don't recognize the name?"

He waited again, one eyebrow cocked upward. Then, he grinned and went on:

"A little before your time, I imagine, but the Farraday gang was notorious in the Southwest some twenty to twenty-five years ago. Bank robbers. Ma and her three sons. Ma doing the planning, and the three men faithfully carrying out her orders. Three of the orneriest, coldest-blooded killers ever to shoot a teller in the back. And their wives and children—they all lived together near the town where I worked—their wives and children were just as ornery as they were. Why—Yes, Frank?"

"N-nothing," I said. "I mean, I thought . . ."

"I know. I was confident that your interest in the oil business and my early days in Oklahoma was something more than casual. But, no, there was no oil on the Farraday property; they lived too far back in the hills. For that matter, I doubt that even had they owned oil-producing land, it would have altered their way of life a whit. They were cruel, vicious, because they wanted to be. It was all they understood—men, women and children. Being a very clannish lot, with little trust in the law, their neighbors protected and put up with them for years. In the end, however, they finally became so outraged that they moved in and massacred the lot of them. Shot them like the swine they were, then burned their dwellings. Wiped out the entire family—supposedly."

Mona. She was part of an outfit like that. No wonder she'd been so ready to kill her own aunt—her grandmother, probably. No wonder that she acted like—

"I said *supposedly*, Frank. Criminal investigation was just emerging from swaddling clothes in those days and, of course, neither Ma nor the various children had police records. A number of bodies were found in the smoldering ruins; also the charred remnants of a quantity of currency. Ergo, and in the absence of proof to the contrary, it was assumed—*believed*, I should say—that the entire family was wiped out, and with them their ill-gotten gains. But you and I know better, don't we, Frank? We are the only ones who do know."

He winked at me, grinning with his puffy little lips drawn back from his teeth. Like a cat that's just had a good meal. He licked his lips slightly, grinning and waiting, and my stomach turned over and over. And the band grew tighter and tighter around my head.

I began to tremble. My mouth opened and I felt a scream crawling up from my throat, and I had to swallow hard to choke it back.

"N-no!" I said. "You've got it all wrong, Stape! I—"

"Dear, dear," he said. "Oh, dear me. You are such a tiresome fellow, Frank."

"I'm telling you! It's the God's truth, Stape. The girl was kidnapped, see. She was actually the daughter of a very wealthy family, and the money was ransom money and—and—"

He laughed out loud. "And you were going to act as custodian of it, eh? Oh, my dear boy, I'm almost embarrassed for you."

"It's true, goddammit!" *It had to be true. Something had to be true besides what—what was true.* "That's why the old woman didn't spend any of the money see? She found out it was marked, and—"

"But it wasn't marked, Frank. I know it. You must know it also, unless you're a much bigger fool than you appear."

"Well-uh-well, then, she found out—she figured out—that the serial numbers had been recorded, and—"

"Oh? Then why, since it was unspendable, did she keep it all these years?"

He was playing with me, laughing at me, having a hell of a time for himself. "Yes, Frank? And why—if the authorities are on the lookout for those serials—why aren't you in custody?"

"Well—" I had to go on. I was talking crap, making a horse's ass of myself, but I had to go on. "Well, there's bound to be something wrong with it. If there wasn't, why didn't she spend it? Why did she go on living like a goddamned hog when—"

"Because she was one, a grasping old sow."

"You don't know," I said. "You don't know that the money isn't hot. She could have found out that—"

"Then, why, as I asked a moment ago, didn't she destroy it?"

"Well—uh—well, because she couldn't! Jesus, you've got a hun— a pretty good wad of dough, how can you destroy it? I couldn't. She couldn't. So she just hung onto it, figuring that maybe some day, somehow, she might be able to shove it—"

"Oh, Frank . . . "

"You don't know," I said. "Goddammit, you can't be sure, Stape!"

"I not only can be, but I am. You see, I had some several dealings with the Farradays at this store I managed. Delivered merchandise to their mountain retreat at considerably above the market prices. There was nothing criminal about our association—nothing provably illegal, I should say—but the company became embarrassed to the point of transferring me to another town . . . However! Enough of personal history. My point is that the Farradays were strictly bank robbers."

"But they might have pulled one kid—"

"Stop it! No more nonsense, Frank . . . How much did you get and where is it?"

I looked down at the floor. I looked up again, keeping my eyes away from the corner where the sample case was.

"She didn't have as much as I thought. Just ten thousand dollars. I can—well, I got it out in the country, see—but I can bring it in the morning."

"Ten thousand? You mean, a hundred thousand, I'm sure. You almost said it a moment ago."

"All right," I said. "So goddammit, there's a hundred thousand. Come on with me and we'll go and get it."

He hesitated. Then he nodded, smiling faintly. "Very well, Frank, but perhaps I should tell you something first. I left a letter with the night clerk at my hotel—a very reliable man, incidentally. He's instructed to mail it if I fail to return by midnight."

His smile spread, and he laughed out loud again.

I thought, *It can't be like this* . . . And I guess I must have said it.

"But it is, Frank; it is like that. And now you will produce the money. Immediately!"

I got up. I brought the case over to the coffee table and snapped it open. I started to reach in for the satchel, digging it out from under the samples, and he brushed my hands away and grabbed it himself.

He opened it. He made a funny purring sound.

"Mmmm. Wonderful ... I hope you won't think I'm greedy if I don't offer to share with you?"

"You've got to," I said. I kept saying it. "You got to, Stape. A—a few grand, well, one grand. Something! Anything! I ki—I did it all, and—"

"So sorry." He shook his head. "But I'll be happy to give you a word of wisdom. You have no problems which money will solve."

"You son-of-a-bitch," I said.

"You really don't, Frank. You'd be just as miserable with the money as without it ... Well, much as I hate to leave such pleasant company ..."

He buttoned his coat, and stood up. He tucked the money satchel under his arm.

"I want that silverware contract back," I said. "By God, you'll never be able to hold that over me."

"The sil—oh, yes, to be sure. And very shrewd of you. You can pick it up in the morning, get your wages to date at the same time."

"My wages," I said.

"Well? No more questions? You're not wondering why I delayed calling you to account until tonight?"

"Get out," I said.

"The girl, dear boy: the clinching bit of proof. I didn't really need it, but—"

"Get out!"

"Of course. But shouldn't you invite her in, Frank? She's just around the corner ... and you do look so lonesome."

TWENTY-ONE

Lonesome, he said. The man said I looked lonesome. And I had all kinds of company. All kinds. All dead. All jumping up in front of me wherever I looked, all laughing and crying and singing in my mind.

All dead. And all for nothing.

All for a dame that had been born rotten, and got more rotten every damned day of her life.

... I met her, and brought her back to the house. I told her about Staples and losing the money. I laid it out cold for her, kind of hoping, you know, that she'd bitch or give me a hard time about it. But she didn't let out a peep. She was sympathetic, sorry on my account, but she acted like it didn't matter to her. As long as she could be with me, that was all that mattered.

I began to think that maybe I might be mistaken about her. To feel that she was the swell kid I'd thought she was in the beginning. It was pretty hard to swallow, and, of course, I couldn't sell myself completely. But I did it enough. Enough to keep from slugging her. Enough to put up with her . . . for the time being.

She was all I had, you see; all I'd got for all I'd done. And I had to have someone with me. I'd almost always had someone with me.

I went out and got some more whiskey—it took just about my last nickel. I came back and we talked and drank. And after a while she talked and I drank. And pretty soon there was no more talk, and only me drinking.

She fell asleep with her head in my lap. I passed out. When morning came, we were still there on the lounge.

I fixed us some coffee and toast—I didn't want her slopping around with my grub. I told her to beat it back to her house and gather up anything she wanted to take with her. She left, hurrying, and I went back into the bedroom.

I stuffed all of Joyce's things into a big pasteboard carton. Clothes, cosmetics and toilet articles: everything. I carried the box out into the alley, and set it down by the trash can. Then, I drove down to the store.

The other collectors had checked out, and Staples was alone. He gave me the silverware contract and I struck a match to it, dropping it to the floor and kicking the ashes to pieces.

"Such a messy fellow," he pouted. "But, I suppose, I shouldn't chide you ... Your money, Frank. I'm making it a full fifty dollars."

I picked up the money, not saying anything. I gave him a slow, hard stare; and then I turned around and started to leave.

"Frank—" There was a worried note in his voice. "What—uh—what are your plans, Frank?"

"What's that to you?" I said.

"But I've always been concerned for you, dear boy. Always. And it's dawned on me that since you'll doubtless want to be moving on ..."

I began to get it. He *was* worried. He wasn't just another hired hand that could pull out without a moment's notice. The books would have to be audited and the stock inventoried before he could leave; and that would take two or three weeks at the inside. And he didn't like the idea of me being in town during that time. I might get desperate, see? Might get drunk and jam myself up with the police ... and do a little talking.

"I don't know," I said. "Why would I want to travel? I figure I'll stay right here."

He gave me a peeved look, but he opened the cash drawer. He took out all the currency inside, counted it and shoved it through the wicket.

"Four hundred and forty-seven dollars, Frank. Almost five hundred with the fifty you have. That should see you well on your way."

"I like it here," I said. "I'm not going anywhere."

"Now, Frank ... "

"Not unless you do a lot better than that," I said. "Hell, make it a grand, anyway. With all you've got—"

"But I don't have it with me. It's put away in a safe place, and it's going to remain there until my resignation takes effect."

"Well . . . well," I said. "Write me a check, then. Give me your check for five hundred."

"Oh . . ." He shook his head, grinning. "Must you really be so obvious? ... No checks. I couldn't oblige you even if I was stupid. It will take just about my entire bank balance to square with the cash drawer."

I was sure he was lying, but there wasn't much I could do about it. He was just a little worried—not actually scared—and I'd played that worry for all it was worth.

I picked up the money, and left.

... I owed two hundred and thirty on the car. I paid it off—I couldn't have a goddamned finance company on my tail—and went back to the house. Mona was there waiting for me. I got my stuff together, and loaded all our baggage into the car. There was quite a bit of it, since I figured I'd better take Joyce's. It wasn't monogramed and it was pretty good stuff, and it might look funny if I left it behind.

I'd always made out pretty well in Omaha. As well, I mean, as I've made out anywhere. So that's where I headed for, and we got there just after dark. We stopped at a diner for a bite to eat. The waitress brought me a newspaper. I glanced at it ... and that was our last stop in Omaha.

I started driving again, and I drove almost night and day. To Des Moines. Down across to Grand Island. Across to Denver ... I sold the car in Denver, a lousy three hundred and twenty-five bucks, and we started traveling by bus.

Yeah, I suppose she wondered what the score was. Or maybe she didn't either. She hadn't been around enough to know when something was screwy and when it wasn't, so maybe she didn't wonder. Anyway, she didn't ask any questions, try to give me a hard time. And it was a damned good thing for her that she didn't.

I'd had it, brother, know what I mean? And it looked like I was going to keep right on getting it. Because Staples had given the cops a bum steer—tole 'em I had a seaman's ticket and probably intended to ship out—but that didn't help much. Nothing helped much. The crew haircut, the horn-rimmed glasses, the mustache. I was still scared as hell, afraid to settle down in one place.

It was lousy, the lousiest stinking luck a guy ever had in his life. It—goddammit, it just wasn't fair! I ask you, now, did you ever hear of coal being moved by anything but regular freight? You're damned right you didn't and neither did anyone else. But that one car—that one car—they had to make an exception out of it. It got hooked onto a manifest, an express freight, and it didn't stop until it got into Kansas City. It was in there at noon the next day, and they started unloading it right away—they couldn't wait, goddamn them. And inside of an hour, the police doctor was posting the body.

Well, that soon, it was easy to fix the time of death. And they knew the body couldn't have been put on the train but one place. So they wired the cops at that place, and the cops started sniffing around, and they found that box of stuff back in the alley by the trash can . . .

I had to keep moving. My money was running out, and I had to keep moving; and if I hadn't been saddled with her—chained to a goddamned tramp—

Well.

Well, she finally started in on me. I didn't have it tough enough, I guess, so she had to make it tougher. Watching me all the time like I was a goddamned freak or something. Not saying anything unless I spoke to her. You know: a lot of little things. Wearing me down little by little.

And stupid! The only thing she could do was bawl, and she never missed a chance at that.

I was walking a little ahead of her that day in Dallas. I'd told her for God's sake, if she wanted to look and act like a goddamned tramp she could walk by herself. So I was ahead of her, like I say, and finally I looked around; and she wasn't there any more. Hardly anyone was on the sidewalk any more.

They were all out on the street about a half block back, crowded around the front of a big truck . . .

TWENTY-TWO

Upward and Onward: The True Story of a Man's Fight Against High Odds and Low Women . . . by Derf Senoj

I was born in New York City of poor but honest parents, and from my earliest recollections I was out working and trying to make something of myself. But from my earliest recollections someone was always trying to give me a hard time. It was that way with everything I did. One way or another, I'd get the blocks put to me; so I will mercifully spare you the sordid details.

I kept thinking that if I had some little helpmeet to dwell with, the unequal struggle would not be so unequal. But I didn't have any more luck that way than I did in the other. Tramps, that's all I got. Five goddamned tramps in a row ... or maybe it was six or seven, but it doesn't matter. It was like they were all the same person.

Well, finally I landed in Oklahoma City, and it looks like at last my luck has changed. Not with money. I was buying the gold, door to door, and how can you make any money when everybody cheats you? But it looked like it had sure changed with women. It not only looked that way, but it was that way. And as far as the money went, she had enough for forty people.

I met her when I was working this swell apartment house there in the City. I sneaked in past the doorman, and hers was the first apartment I hit. Classy? Beautiful? Well, all I can say is that I'd never seen anything like her. I could hardly believe it when she smiled and asked me inside.

I was ashamed to hit her up on the gold. I said I was looking for a party that used to live there, and so on, and I was sure sorry to have bothered her. And—

"Now, now—" She laughed, but she didn't laugh at me, understand. It was nice and sympathetic. "Don't apologize for your job. Of course, I am a little disturbed to see a gentleman of your personality and evident ability doing this kind of—"

"Well," I said, "it's just temporary, see? I got a little down on my luck, and I had to take what I could get."

"How dreadful! You sit right down and I'll fix you a nice drink."

I sat down on about two thousand dollars' worth of lounge. She brought our drinks, and sat down next to me. She smiled at me and kept the conversation going, because naturally I was pretty speechless.

I finished my drink and started to get up. She put her hand on my arm. "Please," she said. "Please don't go. I've been so lonely since my husband died."

I said I was certainly sorry to hear of her husband's death. Her eyes clouded up a little for a moment, and then she shook her head.

"It's lonely without him and n-naturally I didn't want him to die, b-but—but, oh, it's a terrible thing to say but I think I'd actually begun to hate him! He misrepresented himself. He pretended to be everything I wanted, and then after we were married . . ."

"I know what you mean," I said. "I know exactly what you mean, ba—uh—"

"Say it," she whispered, and she turned and threw her arms around me. "Say I'm your baby. Say it, say anything to me, do anything to . . . you like. But j-just don't go away . . ."

And it was like a beautiful dream, dear reader, but I'm
talk about dreams
kidding you negative: that was exactly how I came to meet the lovely Helene, my princess charming. Thus, at last, were two love-hungry souls united.

You will notice that I haven't described her, but I can't. Because she looked so many different ways. When she went out where anyone else could see her, she always looked the same way: the way she looked that first day I met her. But when we were alone, well, if I hadn't known it was her sometimes, I wouldn't have known it was her
a goddamned syphilitic bag
the same woman. She had dozens of different complete outfits— clothes that a girl of eighteen would wear, or a woman of twenty-five, or thirty-five and so on. All complete from house dresses to evening gowns. And she had all of these different kinds of make-up. Powder and lipstick and rouge—dozens of different shades—hairpieces and eyelashes and brows and teethcaps. Even little glass things to slip in over her eyes and change their color. It was kind of a hobby with her, see, making herself up in all those different ways. And right at the start it made me a little uneasy; I got to wondering what was real and what wasn't: And maybe if I saw her as she really
one more bag like all the rest
was, I wouldn't be able to take it. But that was just at first. You see it could be no other way, dear reader: I mean, she had to be
a bag in a fleabag, for Christ's sake. and I couldn't go any
beautiful and classy and all that a man desires in a woman. All the royal rooking I'd got from tramps, I couldn't take any more. And after the long unequal struggle I had at least found my heart's desire.

She'd inherited a pile of dough from her father; but that's

stole her brother-in-law's savings
about all I ever found out about her or him. I never even learned his
name—her maiden name. She acted embarrassed when I mentioned
anything about her background, so I didn't do it more than a time or
two. I figured that the old man had probably made his pile selling
clap medicine or something like that, and naturally she was embarrassed. And it was best to stay off the subject. After all, although I
had always worked my can off and never complained, there were a
few chapters in my own life which I preferred to remain sealed.

Her money was in a bank in another city—just where I
hidden in the mattress
don't know. But she was so embarrassed about her maiden name that
she never cashed any checks there in town, or let the bank send her
any dough. Whenever she ran short, she'd just hop a plane to this city
and draw out what she wanted, and be back the same night.

She'd gone after some dough, the morning this story broke in the
newspapers—a story about some people I used to know. And I
wow! the wine and the hay! yeeoweeeee
laughed so goddamned hard when I read it that I almost busted a rib.
I read it and re-read it, all day long, and each time I laughed
safe now. safe with a bag in a fleabag
harder than ever:

The 20-year-old Stirling kidnap case appeared to be solved today
with the arrest of an ex-store manager and admitted associate of the
notorious Farraday gang.

The suspect is H. J. Staples, 55. More than $90,000 of the $100,000
ransom money was recovered from his swank Sarasota, Fla., hotel
suite.

Staples first came under scrutiny of the authorities about four
months ago when several hundred dollars in kidnap currency was
deposited to the account of a store he then managed. Believing that
the deposit was made as a "feeler," law officials refrained from
arresting him until he put large and thoroughly incriminating sums
into circulation.

Ramona Stirling was the only child of multimillionaire oil-man,
Arthur Stirling, and his semi-invalid wife. Three years old at the

time, Ramona was snatched from the grounds of the family's luxurious Tulsa estate, after her nurse had been lured into the house by a fake telephone call.

The ransom of $100,000 was demanded, and promptly paid. But an inexperienced newscaster revealed that the serial numbers of the currency had been recorded. With the divulging of this information, the Stirlings lost all contact with the kidnapers, and it is generally conceded that the child was murdered.

Mrs. Stirling died less than six weeks after the kidnaping. Her husband went to his grave the following month. In the absence of heirs, the great Stirling fortune was claimed by the state.

The suspect Staples quit his job some three months ago and began traveling about the country, making various small expenditures along the way. At last convinced, apparently, that time had cooled off the "hot" money, he arrived in Florida yesterday and began to splurge. His arrest followed.

Grilled by state, federal and local officials, he told a wildly implausible story of how he came into possession of the money. Full details are not yet available but it is known that his tale involved "Ma" Farraday (of the aforementioned gangsters) and Frank Dillon, a former associate of Staples', who had been sought for several months in connection with the death of his wife and their unborn child. Officials place no credence whatsoever in the suspect's "explanations."

That Staples was once on excellent terms with the gangsters is acknowledged. It is pointed out, however, that the entire Farraday family was wiped out more than two decades ago; and that, this being the case, Staples' statement that Dillon killed "Ma" for the ransom money is nothing short of ridiculous. Moreover, it was pointed out, the Farradays were bank robbers. They were never known to have indulged in any other criminal activity, and it is virtually unbelievable that they would have.

As for Dillon, authorities now believe that he was himself a murder victim and he is no longer being sought as a fugitive. They theorized that he and Mrs. Dillon somehow learned that Staples had the ransom cash, and that the latter killed both. Dillon's body, it was explained, could have been buried in a coal car which was destined for a conveyor-fed blast furnace ...

I laughed and laughed when I read that story. I felt
safe. from what? not the thing I needed to be safe from.
good all day. And then evening came on, and I didn't
and it was just like always only worse. the worst tramp of
laugh any more and I didn't feel good any more.
all, the worst fleabag of all. and I couldn't take it. the end
Because it was quite a tragedy, when you got to
had to be better than this, so we drank the wine. we
thinking about it: and I guess you know dear reader
smoked the hay. we started sniffing the snow. they say
I'm a pretty soft-hearted son-of-a-bitch. Yes, it was a
you can't do it. guzzle the juice and puff the mary and
terrible tragedy and whoever was responsible for it
sniff the c. but we did, we did that and then we went on
ought to be jailed. Making a guy want what he
the h. we started riding the main line, we got sick as
couldn't get. Making him so he couldn't get much, but
bastards but we kept right on and after a while, man oh,
he'd want a lot. Laying it all out for him every place he
man, we didn't know from nothing. we were blind, too
turned—the swell cars and clothes and places to live.
paralyzed to feel, too numb. but everything began to get
never letting him have anything, but always making
beautiful. she was and the room was and I was. it was
him want. Making him feel like a bastard because he
like it ought to be at the end if it's never been that way
didn't have what he couldn't get. Making him hate
before, and we kept digging into the mattress, and the
himself, and if a guy hates himself how can he love
porter kept bringing in the stuff. helene started vomiting
anyone else? Helene came home, my fairy princess,
a lot, but it didn't seem to bother her and it didn't bother
and she saw I was feeling low so she fixed me a big
me any. even the puke was beautiful like everything else.
drink. And right after that I began to get drowsy. I
she was the most beautiful woman in the world and all I
was sleepy; I went and stretched out on the bed, and
wanted was to do something nice for her, show her how

she came in and sat down beside me. She had a big
much I appreciated and loved her. she was all the women
pair of shears in her hand, and she sat snipping the
of the world rolled into one. so it was the very least I could
ends of her hair, staring down at me. And I looked at
do, and I'd have to do it fast. she was in the bathroom
her, my eyes dropping shut. And she made herself
puking. I got up and shoved my foot through the window.
look like Joyce and then like Mona, and then ... all the
it woke me up a little; the cold air, and those jagged
others. She said I'd disappointed her; I'd turned out
splinters of glass. but I probably wouldn't feel anything,
like all her other men. You deceived me, she said.
the load I was carrying and she was entitled to it. I poked
You're no different from the rest, Fred. And you'll
my leg through the window. I straddled it, rocking back
have to pay like the rest. Don't you want me to,
and forth, and it didn't take hardly any time at all. helene
darling. I nodded and she began unfastening and
came to the door of the bathroom, and she began
fumbling and then, then she lowered the shears and
laughing, screaming. I threw myself out the window.
then she was smiling again and letting me see. There, she said, that's
much better, isn't it? And, then, nice as I'd been, she started laughing.
Screaming at me.